James Baldwin

If Beale Street Could Talk

James Baldwin was born in 1924 and educated in New York. He is the author of more than twenty works of fiction and nonfiction, including *Go Tell It on the Mountain*; *Notes of a Native Son*; *Giovanni's Room*; *Nobody Knows My Name*; *Another Country*; *The Fire Next Time*; *Nothing Personal*; *Blues for Mister Charlie*; *Going to Meet the Man*; *The Amen Corner*; *Tell Me How Long the Train's Been Gone*; *One Day When I Was Lost*; *No Name in the Street*; *The Devil Finds Work*; *Little Man, Little Man*; *Just Above My Head*; *The Evidence of Things Not Seen*; *Jimmy's Blues*; and *The Price of the Ticket*. Among the awards he received are a Eugene F. Saxon Memorial Trust Award, a Rosenwald Fellowship, a Guggenheim Fellowship, a *Partisan Review* Fellowship, and a Ford Foundation grant. He was made a Commander of the Legion of Honor in 1986. He died in 1987.

VINTAGE

INTERNATIONAL

Go Tell It on the Mountain (1953)

Notes of a Native Son (1955)

Giovanni's Room (1956)

Nobody Knows My Name (1961)

Another Country (1962)

The Fire Next Time (1963)

Nothing Personal (1964)

Blues for Mister Charlie (1964)

Going to Meet the Man (1965)

The Amen Corner (1968)

Tell Me How Long the Train's Been Gone (1968)

One Day When I Was Lost (1972)

No Name in the Street (1972)

The Devil Finds Work (1976)

Little Man, Little Man (1976)

Just Above My Head (1979)

The Evidence of Things Not Seen (1985)

Jimmy's Blues (1985)

The Price of the Ticket (1985)

if
beale
street
could
talk

if
beale
street
could
talk

A novel

JAMES BALDWIN

Introduction by Brit Bennett

VINTAGE INTERNATIONAL
Vintage Books
A Division of Penguin Random House LLC
New York

FIRST VINTAGE INTERNATIONAL DELUXE EDITION 2024

Copyright © 1974 by James Baldwin
Copyright renewed 2002 by Gloria Baldwin Karefa-Smart
Introduction copyright © 2024 by Brit Bennett

Cataloging-in-Publication Data is on file at the Library of Congress.

Vintage International Deluxe Edition ISBN: 978-0-593-68898-4
Vintage International Trade Paperback ISBN: 978-0-307-27593-6
eBook ISBN: 978-0-8041-4967-9

vintagebooks.com

Printed in the United States of America
10 9 8 7 6 5 4 3 2 1

for YORAN

Mary, Mary,
What you going to name
That pretty little baby?

Introduction to the
Vintage International Edition (2024)

There's a moment early in James Baldwin's magnificent 1974 novel *If Beale Street Could Talk* when Tish finds herself at a little Spanish restaurant in Greenwich Village where she, surprisingly, feels at home. Although she speaks no Spanish, her boyfriend, Fonny, is a regular, so she delights in the friendly waiters and the good food and the kind service that makes her feel welcome in a new place. Later, after tragedy befalls, Tish returns alone to this restaurant as a place of solace, where, out of friendship for Fonny, the waitstaff care for her. In a novel set against the brutality of New York City, this restaurant serves as an early glimpse of how this love story expands beyond its central couple to the community that helps them survive.

The Spanish restaurant is introduced only after we have already learned the novel's devastating premise. The story opens with nineteen-year-old Tish arriving at the jail to tell her childhood love Fonny that she is pregnant. Although she is nervous to share her news, Fonny is overjoyed; the baby, as well as Tish's daily visits, give him hope and keep him tethered to the outside world, even as he faces dire circumstances. It is Tish and her family who struggle throughout the novel to free Fonny, even as Tish faces her impending motherhood.

In *James Baldwin: A Biography*, David Adams Leeming writes that *If Beale Street Could Talk* was inspired, in part, by Baldwin's friendship with Tony Maynard. In 1967, Maynard was arrested in Manhattan for allegedly shooting a white Marine, and imprisoned for six and a half years for a crime he did not commit. In 1974, Maynard was finally freed after a judge determined that prosecutors suppressed evidence that proved their key witnesses' unreliability. The trial lasted three minutes; when he was released on bail, Maynard said, according to the *New York Times*, "It happened so fast." Throughout Maynard's incarceration, Baldwin publicly advocated for his release. According to his biographer, he'd hoped to write a book with Maynard about his experience as a wrongfully incarcerated man. Although that book never came to fruition, Baldwin would instead publish *If Beale Street Could Talk*, a love story that doubles as a searing indictment of the American criminal justice system that ensnared his friend.

The novel earns much of its tension between the interplay of these two types of stories. Through an intricately woven nonchronological timeline, we see the span of Tish and Fonny's love story, a lifelong friendship that unfolds, surprisingly to both of them, into romance. "Fonny liked me so much," Tish thinks, "that it didn't occur to him that he loved me." One of the delights of this novel is the early ease of Tish and Fonny's love, although because the story is presented out of chronological order, even their hopeful courtship feels tragic. When Tish learns that she is pregnant, her joy is tempered by the fact that she does not know if Fonny will ever be able to come home. She is carrying a new life while all too aware of the precariousness of black life itself.

Fonny's legal troubles begin early in the novel. After apartment-hunting in preparation for starting their life together, Tish is assaulted by a white man at a grocery store, and when Fonny defends her, he instead draws the attention of a white police officer. Afterward, a grim Fonny tells Tish that he knows that the incident has made him the humiliated officer's new target. "He wasn't anybody's nigger," Tish thinks. "And that's a crime, in this fucking free country. You're suppose to be somebody's nigger. And if you're nobody's nigger, you're a bad nigger: and that's what the cops decided when Fonny moved downtown."

If Beale Street Could Talk earns its title from the song "Beale Street Blues," set on the Memphis street famously considered a birthplace of the blues. Though the characters never venture to Tennessee, the blues permeate this novel. In *The Spirituals and the Blues: An Interpretation*, James H. Cone writes that the blues "caught the absurdity of black existence in white America" as well as the ability of black people to "transcend trouble without ignoring it." Likewise, *If Beale Street Could Talk* captures this sensibility through the pain facing its characters as well as their attempts to survive. Though Fonny himself is innocent, at the center of his false charges is a real crime. The novel never leaves in doubt the fact that the victim, a young Puerto Rican woman named Victoria, *was* raped; her unwillingness to revisit her trauma is searing and believable. Even though her testimony threatens Fonny's freedom, Baldwin renders her palpable pain, presenting a complex tragedy that has claimed multiple victims.

There is also Daniel, a childhood friend with whom Fonny reunites after Daniel's recent release from prison. His charges were trumped up as well. "They said—they still say—I stole a car," he tells Fonny. "Man, I can't even drive a car." From the beginning, Daniel's loneliness is evident. His father has died, and he lives with an ill mother. When he's arrested for the car theft, he has a little weed in his pockets, so he is offered a lighter sentence in exchange for a guilty plea. "I was alone, baby," he explains to Fonny, "wasn't nobody, and so I entered the guilty plea. Two years!" Daniel's story is a harrowing reminder of the arbitrary ease with which black life can be stolen:

> Maybe I'd feel different if I had done something and got caught. But I didn't do nothing. They were just playing with me, man, because they could. And I'm lucky it was only two years, you dig? Because they can do with you whatever they want. Whatever they want.

Through his long, meditative speeches, Baldwin slowly unravels the trauma Daniel experienced, as well as the horrors awaiting Fonny. On the night that Fonny is arrested, Daniel weeps in his arms as he confides in him about the violence he experienced in prison. "He had seen nine men rape one boy: and he had been raped. He would never, never, never again be the Daniel he had been." Like Victoria, Daniel's life is forever altered by sexual violence, her pain weaponized by the state and his pain enabled by the same.

If Beale Street Could Talk was published in 1974 and spent seven weeks on the bestseller list. But the novel also earned mixed reviews. In the *New York Review of Books*, Joyce Carol Oates praised the novel as a "quite moving and very traditional celebration of love"; the book, however, was panned by Anatole Broyard in the *New York Times* as a "vehemently sentimental love story." Perhaps even more egregiously, Broyard's incurious review hand-wrings about how the novel's nonblack readers might react to the book's brutal indictment of American racial politics. But perhaps what is most liberating about this book is its disinterest in coddling a white audience. In his famous 1955 essay "Everybody's Protest Novel," Baldwin tackles two monumental texts in the American canon—*Uncle Tom's Cabin* by Harriet Beecher Stowe and *Native Son* by Richard Wright—as disingenuous attempts at social critique that ultimately comfort their audience. "They emerge for what they are," he writes, "a mirror of our confusion, dishonesty, panic, trapped and immobilized in the sunlit prison of the American dream. They are fantasies, connecting nowhere with reality, sentimental."

But *If Beale Street Could Talk* avoids this trap through its unflinching characters, bound together by community. If one of Baldwin's gripes with *Native Son* is Bigger Thomas reflecting the "isolation of the Negro within its own group," then *Beale Street* is instead about the necessity of community in survival. Although Fonny has a strained relationship with his pious and hypocritical mother and sisters, he is supported by his father as well as Tish's family. Tish's sister supplies the white lawyer who eventually earns their trust; her father steals from work in order to raise the bail money; and in one of the more thrilling sequences in the book, her mother ventures to Puerto Rico in order to convince the victim to recant her false identification. In contrast, consider Daniel. An alternate version of Fonny, Daniel previews the absurd legal labyrinth Fonny will have to navigate. The difference, however, is that Daniel is "alone, baby," lacking the network that helps Fonny survive.

Black survival, Baldwin suggests, requires more than romantic love; it requires a more complicated and expansive love story. Early on in the novel, when Tish tells her family that she is pregnant, she braces for judgment but instead receives only joy. She feels her father's hand on her belly and thinks, "That child in my belly was also, after all, his child, too, for there would have been no Tish if there had been no Joseph. Our laughter in that kitchen, then, was our helpless response to a miracle." This is the miracle of *If Beale Street Could Talk*, one life nesting inside another, sheltering each other.

BRIT BENNETT
December 2023

Born and raised in Southern California, Brit Bennett graduated from Stanford University and later earned her MFA in fiction at the University of Michigan. Her debut novel, *The Mothers*, was a *New York Times* bestseller and a finalist for both the NBCC John Leonard Prize and the PEN/Robert W. Bingham Prize for Debut Fiction. Her second novel, *The Vanishing Half*, was an instant #1 *New York Times* bestseller, longlisted for the National Book Award, a finalist for the Women's Prize, and named one of the ten best books of the year by *The New York Times*.

ONE

troubled
about
my
soul

I look at myself in the mirror. I know that I was christened Clementine, and so it would make sense if people called me Clem, or even, come to think of it, Clementine, since that's my name: but they don't. People call me Tish. I guess that makes sense, too. I'm tired, and I'm beginning to think that maybe everything that happens makes sense. Like, if it didn't make sense, how could it happen? But that's really a terrible thought. It can only come out of trouble—trouble that doesn't make sense.

Today, I went to see Fonny. That's not *his* name, either, he was christened Alonzo: and it might make sense if people called him Lonnie. But, no, we've always called him Fonny. Alonzo Hunt, that's his name. I've known him all my life, and I hope I'll always know him. But I only call him Alonzo whan I have to break down some real heavy shit to him.

Today, I said, "—Alonzo—?"

And he looked at me, that quickening look he has when I call him by his name.

He's in jail. So where we were, I was sitting on a bench in front of a board, and he was sitting on a bench in front of a board. And we were facing each other through a wall of glass between us. You can't hear anything through this glass, and so you both have a little telephone. You have to talk through that. I don't know why people always look down when they talk through a telephone, but they always do. You have to remember to look up at the person you're talking to.

I always remember now, because he's in jail and I love his eyes and every time I see him I'm afraid I'll never see him again. So I pick up the phone as soon as I get there and I just hold it and I keep looking up at him.

So, when I said, "—Alonzo—?" he looked down and then he looked up and he smiled and he held the phone and he waited.

I hope that nobody has ever had to look at anybody they love through glass.

And I didn't say it the way I meant to say it. I meant to say it in a very offhand way, so he wouldn't be too upset, so he'd understand that I was saying it without any kind of accusation in my heart.

You see: I know him. He's very proud, and he worries a lot, and, when I think about it, I know—he doesn't—that that's the biggest reason he's in jail. He worries too much already, I don't want him to worry about me. In fact, I didn't want to say what I had to say. But I knew I had to say it. He had to know.

And I thought, too, that when he got over being worried, when he was lying by himself at night, when he was all by himself, in the very deepest part of himself, maybe, when he thought about it, he'd be glad. And that might help him.

I said, "Alonzo, we're going to have a baby."

I looked at him. I know I smiled. His face looked as though it were plunging into water. I couldn't touch him. I wanted so to touch him. I smiled again and my hands got wet on the phone and then for a moment I couldn't see him at all and I shook my head and my face was wet and I said, "I'm glad. I'm glad. Don't you worry. I'm glad."

But he was far away from me now, all by himself. I waited for him to come back. I could see it flash across his face: *my* baby? I knew that he would think that. I don't mean that he doubted *me:* but a man thinks that. And for those few seconds while he was out there by himself, away from me, the baby was the only real thing in the world, more real than the prison, more real than me.

I should have said already: we're not married. That means more to him than it does to me, but I understand how he feels. We were going to get married, but then he went to jail.

Fonny is twenty-two. I am nineteen.

He asked the ridiculous question: "Are you sure?"

"No. I ain't sure. I'm just trying to mess with your mind."

Then he grinned. He grinned because, then, he knew.

"What we going to do?" he asked me—just like a little boy.

"Well, we ain't going to drown it. So, I guess we'll have to raise it."

Fonny threw back his head, and laughed, he laughed till tears come down his face. So, then, I felt that the first part, that I'd been so frightened of, would be all right.

"Did you tell Frank?" he asked me.

Frank is his father.

I said, "Not yet."

"You tell your folks?"

"Not yet. But don't worry about them. I just wanted to tell you first."

"Well," he said, "I guess that makes sense. A baby."

He looked at me, then he looked down. "What you going to do, for real?"

"I'm going to do just like I been doing. I'll work up to just about the last month. And then, Mama and Sis will take care for me, you ain't got to worry. And anyway we have you out of here before then."

"You sure about that?" With his little smile.

"Of course I'm sure about that. I'm always sure about that."

I knew what he was thinking, but I can't let myself think about it—not now, watching him. I *must* be sure.

The man came up behind Fonny, and it was time to go. Fonny smiled and raised his fist, like always, and I raised mine and he stood up. I'm always kind of surprised when I see him in here, at how tall he is. Of course, he's lost weight and that may make him seem taller.

He turned around and went through the door and the door closed behind him.

I felt dizzy. I hadn't eaten much all day, and now it was getting late.

I walked out, to cross these big, wide corridors I've come to hate, corridors wider than all the Sahara desert. The Sahara is never empty; these corridors are never empty. If you cross the Sahara, and you fall, by and by vultures circle around you, smelling, sensing, your death. They circle lower and lower: they wait. They know. They know exactly when the flesh is ready, when the spirit cannot fight back. The poor are always crossing the Sahara. And the lawyers and bondsmen and all that crowd circle around the poor, exactly like vultures. Of course, they're not any richer than the poor, really, that's why they've turned into vultures, scavengers, indecent garbage men, and I'm talking about the black cats, too, who, in so many ways, are worse. I think that, personally, I would be ashamed. But I've had to think about it and now I think that maybe not. I don't know what I wouldn't do to get Fonny out of jail. I've never come across any shame down here, except shame like mine, except the shame of the hardworking black ladies, who call me Daughter, and the shame of proud Puerto Ricans, who don't understand what's happened—no one who speaks to them speaks Spanish, for example—and who are ashamed that they have loved ones in jail. But they are wrong to be ashamed. The people responsible for these jails should be ashamed.

And I'm not ashamed of Fonny. If anything, I'm proud. He's a man. You can tell by the way he's taken all this shit that he's a man. Sometimes, I admit, I'm scared—because nobody can take the shit they throw on us forever. But, then, you just have to somehow fix your mind to get from one day to the next. If you think too far ahead, if you even *try* to think too far ahead, you'll never make it.

Sometimes I take the subway home, sometimes I take the bus. Today, I took the bus because it takes a little longer and I had a lot on my mind.

Being in trouble can have a funny effect on the mind. I don't know if I can explain this. You go through some days and you seem to be hearing people and you seem to be talking to them and you seem to be doing your work, or, at least, your work gets done; but you haven't seen or heard a soul and if someone asked you what you have done that day you'd have to think awhile before you could answer. But, at the same time, and even on the self-same day—and this is what is hard to explain—you see people like you never saw them before. They shine as bright as a razor. Maybe it's because you see people differently than you saw them before your trouble started. Maybe you wonder about them more, but in a different way, and this makes them very strange to you. Maybe you get scared and numb, because you don't know if you can depend on people for anything, anymore.

And, even if they wanted to do something, what could they do? I can't say to anybody in this bus, Look, Fonny is in trouble, he's in jail—can you imagine what anybody on this bus would say to me if they knew, from my mouth, that I love somebody in jail?—and I know he's never committed any crime and he's a beautiful person, please help me get him out. Can you imagine what anybody on this bus would say? What would *you* say? I can't say, I'm going to have this baby and I'm scared, too, and I don't want anything to happen to my baby's father, don't let him die in prison, please, oh, please! You can't say that. That means you can't really say anything. Trouble means you're alone. You sit down, and you look out the window and you wonder if you're going to spend the rest of your life going back and forth on this bus. And if you do, what's going to happen to your baby? What's going to happen to Fonny?

And if you ever did like the city, you don't like it anymore. If I ever get out of this, if we ever get out of this, I swear I'll never set foot in downtown New York again.

Maybe I used to like it, a long time ago, when Daddy used to bring me and Sis here and we'd watch the people and the buildings and Daddy would point out different sights to us and we might stop in Battery Park and have ice cream and hot dogs. Those were great days and we were always very happy—but that was because of our father, not because of the city. It was because we knew our father loved us. Now, I can say, because I certainly know it now, the city didn't. They looked at us as though we were zebras —and, you know, some people like zebras and some people don't. But nobody ever asks the zebra.

It's true that I haven't seen much of other cities, only Philadelphia and Albany, but I swear that New York must be the ugliest and the dirtiest city in the world. It must have the ugliest buildings and the nastiest people. It's got to have the worst cops. If any place is worse, it's got to be so close to hell that you can smell the people frying. And, come to think of it, that's exactly the smell of New York in the summertime.

I met Fonny in the streets of this city. I was little, he was not so little. I was around six—somewhere around there—and he was around nine. They lived across the street, him and his family, his mother and two older sisters and his father, and his father ran a tailor shop. Looking back, now, I kind of wonder who he ran the tailor shop *for:* we didn't know anybody who had money to take clothes to the tailor—well, maybe once in a great while. But I don't think *we* could have kept him in business. Of course, as I've been told, people, colored people, weren't as poor then as they had been when my Mama and Daddy were trying to get it together. They weren't as poor then as we had been in the South. But we were certainly poor enough, and we still are.

I never really noticed Fonny until once we got into a fight, after school. This fight didn't really have anything to do with Fonny and me at all. I had a girl friend, named Geneva, a kind of loud, raunchy girl, with her hair plaited tight on her head, with big, ashy knees and long legs and big feet; and she was always into something. Naturally she was my best friend, since I was never into anything. I was skinny and scared and so I followed her and got into all *her* shit. Nobody else wanted me, really, and you *know* that nobody else wanted her. Well, she said that she couldn't stand Fonny. Every time she looked at him, it just made her sick. She was always telling me how ugly he was, with skin just like raw, wet potato rinds and eyes like a Chinaman and all that nappy hair and them thick lips. And so bow-legged he had bunions on his ankle bones; and the way his behind stuck out, his mother must have been a gorilla. I agreed with her because I had to, but I didn't really think he was as bad as all that. I kind of liked his eyes, and, to tell the truth, I thought that if people in China had eyes like that, I wouldn't mind going to China. I had never seen a gorilla, so his behind looked perfectly normal to me, and wasn't, really, when you had to think about it, as big as Geneva's; and it wasn't until much later that I realized that he was, yes, a little bowlegged. But Geneva was always up in Fonny's face. I don't think he ever noticed her at all. He was always too busy with his friends, who were the worst boys on the block. They were always coming down the street, in rags, bleeding, full of lumps, and, just before this fight, Fonny had lost a tooth.

Fonny had a friend named Daniel, a big, black boy, and Daniel had a thing about Geneva something like the way Geneva had a thing about Fonny. And I don't remember how it all started, but, finally, Daniel had Geneva down on the ground, the two of them rolling around, and I was trying to pull Daniel off her and Fonny was pulling on me. I turned around and hit him with the only thing I could get my hands on, I grabbed it out of the garbage can. It was only a stick; but it had a nail in it. The nail raked across his cheek and it broke the skin and the blood started dripping. I couldn't believe my eyes, I was so scared. Fonny put his hand to his face and then looked at me and then looked at his hand and I didn't have any better sense than to drop the stick and run. Fonny ran after me and, to make matters worse, Geneva saw the blood and she started screaming that I'd killed him, I'd killed him! Fonny caught up to me in no time and he grabbed me tight and he spit at me through the hole where his tooth used to be. He caught me right on the mouth, and—it so *humiliated* me, I guess—because he hadn't hit me, or hurt me—and maybe because I sensed what he had not done—that I screamed and started to cry. It's funny. Maybe my life changed in that very moment when Fonny's spit hit me in the mouth. Geneva and Daniel, who had started the whole thing, and didn't have a scratch on them, both began to scream at me. Geneva said that I'd killed him for sure, yes, I'd killed him, people caught the lockjaw and died from rusty nails. And Daniel said, Yes, he knew, he had a uncle down home who died like that. Fonny was listening to all this, while the blood kept dripping and I kept crying. Finally, he must have realized that they were talking about him, and that he was a dead man—or boy—because he started crying, too, and then Daniel and Geneva took him between them and walked off, leaving me there, alone.

And I didn't see Fonny for a couple of days. I was sure he had the lockjaw, and was dying; and Geneva said that just as soon as he was dead, which would be any minute, the police would come and put me in the electric chair. I watched the tailor shop, but everything seemed normal. Mr. Hunt was there, with his laughing, light-brown-skinned self, pressing pants, and telling jokes to whoever was in the shop—there was always someone in the shop—and every once in a while, Mrs. Hunt would come by. She was a Sanctified woman, who didn't smile much, but, still, neither of them acted as if their son was dying.

So, when I hadn't seen Fonny for a couple of days, I waited until the tailor shop seemed empty, when Mr. Hunt was in there by himself, and I went over there. Mr. Hunt knew me, then, a little, like we all knew each other on the block.

"Hey, Tish," he said, "how you doing? How's the family?"

I said, "Just fine, Mr. Hunt." I wanted to say, How's *your* family? which I always *did* say and had planned to say, but I couldn't.

"How you doing in school?" he asked me, after a minute: and I thought he looked at me in a real strange way.

"Oh, all right," I said, and my heart started to beating like it was going to jump out of my chest.

Mr. Hunt pressed down that sort of double ironing board they have in tailor shops—like two ironing boards facing each other—he pressed that down, and he looked at me for a minute and then he laughed and said, "Reckon that big-headed boy of mine be back here pretty soon."

I heard what he said, and I understood—something; but I didn't know what it was I understood.

I walked to the door of the shop, making like I was going out, and then I turned and I said, "What's that, Mr. Hunt?"

Mr. Hunt was still smiling. He pulled the presser down and turned over the pants or whatever it was he had in there, and said, "Fonny. His Mama sent him down to her folks in the country for a little while. Claim he get into too much trouble up here."

He pressed the presser down again. "She don't know what kind of trouble he like to get in down there." Then he looked up at me and he smiled. When I got to know Fonny and I got to know Mr. Hunt better, I realized that Fonny has his smile. "Oh, I'll tell him you come by," he said.

I said, "Say hello to the family for me, Mr. Hunt," and I ran across the street.

Geneva was on my stoop and she told me I looked like a fool and that I'd almost got run over.

I stopped and said, "You a liar, Geneva Braithwaite. Fonny ain't got the lockjaw and he ain't going to die. And I ain't going to jail. Now, you just go and ask his Daddy." And then Geneva gave me such a funny look that I ran up my stoop and up the stairs and I sat down on the fire escape, but sort of in the window, where she couldn't see me.

Fonny came back, about four or five days later, and he came over to my stoop. He didn't have a scar on him. He had two doughnuts. He sat down on my stoop. He said, "I'm sorry I spit in your face." And he gave me one of his doughnuts.

I said, "I'm sorry I hit you." And then we didn't say anything. He ate his doughnut and I ate mine.

People don't believe it about boys and girls that age—people don't believe much and I'm beginning to know why—but, then, we got to be friends. Or, maybe, and it's really the same thing—something else people don't want to know—I got to be his little sister and he got to be my big brother. He didn't like his sisters and I didn't have any brothers. And so we got to be, for each other, what the other missed.

Geneva got mad at me and she stopped being my friend; though, maybe, now that I think about it, without even knowing it, I stopped being *her* friend; because, now—and without knowing what that meant—I had Fonny. Daniel got mad at Fonny, he called him a sissy for fooling around with girls, and he stopped being Fonny's friend—for a long time; they even had a fight and Fonny lost another tooth. I think that anyone watching Fonny then was sure that he'd grow up without a single tooth in his head. I remember telling Fonny that I'd get my mother's scissors from upstairs and go and kill Daniel, but Fonny said I wasn't nothing but a girl and didn't have nothing to do with it.

Fonny had to go to church on Sundays—and I mean, he *had* to go: though he managed to outwit his mother more often than she knew, or cared to know. His mother—I got to know her better, too, later on, and we're going to talk about her in a minute—was, as I've said, a Sanctified woman and if she couldn't save her husband, she was damn sure going to save her child. Because it was *her* child; it wasn't *their* child.

I think that's why Fonny was so bad. And I think that's why he was, when you got to know him, so nice, a really nice person, a really sweet man, with something very sad in him: when you got to know him. Mr. Hunt, Frank, didn't try to claim him but he loved him—loves him. The two older sisters weren't Sanctified exactly, but they might as well have been, and they certainly took after their mother. So that left just Frank and Fonny. In a way, Frank had Fonny all week long, Fonny had Frank all week long. They both knew this and that was why Frank could give Fonny to his mother on Sundays. What Fonny was doing in the street was just exactly what Frank was doing in the tailor shop and in the house. He was being bad. That's why he hold on to that tailor shop as long as he could. That's why, when Fonny came home bleeding, Frank could tend to him; that's why they could, both the father and the son, love me. It's not really a mystery except it's always a mystery about people. I used to wonder, later, if Fonny's mother and father ever made love together. I asked Fonny. And Fonny said:

"Yeah. But not like you and me. I used to hear them. She'd come home from church, wringing wet and funky. She'd act like she was so tired she could hardly move and she'd just fall across the bed with her clothes on—she'd maybe had enough strength to take off her shoes. And her hat. And she'd always lay her handbag down someplace. I can still hear that sound, like something heavy, with silver inside it, dropping heavy wherever she laid it down. I'd hear her say, The Lord sure blessed my soul this evening. Honey, when you going to give your life to the Lord? And, baby, he'd say, and I swear to you he was lying there with his dick getting hard, and, excuse me, baby, but her condition weren't no better, because this, you dig? was like the game you hear two alley cats playing in the alley. Shit. She going to whelp and *mee-e-ow* till times get better, she going to get that cat, she going to run him all *over* the alley, she going run him till he bite her by the neck—by this time he just want to get some sleep really, but she got her chorus going, he's got to stop the music and ain't but one way to do it—he going to bite her by the neck and then she got him. So, my Daddy just lay there, didn't have no clothes on, with his dick getting harder and harder, and my Daddy would say, About the time, I reckon, that the Lord gives *his* life to *me*. And she'd say, Oh, Frank, let me bring you to the Lord. And he'd say, Shit, woman, I'm going to bring the Lord to *you. I'm* the Lord. And she'd start to crying, and she'd moan, Lord, help me help this man. You give him to me. I can't do nothing about it. Oh, Lord, help me. And he'd say, The Lord's going to help you, sugar, just as soon as you get to be a little child again, naked, like a little child. Come on, come to the Lord. And she'd start to crying and calling on Jesus while he started taking all her clothes off—I could hear them kind of rustling and whistling and tearing and falling to the floor and sometimes I'd get my foot caught in one of them things when I was coming through their room in the morning on my way to school—and when he got her naked and got on top of her and she was still crying, Jesus! help me, Lord! my

Daddy would say, You got the Lord now, right here. Where you want your blessing? Where do it hurt? Where you want the Lord's hands to touch you? here? here? or here? Where you want his tongue? Where you want the Lord to enter you, you dirty, dumb black bitch? you bitch. You bitch. You bitch. And he'd slap her, hard, loud. And she'd say, Oh, Lord, help me to bear my burden. And he'd say, Here it is, baby, you going to bear it all right, I know it. You got a friend in Jesus, and I'm going to tell you when he comes. The first time. We don't know nothing about the second coming. Yet. And the bed would shake and she would moan and moan and moan. And, in the morning, was just like nothing never happened. She was just like she had been. She still belonged to Jesus and he went off down the street, to the shop."

And then Fonny said, "Hadn't been for me, I believe the cat would have split the scene. I'll always love my Daddy because he didn't leave me." I'll always remember Fonny's face when he talked about his Daddy.

Then, Fonny would turn to me and take me in his arms and laugh and say, "You remind me a lot of my mother, you know that? Come on, now, and let's sing together, Sinner, do you love my Lord?—And if I don't hear no moaning, I'll know you ain't been saved."

I guess it can't be too often that two people can laugh and make love, too, make love because they are laughing, laugh because they're making love. The love and the laughter come from the same place: but not many people go there.

Fonny asked me, one Saturday, if I could come to church with him in the morning and I said, Yes, though we were Baptists and weren't supposed to go to a Sanctified church. But, by this time, everybody knew that Fonny and I were friends, it was just simply a fact. At school, and all up and down the block, they called us Romeo and Juliet, though this was not because they'd read the play, and here Fonny came, looking absolutely miserable, with his hair all slicked and shining, with the part in his hair so cruel that it looked like it had been put there with a tomahawk or a razor, wearing his blue suit and Sis had got me dressed and so we went. It was like, when you think about it, our first date. His mother was waiting downstairs.

It was just before Easter, so it wasn't cold but it wasn't hot.

Now, although we were little and I certainly couldn't be dreaming of taking Fonny from her or anything like that, and although she didn't really love Fonny, only thought that she was supposed to because she had spasmed him into this world, already, Fonny's mother didn't like me. I could tell from lots of things, such as, for example, I hardly ever went to Fonny's house but Fonny was always at mine; and this wasn't because Fonny and Frank didn't want me in their house. It was because the mother and them two sisters didn't want me. In one way, as I realized later, they didn't think that I was good enough for Fonny —which really means that they didn't think that I was good enough for *them*—and in another way, they felt that I was maybe just exactly what Fonny deserved. Well, I'm dark and my hair is just plain hair and there is nothing very outstanding about me and not even Fonny bothers to pretend I'm pretty, he just says that pretty girls are a terrible drag.

When he says this, I know that he's thinking about his mother—that's why, when he wants to tease me, he tells me I remind him of his mother. I don't remind him of his mother at all, and he knows that, but he also knows that I know how much he loved her: how much he wanted to love her, to be allowed to love her, to have that translation read.

Mrs. Hunt and the girls are fair; and you could see that Mrs. Hunt had been a very beautiful girl down there in Atlanta, where she comes from. And she still had—has—that look, that don't-you-touch-me look, that women who were beautiful carry with them to the grave. The sisters weren't as beautiful as the mother and, of course, they'd never been young, in Atlanta, but they were fair skinned—and their hair was long. Fonny is lighter than me but much darker than they, his hair is just plain nappy and all the grease his mother put into it every Sunday couldn't take out the naps.

Fonny really takes after his father: so, Mrs. Hunt gave me a real sweet patient smile as Fonny brought me out the house that Sunday morning.

"I'm mighty pleased you coming to the house of the Lord this morning, Tish," she said. "My, you look pretty this morning!"

The way she said it made me *know* what I have must looked like other mornings: it made me know what I looked like.

I said, "Good-morning, Mrs. Hunt," and we started down the street.

It was the Sunday morning street. Our streets have days, and even hours. Where I was born, and where my baby will be born, you look down the street and you can almost see what's happening in the house: like, say, Saturday, at three in the afternoon, is a very bad hour. The kids are home from school. The men are home from work. You'd think that this might be a very happy get together, but it isn't. The kids see the men. The men see the kids. And this drives the women, who are cooking and cleaning and straightening hair and who see what men won't see, almost crazy. You can see it in the streets, you can hear it in the way the women yell for their children. You can see it in the way they come down out of the house—in a rush, like a storm—and slap the children and drag them upstairs, you can hear it in the child, you can see it in the way the men, ignoring all this, stand together in front of a railing, sit together in the barbershop pass a bottle between them, walk to the corner to the bar, tease the girl behind the bar, fight with each other, and get very busy, later, with their vines. Saturday afternoon is like a cloud hanging over, it's like waiting for a storm to break.

But, on Sunday mornings the clouds have lifted, the storm has done its damage and gone. No matter what the damage was, everybody's clean now. The women have somehow managed to get it all together, to hold everything together. So, here everybody is, cleaned, scrubbed, brushed, and greased. Later, they're going to eat ham hocks or chitterlings or fried or roasted chicken, with yams and rice and greens or cornbread or biscuits. They're going to come home and fall out and be friendly: and some men wash their cars, on Sundays, more carefully than they wash their foreskins. Walking down the street that Sunday morning, with Fonny walking beside me like a prisoner and Mrs.

Hunt on the other side of me, like a queen making great strides into the kingdom, was like walking through a fair. But now I think that it was only Fonny—who didn't say a word—that made it seem like a fair.

We heard the church tambourines from a block away.

"Sure wish we could get your father to come out to the Lord's house one of these mornings," said Mrs. Hunt. Then she looked at me. "What church do you usually go to, Tish?"

Well, as I've said, we were Baptists. But we didn't go to church very often—maybe Christmas or Easter, days like that. Mama didn't dig the church sisters, who didn't dig her, and Sis kind of takes after Mama, and Daddy didn't see any point in running after the Lord and he didn't seem to have very much respect for him.

I said, "We go to Abyssinia Baptist," and looked at the cracks in the sidewalk.

"That's a very handsome church," said Mrs. Hunt—as though that was the best thing that could possibly be said about it and that that certainly wasn't much.

It was eleven in the morning. Service had just begun. Actually, Sunday school had begun at nine and Fonny was usually supposed to be in church for that; but on this Sunday morning he had been given a special dispensation because of me. And the truth is, too, that Mrs. Hunt was kind of lazy and didn't really like getting up that early to make sure Fonny was in Sunday school. In Sunday school, there wasn't anybody to admire her—her carefully washed and covered body and her snow-white soul. Frank was not about to get up and take Fonny off to Sunday school and the sisters didn't want to dirty their hands on their nappy-headed brother. So, Mrs. Hunt, sighing deeply and praising the Lord, would have to get up and get Fonny dressed. But, of course, if she didn't take him to Sunday school by the hand, he didn't usually get there. And, many times, that woman fell out happy in church without knowing the whereabouts of her only son: "Whatever Alice don't feel like being bothered with," Frank was to say to me, much later, "she leaves in the hands of Lord."

The church had been a post office. I don't know how come the building had had to be sold, or why, come to that, anybody had wanted to buy it, because it still looked like a post office, long and dark and low. They had knocked down some walls and put in some benches and put up the church signs and the church schedules; but the ceiling was that awful kind of wrinkled tin, and they had either painted it brown or they had left it unpainted. When you came in, the pulpit looked a mighty long ways off. To tell the truth, I think the people in the church were just proud that their church was so big and that they had somehow got their hands on it. Of course I was (more or less) used to Abyssinia. It was brighter, and had a balcony. I used to sit in that balcony, on Mama's knees. Every time I think of a certain song, "Uncloudy Day," I'm back in that balcony again, on Mama's knees. Every time I hear "Blessed Quietness," I think of Fonny's church and Fonny's mother. I don't mean that either the song or the church was quiet. But I don't remember ever hearing that song in our church. I'll always associate that song with Fonny's church because when they sang it on that Sunday morning, Fonny's mother got happy.

Watching people get happy and fall out under the

Power is always something to see, even if you see it all the time. But people didn't often get happy in our church: we were more respectable, more civilized, than sanctified. I still find something in it very frightening: but I think this is because Fonny hated it.

That church was so wide, it had three aisles. Now, just to the contrary of what you might think, it's much harder to find the central aisle than it is when there's just one aisle down the middle. You have to have an instinct for it. We entered that church and Mrs. Hunt led us straight down the aisle which was farthest to the left, so that everybody from two aisles over had to turn and watch us. And—frankly— we were something to watch. There was black, long-legged me, in a blue dress, with my hair straightened and with a blue ribbon in it. There was Fonny, who held me by the hand, in a kind of agony, in his white shirt, blue suit, and blue tie, his hair grimly, despairingly shining not so much from the Vaseline in his hair as from the sweat in his scalp; and there was Mrs. Hunt, who, somehow, I don't know how, from the moment we walked through the church doors, became filled with a stern love for her two little heathens and marched us before her to the mercy seat. She was wearing something pink or beige, I'm not quite sure now, but in all that gloom, it showed. And she was wearing one of those awful hats women used to wear which have a veil on them which stops at about the level of the eyebrow or the nose and which always makes you look like you have some disease. And she wore high heels, too, which made a certain sound, something like pistols, and she carried her head very high and noble. She was saved the moment she entered the church, she was Sanctified holy, and I even remember until today how much she made me tremble, all of a sudden, deep inside. It was like there was nothing, nothing, nothing you could ever hope to say to her unless you wanted to pass through the hands of the living God: and He would check it out with her before He answered you. The mercy seat: she led us to the front row and sat us down before it. She made us sit but she knelt, on her knees, I mean, in front of her seat, and bowed her head and covered her eyes, making sure she didn't fuck with that veil. I stole a look at Fonny, but Fonny wouldn't look at me. Mrs. Hunt rose, she faced the entire congregation for a moment and then she, modestly, sat down.

Somebody was testifying, a young man with kind of reddish hair, he was talking about the Lord and how the Lord had dyed all the spots out of his soul and taken all the lust out of his flesh. When I got older, I used to see him around. His name was George: I used to see him nodding on the stoop or on the curb, and he died of an overdose. The congregation amened him to death, a big sister, in the pulpit, in her long white robe, jumped up and did a little shout; they cried, Help him, Lord Jesus, help him! and the moment he sat down, another sister, her name was Rose and not much later she was going to disappear from the church and have a baby—and I still remember the last time I saw her, when I was about fourteen, walking the streets in the snow with her face all marked and her hands all swollen and a rag around her head and her stockings falling down, singing to herself—stood up and started singing, *How did you feel when you come out the wilderness, leaning on the Lord?* Then Fonny did look at me, just for a second. Mrs. Hunt was singing and clapping her hands. And a kind of fire in the congregation mounted.

Now, I began to watch another sister, seated on the other side of Fonny, darker and plainer than Mrs. Hunt but just as well dressed, who was throwing up her hands and crying, Holy! Holy! Holy! Bless your name, Jesus! Bless your name, Jesus! And Mrs. Hunt started crying out and seemed to be answering her: it was like they were trying to outdo each other. And the sister was dressed in blue, dark, dark blue and she was wearing a matching blue hat, the kind of hat that sits back—like a skull cap—and the hat had a white rose in it and every time she moved it moved, every time she bowed the white rose bowed. The white rose was like some weird kind of light, especially since she was so dark and in such a dark dress. Fonny and I just sat there between them, while the voices of the congregation rose and rose and rose around us, without any mercy at all. Fonny and I weren't touching each other and we didn't look at each other and yet we were holding on to each other, like children in a rocking boat. A boy in the back, I got to know him later, too, his name was Teddy, a big brown-skinned boy, heavy everywhere except just where he should have been, thighs, hands, behind, and feet, something like a mushroom turned upside down, started singing, "Blessed quietness, holy quietness."

"*What assurance in my soul*" sang Mrs. Hunt.

"*On the stormy sea,*" sang the dark sister, on the other side of Fonny.

"*Jesus speaks to me,*" sang Mrs. Hunt.

"*And the billows* cease *to roll!*" sang the dark sister.

Teddy had the tambourine, and this gave the cue to the piano player—I never got to know him: a long dark, evil-looking brother, with hands made for strangling; and with these hands he attacked the keyboard like he was beating the brains out of someone he remembered. No doubt, the congregation had their memories, too, and they went to pieces. The church began to rock. And rocked me and Fonny, too, though they didn't know it, and in a very different way. Now, we knew that nobody loved us: or, now, we knew who did. Whoever loved us was not here.

It's funny what you hold on to to get through terror when terror surrounds you. I guess I'll remember until I die that black lady's white rose. Suddenly, it seemed to stand straight up, in that awful place, and I grabbed Fonny's hand—I didn't know I'd grabbed it; and, on either side of us, all of a sudden, the two women were dancing—shouting: the holy dance. The lady with the rose had her head forward and the rose moved like lightning around her head, our heads, and the lady with the veil had her head back: the veil which was now far above her forehead, which framed that forehead, seemed like the sprinkling of black water, baptizing us and sprinkling her. People moved around us, to give them room, and they danced into the middle aisle. Both of them held their handbags. Both of them wore high heels.

Fonny and I never went to church again. We have never talked about our first date. Only, when I first had to go and see him in the Tombs, and walked up those steps and into those halls, it was just like walking into church.

Now that I had told Fonny about the baby, I knew I had to tell: Mama and Sis—but her real name is Ernestine, she's four years older than me—and Daddy and Frank. I got off the bus and I didn't know which way to go—a few blocks west, to Frank's house, or one block east, to mine.

But I felt so funny, I thought I'd better get home. I really wanted to tell Frank before I told Mama. But I didn't think I could walk that far.

My Mama's a kind of strange woman—so people say —and she was twenty-four when I was born, so she's past forty now. I must tell you, I love her. I think she's a beautiful woman. She may not be beautiful to look at—whatever the fuck *that* means, in this kingdom of the blind. Mama's started to put on a little weight. Her hair is turning gray, but only way down on the nape of her neck, in what her generation called the "kitchen," and in the very center of her head—so she's gray, visibly, only if she bows her head or turns her back, and God knows she doesn't often do either. If she's facing you, she's black on black. Her name is Sharon. She used to try to be a singer, and she was born in Birmingham; she managed to get out of that corner of hell by the time she was nineteen, running away with a traveling band, but, more especially, with the drummer. That didn't work out, because, as she says,

"I don't know if I ever loved him, really. I was young but I think now that I was younger than I should have been, for my age. If you see what I mean. Anyway, I know I wasn't woman enough to help the man, to give him what he needed."

He went one way and she went another and she ended up in Albany, of all places, working as a barmaid. She was twenty and had come to realize that, though she had a voice, she wasn't a singer; that to endure and embrace the life of a singer demands a whole lot more than a voice. This meant that she was kind of lost. She felt herself going under; people were going under around her, every day; and Albany isn't exactly God's gift to black folks, either.

Of course, I must say that I don't think America is God's gift to anybody—if it is, God's days have *got* to be numbered. That God these people say they serve—and *do* serve, in ways that they don't know—has got a very nasty sense of humor. Like you'd beat the shit out of Him, if He was a man. Or: if *you* were.

In Albany, she met Joseph, my father, and she met him in the bus stop. She had just quit her job and he had just quit his. He's five years older than she is and he had been a porter in the bus station. He had come from Boston and he was really a merchant seaman; but he had sort of got himself trapped in Albany mainly because of this older woman he was going with then, who really just didn't dig him going on sea voyages. By the time Sharon, my mother, walked into that bus station with her little cardboard suitcase and her big scared eyes, things were just about ending between himself and this woman—Joseph didn't like bus stations—and it was the time of the Korean war, so he knew that if he didn't get back to sea soon, he'd be in the army and he certainly would not have dug *that*. As sometimes happens in life, everything came to a head at the same time: and here came Sharon.

He says, and I believe him, that he knew he wasn't going to let her out of his sight the moment he saw her walk away from the ticket window and sit down by herself on a bench and look around her. She was trying to look tough and careless, but she just looked scared. He says he wanted to laugh, and, at the same time, something in her frightened eyes made him want to cry.

He walked over to her, and he wasted no time.

"Excuse me, Miss. Are you going to the city?"

"To New York City, you mean?"

"Yes, Miss. To New York—city."

"Yes," she said, staring at him.

"I am too," he said, having just at that minute decided it, but being pretty sure that he had the money for a ticket on him, "but I don't know the city real well. Do you know it?"

"Why, no, not too well," she said, looking more scared than ever because she really didn't have any idea who this nut could be, or what he was after. She'd been to New York a few times, with her drummer.

"Well, I've got a uncle lives there," he said, "and he give me his address and I just wonder if you know where it is." He hardly knew New York at all, he'd always worked mainly out of San Francisco, and he gave Mama an address just off the top of his head, which made her look even more frightened. It was an address somewhere down off Wall Street.

"Why, yes," she said, "but I don't know if any colored people live down there." She didn't dare tell this maniac that *nobody* lived down there, there wasn't a damn thing down there but cafeterias, warehouses, and office buildings. "Only white people," she said, and she was kind of looking for a place to run.

"That's right," he said, "my uncle's a white man," and he sat down next to her.

He had to go to the ticket window to get his ticket, but he was afraid to walk away from her yet, he was afraid she'd disappear. And now the bus came, and she stood up.

So he stood up and picked up her bag and said, "Allow me," and took her by the elbow and marched her over to the ticket window and she stood next to him while he bought his ticket. There really wasn't anything else that she could do, unless she wanted to start screaming for help; and she couldn't, anyway, stop him from getting on the bus. She hoped she'd figure out something before they got to New York.

Well, that was the last time my Daddy ever saw that bus station, and the very last time he carried a stranger's bags.

She hadn't got rid of him by the time they got to New York, of course; and he didn't seem to be in any great hurry to find his white uncle. They got to New York and he helped her get settled in a rooming house, and he went to the Y. And he came to get her the next morning, for breakfast. Within a week, he had married her and gone back to sea and my mother, a little stunned, settled down to live.

She'll take the news of the baby all right, I believe, and so will Sis Ernestine. Daddy may take it kind of rough but that's just because he doesn't know as much about his daughter as Mama and Ernestine do. Well. He'll be worried, too, in another way, and he'll show it more.

Nobody was home when I finally made it up to that top floor of ours. We've lived here for about five years, and it's not a bad apartment, as housing projects go. Fonny and I had been planning to fix up a loft down in the East Village, and we'd looked at quite a few. It just seemed better for us because we couldn't really afford to live in a project, and Fonny hates them and there'd be no place for Fonny to work on his sculpture. The other places in Harlem are even worse than the projects. You'd never be able to start your new life in those places, you remember them too well, and you'd never want to bring up your baby there. But it's something, when you think about it, how many babies *were* brought into those places, with rats as big as cats, roaches the size of mice, splinters the size of a man's finger, and somehow survived it. You don't want to think about those who didn't; and, to tell the truth, there's always something very sad in those who did, or do.

I hadn't been home more than five minutes when Mama walked through the door. She was carrying a shopping bag and she was wearing what I call her shopping hat, which is a kind of floppy beige beret.

"How you doing, Little One?" she smiled, but she gave me a sharp look, too. "How's Fonny?"

"He's just the same. He's fine. He sends his love."

"Good. You see the lawyer?"

"Not today. I have to go on Monday—you know—after work."

"He been to see Fonny?"

"No."

She sighed and took off her hat, and put it on the TV set. I picked up the shopping bag and we walked into the kitchen. Mama started putting things away.

I half sat, half leaned, on the sink, and I watched her. Then, for a minute there, I got scared and my belly kind of turned over. Then, I realized that I'm into my third month, I've *got* to tell. Nothing shows yet, but one day Mama's going to give me another sharp look.

And then, suddenly, half leaning, half sitting there, watching her—she was at the refrigerator, she looked critically at a chicken and put it away, she was kind of humming under her breath, but the way you hum when your mind is concentrated on something, something painful, just about to come around the corner, just about to hit you—I suddenly had this feeling that she already knew, had known all along, had only been waiting for me to tell her.

I said, "Mama—?"

"Yeah, Little Bit?" Still humming.

But I didn't say anything. So, after a minute, she closed the refrigerator door and turned and looked at me.

I started to cry. It was her look.

She stood there for a minute. She came and put a hand on my forehead and then a hand on my shoulder. She said, "Come on in my room. Your Daddy and Sis be here soon."

We went into her room and sat down on the bed and Mama closed the door. She didn't touch me. She just sat very still. It was like she had to be very together because I had gone to pieces.

She said, "Tish, I declare. I don't think you got nothing to cry about." She moved a little. "You tell Fonny?"

"I just told him today. I figured I should tell him first."

"You did right. And I bet he just grinned all over his face, didn't he?"

I kind of stole a look at her and I laughed, "Yes. He sure did."

"You must—let's see—you about three months gone?"

"Almost."

"What you crying about?"

Then she did touch me, she took me in her arms and she rocked me and I cried.

She got me a handkerchief and I blew my nose. She walked to the window and she blew hers.

"Now, listen," she said, "you got enough on your mind without worrying about being a bad girl and all that jive-ass shit. I sure hope I raised you better than that. If you was a bad girl, you wouldn't be sitting on that bed, you'd long been turning tricks for the warden."

She came back to the bed and sat down. She seemed to be raking her mind for the right words.

"Tish," she said, "when we was first brought here, the white man he didn't give us no preachers to say words over us before we had our babies. And you and Fonny be together right now, married or not, wasn't for that same damn white man. So, let me tell you what you got to do. You got to think about that baby. You got to hold on to that baby, don't care what else happens or don't happen. *You* got to do that. Can't nobody else do that for you. And the rest of us, well, we going to hold on to you. And we going to get Fonny out. Don't you worry. I know it's hard —but don't you worry. And that baby be the best thing that ever happened to Fonny. He needs that baby. It going to give him a whole lot of courage."

She put one finger under my chin, a trick she has sometimes, and looked me in the eyes, smiling.

"Am I getting through to you, Tish?"

"Yes, Mama. Yes."

"Now, when your Daddy and Ernestine get home, we going to sit at the table together, and *I'll* make the family announcement. I think that might be easier, don't you?"

"Yes. Yes."

She got up from the bed.

"Take off them streets clothes and lie down for a minute. I'll come get you."

She opened the door.

"Yes, Mama—Mama?"

"Yes, Tish?"

"Thank you, Mama."

She laughed. "Well, Tish, daughter, I do not know what you thanking me for, but you surely more than welcome."

She closed the door and I heard her in the kitchen. I took off my coat and my shoes and lay back on the bed. It was the hour when darkness begins, when the sounds of the night begin.

The doorbell rang. I heard Mama yell, "Be right there!" and then she came into the room again. She was carrying a small water glass with a little whiskey in it.

"Here. Sit up. Drink this. Do you good."

Then she closed the bedroom door behind her and I heard her heels along the hall that leads to the front door. It was Daddy, he was in a good mood, I heard his laugh.

"Tish home yet?"

"She's taking a little nap inside. She was kind of beat."

"She see Fonny?"

"Yeah. She saw Fonny. She saw the inside of the Tombs, too. That's why I made her lie down."

"What about the lawyer?"

"She going to see him Monday."

Daddy made a sound, I heard the refrigerator door open and close, and he poured himself a beer.

"Where's Sis?"

"She'll be here. She had to work late."

"How much you think them damn lawyers is going to cost us, before this thing is over?"

"Joe, you know damn well ain't no point in asking me that question."

"Well. They sure got it made, the rotten motherfuckers."

"Amen to that."

By now, Mama had poured herself some gin and orange juice and was sitting at the table, opposite him. She was swinging her foot; she was thinking ahead.

"How'd it go today?"

"All right."

Daddy works on the docks. He doesn't go to sea anymore. *All right* means that he probably didn't have to curse out more than one or two people all day long, or threaten anybody with death.

Fonny gave Mama one of his first pieces of sculpture. This was almost two years ago. Something about it always makes me think of Daddy. Mama put it by itself on a small table in the living room. It's not very high, it's done in black wood. It's of a naked man with one hand at his forehead and the other half hiding his sex. The legs are long, very long, and very wide apart, and one foot seems planted, unable to move, and the whole motion of the figure is torment. It seemed a very strange figure for such a young kid to do, or, at least, it seemed strange until you thought about it. Fonny used to go to a vocational school where they teach kids to make all kinds of shitty, really useless things, like card tables and hassocks and chests of drawers which nobody's ever going to buy because who buys handmade furniture? The rich don't do it. They say the kids are dumb and so they're teaching them to work with their hands. Those kids aren't dumb. But the people who run these schools want to make sure that they don't get smart: they are really teaching the kids to be slaves. Fonny didn't go for it at all, and he split, taking most of the wood from the workshop with him. It took him about a week, tools one day, wood the next; but the wood was a problem because you can't put it in your pocket or under your coat; finally, he and a friend broke in the school after dark, damn near emptied the woodwork shop, and loaded the wood into the friend's brother's car. They hid some of the wood in the basement of a friendly janitor, and Fonny brought the tools to my house, and some of that wood is still under my bed.

Fonny had found something that he could do, that he wanted to do, and this saved him from the death that was waiting to overtake the children of our age. Though the death took many forms, though people died early in many different ways, the death itself was very simple and the cause was simple, too: as simple as a plague: the kids had been told that they weren't worth shit and everything they saw around them proved it. They struggled, they struggled, but they fell, like flies, and they congregated on the garbage heaps of their lives, like flies. And perhaps I clung to Fonny, perhaps Fonny saved *me* because he was just about the only boy I knew who wasn't fooling around with the needles or drinking cheap wine or mugging people or holding up stores—and he never got his hair conked: it just stayed nappy. He started working as a short-order cook in a barbecue joint, so he could eat, and he found a basement where he could work on his wood and he was at our house more often than he was at his own house.

At his house, there was always fighting. Mrs. Hunt couldn't stand Fonny, or Fonny's ways, and the two sisters sided with Mrs. Hunt—especially because, now, they were in terrible trouble. They had been raised to be married but there wasn't anybody around them good enough for them. They were really just ordinary Harlem girls, even though they'd made it as far as City College. But absolutely nothing was happening for them at City College—nothing: the brothers with degrees didn't want them; those who wanted their women black wanted them black; and those who wanted their women white wanted them white. So, there they were, and they blamed it all on Fonny. Between the mother's prayers, which were more like curses, and the sisters' tears, which were more like orgasms, Fonny didn't stand a chance. Neither was Frank a match for these three hags. He just got angry, and you can just about imagine the shouting that went on in that house. And Frank had started drinking. I couldn't blame him. And sometimes he came to our house, too, pretending that he was looking for Fonny. It was much worse for him than it was for Fonny; and he had lost the tailor shop and was working in the garment center. He had started to depend on Fonny now, the way Fonny had once depended on him. Neither of them, anyway, as you can see, had any other house they could go to. Frank went to bars, but Fonny didn't like bars.

That same passion which saved Fonny got him into trouble, and put him in jail. For, you see, he had found his center, his own center, inside him: and it showed. He wasn't anybody's nigger. And that's a crime, in this fucking free country. You're suppose to be *somebody's* nigger. And if you're nobody's nigger, you're a bad nigger: and

that's what the cops decided when Fonny moved downtown.

Ernestine has come in, with her bony self. I can hear
her teasing Daddy.

She works with kids in a settlement house way downtown—kids up to the age of fourteen or so, all colors, boys
and girls. It's very hard work, but she digs it—I guess if
she didn't dig it, she couldn't do it. It's funny about people.
When Ernestine was little she was as vain as vain could be.
She always had her hair curled and her dresses were always clean and she was always in front of that damn mirror, like she just could not believe how beautiful she was.
I hated her. Since she was nearly four years older than me,
she considered me beneath her notice. We fought like cats
and dogs, or maybe it was more like two bitches.

Mama tried not to worry too much about it. She figured
that Sis—*I* called her Sis as a way of calling her out of her
name and also, maybe, as a way of claiming her—was
probably cut out for show business, and would end up on
the stage. This thought did not fill her heart with joy: but
she had to remember, my mother, Sharon, that she had
once tried to be a singer.

All of a sudden, it almost seemed like from one day
to the next, all that changed. Sis got tall, for one thing, tall
and skinny. She took to wearing slacks and tying up her
hair and she started reading books like books were going
out of style. Whenever I'd come home from school and
she was there, she'd be curled up on something, or lying on
the floor, reading. She stopped reading newspapers. She
stopped going to the movies. "I don't need no more of the

white man's lying shit," she said. "He's fucked with my mind enough already." At the same time, she didn't become rigid or unpleasant and she didn't talk, not for a long time anyway, about what she read. She got to be much nicer to me. And her face began to change. It became bonier and more private, much more beautiful. Her long narrow eyes darkened with whatever it was they were beginning to see.

She gave up her plans for going to college, and worked for a while in a hospital. She met a little girl in that hospital, the little girl was dying, and, at the age of twelve, she was already a junkie. And this wasn't a black girl. She was Puerto Rican. And then Ernestine started working with children.

"Where's Jezebel?"

Sis started calling me Jezebel after I got my job at the perfume center of the department store where I work now. The store thought that it was very daring, very progressive, to give this job to a colored girl. I stand behind that damn counter all day long, smiling till my back teeth ache, letting tired old ladies smell the back of my hand. Sis claimed that I came home smelling like a Louisiana whore.

"She's home. She's lying down."

"She all right?"

"She's tired. She went to see Fonny."

"How's Fonny taking it?"

"Taking it."

"Lord. Let me make myself a drink. You want me to cook?"

"No. I'll get into the pots in a minute."

"She see Mr. Hayward?"

Arnold Hayward is the lawyer. Sis found him for me

through the settlement house, which has beeen forced, after all, to have some dealings with lawyers.

"No. She's seeing him on Monday, after work."

"You going with her?"

"I think I better."

"Yeah. I think so, too—Daddy, you better stop putting down that beer, you getting to be as big as a house.—And I'll call him from work, before you all get there.—You want a shot of gin in that beer, old man?"

"Just put it on the side, daughter dear, before I stand up."

"Stand up!—Here!"

"And tan your hide. You better listen to Aretha when she sings 'Respect.'—You know, Tish says she thinks that lawyer wants more money."

"Daddy, we paid him his retainer, that's why ain't none of us got no clothes. And I know we got to pay expenses. But he ain't supposed to get no more *money* until he brings Fonny to trial."

"He says it's a tough case."

"Shit. What's a lawyer for?"

"To make money," Mama said.

"Well. Anybody talk to the Hunts lately?"

"They don't want to know nothing about it, you know that. Mrs. Hunt and them two camellias is just in disgrace. And poor Frank ain't got no money."

"Well. Let's not talk too much about it in front of Tish. We'll work it out somehow."

"Shit. We got to work it out. Fonny's like one of us."

"He *is* one of us," said Mama.

I turned on the lights in Mama's bedroom, so they'd

know I was up, and I looked at myself in the mirror. I kind of patted my hair and I walked into the kitchen.

"Well," said Sis, "although I cannot say that your beauty rest did you a hell of a lot of good, I *do* admire the way you persevere."

Mama said that if we wanted to eat, we'd better get our behinds out of her kitchen, and so we went into the living room.

I sat on the hassock, leaning on Daddy's knee. Now, it was seven o'clock and the streets were full of noises. I felt very quiet after my long day, and my baby began to be real to me. I don't mean that it hadn't been real before; but, now, in a way, I was alone with it. Sis had left the lights very low. She put on a Ray Charles record and sat down on the sofa.

I listened to the music and the sounds from the streets and Daddy's hand rested lightly on my hair. And everything seemed connected—the street sounds, and Ray's voice and his piano and my Daddy's hand and my sister's silhouette and the sounds and the lights coming from the kitchen. It was as though we were a picture, trapped in time: this had been happening for hundreds of years, people sitting in a room, waiting for dinner, and listening to the blues. And it was as though, out of these elements, this patience, my Daddy's touch, the sounds of my mother in the kitchen, the way the light fell, the way the music continued beneath everything, the movement of Ernestine's head as she lit a cigarette, the movement of her hand as she dropped the match into the ashtray, the blurred human voices rising from the street, out of this rage and a steady, somehow triumphant sorrow, my baby was slowly being formed. I wondered if it would have Fonny's eyes. As someone had wondered, not, after all, so very long ago, about the eyes of Joseph, my father, whose hand rested on my head. What struck me suddenly, more than anything else, was something I knew but hadn't looked at: this was Fonny's baby and mine, we had made it together, it was both of us. I didn't know either of us very well. What would both of us be like? But this, somehow, made me think of Fonny and made me smile. My father rubbed his hand over my forehead. I thought of Fonny's touch, of Fonny, in my arms, his breath, his touch, his odor, his weight, that terrible and beautiful presence riding into me and his breath being snarled, as if by a golden thread, deeper and deeper in his throat as he rode—as he rode deeper and deeper not so much into me as into a kingdom which lay just behind his eyes. He worked on wood that way. He worked on stone that way. If I had never seen him work, I might never have known he loved me.

It's a miracle to realize that somebody loves you.

"Tish?"

Ernestine, gesturing with her cigarette.

"Yes."

"What time you seeing the lawyer on Monday?"

"After the six o'clock visit. I'll be there about seven. He says he's got to work late, anyway."

"If he says anything about more money, you tell him to call me, you hear?"

"I don't know what good that's going to do, if he wants more money, he wants more money——"

"You do like your sister tells you," Daddy said.

"He won't talk to you," Ernestine said, "the way he'll talk to me, can you dig it?"

"Yes," I said, finally, "I can dig it." But, for reasons I couldn't explain, something in her voice frightened me to death. I felt the way I'd felt all day, alone with my trouble. Nobody could help me, not even Sis. Because she was certainly determined to help me, I knew that. But maybe I realized that she was frightened, too, although she was trying to sound calm and tough. I realized that she knew a whole lot about it because of the kids downtown. I wanted to ask her how it worked. I wanted to ask her *if* it worked.

When there's nobody but us we eat in the kitchen, which is maybe the most important room in our house, the room where everything happens, where things begin and take their shape and end. Now, when supper was over that night, Mama went to the cupboard and came back with an old bottle, a bottle she's had for years, of very old French brandy. They came from her days as a singer, her days with the drummer. This was the last bottle, it hadn't been opened yet. She put the bottle on the table, in front of Joseph, and she said, "Open it." She got four glasses and then she stood there while he opened it. Ernestine and Joseph looked like they just couldn't guess what had got into Mama: but I knew what she was doing, and my heart jumped up.

Daddy got the bottle open. Mama said, "You the man of the house, Joe. Start pouring."

It's funny about people. Just before something happens, you almost know what it is. You *do* know what it is, I believe. You just haven't had the time—and now you *won't* have the time—to say it to yourself. Daddy's face changed in a way I can't describe. His face became as definite as stone, every line and angle suddenly seemed chiseled, and his eyes turned a blacker black. He was waiting—suddenly, helplessly—for what was already known to be translated, to enter reality, to be born.

Sis watched Mama with her eyes very calm, her eyes very long and narrow, smiling a little.

No one looked at me. I was there, then, for them, in a way that had nothing to do with me. I was there, then, for them, like Fonny was present, like my baby, just beginning now, out of a long, long sleep, to turn, to listen, to awaken, somewhere beneath my heart.

Daddy poured and Mama gave us each a glass. She looked at Joseph, then at Ernestine, then at me—she smiled at me.

"This is sacrament," she said, "and, no, I ain't gone crazy. We're drinking to a new life. Tish is going to have Fonny's baby." She touched Joseph. "Drink," she said.

Daddy wet his lips, staring at me. It was like no one could speak before he spoke. I stared at him. I didn't know what he was going to say. Joseph put his glass down. Then he picked it up again. He was trying to speak; he wanted to speak; but he couldn't. And he looked at me as if he was trying to find out something, something my face would tell him. A strange smile wavered just around his face, not yet *in* his face, and he seemed to be traveling backward and forward at once, in time. He said, "That's a hell of a note." Then he drank some more brandy, and he said, "Ain't you going to drink to the little one, Tish?" I swallowed a little brandy, and I coughed and Ernestine patted me on the back. Then, she took me in her arms. She had tears on her face. She smiled down at me—but she didn't say anything.

"How long this been going on?" Daddy asked.

"About three months," Mama said.

"Yeah. That's what I figured," said Ernestine, surprising me.

"Three months!" Daddy said: as though five months or two months would have made some kind of difference and made more sense.

"Since March," I said. Fonny had been arrested in March.

"While you two was running around looking at places, so you could get married," Daddy said. His face was full of questions, and he would have been able to ask these questions of his son—or, at least, I think that a black man can: but he couldn't ask these questions of his daughter. For a moment, I was almost angry, then I wasn't. Fathers and sons are one thing. Fathers and daughters are another.

It doesn't do to look too hard into this mystery, which is as far from being simple as it is from being safe. We don't know enough about ourselves. I think it's better to know that you don't know, that way you can grow with the mystery as the mystery grows in you. But, these days, of course, everybody knows everything, that's why so many people are so lost.

But I wondered how Frank would take the news that his son, Fonny, was about to be a father. Then I realized that the first thing everybody thought was, *But Fonny's in jail!* Frank would think that: that would be his first thought. Frank would think, if anything happens, my boy won't never see his baby. And Joseph thought, If anything happens, my little girl's baby won't have no father. Yes. That was the thought, unspoken, which stiffened the air in our kitchen. And I felt that I should say something. But

I was too tired. I leaned against Ernestine's shoulder. I had nothing to say.

"You sure you want this baby, Tish?" my father asked me.

"Oh, yes," I said, "and Fonny wants it, too! It's *our baby*," I said. "Don't you see? And it's not Fonny's fault that he is in jail, it's not as though he ran away, or anything. And—" this was the only way I could answer the questions he hadn't asked—"we've always been best friends, ever since we were little, you know that. And we'd be married now, if—if—!"

"Your father know that," Mama said. "He's only worried about you."

"Don't you go thinking I think you a bad girl, or any foolishness like that," Daddy said. "I just asked you that because you so young, that's all, and——"

"It's rough, but we'll make it," Ernestine said.

She knows Daddy better than I do. I think it's because she's felt since we were children that our Daddy maybe loved me more than he loves her. This isn't true, and she knows that now—people love different people in different ways—but it must have seemed that way to her when we were little. I look as though I just can't make it, she looks like can't nothing stop her. If you look helpless, people react to you in one way and if you look strong, or just come on strong, people react to you in another way, and, since you don't see what they see, this can be very painful. I think that's maybe why Sis was always in front of that damn mirror all the time, when we were kids. She was saying, *I don't care. I got me.* Of course, this only made her come on stronger than ever, which was the last effect she desired: but that's the way we are and that's how we can sometimes get so fucked up. Anyway, she's past all that. She knows who she is, or, at least, she knows who she damn well isn't; and since she's no longer terrified of uprisings in those forces which she lives with and has learned how to use and subdue, she can walk straight ahead into anything; and so she can cut Daddy off when he's talking—which I can't do. She moved away from me a little and put my glass in my hand. "Unbow your head, sister," she said, and raised her glass and touched mine. "Save the children," she said, very quietly, and drained her glass.

Mama said, "To the newborn," and Daddy said, "I hope it's a boy. That'd tickle old Frank to pieces, I bet." Then he looked at me. "Do you mind," he asked me, "if I'm the one to tell him, Tish?"

I said, "No. I don't mind."

"Well, then!" he said, grinning, "maybe I'll go on over there now."

"Maybe you better phone first," Mama said. "He don't stay home a whole lot, you know."

"I sure would like to be the one to tell them sisters," said Ernestine.

Mama laughed, and said, "Joe, why don't you just call up and ask them all over here? Hell, it's Saturday night and it ain't late and we still got a lot of brandy in the bottle. And, now that I think about it, it's really the best way to do it."

"That's all right with you, Tish?" Daddy asked me.

"It's got to be done," I said.

So, Daddy stood up, after watching me for a moment, and walked into the living room, to the phone. He could have used the wall phone in the kitchen but he had that kind of grim smile on his face which he has when he knows he's got business to take care of and when he wants to make sure you know enough to stay out of it.

We listened to him dialing the number. That was the only sound in the house. Then, we could hear the phone at the other end, ringing. Daddy cleared his throat.

We heard, "Mrs. Hunt—? Oh. Good evening, Mrs. Hunt. This is Joe Rivers talking. I just wondered if I could please speak to Frank, if he's home—Thank you, Mrs. Hunt."

Mama grunted, and winked at Sis.

"Hey!—How you doing? Yeah, this is Joe. I'm all right, man, hanging in, you know—say, listen—oh, yeah, Tish saw him this afternoon, man, he's fine.—Yeah—As a matter of *fact*, man, we got a whole *lot* to talk about, that's why I'm calling you.—I can't go into all that over the phone, man. Listen. It concerns all of us—Yes.—Listen. Don't give me all that noise. You all just jump in the car and come on over here. Now. Yeah. That's right. *Now* —What?—Look, man, I said it concerns *all* of us.—Ain't nobody here dressed neither, she can come in her fucking *bathrobe* for all I care.—Shut up, you sick mother. I'm try- ing to be nice. Shit. Don't be bitter—Just dump her in the back seat of the *car,* and *drive,* now, come on, man. This is *serious.*—Hey. Pick up a six pack, I'll pay you when you get here.—Yeah.—Look. Will you hang up this phone and get your ass, I mean your *collective* ass, on over here, man? —In a minute. Bye."

He came back into the kitchen, smiling.

"Mrs. Hunt is getting dressed," he said, and sat down.

Then he looked over at me. He smiled—a wonderful smile. "Come on over here, Tish," he said, "and sit down on your Daddy's knee."

I felt like a princess. I swear I did. He took me in his arms and settled me on his lap and kissed me on the forehead and rubbed his hand, at first roughly and then very gently through my hair. "You're a good girl, Clementine," he said. "I'm proud of you. Don't you forget that."

"She ain't going to forget it," said Ernestine. "I'll whip her ass."

"But she's *pregnant!*" Mama cried, and took a sip of her cognac and then we all cracked up. My father's chest shook with laughter, I felt his chest rising and falling between my shoulder blades, and this laughter contained a furious joy, an unspeakable relief: in spite of all that hung above our heads. I was his daughter, all right: I had found someone to love and I was loved and he was released and verified. That child in my belly was also, after all, *his* child, too, for there would have been no Tish if there had been no Joseph. Our laughter in that kitchen, then, was our helpless response to a miracle. That baby was our baby, it was on its way, my father's great hand on my belly held it and warmed it: in spite of all that hung above our heads, that child was promised safety. Love had sent it, spinning out of us, to us. Where that might take us, no one knew: but, now, my father, Joe, was ready. In a deadlier and more profound way than his daughters were, this child was the seed of his loins. And no knife could cut him off from life until that child was born. And I almost felt the child feel this, that child which had no movement yet—I almost felt it leap against my father's hand, kicking upward against my ribs. Something in me sang and hummed and then I felt the deadly morning sickness and I dropped my head onto my father's shoulder. He held me. It was very silent. The nausea passed.

Sharon watched it all, smiling, swinging her foot, thinking ahead. Again, she winked at Ernestine.

"Shall we," asked Ernestine, rising, "dress for Mrs. Hunt?"—and we all cracked up again.

"Look. We got to be nice," said Joseph.

"We'll be nice," said Ernestine. "Lord knows we'll be nice. You *raised* us right. You just didn't never buy us no *clothes.*" She said to Mama, "But Mrs. Hunt, now, and them sisters, they got *wardrobes*—! Ain't no sense in trying to compete with them," she said despairingly, and sat down.

"I didn't run no tailor shop," said Joseph, and looked into my eyes, and smiled.

The very first time Fonny and I made love was strange. It was strange because we had both seen it coming. That is not exactly the way to put it. We had *not* seen it coming. Abruptly, it was there: and then we knew that it had always been there, waiting. We had not seen the moment. But the moment had seen us, from a long ways off—sat there, waiting for us—utterly free, the moment, playing cards, hurling thunderbolts, cracking spines, tremendously waiting for us, dawdling home from school, to keep our appointment.

Look. I dumped water over Fonny's head and scrubbed Fonny's back in the bathtub, in a time that seems a long time ago now. I swear I don't remember seeing his sex, and yet, of course, I must have. We never played doctor—and yet, I had played this rather terrifying game with other boys and Fonny had certainly played with other girls, and boys. I don't remember that we ever had any curiosity concerning each other's bodies at all—due to the cunning of that watching moment which knew we were approaching. Fonny loved me too much, we needed each other too much. We were a part of each other, flesh of each other's flesh—which meant that we so took each other for granted that we never thought of the flesh. He had legs, and I had legs—that wasn't all we knew but that was all we used. They brought us up the stairs and down the stairs and, always, to each other.

But that meant that there had never been any occasion for shame between us. I was flatchested for a very long time. I'm only beginning to have real breasts now, because of the baby, in fact, and I still don't have any hips. Fonny liked me so much that it didn't occur to him that he loved me. I liked him so much that no other boy was real to me. I didn't see them. I didn't know what this meant. But the waiting moment, which had spied us on the road, and which was waiting for us, knew.

Fonny kissed me good-night one night when he was twenty-one and I eighteen, and I felt his sex jerk against me and he moved away. I said good-night and I ran up the stairs and he ran down the stairs. And I couldn't sleep that night: something had happened. And he didn't come around, I didn't see him, for two or three weeks. That was when he did that wood figure which he gave to Mama.

The day he gave it to her was a Saturday. After he gave the figure to Mama we left the house and we walked around. I was so happy to see him, after so long, that I was ready to cry. And everything was different. I was walking through streets I had never seen before. The faces around me, I had never seen. We moved in a silence which was music from everywhere. Perhaps for the first time in my life, I was happy and knew that I was happy, and Fonny held me by the hand. It was like that Sunday morning, so long ago, when his mother had carried us to church.

Fonny had no part in his hair now—it was heavy all over his head. He had no blue suit, he had no suit at all. He was wearing an old black and red lumber jacket and old gray corduroy pants. His heavy shoes were scuffed; and he smelled of fatigue.

He was the most beautiful person I had seen in all my life.

He has a slow, long-legged, bowlegged walk. We walked down the stairs to the subway train, he holding me by the hand. The train, when it came, was crowded, and he put an arm around me for protection. I suddenly looked up into his face. No one can describe this, I really shouldn't try. His face was bigger than the world, his eyes deeper than the sun, more vast than the desert, all that had ever happened since time began was in his face. He smiled: a little smile. I saw his teeth: I saw exactly where the missing tooth had been, that day he spat in my mouth. The train rocked, he held me closer, and a kind of sigh I'd never heard before stifled itself in him.

It's astounding the first time you realize that a stranger has a body—the realization that he has a body makes him a stranger. It means that you have a body, too. You will live with this forever, and it will spell out the language of your life.

And it was absolutely astonishing to me to realize that I was a virgin. I really was. I suddenly wondered how. I wondered why. But it was because I had always, without ever thinking about it, known that I would spend my life with Fonny. It simply had not entered my mind that my life could do anything else. This meant that I was not merely a virgin; I was still a child.

We got off the train at Sheridan Square, in the Village. We walked east along West Fourth Street. Since it was Saturday, the streets were crowded, unbalanced with the weight of people. Most of them were young, they had to be young, you could see that: but they didn't seem young to me. They frightened me, I could not, then, have said why. I thought it was because they knew so much more than me. And they did. But, in another way, which I'm only beginning to understand now, they didn't. They had it all together: the walk, the sound, the laughter, the untidy clothes —clothes which were copies of a poverty as unimaginable for them as theirs was inexpressibly remote from me. There were many blacks and white together: it was hard to tell which was the imitation. They were so free that they believed in nothing; and didn't realize that this illusion was their only truth and that they were doing exactly as they had been told.

Fonny looked over at me. It was getting to be between six and seven.

"You all right?"

"Sure. You?"

"You want to eat down here or you want to wait till we get back uptown or you want to go to the movies or you want a little wine or a little pot or a beer or a cup of coffee? Or you just want to walk a little more before you make up your mind?" He was grinning, warm and sweet, and pulling a little against my hand, and swinging it.

I was very happy, but I was uncomfortable, too. I had never been uncomfortable with him before.

"Let's walk to the park first." I somehow wanted to stay outside awhile.

"Okay." And he still had that funny smile on his face, like something wonderful had just happened to him and no one in the world knew anything about it yet, but him. But he would tell somebody soon, and it would be me.

We crossed crowded Sixth Avenue, all kinds of people out hunting for Saturday night. But nobody looked at us, because we were together and we were both black. Later, when I had to˙walk these streets alone, it was different, the people were different, and I was certainly no longer a child.

"Let's go this way," he said, and we started down Sixth Avenue, toward Bleecker Street. We started down Bleecker and Fonny stared for a moment through the big window of the San Remo. There was no one in there that he knew, and the whole place looked tired and discouraged, as though wearily about to shave and get dressed for a terrible evening. The people under the weary light were veterans of indescribable wars. We kept walking. The streets were very crowded now, with youngsters, black and white, and cops. Fonny held his head a little higher, and his grip tightened on my hand. There were lots of kids on the sidewalk, before the crowded coffee shop. A jukebox was playing Aretha's "That's Life." It was strange. Everyone was in the streets, moving and talking, like people do everywhere, and yet none of it seemed to be friendly. There was something hard and frightening about it: the way that something which looks real, but isn't, can send you screaming out of your mind. It was just like scenes uptown, in a way, with the older men and women sitting on the stoops; with small children running up and down the block, cars moving slowly through this maelstrom, the cop car parked on the corner, with the two cops in it, other cops swaggering slowly along the sidewalk. It was like scenes uptown, in a way, but with something left out, or something put in, I couldn't tell: but it was a scene that frightened me. One had to make one's way carefully here, for all these people were blind. We were jostled, and Fonny put his arm around my shoulder. We passed Minetta Tavern, crossed Minetta Lane, passed the newspaper stand on the next corner, and crossed diagonally into the park, which seemed to huddle in the shadow of the heavy new buildings of NYU and the high new apartment buildings on the east and the north. We passed the men who had been playing chess in the lamplight for generations, and people walking their dogs, and young men with bright hair and very tight pants, who looked quickly at Fonny and resignedly at me. We sat down on the stone edge of the dry fountain, facing the arch. There were lots of people around us, but I still felt this terrible lack of friendliness.

"I've slept in this park sometimes," said Fonny. "It's not a good idea." He lit a cigarette. "You want a cigarette?"

"Not now." I had wanted to stay outside for a while. But now I wanted to get in, away from these people, out of the park. "Why did you sleep in the park?"

"It was late. I didn't want to wake up my folks. And I didn't have no bread."

"You could have come to *our* house."

"Well. I didn't want to wake up none of *you* neither." He put his cigarettes back into his pocket. "But I got me a pad down here now. I'll show it to you later, you want to see it." He looked at me. "You getting cold and tired, I'll get you something to eat, okay?"

"Okay. You got money?"

"Yeah, I hustled me up a little change, baby. Come on."

We did a lot of walking that night, because now Fonny took me way west, along Greenwich, past the Women's House of Detention, to this little Spanish restaurant, where Fonny knew all the waiters and they all knew him. And these people were different from the people in the street, their smiles were different, and I felt at home. It was Saturday, but it was early, and they put us at a small table in the back—not as though they didn't want people to see us but as though they were glad we'd come and wanted us to stay as long as possible.

I hadn't had much experience in restaurants, but Fonny had; he spoke a little Spanish, too, and I could see that the waiters were teasing him about me. And then I remembered, as I was being introduced to our waiter, Pedrocito—which meant that he was the youngest—that we had been called on the block, Romeo and Juliet, people had always teased us. But not like this.

Some days, days I took off, when I could see him in the middle of the day, and then, again, at six, I'd walk from Centre Street to Greenwich, and I'd sit in the back and they'd feed me, very silently and carefully making sure that I ate—something; more than once, Luisito, who had just arrived from Spain and who could barely speak English, took away the cold omelette which he had cooked and which I had not touched and brought me a new, hot one, saying, "Señorita—? *Por favor.* He and the *muchacho* need your strength. He will not forgive us, if we let you starve. We are his friends. He trusts us. You must trust us, too." He would pour me a little red wine. "Wine is good. *Slow*-ly." I would take a sip. He would smile, but he would not move until I began to eat. Then, "It will be a boy," he said, and grinned and moved away. They got me through many and many a terrible day. They were the very nicest people I had met in all New York; they cared. When the going got rough, when I was heavy, with Joseph, and Frank, and Sharon working, and Ernestine in battle, they would arrange to have errands in the neighborhood of the Tombs, and, as though it were the most natural thing in the world—which it was, for them—drive me to their restaurant, and then they would drive me back down for the six o'clock visit. I will never forget them, never: they knew.

But on this particular Saturday night, we did not know; Fonny did not know, and we were happy, all of us. I had one margherita, though we all knew that this was against the goddam motherfucking shit-eating *law,* and Fonny had a whiskey because at twenty-one you have a legal right to drink. His hands are big. He took my hands and put his hands in mine. "I want to show you something later," he said. I could not tell whose hands were trembling, which hands were holding. "Okay," I said. He had ordered paella and when it came we unjoined our hands and Fonny, elaborately, served me. "Next time it's your turn," he said, and we laughed and began to eat. And we had wine. And there were candles. And other people came, looking at us strangely, but, "We know the cats who own the joint," Fonny said, and we laughed again, and we were safe.

I had never seen Fonny outside of the world in which I moved. I had seen him with his father and his mother and his sisters, and I had seen him with us. But I'm not sure, now that I think about it, that I had ever really seen him with *me:* not until this moment when we were leaving the restaurant and all the waiters were laughing and talking with him, in Spanish and in English, and Fonny's face opened in a way I'd never seen it open and that laugh of his came rumbling up from his balls, from *their* balls— I had certainly never seen him, anyway, in the world in which *he* moved. Perhaps it was only now that I saw him with me, for he was turned away from me, laughing, but he was holding on to my hand. He was a stranger to me, but joined. I had never seen him with other men. I had never seen the love and respect that men can have for each other.

I've had time since to think about it. I think that the first time a woman sees this—though I was not yet a woman—she sees it, first of all, only because she loves the man: she could not possibly see it otherwise. It can be a very great revelation. And, in this fucked up time and place, many women, perhaps most women, feel, in this warmth and energy, a threat. They think that they feel locked out. The truth is that they sense themselves in the presence, so to speak, of a language which they cannot decipher and therefore cannot manipulate, and, however they make a thing about it, so far from being locked out, are appalled by the apprehension that they are, in fact, forever locked in. Only a man can see in the face of a woman the girl she was. It is a secret which can be revealed only to a particular man, and, then, only at his insistence. But men have no secrets, except from women, and never grow up in the way that women do. It is very much harder, and it takes much longer, for a man to grow up, and he could never do it at all without women. This is a mystery which can terrify and immobilize a woman, and it is always the key to her deepest distress. She must watch and guide, but he must lead, and he will always appear to be giving far more of his real attention to his comrades than he is giving to her. But that noisy, outward openness of men with each other enables them to deal with the silence and secrecy of women, that silence and secrecy which contains the truth of a man, and releases it. I suppose that the root of the resentment—a resentment which hides a bottomless terror —has to do with the fact that a woman is tremendously controlled by what the man's imagination makes of her— literally, hour by hour, day by day; so she becomes a woman. But a man exists in his own imagination, and can never be at the mercy of a woman's.—Anyway, in this fucked up time and place, the whole thing becomes ridiculous when you realize that women are supposed to be more imaginative than men. This is an idea dreamed up by men, and it proves exactly the contrary. The truth is that dealing with the reality of men leaves a woman very little time, or need, for imagination. And you can get very fucked up, here, once you take seriously the notion that a man who is not afraid to trust his imagination (which is all that men have ever trusted) is effeminate. It says a lot about this country, because, of course, if all you want to do is make money, the very last thing you need is imagination. Or women, for that matter: or men.

"A very good night, Señorita!" cried the patriarch of the house, and Fonny and I were in the streets again, walking.

"Come and see my pad," said Fonny. "It ain't far."

It was getting to be between ten and eleven.

"Okay," I said.

I didn't know the Village, then—I do, now; then, everything was surprising. Where we were walking was much darker and quieter than on Sixth Avenue. We were near the river, and we were the only people in the street. I would have been afraid to walk this street alone.

I had the feeling that I maybe should call home, and I started to say this to Fonny, but I didn't.

His pad was in a basement on Bank Street. We stopped beside a low, black metal railing, with spikes. Fonny opened a gate, very quietly. We walked down four steps, we turned left, facing a door. There were two windows to the right of us. Fonny put his key in the lock, and the door swung inside. There was a weak yellow light above us. Fonny pushed me in before him and closed the door behind us and led me a few paces down a dark, narrow hall. He opened another door, and switched on the light.

It was a small, low room, those were the windows facing the gate. It had a fireplace. Just off the room was a tiny kitchenette and a bathroom. There was a shower; there wasn't any bathtub. In the room, there was a wooden stool and a couple of hassocks and a large wooden table and a small one. On the small table, there were a couple of empty beer cans and on the large table, tools. The room smelled of wood and there was raw wood all over the room. In the far corner, there was a mattress on the floor, covered with a Mexican shawl. There were Fonny's pencil sketches pinned on the wall, and a photograph of Frank.

We were to spend a long time in this room: our lives.

When the doorbell rang, it was Ernestine who went to the door, and Mrs. Hunt who entered first. She was dressed in something which looked very stylish until you looked at it. It was brown, it was shiny, it made one think of satin; and it had somehow white lace fringes at the knees, I think, and the elbows, and—I think—at the waist; and she was wearing a kind of scoop hat, an upside down coal scuttle, which hardened her hard brow.

She was wearing heels, she was gaining weight. She was fighting it, not successfully. She was frightened: in spite of the power of the Holy Ghost. She entered smiling, not quite knowing at what, or at whom, being juggled, so to speak, between the scrutiny of the Holy Ghost and her unsteady recollection of her mirror. And something in the way that she walked in and held out her hand, something in that smile of hers, which begged for mercy at the same time that it could not give it, made her quite wonderful for me. She was a woman I had never seen before. Fonny had been in her belly. She had carried him.

Behind her were the sisters, who were quite another matter. Ernestine, very hearty and upbeat at the door ("Only way to get to see you people is to call an emergency summit meeting! Now, don't you know that ain't right? Come on *in* this house!") had shuttled Mrs. Hunt past her, into Sharon's orbit: and Sharon, full of grace, delivered her, not quite, to Joseph, who had his arm around me. Something in the way my father held me and something in his smile frightened Mrs. Hunt. But I began to see that she had always been frightened.

Though the sisters were Fonny's sisters, I had never thought of them as his sisters. Well. That's not true. If they had not been Fonny's sisters, I would never have noticed them at all. Because they were his sisters, and I knew that they didn't really like Fonny, I hated them. *They* didn't hate *me*. They didn't hate anybody, and that was what was wrong with them. They smiled at an invisible host of stricken lovers as they entered our living room, and Adrienne, the oldest, who was twenty-seven, and Sheila, who was twenty-four, went out of their way to be very sweet with raggedy-assed me, just like the missionaries had told them. All they really saw was that big black hand of my father's which held them at the waist—of course, my Daddy was really holding *me* at the waist, but it was somehow like it was them. They did not know whether they disapproved of its color, its position, or its shape: but they certainly disapproved of its power of touch. Adrienne was too old for what she was wearing, and Sheila was too young. Behind them, here came Frank, and my father loosened his hold on me a little. We clattered and chattered into the living room.

Mr. Hunt looked very tired, but he still had that smile. He sat down on the sofa, near Adrienne, and he said, "So you saw my big-headed boy today, did you?"

"Yes. He's fine. He sends his love."

"They ain't giving him too hard a time?—I just ask

you like that because, you know, he might say things to you he wouldn't say to me."

"Lovers' secrets," said Adrienne, and crossed her legs, and smiled.

I didn't see any reason at all to deal with Adrienne, at least not yet; neither did Mr. Hunt, who kept watching me.

I said, "Well. He hates it, you can see that. And he should. But he's very strong. And he's doing a lot of reading and studying." I looked at Adrienne. "He'll be all right. But we have to get him out of there."

Frank was about to say something when Sheila said, sharply, "If he'd done his reading and studying when he should have, he wouldn't be *in* there."

I started to say something, but Joseph said, quickly, "You bring that six-pack, man? Or, I got some gin and we got whiskey and we got some brandy." He grinned. "Ain't got no Thunderbird, though." He turned to Mrs. Hunt. "I'm sure you ladies won't mind—?"

Mrs. Hunt smiled. "Mind? Frank does not care if we *mind*. He will go right on and do what pleases *him*. He ain't never thought about nobody else."

"Mrs. Hunt," said Sharon, "what can I get you, sugar? I can offer you some tea, or coffee—and we got ice cream—and Coca-Cola."

"—and Seven-Up," said Ernestine. "I can make you a kind of ice-cream soda. Come on, Sheila, you want to help me? Sit down, Mama. We'll get it together."

She dragged Sheila into the kitchen.

Mama sat down next to Mrs. Hunt.

"Lord," she said, "the time sure flies. We ain't hardly seen each other since this trouble started."

"Don't say a *word*. I have been running myself *sick*, all up and down the Bronx, trying to get the very best legal advice I can *find*—from some of the people I used to work for, you know—one of them is a city *council*man and he knows just *everybody* and he can *pull* some strings—people just *got* to listen to him, you know. But it's been taking up *all* of my time and the doctor says I *must* be careful, he says I'm putting an awful strain on my heart. He says, Mrs. Hunt, you got to remember, don't care how much that boy wants his freedom, he wants his mother, too. But, look like, it don't matter to me. I ain't worried about *me*. The *Lord* holds *me* up. I just pray and pray and pray that the Lord will bring my boy to the light. That's all I pray for, every day and every night. And then, sometimes I think that maybe this is the *Lord's* way of making my boy think on his sins and surrender his soul to Jesus—"

"You might be right," said Sharon. "The Lord sure works in mysterious ways."

"Oh, *yes!*" said Mrs. Hunt. "Now, He may *try* you. But He ain't never left none of His children alone."

"What you think," Sharon asked, "of the lawyer, Mr. Hayward, that Ernestine found?"

"I haven't seen him yet. I just have not had time to get downtown. But I know Frank saw him——"

"What do you think, Frank?" Sharon asked.

Frank shrugged. "It's a white boy who's been to a law school and he got them degrees. Well, you know. I ain't got to tell you what that means: it don't mean shit."

"Frank, you're talking to a woman," said Mrs. Hunt.

"I'm hip, and it's a mighty welcome change—like I was saying, it don't mean shit and I ain't sure we're going to stay with him. On the other hand, as white boys go, he's not so bad. He's not as full of shit now, because he's hungry, as he may be later, when he's full. Man," he said to Joseph, "you know I don't want my boy's life in the hands of these white, ball-less motherfuckers. I swear to Christ, I'd rather be boiled alive. That's my only son, man, *my only son.* But we all in the hands of white men and I know some very hincty black cats I wouldn't trust, neither."

"But I keep trying to tell you, I keep trying to *tell* you," cried Mrs. Hunt, "that it's that negative attitude which is so dangerous! You're so full of *hate!* If you give people hatred, they will give it back to you! Every time I hear you talk this way, my heart breaks and I tremble for my son, sitting in a dungeon which only the love of God can bring him out of—Frank, if you love your son, give up this hatred, give it up. It will fall on your son's head, it will kill him."

"Frank's not talking hatred, Mrs. Hunt," Sharon said. "He's just telling the truth about life in this country, and it's only natural for him to be upset."

"I trust in God," said Mrs. Hunt. "I know He cares for me."

"I don't know," Frank said, "how God expects a man to act when his son is in trouble. *Your* God crucified *His* son and was probably glad to get rid of him, but I ain't like that. I ain't hardly going out in the street and kiss the first white cop I see. But I'll be a *very* loving motherfucker the day my son walks out of that hellhole, free. I'll be a *loving* motherfucker when I hold my son's head between my hands again, and look into his eyes. Oh! I'll be *full* of love, *that* day!" He rose from the sofa, and walked over to his wife. "And if it don't go down like that, you can bet I'm going to blow some heads off. And if you say a word to me about that Jesus you been making it with all these years, I'll blow your head off first. You was making it with that white Jew bastard when you should have been with your son."

Mrs. Hunt put her head in her hands, and Frank slowly crossed the room again, and sat down.

Adrienne looked at him and she started to speak, but she didn't. I was sitting on the hassock, near my father. Adrienne said, "Mr. Rivers, exactly what is the purpose of this meeting? You haven't called us all the way over here just to watch my father insult my mother?"

"Why not?" I said. "It's Saturday night. You can't tell what people won't do, if they get bored enough. Maybe we just invited you over to liven things up."

"I can believe," she said, "that you're that malicious. But I can't believe you're that stupid."

"I haven't seen you *twice* since your brother went to jail," I said, "and I ain't *never* seen you down at the Tombs. Fonny told me he saw you once, and you was in a hurry then. And you ain't said a word about it on your job, I bet—have you? And you ain't said a word about it to none of them white-collars ex-antipoverty-program pimps and hustlers and faggots you run with, have you? And you sitting on that sofa right now, thinking you finer than Elizabeth Taylor, and all upset because you got some half-honky chump waiting for you somewhere and you done had to take time out to find out something about your brother." Mrs. Hunt was staring at me with terrible eyes. A cold bitter smile played on Frank's lips: he looked down.

Adrienne looked at me from a great distance, adding one more tremendous black mark against her brother's name, and, finally, as I had known all along she wished to do, lit a cigarette. She blew the smoke carefully and delicately into the air, and seemed to be resolving, in silence, that she would never again, for *any* reason, allow herself to be trapped among people so unspeakably inferior to herself.

Sheila and Ernestine reentered, Sheila looking rather frightened, Ernestine looking grimly pleased. She served Mrs. Hunt her ice cream, set down a Coke near Adrienne, gave Joseph a beer, gave Frank a Seven-Up, with gin, gave Sheila a Coke, gave Sharon a Seven-Up, with gin, gave me a brandy, and took a highball for herself. "Happy landings," she said cheerfully, and she sat down and everybody else sat down.

There was, then, this funny silence: and everyone was staring at me. I felt Mrs. Hunt's eyes, more malevolent, more frightened, than ever. She was leaning forward, one hand tight on the spoon buried in her ice cream. Sheila looked terrified. Adrienne's lips curled in a contemptuous smile, and she leaned forward to speak, but her father's hand, hostile, menacing, rose to check her. She leaned back. Frank leaned forward.

My news was, after all, for him. And, looking at him, I said, "I called this summit meeting. I had Daddy ask you all to come over so I could tell you what I had to tell Fonny this afternoon. Fonny's going to be a father. We're going to have a baby."

Frank's eyes left mine, to search my father's. Both men then went away from us, sitting perfectly still, on the chair, on the sofa: they went away together, and they made a strange journey. Frank's face, on this journey, was awful, in the Biblical sense. He was picking up stones and putting them down, his sight forced itself to stretch itself, beyond horizons he had never dreamed of. When he returned, still in company with my father, his face was very peaceful. "You and me going to go out and get drunk," he told Joseph. Then he grinned, looking, almost, just like Fonny, and he said, "I'm glad, Tish. I'm mighty glad."

"And who," asked Mrs. Hunt, "is going to be responsible for this baby?"

"The father and the mother," I said.

Mrs. Hunt stared at me.

"You can bet," Frank said, "that it won't be the Holy Ghost."

Mrs. Hunt stared at Frank, then rose, and started walking toward me; walking very slowly, and seeming to hold her breath. I stood up, and moved to the center of the room, holding mine.

"I guess you call your lustful action love," she said. "I don't. I always knew that you would be the destruction of my son. You have a demon in you—I always knew it. My God caused me to know it many a year ago. The Holy Ghost will cause that child to shrivel in your womb. But my son will be forgiven. *My* prayers will save him."

She was ridiculous and majestic; she was testifying. But Frank laughed and walked over to her, and, with the back of his hand, knocked her down. Yes. She was on the floor, her hat way on the back of her head and her dress up above her knees and Frank stood over her. She did not make a sound, nor did he.

"Her *heart!*" murmured Sharon; and Frank laughed again.

He said, "I think you'll find it's still pumping. But I wouldn't call it a heart." He turned to my father. "Joe, let the women take care of her, and come with me." And, as my father hesitated, "Please. Please, Joe. Come on."

"Go on with him," Sharon said. "Go on."

Sheila knelt beside her mother. Adrienne stubbed out her cigarette in the ashtray, and stood up. Ernestine came out of the bathroom with rubbing alcohol and knelt beside Sheila. She poured the alcohol onto the cotton and rubbed Mrs. Hunt's temples and forehead, carefully taking the hat completely off and handing it to Sheila.

"Go on, Joe," said Sharon. "We don't need you here."

The two men walked out, the door closed behind them, and now there were these six women who had to deal with each other, if only for a moment. Mrs. Hunt slowly stood up and moved to her chair and sat down. And before she could say anything, I said, "That was a terrible thing you said to me. It was the most terrible thing I've heard in all my life."

"My father didn't have to slap her," said Adrienne. "She *does* have a weak heart."

"She got a weak head," said Sharon. She said to Mrs. Hunt, "The Holy Ghost done softened your brain, child. Did you forget it was Frank's grandchild you was cursing? And of course it's *my* grandchild, too. I know some men and some women would have cut that weak heart out of your body and gladly gone to hell to pay for it. You want some tea, or something? You really ought to have some brandy, but I reckon you too holy for that."

"I don't think you have the right to sneer at my mother's faith," said Sheila.

"Oh, don't give me that bullshit," Ernestine said. "You

so shamed you got a Holy Roller for a mother, you don't know what to do. You don't sneer. You just say it shows she's got 'soul,' so other people won't think it's catching—and also so they'll see what a bright, bright girl *you* are. You make me sick."

"*You* make *me* sick," said Adrienne. "Maybe my mother didn't say it exactly like she *should* have said it—after all, she's very upset! And she *does* have soul! And what do you funky niggers think *you've* got? She only asked one question, *really*—" She put up one hand to keep Ernestine from interrupting her—"She said, Who's going to raise this baby? And who *is*? Tish ain't got no education and God knows she ain't got nothing else and Fonny ain't *never* been worth a damn. You know that yourself. Now. Who *is* going to take care of this baby?"

"*I* am," I said, "you dried up yellow cunt, and you keep on talking, I'm going to take mighty good care of *you*."

She put her hands on her hips, the fool, and Ernestine moved between us, and said, very sweetly, "Adrienne? Baby? May I tell you something, lumps? Sweetie? Sweetie-pie?" She put one hand very lightly against Adrienne's cheek. Adrienne quivered but did not move. Ernestine let her hand rest and play for a moment. "Oh, sugar. From the very first day I laid eyes on your fine person, I got hung up on your Adam's apple. I been dreaming about it. You know what I mean—? When you get hung up on something? You ain't never really been hung up on anything or anybody, have you? You ain't never watched your Adam's apple move, have you? *I* have. I'm watching it right now. Oh. It's delicious. I just can't tell, sweetie, if I want to tear it out with my fingers or my teeth—ooh!—or carve it out, the way you carve a stone from a peach. It is a thing of *beauty*. Can you dig where I'm coming from, sugar?—But if you touch my sister, I'm going to have to make up my mind pretty quick. So"—she moved away from Adrienne—"touch her. Go on, please. Take these chains from my heart and set me free."

"I knew we shouldn't have come," Sheila said. "I knew it."

Ernestine stared at Sheila until Sheila was forced to raise her eyes. Then, Ernestine laughed, and said, "My. I must have a dirty mind, Sheila. I didn't know that you could even *say* that word."

Then real hatred choked off the air. Something bottomless occurred which had nothing to do with what seemed to be occurring in the room. I suddenly felt sorry for the sisters—but Ernestine didn't. She stood where she stood, one hand on her waist, one hand hanging free, moving only her eyes. She was wearing gray slacks and an old blouse and her hair was untidy on her head and she wore no makeup. She was smiling. Sheila looked as though she could hardly breathe or stand, as though she wanted to run to her mother, who had not moved from her chair. Adrienne, whose hips were wide, wore a white blouse and a black, flaring, pleated skirt and a short, tight, black jacket and low heels. Her hair was parted in the middle and tied with a white ribbon at the nape of her neck. Her hands were no longer on her hips. Her skin, which was just a shade too dark to be high yellow, had darkened and mottled. Her forehead seemed covered with oil. Her eyes had darkened with her skin and the skin was rejecting the makeup by denying it any moisture. One saw that she was not really very pretty, that the face and the body would coarsen and thicken with time.

"Come," she said to Sheila, "away from these foul-mouthed people," and she had a certain dignity as she said it.

They both walked to their mother, who was, I could suddenly see, the witness to, and guardian of their chastity.

Mrs. Hunt rose, then, oddly peaceful.

"I sure hope," she said, "that you're pleased with the way you raised your daughters, Mrs. Rivers."

Sharon was peaceful, too, but there was a kind of startled wonder in it: she stared at Mrs. Hunt and said nothing. And Mrs. Hunt added, "These girls won't be bringing *me* no bastards to feed, I can guarantee you that."

"But the child that's coming," said Sharon, after a moment, "is your grandchild. I don't understand you. It's your *grandchild*. What difference does it make how it gets here? The child ain't got nothing to do with that—don't none of us have nothing to do with *that!*"

"That child," said Mrs. Hunt, and she looked at me for a moment, then started for the door, Sharon watching her all the while, "that child——"

I let her get to the door. My mother moved, but as though in a dream, to swing the locks; but I got there before her; I put my back against the door. Adrienne and Sheila were behind their mother.

Sharon and Ernestine did not move.

"That child," I said, "is in my belly. Now, you raise your knee and kick it out—or with them high heel shoes. You don't want this child? Come on and kill it now. I dare you." I looked her in the eyes. "It won't be the first child you tried to kill." I touched her upside down coal scuttle hat. I looked at Adrienne and Sheila. "You did pretty well with the first two—" and then I opened the door, but I didn't move—"okay, you try it again, with Fonny. I dare you."

"May we," asked Adrienne, with what she hoped was ice in her voice, "leave now?"

"Tish," said Sharon; but she did not move.

Ernestine moved past me, moving me away from the door and delivering me to Sharon. "Ladies," she said, and moved to the elevator and pressed the button. She was past a certain fury now. When the elevator arrived and the door opened, she merely said, ushering them in, but holding the door open with one shoulder, "Don't worry. We'll never tell the baby about you. There's no way to tell a baby how obscene human beings can be!" And, in another tone of voice, a tone I'd never heard before, she said, to Mrs. Hunt, "Blessed be the next fruit of thy womb. I hope it turns out to be uterine cancer. And I mean that." And, to the sisters, "If you come anywhere near this house again in life, *I will kill you.* This child is not your child—you have just said so. If I hear that you have so much as crossed a playground and *seen* the child, you won't live to get any *kind* of cancer. Now. I am not my sister. Remember that. My sister's nice. I'm not. My father and my mother are nice. I'm not. I can tell you why Adrienne can't get fucked —you want to hear it? I could tell you about Sheila, too, and all those cats she jerks off in their handkerchiefs, in cars and movies—now, you want to hear *that?*" Sheila began to cry and Mrs. Hunt moved to close the elevator door. Ernestine laughed, and, with one shoulder, held it open and her voice changed again. "You just cursed the child in my sister's womb. Don't you *never* let me see you again, you broken down half-white bride of Christ!" And she spat in Mrs. Hunt's face, and then let the elevator door close. And she yelled down the shaft, "That's your flesh and blood you were cursing, you sick, filthy dried-up cunt! And you carry that message to the Holy Ghost and if He don't like it you tell Him I said He's a faggot and He better not come nowhere near me."

And she came back into the house, with tears running down her face, and walked to the table and poured herself a drink. She lit a cigarette; she was trembling.

Sharon, in all this, had said nothing. Ernestine had delivered me to her, but Sharon had not, in fact, touched me. She had done something far more tremendous; which was, mightily, to hold me and keep me still; without touching me.

"Well," she said, "the men are going to be out for a while. And Tish needs her rest. So let's go on to sleep."

But I knew that they were sending me to bed so that they could sit up for a while, without me, without the men, without anybody, to look squarely in the face the fact that Fonny's family didn't give a shit about him and were not going to do a thing to help him. *We* were his family now, the only family he had: and now everything was up to us.

I walked into my bedroom very slowly and I sat down on the bed for a minute. I was too tired to cry. I was too tired to feel anything. In a way, Sis Ernestine had taken it all on herself, everything, because she wanted the child to make its journey safely and get here well: and that meant that I had to sleep.

So I undressed and curled up on the bed. I turned the way I'd always turned toward Fonny, when we were in bed together. I crawled into his arms and he held me. And he was so present for me that, again, I could not cry. My tears would have hurt him too much. So he held me and I whispered his name, while I watched the streetlights playing on the ceiling. Dimly, I could hear Mama and Sis in the kitchen, making believe that they were playing gin rummy.

That night, in the room on Bank Street, Fonny took the Mexican shawl off the pallet he had on the floor and draped it over my head and shoulders. He grinned and stepped back. "I be damned," he said, "there *is* a rose in Spanish Harlem." He grinned again. "Next week, I'm going to get you a rose for your hair." Then, he stopped grinning and a kind of stinging silence filled the room and filled my ears. It was like nothing was happening in the world but us. I was not afraid. It was deeper than fear. I could not take my eyes away from his. I could not move. If it was deeper than fear, it was not yet joy. It was wonder.

He said, not moving, "We're grown up now, you know?"

I nodded.

He said, "And you've always been—*mine*—no?"

I nodded again.

"And you know," he said, still not moving, holding me with those eyes, "that I've always been yours, right?"

I said, "I never thought about it that way."

He said, "Think about it now, Tish."

"I just know that I love you," I said, and I started to

cry. The shawl seemed very heavy and hot and I wanted
to take it off, but I couldn't.

Then he moved, his face changed, he came to me and
took the shawl away and flung it into a corner. He took
me in his arms and he kissed my tears and then he kissed
me and then we both knew something which we had not
known before.

"I love you, too," he said, "but *I* try not to cry about it."
He laughed and he made me laugh and then he kissed me
again, harder, and he stopped laughing. "I want you to
marry me," he said. I must have looked surprised, for he
said, "That's right. I'm yours and you're mine and that's
it, baby. But I've got to try to explain something to you."

He took me by the hand and led me to his worktable.

"This is where my life is," he said, "my real life." He
picked up a small piece of wood, it was about the size of
two fists. There was the hope of an eye gouged into it, the
suggestion of a nose—the rest was simply a lump of somehow breathing wood. "This might turn out all right one
day," he said, and laid it gently down. "But I think I might
already have fucked it up." He picked up another piece,
the size of a man's thigh. A woman's torso was trapped in
it. "I don't know a thing about her yet," he said, and put
it down, again very gently. Though he held me by one
shoulder and was very close to me, he was yet very far
away. He looked at me with his little smile. "Now, listen,"
he said, "I ain't the kind of joker going to give you a hard
time running around after other chicks and shit like that. I
smoke a little pot but I ain't never popped no needles and
I'm really very square. But—" he stopped and looked at
me, very quiet, very hard: there was a hardness in him I

had barely sensed before. Within this hardness moved his love, moved as a torrent or as a fire moves, above reason, beyond argument, not to be modified in any degree by anything life might do. I was his, and he was mine—I suddenly realized that I would be a very unlucky and perhaps a dead girl should I ever attempt to challenge this decree.

"But," he continued—and he moved away from me; his heavy hands seemed to be attempting to shape the air— "I live with wood and stone. I got stone in the basement and I'm working up here all the time and I'm looking for a loft where I can really work. So, all I'm trying to tell you, Tish, is I ain't offering you much. I ain't got no money and I work at odd jobs—just for bread, because I ain't about to go for none of their jive-ass okey-doke—and that means that you going to have to work, too, and when you come home most likely I'll just grunt and keep on with my chisels and shit and maybe sometimes you'll think I don't even know you're there. But don't ever think that, ever. You're with me all the time, all the time, without you I don't know if I could make it at all, baby, and when I put down the chisel, I'll always come to you. I'll always come to you. I need you. I love you." He smiled. "Is that all right, Tish?"

"Of course it's all right with me," I said. I had more to say, but my throat wouldn't open.

He took me by the hand, then, and he led me to the pallet on the floor. He sat down beside me, and he pulled me down so that my face was just beneath his, my head was in his lap. I sensed a certain terror in him. He knew that I could feel his sex stiffening and beginning to rage against the cloth of his pants and against my jawbone; he wanted me to feel it, and yet he was afraid. He kissed my face all over, and my neck, and he uncovered my breasts and put his teeth and tongue there and his hands were all over my body. I knew what he was doing, and I didn't know. I was in his hands, he called me by the thunder at my ear. I was in his hands: I was being changed; all that I could do was cling to him. I did not realize, until I realized it, that I was also kissing him, that everything was breaking and changing and turning in me and moving toward him. If his arms had not held me, I would have fallen straight downward, backward, to my death. My life was holding me. My life was claiming me. I heard, I felt his breath, as for the first time: but it was as though his breath were rising up out of me. He opened my legs, or I opened them, and he kissed the inside of my thighs. He took off all my clothes, he covered my whole body with kisses, and then he covered me with the shawl and then he went away.

The shawl scratched. I was cold and hot. I heard him in the bathroom. I heard him pull the chain. When he came back, he was naked. He got under the shawl, with me, and stretched his long body on top of mine, and I felt his long black heavy sex throbbing against my navel.

He took my face in his hands, and held it, and he kissed me.

"Now, don't be scared," he whispered. "Don't be scared. Just remember that I belong to you. Just remember that I wouldn't hurt you for nothing in this world. You just going to have to get used to me. And we got all the time in the world."

It was getting to be between two and three: he read my mind. "Your Mama and Daddy know you're with me," he said, "and they know I won't let nothing happen to you." Then, he moved down and his sex moved against my opening. "Don't be scared," he said again. "Hold on to me."

I held on to him, in an agony; there was nothing else in the world to hold on to; I held him by his nappy hair. I could not tell if he moaned or if I moaned. It hurt, it hurt, it didn't hurt. It was a strange weight, a presence coming into me—into a me I had not known was there. I almost screamed, I started to cry: it hurt. It didn't hurt. Something began, unknown. His tongue, his teeth on my breasts, hurt. I wanted to throw him off, I held him tighter and still he moved and moved and moved. I had not known there was so much of him. I screamed and cried against his shoulder. He paused. He put both hands beneath my hips. He moved back, but not quite out, I hung nowhere for a moment, then he pulled me against him and thrust in with all his might and something broke in me. Something broke and a scream rose up in me but he covered my lips with his lips, he strangled my scream with his tongue. His breath was in my nostrils, I was breathing with his breath and moving with his body. And now I was open and helpless and I felt him everywhere. A singing began in me and his body became sacred—his buttocks, as they quivered and rose and fell, and his thighs between my thighs and the weight of his chest on mine and that stiffness of his which stiffened and grew and throbbed and brought me to another place. I wanted to laugh and cry. Then, something absolutely new began, I laughed and I cried and I called his name. I held him closer and closer and I strained to receive it all, all, all of him. He paused and he kissed me and kissed me. His head moved all over my neck and my breasts. We could hardly breathe: if we did not breathe again soon, I knew we would die. Fonny moved again, at first very slowly, and then faster and faster. I felt it coming, felt myself coming, going over the edge, everything in me flowing down to him, and I called his name over and over while he growled my name in his throat, thrusting now with no mercy—caught his breath sharply, let it out with a rush and a sob and then pulled out of me, holding me tight, shooting a boiling liquid all over my belly and my chest and my chin.

Then we lay still, glued together, for a long time.

"I'm sorry," he said, finally, shyly, into the long silence, "to have made such a mess. But I guess you don't want to have no baby right away and I didn't have no protection on me."

"I think I made a mess, too," I said. "It was the first time. Isn't there supposed to be blood?"

We were whispering. He laughed a little. "I had a hemorrhage. Shall we look?"

"I like lying here like this, with you."

"I do too." Then, "Do you like me, Tish?" He sounded like a little boy. "I mean—when I make love to you—do you like it?"

I said, "Oh, come on. You just want to hear me say it."

"That's true. So—?"

"So what?"

"So why don't you go ahead and say it?" And he kissed me.

I said, "It was a little bit like being hit by a truck"—he laughed again—"but it was the most beautiful thing that ever happened to me."

"For me, too," he said. He said it in a very wondering way, almost as though he were speaking of someone else. "No one ever loved me like that before."

"Have you had a lot of girls?"

"Not so many. And nobody for you to worry about."

"Do I know any of them?"

He laughed. "You want me to walk you down the street and point them out to you? Now, you know that wouldn't be nice. And, now that I've got to know you just a little better, I don't believe it would be safe." He snuggled up to me and put his hand on my breast. "You got a wildcat in you, girl. Even if I had the time to go running after other foxes, I sure wouldn't have the energy. I'm really going to have to start taking my vitamins."

"Oh, shut up. You're disgusting."

"Why am I disgusting? I'm only talking about my *health*. Don't you care nothing about my *health*? And they're *chocolate covered*—vitamins, I mean."

"You're crazy."

"Well," he conceded cheerfully, "I'm crazy about you. You want we should check the damage before this stuff hardens into cement?"

He turned on the light and we looked down at ourselves and our bed.

Well, we were something of a sight. There was blood, quite a lot of it—or it seemed like a lot to me, but it didn't frighten me at all, I felt proud and happy—on him and on the bed and on me; his sperm and my blood were slowly creeping down my body, and his sperm was on him and on me; and, in the dim light and against our dark bodies, the effect was as of some strange anointing. Or, we might have just completed a tribal rite. And Fonny's body was a total mystery to me—the body of one's lover always is, no matter how well one gets to know it: it is the changing envelope which contains the gravest mystery of one's life. I stared at his heavy chest, his flat belly, the belly button, the spinning black hair, the heavy limp sex: he had never been circumcized. I touched his slim body and I kissed him on the chest. It tasted of salt and some pungent, unknown bitter spice—clearly, as others might put it, it would become an acquired taste. One hand on my hand, one hand on my shoulder, he held me very close. Then he said, "We've got to go. I better get you home before dawn."

It was half past four.

"I guess so," I said, and we got up and walked into the shower. I washed his body and he washed mine and we laughed a lot, like children, and he warned me if I didn't take my hands off him we might never get uptown and then my Daddy might jump salty and, after all, Fonny said, he had a lot to talk to my Daddy about and he had to talk to him right away.

Fonny got me home at seven. He held me in his arms in the almost empty subway all the way uptown. It was Sunday morning. We walked our streets together, hand in hand; not even the church people were up yet; and the people who were still up, the few people, didn't have eyes for us, didn't have eyes for anybody, or anything.

We got to my stoop and I thought Fonny would leave me there and I turned to kiss him away, but he took me by the hand and said, "Come on," and we walked up the stairs. Fonny knocked on the door.

Sis opened it, her hair tied up, wearing an old green bathrobe. She looked as evil as she could be. She looked from me to Fonny and back again. She didn't exactly want to, but she smiled.

"You're just in time for coffee," she said, and moved back from the door, to let us in.

"We——" I started to say; but Fonny said, "Good-morning, Miss Rivers"—and something in his tone made Sis look at him sharply and come full awake—"I'm sorry we coming in so late. Can I speak to Mr. Rivers, please? It's important."

He still held me by the hand.

"It might be easier to see him," Sis said, "if you come inside, out of the hall."

"We——" I started again, intending to make up God knows what excuse.

"Want to get married," Fonny said.

"Then you'd really better have some coffee," Sis said, and closed the door behind us.

Sharon now came into the kitchen, and she was some-what more together than Sis—that is, she was wearing slacks, and a sweater, and she had knotted her hair in one braid and skewered it to the top of her skull.

"Now, where have you two been," she began, "till this hour of the morning? Don't you know better than to be behaving like that? I declare. We was just about to start calling the police."

But I could see, too, that she was relieved that Fonny was sitting in the kitchen, beside me. That meant some-thing very important, and she knew it. It would have been a very different scene, and she would have been in very different trouble if I had come upstairs alone.

"I'm sorry, Mrs. Rivers," Fonny said. "It's all my fault.

I hadn't seen Tish for a few weeks and we had a lot to talk about—*I* had a lot to talk about—and—" he gestured— "I kept her out."

"Talking?" Sharon asked.

He did not quite flinch; he did not drop his eyes. "We want to get married," he said. "That's how come I kept her out so late." They watched each other. "I love Tish," he said. "That's why I stayed away so long. I even—" he looked briefly at me—"went to see other girls—and—I did all kind of things, to kind of get it out of my mind." He looked at me again. He looked down. "But I could see I was just fooling myself. I didn't love nobody else but her. And then I got scared that maybe she'd go away or somebody else would come along and take her away and so I came back." He tried to grin. "I came running back. And I don't want to have to go away again." Then, "She's always been my girl, you know that. And—I am not a bad boy. You know that. And—you're the only family I've ever had."

"That," Sharon grumbled, "is why I can't figure out why you calling me Mrs. Rivers, all of a sudden." She looked at me. "Yeah. I hope you realize, Miss, that you ain't but eighteen years old."

"*That* argument," said Sis, "and a subway token, will get you from here to the corner. If *that* far!" She poured the coffee. "Actually, it's the older sister who is expected to marry first. But we have never stood on ceremony in *this* house."

"What do *you* think about all this?" Sharon asked her.

"Me? I'm delighted to be rid of the little brat. I never *could* stand her. I *could* never see what all the rest of you saw in her, I swear." She sat down at the table and grinned. "Take some sugar, Fonny. You are going to need it, believe me, if you intend to tie yourself up with my sweet, *sweet* little sister."

Sharon went to the kitchen door, and yelled, "Joe! Come on out here! Lightning's done struck the poor-house! Come on, now, I mean it."

Fonny took my hand.

Joseph came into the kitchen, in slippers, old corduroy pants, and a T-shirt. I began to realize that no one in this house had really been to sleep. Joseph saw me first. He really did not see anyone else. And, since he was both furious and relieved, his tone was very measured. "I'd like you to tell me exactly •what you mean, young lady, by walking in here this hour of the morning. If you want to leave home, then you leave home, you hear? But, as long as you in *my* house, you got to respect it. You hear me?"

Then he saw Fonny, and Fonny let go my hand, and stood up.

He said, "Mr. Rivers, please don't scold Tish. It's all my fault, sir. I kept her out. I had to talk to her. Please. Mr. Rivers. Please. I asked her to marry me. That's what we were doing out so long. We want to get married. That's why I'm here. You're her father. You love her. And so I know you know—you *have* to know—that *I* love her. I've loved her all my life. You know that. And if I didn't love her, I wouldn't be standing in this room now—would I? I could have left her on the stoop and run away again. I know you might want to beat me up. But I love her. That's all I can tell you."

Joseph looked at him.

"How old are you?"

"I'm twenty-one, sir."

"You think that's old enough to get married?"

"I don't know, sir. But it's old enough to know who you love."

"You think so?"

Fonny straightened. "I know so."

"How you going to feed her?"

"How did you?"

We, the women, were out of it now, and we knew it. Ernestine poured Joseph a cup of coffee and pushed it in his direction.

"You got a job?"

"I load moving vans in the daytime and I sculpt at night. I'm a sculptor. We know it won't be easy. But I'm a real artist. And I'm going to be a very good artist— maybe, even, a great one." And they stared at each other again.

Joseph picked up his coffee, without looking at it, and sipped it without tasting it.

"Now, let me get this straight. You asked my little girl to marry you, and she said——"

"Yes," said Fonny.

"And you come here to tell me or to ask my permission?"

"Both, sir," said Fonny.

"And you ain't got no kind of——"

"Future," Fonny said.

Both men, again, then measured each other. Joseph put his coffee down. Fonny had not touched his.

"What would you do in my place?" Joseph asked.

I could feel Fonny trembling. He could not help it—his hand touched my shoulder lightly, then moved away. "I'd ask my daughter. If she tells you she don't love me, I'll go away and I won't never bother you no more."

Joseph looked hard at Fonny—a long look, in which one watched skepticism surrender to a certain resigned tenderness, a self-recognition. He looked as though he wanted to knock Fonny down; he looked as though he wanted to take him in his arms.

Then Joseph looked at me.

"Do you love him? You want to marry him?"

"Yes." I had not known my voice could sound so strange. "Yes. Yes." Then, I said, "I'm very much your daughter, you know, and very much my mother's daughter. So, you ought to know that I mean no when I say no and I mean yes when I say yes. And Fonny came here to ask for your permission, and I love him for that. *I* very much want your permission because I love you. But I am not going to marry *you*. I am going to marry Fonny."

Joseph sat down.

"When?"

"As soon as we get the bread together," Fonny said.

Joseph said, "You and me, son, we better go into the other room."

And so they went away. We did not say anything. There was nothing for us to say. Only, Mama said, after a moment, "You sure you love him, Tish? You're sure?"

"Mama," I said, "why do you ask me that?"

"Because she's been secretly hoping that you'd marry Governor Rockefeller," Ernestine said.

For a moment Mama looked at her, hard; then she

laughed. Ernestine, without knowing it, or meaning to, had come very close to the truth—not the literal truth, but the truth: for the dream of safety dies hard. I said, "You know that dried-up cracker ass-hole is much too old for me."

Sharon laughed again. "That is not," she said, "the way he sees *himself*. But I guess I just would not be able to swallow the way he would see *you*. So. We can close the subject. You going to marry Fonny. All right. When I really think about it"—and now she paused, and, in a way, she was no longer Sharon, my mother, but someone else; but that someone else was, precisely, my mother, Sharon— "I guess I'm real pleased." She leaned back, arms folded, looking away, thinking ahead. "Yeah. He's real. He's a man."

"He's not a man yet," said Ernestine, "but he's going to become a man—that's why you sitting there, fighting them tears. Because that means that your youngest daughter is about to become a woman."

"Oh, shut up," Sharon said. "Wish to God you'd get married to somebody, then I'd be able to bug *you* half to death, instead of the other way around."

"You'd miss me, too," said Ernestine, very quietly, "but I don't think I'm ever going to marry. Some people do, you know—Mama?—and some people don't." She stood up and kind of circled the room and sat down again. We could hear Fonny's voice and Joseph's voice, in the other room, but we couldn't hear what they were saying—also, we were trying very hard *not* to hear. Men are men, and sometimes they must be left alone. Especially if you have the sense to realize that if they're locked in a room together, where they may not especially want to be, they are locked in because of their responsibility for the women outside.

"Well I can understand that," said Sharon—very steadily, and without moving.

"The only trouble," Ernestine said, "is that sometimes you would *like* to belong to somebody."

"But," I said—I had not known I was going to say it —"it's very frightening to belong to somebody."

And perhaps until the moment I heard myself say this, I had not realized that this is true.

"Six in one," said Ernestine, and smiled, "half dozen in the other."

Joseph and Fonny came back from the other room.

"Both of you are crazy," Joseph said, "but there's nothing I can do about *that*." He watched Fonny. He smiled—a smile both sweet and reluctant. Then, he looked at me. "But—Fonny's right—somebody was bound to come along some day and take you away. I just didn't think it would happen so soon. But—like Fonny says, and it's true —you've always been together, from childhood on. And you ain't children no more." He took Fonny by the hand and led Fonny to me, and he took me by the hand and he pulled me to my feet. He put my hand in Fonny's hand. "Take care of each other," he said. "You going to find out that it's more than a notion."

Tears were standing in Fonny's eyes. He kissed my father. He let go my hand. He moved to the door. "I've got to get home," he said, "and tell my Daddy." His face changed, he looked at me, he kissed me across the space dividing us. "He'll be mighty happy," he said. He opened the door. He said to Joseph, "We be back here around six this evening, okay?"

"Okay," said Joseph, and now he was smiling all over his face.

Fonny went on out the door. Two or three days later, Tuesday or Wednesday, we went downtown together again and started seriously looking around for our loft.

And *that* was going to turn out to be a trip and a half.

Mr. Hayward was in his office on the Monday, just as he had said he would be. I got there about seven fifteen, and Mama was with me.

Mr. Hayward is about thirty-seven, I would guess, with gentle brown eyes and thinning brown hair. He's very, very tall, and he's big; and he's nice enough, or he seems nice enough, but I'm just not comfortable with him. I don't know if it's fair to blame him for this. I'm not really comfortable with anybody these days, and I guess I certainly wouldn't be comfortable with a lawyer.

He stood up as we came in, and put Mama in the big chair and me in the smaller one and sat down again behind his desk.

"How are you ladies today? Mrs. Rivers? And how are you, Tish? Did you see Fonny?"

"Yes. At six o'clock."

"And how is he?"

That always seemed a foolish question to me. How *is* a man if he's fighting to get out of prison? But then, too, I had to force myself to see, from another point of view, that it was an important question. For one thing, it was the question I was living with; and, for another, knowing "how" Fonny was might make a very important difference for Mr. Hayward, and help him with his case. But I also resented having to tell Mr. Hayward anything at all about Fonny. There was so much that I felt he should already have known. But maybe I'm being unfair about that, too.

"Well, let's put it this way, Mr. Hayward. He hates being in there, but he's trying not to let it break him."

"When we going to get him out?" asked Mama.

Mr. Hayward looked from Mama to me, and smiled—a painful smile, as though he had just been kicked in the balls. He said, "Well, as you ladies know, this is a very difficult case."

"That's why my sister hired *you*," I said.

"And you are beginning to feel now that her confidence was misplaced?" He was still smiling. He lit a cigar.

"No," I said, "I wouldn't say that."

I wouldn't have dared to say that—not yet, anyway—because I was afraid of having to look for another lawyer, who might easily be worse.

"We liked having Fonny around," Mama said, "and we just kind of miss him."

"I can certainly understand that," he said, "and I'm doing all I can to get him back to you, just as fast as I can. But, as you ladies know, the very greatest difficulty has been caused by the refusal of Mrs. Rogers to reconsider her testimony. And now she has disappeared."

"Disappeared?" I shouted, "how can she just disappear?"

"Tish," he said, "this is a very big city, a very big country—even, for that matter, a very big world. People *do* disappear. I don't think that *she* has gone very far—they certainly do not have the means for a long journey. But her family may have returned her to Puerto Rico. In any case, in order to find her, I will need special investigators, and—"

"That means money," Mama said.

"Alas," said Mr. Hayward. He stared at me from behind his cigar, an odd, expectant, surprisingly sorrowful look.

I had stood up; now I sat down. "That filthy bitch," I said, "that filthy bitch."

"How *much* money?" Mama asked.

"I am trying to keep it as low as possible," said Mr. Hayward, with a shy, boyish smile, "but special investigators are—*special,* I'm afraid, and they know it. If we're lucky, we'll locate Mrs. Rogers in a matter of days, or weeks. If not"—he shrugged—"well, for the moment, let's just assume we'll be lucky." And he smiled again.

"Puerto Rico," Mama said heavily.

"We don't *know* that she has returned there," Mr. Hayward said, "but it *is* a very vivid possibility. Anyway, she and her husband disappeared some days ago from the apartment on Orchard Street, leaving no forwarding address. We have not been able to contact the other relatives, the aunts and uncles, who, anyway, as you know, have never been very cooperative."

"But doesn't it make it look bad for her story," I asked, "to just disappear like that? She's the key witness in this case."

"Yes. But she is a distraught, ignorant, Puerto Rican woman, suffering from the aftereffects of rape. So her behavior is not incomprehensible. You see what I mean?" He looked at me hard, and his voice changed. "And she is only *one* of the key witnesses in this case. You have forgotten the testimony of Officer Bell—*his* was the really authoritative identification of the rapist. It is Bell who swears that he *saw* Fonny running away from the scene of the crime. And I have always been of the opinion—you will remember that we discussed this—that it is *his* testimony which Mrs. Rogers continually repeats——"

"If he saw Fonny at the scene of the crime, then why did he have to wait and come and get him out of the *house?*"

"Tish," Mama said. "Tish." Then, "You mean—let me get you straight now—that it's that Officer Bell who tells her what to say? You mean *that?*"

"Yes," said Mr. Hayward.

I looked at Hayward. I looked around the room. We were way downtown, near Broadway, not far from Trinity Church. The office was of dark wood, very smooth and polished. The desk was wide, with two telephones, a button kept flashing. Hayward ignored it, watching me. There were trophies and diplomas on the walls, and a large photograph of Hayward, Senior. On the desk, framed, were two photographs, one of his wife, smiling, and one of his two small boys. There was no connection between this room, and me.

Yet, here I was.

"You're saying," I said, "that there's no way of getting at the truth in this case?"

"No. I am not saying that." He re-lit his cigar. "The truth of a case doesn't matter. What matters is—who wins."

Cigar smoke filled the room. "I don't mean," he said, carefully, "that *I* doubt the truth. If I didn't believe in Fonny's innocence, I would never have taken the case. I know something about Officer Bell, who is a racist and a liar—I have told him that to his face, so you can feel perfectly free to quote me, to anyone, at any time you wish—and I know something about the D.A. in charge of this case, who is worse. Now. You and Fonny insist that you were together, in the room on Bank Street, along with an old friend, Daniel Carty. Your testimony, as you can imagine, counts for nothing, and Daniel Carty has just been arrested by the D.A.'s office and is being held incommunicado. I have not been allowed to see him." Now, he rose and paced to the window. "What they are doing is really against the law—but—Daniel has a record, as you know. They, obviously, intend to make him change his testimony. And—I do not *know* this, but I am willing to bet—that that is how and why Mrs. Rogers has disappeared." He paced back to his desk, and sat down. "So. You see." He looked up at me. "I will make it as easy as I can. But it will still be very hard."

"How soon do you need the money?" Mama asked.

"I have begun the operation already," he said, "of tracing the lady. I will need the money as soon as you can get it. I will also force the D.A.'s office to allow me to see Daniel Carty, but they will throw every conceivable obstacle in my way——"

"So we're trying," Mama said, "to buy time."

"Yes," he said.

Time: the word tolled like the bells of a church. Fonny was doing: *time.* In six months *time,* our baby would be

here. Somewhere, in time, Fonny and I had met: somewhere, in time, we had loved; somewhere, no longer in
time, but, now, totally, at time's mercy, we loved.

Somewhere in time, Fonny paced a prison cell, his hair
growing—nappier and nappier. Somewhere, in time, he
stroked his chin, itching for a shave, somewhere, in time,
he scratched his armpits, aching for a bath. Somewhere in
time he looked about him, knowing that he was being lied
to, in time, with the connivance of time. In another time,
he had feared life: now, he feared death—somewhere in
time. He awoke every morning with Tish on his eyelids
and fell asleep every night with Tish tormenting his navel.
He lived, now, in time, with the roar and the stink and the
beauty and horror of innumerable men: and he had been
dropped into this inferno in the twinkling of an eye.

Time could not be bought. The only coin time ac-
cepted was life. Sitting on the leather arm of Mr. Hayward's chair, I looked through the vast window, way
down, on Broadway, and I began to cry.

"Tish," said Hayward, helplessly.

Mama came and took me in her arms.

"Don't do us like that," she said. "Don't do us like
that."

But I couldn't stop. It just seemed that we would
never find Mrs. Rogers; that Bell would never change his
testimony; that Daniel would be beaten until he changed
his. And Fonny would rot in prison, Fonny would die
there—and I—I could not live without Fonny.

"Tish," Mama said, "you a woman now. You *got* to
be a woman. We are in a rough situation—but, if you really
want to think about it, ain't nothing new about that. That's

just exactly, daughter, when *you do not give up*. You *can't* give up. We got to get Fonny out of there. *I don't care what we have to do to do it*—you understand me, daughter? This shit has been going on long enough. Now. You start thinking about it any other way, you just going to make yourself sick. *You* can't get sick *now*—you know that—I'd rather for the state to kill him than for *you* to kill him. So, come on, now—we going to get him *out.*"

She moved away from me. I dried my eyes. She turned back to Hayward.

"You don't have an address for that child in Puerto Rico, do you?"

"Yes." He wrote it out on a piece of paper, and handed it to her. "We're sending somebody down there this week."

Mama folded the piece of paper, and put it in her purse.

"How soon do you think you'll be able to see Daniel?"

"I intend," he said, "to see him tomorrow, but I'm going to have to raise all kinds of hell to do it."

"Well," Mama said, "just as long as you do it."

She came back to me.

"We'll put our heads together, at home, Mr. Hayward, and start working it on out, and I'll have Ernestine call you early tomorrow morning. All right?"

"That's fine. Please give Ernestine my regards." He put down his cigar, and came and put one clumsy hand on my shoulder. "My dear Tish," he said. "Please hold on. Please hold on. I swear to you that we will win, that Fonny will have his freedom. No, it will not be easy. But neither will it be as insurmountable as it seems to you today."

"Tell her," Mama said.

"Now—when I go to see Fonny, the first question he

always asks is always about you. And I always say, Tish? she's fine. But he watches my face, to make sure I'm not lying. And I'm a very bad liar. I'm going to see him to-morrow. What shall I tell him?"

I said, "Tell him I'm fine."

"Do you think you can manage to give us a little smile?—to go with the message. I could carry it with me. He'd like that."

I smiled, and he smiled, and something really human happened between us, for the first time. He released my shoulder, and walked over to Mama. "Could you have Ernestine call me around ten? or even earlier, if possible. Otherwise, she may not be able to get me before six."

"Will do. And thank you very much, Mr. Hayward."

"You know something—? I wish you'd drop the mister."

"Well—okay. Hayward. Call me Sharon."

"That *I* will do. And I hope that we become friends, out of all this."

"I'm sure we will," Mama said. "Thank you again. 'Bye now."

"Good-bye. Don't forget what I said, Tish."

"I won't. I promise. Tell Fonny I'm fine."

"*That's* my girl. Or, rather"—and he looked more boy-ish than ever—"Fonny's girl." And he smiled. He opened the door for us. He said, "Good-bye."

We said, "Good-bye."

Fonny had been walking down Seventh Avenue, on a Saturday afternoon, when he ran into Daniel again. They had not seen each other since their days in school.

Time had not improved Daniel. He was still big, black,

and loud; at the age of twenty-three—he is a little older than Fonny—he was already running out of familiar faces. So, they grabbed each other on the avenue—after a moment of genuine shock and delight—howling with laughter, beating each other around the head and shoulders, children again, and, though Fonny doesn't like bars, sat themselves down at the nearest one, and ordered two beers.

"Wow! What's happening?" I don't know which of them asked the question, or which of them asked it first: but I can see their faces.

"Why you asking *me,* man?"

"Because, like the man says about Mt. Everest, you're *there.*"

"Where?"

"No kidding, man—how you making it?"

"I gotta slave for the Jew in the garment center, pushing a hand truck, man, riding up and down in them elevators."

"How your folks?"

"Oh, my Daddy passed, man, while ago. I'm still at the same place, with my Mama. Her varicose veins come down on her, though. So"—and Daniel looked down into his beer.

"What you doing—I mean, now?"

"You mean, this minute?"

"I mean, you any plans, man, you hung up, or can you come on and hang out with me? I mean, right now—?"

"I ain't doing nothing."

Fonny swallowed his beer, and paid the man. "Come on. We got some beer at the pad. Come *on.* You remember Tish?"

"Tish?—"

"*Yeah,* Tish. Skinny little Tish. *My* girl."

"Skinny little Tish?"

"*Yeah.* She's *still* my girl. We going to get married, man. Come on, and let me show you the pad. And she'll fix us something to eat—come *on,* I told you we got beer at the house."

And, though he certainly shouldn't be spending the money, he pushes Daniel into a cab and they roll on down to Bank Street: where I am not expecting them. But Fonny is big and cheerful, overjoyed; and the truth is that I recognize Daniel by the light in Fonny's eyes. For, it is not so much that time has not improved him: I can see to what extent he has been beaten. This is not because I am perceptive, but because I am in love with Fonny. Neither love nor terror makes one blind: indifference makes one blind. And I could not be indifferent to Daniel because I realized, from Fonny's face, how marvelous it was for him to have scooped up, miraculously, from the swamp waters of his past, a friend.

But it means that I must go out, shopping, and so out I go, leaving them alone. We have a record player. As I go out, Fonny is putting on "Compared To What," and Daniel is squatting on the floor, drinking beer.

"So, you really going to get married?" Daniel asks—both wistful and mocking.

"Well, yeah, we looking for a place to live—we looking for a loft because that don't cost no whole lot of bread, you know, and that way I can work without Tish being bugged to death. This room ain't big enough for one, ain't no question about its being big enough for two, and I got all my work here, and in the basement." He is rolling a cigarette as he says this, for him and for Daniel, squatting opposite him. "They got lofts standing empty all over the East Side, man, and don't nobody want to rent them, except freaks like me. And they all fire traps and some of them ain't even got no toilets. So, you figure like finding a loft ain't going to be no sweat." He lights the cigarette, takes a drag, and hands it to Daniel. "But, man—this country really do not like niggers. They do not like niggers so bad, man, they will rent to a leper first. I swear." Daniel drags on the cigarette, hands it back to Fonny—*Tired old ladies kissing dogs!* cries the record player—who drags on it, takes a sip of his beer and hands it back. "Sometimes Tish and I go together, sometimes she goes alone, sometimes I go alone. But it's always the same story, man." He stands up. "And now I can't let Tish go alone no more because, dig, last week we thought we *had* us a loft, the cat had promised it to her. But he had not seen *me*. And he figures a black chick by herself, way downtown, looking for a loft, well, he *know* he going to make it with *her*. *He* thinks she's propositioning him, that's what he *really* thinks. And Tish comes to tell me, just so proud and happy"—he sits down again—"and we go on over there. And when the cat sees me, he says there's been some great misunderstanding, he *can't* rent the loft because he's got all these relatives coming in from Rumania like in half an hour and he got to give it to *them*. Shit. And I *told* him he was full of shit and he threatened to call the cops on my ass." He takes the cigarette from Daniel. "I'm really going to have to try to figure out some way of getting some bread together and getting out of this fucking country."

"How you going to do that?"

"I don't know yet," says Fonny. "Tish can't swim." He gives the cigarette back to Daniel, and they whoop and rock with laughter.

"Maybe you could go first," says Daniel, soberly.

The cigarette and the record are finished.

"No," says Fonny, "I don't think I want to do that." Daniel watches him. "I'd be too scared."

"Scared of what?" asks Daniel—though he really knows the answer to this question.

"Just scared," says Fonny—after a long silence.

"Scared of what might happen to Tish?" Daniel asks.

There is another long silence. Fonny is staring out the window. Daniel is staring at Fonny's back.

"Yes," Fonny says, finally. Then, "Scared of what might happen to both of us—without each other. Like Tish ain't got no sense at all, man—she trusts everybody. She walk down the street, swinging that little behind of hers, and she's *surprised,* man, when some cat tries to jump her. She don't see what I see." And silence falls again, Daniel watching him, and Fonny says, "I know I might seem to be a weird kind of cat. But I got two things in my life, man—I got my wood and stone and I got Tish. If I lose them, I'm lost. I know that. You know"—and now he turns to face Daniel—"whatever's in me I didn't put there. And I can't take it out."

Daniel moves to the pallet, leans against the wall. "I don't know if you so *weird*. I know you lucky. I ain't got nothing like that. Can I have another beer, man?"

"Sure," Fonny says, and goes to open two more cans. He hands one to Daniel and Daniel takes a long swallow before he says, "I just come out the slammer, baby. Two years."

Fonny says nothing—just turns and looks.

Daniel says nothing; swallows a little more beer.

"They said—they still *say*—stole a car. Man, I can't even *drive* a car, and I tried to make my lawyer—but he was really *their* lawyer, dig, he worked for the city—prove that, but he didn't. And, anyway, I wasn't in no car when they picked me up. But I had a little grass on me. I was on my stoop. And so they come and picked me up, like that, you know, it was about midnight, and they locked me up and then the next morning they put me in the lineup and somebody said it was *me* stole the car—that car I ain't seen yet. And so—you know—since I had that weed on me, they had me anyhow and so they said if I would plead guilty they'd give me a lighter sentence. If I *didn't* plead guilty, they'd throw me the book. Well"—he sips his beer again—"I was alone, baby, wasn't nobody, and so I entered the guilty plea. Two years!" He leans forward, staring at Fonny. "But, then, it sounded a whole lot better than the marijuana charge." He leans back and laughs and sips his beer and looks up at Fonny. "It wasn't. I let them fuck over me because I was scared and dumb and I'm sorry now." He is silent. Then, "Two years!"

"By the balls," says Fonny.

"Yes," says Daniel—after the loudest and longest silence either of them has ever known.

When I come back in, they are both sitting there, a little high, and I say nothing and I move about in the tiny space of the kitchenette as quietly as I can. Fonny comes in for a moment and rubs up against me from behind and hugs me and kisses the nape of my neck. Then, he returns to Daniel.

"How long you been out?"

"About three months." He leaves the pallet, walks to the window. "Man, it was bad. Very bad. And it's bad now. Maybe I'd feel different if I had done something and got caught. But I didn't do nothing. They were just playing with me, man, because they could. And I'm lucky it was only two years, you dig? Because they can do with you whatever they want. *Whatever they want.* And they dogs, man. I really found out, in the slammer, what Malcolm and them cats was talking about. The white man's *got* to be the devil. He sure ain't a man. Some of the things I saw, baby, I'll be dreaming about until the day I die."

Fonny puts one hand on Daniel's neck. Daniel shudders. Tears stream down his face.

"I know," Fonny says, gently, "but try not to let it get to you too tough. You out now, it's over, you young."

"Man, I know what you're saying. And I appreciate it. But you don't know—the worst thing, man, the *worst* thing —is that they can make you so fucking *scared*. Scared, man. *Scared.*"

Fonny says nothing, simply stands there, with his hand on Daniel's neck.

I yell, from the kitchen, "You cats hungry?"

"Yeah," Fonny yells back, "we starving. *Move* it!"

Daniel dries his eyes and comes to the door of the kitchenette and smiles at me.

"It's nice to see you, Tish. You sure ain't gained no weight, have you?"

"You hush. I'm skinny because I'm *poor.*"

"Well, I sure don't know why you didn't pick yourself a rich husband. You ain't *never* going to gain no weight *now.*'"

"Well, if you skinny, Daniel, you can move faster and

when you in a tight place, you got a better chance of getting out of it. You see what I mean."

"You sound like you got it figured. You learn all that from Fonny?"

"I learned *some* things from Fonny. But I also have a swift, natural intelligence—haven't you been struck by it?"

"Tish, I been struck by so many things that I really have not had time to do you justice."

"You're not the only one. And I can't really blame you. I'm so remarkable, I sometimes have to pinch myself."

Daniel laughs. "I'd like to see that. Where?"

Fonny mutters, "She's so remarkable, I sometimes have to go up side her head."

"He beats you, too?"

"Ah! what *can* I do—? *All my life is just despair, but I don't care*—"

Suddenly we are singing,

> *When he takes me in his arms,*
> *The world is bright, all right.*
> *What's the difference if I say*
> *I'll go away*
> *When I know I'll come back*
> *On my knees someday*
> *For, whatever my man is*
> *I am his,*
> *Forevermore!*

Then, we are laughing. Daniel sobers, looking within, suddenly very far away. "Poor Billie," he says, "they beat the living crap out of *her*, too."

"Man," Fonny says, "we just have to move it from day

to day. If you think too much about it, you really *are* fucked, can't move at all."

"Let's eat," I say. "Come on."

I have prepared what I know Fonny likes: ribs and cornbread and rice, with gravy, and green peas. Fonny puts on the record player, low: Marvin Gaye's "What's Going On."

"Maybe Tish can't gain no weight," says Daniel, after a moment, "but *you* sure will. You folks mind if I drop by more often—say, around this time?"

"Feel free," says Fonny, cheerfully, and winks at me. "Tish ain't very good looking, but she can sure get the pots together."

"I'm happy to know I have some human use," I tell him, and he winks at me again, and starts chewing on a rib.

Fonny: chews on the rib, and watches me: and, in complete silence, without moving a muscle, we are laughing with each other. We are laughing for many reasons. We are together somewhere where no one can reach us, touch us, joined. We are happy, even, that we have food enough for Daniel, who eats peacefully, not knowing that we are laughing, but sensing that something wonderful has happened to us, which means that wonderful things happen, and that maybe something wonderful will happen to *him*. It's wonderful, anyway, to be able to help a person to have that feeling.

Daniel stays with us till midnight. He's a little afraid to leave, afraid, in fact, to hit those streets, and Fonny realizes this and walks him to the subway. Daniel, who cannot abandon his mother, yet longs to be free to confront his life; is terrified at the same time of what that life may bring, is terrified of freedom; and is struggling in a trap. And Fonny, who is younger, struggles now to be older, in order to help his friend toward his deliverance. *Didn't my Lord deliver Daniel? And why not every man?*

The song is old, the question unanswered.

On their walk that night, and many nights thereafter, Daniel tried to tell Fonny something about what had happened to him, in prison. Sometimes he was at the house, and so I heard it, too; sometimes, he and Fonny were alone. Sometimes, when Daniel spoke, he cried—sometimes, Fonny held him. Sometimes, I did. Daniel brought it out, or forced it out, or tore it out of himself as though it were torn, twisted, chilling metal, bringing with it his flesh and his blood—he tore it out of himself like a man trying to be cured:

"You don't know what's happening to you, at first. No way to know it. They come and got me off my stoop and they searched me. When I thought about it later, I realized that I didn't really know *why*. I was always on that stoop, me and the other cats, and they was always passing by, and, while *I* wasn't never on no shit, they knew some of the other cats has to be—you *know* they knew it. And they could see the dudes scratching and nodding. I think they dug that. When I thought about it later, I thought to myself, the motherfuckers really dig that shit. They go on into headquarters and report, Everything's cool, sir. We escorted the French connection while he made his rounds and the shit's been delivered and the niggers is out of it.

But this night I was by myself, about to go on in, and they stopped the car and yelled at me and pushed me into the hallway and searched me. *You* know how they do it."

I *don't* know. But Fonny nods, his face still, his eyes very dark.

"And I had just picked up this grass, it was in my ass-pocket. And so they pulled it out, man, do they *love* to pat your ass, and one of them give it to the other and one of them handcuffed me and pushed me into the car. And I hadn't known it was going to come to that, maybe I was a little high, maybe I hadn't had time to think, but, baby, when that man put his handcuffs on me and pushed me down the steps and on into the car and then that car started moving, I wanted to scream for my Mama. And then I started getting scared, because she can't hardly do nothing for herself, and she'd start to worrying about me, and wouldn't nobody know where I was! They took me down to the precinct and they booked me on a narcotics charge and they took everything I had off of me and I started to ask, Can I make a phone call? and then I realized that I didn't really have nobody to call, except my Mama, and who *she* going to call this hour of night? I just hoped she was sleeping, you know, like she had just figured that I was out late, and, by time she woke up in the morning and realized I wasn't there that maybe I'd have figured out—something. They put me in this little cell with about four or five other cats, they was just nodding and farting, and I sat there and I tried to get my mind together. Because what the fuck am I going to do? I ain't got nobody to call—I really *don't,* except maybe that Jew I work for; he a nice enough dude, but, man, he ain't hardly going to dig it. What I'm really trying to figure is how I can get somebody *else* to call my Mama, somebody who's cool, who can cool *her,* somebody who can *do* something. But I can't think of nobody.

"Morning came and they put us in the wagon. There's this old white motherfucker they picked up off the Bowery —I guess—he done vomited all over himself and he's looking down at the floor and he's singing. He can't sing, but he sure is stinking. And, man, I'm sure grateful I ain't on no shit because now one of the brothers is started to moan, he got his arms wrapped around himself, and sweat is starting to pour off that cat, like water down a scrubbing board. I ain't much older than he is, and I sure wish I could help him but I know I can't do nothing. And I think to myself, Now, the cops who put him in this wagon know that this dude is *sick*. I *know* they know it. He ain't supposed to be in here—and him not hardly much more than a kid. But the mothers who put him in this wagon, man, they was coming in their pants while they did it. I don't believe there's a white man in this country, baby, who can even *get* his dick hard, without he hear some nigger moan.

"Well, we get on down there. And I still ain't thought of nobody to call. I want to shit and I want to die, but I know I can't do neither. I figure they'll let me shit when they get ready, in the meantime I just got to hold it best I can, and it just pure foolishness for me to think of wanting to die because they can kill me any time they want to and maybe I'll die today. Before I shit. And then I think of my Mama again. I *know* she worried by now."

Sometimes Fonny held him, sometimes I did. Sometimes, he stood at the window, with his back to us.

"I can't really tell you much more about it—maybe

there's a whole lot of shit that I won't never be *able* to tell nobody. They had me on the grass, and so they nailed me on the car—that car I ain't seen yet. I guess they just happened to need a car thief that day. Sure wish I knew whose car it was. I hope it wasn't no black dude's car, though."

Then, sometimes, Daniel would grin, sometimes he would dry his eyes. We would eat and drink together. Daniel was trying very hard to get past something, something unnamable: he was trying as hard as a man can try. And sometimes I held him, sometimes Fonny: we were all he had.

On the Tuesday after the Monday that I saw Hayward, I saw Fonny at the six o'clock visit. I had never seen him so upset before.

"What the fuck we going to do about Mrs. Rogers? Where the fuck did she go?"

"I don't know. But we'll find her."

"How you going to find her?"

"We're sending people to Puerto Rico. We think that's where she went."

"And suppose she went to Argentina? or Chile? or China?"

"Fonny. Please. How's she going to get that far?"

"They can give her the money, to go anywhere!"

"Who?"

"The D.A.'s office, that's who!"

"Fonny——"

"You don't believe me? You don't think they can do it?"

"I don't think they have."

"How you going to get the money to find her?"

"We're all working, all of us."

"Yeah. My Daddy's working in the garment center, you're working in a department store, *your* Daddy's working on the waterfront——!"

"Fonny. Listen——"

"Listen to what? What we going to do about that fucking lawyer? He don't give a shit about me, he don't give a shit about *nobody!* You want me to die in here? You know what's going on in here? You know what's happening to me, to *me, to me,* in *here?*"

"Fonny. Fonny. Fonny."

"I'm sorry, baby. I don't mean none of that for you. I'm sorry. I love you, Tish. I'm sorry."

"I love you, Fonny. I love you."

"How's the baby coming?"

"It's growing. It'll start showing more next month."

We stared at each other.

"Get me out of here, baby. Get me out of here. Please."

"I promise. I promise. I promise."

"Don't cry. I'm sorry I yelled. I wasn't yelling at you, Tish."

"I know."

"Please don't cry. Please don't cry. It's bad for the baby."

"All right."

"Give us a smile, Tish."

"Is that all right?"

"You can do better than that."

"Is this better?"

"Yeah. Give us a kiss."

I kissed the glass. He kissed the glass.

"You still love me?"

"I'll always love you, Fonny."

"I love you. I miss you. I miss everything about you, I miss everything we had together, everything we did together, walking and talking and making love—oh, baby, get me out of here."

"I will. Hold on."

"I promise.—Later."

"Later."

He followed the guard into the unimaginable inferno, and I stood up, my knees and elbows shaking, to cross the Sahara again.

That night I dreamed, I dreamed all night, I had terrible dreams. In one of these dreams, Fonny was driving a truck, a great big truck, very fast, too fast, down the highway, and he was looking for me. But he didn't see me. I was behind the truck, calling out his name, but the roar of the motor drowned my voice. There were two turnings off this highway, and they both looked exactly alike. The highway was on a cliff, above the sea. One of the turnings led to the driveway of our house; the other led to the cliff's edge and a drop straight down to the sea. He was driving too fast, too fast! I called his name as loud as I could and, as he began to turn the truck, I screamed again and woke up.

The light was on, and Sharon was standing above me. I cannot describe her face. She had brought in a cold, wet towel and she wiped my brow and my neck. She leaned down and kissed me.

Then, she straightened and looked into my eyes.

"I know I can't help you very much right now—God knows what I wouldn't give if I could. But I know about suffering; if that helps. I know that it ends. I ain't going to tell you no lies, like it always ends for the better. Sometimes it ends for the worse. You can suffer so bad that you can be driven to a place where you can't ever suffer again: and that's worse."

She took both my hands and held them tightly between her own. "Try to remember that. And: the only way *anything* ever gets done is when you make up your mind to do it. I know a lot of our loved ones, a lot of our men, have died in prison: but not *all* of them. You remember that. And: you ain't really alone in that bed, Tish. You got that child beneath your heart and we're all counting on you, Fonny's counting on *you*, to bring that child here safe and well. You the only one who can do it. But you're strong. Lean on your strength."

I said, "Yes. Yes, Mama." I knew I didn't have any strength. But I was going to have to find some, somewhere.

"Are you all right now? Can you sleep?"

"Yes."

"I don't want to sound foolish. But, just remember, love brought you here. If you trusted love this far, don't panic now."

And, again, she kissed me and she turned out the light and she left me.

I lay there—wide awake; and very frightened. *Get me out of here.*

I remembered women I had known, but scarcely

looked at, who had frightened me; because they knew how to use their bodies in order to get something that they wanted. I now began to realize that my judgment of these women had had very little to do with morals. (And I now began to wonder about the meaning of this word.) My judgment had been due to my sense of how little they appeared to want. I could not conceive of peddling myself for so low a price.

But, for a higher price? for Fonny?

And I fell asleep; for a while; and then I woke up. I had never been so tired in my life. I ached all over. I looked at the clock and I realized that it would soon be time to get up and go to work, unless I called in sick. But I could not call in sick.

I got dressed and went out to the kitchen, to have tea with Mama. Joseph and Ernestine had already gone. Mama and I sipped our tea in almost total silence. Something was turning over and over and over, in my mind: I could not speak.

I came down into the streets. It was a little past eight o'clock. I walked these morning streets; these streets are never empty. I passed the old blind black man on the corner. Perhaps I had seen him all my life. But I wondered about his life, for the first time, now. There were about four kids, all junkies, standing on the corner, talking. Some women were rushing to work. I tried to read their faces. Some women were finally going to get a little rest, and they headed off the avenue, to their furnished rooms. Every side street was piled high with garbage, and garbage was piled high before every stoop along the avenue. I thought, If I'm going to peddle ass, I better not try it up here. It would take just as long as scrubbing floors, and be a lot more painful. What I was really thinking was, I know I can't do it before the baby comes, but, if Fonny's not out by then, maybe I'll have to try it. Maybe I better get ready. But there was something else turning over, at the bottom of my mind, which I knew I didn't have the courage to look at yet.

Get ready, how? I walked down the steps and pushed through the turnstile and stood on the subway platform, with the others. When the train came, I pushed in, with the others, and I leaned against a pole, while their breath and smell rolled over me. Cold sweat covered my forehead and began to trickle down my armpits and my back. I hadn't thought of it before, because I knew I had to keep on working up to just about the last minute; but now I began to wonder just how, as I became heavier and sicker, I was going to *get* to work. If I should pass out, these people, getting on and getting off, would simply trample me and the baby to death. *We're counting on you—Fonny's counting on you—Fonny's counting on* you, *to bring that baby here, safe and well*. I held the white bar more firmly. My freezing body shook.

I looked around the subway car. It was a little like the drawings I had seen of slave ships. Of course, they hadn't had newspapers on the slave ships, hadn't needed them yet; but, as concerned space (and also, perhaps, as concerned intention) the principle was exactly the same. A heavy man, smelling of hot sauce and toothpaste, breathed heavily into my face. It wasn't his fault that he had to breathe, or that my face was there. His body pressed against me, too, very hard, but this did not mean that he was thinking of rape, or thinking of me at all. He was probably wondering only—and that, dimly—how he was going to get through another day on his job. And he certainly did not see me.

And, when a subway car is packed—unless it's full of people who know each other, going on a picnic, say—it is almost always silent. It's as though everybody is just holding his breath, waiting to get out of there. Each time the train comes into a station, and some of the people push you aside, in order to get out—as happened now, for example, with the man who smelled of hot sauce and toothpaste—a great sigh seems to rise; stifled immediately by the people who get on. Now, a blond girl, carrying a bandbox, was breathing her hangover into my face. My stop came, and I got off, climbed the steps and crossed the street. I went into the service entrance and punched the clock, put my street clothes away and went out to my counter. I was a little late for the floor, but I'd clocked in on time.

The floor manager, a white boy, young, nice enough, gave me a mock scowl as I hurried to my place.

It isn't only old white ladies who come to that counter to smell the back of my hand. Very rarely does a black cat come anywhere near this counter, and if, or when, he does, his intentions are often more generous and always more precise. Perhaps, for a black cat, I really do, too closely, resemble a helpless baby sister. He doesn't want to see me turn into a whore. And perhaps some black cats come closer, just to look into my eyes, just to hear my voice, to check out what's happening. And they never smell the back of my hand: a black cat puts out *his* hand, and you spray it, and he carries the back of his own hand to his own nostrils. And he doesn't bother to pretend that he's come to buy perfume. Sometimes, he does—buy some perfume; most often he doesn't. Sometimes the hand he has brought down from his nostrils clenches itself into a secret fist, and, with that prayer, that salutation, he moves away. But a white man will carry your hand to his nostrils, he will hold it there. I watched everybody, all day long, with something turning over and over and over, in my mind. Ernestine came to pick me up at the end of the day. She said that Mrs. Rogers had been located, in Santurce, Puerto Rico; and someone of us would have to go there.

"With Hayward?"

"No. Hayward's got to deal with Bell, and the D.A. here. Anyway, you can see that, for many, many reasons, Hayward *can't* go. He'd be accused of intimidating a witness."

"But that's what *they're* doing—!"

"Tish"—we were walking up Eighth Avenue, toward Columbus Circle—"it would take us until your baby is voting age to prove *that*."

"Are we going to take the subway, or the bus?"

"We're going to sit down somewhere until this rush hour's over. You and me, we've got to talk anyway, before we talk to Mama and Daddy. They don't know yet. I haven't talked to them yet."

And I realize how much Ernestine loves me, at the same time that I remember that she is, after all, only four years older than I.

Mrs. Victoria Rogers, née Victoria Maria San Felipe Sanchez, declares that on the evening of March 5, between

*the hours of eleven and twelve, in the vestibule of her home,
she was criminally assaulted by a man she now knows to
have been Alonzo Hunt, and was used by the aforesaid
Hunt in the most extreme and abominable sexual manner,
and forced to undergo the most unimaginable sexual per-
versions.*

I have never seen her. I know only that an American-
born Irishman, Gary Rogers, an engineer, went to Puerto
Rico about six years ago, and there met Victoria, who was
then about eighteen. He married her, and brought her to
the mainland. His career did not go up, but down; he
seems to have become embittered. In any case, having
pumped three children out of her, he left. I know nothing
about the man with whom she was living on Orchard
Street, with whom, presumably, she had fled to Puerto Rico.
The children are, presumably, somewhere on the mainland,
with her relatives. Her "home" is Orchard Street. She lived
on the fourth floor. If the rape took place in the "vestibule,"
then she was raped on the ground floor, under the staircase.
It could have taken place on the fourth floor, but it seems
unlikely; there are four apartments on that floor. Orchard
Street, if you know New York, is a very long way from
Bank Street. Orchard Street is damn near in the East River
and Bank Street is practically in the Hudson. It is not possible
to run from Orchard to Bank, particularly not with the
police behind you. Yet, Bell *swears* that he saw Fonny "run
from the scene of the crime." This is possible only if Bell
were off duty, for his "beat" is on the West Side, not the
East. Yet, Bell could arrest Fonny out of the house on
Bank Street. It is then up to the accused to prove, and pay

for proving, the irregularity and improbability of this sequence of events.

Ernestine and I had sat down in the last booth of a bar off Columbus.

Ernestine's way with me, and with all her children, is to drop something heavy on you and then lean back, calculating how you'll take it. She's got to know that, in order to calculate her own position: the net's got to be in place.

Now, maybe because I had spent so much of the day, and the night before, with my terrors—and my calculations—concerning the possible sale of my body, I began to see the reality of rape.

I asked, "Do you think she really was raped?"

"Tish. I don't know what's going on in that busy, ingrown mind of yours, but that question has no bearing on anything. As far as our situation is concerned, baby, she was raped. That's it." She paused and sipped her drink. She sounded very calm, but her forehead was tense, intelligent, with terror. "I think, in fact, that she was raped and that she has absolutely no idea who did it, would probably not even recognize him if he passed her on the street. I may sound crazy, but the mind works that way. She'd recognize him if he raped her *again*. But then it would no longer be rape. If you see what I mean."

"I see what you mean. But why does she accuse Fonny?"

"Because Fonny was presented to her as the rapist and it was much easier to say yes than to try and relive the whole damn thing again. This way, it's over, for her. Except for the trial. But, then, it's really over. For her."

"And for us, too?"

"No." She looked at me very steadily. It may seem a funny thing to say, but I found myself admiring her guts. "It won't be over for us." She spoke very carefully, watching me all the while. "There's a way in which it may never be over, for us. But we won't talk about that now. Listen. We have to think about it very seriously, and in another way. That's why I wanted to have a drink alone with you, before we went home."

"What are you trying to tell me?" I was suddenly very frightened.

"Listen. I don't think that we can get her to change her testimony. You've got to understand: she's not lying."

"What are you trying to tell me? What the fuck do you mean, she's not lying?"

"Will you listen to me? Please? Of course, she's *lying*. *We* know she's lying. But—*she's*—not—*lying*. As far as she's concerned, Fonny raped her and that's that, and now she hasn't got to deal with it anymore. It's over. For her. If she changes her testimony, she'll go mad. Or become another woman. And you know how often people go mad, and how rarely they change."

"So—what are we to do?"   .

"We have to disprove the state's case. There's no point in saying that we have to make *them* prove it, because, as far as they're concerned, the accusation *is* the proof and that's exactly the way those nuts in the jury box will take it, quiet as it's kept. *They're* liars, too—and *we* know they're liars. But *they* don't."

I remembered, for some reason, something someone had said to me, a long time ago—it might have been Fonny: *A fool never says he's a fool.*

"We can't disprove it. Daniel's in jail."

"Yes. But Hayward is seeing him tomorrow."

"That don't mean nothing. Daniel is still going to change his testimony, I bet you."

"He may. He may not. But I have another idea."

There we sat, in this dirty bar, two sisters, trying to be cool.

"Let's say the worst comes to the worst. Mrs. Rogers will not change her testimony. Let's say Daniel changes his. That leaves only Officer Bell, doesn't it?"

"Yes. And so what?"

"Well—I have a file on him. A long file. I can prove that he murdered a twelve-year-old black boy, in Brooklyn, two years ago. That's how come he was transferred to Manhattan. I know the mother of the murdered boy. And I know Bell's wife, who hates him."

"She can't testify against him."

"She hasn't got to testify against him. She just has to sit in that courtroom, and watch him—"

"I don't see how this helps us—at *all*——"

"I know you don't. And you may be right. But, if worse comes to worst, and it's always better to assume that it will—come to worst—then our tactic has to be to shatter the credibility of the state's only witness."

"Ernestine," I said, "you're dreaming."

"I don't think I am. I'm gambling. If I can get those two women, one white and one black, to sit in that courtroom, and if Hayward does his work right, we ought to be able to shatter the case, on cross-examination. Remember, Tish, that, after all, it isn't very much of a case. If Fonny were white, it wouldn't be a case at all."

Well. I understand what she means. I know where she's

coming from. It's a long shot. But, in our position, after all, only the long shot counts. We don't have any other: that's it. And I realize, too, that if we thought it were feasible, we might very well be sitting here, cool, very cool, discussing ways and means of having Bell's head blown off. And, when it was done, we'd shrug and have another drink: that's it. People don't know.

"Yes. Okay. What about Puerto Rico?"

"That's one of the reasons I wanted to talk to you. Before we talk to Mama and Daddy. Look. *You* can't go. You've got to be here. For one thing, without you, Fonny will panic. I don't see how *I* can go. I've got to keep lighting firecrackers under Hayward's ass. Obviously, a man can't go. Daddy can't go, and God knows Frank can't go. That leaves—Mama."

"Mama—?"

"Yes."

"She don't want to go to Puerto Rico."

"That's right. And she hates planes. But she wants your baby's father out of jail. Of course she doesn't want to go to Puerto Rico. But she'll go."

"And what do you think she can *do?*"

"She can do something no special investigator can do. She may be able to break through to Mrs. Rogers. Maybe not—but if she can, we're ahead. And if not—well, we haven't lost anything, and, at least, we'll know we've tried."

I watch her forehead. Okay.

"And what about Daniel?"

"I told you. Hayward is seeing him tomorrow. He *may* have been able to see him today. He's calling us tonight."

I lean back. "Some shit."

"Yeah. But we in it now."

Then, we are silent. I realize, for the first time, that the bar is loud. And I look around me. It's actually a terrible place and I realize that the people here can only suppose that Ernestine and I are tired whores, or a Lesbian couple, or both. Well. We are certainly in it now, and it may get worse. It will, certainly—and now something almost as hard to catch as a whisper in a crowded place, as light and as definite as a spider's web, strikes below my ribs, stunning and astonishing my heart—get worse. But that light tap, that kick, that signal, announces to me that what can get worse can get better. Yes. It will get worse. But the baby, turning for the first time in its incredible veil of water, announces its presence and claims me; tells me, in that instant, that what can get worse can get better; and that what can get better can get worse. In the meantime—forever —it is entirely up to me. The baby cannot get here without me. And, while I may have known this, in one way, a little while ago, now the baby knows it, and tells me that while it will certainly be worse, once it leaves the water, what gets worse can also get better. It will be in the water for a while yet: but it is preparing itself for a transformation. And so must I.

I said, "It's all right. I'm not afraid."

And Ernestine smiled, and said, "Let's move it then."

Joseph and Frank, as we learn later, have also been sitting in a bar, and this is what happened between them:

Joseph has a certain advantage over Frank—though it is only now that he begins to realize, or, rather, suspect it—in that he has no sons. He has always wanted a son; this fact cost Ernestine far more than it cost me; for, by the time I came along, he was reconciled. If he had had sons, they might very well be dead, or in jail. And they both know, facing each other in the booth of a bar on Lenox Avenue, that it is a miracle that Joseph's daughters are not on the block. Both of them know far more than either of them would like to know, and certainly far more than either can say, concerning the disasters which have overtaken the women in Frank's house.

And Frank looks down, holding his drink tightly between both hands: *he* has a son. And Joseph sips his beer and watches him. That son is also *his* son now, and that makes Frank his brother.

They are both grown men, approaching fifty, and they are both in terrible trouble.

Neither of them look it. Joseph is much darker than Frank, black, deep-set, hooded eyes, stern, still, a high forehead in which one vein beats, leftward, a forehead so high that it can make you think of cathedrals. His lips are always a little twisted. Only those who know him—only those who love him—know when this twist signals laughter, love, or fury. The key is to be found in the pulsing vein in the forehead. The lips change very little, the eyes change all the time: and when Joseph is happy, and when he laughs, something absolutely miraculous is happening. He then looks, I swear to you,—and his hair is beginning to turn gray,—about thirteen years old. I thought once, I'm certainly glad I didn't meet him when he was a young man and then I thought, But you're his daughter, and then I dropped into a paralyzed silence, thinking: Wow.

Frank is light, thinner. I don't think that you can describe my father as handsome; but you can describe Frank that way. I don't mean to be putting him down when I say that because that face has paid, and is paying, a dreadful price. People make you pay for the way you look, which is also the way *you* think you look, and what time writes in a human face is the record of that collision. Frank has survived it, barely. His forehead is lined like the palm of a hand—unreadable; his graying hair is thick and curls violently upward from the widow's peak. His lips are not as thick as Joseph's and do not dance that way, are pressed tightly together, as though he wished they would disappear. His cheekbones are high, and his large dark eyes slant upward, like Fonny's—Fonny has his father's eyes.

Joseph certainly cannot realize this in the way that his daughter knows it. But he stares at Frank in silence, and forces Frank to raise his eyes.

"What we going to do?" Frank asks.

"Well, the first thing we got to do," says Joseph, resolutely, "is to stop blaming each other, and stop blaming ourselves. If we can't do that, man, we'll never get the boy out because *we'll* be so fucked up. And we cannot fuck up now, baby, and I know you hear where I'm coming from."

"Man, what," asks Frank—with his little smile—"we going to do about the money?"

"You ever have any money?" Joseph asks.

Frank looks up at him and says nothing—merely questions him with his eyes.

Joseph asks again, "You ever have any money?"

Frank says, finally, "No."

"Then, why you worried about it now?"

Frank looks up at him again.

"You raised them somehow, didn't you? You fed them somehow—didn't you? If we start to worrying about money now, man, we going to be fucked and we going to lose our children. That white man, baby, and may his balls shrivel and his ass-hole rot, he *want* you to be worried about the money. That's his whole game. But if we got to where we are without money, we can get further. I ain't worried about they money—they ain't got no right to it anyhow, they stole it from us—they ain't never met nobody they didn't lie to and steal from. Well, I can steal, too. *And* rob. How you think I raised my daughters? Shit."

But Frank is not Joseph. He stares down again, into his drink.

"What you think is going to happen?"

"What we *make* happen," says Joseph—again, with resolution.

"That's easy to say," says Frank.

"Not if you mean it," says Joseph.

There is a long silence into which neither man speaks. Even the jukebox is silent.

"I guess," Frank says, finally, "I love Fonny more than I love anybody in this world. And it makes me ashamed, man, I swear, because he was a real sweet manly little boy, wasn't scared of nothing—except maybe his Mama. He didn't understand his Mama." Frank stops. "And I don't know what I should have done. I ain't a woman. And there's some things only a woman can do with a child. And I thought she loved him—like I guess I thought, one time, she loved me." Frank sips his drink, and he tries to smile.

"I don't know if I was ever any kind of father to him—any kind of *real* father—and now he's in jail and it ain't his fault and I don't even know how I'm going to get him out. I'm sure one hell of a man."

"Well," says Joseph, "*he* sure think you are. He loves you, and he respects you—now, you got to remember that *I* might know that much better than you. Tell you something else. Your baby son is the father of my baby daughter's baby. Now, how you going to sit here and act like can't nothing be done? We got a child on the way here, man. You want me to beat the shit out of you?" He says this with ferocity; but, after a moment, he smiles. "I know," he says, then, carefully, "I know. But I know some hustles and you know some hustles and these are our children and we got to set them free." Joseph finishes his beer. "So, let's drink up, man, and go on in. We got a whole lot of shit to deal with, in a hurry."

Frank finishes his drink, and straightens his shoulders. "You right, old buddy. Let's make it."

The date for Fonny's trial keeps changing. This fact, paradoxically, forces me to realize that Hayward's concern is genuine. I don't think that he very much cared, in the beginning. He had never taken a case like Fonny's before, and it was Ernestine, acting partly out of experience but mainly out of instinct, who had bludgeoned him into it. But, once into it, the odor of shit rose high; and he had no choice but to keep on stirring it. It became obvious at once, for example, that the degree of his concern for his client—or the fact that he had any genuine concern for his client at all—placed him at odds, at loggerheads, with the keepers of the keys and seals. He had not expected this, and at first it bewildered, then frightened, then angered him. He swiftly understood that he was between the carrot and the stick: he couldn't avoid the stick but he had to make it clear, finally, that he'd be damned if he'd go for the carrot. This had the effect of isolating, indeed of branding him, and, as this increased Fonny's danger, it also increased Hayward's responsibility. It did not help that I distrusted him, Ernestine harangued him, Mama was laconic, and, for Joseph, he was just another white boy with a college degree.

Although, naturally, in the beginning, I distrusted him, I am not really what you can call a distrustful person: and, anyway, as time wore on, with each of us trying to hide our terror from the other, we began to depend more and more on one another—we had no choice. And I began to see, as time wore on, that, for Hayward, the battle increasingly became a private one, involving neither gratitude nor public honor. It was a sordid, a banal case, this rape by a black boy of an ignorant Puerto Rican woman—what was he getting so excited about? And so his colleagues scorned and avoided him. This fact introduced yet other dangers, not least of them the danger of retreating into the self-pitying and quixotic. But Fonny was too real a presence, and Hayward too proud a man for that.

But the calendars were full—it would take about a thousand years to try all the people in the American prisons, but the Americans are optimistic and still hope for time—and sympathetic or merely intelligent judges are as rare as snowstorms in the tropics. There was the obscene power and the ferocious enmity of the D.A.'s office. Thus, Hayward walked a chalk line, maneuvering very hard to bring Fonny before a judge who would really listen to the case. For this, Hayward needed charm, patience, money, and a backbone of tempered steel.

He managed to see Daniel, who has been beaten. He cannot arrange for his release because Daniel has been booked on a narcotics charge. Without becoming Daniel's lawyer, he cannot visit him. He suggests this to Daniel, but Daniel is evasive and afraid. Hayward suspects that Daniel has also been drugged and he does not know if he dares bring Daniel to the witness stand, or not.

So. There we are. Mama begins letting out my clothes, and I go to work wearing jackets and slacks. But it's clear that I'm not going to be able to keep working much longer: I've got to be able to visit Fonny every instant that I can. Joseph is working overtime, double time, and so is Frank. Ernestine has to spend less time with her children because she has taken a job as part-time private secretary to a very rich and eccentric young actress, whose connections she intends to intimidate, and use. Joseph is coldly, systematically, stealing from the docks, and Frank is stealing from the garment center and they sell the hot goods in Harlem, or in Brooklyn. They don't tell us this, but we know it. They don't tell us because, if things go wrong, we can't be accused of being accomplices. We cannot penetrate their silence, we must not try. Each of these men would gladly go to jail, blow away a pig, or blow up a city, to save their progeny from the jaws of this democratic hell.

Now, Sharon must begin preparing for her Puerto Rican journey, and Hayward briefs her:

"She is not actually in Santurce, but a little beyond it, in what might once have been called a suburb, but which is now far worse than what we would call a slum. In Puerto Rico, I believe it is called a *favella*. I have been to Puerto Rico once, and so I will not try to describe a *favella*. And I am sure, when you return, that you will not try to describe it, either."

Hayward looks at her, at once distant and intense, and hands her a typewritten sheet of paper. "This is the address. But I think that you will understand, almost as soon as you get where you are going, that the word 'address' has almost no meaning—it would be more honest to say: this is the neighborhood."

Sharon, wearing her floppy beige beret, looks at it.

"There's no phone," says Hayward, "and, anyway, a phone is the very last thing you need. You might as well send up flares. But it isn't hard to find. Just follow your nose."

They stare at each other.

"Now," says Hayward, with his really painful smile, "just to make things easier for you, I must tell you that we are not really certain under which name she is living. Her maiden name is Sanchez—but that's a little like looking for a Mrs. Jones or a Mr. Smith. Her married name is Rogers; but I am sure that that appears only on her passport. The name of what we must call her common-law husband"— and now he pauses to look down at another sheet of paper, and then at Sharon and then at me—"is Pietro Thomasino Alvarez."

He hands Sharon this piece of paper; and, again, Sharon studies it.

"And," says Hayward, "take this with you. I hope it will help. She still looks this way. It was snapped last week."

And he hands Sharon a photograph, slightly larger than passport size.

I have never seen her. I stand, to peer over Sharon's shoulder. She is blond—but are Puerto Ricans blond? She is smiling up into the camera a constipated smile; yet, there is life in the eyes. The eyes and the eyebrows are dark, and the dark shoulders are bare.

"This from a night club?" Sharon asks; and, "Yes," Hayward answers, she watching him, he watching her: and:

"Does she work there?" Sharon asks.

"No," says Hayward. "But Pietro does."

I keep studying, over my mother's shoulder, the face of my most mortal enemy.

Mama turns the photograph over, and holds it in her lap.

"And how old is this Pietro?"

"About—twenty-two," says Hayward.

And just exactly like, as the song puts it, *God arose! In a windstorm! And he troubled everybody's mind!* silence fell in the office. Mama leans forward, thinking ahead.

"Twenty-two," she says, slowly.

"Yes," says Hayward. "I'm afraid that detail may present us with a brand new ball game."

"What do you want me to do exactly?" Sharon asks.

"Help me," Hayward says.

"Well," says Sharon, after a moment, opening her purse, then opening her wallet, carefully placing the bits of paper in her wallet, closing the wallet, burying the wallet in the depths of her purse, and snapping shut the purse, "then I'll be leaving sometime tomorrow. I'll call, or have somebody call, before I go. Just so you'll know where I am."

And she rises, and Hayward rises, and we walk to the door.

"Do you have a photograph of Fonny with you?" Hayward asks.

"*I* do," I say.

And I open my bag and find my wallet. I actually have two photographs, one of Fonny and me leaning against the railing of the house on Bank Street. His shirt is open to the belly button, he has one arm around me, and we are both laughing. The other is of Fonny alone, sitting in the house near the record player, somber and peaceful; and it's my favorite photograph of him.

Mama takes the photographs, hands them to Hayward, who studies them. Then she takes them back from Hayward.

"These the only ones you got?" she asks me.

"Yes," I say.

She hands me back the photograph of Fonny alone. She puts the one of Fonny and me into her wallet, which again descends into the bottom of her purse. "This one ought to get it," she says. "After all, it *is* my daughter, and *she* ain't been raped." She shakes hands with Hayward. "Keep your fingers crossed, son, and let's hope the old lady can bring home the goods."

She turns toward the door. But Hayward checks her again.

"The fact that you are going to Puerto Rico makes me feel better than I have felt for weeks. But: I must also tell you that the D.A.'s office is in constant touch with the Hunt family—that is, the mother and the two sisters—and their position appears to be that Fonny has always been incorrigible and worthless."

Hayward pauses, and looks steadily at us both.

"Now: if the state can get three respectable black women to depose, or to testify, that their son and brother has always been a dangerously antisocial creature, this is a very serious blow for us."

He pauses again, and he turns toward the window.

"As a matter of fact—for Galileo Santini is not a stupid man—it might be vastly more effective if he does not call them as character witnesses, for then they cannot be cross-examined—he need merely convey to the jury that these respectable churchgoing women are prostrate with shame and grief. And the father can be dismissed as a hard-drinking good-for-nothing, a dreadful example to his son—especially as he has publicly threatened to blow Santini's head off."

He turns from the window, to watch us very carefully.

"I think I will probably call on you, Sharon, and on Mr. Rivers, as character witnesses. But you see what we are up against."

"It's always better," says Sharon, "to know than not to know."

Hayward claps Sharon gently on the shoulder. "So try to bring home the goods."

I think to myself: and I will take care of those sisters, and that mother. But I don't say anything, except "Thanks, Hayward. Good-bye."

And Sharon says, "Okay. Got you. Good-bye." And we walk down the hall to the elevator.

I remember the night the baby was conceived because it was the night of the day we finally found our loft. And this cat, whose name was Levy, really was going to rent it to us, he wasn't full of shit. He was an olive-skinned, curly-haired, merry-faced boy from the Bronx, about thirty-three, maybe, with big, kind of electrical black eyes, and he dug us. He dug people who loved each other. The loft was off Canal Street, and it was big and in pretty good condition. It had two big windows on the street, and the two back windows opened onto a roof, with a railing. There was a room for Fonny to work, and, with all the windows open, you wouldn't die of heat prostration in the summertime. We were very excited about the roof because you could have dinner on it, or serve drinks, or just sit there in the evenings, if you wanted to, with your arms around each other. "Hell," Levy said, "drag out the blankets and sleep on it." He smiled at Fonny. "Make babies on it. That's how *I* got here." What I most remember about him is that he didn't make either of us feel self-conscious. We all laughed together. "You two should have some beautiful babies," he said, "and, take it from me, kids, the world damn sure needs them."

He asked us for only one month in advance, and, about a week later, I took the money over to him. And then, when Fonny got into trouble, he did something very strange, and, I think, very beautiful. He called me and he said that I could have the money back, anytime I wanted it. But, he said, he wouldn't rent that loft to anybody but us. "I can't," he said. "The bastards. That loft stays empty until your man gets out of jail, and I ain't just whistling Dixie, honey." And he gave me his number and asked me please to let him know if there was anything at all he could do. "I want you kids to have your babies. I'm funny that way."

Levy explained and exhibited the somewhat complicated structure of locks and keys. Our loft was the top, up three or four stories. The stairs were steep. There was a set of keys for our loft, which had double locks. Then, there was the door at the top of the steps, which locked us away from the rest of the building.

"Man," Fonny asked, "what do we do in case of fire?"

"Oh," said Levy, "I forgot," and he unlocked the doors again and we went back into the loft. He took us onto the roof and led us to the edge, where the railing was. On the far right of the roof the railing opened, extending itself into a narrow catwalk. This railing led to the metal steps, by which steps one descended into the courtyard. Once in this courtyard, which seemed to be closed in by walls, one might wonder what on earth to do: it was something of a trap. Still, one would not have had to leap from the burning building. Once on the ground, one had to hope, merely, not to be buried beneath the flaming, crashing walls.

"Well," said Fonny, carefully holding me by one elbow, and leading me back onto the roof, "I can dig that." We again went through the ritual of the locking of the doors, and descended into the street. "Don't worry about the neighbors," Levy said, "because, after five or six o'clock, you won't have any. All you got between you and the street are small, failing sweatshops."

And we got into the streets and he showed us how to lock and unlock the street door.

"Got it?" he asked Fonny.

"Got it," Fonny said.

"Come on. I'll buy you a milk shake."

And we had three milk shakes on the corner, and Levy shook hands, and left us, saying that he had to get home to his wife and kids—two boys, one aged two, one aged three and a half. But before he left us, he said, "Look. I told you not to worry about the neighbors. But watch out for the cops. They're murder."

One of the most terrible, most mysterious things about a life is that a warning can be heeded only in retrospect: too late.

Levy left us, and Fonny and I walked, hand in hand, up the broad, bright, crowded streets, toward the Village, toward our pad. We talked and talked and laughed and laughed. We crossed Houston and started up Sixth Avenue —Avenue of the Americas!—with all those fucking flags on it, which we didn't see. I wanted to stop at one of the markets on Bleecker Street, to buy some tomatoes. We crossed the Avenue of the Americas and started west, on Bleecker. Fonny had one hand around my waist. We stopped at a vegetable stand. I started looking.

Fonny hates shopping. He said, "Wait one minute. I'm going to buy some cigarettes," and he went up the street, just around the corner.

I started picking out the tomatoes, and I remember that I was kind of humming to myself. I started looking around for a scale and for the man or the woman who would weigh the tomatoes for me and tell me what I owed.

Fonny is right about me when he says I'm not very bright. When I first felt this hand on my behind, I thought it was Fonny: then I realized that Fonny would never, never touch me that way, in public.

I turned, my six tomatoes in both hands, and found myself facing a small, young, greasy Italian punk.

"I can sure dig a tomato who digs tomatoes," he said, and he licked his lips, and smiled.

Two things happened in me, all at the same time— three. This was a very crowded street. I knew that Fonny would be back at any moment. I wanted to smash my tomatoes in the boy's face. But no one had really noticed us yet, and I didn't want Fonny to get into a fight. I saw a white cop coming slowly up the street.

I realized that I was black and that the crowded streets were white and so I turned away and walked into the shop, still with my tomatoes in my hands. I found a scale and I put the tomatoes on the scale and I looked around for someone to weigh them, so that I could pay and get out of this store before Fonny came back from around the corner. The cop was now on the other side of the street; and the boy had followed me into the store.

"Hey, sweet tomato. *You* know I dig tomatoes."

And now people *were* watching us. I did not know what to do—the only thing to do was to get out of there before Fonny turned the corner. I tried to move: but the boy blocked my way. I looked around, for someone to help me—people were staring, but no one moved. I decided, in despair, to call the cop. But, when I moved, the boy grabbed my arm. He was, really, probably, just a broken-down junkie—but when he grabbed my arm, I slapped his face and I spat in it: and exactly at that moment, Fonny entered the store.

Fonny grabbed the boy by the hair, knocked him to the ground, picked him up and kicked him in the balls and dragged him to the sidewalk and knocked him down again. I screamed and held on to Fonny with all my might, for I saw that the cop, who had been on the far corner, was now crossing the street, on the run; and the white boy lay bleeding and retching in the gutter. I was sure that the cop intended to kill Fonny; but he could not kill Fonny if I could keep my body between Fonny and this cop; and with all my strength, with all my love, my prayers, and armed with the knowledge that Fonny was not, after all, going to knock *me* to the ground, I held the back of my head against Fonny's chest, held both his wrists between my two hands, and looked up into the face of this cop. I said, "That man—there—attacked me. Right in this store. Right now. Everybody saw it."

No one said a word.

The cop looked at them all. Then, he looked back at me. Then, he looked at Fonny. I could not see Fonny's face. But I could see the cop's face: and I knew that I must not move, nor, if I could possibly help it, allow Fonny to move.

"And where were you," the cop elaborately asked Fonny, "while all this"—his eyes flicked over me in exactly the same way the boy's eyes had—"while all this was going on between junior, there, and"—his eyes took me in again —"and your girl?"

"He was around the corner," I said, "buying cigarettes." For I did not want Fonny to speak.

I hoped that he would forgive me, later.

"Is that so, boy?"

I said, "He's not a boy. Officer."

Now, he looked at me, really looked at me for the first time, and, therefore, for the first time, he really looked at Fonny.

Meanwhile, some people had got junior to his feet.

"You live around here?" the cop asked Fonny.

The back of my head was still on Fonny's chest, but he had released his wrists from my hands.

"Yes," Fonny said, "on Bank Street," and he gave the officer the address.

I knew that, in a moment, Fonny would push me away.

"We're going to take you down, boy," the cop said, "for assault and battery."

I do not know what would now have happened if the Italian lady who ran the store had not spoken up. "Oh, no," she said, "I know both these young people. They shop here very often. What the young lady has told you is the truth. I saw them both, just now, when they came, and I watched her choose her tomatoes and her young man left her and he said he would be right back. I was busy, I could not get to her right away; her tomatoes are still on the scale. And that little good-for-nothing shit over there, he *did* attack her. And he has got exactly what he deserved. What would *you* do if a man attacked *your* wife? if you have one." The crowd snickered, and the cop flushed. "I saw exactly what happened. I am a witness. And I will swear to it."

She and the cop stared at each other.

"Funny way to run a business," he said, and licked his lower lip.

"*You* will not tell *me* how to run my business," she

said. "I was on this street before you got here and I will be here when you are gone. Take," she said, gesturing toward the boy now sitting on the curbstone, with some of his friends around him, "that miserable urchin away with you, to Bellevue, or to Rikers' Island—or drop him in the river, he is of no earthly use to anyone. But do not try to frighten *me—basta!*"

I notice, for the first time, that Bell's eyes are blue and that what I can see of his hair is red.

He looks again at me and then again at Fonny.

He licks his lips again.

The Italian lady reenters the store and takes my tomatoes off the scale and puts them in a bag.

"Well," says Bell, staring at Fonny, "be seeing you around."

"You may," says Fonny, "and then again, you may not."

"Not," says the Italian lady, coming back into the street, "if they, or I, see you first." She turns me around and puts the bag of tomatoes into my hands. She is standing between myself and Bell. She stares into my eyes. "You have a good man," she says. "Take him home. Away from these diseased pigs." I look at her. She touches my face. "I have been in America a long time," she says. "I hope I do not die here."

She goes back into her store. Fonny takes the tomatoes from me, and holds the bag in the crook of one arm; the other arm he entwines through mine, interlocking his fingers through mine. We walk slowly away, toward our pad.

"Tish," says Fonny—very quietly; with a dreadful quietness.

I almost know what he is going to say.

"Yes?"

"Don't ever try to protect me again. Don't do that."

I know I am saying the wrong thing: "But you were trying to protect *me*."

"It's not," he says, with the same terrifying quietness, "the same thing, Tish."

And he suddenly takes the bag of tomatoes and smashes them against the nearest wall. Thank God the wall is blank, thank God it is now beginning to be dark. Thank God tomatoes spatter but do not ring.

I know what he is saying. I know he is right. I know I must not say anything. Thank God, he does not let go my hand. I look down at the sidewalk, which I cannot see. I hope he cannot hear my tears.

But he does.

He stops and turns me to him, and he kisses me. He pulls away and looks at me and kisses me again.

"Don't think I don't know you love me. You believe we going to make it?"

Then, I am calm. There are tears on his face, his or mine, I don't know. I kiss him where our tears fall. I start to say something. He puts one finger on my lips. He smiles his little smile.

"Hush. Don't say a word. I'm going to take you out to dinner. At our Spanish place, you remember? Only, this time, it's got to be on credit."

And he smiles and I smile and we keep on walking.

"We have no money," Fonny says to Pedrocito, when we enter the restaurant, "but we are very hungry. And I will have some money in a couple of days."

"In a couple of days," says Pedrocito, furiously, "that is

what they all say! And, furthermore"—striking an incredulous hand to his forehead—"I suppose that you would like to eat *sitting down!*"

"Why, yes," says Fonny, grinning, "if you could arrange it, that would be nice."

"At a *table,* no doubt?" And he stares at Fonny as though he simply cannot believe his eyes.

"Well—I would—yeah—like a table—"

"Ah!" But, "Good evening, Señorita," Pedrocito now says, and smiles at me. "It is for her I do it, you know," he informs Fonny. "It is clear that you do not feed her properly." He leads us to a table and sits us down. "And now, no doubt," he scowls, "you would like two margheritas?"

"Caught me again," says Fonny, and he and Pedrocito laugh and Pedrocito disappears.

Fonny takes my hand in his.

"Hello," he says.

I say, "Hello."

"I don't want you to feel bad about what I said to you before. You a fine, tough chick and I know, hadn't been for you, my brains might be being spattered all over that precinct basement by now."

He pauses, and he lights a cigarette. I watch him.

"So, I don't mean that you did nothing wrong. I guess you did the only thing you could have done. But you got to understand where I'm coming from."

He takes my hands between his again.

"We live in a nation of pigs and murderers. I'm scared every time you out of my sight. And maybe what happened just now was my fault, because I should never have left you

: *141* :

alone at that vegetable stand—but I was just so happy, you know, about the loft—I wasn't thinking—"

"Fonny, I've been to that vegetable stand a hundred times, and nothing like that ever happened before. I've got to take care of you—of us. You can't go everywhere I go. How is it *your* fault? That was just some broken-down junkie—"

"Some broken-down white American," Fonny says.

"Well. It's still not *your* fault."

He smiles at me.

"They got us in a trick bag, baby. It's hard, but I just want for you to bear in mind that they can make us lose each other by putting me in the shit—or, they can try to make us lose each other by making *you* try to protect me from it. You see what I mean?"

"Yes," I say, finally, "I see what you mean. And I know that that's true."

Pedrocito returns, with our margheritas.

"We have a specialty tonight," he announces, "very, *very* Spanish, and we are trying it out on all those customers who think Franco is a great man." He looks at Fonny quizzically. "I suppose that you do not exactly qualify—so, for you, I will remove the arsenic. Without the arsenic, it is a little less strong, but it is actually very good, I think you will like it. Do you trust me not to poison you? Anyway, it would be very foolish of me to poison you before you pay your *tremendous* bill. We would immediately go bankrupt." He turns to me. "Will you trust me, Señorita? I assure you that we will prepare it with love."

"Now, watch it, Pete," says Fonny.

"Oh, your mind is like a sewer, you do not deserve so beautiful a girl." And he disappears again.

"That cop," Fonny says, "that cop."

"What about that cop?" But I am suddenly, and I don't know why, as still and as dry as a stone: with fear.

"He's going to try to get me," Fonny says.

"How? You didn't do anything wrong. The Italian lady said so, and she said that she would swear to it."

"That's why he's going to try to get me," Fonny says. "White men don't like it at *all* when a white lady tells them, You a boatful of motherfuckers, and the black cat was right, and you can kiss my ass." He grins. "Because that's what she told him. In front of a whole lot of people. And he couldn't do shit. And he ain't about to forget it."

"Well," I say, "we'll soon be moving downtown, to our loft."

"That's right," he says, and smiles again. Pedrocito arrives, with our specialties.

When two people love each other, when they really love each other, everything that happens between them has something of a sacramental air. They can sometimes seem to be driven very far from each other: I know of no greater torment, no more resounding void—*When your lover has gone!* But tonight, with our vows so mysteriously menaced, and with both of us, though from different angles, placed before this fact, we were more profoundly together than we had ever been before. *Take care of each other,* Joseph had said. *You going to find out it's more than a notion.*

After dinner, and coffee, Pedrocito offered us brandy, and then he left us, in the nearly empty restaurant. Fonny and I just sat there and sipped our brandy, talking a little, holding hands—digging each other. We finished our brandy. Fonny said, "Shall we go?"

"Yes," I said. For I wanted to be alone with him, in his arms.

He signed the check; the last check he was ever to sign there. I have never been allowed to pay it—it has been, they say, misplaced.

We said good-night, and we walked home, with our arms around each other.

There was a patrol car parked across the street from our house, and, as Fonny opened our gate and unlocked our door, it drove off. Fonny smiled, but said nothing. I said nothing.

The baby was conceived that night. I know it. I know it from the way Fonny touched me, held me, entered me. I had never been so open before. And when he started to pull out, I would not let him, I held on to him as tightly as I could, crying and moaning and shaking with him, and felt life, life, his life, inundating me, entrusting itself to me.

Then, we were still. We did not move, because we could not. We held each other so close that we might indeed have been one body. Fonny caressed me and called my name and he fell asleep. I was very proud. I had crossed my river. Now, we were one.

Sharon gets to Puerto Rico on an evening plane. She knows exactly how much money she has, which means that she knows how rapidly she must move against time—which is inexorably moving against her.

She steps down from the plane, with hundreds of

others, and crosses the field, under the blue-black sky; and something in the way the stars hang low, something in the way the air caresses her skin, reminds her of that Birmingham she has not seen in so long.

She has brought with her only a small overnight bag, so she need not wait in line for her luggage. Hayward has made a reservation for her in a small hotel in San Juan; and he has written the address on a piece of paper.

He has warned her that it may not be so easy to find a taxi.

But he has not, of course, been able to prepare her for the stunning confusion which reigns at the San Juan airport. So, Sharon stands still for a moment, trying to sort things out.

She is wearing a green summer dress, my mother, and a wide-brimmed, green cloth hat; her handbag over her shoulder, her overnight bag in her hand; she studies the scene.

Her first impression is that everyone appears to be related to each other. This is not because of the way they look, nor is it a matter of language: it is because of the way they relate to each other. There are many colors here, but this does not, at least at the airport, appear to count for very much. Whoever is speaking is shouting—that is the only way to be heard; and everyone is determined to be heard. It is quite impossible to guess who is leaving, who arriving. Entire families appear to have been squatting there for weeks, with all their earthly possessions piled around them—not, Sharon notes, that these possessions towered very high. For the children, the airport appears to be merely a more challenging way of playing house.

Sharon's problems are real and deep. Since she cannot

allow these to become desperate, she must now rely on what she can establish of illusion: and the key to illusion is complicity. The world sees what it wishes to see, or, when the chips are down, what you tell it to see: it does not wish to see who, or what, or why you are. Only Sharon knows that she is my mother, only she knows what she is doing in San Juan, with no one to meet her. Before speculation rises too high, she must make it clear that she is a visitor, from up the road—from North America: who, through no fault of her own, speaks no Spanish.

Sharon walks to the Hertz desk, and stands there, and smiles, somewhat insistently, at one of the young ladies behind the desk.

"Do you speak English?" she asks the young lady.

The young lady, anxious to prove that she does, looks up, determined to be helpful.

Sharon hands her the address of the hotel. The young lady looks at it, looks back at Sharon. Her look makes Sharon realize that Hayward has been very thoughtful, and that he has placed her in a very respected, respectable hotel.

"I am very sorry to bother you," says Sharon, "but I do not speak any Spanish, and I have had to come here unexpectedly." She pauses, giving no explanation. "And I do not drive. I wondered if I could rent a car, with a driver, or, if not, if you could tell me exactly how to get a taxi—?" Sharon makes a helpless gesture. "You see—?"

She smiles, and the young lady smiles. She looks again at the paper, looks around the airport, narrowing her eyes.

"One moment, Señora," she says.

She leaves her phone off the hook, swings open the small gate, closes it behind her, and disappears.

She reappears very quickly, with a boy of about eighteen. "This is your taxi driver," she says. "He will take you where you are going." She reads the address aloud, and gives the piece of paper back to Sharon. She smiles. "I hope you will enjoy your visit, Señora. If you need anything—allow me?" She gives Sharon her card. "If you need anything, please do not hesitate to call on me."

"Thank you," says Sharon. "Thank you very much. You have been beautiful."

"It was nothing. Jaime," she says, authoritatively, "take the lady's bag."

Jaime does so, and Sharon says good-night, and follows Jaime.

Sharon thinks, *One down!* and begins to be frightened.

But she has to make her choices very quickly. On the way into town, she decides—because he is there—to make friends with Jaime, and to depend, or to seem to depend, on him. He knows the town, and he can drive. It is true that he is terribly young. But that could turn out to be a plus. Someone older, knowing more, might turn out to be a terrible hassle. Her idea is to case the nightclub, to see Pietro, and, possibly, Victoria, without saying anything to them. But it is not a simple matter for a lone woman, black or white, to walk, unescorted, into a nightclub. Furthermore, for all she knows, this nightclub may be a whorehouse. Her only option is to play the American tourist, wide-eyed—but she is black, and this is Puerto Rico.

Only she knows that she's my mother, and about to

become a grandmother; only she knows that she is past forty; only she knows what she is doing here.

She tips Jaime when they arrive at the hotel. Then, as her bag is carried into the hotel, she looks suddenly at her watch. "My God," she says, "do you think you could wait for me, just for a minute, while I register? I had no *idea* it was so late. I promised to meet someone. I won't be a moment. The boy will carry the bag up. Will that be all right?"

Jaime is a somewhat muddy-faced boy, with brilliant eyes, and a sullen smile. He is entirely intrigued by this improbable North American lady—intrigued because he knows, through unutterably grim experience, that, though she may be in trouble, and certainly has a secret, she is not attempting to do him any violence. He understands that she needs him—the taxi—for something; but that is not his affair. He does not know he knows it—the thought has not consciously entered his mind—but he knows she is a mother. He has a mother. He knows one when he sees one. He knows, again without knowing that he knows it, that he can be of service to her tonight. His courtesy is as real as her trouble. And so he says, gravely, that, of course, he will take the Señora wherever she wishes and wait for her as long as she likes.

Sharon cheats on him, a little. She registers, goes up in the elevator with the bellboy, tips him. She cannot decide whether to wear her hat, or not. Her problem is both trivial and serious, but she has never had to confront it before. Her problem is that she does not look her age. She takes her hat off. She puts it back on. Does the hat make her look younger, or older? At home, she looks her age (whatever that age is) because everybody knows her age. She looks her age because she knows her role. But, now, she is about to enter a nightclub, in a strange town, for the first time in twenty years, alone. She puts the hat on. She takes it off. She realizes that panic is about to overtake her, and so she throws the hat onto the night table, scrubs her face in cold water as harshly as she once scrubbed mine, puts on a high-necked white blouse and a black skirt and black high-heeled shoes, pulls her hair cruelly back from her forehead, knots it, and throws a black shawl over her head and shoulders. The intention of all this is to make her look elderly. The effect is to make her look juvenile. Sharon curses, but the taxi is waiting. She grabs her handbag, runs to the elevator, walks swiftly through the lobby, and gets to the taxi. She, certainly, anyway, Jaime's brilliant eyes inform her, looks like a Yankee—or a *gringo*—tourist.

The nightclub is located in what was certainly a backwater, if not, indeed, a swamp, before the immense hotel which houses it was built. It is absolutely hideous, so loud, so blatant, so impervious and cruel, that, facing it causes mere vulgarity to seem an irrecoverable state of grace. Sharon is now really frightened, her hands are shaking. She lights a cigarette.

"I must find someone," she says, to Jaime. "I will not be long."

She has no way of realizing, at that moment, that the entire militia would have trouble driving Jaime away. Sharon has now become his property. This lady, he knows, is in deep trouble. And it is not an ordinary trouble: because this *is* a lady.

"Certainly, Señora," says Jaime, with a smile, and gets out of the cab, and comes to open the door for her.

"Thank you," Sharon says, and walks quickly toward the garish doors, wide open. There is no doorman visible. But there will certainly be a doorman inside.

Now, it must all be played by ear. And all that holds her up, my mother, who once dreamed of being a singer, is her private knowledge of what she is doing in this place.

She enters, in fact, the hotel lobby, keys, registration, mail, cashier, bored clerks (mainly white, and decidedly pale) with no one paying her the slightest attention. She walks as though she knows exactly where she is going. The nightclub is on the left, down a flight of stairs. She turns left, and walks down the stairs.

No one has stopped her yet.

"Señorita—?"

She has never seen a photograph of Pietro. The man before her is bland and swarthy. The light is too dim (and her surroundings too strange) for her to be able to guess his age; he does not seem unfriendly. Sharon smiles.

"Good evening. I hope I'm in the right place. This is ——?" and she stammers the name of the nightclub.

"Sí, Señorita."

"Well—I'm supposed to meet a friend here, but the flight I meant to take was overbooked, and so I was forced to take an earlier one. So, I'm a little early. Could you hide me at a table, in a corner, somewhere?"

"Certainly. With pleasure." He leads her through the crowded room. "What is the name of your friend?"

Her mind dries up, she must go for broke. "It's actually more in the nature of business. I am waiting for a Señor Alvarez. I am Mrs. Rivers. From New York."

"Thank you." He seats her at a table, against the wall. "Will you have a drink while waiting?"

"Yes. Thank you. A screwdriver."

He bows, whoever he is, and walks away.

Two down! thinks Sharon. And she is now very calm.

This is a nightclub, and so the music is—"live." Sharon's days with the drummer come back to her. Her days as a singer come back to her. They do not, as she is to make very vivid to me, much later, come back with the rind of regret. She and the drummer lost each other—that was that; she was not equipped to be a singer, and that was that. Yet, she remembers what she and the drummer and the band attempted, she knows from whence they came. If I remember "Uncloudy Day" because I remember myself sitting on my mother's knee when I first heard it, she remembers "My Lord and I": *And so, we'll walk together, my Lord and I.* That song is Birmingham, her father and her mother, the kitchens, and the mines. She may never, in fact, ever have particularly liked that particular song, but she knows about it, it is a part of her. She slowly realizes that this is the song, which, to different words, if words indeed there are, the young people on the bandstand are belting, or bolting out. And they know nothing at all about the song they are singing: which causes Sharon to wonder if they know anything about themselves at all. This is the first time that Sharon has been alone in a very long time. Even now, she is alone merely physically, in the same way, for example, that she is alone when she goes shopping for her family. Shopping, she must listen, she must look, say yes to this, say no to that, she must choose: she has a family to feed. She cannot poison them, because she loves them. And now she finds herself listening to a sound she has never heard before. If she were shopping, she could not take this home and put it on the family table for it would not nourish them. *My gal and I!* cries the undernourished rock singer, whipping himself into an electronic orgasm. But no one who had ever had a lover, a mother or father, or a Lord, could sound so despairingly masturbatory. For it is despair that Sharon is hearing, and despair, whether or not it can be taken home and placed on the family table, must always be respected. Despair can make one monstrous, but it can also make one noble: and here these children are, in the arena, up for grabs. Sharon claps for them, because she prays for them. Her screwdriver comes, and she smiles up at a face she cannot see. She sips her drink. She stiffens: the children are about to go into their next number: and she looks up into another face she cannot see.

The children begin their number, loud: "I Can't Get No Satisfaction."

"You Mrs. Rivers? You waiting for me?"

"I think so. Won't you sit down?"

He sits down, facing her. Now, she sees him.

Again—thinking of me, and Fonny, and the baby, cursing herself for being so inept, knowing herself to be encircled, trapped, her back to the wall, his back to the door—she yet must go for broke.

"I was told that a certain Mr. Pietro Alvarez worked here. Are you Pietro Alvarez?"

She sees him. And yet, of course, at the same time, she doesn't.

"Maybe. What you want to see him about?"

Sharon wants a cigarette, but she is afraid her hand

will tremble. She picks up her screwdriver in both hands, and sips it, slowly, rather thanking God, now, for the shawl, which she can maneuver to shadow her face. If she can see him, he can also see her. She is silent for a moment. Then she puts down her drink and she picks up a cigarette.

"May I have a light, please?"

He lights it. She takes off the shawl.

"I do not especially want to see Mr. Alvarez. I want to see Mrs. Victoria Rogers. I am the mother-in-law, to be, of the man she has accused of raping her, and who is now in prison, in New York."

She watches him. He watches her. Now, she begins to see him.

"Well, lady, you got one hell of a son-in-law, let me tell you that."

"I also have one hell of a daughter. Let *me* tell you *that*."

The moustache he has grown to make him look older twitches. He runs his hands through his thick black hair.

"Look. The kid's been through enough. More than enough. Leave her alone."

"A man is about to die, for something he didn't do. Can we leave *him* alone?"

"What makes you think he didn't do it?"

"*Look at me!*"

The children on the bandstand finish their set, and go off, and, immediately, the jukebox takes over: Ray Charles, "I Can't Stop Loving You."

"What you want me to look at you for?"

The waiter comes.

"What are you drinking? Señor?" Sharon put out her cigarette, and immediately lights another.

"It's on me. Give me the usual. And give the lady what she's drinking."

The waiter goes.

"Look at me."

"I'm looking at you."

"Do you think I love my daughter?"

"Frankly—it's hard to believe you *have* a daughter."

"I'm about to become a grandmother."

"From—?"

"Yes."

He is young, very, very young, but also very old; but not old in the way that she had expected him to be. She had expected the age of corruption. She is confronting the age of sorrow. She is confronting torment.

"Do you think that I would marry my daughter to a rapist?"

"You might not know."

"Look at me again."

And he does. But it does not help him.

"Look. I wasn't there. But Victoria swears it was him. And she's been through shit, baby, she's been through some *shit,* and I don't want to put her through no more! I'm sorry, lady, but I don't care what happens to your daughter—" He stops. "She's going to have a baby?"

"Yes."

"What you want from me? Can't you leave us alone? We just want to be left alone."

Sharon says nothing.

"Look. I ain't no American. You got all them lawyers and folks up there, why you coming to me? Shit—I'm sorry, but I ain't nothing. I'm an Indian, wop, spic, spade —name it, that's me. I got my little thing going here, and I got Victoria, and, lady, I don't want to put her through no more shit; I'm sorry, lady, but I really just can't help you."

He starts to rise—he does not want to cry before her. Sharon takes his wrist. He sits down, one hand before his face.

Sharon takes out her wallet.

"Pietro—I can call you that, because I am old enough to be your mother. My son-in-law is your age."

He leans his head on one hand, and looks at her.

Sharon hands him the photograph of Fonny and myself.

"Look at it."

He does not want to, but he does.

"Are you a rapist?"

He looks up at her.

"Answer me. Are you?"

The dark eyes, in the stolid face, staring, now directly into my mother's eyes, make the face electrical, light a fire in the darkness of a far-off hill: he has heard the question.

"Are you?"

"No."

"Do you think I have come here to make you suffer?"

"No."

"Do you think I am a liar?"

"No."

"Do you think I am crazy?—we are all a little crazy, I know. But *really* crazy?"

"No."

"Then, will you take this photograph home, to Victoria, and ask her really to think about it, really to study it? Hold her in your arms. Do that. I am a woman. I know that she was raped, and I know—well—I know what women know. But I also *know* that Alonzo did not rape her. And I say that, to you, because I know that you know what men know. *Hold her in your arms."* She stares at him an instant; he stares at her. "And—will you call me tomorrow?" She gives him the name and the phone number of the hotel. He writes it down. "Will you?"

He looks at her, now very hard and cold. He looks at the phone number. He looks at the photograph.

He pushes both toward Sharon.

"No," he says, and rises, and leaves.

Sharon sits there. She listens to the music. She watches the dancers. She forces herself to finish her second, unwanted drink. She cannot believe that what is happening is actually happening. But it *is* happening. She lights a cigarette. She is acutely aware, not merely of her color, but of the fact that in the sight of so many witnesses, her position, ambiguous upon her entrance, is now absolutely clear: the twenty-two-year-old boy she has traveled so far to see has just walked out on her. She wants to cry. She also wants to laugh. She signals for the waiter.

"Sí—?"

"What do I owe you?"

The waiter looks bewildered. "But nothing, Señora. Señor Alvarez has made himself responsible."

She realizes that his eyes hold neither pity, nor scorn. This is a great shock to her, and it brings tears to her eyes. To hide this, she bows her head and arranges her shawl. The waiter moves away. Sharon leaves five dollars on the table. She walks to the door. The bland, swarthy man opens it for her.

"Thank you, Señora. Good-night. Your taxi is waiting for you. Please come again."

"Thank you," my mother says, and smiles, and walks up the stairs.

She walks through the lobby. Jaime is leaning against the taxi. His face brightens when he sees her, and he opens the door for her.

"What time will you need me tomorrow?" he asks her.

"Is nine o'clock too early?"

"But, no." He laughs. "I am always up before six."

The car begins to move.

"Beautiful," says Sharon—swinging her foot, thinking ahead.

And the baby starts kicking, waking me up at night. Now that Mama is in Puerto Rico, it is Ernestine and Joseph who keep watch over me. I am afraid to quit my job, because I know we need the money. This means that I very often miss the six o'clock visit.

It seems to me that if I quit my job, I'll be making the six o'clock visit forever. I explain this to Fonny, and he says he understands, and, in fact, he does. But understanding doesn't help him at six o'clock. No matter what you understand, you can't help waiting: for your name to be called, to be taken from your cell and led downstairs. If you have visitors, or even if you have only one visitor, but that visitor is constant, it means that someone outside cares about you. And this can get you through the night, into the day. No matter what you may understand, and *really* understand, and no matter what you may tell yourself, if no one comes to see you, you are in very bad trouble. And trouble, here, means danger.

Joseph puts it to me very squarely, one Sunday morning. I have been more than usually sick that morning, and Joseph has had to tend to me because Ernestine has a rush job at the home of the actress. I cannot imagine what this thing inside of me is doing, but it appears to have acquired feet. Sometimes it is still, for days on end, sleeping perhaps, but more probably plotting—plotting its escape. Then, it turns, beating the water, churning, obviously becoming unspeakably bored in this element, and wanting out. We are beginning to have a somewhat acrid dialogue, this thing and I—it kicks, and I smash an egg on the floor, it kicks, and suddenly the coffeepot is upside down on the table, it kicks, and the perfume on the back of my hand brings salt to the roof of my mouth, and my free hand weighs on the heavy glass counter, with enough force to crack it in two. Goddammit. Be patient. I'm doing the best I can—and it kicks again, delighted to have elicited so furious a response. Please. Be still. And then, exhausted, or, as I suspect, merely cunning, it *is* still, having covered my forehead with sweat, and having caused me to vomit up my breakfast, and go to the bathroom—uselessly—about four or five times. But it really *is* very cunning, it intends to live: it never moves while I am riding the subway, or when I am crossing a crowded street. But it grows heavier and heavier, its claims become more absolute with every hour. It is, in fact, staking its claim. The message is that it does not so much belong to *me*—though there is another, gentler kick, usually at night, signifying that it has no objection to belonging to me, that we may even grow to be fond of each other—as *I* belong to *it*. And then it hauls off again, like Muhammad Ali, and I am on the ropes.

I do not recognize my body at all, it is becoming absolutely misshapen. I try not to look at it, because I simply do not recognize it. Furthermore, I sometimes take something off in the evening, and have difficulty getting back into it in the morning. I can no longer wear high heels, they distort my sense of balance as profoundly as one's vision is distorted if one is blind in one eye. I have never had breasts, or a behind, but I am beginning to have them now. It seems to me that I am gaining weight at the rate of about three hundred pounds an hour, and I do not dare speculate on what I will probably look like by the time this thing inside of me finally kicks itself out. Lord. And yet, we are beginning to know each other, this thing, this creature, and I, and sometimes we are very, very friendly. It has something to say to me, and I must learn to listen— otherwise, I will not know what to say when it gets here. And Fonny would never forgive me for that. After all, it was I who wanted this baby, more than he. And, at a depth beneath and beyond all our troubles, I am very happy. I can scarcely smoke at all anymore, *it* has seen to that. I have acquired a passion for cocoa, and doughnuts, and brandy is the only alcohol which has any taste at all. So, Ernestine casually brings over a few bottles from the actress's house. "She'll never miss them, baby. The way *they* drink?"

On this Sunday morning, Joseph serves me my third

cup of cocoa, the previous two having been kicked right back up, and sits down at the table before me, very stern.

"Do you want to bring this baby here, or not?"

The way he looks at me, and the way he sounds, scares me half to death.

"Yes," I say, "I do."

"And you love Fonny?"

"Yes. I do."

"Then, I'm sorry, but you going to have to quit your job."

I watch him.

"I know you worried about the money. But you let *me* worry about that. I got more experience. Anyway, you ain't making no damn money. All you doing is wearing yourself out, and driving Fonny crazy. You keep on like you going, you going to lose that baby. You lose that baby, and Fonny won't want to live no more, and you'll be lost and then I'll be lost, everything is lost."

He stands up and walks to the window, his back to me. Then, he faces me again. "I'm serious, Tish."

I say, "I know you are."

Joseph smiles. "Listen, little girl. We got to take care of each other in this world, right? Now: there are some things I can do that you can't do. That's all. There's things *I* can do that *you can't do*—and things *you* can do that *I* can't do, just like I can't have your baby for you. I would if I could. There's nothing I wouldn't do for you—you know that?" And he watches me, still smiling.

"Yes. I know that."

"And there are things *you* can do for Fonny that I can't do—right?"

"Yes."

Joseph walks up and down the kitchen. "Young folks hate to hear this—*I* did, when I was young—but you *are* young. Child, I wouldn't lose neither one of you for all the goddamn coffee in Brazil—but you young. Fonny ain't hardly much more than a boy. And he's in trouble no boy should be in. And you all he's got, Tish. You are *all* he's got. I'm a man, and I know what I'm talking about. You understand me?"

"Yes."

He sits down before me again. "You got to see him every day, Tish. Every day. You take care of Fonny. We'll take care of the rest. All right?"

"All right."

He kisses my tears.

"Get that baby here, safe and sound. We'll get Fonny out of jail. I promise. Do *you* promise?"

I smile, and I say, "Yes. I promise."

The next morning, I am, anyway, far too ill to be able to go to work and Ernestine calls the store to tell them so. She says that she, or I, will be coming in to collect my paycheck in the next few days.

So, that is that, and here we go. There is a level on which, if I'm to be honest, I must say that I absolutely hated it—: having nothing to do. But this forced me to recognize, finally, that I had clung to my job in order to avoid my trouble. Now, I was alone, with Fonny, my baby, and me.

But Joseph was right, and Fonny is radiant. On the days I do not see Hayward, I see Fonny twice a day. I am always there for the six o'clock visit. And Fonny knows that I will be there. It is very strange, and I now begin to learn a very strange thing. My presence, which is of no practical value whatever, which can even be considered, from a practical point of view, as a betrayal, is vastly more important than any practical thing I might be doing. Every day, when he sees my face, he knows, again, that I love him—and God knows I do, more and more, deeper and deeper, with every hour. But it isn't only that. It means that others love him, too, love him so much that they have set me free to be there. He is not alone; we are not alone. And if I am somewhat terrified by the fact that I no longer have anything which can be called a waistline, he is delighted. "Here she come! Big as *two* houses! You sure it ain't twins? or triplets? Shit, we *might* make history."

Throwing back his head, holding on to the telephone, looking me in the eye, laughing.

And I understand that the growth of the baby is connected with his determination to be free. So. I don't care if I get to be as big as two houses. The baby wants out. Fonny wants out. And we are going to make it: in time.

Jaime is prompt, and Sharon is in the *favella* by nine thirty. Jaime knows the location, roughly, of the particular dwelling, but he does not know the lady—at least, he is not sure that he does. He is still thinking about it when Sharon steps out of the taxi.

Hayward had tried to warn Sharon by telling her that he had never been able to describe a *favella* and that he very much doubted, if, after her visit, she would wish to try. It is bitter. The blue sky above, and the bright sun; the blue sea, here, the garbage dump, there. It takes a moment to realize that the garbage dump *is* the *favella*. Houses are built on it—dwellings; some on stilts, as though attempting to rise above the dung heap. Some have corrugated metal roofs. Some have windows. All have children.

Jaime walks beside Sharon, proud to be her protector, uneasy about the errand. The smell is fantastic—but the children, sliding up and down their mountain, making the air ring, dark, half naked, with their brilliant eyes, their laughter, splashing into and out of the sea, do not seem to care.

"This ought to be the place," Jaime says, and Sharon steps through an archway into a crumbling courtyard. The house which faces her must have been, at some point in time, an extremely important private dwelling. It is not private now. Generations of paint flake off the walls, and the sunlight, which reveals every stain and crack, does not deign to enter the rooms: some of which are shuttered, to the extent, that is, that the shutters hold. It is louder than an untrained orchestra in rehearsal and the sound of infants and children is the theme: tremendously developed, in extraordinary harmonies, in the voices of the elders. There seem to be doors everywhere—low, dark, and square.

"I think it might be here," Jaime says, nervously, and he points to one of the doors. "On the third floor. I think. You say she is blond?"

Sharon looks at him. He is absolutely miserable: he does not want her to go upstairs alone.

She touches his face, and smiles: he suddenly reminds her of Fonny, brings back to her why she is here.

"Wait for me," she says. "Don't worry. I won't be long."

And she walks through the door and climbs the steps as though she knows exactly where she is going. There are four doors on the third floor. There are no names on any of them. One of them is a little open, and she knocks on it— opening it a little further as she knocks.

"Mrs. Rogers—?"

A very thin girl, with immense dark eyes in a dark face, wearing a flowered housedress, barefoot, steps into the middle of the room. Her curly hair is a muddy blond: high cheekbones, thin lips, wide mouth: a gentle, vulnerable, friendly face. A gold crucifix burns against her throat.

She says, "Señora—?" and then stands still, staring at Sharon with her great eyes, frightened.

"Señora—?"

For Sharon has said nothing, merely stands in the doorway, watching her.

The girl's tongue moistens her lips. She says, again, "Señora—?"

She does not look her age. She looks like a little girl. Then she moves and the light strikes her differently and Sharon recognizes her.

Sharon leans against the open door, really afraid for a moment that she will fall.

"Mrs. Rogers—?"

The girl's eyes narrow, her lips curl.

"No, Señora. You are mistaken. I am Sanchez."

They watch each other. Sharon is still leaning against the door.

The girl makes a movement toward the door, as though to close it. But she does not wish to push Sharon. She does not want to touch her. She takes one step, she stops; she touches the crucifix at her throat, staring at Sharon. Sharon cannot read the girl's face. There is concern in it, not unlike Jaime's concern. There is terror in it, too, and a certain covered terrified sympathy.

Sharon, still not absolutely certain that she can move, yet senses that whether she can move or not, it is better not to change her position against the open door. It gives her some kind of advantage.

"Excuse me, Señora, but I have work to do—if you please? I don't know any Mrs. Rogers. Maybe in one of the other places around here—?" She smiles faintly and looks toward the open window. "But there are so many. You will be looking for a long time."

She looks at Sharon, with bitterness. Sharon straightens and they are, abruptly, looking each other in the eye—each held, now, by the other.

"I have a photograph of you," says Sharon.

The girl says nothing. She attempts to look amused.

Sharon takes out the photograph and holds it up. The girl walks toward the door. As she advances, Sharon moves from the door, into the room.

"Señora—! I have told you that I have my work to do." She looks Sharon up and down. "I am not a North American lady."

"I am not a lady. I am Mrs. Rivers."

"And I am Mrs. Sanchez. What do you want with me? I do not know you."

"I know you don't *know* me. Maybe you never even heard of me." Something happens in the girl's face, she tightens her lips, rummages in the pocket of her housecoat for her cigarettes, blowing the smoke insolently toward

Sharon. Yet, "Will you have a cigarette, Señora?" and she extends the package toward Sharon.

There is a plea in the girl's eyes, and Sharon, with a shaking hand, takes the cigarette and the girl lights it for her. She puts the package back into the pocket of her housecoat.

"I know you don't know me. But I think you must have heard of me."

The girl looks briefly at the photograph in Sharon's hand; looks at Sharon; and says nothing.

"I met Pietro last night."

"Ah! And did he give you the photograph?"

She had meant this as sarcasm; realizes that she made a mistake; still—her defiant eyes seem to say, staring into Sharon's—there are so many Pietros!

"No. I got it from the lawyer for Alonzo Hunt—the man you say raped you."

"I don't know what you're talking about."

"I think you do."

"Look. I ain't got nothing against nobody. But I got to ask you to get out of here."

She is trembling, and close to tears. She holds both dark hands clenched tightly before her, as though to prevent herself from touching Sharon.

"I'm here to try to get a man out of *prison*. That man is going to marry my daughter. And he did not rape you."

She takes out the photograph of me and Fonny.

"Look at it." •

The girl turns away, again toward the window; sits down on the unmade bed, still staring out of the window.

Sharon approaches her.

"Look at it. Please. The girl is my daughter. The man with her is Alonzo Hunt. Is this the man who raped you?"

The girl will not look at the photograph, or at Sharon.

"Is this the man who raped you?"

"One thing I can tell, lady—you ain't never been raped." She looks down at the photograph, briefly, then up at Sharon, briefly. "It looks like him. But he wasn't laughing."

After a moment, Sharon asks, "May I sit down?"

The girl says nothing, only sighs and folds her arms. Sharon sits beside her, on the bed.

There must be two thousand transistor radios playing all around them, and all of them are playing B.B. King. Actually, Sharon cannot tell what the radios are playing, but she recognizes the beat: it has never sounded louder, more insistent, more plaintive. It has never before sounded so determined and dangerous. This beat is echoed in the many human voices, and corroborated by the sea—which shines and shines beyond the garbage heap of the *favella*.

Sharon sits and listens, listens like she never has before. The girl's face is turned toward the window. Sharon wonders what she is hearing, what she is seeing. Perhaps she is not seeing or hearing anything. She sits with a stubborn, still helplessness, her thin hands limp between her knees, like one who has been caught in traps before.

Sharon watches her fragile back. The girl's curly hair is beginning to dry out, and is dark at the roots. The beat of the music rises higher, becoming almost unbearable, beginning to sound inside Sharon's head, and causing her to feel that her mind is about to crack.

She is very close to tears now, she cannot tell herself

why. She rises from the bed, and walks toward the music. She looks at the children, and watches the sea. In the distance there is an archway, not unlike the archway through which she has walked, abandoned by the Moors. She turns and looks at the girl. The girl is looking down at the floor.

"Were you born here?" Sharon asks her.

"Look, lady, before you go any further, just let me tell you, you can't do nothing to me, I ain't alone and helpless here, I got friends, just let me tell you!"

And she flashes up at Sharon a furious, frightened, doubting look. But she does not move.

"I'm not trying to do anything to you. I'm just trying to get a man out of jail."

The girl turns on the bed, putting her back to Sharon.

"An innocent man," Sharon adds.

"Lady, I think you in the wrong place, I really do. Ain't no reason to talk to me. Ain't nothing I can do!"

Sharon begins searching:

"How long were you in New York?"

The girl flicks her cigarette out of the window. "Too long."

"Did you leave your children there?"

"Listen. Leave my children out of this."

It is getting hot in the room, and Sharon takes off her light cloth jacket and sits down again on the bed.

"I," she says, carefully, "am a mother, too."

The girl looks at her, attempting a scornful distance. But, though she and envy are familiars, scorn is unknown to her.

"Why did you come back here?" Sharon asks her.

This is not the question which the girl had expected. In

fact, it is not the question which Sharon had intended to ask.

And they look at each other, the question shimmering between them the way the light changes on the sea.

"You said you're a mother," the girl says, finally, and rises and walks again to the window.

This time, Sharon follows her, and they stare out at the sea together. In a way, with the girl's sullen answer, Sharon's mind begins to clear. In the girl's answer she reads a plea: she begins to speak to her differently.

"Daughter. In this world, terrible things happen to you, and we can all do some terrible things." She is carefully looking out of the window; she is watching the girl. "I was a woman before you got to be a woman. Remember that. But"—and she turns to Victoria, she pulls the girl toward her, the thin wrists, the bony hands, the folded arms, touching her, lightly: she tries to speak as though she were speaking to me—"you pay for the lies you tell." She stares at the girl. The girl stares at her. "You've put a man in jail, daughter, a man you've never seen. He's twenty-two years old, daughter, he wants to marry *my* daughter— and—" Victoria's eyes meet hers again—"he's black." She lets the girl go, and turns back to the window. "Like us."

"I *did* see him."

"You saw him in the police lineup. That's the *first* time you saw him. And the *only* time."

"What makes *you* so sure?"

"Because I've known him all his life."

"Hah!" says Victoria, and tries to move away. Tears rise in the dark, defeated eyes. "If you knew how many women I've heard say that. They didn't see him—when *I* saw him—when he came to *me!* They *never* see that. Respectable *women*—like you!—they never see that." The tears begin to roll down her face. "You might have known a nice little boy, and he might be a nice man—with *you!* But you don't know the man who did—who did—what he did to me!"

"But, are you," Sharon asks, "sure that *you* know him?"

"*Yes,* I'm sure. They took me down there and they asked me to pick him out and I picked him out. That's all."

"But you were—it happened—in the dark. You saw Alonzo Hunt—in the lights."

"There's lights in the hallway. I saw enough."

Sharon grabs her again, and touches the crucifix.

"Daughter, daughter. In the name of God."

Victoria looks down at the hand on the cross, and screams: a sound like no sound Sharon has ever heard before. She breaks away from Sharon, and runs to the door, which has remained open all this time. She is screaming and crying, "Get out of here! Get out of here!"

Doors open. People begin to appear. Sharon hears the taxi horn. *One: two: one: two: one: two: three: one: two: three.* Victoria is now screaming in Spanish. One of the older women in the hall comes to the door, and takes Victoria in her arms. Victoria collapses, weeping, into this woman's breasts; and the woman, without a look at Sharon, leads her away. But everyone else, gathering, is staring at Sharon and now the lonely sound Sharon hears is the horn of Jaime's taxi.

They are staring at her, at her clothes; there is nothing she can say to them; she moves into the hallway, toward them. Her light summer jacket is over her arm, she is holding her handbag, she has the photograph of Fonny and me in one hand. She gets past them slowly, and, slowly, gets down the staring stairs. There are people on every landing. She gets out of the courtyard, into the street. Jaime opens the taxi door for her. She gets in, he slams the door, and, without a word, he drives her away.

In the evening, she goes to the club. But, the doorman informs her, Señor Alvarez will not be there this evening, that there are no tables for single women, and that, anyway, the club is full.

The mind is like an object that picks up dust. The object doesn't know, any more then the mind does, why what clings to it clings. But once whatever it is lights on you, it doesn't go away; and so, after that afternoon at the vegetable stand, I saw Bell everywhere, and all the time.

I did not know his name then. I discovered his name on the night I asked him for it. I had already memorized his badge number.

I had certainly seen him before that particular afternoon, but he had been just another cop. After that afternoon, he had red hair and blue eyes. He was somewhere in his thirties. He walked the way John Wayne walks, striding out to clean up the universe, and he believed all that shit: a wicked, stupid, infantile motherfucker. Like his heroes, he was kind of pinheaded, heavy gutted, big assed, and his eyes were as blank as George Washington's eyes. But I was beginning to learn something about the blankness of those eyes. What I was learning was beginning to frighten me to death. If you look steadily into that un-blinking blue, into that pinpoint at the center of the eye, you discover a bottomless cruelty, a viciousness cold and icy. In that eye, you do not exist: if you are lucky. *If* that eye, from its height, has been forced to notice you, if you *do* exist in the unbelievably frozen winter which lives behind that eye, you are marked, marked, marked, like a man in a black overcoat, crawling, fleeing, across the snow. The eye resents your presence in the landscape, cluttering up the view. Presently, the black overcoat will be still, turning red with blood, and the snow will be red, and the eye re-sents this, too, blinks once, and causes more snow to fall, covering it all. Sometimes I was with Fonny when I crossed Bell's path, sometimes I was alone. When I was with Fonny, the eyes looked straight ahead, into a freezing sun. When I was alone, the eyes clawed me like a cat's claws, raked me like a rake. These eyes look only into the eyes of the conquered victim. They cannot look into any other eyes. When Fonny was alone, the same thing hap-pened. Bell's eyes swept over Fonny's black body with the unanswerable cruelty of lust, as though he had lit the blow-torch and had it aimed at Fonny's sex. When their paths crossed, and I was there, Fonny looked straight at Bell, Bell looked straight ahead. *I'm going to fuck you, boy,* Bell's eyes said. *No, you won't,* said Fonny's eyes. *I'm going to get my shit together and haul ass out of here.*

I was frightened because, in the streets of the Village, I realized that we were entirely alone. Nobody cared about us except us; or, whoever loved us was not there.

Bell spoke to me once. I was making it to Fonny's, late, from work. I was surprised to see him because I had got off the subway at Fourteenth Street and Eighth Avenue, and he was usually in the neighborhood of Bleecker and MacDougal. I was huffing and puffing down the avenue, carrying a package of odds and ends I had lifted from the Jew, when I saw him walking slowly up the avenue, toward me. For a minute, I was frightened because my package— which had things like glue and staples and watercolors and paper and tacks and nails and pens—was hot. But he couldn't know that, and I already hated him too much to care. I walked toward him, he walked toward me. It was beginning to be dark, around seven, seven thirty. The streets were full, homeward men, leaning drunkards, flee-ing women, Puerto Rican kids, junkies: here came Bell.

"Can I carry that for you?"

I almost dropped it. In fact, I almost peed on myself. I looked into his eyes.

"No," I said, "thanks very much," and I tried to keep moving, but he was standing in my way.

I looked into his eyes again. This may have been the very first time I ever really looked into a white man's eyes. It stopped me, I stood still. It was not like looking into a man's eyes. It was like nothing I knew, and—therefore— it was very powerful. It was seduction which contained the promise of rape. It was rape which promised debasement and revenge: on both sides. I wanted to get close to him, to enter into him, to open up that face and change it and de-stroy it, descend into the slime with him. Then, we would both be free: I could almost hear the singing.

"Well," he said, in a very low voice, "you ain't got far to go. Sure wish I could carry it for you, though."

I can still see us on that hurrying, crowded, twilight

avenue, me with my package and my handbag, staring at him, he staring at me. I was suddenly his: a desolation entered me which I had never felt before. I watched his eyes, his moist, boyish, despairing lips, and felt his sex stiffening against me.

"I ain't a bad guy," he said. "Tell your friend. You ain't got to be afraid of me."

"I'm not afraid," I said. "I'll tell him. Thanks."

"Good-night," he said.

"Good-night," I answered, and I hurried on my way.

I never told Fonny about it. I couldn't. I blotted it out of my mind. I don't know if Bell ever spoke to Fonny—I doubt it.

On the night that Fonny was arrested, Daniel was at the house. He was a little drunk. He was crying. He was talking, again, about his time in prison. He had seen nine men rape one boy: and *he* had been raped. He would never, never, never again be the Daniel he had been. Fonny held him, held him up just before he fell. I went to make the coffee.

And then they came knocking at the door.

TWO

zion

Fonny is working on the wood. It is a soft, brown wood, it stands on his worktable. He has decided to do a bust of me. The wall is covered with sketches. I am not there.

His tools are on the table. He walks around the wood, terrified. He does not want to touch it. He knows that he must. But he does not want to defile the wood. He stares and stares, almost weeping. He wishes that the wood would speak to him; he is waiting for the wood to speak. Until it speaks, he cannot move. I am imprisoned somewhere in the silence of that wood, and so is he.

He picks up a chisel, he puts it down. He lights a cigarette, sits down on his work stool, stares, picks up the chisel again.

He puts it down, goes into the kitchen to pour himself a beer, comes back with the beer, sits down on the stool again, stares at the wood. The wood stares back at him.

"You cunt," says Fonny.

He picks up the chisel again, and approaches the waiting wood. He touches it very lightly with his hand, he caresses it. He listens. He puts the chisel, teasingly, against it. The chisel begins to move. Fonny begins.

And wakes up.

He is in a cell by himself, at the top of the prison. This is provisional. Soon, he will be sent downstairs, to a larger cell, with other men. There is a toilet in the corner of the cell. It stinks.

And Fonny stinks.

He yawns, throwing his arms behind his head, and turns, furiously, on the narrow cot. He listens. He cannot tell what time it is, but it does not matter. The hours are all the same, the days are all the same. He looks at his shoes, which have no laces, on the floor beside the cot. He tries to give himself some reason for being here, some reason to move, or not to move. He knows that he must do something to keep himself from drowning in this place, and every day he tries. But he does not succeed. He can neither retreat into himself nor step out of himself. He is righteously suspended, he is still. He is still with fear. He rises, and walks to the corner, and pees. The toilet does not work very well, soon it will overflow. He does not know what he can do about it. He is afraid, up here, alone. But he is also afraid of the moment when he will be moved downstairs, with the others, whom he sees at mealtimes, who see him. He knows who they are, he has seen them all before, were they to encounter each other outside he would know what to say to them. Here, he knows nothing, he is dumb, he is absolutely terrified. Here, he is at everyone's mercy, and he is also at the mercy of this stone and steel. Outside, he is not young. Here, he realizes that he is young, very young, too young. And—will he grow old here?

He stares through the small opening in the cell door into what he can see of the corridor. Everything is still and silent. It must be very early. He wonders if today is the day he will be taken to the showers. But he does not know what day it is, he cannot remember how long ago it was that he was taken to the showers. I'll ask somebody today, he thinks, and then I'll remember. I've got to make myself remember. I can't let myself go like this. He tries to remember everything he has ever read about life in prison. He can remember nothing. His mind is as empty as a shell; rings, like a shell, with a meaningless sound, no questions, no answers, nothing. And he stinks. He yawns again, he scratches himself, he shivers, with a mighty effort he stifles a scream, grabs the bars of the high window and looks up into what he can see of the sky. The touch of the steel calms him a little; the cool, rough stone against his skin comforts him a little. He thinks of Frank, his father. He thinks of me. He wonders what we are doing now, at this very moment. He wonders what the whole world, his world, is doing without him, why he has been left alone here, perhaps to die. The sky is the color of the steel; the heavy tears drip down Fonny's face, causing the stubble on his face to itch. He cannot muster his defenses because he can give himself no reason for being here.

He lies back down on the cot. He has five cigarettes left. He knows that I will bring him cigarettes this evening. He lights a cigarette, staring up at the pipes on the ceiling. He shakes. He tries to put his mind at ease. *Just one more day. Don't sweat it. Be cool.*

He drags on the cigarette. His prick hardens. Absently, he strokes it, through his shorts; it is his only friend. He clenches his teeth, and resists, but he is young and he is lonely, he is alone. He strokes himself gently, as though in prayer, closing his eyes. His rigid sex responds, burning, and Fonny sighs, dragging on the cigarette again. He pauses, but his hand will not be still—cannot be still. He catches his lower lip in his teeth, wishing—but the hand will not be still. He lifts himself out of his shorts and pulls the blanket up to his chin. The hand will not be still, it tightens, it tightens, moving faster, and Fonny sinks and rises. Oh. He tries to think of no one, he tries not to think of me, he does not wish me to have any connection with this cell, or with this act. Oh. And he turns, rising, writhing, his belly beginning to shake. Oh: and great tears gather behind his eyes. He does not want it to end. It must end. Oh. Oh. Oh. He drops his cigarette on the stone floor, he surrenders totally, he pretends that human arms are holding him, he moans, he nearly screams, his thickening, burning sex causes him to arch his back, and his limbs stiffen. Oh. He does not want it to end. It must end. He moans. It is unbelievable. His sex trickles, spurts, explodes, all over his hand and his belly and his balls, he sighs; after a long moment he opens his eyes and the cell comes crashing down on him, steel and stone, making him know he is alone.

He is brought down to see me at six o'clock.

He remembers to pick up the phone.

"Hey!" And he grins. "How you doing, baby? Tell me something."

"You know I ain't got nothing to tell. How you?"

He kisses the glass. I kiss the glass.

But he does not look well.

"Hayward's coming to see you tomorrow morning. He thinks he's got a date fixed for the trial."

"For when?"

"Soon. Very soon."

"What do you mean by soon? Tomorrow? Next month? Next year?"

"Would I tell you, Fonny, if I didn't know it was soon? Would I? And Hayward *told* me I could tell you."

"Before the baby gets here?"

"Oh, yes, before the baby gets here."

"When is it due?"

"Soon."

His face changes then, and he laughs. He makes a mock menacing gesture with one fist.

"How is it? the baby."

"Alive and kicking. Believe me."

"Whipping your ass, huh?" He laughs again. "Old Tish."

And again his face changes, another light comes into it, he is very beautiful.

"You seen Frank?"

"Yes. He's been doing a lot of overtime. He'll be here tomorrow."

"He coming with you?"

"No. He's coming with Hayward, in the morning."

"How is he?"

"He's fine, baby."

"And my two funky sisters?"

"They're like they've always been."

"Not married yet?"

"No, Fonny. Not yet."

I wait for the next question:

"And my Mama?"

"I haven't seen her. Naturally. But she seems to be all right."

"Her weak heart ain't done her in yet, huh? Your Mama back from Puerto Rico?"

"Not yet. But we expect her any minute."

His face changes again.

"But—if that chick still says I raped her—I'm going to be here for a while."

I light a cigarette, and I put it out. The baby moves, as though it is trying to get a glimpse of Fonny.

"Mama thinks that Hayward can destroy her testimony. She seems to be a kind of hysterical woman. She's a part-time whore, anyway—that doesn't help her case. And—you were the blackest thing in the lineup that morning. There were some white cats and a Puerto Rican and a couple of light brown brothers—but you were the only *black* man."

"I don't know how much that's going to mean."

"Well, one thing it *can* mean is that the case can be thrown out of court. She says she was raped by a black man, and so they put *one* black man in a lineup with a whole lot of pale dudes. And so, naturally, she says it was you. If she was looking for a black cat, she *knows* it can't be none of the others."

"What about Bell?"

"Well, he's already killed one black kid, just like I told you. And Hayward will make sure that the jury knows that."

"Shit. If the jury knows that, they'll probably want to give him a medal. He's keeping the streets safe."

"Fonny, don't think like that. Baby. We agreed when this shit started, that we'd just have to move it from day to day and not blow our cool and not try to think too far ahead. I know exactly what you mean, sweetheart, but there's no point in thinking about it like that——"

"Do you miss me?"

"Oh, God, yes. That's why you can't blow your cool. I'm waiting for you, the baby's waiting for you!"

"I'm sorry, Tish. I'm sorry. I'll get it together. I really will. But, sometimes it's hard, because I ain't got no business here—you know? And things are happening inside me that I don't really understand, like I'm beginning to see things I never saw before. I don't have any words for those things, and I'm scared. I'm not as tough as I thought I was. I'm younger than I thought I was. But I'll get it together. I promise you. I promise. Tish. I'll be better when I come out than I was when I came in. I promise. I know it. Tish. Maybe there's something I had to see, and—I couldn't have seen it without coming in here. Maybe. Maybe that's it. Oh, Tish—do you love me?"

"I love you. I love you. You *have* to know I love you, just like you know that nappy hair is growing on your head."

"Do I look awful?"

"Well, I wish I could get my hands on you. But you're beautiful to me."

"I wish I could get my hands on you, too."

A silence falls, and we look at each other. We are looking at each other when the door opens behind Fonny, and the man appears. This is always the most awful moment, when Fonny has to rise and turn, I have to rise and turn. But Fonny is cool. He stands, and raises his fist.

He smiles, and stands there for a moment, looking me dead in the eye. Something travels from him to me, it is love and courage. Yes. Yes. We are going to make it, somehow. Somehow. I stand, and smile, and raise my fist. He turns into the inferno. I walk toward the Sahara.

The miscalculations of this world are vast. The D.A.'s office, the prosecution, the state—*The People versus Alonzo Hunt!*—has managed to immobilize, isolate, or intimidate, every witness for Alonzo Hunt. But it has fucked itself up, too, as a thinned Sharon informs us on the night that Ernestine borrows the actress's car, and chauffeur, to bring Mama home from Kennedy Airport:

"I waited for another two days. I thought, it can't go down like that. The deal can *not* go down like that. Jaime said that it could, it *would* go down like that. By this time, the story was all over the island. Everybody knew it. Jaime knew more about it than I knew myself. He said that I was being followed everywhere, that *we* were being followed everywhere, and, one night, in the taxi, he proved it. I'll tell you about that another day."

Mama's face: she, too, is seeing something she never saw before.

"I couldn't go around anymore. For the last two days, Jaime got to be my spy, really. They knew his taxi better than they knew him, if you see what I mean. People always know the outside better than they know the inside. If they saw Jaime's taxi coming, well, that was Jaime. They didn't look inside."

Sharon's face: and Joseph's face.

"So, he borrowed somebody else's car. That way, they

didn't see him coming. By the time they *did* see him, it didn't make any difference, since he wasn't with me. He was part of the landscape, like the sea, like the garbage heap, he was something they had known all their lives. They didn't have to look at him. I had never seen it like that before. Maybe they didn't *dare* look at him, like they don't look at the garbage dump. Like they don't look at themselves—like *we* don't look. I had never seen it like that before. Never. I don't speak no Spanish and they don't speak no English. But we on the same garbage dump. For the same reason."

She looks at me.

"For the same reason. I had never thought about it like that before. Who*ever* discovered America *deserved* to be dragged home, in chains, to die."

She looks at me again.

"You get that baby here, you hear me?" And she smiles. She smiles. She is very close to me. And she is very far away. "We ain't going to let nobody put chains on that baby. That's all."

She rises, and paces the kitchen. We watch her: she *has* lost weight. She holds a gin and orange juice in her hand. I know that she has not yet unpacked. I realize, because I watch her fighting her tears, that she is, really, after all, young.

"Anyway. He was there, Jaime was there, when they carried the chick away. She was screaming. She was having a miscarriage. Pietro carried her down the steps, in his arms. She had already started to bleed."

She sips her drink. She stands at our window, very much alone.

"She was carried to the mountains, someplace called *Barranguitas*. You got to know where it is, to get there. Jaime says that she will never be seen again."

There goes the trial, the prosecution having fucked itself out of its principal witness. We have a slim hope, still, in Daniel, but not one of us can see him, even if we knew where he could be found. He has been transferred to a prison upstate: Hayward is checking it out, Hayward is on the case.

The prosecution will ask for time. We will ask that the charge be dropped, and the case dismissed: but must be prepared to settle for bail: if the state will concede it: if we can raise it.

"All right," says Joseph, stands, walks to the window, stands next to Sharon, but does not touch her. They watch their island.

"You okay?" asks Joseph, and lights a cigarette, and hands it to her.

"Yeah. I'm okay."

"Then, let's go on in. You tired. And you been gone a while."

"Good-night," says Ernestine, firmly, and Sharon and Joseph, their arms around each other, walk down the hall, to their room. In a way, *we* are their elders now. And the baby kicks again. Time.

But the effect of all this on Frank is cataclysmic, is absolutely disastrous, and it is Joseph who has to bring him the news. Their hours are, furthermore, now so erratic that he has to bring the news to the house.

Without a word, he has managed to forbid both Ernestine and myself from saying a word to the Hunts.

It is about midnight.

Mrs. Hunt is in bed. Adrienne and Sheila have just come in, and, standing in the kitchen, in their nightgowns, are giggling and sipping Ovaltine. Adrienne's behind is spreading, but there is no hope for Sheila at all. Sheila has been told that she resembles a nothing actress, Merle Oberon, whom she has encountered on the Late Late Show, and so she has clipped her eyebrows with the same intention, but not to the same effect. The Oberon chick was paid, at least, for her disquieting resemblance to an egg.

Joseph must be on the docks in the early morning, and so he has no time to waste. Neither does Frank, who must also be downtown, early.

Frank puts a beer before Joseph, pours a little wine for himself. Joseph takes a sip of his beer. Frank sips his wine. They watch each other for a rather awful moment, aware of the girls' laughter in the kitchen. Frank wants to make the laughter stop, but he cannot take his eyes from Joseph's eyes.

"Well—?" says Frank.

"Brace yourself. I'm going to hit you hard. The trial's been postponed because the Puerto Rican chick, dig, has lost her baby and look like she's flipped her wig, too, lost her mind, man, anyway she in the hills of Puerto Rico someplace and she can't be moved and can't nobody see her, she can't come to New York now, no *way* and so the City wants the trial postponed—until she *can*." Frank says nothing. Joseph says, "You understand what I'm saying?"

Frank sips his wine, and says, quietly, "Yeah. I understand."

They hear the girls' low voices in the kitchen: this

sound is about to drive both men insane.

Frank says, "You telling me that they going to keep Fonny in jail until this chick comes to her senses." He sips his wine again, looks at Joseph. "Is that right?"

Something in Frank's aspect is beginning to terrify Joseph, but he does not know what it is.

"Well—that's what they *want* to do. But we might be able to get him out, on bail."

Frank says nothing. The girls giggle, in the kitchen.

"How much bail?"

"We don't know. It ain't been set yet." He sips his beer, more and more frightened, obscurely, but profoundly.

"When is it going to be set?"

"Tomorrow. The day after." He has to say it: *"If—"*

"If what?"

"If they accept our plea, man. They ain't *got* to let us have no bail." There is something else he has to say. "And —I don't think this will happen, but it's better to look at it from the *worst* side—they *might* try to make the charge against Fonny heavier because the chick's lost her baby, and seems to have flipped her wig."

Silence: the girlish laughter from the kitchen.

Joseph scratches one armpit, watching Frank. Joseph is more and more uneasy.

"So," says Frank, finally, with an icy tranquility, "we're fucked."

"What makes you say that, man? It's rough, I agree, but it ain't yet over."

"Oh, *yes,*" says Frank, "it's over. They got him. They ain't going to let him go till they get ready. And they ain't ready yet. And ain't nothing we can do about it."

Joseph shouts, out of his fear, "We *got* to do something about it!" He hears his voice, banging against the walls, against the girlish laughter from the kitchen.

"What: can we do about it?"

"If they give us bail, get the change together—"

"How?"

"Man, I don't know how! I just know we have to do it!"

"And if they don't give us bail?"

"We get him *out!* I don't care what we have to do to get him out!"

"I don't, neither! But what can we *do?*"

"*Get him out.* That's what we have to do. We both know he ain't *got* no business in there. Them lying motherfuckers, they know it, too." He stands. He is trembling. The kitchen is silent. "Look. I know what you're saying. You're saying they got us by the balls. Okay. But that's our flesh and blood, baby: *our flesh and blood.* I don't know *how* we going to do it. I just know we have to do it. I know you ain't scared for you, and God knows I ain't scared for me. That boy is got to come out of there. That's all. And we got to get him out. That's all. And the first thing we got to do, man, is just not to lose our nerve. We can't let these cunt-faced white-assed motherfuckers get away with this shit no longer." He subsides, he sips his beer. "They been killing our children long enough."

Frank looks toward the open kitchen door, where his two daughters stand.

"Is everything all right?" Adrienne asks.

Frank hurls his glass of wine onto the floor, it rings and shatters. "You two dizzy off-white cunts, get the fuck out of my face, you hear? *Get the fuck out of my face.* If you was any kind of women you'd be peddling pussy on the block to get your brother out of jail instead of giving it away for free to all them half-assed faggots who come sniffing around you with a book under their arm. Go to bed! *Get out of my face!*"

Joseph watches the daughters. He sees something very strange, something he had never thought of: he sees that Adrienne loves her father with a really desperate love. She knows he is in pain. She would soothe it if she could, she does not know how. She would give anything to know how. She does not know that she reminds Frank of her mother.

Without a word, she drops her eyes and turns away, and Sheila follows her.

The silence is enormous—it spreads and spreads. Frank puts his head in his hands. Then, Joseph sees that Frank loves his daughters.

Frank says nothing. Tears drop onto the table, trickling down from the palms with which he has covered his face. Joseph watches: the tears drip from the palm, onto the wristbone, to splash—with a light, light, intolerable sound—on the table. Joseph does not know what to say—yet:

"This ain't no time for crying, man," he says. He finishes his beer. He watches Frank. "You all right?"

Frank says, finally, "Yeah. I'm all right."

Joseph says, "Get some sleep. We got to move it early in the morning. I'll talk to you end of the day. You got it?"

"Yeah," says Frank. "I got it."

When Fonny learns that the trial has been postponed, and learns why, and what effect Victoria's disaster may have on his own—it is I who tell him—something quite strange, altogether wonderful, happens in him. It is not that he gives up hope, but that he ceases clinging to it.

"Okay," is all he says.

I seem to see his high cheekbones for the first time, and perhaps this is really true, he has lost so much weight. He looks straight at me, into me. His eyes are enormous, deep and dark. I am both relieved and frightened. He has moved —not away from me: but he has moved. He is standing in a place where I am not.

And he asks me, staring at me with those charged, enormous eyes,

"You all right?"

"Yes. I'm all right."

"The baby all right?"

"Yes. The baby's fine."

He grins. It is, somehow, a shock. I will always see the space where the missing tooth has been.

"Well. I'm all right, too. Don't you worry. I'm coming home. I'm coming home, to you. I want you in my arms. I want your arms around me. I've got to hold our baby in my arms. It's got to be. You keep the faith."

He grins again, and everything inside me moves. Oh, love. Love.

"Don't you worry. I'll be home."

He grins again, and stands, and salutes me. He looks at me, hard, with a look I have never seen on any face before. He touches himself, briefly, he bends to kiss the glass, I kiss the glass.

Now, Fonny knows why he is here—why he is where he is; now, he dares to look around him. He is not here for anything he has done. He has always known that, but now he knows it with a difference. At meals, in the showers, up and down the stairs, in the evening, just before everyone is locked in again, he looks at the others, he listens: what have *they* done? Not much. To do much is to have the power to place these people where they are, and keep them where they are. These captive men are the hidden price for a hidden lie: the righteous must be able to locate the damned. To do much is to have the power and the necessity to dictate to the damned. But that, thinks Fonny, works both ways. *You're in or you're out. Okay. I see. Mother-fuckers. You won't hang me.*

I bring him books, and he reads. We manage to get him paper, and he sketches. Now that he knows where he is, he begins to talk to the men, making himself, so to speak, at home. He knows that anything may happen to him here. But, since he knows it, he can no longer turn his back: he has to face it, even taunt it, play with it, dare.

He is placed in solitary for refusing to be raped. He loses a tooth, again, and almost loses an eye. Something hardens in him, something changes forever, his tears freeze in his belly. But he has leaped from the promontory of despair. He is fighting for his life. He sees his baby's face before him, he has an appointment he must keep, and he will be here, he swears it, sitting in the shit, sweating and stinking, when the baby gets here.

Hayward arranges the possibility of bail for Fonny. But it is high. And here comes the summer: time.

On a day that I will never forget, Pedrocito drove me home from the Spanish restaurant, and, heavy, heavy, heavy, I got to my chair and I sat down.

The baby was restless, and I was scared. It was almost time. I was so tired, I almost wanted to die. For a long time, because he was in solitary, I had not been able to see Fonny. I had seen him on this day. He was so skinny; he was so bruised: I almost cried out. To whom, where? I saw this question in Fonny's enormous, slanted black eyes —eyes that burned, now, like the eyes of a prophet. Yet, when he grinned, I saw, all over again, my lover, as though for the first time.

"We got to get some meat on your bones," I said. "Lord, have mercy."

"Speak up. He can't hear you." But he said it with a smile.

"We almost got the money to bail you out."

"I figured you would."

We sat, and we just looked at each other. We were making love to each other through all that glass and stone and steel.

"Listen, I'll soon be out. I'm coming home because I'm glad I came, can you dig that?"

I watched his eyes.

"Yes," I said.

"Now. I'm an artisan," he said. "Like a cat who makes —tables. I don't like the word artist. Maybe I never did. I sure the fuck don't know what it means. I'm a cat who works from his balls, with his hand. I know what it's about now. I think I really do. Even if I go under. But I don't think I will. Now."

He is very far from me. He is with me, but he is very far away. And now he always will be.

"Where you lead me," I said, "I'll follow."

He laughed. "Baby. Baby. Baby. I love you. And I'm

going to *build* us a table and a whole lot of folks going to be eating off it for a long, *long* time to come."

From my chair, I looked out my window, over these dreadful streets.

The baby asked,

Is there not one righteous among them?

And kicked, but with a tremendous difference, and I knew that my time was almost on me. I remember that I looked at my watch: it was twenty to eight. I was alone, but I knew that someone, soon, would be coming through the door. The baby kicked again, and I caught my breath, and I almost cried, and the phone rang.

I crossed the room, heavy, heavy, heavy, and I picked it up.

"Hello—?"

"Hello—Tish? This is Adrienne."

"How are you, Adrienne?"

"Tish—have you seen my father? Is Frank there?"

Her voice almost knocked me down. I had never heard such terror.

"No. Why?"

"When did you see him last?"

"Why—I *haven't* seen him. I know he's seen Joseph. But *I* haven't seen him."

Adrienne was weeping. It sounded horrible over the phone.

"Adrienne! What's the matter? What's the *matter?*"

And I remember that at that moment everything stood still. The sun didn't move and the earth didn't move, the sky stared down, waiting, and I put my hand on my heart to make it start beating again.

"Adrienne! *Adrienne!*"

"Tish—my Daddy was fired from his job, two days ago—they said he was stealing, and they threatened to put him in jail—and he was all upset, because of Fonny and all, and he was drunk when he came home and he cursed everybody out and then he went out the door and ain't nobody seen him since—Tish—don't you know where my father is?"

"Adrienne, baby, I don't. I swear to God, I don't. I haven't seen him."

"Tish, I know you don't like me——"

"Adrienne, you and me, we had a little fight, but that's all right. That's normal. That don't mean I don't like you. I would surely never do anything to hurt you. You're Fonny's *sister*. And if I love him, I *got* to love you. Adrienne—?"

"If you see him—will you call me?"

"Yes. Yes. Yes, of course."

"Please. Please. Please. I'm scared," said Adrienne, in a low, different altogether tone of voice, and she hung up.

I put down the phone and the key turned in the lock and Mama came in.

"Tish, what's the matter with you?"

I got back to my chair and I sat down in it.

"That was Adrienne. She's looking for Frank. She said that he was fired from his job, and that he was real upset. And Adrienne—that poor child sounds like she's gone to pieces. Mama"—and we stared at each other; my mother's face was as still as the sky—"has Daddy seen him?"

"I don't know. But Frank ain't been by here."

She put her bag down on top of the TV set and came over and put her hand on my brow.

"How you feeling?"

"Tired. Funny."

"You want me to get you a little brandy?"

"Yes. Thank you, Mama. That might be a good idea. It might help to settle my stomach."

She went into the kitchen and came back with the brandy and put it in my hand.

"Your stomach upset?"

"A little. It'll go away."

I sipped the brandy, and I watched the sky. She watched me for a moment, then she went away again. I watched the sky. It was as though it had something to say to me. I was in some strange place, alone. Everything was still. Even the baby was still.

Sharon came back.

"You see Fonny today?"

"Yes."

"And how was he?"

"He's beautiful. They beat him up, but they didn't beat him—if you see what I mean. He's beautiful."

But I was so tired, I remember that I could hardly speak. Something was about to happen to me. That was what I felt, sitting in that chair, watching the sky—and I couldn't move. All I could do was wait.

Until my change comes.

"I think Ernestine's got the rest of the money," Sharon said, and smiled. "From her actress."

Before I could say anything, the doorbell rang, and Sharon went to the door. Something in her voice, at the door, made me stand straight up and I dropped the brandy glass on the floor. I still remember Sharon's face, she was standing behind my father, and I remember my father's face.

Frank had been found, he told us, way, way, way up the river, in the woods, sitting in his car, with the doors locked, and the motor running.

I sat down in my chair.

"Does Fonny know?"

"I don't think so. Not yet. He won't know till morning."

"I've got to tell him."

"You can't get there till morning, daughter."

Joseph sat down.

Sharon asked me, sharply, "How you feeling, Tish?"

I opened my mouth to say—I don't know what. When I opened my mouth, I couldn't catch my breath. Everything disappeared, except my mother's eyes. An incredible intelligence charged the air between us. Then, all I could see was Fonny. And then I screamed, and my time had come.

Fonny is working on the wood, on the stone, whistling, smiling. And, from far away, but coming nearer, the baby cries and cries and cries and cries and cries and cries and cries and cries, cries like it means to wake the dead.

[Columbus Day] Oct. 12, 1973
St. Paul de Vence

I AM NOT YOUR NEGRO

A Companion Edition to the Documentary Film Directed by Raoul Peck

To compose his stunning documentary film *I Am Not Your Negro*, acclaimed filmmaker Raoul Peck mined James Baldwin's published and unpublished oeuvre, selecting passages from his books, essays, letters, notes, and interviews that are every bit as incisive and pertinent now as they have ever been. Weaving these texts together, Peck brilliantly imagines the book that Baldwin never wrote. In his final years, Baldwin had envisioned a book about his three assassinated friends, Medgar Evers, Malcolm X, and Martin Luther King, Jr. His deeply personal notes for the project have never before been published. Peck's film uses them to jump through time, juxtaposing Baldwin's private words with his public statements in a blazing examination of the tragic history of race in America.

Literature

GO TELL IT ON THE MOUNTAIN

Go Tell It on the Mountain, originally published in 1953, is Baldwin's first major work, a novel that has established itself as an American classic. With lyrical precision, psychological directness, resonating symbolic power, and a rage that is at once unrelenting and compassionate, Baldwin chronicles a fourteen-year-old boy's discovery one Saturday in March 1935 of the terms of his identity as the stepson of the minister of a Pentecostal storefront church in Harlem. Baldwin's rendering of his protagonist's spiritual, sexual, and moral struggle toward self-invention opened new possibilities in the American language and in the way Americans understand themselves.

Fiction

TELL ME HOW LONG THE TRAIN'S BEEN GONE

At the height of his theatrical career, the actor Leo Proudhammer is nearly felled by a heart attack. As he hovers between life and death, Baldwin shows the choices that have made him enviably famous and terrifyingly vulnerable. For between Leo's childhood on the streets of Harlem and his arrival into the intoxicating world of the theater lies a wilderness of desire and loss, shame and rage. An adored older brother vanishes into prison. There are love affairs with a white woman and a younger black man, each of whom will make irresistible claims on Leo's loyalty. *Tell Me How Long the Train's Been Gone* is overpowering in its vitality and extravagant in the intensity of its feeling.

Fiction/Literature

GIOVANNI'S ROOM

Set in the 1950s Paris of American expatriates, liaisons, and violence, a young man finds himself caught between desire and conventional morality. With a sharp, probing imagination, James Baldwin's now-classic narrative delves into the mystery of loving and creates a moving, highly controversial story of death and passion that reveals the unspoken complexities of the human heart.

Fiction

THE AMEN CORNER

In his first work for the theater, James Baldwin brought all the fervor and majestic rhetoric of the storefront churches of his childhood along with an unwavering awareness of the price those churches exacted from their worshippers. For years Sister Margaret Alexander has moved her Harlem congregation with a mixture of personal charisma and ferocious piety. But when Margaret's estranged husband, a scapegrace jazz musician, comes home to die, she is in danger of losing both her standing in the church and the son she has tried to keep on the godly path.

Drama

THE DEVIL FINDS WORK

Baldwin's personal reflections on movies gathered here in a
book-length essay are also a probing appraisal of American
racial politics. Offering an incisive look at racism in
American movies and a vision of America's self-delusions
and deceptions, Baldwin challenges the underlying assumptions in such films as *In the Heat of the Night*, *Guess
Who's Coming to Dinner*, and *The Exorcist*. Here are our
loves and hates, biases and cruelties, fears and ignorance
reflected by the films that have entertained us and shaped
our consciousness. *The Devil Finds Work* showcases the
stunning prose of a writer whose passion never diminished
his struggle for equality, justice, and social change.

Essays/Film Criticism

ALSO AVAILABLE

Another Country
Blues for Mister Charlie
The Cross of Redemption
The Fire Next Time
Going to Meet the Man
No Name in the Street
Nobody Knows My Name
One Day When I Was Lost
Vintage Baldwin

VINTAGE INTERNATIONAL
Available wherever books are sold.
vintagebooks.com

"The best essayist in this country—a man whose power has always been in his reasoned, biting sarcasm; his insistence on removing layer by layer the hardened skin with which Americans shield themselves from their country."   —*The New York Times Book Review*

"More eloquent than W. E. B. Du Bois, more penetrating than Richard Wright."   —*The Atlantic*

"Baldwin's way of seeing, his clarity, precision, and eloquence are unique. . . . He manages to be concrete, particular . . . yet also transcendent, arching above the immediacy of an occasion or crisis. He speaks as great black gospel music speaks, through metaphor, parable, rhythm."   —John Edgar Wideman

"He has not himself lost access to the sources of his being—which is what makes him read and awaited by perhaps a wider range of people than any other major American writer."   —*The Nation*

"[Baldwin is] among the most penetrating and perceptive of American thinkers."   —*The New Republic*

"To be James Baldwin is to touch on so many hidden places in Europe, America, the Negro, the white man—to be forced to understand so much."   —Alfred Kazin

"He has become one of the few writers of our time."   —Norman Mailer

"Baldwin is biting and insightful. . . . [He] shows a masterful sweep of language and ideas and feelings that continues to resonate."   —*Booklist*

JAMES BALDWIN

Giovanni's Room

James Baldwin was born in 1924 and educated in New York. He is the author of more than twenty works of fiction and nonfiction, including *Go Tell It on the Mountain*; *Notes of a Native Son*; *Giovanni's Room*; *Nobody Knows My Name*; *Another Country*; *The Fire Next Time*; *Nothing Personal*; *Blues for Mister Charlie*; *Going to Meet the Man*; *The Amen Corner*; *Tell Me How Long the Train's Been Gone*; *One Day When I Was Lost*; *No Name in the Street*; *The Devil Finds Work*; *Little Man, Little Man*; *Just Above My Head*; *The Evidence of Things Not Seen*; *Jimmy's Blues*; and *The Price of the Ticket*. Among the awards he received are a Eugene F. Saxon Memorial Trust Award, a Rosenwald Fellowship, a Guggenheim Fellowship, a *Partisan Review* Fellowship, and a Ford Foundation grant. He was made a Commander of the Legion of Honor in 1986. He died in 1987.

INTERNATIONAL

Books by
JAMES BALDWIN

JAMES BALDWIN

Giovanni's Room

A NOVEL

Introduction by
KEVIN YOUNG

VINTAGE INTERNATIONAL
Vintage Books
A Division of Penguin Random House LLC
New York

FIRST VINTAGE INTERNATIONAL DELUXE EDITION 2024

Vintage is a registered trademark and Vintage International
and colophon are trademarks of Penguin Random House LLC.

Cataloging-in-Publication Data is on file at the Library of Congress.

Vintage International Deluxe Edition ISBN: 978-0-593-68896-0
Vintage International Trade Paperback ISBN: 978-0-345-80656-7
eBook ISBN: 978-0-345-80657-4

vintagebooks.com

Printed in the United States of America
10   9   8   7   6   5   4   3   2   1

FOR LUCIEN

I am the man, I suffered, I was there.
                              —Whitman

Introduction to the
Vintage International Edition (2024)

I first read *Giovanni's Room* in the Europe that James Baldwin had decided to move to in 1948. He would later say he left America in order to save his life; this novel was one of the ways he did so. My sojourn, undertaken five years after Baldwin died in 1987 and nearly forty years after he wrote the book, was of the kind recent college graduates take—no Grand Tour or expatriate escape, it was more backpacking and Eurorailing for weeks on end. Still, like Baldwin, I depended on the kindness of friends—managing never to encounter a hostel or hotel, I was fortunate enough to crash on friends' couches or in their families' guest rooms from Barcelona to Paris, Geneva to Zurich, Berlin to London. It was—like Baldwin, I learned later—writing that got me there.

In London I bounced between the flat of friends of my good friend and travel companion Philippe Wamba—a terrific writer killed in a car accident in Kenya a decade later—and another former college friend, a woman who went by Lucien. We drank in pubs and went to dub clubs and ate at friends' houses, who were Pakistani and Australian, Jamaican and British, biracial and African, all of whom called themselves Black, which then was a stance as much as a color. *We Black People created all the world's music*, an Australian-born Pakistani newfound friend declared, and I knew I was no longer in the Kansas that had partly raised me. A place where, when I asked my beloved English high school teacher whether I should read a writer I'd heard of named James Baldwin, she told me there was no need to bother.

It was hard to leave the kind of rich fellowship I found in London-town, but I decided to go back to Paris, alone. Before my departure I was staying with Lucien when I bought the paperback of *Giovanni's Room* I still have, knowing only it was a book of Paris and exile, which I knew mainly as a feeling. Because of my teacher's reticence, let's call it, I came to Baldwin late and chiefly by myself: I read his third novel, *Another Country*, in college till the paperback split its spine, and had devoured his essays as I came across them. But Baldwin provided me one of my first and finest examples of the artist as autodidact, the self-taught scholar, so even that seemed fitting. Moreover, I well understood the "Stranger in the Village" Baldwin wrote of around the same time as *Giovanni's Room*—if not a stranger, then sometimes I felt strange at home and abroad. Whenever we crossed borders in Europe, just to be safe, Philippe and I would tuck our garlands of dreads under our ball caps.

Opening the book, I found an epigraph from Walt Whitman: *I am the man, I suffered, I was there*. This struck me then and now as a deeply American sentiment, in which a trading of selves was part and parcel of an expansive American "I." Knowing too that Whitman's epigraph was speaking in that moment of feeling one with the American slave was profound then and still seems so despite Whitman's other damning racist views.

Then I turned the page to the dedication: *For Lucien.* I showed my friend, she of the same name; we both gasped. Everything then felt fated.

Baldwin's second novel, and still one of my favorite books, *Giovanni's Room* is about being someone else—or at least wanting to be. Baldwin writes in the first person as a young white man who describes himself self-consciously in the first paragraph as being blond, so there is little doubt. As an American, our narrator is foreign but also not exactly a stranger, though he's speaking from a house not his in the South of France: "My face is like a face you have seen many times. My ancestors conquered a continent, pushing across death-laden plains, until they came to an ocean which faced away from Europe into a darker past." The narrator, whose name we learn later is David, is an American in France remembering the City of Light while having a dark night of the soul—just one of the many paradoxes that animate the book.

It is a book of choices but filled with destiny and doom. *Giovanni's Room* begins not at the beginning but at the end, with David telling us about the failure of his relationship with his fiancée, Hella, whom he didn't really love; and his passionate affair with Giovanni, whom David, along with much of society, believes he shouldn't love. Within just a few pages, David also recalls an early love, Joey, with whom he had a brief but crucial encounter that he then denied in all senses, one that parallels his onetime innocence and current guilt he feels about Giovanni and about Hella. He's guilty too about an America he had to leave to find love and a Paris where he couldn't quite find love—or at least keep it. "People are too various to be treated so lightly," he tells us, his captive audience. "I am too various to be trusted." Even the multitudes of self that Whitman sang of are for David a curse.

Paris also is a character David both loves and regrets. As the City of Love, its freedoms—from sexuality and from American history, personal and otherwise—prove a burden. "These nights were being acted out under a foreign sky, with no one to watch, no penalties attached—it was this last fact which was our undoing, for nothing is more unbearable, once one has it, than freedom." *Giovanni's Room* evokes *le milieu*, the cafés and gay bars, *habitués* and underground haunts, with an ease that confirms Baldwin's writerly skill and David's familiarity with the scene. Both observant and hypercritical, David takes no small pleasure in describing the theater of the all-night bars, describing the patrons and barkeeps as "a troupe, who would now play various roles in a play they knew very well," one scripted by hunger and desire, money or the lack of it. Yet, while self-conscious, David is also, we come to know, deluded. His recollections are awash in metaphors, analogues, dreamscapes, and nightmares, seeking a sound to match the *noir* mood. "It was like holding in my hand some rare, exhausted, nearly doomed bird which I had miraculously happened to find," he says of his first love. "Out of this astounding, intolerable pain came joy."

This is the blues, sung only as Baldwin could—taking his own pain and joys, his freedom and constraints, his very life, to make something imagined and sound.

In his essays, Baldwin wrote that it was only once he went to Europe that he was able to fully hear the blues of Bessie Smith. In America, the place where the blues began—the place that made the blues necessary, where Black folks took their pain and turned it, if not into joy, then a juke—the blues were effectively off limits to him. Some of this was his church raising. But it was also the blues' unapologetic Blackness, their sorrows paired with unbridled raptures. Baldwin brought with him abroad only two books, the Bible and Shakespeare, and the blues united the two with a secular vision of suffering and redemption.

It was painter and mentor Beauford Delaney who introduced Baldwin to Bessie's music, providing him what one of Baldwin's biographers, David Leeming, calls "a Bessie Smith blues lesson." Later, while Baldwin was beginning to conceive *Giovanni's Room* at artist retreats MacDowell and Yaddo on one of his returns to the States in the early 1950s, Delaney wrote him about "the misery of which the jewel of life is formed." Baldwin had the model of Delaney, a committed artist and himself a preacher's kid, also gay, whose life was a blues-style resistance. Delaney had found his way in the bohemia of Greenwich Village, and soon Baldwin joined the neighborhood's tradition of liberation; later it was Delaney who followed Baldwin to Paris, where he painted with his signature yellow undertones through his own personal sorrows.

Baldwin manages to craft real characters in this novel who are also the stuff of myth. This starts with Giovanni, an Italian living precariously in France with a work permit from a lecherous bar owner; the character is based in part on the real-life Lucien Happersberger of the dedication, whom Baldwin met in Paris. Born in Switzerland, Lucien was Baldwin's onetime lover and lifelong confidant and friend; it was at his family place where Baldwin finished *Go Tell It on the Mountain*.

Baldwin also makes use of classical European myth. There's David's stepmother who "might have been working on the same scarf, or sweater, or God knows what, all the years I knew her," who evokes both the Fates knitting and Penelope's waiting for Odysseus to return, unraveling each night the tapestry she crafted by day; and the bar matrons, "those absolutely inimitable and indomitable ladies, produced only in the city of Paris, but produced there in great numbers, who would be as outrageous and unsettling in any other city as a mermaid on a mountaintop." Sirens and Fates: no wonder that David in his self-exile finds himself "abruptly, intolerably, with a longing to go home" while also seeing himself "sharply, as a wanderer, an adventurer, rocking through the world, unanchored," a modern Odysseus. Fate also helps explain how from their first meeting, David and Giovanni almost instantly seem sides of a coin destined for bad luck. Though bartenders are often a philosophizing sort, Giovanni is a potent cocktail of cynical and curious—he is remarkably open and even disarming of David upon their first meeting, which consists of intense discussions about the difference between New York and Paris, innocence and naivete, time and doom.

But there's also something else. Baldwin evokes color often in *Giovanni's Room*, but he shies away from Blackness. The decision to write only of and as white characters seems his boldest choice, and now seems completely right. It is clear that in doing so Baldwin means not to confuse sexuality with Blackness, too often stereotyped as hypersexual. He would later find the words to evoke Black, interracial, and queer relationships in the epic *Another Country*, but in this short novel he means us to pay strict attention to the specificity, that rightly or wrongly, he is able to ascribe to David—whose tragic flaws aren't simply race or sexuality, but love.

Writing as a white speaker is something Baldwin seems to be taking joy from, being an integral part of the rhetorical flourish in his essays at the time. For the most part gathered in *Notes of a Native Son*, released the year before, essays like "Many Thousands Gone" and "Everybody's Protest Novel" make the "everybody" rhetorically American, if not white, while considering the injustice visited upon Black lives and the response to it by the protest novel. Baldwin wishes to avoid this protest tradition, from *Uncle Tom's Cabin* to *Native Son*, while forging a new path to talk about race and justice. His is the whiteness of the whale—participating in the American tradition found in the novel and in society, from *Moby-Dick* to *The Scarlet Letter* to *Adventures of Huckleberry Finn*, *The Great Gatsby* to *To Kill a Mockingbird*, that marries symbol and sexuality and guilt, casting whiteness as a source of shadow. Indeed, Giovanni's alienation, "darkness," and desire for acceptance by David and society, reads as a metaphor for Blackness itself. For Leeming, "David is representative of the outlook and failure of white America, and Giovanni is just as clearly the embodiment of what Baldwin sees as the outlook of the black man."

Once called *One for My Baby* or *A Fable for My Children*, *Giovanni's Room* is both a fable and a love song, seeking to make the strange familiar and the familiar strange in only the way Baldwin could. With "my baby" and "my children" giving way to a story that claims to belong to Giovanni; by moving from a familiar American self to a foreign, imagined one; by the very act of calling it *Giovanni's Room*, Baldwin made the story his own.

Born in Harlem in 1924, Baldwin grew up in and around the Schomburg Center for Research in Black Culture, first established in 1925 as The New York Public Library's Negro Division of Literature, History and Prints as part of its 135th Street branch. For Baldwin the eventual Schomburg Center became central, as it has for so many, to his cultural and literary imagination. "I went to the 135th Street library at least three or four times a week, and I read everything there. I mean, every single book in that library," Baldwin said later. "In some blind and instinctive way, I knew that what was happening in those books was also happening all around me. And I was trying to make a connection between the books and the life I saw and the life I lived." This life was one that others lived too, a lesson Baldwin learned sooner than some. "You think your pain and your heartbreak are unprecedented in the history of the world, but then you read," he wrote. "It was books that taught me that the things that tormented me most were the very things that connected me with all the people who were alive, who had ever been alive." *I was the man, I suffered, I was there.*

In 2017, almost immediately after I began my former position as the director of the Schomburg Center, the Center was named a National Historic Landmark; shortly after, the Schomburg Center acquired the Baldwin papers forty years after his death, made up of thirty linear feet of papers dating to 1938, housed in the very place he had read deeply and, dare I say, Blackly. In the archives that opened just months later, there is Baldwin's steady hand and, moreover, his steady eye. Never have I seen drafts so full-throated and fully developed. Handwritten pages feel like fully realized oratory; sentences in typescripts bear occasional carets and edits, but even the rare strikeouts and removed passages appear like vintage Baldwin. His voice, from the start, was there, unmistakable, and his own, a mix of pulpit and literature, of all he read and felt and found.

One gets the sense that for Baldwin, literature was an inheritance he never once questioned, just quested after. He had no choice, it would seem, being self-taught in a world built to ignore him. Suffering was a given, but what you did with it? That was yours, or could be. Bessie and Beauford and the Bible taught him that. Paris and Greenwich Village, Delaney and other Black mentors like Richard Wright and Langston Hughes, all underscored for Baldwin that his was not a solo act. Despite what some accounts say, it is important to remember that Baldwin was neither first nor alone in his journeys as a Black thinker and writer. At the turn of the twentieth century, the Village had a Black area nicknamed Little Africa, one of many in New York either gentrified or erased entirely, as Seneca Village had been in what's now Central Park. There was also a coterie of African American expatriates in Paris before and after the Great War whose tradition he found himself in, from Henry Ossawa Tanner to Josephine Baker to Augusta Savage; and in the postwar period when he first moved to Paris, he found Black friends and cohorts at outposts in Montmartre and Saint-Germain-des-Prés, where he could often be found at Café de Flore.

Born in a Harlem once inhabited by the Lenape and built up by the Dutch that was now chiefly Black, Baldwin was well aware that places could change, could change you, and could serve as allegories for a nation and a moment. Paris served in that way for him, as a site of both refuge and increasing familiarity, which is to say, Blackness.

Written in the early 1950s and published in 1956, *Giovanni's Room* sold briskly from the start, earning positive reviews that matched its prepublication publicity. *The New York Times* wrote of the novel's "dignity and intensity." While the first edition and other, later, paperbacks would be subtle, at least on the cover, the first paperback from Signet in 1959 suggested something more scandalous: a man, presumably Giovanni, in a deeply unbuttoned blue shirt, wine bottle on the floor, bed in the background. The bed frame is not the only thing that's wrought. "A daring novel that treats a controversial subject with honesty and compassion," the front reads; the back is less subtle, describing a "Tormented Triangle" in which Baldwin, "with resourcefulness, subtlety and unusual candor," portrays the "thoughts of a young man who is engaged to a girl and attracted to another man."

Again, Baldwin was not alone. The paperback of *Giovanni's Room* participates in a pulp tradition of making tame stories scandalous, and making scandalous stories sell. Many Black classics from the 1940s onward got the pulp treatment, from Ann Petry's *The Street* (1946) to the work of fellow expat Chester Himes. Somehow Ralph Ellison's *Invisible Man* (1952) would be depicted on its cover as a young man, not the haint he spoke of himself as.

In turn, the queer novel tradition traces back to the early 1930s, often in Paris, in which stories could be published, or set, that suggested libertine fantasy or the facts of gay life. In many gay novels in English at the time, one might speak their love's name only disapprovingly. There was Blair Niles's *Strange Brother* (1931), set in Harlem, and Lew Levenson's *Butterfly Man* (1934), about a Texas innocent lured astray, which not only ended in death for the gay main character, but suicide. André Tellier's *Twilight Men* (1931) reversed the expatriate trend by telling of a Frenchman who experiences the temptations of Greenwich Village, then threw in a murder before the suicide. The fact that many of these proved underground classics despite their damning stance—with many reprinted as paperbacks or pulps in the repressed 1950s, including *Stranger Brother* and *Butterfly Man*—is chiefly a sign of their scarcity.

But not all were tragic. Charles Henri Ford and Parker Tyler collaborated on an early, important novel called *The Young and Evil*, published in Paris in 1933, regularly called "the first gay novel" given its undaunted spirit. Euphemizing homosexuality as *twilight* or *torchlight* or *butterfly* or *strange*, most such books seemed to come up with new names for "gay," which was still underground slang—recording a sexuality that is often so coded or vilified as to be indirect at best. Poetry from Whitman onward had an easier time of it. By invoking Whitman in his epigraph, Baldwin wasn't just signifying on Americanness, or whiteness, but on gay identity.

There were also examples from the Harlem Renaissance, whose younger members embraced sexuality in all its forms, as they did their Blackness. Indeed, celebrated Harlem poet Countee Cullen was Baldwin's French teacher at Frederick Douglass Junior High School. "Baldwin learned his first bit of French, a language in which he later became fluent, in Countee Cullen's French class at Frederick Douglass, and he always said that his dream of going to France originated with Cullen," writes Leeming. Where Cullen could be evocative in his poetry, he also wrote in ways coded and quiet as kept. There were also more out examples like writer and artist Richard Bruce Nugent, who said of the Harlem Renaissance, "Harlem was very much like the Village. People did what they wanted to do with whom they wanted to do it. . . . Nobody was in the closet. There wasn't any closet." In Cullen's last interview, conducted by Baldwin in 1942 for the DeWitt Clinton literary magazine *The Magpie*—the same magazine Cullen had edited as a student twenty years before—Baldwin was connected to a tradition of Black excellence and exploration.

In the end, Baldwin, unlike his character David, wasn't alone—or in denial. This doesn't mean he wasn't ever lonely, or often despairing, even at times suicidal. Rather, he crafted a world in his writing and in France, where he could be more himself than at home, in the Harlem of his birth or the America of his inheritance. Yet he well understood he took all his inheritances with him, everywhere he went.

Much of the power in Baldwin's novel comes from its remaining, in the end, hard to categorize. Thoughtful and visceral, hopeful and tragic, fated yet filled with forethought, *Giovanni's Room* is a jewel box of misery but also joy. Like the blues, it too is a journeyman; as a *nouveau noir*, it is filled with light. The novel is cinematic in its scope and also its focus, with startling dialogue that both suggests Baldwin the playwright's power and makes the several attempts to film it unsurprising. (There are a number of unrealized screenplays based on the novel found in the Baldwin archives.) *Giovanni's Room* provides an occasion for some of the most profound entries in Baldwin's philosophy—things David says in the novel about America or innocence or finding oneself are often attributed to Baldwin—but has the requisite plot, action, and death of a pulp.

"Perhaps, as we say in America, I wanted to find myself," goes one well-known passage. "This is an interesting phrase, not current as far as I know in the language of any other people, which certainly does not mean what it says but betrays a nagging suspicion that something has been misplaced. I think now that if I had had any intimation that the self I was going to find would turn out to be only the same self from which I had spent so much time in flight, I would have stayed at home." Such philosophy only makes it a tragedy, not a comedy, and Baldwin wouldn't be as interested in those (except on the silver screen). "Perhaps everybody has a garden of Eden, I don't know; but they have scarcely seen their garden before they see the flaming sword," David tells us. "Then, perhaps, life only offers the choice of remembering the garden or forgetting it. Either, or: it takes strength to remember, it takes another kind of strength to forget, it takes a hero to do both." *Perhaps* is one of David's favorite words, only adding to his waverings.

Above all, *Giovanni's Room* is a love story. To describe its plot not only fails to do it justice but reminds us how in other hands the subject matter would be (and had been) just another cult entry or pulp oddity. Instead, *Giovanni's Room* is a remarkable statement about the writer's values—and willingness to take on anything. Even whiteness. And in a lifetime of writing, Baldwin evoked love almost as much as he did America and history. "The world is held together," he said, "really it is held together, by the love and the passion of a very few people." It is love that Baldwin saw as the antidote to our woes. Baldwin would test this theory in his critiques of America, a country he loved but chose not to live in; in his celebrations of Blackness, which he had to go to Switzerland and France and Turkey to fully embody; and in his nonfiction and fiction, in which from *Go Tell It on the Mountain* to *Another Country* to *If Beale Street Could Talk* to *The Price of the Ticket*, he made love a central theme.

In carrying Baldwin's books in both my hands and now in my memory, crossing borders real and imagined, I am struck by how our need for Baldwin, his wisdom, insight, and indeed prophecy, is a love story too. And an act of faith.

Long after I read *Giovanni's Room* but well before I was fortunate enough to steward his work in archives and museums, I found a first edition of *Giovanni's Room*. Now in my collection, this copy is signed by Baldwin to fellow writer and onetime Harlemite Owen Dodson. Baldwin's inscription seems to speak to me, to all of us, with words that resonate much like the dedication to *Giovanni's Room* did when I first read it: *With Love, Jimmy. Keep the faith.*

KEVIN YOUNG

2024

Kevin Young is the author of fifteen books of poetry and prose, including *Stones*, shortlisted for the T. S. Eliot Prize; *Blue Laws: Selected & Uncollected Poems 1995–2015*, longlisted for the National Book Award; *Book of Hours*, winner of the Lenore Marshall Poetry Prize from the Academy of American Poets; *Jelly Roll: a blues*, a finalist for both the National Book Award and the Los Angeles Times Book Prize for Poetry; *Emile and the Field*, named one of the "Best Children's Books of the Year" by the *New York Times*; and *The Grey Album*, winner of the Graywolf Press Nonfiction Prize and the PEN Open Book Award, a *New York Times* Notable Book, and a finalist for the National Book Critics Circle Award for criticism. The poetry editor of *The New Yorker*, Young is the editor of nine other volumes, most recently the acclaimed anthology *African American Poetry: 250 Years of Struggle & Song*. He is a member of the American Academy of Arts and Sciences, the American Academy of Arts and Letters, the Society of American Historians, and was named a Chancellor of the Academy of American Poets in 2020. He lives and works in Washington, D.C.

PART ONE

O N E

I STAND AT THE window of this great house in the south of France as night falls, the night which is leading me to the most terrible morning of my life. I have a drink in my hand, there is a bottle at my elbow. I watch my reflection in the darkening gleam of the window pane. My reflection is tall, perhaps rather like an arrow, my blond hair gleams. My face is like a face you have seen many times. My ancestors conquered a continent, pushing across death-laden plains, until they came to an ocean which faced away from Europe into a darker past.

I may be drunk by morning but that will not do any good. I shall take the train to Paris anyway. The train will be the same, the people, struggling for comfort and, even, dignity on the straight-backed, wooden, third-class seats will be the same, and I will be the same. We will ride through the same changing countryside north-ward, leaving behind the olive trees and the sea and all of the glory of the stormy southern sky, into the mist and rain of Paris. Someone will offer to share a sandwich with me, someone will offer me a sip of wine, someone will ask me for a match. People will be roaming the corridors outside, looking out of windows, looking in at us. At each stop, recruits in their baggy brown uniforms and colored hats will open the compartment door to ask *Complet?* We will all nod Yes, like conspirators, smiling faintly at each other as they continue through the train. Two or three of them will end up before our compartment door, shouting at each other in their heavy, ribald voices, smoking their dreadful army cigarettes. There will be a girl sitting opposite me who will wonder why I have not been flirting with her, who will be set on edge by the presence of the recruits. It will all be the same, only I will be stiller.

And the countryside is still tonight, this countryside reflected through my image in the pane. This house is just outside a small summer resort—which is still empty, the season has not yet begun. It is on a small hill, one can look down on the lights of the town and hear the thud of the sea. My girl, Hella, and I rented it in Paris, from photographs, some months ago. Now she has been gone a week. She is on the high seas now, on her way back to America.

I can see her, very elegant, tense, and glittering, surrounded by the light which fills the salon of the ocean liner, drinking rather too fast, and laughing, and watching the men. That was how I met her, in a bar in Saint-Germain-des-Prés, she was drinking and watching, and that was why I liked her, I thought she would be fun to have fun with. That was how it began, that was all it meant to me; I am not sure now, in spite of everything, that it ever really meant more than that to me. And I don't think it ever really meant more than that to her—at least not until she made that trip to Spain and, finding herself there, alone, began to wonder, perhaps, if a lifetime of drinking and watching the men was exactly what she wanted. But it was too late by that time. I was already with Giovanni. I had asked her to marry me before she went away to Spain; and she laughed and I laughed but that, somehow, all the same, made it more serious for me, and I persisted; and then she said she would have to go away and think about it. And the very last night she was here, the very last time I saw her, as she was packing her bag, I told her that I had loved her once and I made myself believe it. But I wonder if I had. I was thinking, no doubt, of our nights in bed, of the peculiar innocence and confidence, which will never come again, which had made those nights so delightful, so unrelated to past, present, or anything to come, so unrelated, finally, to my life since it was not necessary for me to take any but the most mechanical responsibility for them. And these nights were being acted out under a foreign sky, with no one to watch, no penalties attached—it was this last fact which was our undoing, for nothing is more unbearable, once one has it, than freedom. I suppose this was why I asked her to marry me: to give myself something to be moored to. Perhaps this was why, in Spain, she decided that she wanted to marry me. But people can't, unhappily, invent their mooring posts, their lovers and their friends, anymore than they can invent their parents. Life gives these and also takes them away and the great difficulty is to say Yes to life.

I was thinking, when I told Hella that I had loved her, of those days before anything awful, irrevocable, had happened to me, when an affair was nothing more than an affair. Now, from this night, this coming morning, no matter how many beds I find myself in between now and my final bed, I shall never be able to have any more of those boyish, zestful affairs—which are, really, when one thinks of it, a kind of higher, or, anyway, more pretentious masturbation. People are too various to be treated so lightly. I am too various to be trusted. If this were not so I would not be alone in this house tonight. Hella would not be on the high seas. And Giovanni would not be about to perish, sometime between this night and this morning, on the guillotine.

———

I repent now—for all the good it does—one particular lie among the many lies I've told, told, lived, and believed. This is the lie which I told to Giovanni but never succeeded in making him believe, that I had never slept with a boy before. I had. I had decided that I never would again. There is something fantastic in the spectacle I now present to myself of having run so far, so hard, across the ocean even, only to find myself brought up short once more before the bulldog in my own backyard—the yard, in the meantime, having grown smaller and the bulldog bigger.

I have not thought of that boy—Joey—for many years; but I see him quite clearly tonight. It was several years ago. I was still in my teens, he was about my age, give or take a year. He was a very nice boy, too, very quick and dark, and always laughing. For a while he was my best friend. Later, the idea that such a person *could* have been my best friend was proof of some horrifying taint in me. So I forgot him. But I see him very well tonight.

It was in the summer, there was no school. His parents had gone someplace for the weekend and I was spending the weekend at his house, which was near Coney Island, in Brooklyn. We lived in Brooklyn too, in those days, but in a better neighborhood than Joey's. I think we had been lying around the beach, swimming a little and watching the near-naked girls pass, whistling at them and laughing. I am sure that if any of the girls we whistled at that day had shown any signs of responding, the ocean would not have been deep enough to drown our shame and terror. But the girls, no doubt, had some intimation of this, possibly from the way we whistled, and they ignored us. As the sun was setting we started up the boardwalk towards his house, with our wet bathing trunks on under our trousers.

And I think it began in the shower. I know that I felt something—as we were horsing around in that small, steamy room, stinging each other with wet towels—which I had not felt before, which mysteriously, and yet aimlessly, included him. I remember in myself a heavy reluctance to get dressed: I blamed it on the heat. But we did get dressed, sort of, and we ate cold things out of his icebox and drank a lot of beer. We must have gone to the movies. I can't think of any other reason for our going out and I remember walking down the dark, tropical Brooklyn streets with heat coming up from the pavements and banging from the walls of houses with enough force to kill a man, with all the world's grownups, it seemed, sitting shrill and dishevelled on the stoops and all the world's children on the sidewalks or in the gutters or hanging from fire escapes, with my arm around Joey's shoulder. I was proud, I think, because his head came just below my ear. We were walking along and Joey was making dirty wisecracks and we were laughing. Odd to remember, for the first time in so long, how good I felt that night, how fond of Joey.

When we came back along those streets it was quiet; we were quiet too. We were very quiet in the apartment and sleepily got undressed in Joey's bedroom and went to bed. I fell asleep—for quite a while, I think. But I woke up to find the light on and Joey examining the pillow with great, ferocious care.

"What's the matter?"

"I think a bedbug bit me."

"You slob. You got bedbugs?"

"I think one bit me."

"You ever have a bedbug bite you before?"

"No."

"Well, go back to sleep. You're dreaming."

He looked at me with his mouth open and his dark eyes very big. It was as though he had just discovered that I was an expert on bedbugs. I laughed and grabbed his head as I had done God knows how many times before, when I was playing with him or when he had annoyed me. But this time when I touched him something happened in him and in me which made this touch different from any touch either of us had ever known. And he did not resist, as he usually did, but lay where I had pulled him, against my chest. And I realized that my heart was beating in an awful way and that Joey was trembling against me and the light in the room was very bright and hot. I started to move and to make some kind of joke but Joey mumbled something and I put my head down to hear. Joey raised his head as I lowered mine and we kissed, as it were, by accident. Then, for the first time in my life, I was really aware of another person's body, of another person's smell. We had our arms around each other. It was like holding in my hand some rare, exhausted, nearly doomed bird which I had miraculously happened to find. I was very frightened; I am sure he was frightened too, and we shut our eyes. To remember it so clearly, so painfully tonight tells me that I have never for an instant truly forgotten it. I feel in myself now a faint, a dreadful stirring of what so overwhelmingly stirred in me then, great thirsty heat, and trembling, and tenderness so painful I thought my heart would burst. But out of this astounding, intolerable pain came joy; we gave each other joy that night. It seemed, then, that a lifetime would not be long enough for me to act with Joey the act of love.

But that lifetime was short, was bounded by that night—it ended in the morning. I awoke while Joey was still sleeping, curled like a baby on his side, toward me. He looked like a baby, his mouth half open, his cheek flushed, his curly hair darkening the pillow and half hiding his damp round forehead and his long eyelashes glinting slightly in the summer sun. We were both naked and the sheet we had used as a cover was tangled around our feet. Joey's body was brown, was sweaty, the most beautiful creation I had ever seen till then. I would have touched him to wake him up but something stopped me. I was suddenly afraid. Perhaps it was because he looked so innocent lying there, with such perfect trust; perhaps it was because he was so much smaller than me; my own body suddenly seemed gross and crushing and the desire which was rising in me seemed monstrous. But, above all, I was suddenly afraid. It was borne in on me: *But Joey is a boy.* I saw suddenly the power in his thighs, in his arms, and in his loosely curled fists. The power and the promise and the mystery of that body made me suddenly afraid. That body suddenly seemed the black opening of a cavern in which I would be tortured till madness came, in which I would lose my manhood. Precisely, I wanted to know that mystery and feel that power and have that promise fulfilled through me. The sweat on my back grew cold. I was ashamed. The very bed, in its sweet disorder, testified to vileness. I wondered what Joey's mother would say when she saw the sheets. Then I thought of my father, who had no one in the world but me, my mother having died when I was little. A cavern opened in my mind, black, full of rumor, suggestion, of half-heard, half-forgotten, half-understood stories, full of dirty words. I thought I saw my future in that cavern. I was afraid. I could have cried, cried for shame and terror, cried for not understanding how this could have happened to me, how this could have happened *in* me. And I made my decision. I got out of bed and took a shower and was dressed and had breakfast ready when Joey woke up.

I did not tell him my decision; that would have broken my will. I did not wait to have breakfast with him but only drank some coffee and made an excuse to go home. I knew the excuse did not fool Joey; but he did not know how to protest or insist; he did not know that this was all he needed to have done. Then I, who had seen him that summer nearly every day till then, no longer went to see him. He did not come to see me. I would have been very happy to see him if he had, but the manner of my leave-taking had begun a constriction, which neither of us knew how to arrest. When I finally did see him, more or less by accident, near the end of the summer, I made up a long and totally untrue story about a girl I was going with and when school began again I picked up with a rougher, older crowd and was very nasty to Joey. And the sadder this made him, the nastier I became. He moved away at last, out of the neighborhood, away from our school, and I never saw him again.

I began, perhaps, to be lonely that summer and began, that summer, the flight which has brought me to this darkening window.

And yet—when one begins to search for the crucial, the definitive moment, the moment which changed all others, one finds oneself pressing, in great pain, through a maze of false signals and abruptly locking doors. My flight may, indeed, have begun that summer—which does not tell me where to find the germ of the dilemma which resolved itself, that summer, into flight. Of course, it is somewhere before me, locked in that reflection I am watching in the window as the night comes down outside. It is trapped in the room with me, always has been, and always will be, and it is yet more foreign to me than those foreign hills outside.

We lived in Brooklyn then, as I say; we had also lived in San Francisco, where I was born, and where my mother lies buried, and we lived for awhile in Seattle, and then in New York—for me, New York is Manhattan. Later on, then, we moved from Brooklyn back to New York and by the time I came to France my father and his new wife had graduated to Connecticut. I had long been on my own by then, of course, and had been living in an apartment in the east sixties.

We, in the days when I was growing up, were my father and his unmarried sister and myself. My mother had been carried to the graveyard when I was five. I scarcely remember her at all, yet she figured in my nightmares, blind with worms, her hair as dry as metal and brittle as a twig, straining to press me against her body; that body so putrescent, so sickening soft, that it opened, as I clawed and cried, into a breach so enormous as to swallow me alive. But when my father or my aunt came rushing into my room to find out what had frightened me, I did not dare describe this dream, which seemed disloyal to my mother. I said that I had dreamed about a graveyard. They concluded that the death of my mother had had this unsettling effect on my imagination and perhaps they thought that I was grieving for her. And I may have been, but if that is so, then I am grieving still.

My father and my aunt got on very badly and, without ever knowing how or why I felt it, I felt that their long battle had everything to do with my dead mother. I remember when I was very young how, in the big living room of the house in San Francisco, my mother's photograph, which stood all by itself on the mantelpiece, seemed to rule the room. It was as though her photograph proved how her spirit dominated that air and controlled us all. I remember the shadows gathering in the far corners of that room, in which I never felt at home, and my father washed in the gold light which spilled down on him from the tall lamp which stood beside his easy chair. He would be reading his newspaper, hidden from me behind his newspaper, so that, desperate to conquer his attention, I sometimes so annoyed him that our duel ended with me being carried from the room in tears. Or I remember him sitting bent forward, his elbows on his knees, staring towards the great window which held back the inky night. I used to wonder what he was thinking. In the eye of my memory he always wears a grey, sleeveless sweater and he has loosened his tie, and his sandy hair falls forward over a square, ruddy face. He was one of those people who, quick to laugh, are slow to anger; so that their anger, when it comes, is all the more impressive, seeming to leap from some unsuspected crevice like a fire which will bring the whole house down.

And his sister Ellen, a little older than he, a little darker, always overdressed, overmade-up, with a face and figure beginning to harden, and with too much jewelry everywhere, clanging and banging in the light, sits on the sofa, reading; she read a lot, all the new books, and she used to go to the movies a great deal. Or she knits. It seems to me that she was always carrying a great bag full of dangerous-looking knitting needles, or a book, or both. And I don't know what she knitted, though I suppose she must, at least occasionally, have knitted something for my father, or me. But I don't remember it, anymore than I remember the books she read. It might always have been the same book and she might have been working on the same scarf, or sweater, or God knows what, all the years I knew her. Sometimes she and my father played cards—this was rare; sometimes they talked together in friendly, teasing tones, but this was dangerous. Their banter nearly always ended in a fight. Sometimes there was company and I was often allowed to watch them drink their cocktails. Then my father was at his best, boyish and expansive, moving about through the crowded room with a glass in his hand, refilling people's drinks, laughing a lot, handling all the men as though they were his brothers, and flirting with the women. Or no, not flirting with them, strutting like a cock before them. Ellen always seemed to be watching him as though she were afraid he would do something awful, watched him and watched the women and, yes, she flirted with the men in a strange, nerve-wracking kind of way. There she was, dressed, as they say, to kill, with her mouth redder than any blood, dressed in something which was either the wrong color, or too tight, or too young, the cocktail glass in her hand threatening, at any instant, to be reduced to shards, to splinters, and that voice going on and on like a razor blade on glass. When I was a little boy and I watched her in company, she frightened me.

But no matter what was happening in that room, my mother was watching it. She looked out of the photograph frame, a pale, blonde woman, delicately put together, dark-eyed, and straight-browed, with a nervous, gentle mouth. But something about the way the eyes were set in the head and stared straight out, something very faintly sardonic and knowing in the set of the mouth suggested that, somewhere beneath this tense fragility was a strength as various as it was unyielding and, like my father's wrath, dangerous because it was so entirely unexpected. My father rarely spoke of her and when he did he covered, by some mysterious means, his face; he spoke of her only as my mother and, in fact, as he spoke of her, he might have been speaking of his own. Ellen spoke of my mother often, saying what a remarkable woman she had been, but she made me uncomfortable. I felt that I had no right to be the son of such a mother.

Years later, when I had become a man, I tried to get my father to talk about my mother. But Ellen was dead, he was about to marry again. He spoke of my mother, then, as Ellen had spoken of her and he might, indeed, have been speaking of Ellen.

They had a fight one night when I was about thirteen. They had a great many fights, of course; but perhaps I remember this one so clearly because it seemed to be about me.

I was in bed upstairs, asleep. It was quite late. I was suddenly awakened by the sound of my father's footfalls on the walk beneath my window. I could tell by the sound and the rhythm that he was a little drunk and I remember that at that moment a certain disappointment, an unprecedented sorrow entered into me. I had seen him drunk many times and had never felt this way—on the contrary, my father sometimes had great charm when he was drunk— but that night I suddenly felt that there was something in it, in him, to be despised.

I heard him come in. Then, at once, I heard Ellen's voice.

"Aren't you in bed yet?" my father asked. He was trying to be pleasant and trying to avoid a scene, but there was no cordiality in his voice, only strain and exasperation.

"I thought," said Ellen, coldly, "that someone ought to tell you what you're doing to your son."

"What I'm doing to my son?" And he was about to say something more, something awful; but he caught himself and only said, with a resigned, drunken, despairing calm: "What are you talking about, Ellen?"

"Do you really think," she asked—I was certain that she was standing in the center of the room, with her hands folded before her, standing very straight and still—"that you're the kind of man he ought to be when he grows up?" And, as my father said nothing: "He *is* growing up, you know." And then, spitefully, "Which is more than I can say for you."

"Go to bed, Ellen," said my father—sounding very weary.

I had the feeling, since they were talking about me, that I ought to go downstairs and tell Ellen that whatever was wrong between my father and myself we could work out between us without her help. And, perhaps—which seems odd—I felt that she was disrespectful of *me*. For I had certainly never said a word to her about my father.

I heard his heavy, uneven footfalls as he moved across the room, towards the stairs.

"Don't think," said Ellen, "that I don't know where you've been."

"I've been out—drinking—" said my father, "and now I'd like to get a little sleep. Do you mind?"

"You've been with that girl, Beatrice," said Ellen. "That's where you always are and that's where all your money goes and all your manhood and self-respect, too."

She had succeeded in making him angry. He began to stammer. "If you think—if you *think*—that I'm going to stand—stand—stand here—and argue with *you* about my private life—*my* private life!—if you think I'm going to argue with *you* about it, why, you're out of your mind."

"I certainly don't care," said Ellen, "what you do with yourself. It isn't *you* I'm worried about. It's only that you're the only person who has any authority over David. I don't. And he hasn't got any mother. And he only listens to me when he thinks it pleases you. Do you really think it's a good idea for David to see you staggering home drunk all the time? And don't fool yourself," she added, after a moment, in a voice thick with passion, "don't fool yourself that he doesn't know where you're coming from, don't think he doesn't know about your women!"

She was wrong. I don't think I did know about them—or I had never thought about them. But from that evening, I thought about them all the time. I could scarcely ever face a woman without wondering whether or not my father had, in Ellen's phrase, been "interfering" with her.

"I think it barely possible," said my father, "that David has a cleaner mind than yours."

The silence, then, in which my father climbed the stairs was by far the worst silence my life had ever known. I was wondering what they were thinking—each of them. I wondered how they looked. I wondered what I would see when I saw them in the morning.

"And listen," said my father suddenly, from the middle of the staircase, in a voice which frightened me, "all I want for David is that he grow up to be a man. And when I say a man, Ellen, I don't mean a Sunday school teacher."

"A man," said Ellen, shortly, "is not the same thing as a bull. Good-night."

"Good-night," he said, after a moment.

And I heard him stagger past my door.

From that time on, with the mysterious, cunning, and dreadful intensity of the very young, I despised my father and I hated Ellen. It is hard to say why. I don't know why. But it allowed all of Ellen's prophecies about me to come true. She had said that there would come a time when nothing and nobody would be able to rule me, not even my father. And that time certainly came.

It was after Joey. The incident with Joey had shaken me profoundly and its effect was to make me secretive and cruel. I could not discuss what had happened to me with anyone, I could not even admit it to myself; and, while I never thought about it, it remained, nevertheless, at the bottom of my mind, as still and as awful as a decomposing corpse. And it changed, it thickened, it soured the atmosphere of my mind. Soon it was I who came staggering home late at night, it was I who found Ellen waiting up for me, Ellen and I who wrangled night in and night out.

My father's attitude was that this was but an inevitable phase of my growing up and he affected to take it lightly. But beneath his jocular, boys-together air, he was at a loss, he was frightened. Perhaps he had supposed that my growing up would bring us closer together—whereas, now that he was trying to find out something about me, I was in full flight from him. I did not *want* him to know me. I did not want anyone to know me. And then, again, I was undergoing with my father what the very young inevitably undergo with their elders: I was beginning to judge him. And the very harshness of this judgment, which broke my heart, revealed, though I could not have said it then, how much I had loved him, how that love, along with my innocence, was dying.

My poor father was baffled and afraid. He was unable to believe that there could be anything seriously wrong between us. And this was not only because he would not then have known what to do about it; it was mainly because he would then have had to face the knowledge that he had left something, somewhere, undone, something of the utmost importance. And since neither of us had any idea of what this so significant omission could have been, and since we were forced to remain in tacit league against Ellen, we took refuge in being hearty with each other. We were not like father and son, my father sometimes proudly said, we were like buddies. I think my father sometimes actually believed this. I never did. I did not want to be his buddy; I wanted to be his son. What passed between us as masculine candor exhausted and appalled me. Fathers ought to avoid utter nakedness before their sons. I did not want to know—not, anyway, from his mouth—that his flesh was as unregenerate as my own. The knowledge did not make me feel more like his son—or buddy—it only made me feel like an interloper, and a frightened one at that. He thought we were alike. I did not want to think so. I did not want to think that my life would be like his, or that my mind would ever grow so pale, so without hard places and sharp, sheer drops. He wanted no distance between us; he wanted me to look on him as a man like myself. But I wanted the merciful distance of father and son, which would have permitted me to love him.

One night, drunk, with several other people on the way back from an out-of-town party, the car I was driving smashed up. It was entirely my fault. I was almost too drunk to walk and had no business driving; but the others did not know this, since I am one of those people who can look and sound sober while practically in a state of collapse. On a straight, level piece of highway something weird happened to all my reactions, and the car sprang suddenly out of my control. And a telephone pole, foam-white, came crying at me out of the pitch darkness; I heard screams and then a heavy, roaring, tearing sound. Then everything turned absolutely scarlet and then as bright as day and I went into a darkness I had never known before.

I must have begun to wake up as we were being moved to the hospital. I dimly remember movement and voices, but they seemed very far away, they seemed to have nothing to do with me. Then, later, I woke up in a spot which seemed to be the very heart of winter, a high, white ceiling and white walls, and a hard, glacial window, bent, as it seemed, over me. I must have tried to rise, for I remember an awful roaring in my head, and then a weight on my chest and a huge face over me. And as this weight, this face, began to push me under again, I screamed for my mother. Then it was dark again.

When I came to myself at last, my father was standing over my bed. I knew he was there before I saw him, before my eyes focused and I carefully turned my head. When he saw that I was awake, he carefully stepped closer to the bed, motioning to me to be still. And he looked very old. I wanted to cry. For a moment we just stared at each other.

"How do you feel?" he whispered, finally.

It was when I tried to speak that I realized I was in pain and immediately I was frightened. He must have seen this in my eyes, for he said in a low voice, with a pained, a marvellous intensity, "Don't worry, David. You're going to be all right. You're going to be all right."

I still could not say anything. I simply watched his face.

"You kids were mighty lucky," he said, trying to smile. "You're the one got smashed up the most."

"I was drunk," I said at last. I wanted to tell him everything— but speaking was such agony.

"Don't you know," he asked, with an air of extreme bafflement—for this was something he could allow himself to be baffled about—"better than to go driving around like that when you're drunk? You know better than that," he said, severely, and pursed his lips. "Why you could all have been killed." And his voice shook.

"I'm sorry," I said, suddenly. "I'm sorry." I did not know how to say what it was I was sorry for.

"Don't be sorry," he said. "Just be careful next time." He had been patting his handkerchief between his palms; now he opened his handkerchief and reached out and wiped my forehead. "You're all I've got," he said then, with a shy, pained grin. "Be careful."

"Daddy," I said. And began to cry. And if speaking had been agony, this was worse and yet I could not stop.

And my father's face changed. It became terribly old and at the same time absolutely, helplessly young. I remember being absolutely astonished, at the still, cold center of the storm which was occurring in me, to realize that my father had been suffering, was suffering still.

"Don't cry," he said, "don't cry." He stroked my forehead with that absurd handkerchief as though it possessed some healing charm. "There's nothing to cry about. Everything's going to be all right." He was almost weeping himself. "There's nothing wrong, is there? I haven't done anything wrong, have I?" And all the time he was stroking my face with that handkerchief, smothering me.

"We were drunk," I said. "We were drunk." For this seemed, somehow, to explain everything.

"Your Aunt Ellen says it's my fault," he said. "She says I never raised you right." He put away, thank heaven, that handkerchief, and weakly straightened his shoulders. "You got nothing against me, have you? Tell me if you have?"

My tears began to dry, on my face and in my breast. "No," I said, "no. Nothing. Honest."

"I did the best I could," he said. "I really did the best I could." I looked at him. And at last he grinned and said, "You're going to be on your back for awhile but when you come home, while you're lying around the house, we'll talk, huh? and try to figure out what the hell we're going to do with you when you get on your feet. OK?"

"OK," I said.

For I understood, at the bottom of my heart, that we had never talked, that now we never would. I understood that he must never know this. When I came home he talked with me about my future but I had made up my mind. I was not going to go to college, I was not going to remain in that house with him and Ellen. And I ma-neuvered my father so well that he actually began to believe that my finding a job and being on my own was the direct result of his advice and a tribute to the way he had raised me. Once I was out of the house of course, it became much easier to deal with him and he never had any reason to feel shut out of my life for I was always able, when talking about it, to tell him what he wished to hear. And we got on quite well, really, for the vision I gave my father of my life was exactly the vision in which I myself most desperately needed to believe.

For I am—or I was—one of those people who pride themselves on their willpower, on their ability to make a decision and carry it through. This virtue, like most virtues, is ambiguity itself. People who believe that they are strong-willed and the masters of their destiny can only continue to believe this by becoming specialists in self-deception. Their decisions are not really decisions at all—a real decision makes one humble, one knows that it is at the mercy of more things than can be named—but elaborate systems of evasion, of illusion, designed to make themselves and the world appear to be what they and the world are not. This is certainly what my decision, made so long ago in Joey's bed, came to. I had decided to allow no room in the universe for something which shamed and frightened me. I succeeded very well—by not looking at the universe, by not looking at myself, by remaining, in effect, in constant motion. Even constant motion, of course, does not prevent an occasional mysterious drag, a drop, like an airplane hitting an air pocket. And there were a number of those, all drunken, all sordid, one very frightening such drop while I was in the Army which involved a fairy who was later court-martialed out. The panic his punishment caused in me was as close as I ever came to facing in myself the terrors I sometimes saw clouding another man's eyes.

What happened was that, all unconscious of what this ennui meant, I wearied of the motion, wearied of the joyless seas of alcohol, wearied of the blunt, bluff, hearty, and totally meaningless friendships, wearied of wandering through the forests of desperate women, wearied of the work, which fed me only in the most brutally literal sense. Perhaps, as we say in America, I wanted to find myself. This is an interesting phrase, not current as far as I know in the language of any other people, which certainly does not mean what it says but betrays a nagging suspicion that something has been misplaced. I think now that if I had had any intimation that the self I was going to find would turn out to be only the same self from which I had spent so much time in flight, I would have stayed at home. But, again, I think I knew, at the very bottom of my heart, exactly what I was doing when I took the boat for France.

T W O

I MET GIOVANNI DURING my second year in Paris, when I had no money. On the morning of the evening that we met I had been turned out of my room. I did not owe an awful lot of money, only around six thousand francs, but Parisian hotel-keepers have a way of smelling poverty and then they do what anybody does who is aware of a bad smell; they throw whatever stinks outside.

My father had money in his account which belonged to me but he was very reluctant to send it because he wanted me to come home—to come home, as he said, and settle down, and whenever he said that I thought of the sediment at the bottom of a stagnant pond. I did not, then, know many people in Paris and Hella was in Spain. Most of the people I knew in Paris were, as Parisians sometimes put it, of *le milieu* and, while this milieu was certainly anxious enough to claim me, I was intent on proving, to them and to myself, that I was not of their company. I did this by being in their

company a great deal and manifesting toward all of them a tolerance which placed me, I believed, above suspicion. I had written to
friends for money, of course, but the Atlantic Ocean is deep and
wide and money doesn't hurry from the other side.

So I went through my address book, sitting over a tepid coffee in
a boulevard cafe, and decided to call up an old acquaintance who
was always asking me to call, an aging, Belgian-born, American
businessman named Jacques. He had a big, comfortable apartment
and lots of things to drink and lots of money. He was, as I knew he
would be, surprised to hear from me and before the surprise and
the charm wore off, giving him time to become wary, he had invited me for supper. He may have been cursing as he hung up, and
reaching for his wallet, but it was too late. Jacques is not too bad.
Perhaps he is a fool and a coward but almost everybody is one or the
other and most people are both. In some ways I liked him. He was
silly but he was so lonely; anyway, I understand now that the contempt I felt for him involved my self-contempt. He could be unbelievably generous, he could be unspeakably stingy. Though he
wanted to trust everybody, he was incapable of trusting a living
soul; to make up for this, he threw his money away on people; inevitably, then, he was abused. Then he buttoned his wallet, locked his
door, and retired into that strong self-pity which was, perhaps, the
only thing he had which really belonged to him. I thought for a
long while that he, with his big apartment, his well-meant promises, his whiskey, his marijuana, his orgies, had helped to kill Giovanni. As, indeed, perhaps he had. But Jacques' hands are certainly
no bloodier than mine.

I saw Jacques, as a matter of fact, just after Giovanni was sen-
tenced. He was sitting bundled up in his greatcoat on the terrace of
a cafe, drinking a *vin chaud*. He was alone on the terrace. He called
me as I passed.

He did not look well, his face was mottled, his eyes, behind his glasses, were like the eyes of a dying man who looks everywhere for healing.

"You've heard," he whispered, as I joined him, "about Giovanni?"

I nodded yes. I remember the winter sun was shining and I felt as cold and distant as the sun.

"It's terrible, terrible, terrible," Jacques moaned. "Terrible."

"Yes," I said. I could not say anything more.

"I wonder why he did it," Jacques pursued, "why he didn't ask his friends to help him." He looked at me. We both knew that the last time Giovanni had asked Jacques for money, Jacques had refused. I said nothing. "They say he had started taking opium," Jacques said, "that he needed the money for opium. Did you hear that?"

I had heard it. It was a newspaper speculation which, however, I had reasons of my own for believing, remembering the extent of Giovanni's desperation, knowing how far this terror, which was so vast that it had simply become a void, had driven him. "Me, I want to escape," he had told me, "*Je veux m'evader*—this dirty world, this dirty body. I never wish to make love again with anything more than the body."

Jacques waited for me to answer. I stared out into the street. I was beginning to think of Giovanni dying—where Giovanni had been there would be nothing, nothing forever.

"I hope it's not my fault," Jacques said at last. "I didn't give him the money. If I'd known—I would have given him everything I had."

But we both knew this was not true.

"You two together," Jacques suggested, "you weren't happy together?"

"No," I said. I stood up. "It might have been better," I said, "if he'd stayed down there in that village of his in Italy and planted his olive trees and had a lot of children and beaten his wife. He used to love to sing," I remembered suddenly, "maybe he could have stayed down there and sung his life away and died in bed."

Then Jacques said something that surprised me. People are full of surprises, even for themselves, if they have been stirred enough. "Nobody can stay in the garden of Eden," Jacques said. And then: "I wonder why."

I said nothing. I said goodbye and left him. Hella had long since returned from Spain and we were already arranging to rent this house and I had a date to meet her.

I have thought about Jacques' question since. The question is banal but one of the real troubles with living is that living is so banal. Everyone, after all, goes the same dark road—and the road has a trick of being most dark, most treacherous, when it seems most bright—and it's true that nobody stays in the garden of Eden. Jacques' garden was not the same as Giovanni's, of course. Jacques' garden was involved with football players and Giovanni's was involved with maidens—but that seems to have made so little difference. Perhaps everybody has a garden of Eden, I don't know; but they have scarcely seen their garden before they see the flaming sword. Then, perhaps, life only offers the choice of remembering the garden or forgetting it. Either, or: it takes strength to remember, it takes another kind of strength to forget, it takes a hero to do both. People who remember court madness through pain, the pain of the perpetually recurring death of their innocence; people who forget court another kind of madness, the madness of the denial of pain and the hatred of innocence; and the world is mostly divided between madmen who remember and madmen who forget. Heroes are rare.

Jacques had not wanted to have supper in his apartment because his cook had run away. His cooks were always running away. He was always getting young boys from the provinces, God knows how, to come up and be cooks; and they, of course, as soon as they were able to find their way around the capital, decided that cooking was the last thing they wanted to do. They usually ended up going back to the provinces, those, that is, who did not end up on the streets, or in jail, or in Indochina.

I met him at a rather nice restaurant on the rue de Grenelle and arranged to borrow ten thousand francs from him before we had finished our aperitifs. He was in a good mood and I, of course, was in a good mood too, and this meant that we would end up drinking in Jacques' favorite bar, a noisy, crowded, ill-lit sort of tunnel, of dubious—or perhaps not dubious at all, of rather too emphatic—reputation. Every once in a while it was raided by the police, apparently with the connivance of Guillaume, the *patron*, who always managed, on the particular evening, to warn his favorite customers that if they were not armed with identification papers they might be better off elsewhere.

I remember that the bar, that night, was more than ordinarily crowded and noisy. All of the habitués were there and many strangers, some looking, some just staring. There were three or four very chic Parisian ladies sitting at a table with their gigolos or their lovers or perhaps simply their country cousins, God knows; the ladies seemed extremely animated, their males seemed rather stiff; the ladies seemed to be doing most of the drinking. There were the usual paunchy, bespectacled gentlemen with avid, sometimes despairing eyes, the usual, knife-blade lean, tight-trousered boys. One could never be sure, as concerns these latter, whether they were after money or blood or love. They moved about the bar incessantly, cadging cigarettes and drinks, with something behind their eyes at once terribly vulnerable and terribly hard. There were, of course, *les folles,* always dressed in the most improbable combinations, screaming like parrots the details of their latest love affairs—their love affairs always seemed to be hilarious. Occasionally one would swoop in, quite late in the evening, to convey the news that he—

but they always called each other "she"—had just spent time with a celebrated movie star, or boxer. Then all of the others closed in on this newcomer and they looked like a peacock garden and sounded like a barnyard. I always found it difficult to believe that they ever went to bed with anybody, for a man who wanted a woman would certainly have rather had a real one and a man who wanted a man would certainly not want one of *them*. Perhaps, indeed, that was why they screamed so loud. There was the boy who worked all day, it was said, in the post office, who came out at night wearing makeup and earrings and with his heavy blond hair piled high. Sometimes he actually wore a skirt and high heels. He usually stood alone unless Guillaume walked over to tease him. People said that he was very nice, but I confess that his utter grotesqueness made me uneasy; perhaps in the same way that the sight of monkeys eating their own excrement turns some people's stomachs. They might not mind so much if monkeys did not—so grotesquely—resemble human beings.

This bar was practically in my *quartier* and I had many times had breakfast in the nearby workingman's cafe to which all the nightbirds of the neighborhood retired when the bars closed. Sometimes I was with Hella; sometimes I was alone. And I had been in this bar, too, two or three times; once very drunk, I had been accused of causing a minor sensation by flirting with a soldier. My memory of that night was, happily, very dim, and I took the attitude that no matter how drunk I may have been, I could not possibly have done such a thing. But my face was known and I had the feeling that people were taking bets about me. Or, it was as though they were the elders of some strange and austere holy order and were watching me in order to discover, by means of signs I made but which only they could read, whether or not I had a true vocation.

Jacques was aware, I was aware, as we pushed our way to the bar—it was like moving into the field of a magnet or like approaching a small circle of heat—of the presence of a new barman. He stood, insolent and dark and leonine, his elbow leaning on the cash register, his fingers playing with his chin, looking out at the crowd. It was as though his station were a promontory and we were the sea.

Jacques was immediately attracted. I felt him, so to speak, preparing himself for conquest. I felt the necessity for tolerance.

"I'm sure," I said, "that you'll want to get to know the barman. So I'll vanish anytime you like."

There was, in this tolerance of mine, a fund, by no means meagre, of malicious knowledge—I had drawn on it when I called him up to borrow money. I knew that Jacques could only hope to conquer the boy before us if the boy was, in effect, for sale; and if he stood with such arrogance on an auction block he could certainly find bidders richer and more attractive than Jacques. I knew that Jacques knew this. I knew something else: that Jacques' vaunted affection for me was involved with desire, the desire, in fact, to be rid of me, to be able, soon, to despise me as he now despised that army of boys who had come, without love, to his bed. I held my own against this desire by pretending that Jacques and I were friends, by forcing Jacques, on pain of humiliation, to pretend this. I pretended not to see, although I exploited it, the lust not quite sleeping in his bright, bitter eyes and, by means of the rough, male candor with which I conveyed to him his case was hopeless, I compelled him, endlessly, to hope. And I knew, finally, that in bars such as these I was Jacques' protection. As long as I was there the world could see and he could believe that he was out with me, his friend, he was not there out of desperation, he was not at the mercy of whatever adventurer chance, cruelty, or the laws of actual and emotional poverty might throw his way.

"You stay right here," said Jacques. "I'll look at him from time to time and talk to you and that way I'll save money—and stay happy, too."

"I wonder where Guillaume found him," I said.

For he was so exactly the kind of boy that Guillaume always dreamed of that it scarcely seemed possible that Guillaume could have found him.

"What will you have?" he now asked us. His tone conveyed that, though he spoke no English, he knew that we had been speaking about him and hoped we were through.

"Une fine à l'eau," I said; and *"un cognac sec,"* said Jacques, both speaking too quickly, so that I blushed and realized by a faint merriment on Giovanni's face as he served us that he had seen it.

Jacques, wilfully misinterpreting Giovanni's nuance of a smile, made of it an opportunity. "You're new here?" he asked in English.

Giovanni almost certainly understood the question, but it suited him better to look blankly from Jacques to me and then back again at Jacques. Jacques translated his question.

Giovanni shrugged. "I have been here a month," he said.

I knew where the conversation was going and I kept my eyes down and sipped my drink.

"It must," Jacques suggested, with a sort of bludgeoning insistence on the light touch, "seem very strange to you."

"Strange?" asked Giovanni. "Why?"

And Jacques giggled. I was suddenly ashamed that I was with him. "All these men"—and I knew that voice, breathless, insinuating, high as no girl's had ever been, and hot, suggesting, somehow, the absolutely motionless, deadly heat which hangs over swamp ground in July—"all these men," he gasped, "and so few women. Doesn't that seem strange to you?"

"Ah," said Giovanni, and turned away to serve another customer, "no doubt the women are waiting at home."

"I'm sure one's waiting for you," insisted Jacques, to which Giovanni did not respond.

"Well. That didn't take long," said Jacques, half to me, half to the space which had just held Giovanni. "Aren't you glad you stayed? You've got me all to yourself."

"Oh, you're handling it all wrong," I said. "He's mad for you. He just doesn't want to seem too anxious. Order him a drink. Find out where he likes to buy his clothes. Tell him about that cunning little Alfa Romeo you're just dying to give away to some deserving bartender."

"*Very* funny," said Jacques.

"Well," I said, "faint heart never won fair athlete, that's for sure."

"Anyway, I'm sure he sleeps with girls. They always do, you know."

"I've heard about boys who do that. Nasty little beasts."

We stood in silence for awhile.

"Why don't *you* invite him to have a drink with us?" Jacques suggested.

I looked at him.

"Why don't *I?* Well, you may find this hard to believe, but, actually, I'm sort of queer for girls myself. If that was his sister looking so good, I'd invite *her* to have a drink with us. I don't spend money on men."

I could see Jacques struggling not to say that I didn't have any objection to allowing men to spend money on *me;* I watched his brief struggle with a slight smile, for I knew he couldn't say it; then he said, with that cheery, brave smile of his:

"I was not suggesting that you jeopardize, even for a moment, that"—he paused—"that *immaculate* manhood which is your pride and joy. I only suggested that *you* invite him because he will almost certainly refuse if *I* invite him."

"But man," I said, grinning, "think of the confusion. He'll think that *I'm* the one who's lusting for his body. How do we get out of that?"

"If there should be any confusion," said Jacques, with dignity, "I will be happy to clear it up."

We measured each other for a moment. Then I laughed. "Wait till he comes back this way. I hope he orders a magnum of the most expensive champagne in France."

I turned, leaning on the bar. I felt, somehow, elated. Jacques, beside me, was very quiet, suddenly very frail and old, and I felt a quick, sharp, rather frightened pity for him. Giovanni had been out on the floor, serving the people at tables, and he now returned with a rather grim smile on his face, carrying a loaded tray.

"Maybe," I said, "it would look better if our glasses were empty."

We finished our drinks. I set down my glass.

"Barman?" I called.

"The same?"

"Yes." He started to turn away. "Barman," I said, quickly, "we would like to offer you a drink, if we may."

"*Eh, bien!*" said a voice behind us, "*c'est fort ça!* Not only have you finally—thank heaven!—corrupted this great American football player, you use him now to corrupt *my* barman. *Vraiment, Jacques! At your age!*"

It was Guillaume standing behind us, grinning like a movie star, and waving that long white handkerchief which he was never, in the bar at any rate, to be seen without. Jacques turned, hugely delighted to be accused of such rare seductiveness, and he and Guillaume fell into each other arms like old theatrical sisters.

"*Eh bien, ma chérie, comment vas-tu?* I have not seen you for a long time."

"But I have been awfully busy," said Jacques.

"I don't doubt it! Aren't you ashamed, *vieille folle?*"

"*Et toi?* You certainly don't seem to have been wasting your time."

And Jacques threw a delighted look in the direction of Giovanni, rather as though Giovanni were a valuable racehorse or a rare bit of china. Guillaume followed the look and his voice dropped.

"*Ah, ça, mon cher, c'est strictement du* business, *comprends-tu?*"

They moved a little away. This left me surrounded, abruptly, with an awful silence. At last I raised my eyes and looked at Giovanni, who was watching me.

"I think you offered me a drink," he said.

"Yes," I said. "I offered you a drink."

"I drink no alcohol while I work, but I will take a Coca-Cola." He picked up my glass. "And for you—it is the same?"

"The same." I realized that I was quite happy to be talking with him and this realization made me shy. And I felt menaced since Jacques was no longer at my side. Then I realized that I would have to pay, for this round anyway; it was impossible to tug Jacques' sleeve for the money as though I were his ward. I coughed and put my ten thousand franc note on the bar.

"You are rich," said Giovanni, and set my drink before me.

"But no. No. I simply have no change."

He grinned. I could not tell whether he grinned because he thought I was lying or because he knew I was telling the truth. In silence he took the bill and rang it up and carefully counted out my change on the bar before me. Then he filled his glass and went back to his original position at the cash register. I felt a tightening in my chest.

"*À la votre,*" he said.

"*À la votre.*" We drank.

"You are an American?" he asked at last.

"Yes," I said. "From New York."

"Ah! I am told that New York is very beautiful. Is it more beautiful than Paris?"

"Oh, no," I said, "*no* city is more beautiful than Paris—"

"It seems the very suggestion that one *could* be is enough to make you very angry," grinned Giovanni. "Forgive me. I was not trying to be heretical." Then, more soberly and as though to appease me, "You must like Paris very much."

"I like New York, too," I said, uncomfortably aware that my voice had a defensive ring, "but New York is very beautiful in a very different way."

He frowned. "In what way?"

"No one," I said, "who has never seen it can possibly imagine it. It's very high and new and electric—exciting." I paused. "It's hard to describe. It's very—twentieth century."

"You find that Paris is *not* of this century?" he asked with a smile.

His smile made me feel a little foolish. "Well," I said, "Paris is *old*, is many centuries. You feel, in Paris, all the time gone by. That isn't what you feel in New York—" He was smiling. I stopped.

"What do you feel in New York?" he asked.

"Perhaps you feel," I told him, "all the time to come. There's such power there, everything is in such movement. You can't help wondering—*I* can't help wondering—what it will all be like—many years from now."

"Many years from now? When we are dead and New York is old?"

"Yes," I said. "When everyone is tired, when the world—for Americans—is not so new."

"I don't see why the world is so new for Americans," said Giovanni. "After all, you are all merely emigrants. And you did not leave Europe so very long ago."

"The ocean is very wide," I said. "We have led different lives than you; things have happened to us there which have never happened here. Surely you can understand that this would make us a different people?"

"Ah! If it had only made you a different people!" he laughed. "But it seems to have turned you into another species. You are not, are you, on another planet? For I suppose that would explain everything."

"I admit," I said with some heat—for I do not like to be laughed at—"that we may sometimes give the impression that we think we are. But we are not on another planet, no. And neither, my friend, are you."

He grinned again. "I will not," he said, "argue that most unlucky fact."

We were silent for a moment. Giovanni moved to serve several people at either end of the bar. Guillaume and Jacques were still talking. Guillaume seemed to be recounting one of his interminable anecdotes, anecdotes which invariably pivoted on the hazards of business or the hazards of love, and Jacques' mouth was stretched in a rather painful grin. I knew that he was dying to get back to the bar.

Giovanni placed himself before me again and began wiping the bar with a damp cloth. "The Americans are funny. You have a funny sense of time—or perhaps you have no sense of time at all, I can't tell. Time always sounds like a parade *chez vous*—a *triumphant* parade, like armies with banners entering a town. As though, with enough time, and that would not need to be so very much for Americans, *n'est-ce pas?*" and he smiled, giving me a mocking look, but I said nothing. "Well then," he continued, "as though with enough time and all that fearful energy and virtue you people have, everything will be settled, solved, put in its place. And when I say everything," he added, grimly, "I mean all the serious, dreadful things, like pain and death and love, in which you Americans do not believe."

"What makes you think we don't? And what do you believe?"

"I don't believe in this nonsense about time. Time is just common, it's like water for a fish. Everybody's in this water, nobody gets out of it, or if he does the same thing happens to him that happens to the fish, he dies. And you know what happens in this water, time? The big fish eat the little fish. That's all. The big fish eat the little fish and the ocean doesn't care."

"Oh, please," I said. "I don't believe *that*. Time's hot water and we're not fish and you can choose to be eaten and also not to eat— not to eat," I added quickly, turning a little red before his delighted and sardonic smile, "the little fish, of course."

"To choose!" cried Giovanni, turning his face away from me and speaking, it appeared, to an invisible ally who had been eavesdropping on this conversation all along. "To *choose*!" He turned to me again. "Ah, you are really an American. *J'adore votre enthousiasme!*"

"I adore yours," I said, politely, "though it seems to be a blacker brand than mine."

"Anyway," he said mildly, "I don't see what you can do with little fish except eat them. What else are they good for?"

"In my country," I said, feeling a subtle war within me as I said it, "the little fish seem to have gotten together and are nibbling at the body of the whale."

"That will not make them whales," said Giovanni. "The only result of all that nibbling will be that there will no longer be any grandeur anywhere, not even at the bottom of the sea."

"Is *that* what you have against us? That we're not grand?"

He smiled—smiled like someone who, faced with the total inadequacy of the opposition, is prepared to drop the argument. *"Peut-être."*

"You people are impossible," I said. "You're the ones who killed grandeur off, right here in this city, with paving stones. Talk about little fish—!" He was grinning. I stopped.

"Don't stop," he said, still grinning. "I am listening."

I finished my drink. "You people dumped all this *merde* on us," I said, sullenly, "and now you say we're barbaric because we stink."

My sullenness delighted him. "You're charming," he said. "Do you always speak like this?"

"No," I said, and looked down. "Almost never."

There was something in him of the coquette. "I am flattered then," he said, with a sudden, disconcerting gravity, which contained, nevertheless, the very faintest hint of mockery.

"And you," I said, finally, "have you been here long? Do you like Paris?"

He hesitated a moment and then grinned, suddenly looking rather boyish and shy. "It's cold in the winter," he said. "I don't like that. And Parisians—I do not find them so very friendly, do you?" He did not wait for my answer. "They are not like the people I knew when I was younger. In Italy we are friendly, we dance and sing and make love—but these people," and he looked out over the bar, and then at me, and finished his Coca-Cola, "these people, they are cold, I do not understand them."

"But the French say," I teased, "that the Italians are too fluid, too volatile, have no sense of measure—"

"Measure!" cried Giovanni, "ah, these people and their measure! They measure the gram, the centimeter, these people, and they keep piling all the little scraps they save, one on top of the other, year in and year out, all in the stocking or under the bed— and what do they get out of all this measure? A country which is falling to pieces, measure by measure, before their eyes. Measure. I do not like to offend your ears by saying all the things I am sure these people measure before they permit themselves any act whatever. May I offer you a drink now," he asked suddenly, "before the old man comes back? Who is he? Is he your uncle?"

I did not know whether the word "uncle" was being used euphemistically or not. I felt a very urgent desire to make my position clear but I did not know how to go about it. I laughed. "No," I said, "he is not my uncle. He is just somebody I know."

Giovanni looked at me. And this look made me feel that no one in my life had ever looked at me directly before. "I hope he is not very dear to you," he said, with a smile, "because I think he is silly. Not a bad man, you understand— just a little silly."

"Perhaps," I said, and at once felt like a traitor. "He's not bad," I added quickly, "he's really a pretty nice guy." That's not true, either, I thought, he's far from being a nice guy. "Anyway," I said, "he's certainly not very dear to me," and felt again, at once, this strange tightening in my chest and wondered at the sound of my voice.

Carefully now, Giovanni poured my drink. *"Vive l' Amérique,"* he said.

"Thank you," I said, and lifted my glass, *"vive le vieux continent."*

We were silent for a moment.

"Do you come in here often?" asked Giovanni suddenly.

"No," I said, "not very often."

"But you will come," he teased, with a wonderful, mocking light on his face, "more often *now?*"

I stammered: "Why?"

"Ah!" cried Giovanni. "Don't you know when you have made a friend?"

I knew I must look foolish and that my question was foolish too: "So soon?"

"Why no," he said, reasonably, and looked at his watch, "we can wait another hour if you like. We can become friends then. Or we can wait until closing time. We can become friends *then.* Or we can wait until tomorrow, only that means that you must come in here tomorrow and perhaps you have something else to do." He put his watch away and leaned both elbows on the bar. "Tell me," he said, "what is this thing about time? Why is it better to be late than early? People are always saying, we must wait, we must wait. What are they waiting for?"

"Well," I said, feeling myself being led by Giovanni into deep and dangerous water, "I guess people wait in order to make sure of what they feel."

"In order to make *sure!*" He turned again to that invisible ally and laughed again. I was beginning, perhaps, to find his phantom a little unnerving but the sound of his laughter in that airless tunnel was the most incredible sound. "It's clear that you are a true philosopher." He pointed a finger at my heart. "And when you have waited—has it made you sure?"

For this I could simply summon no answer. From the dark, crowded center of the bar someone called *"Garçon!"* and he moved away from me, smiling. "You can wait now. And tell me how sure you have become when I return."

And he took his round metal tray and moved out into the crowd. I watched him as he moved. And then I watched their faces, watching him. And then I was afraid. I knew that they were watching, had been watching both of us. They knew that they had witnessed a beginning and now they would not cease to watch until they saw the end. It had taken some time but the tables had been turned; now I was in the zoo, and they were watching.

I stood at the bar for quite a while alone, for Jacques had escaped from Guillaume but was now involved, poor man, with two of the knife-blade boys. Giovanni came back for an instant and winked.

"Are you sure?"

"You win. You're the philosopher."

"Oh, you must wait some more. You do not yet know me well enough to say such a thing."

And he filled his tray and disappeared again.

Now someone whom I had never seen before came out of the shadows toward me. It looked like a mummy or a zombie—this was the first, overwhelming impression—of something walking after it had been put to death. And it walked, really, like someone who might be sleepwalking or like those figures in slow motion one sometimes sees on the screen. It carried a glass, it walked on its toes, the flat hips moved with a dead, horrifying lasciviousness. It seemed to make no sound; this was due to the roar of the bar, which was like the roaring of the sea, heard at night, from far away. It glittered in the dim light; the thin, black hair was violent with oil, combed forward, hanging in bangs; the eyelids gleamed with mascara, the mouth raged with lipstick. The face was white and thoroughly bloodless with some kind of foundation cream; it stank of powder and a gardenia-like perfume. The shirt, open coquettishly to the navel, revealed a hairless chest and a silver crucifix; the shirt was covered with round, paper-thin wafers, red and green and orange and yellow and blue, which stormed in the light and made one feel that the mummy might, at any moment, disappear in flame. A red sash was around the waist, the clinging pants were a surprisingly sombre grey. He wore buckles on his shoes.

I was not sure that he was coming towards me, but I could not take my eyes away. He stopped before me, one hand on his hip, looked me up and down, and smiled. He had been eating garlic and his teeth were very bad. His hands, I noticed, with an unbelieving shock, were very large and strong.

"*Eh bien,*" he said, "*il te plaît?*"

"*Comment?*" I said.

I really was not sure I had heard him right, though the bright, bright eyes, looking, it seemed, at something amusing within the recess of my skull, did not leave much room for doubt.

"You like him—the barman?"

I did not know what to do or say. It seemed impossible to hit him; it seemed impossible to get angry. It did not seem real, he did not seem real. Besides—no matter what I said, those eyes would mock me with it. I said, as drily as I could:

"How does that concern you?"

"But it concerns me not at all, darling. *Je m'en fou.*"

"Then please get the hell away from me."

He did not move at once, but smiled at me again. *"Il est danger-eux, tu sais.* And for a boy like you—he is *very* dangerous."

I looked at him. I almost asked him what he meant. "Go to hell," I said, and turned my back.

"Oh, no," he said—and I looked at him again. He was laughing, showing all his teeth—there were not many. "Oh, no," he said, "I go not to hell," and he clutched his crucifix with one large hand. "But you, my dear friend—I fear that you shall burn in a very hot fire." He laughed again. "Oh, such fire!" He touched his head. "Here." And he writhed, as though in torment. "Every*where.*" And he touched his heart. "And here." And he looked at me with malice and mockery and something else; he looked at me as though I were very far away. "Oh, my poor friend, so young, so strong, so hand-some—will you not buy me a drink?"

"Va te faire foutre."

His face crumpled in the sorrow of infants and of very old men—the sorrow, also, of certain, aging actresses who were re-nowned in their youth for their fragile, childlike beauty. The dark eyes narrowed in spite and fury and the scarlet mouth turned down like the mask of tragedy. *"T'aura du chagrin,"* he said. "You will be very unhappy. Remember that I told you so."

And he straightened, as though he were a princess and moved, flaming, away through the crowd.

Then Jacques spoke, at my elbow. "Everyone in the bar," he said, "is talking about how beautifully you and the barman have hit it off." He gave me a radiant and vindictive smile. "I trust there has been no confusion?"

I looked down at him. I wanted to do something to his cheerful, hideous, worldly face which would make it impossible for him ever again to smile at anyone the way he was smiling at me. Then I wanted to get out of this bar, out into the air, perhaps to find Hella, my suddenly so sorely menaced girl.

"There's been no confusion," I snapped. "Don't you go getting confused, either."

"I think I can safely say," said Jacques, "that I have scarcely ever been less confused than I am at this moment." He had stopped smiling; he gave me a look which was dry, bitter, and impersonal. "And, at the risk of losing forever your so remarkably candid friendship, let me tell you something. Confusion is a luxury which only the very, very young can possibly afford and you are not that young anymore."

"I don't know what you're talking about," I said. "Let's have another drink."

I felt that I had better get drunk. Now Giovanni went behind the bar again and winked at me. Jacques' eyes never left my face. I turned rudely from him and faced the bar again. He followed me.

"The same," said Jacques.

"Certainly," said Giovanni, "that's the way to do it." He fixed our drinks. Jacques paid. I suppose I did not look too well, for Giovanni shouted at me playfully, "Eh? Are you drunk already?"

I looked up and smiled. "You know how Americans drink," I said. "I haven't even started yet."

"David is far from drunk," said Jacques. "He is only reflecting bitterly that he must get a new pair of suspenders."

I could have killed Jacques. Yet it was only with difficulty that I kept myself from laughing. I made a face to signify to Giovanni that the old man was making a private joke, and he disappeared again. That time of evening had come when great batches of people were leaving and great batches were coming in. They would all encounter each other later anyway, in the last bar, all those, that is, unlucky enough to be searching still at such an advanced hour.

I could not look at Jacques—which he knew. He stood beside

me, smiling at nothing, humming a tune. There was nothing I could say. I did not dare to mention Hella. I could not even pretend to myself that I was sorry she was in Spain. I was glad. I was utterly, hopelessly, horribly glad. I knew I could do nothing whatever to stop the ferocious excitement which had burst in me like a storm. I could only drink, in the faint hope that the storm might thus spend itself without doing any more damage to my land. But I was glad. I was only sorry that Jacques had been a witness. He made me ashamed. I hated him because he had now seen all that he had waited, often scarcely hoping, so many months to see. We had, in effect, been playing a deadly game and he was the winner. He was the winner in spite of the fact that I had cheated to win.

I wished, nevertheless, standing there at the bar, that I had been able to find in myself the force to turn and walk out—to have gone over to Montparnasse perhaps and picked up a girl. Any girl. I could not do it. I told myself all sorts of lies, standing there at the bar, but I could not move. And this was partly because I knew that it did not really matter anymore; it did not even matter if I never spoke to Giovanni again; for they had become visible, as visible as the wafers on the shirt of the flaming princess, they stormed all over me, my awakening, my insistent possibilities.

That was how I met Giovanni. I think we connected the instant that we met. And remain connected still, in spite of our later *séparation de corps,* despite the fact that Giovanni will be rotting soon in unhallowed ground near Paris. Until I die there will be those moments, moments seeming to rise up out of the ground like Macbeth's witches, when his face will come before me, that face in all its changes, when the exact timbre of his voice and tricks of his speech will nearly burst my ears, when his smell will overpower my nostrils. Sometimes, in the days which are coming—God grant me the grace to live them—in the glare of the grey morning, sourmouthed, eyelids raw and red, hair tangled and damp from my stormy sleep, facing, over coffee and cigarette smoke, last night's impenetrable, meaningless boy who will shortly rise and vanish like the smoke, I will see Giovanni again, as he was that night, so vivid, so winning, all of the light of that gloomy tunnel trapped around his head.

THREE

AT FIVE O'CLOCK in the morning Guillaume locked the door of the bar behind us. The streets were empty and grey. On a corner near the bar a butcher had already opened his shop and one could see him within, already bloody, hacking at the meat. One of the great, green Paris buses lumbered past, nearly empty, its bright electric flag waving fiercely to indicate a turn. A *garçon de cafe* spilled water on the sidewalk before his establishment and swept it into the gutter. At the end of the long, curving street which faced us were the trees of the boulevard and straw chairs piled high before cafes and the great stone spire of Saint-Germain-des-Prés—the most magnificent spire, as Hella and I believed, in Paris. The street beyond the *place* stretched before us to the river and, hidden beside and behind us, meandered to Montparnasse. It was named for an adventurer who sowed a crop in Europe which is being harvested until today. I had often walked this street, sometimes, with Hella, towards the river, often, without her, towards the girls of Montparnasse. Not very long ago either, though it seemed, that morning, to have occurred in another life.

We were going to Les Halles for breakfast. We piled into a taxi, the four of us, unpleasantly crowded together, a circumstance which elicited from Jacques and Guillaume, a series of lewd speculations. This lewdness was particularly revolting in that it not only failed of wit, it was so clearly an expression of contempt and self-contempt; it bubbled upward out of them like a fountain of black water. It was clear that they were tantalizing themselves with Giovanni and me and this set my teeth on edge. But Giovanni leaned back against the taxi window, allowing his arm to press my shoulder lightly, seeming to say that we should soon be rid of these old men and should not be distressed that their dirty water splashed— we would have no trouble washing it away.

"Look," said Giovanni, as we crossed the river. "This old whore, Paris, as she turns in bed, is very moving."

I looked out, beyond his heavy profile, which was grey—from fatigue and from the light of the sky above us. The river was swollen and yellow. Nothing moved on the river. Barges were tied up along the banks. The island of the city widened away from us, bearing the weight of the cathedral; beyond this, dimly, through speed and mist, one made out the individual roofs of Paris, their myriad, squat chimney stacks very beautiful and varicolored under the pearly sky. Mist clung to the river, softening that army of trees, softening those stones, hiding the city's dreadful corkscrew alleys and dead-end streets, clinging like a curse to the men who slept beneath the bridges—one of whom flashed by beneath us, very black and lone, walking along the river.

"Some rats have gone in," said Giovanni, "and now other rats come out." He smiled bleakly and looked at me; to my surprise, he took my hand and held it. "Have you ever slept under a bridge?" he asked. "Or perhaps they have soft beds with warm blankets under the bridges in your country?"

I did not know what to do about my hand; it seemed better to do nothing. "Not yet," I said, "but I may. My hotel wants to throw me out."

I had said it lightly, with a smile, out of a desire to put myself, in terms of an acquaintance with wintry things, on an equal footing with him. But the fact that I had said it as he held my hand made it sound to me unutterably helpless and soft and coy. But I could not say anything to counteract this impression: to say anything more would confirm it. I pulled my hand away, pretending that I had done so in order to search for a cigarette.

Jacques lit it for me.

"Where do you live?" he asked Giovanni.

"Oh," said Giovanni, "out. Far out. It is almost not Paris."

"He lives in a dreadful street, near *Nation*," said Guillaume, "among all the dreadful bourgeoisie and their piglike children."

"You failed to catch the children at the right age," said Jacques. "They go through a period, all too brief, *hélas!* when a pig is perhaps the *only* animal they do not call to mind." And, again to Giovanni: "In a hotel?"

"No," said Giovanni, and for the first time he seemed slightly uncomfortable. "I live in a maid's room."

"With the maid?"

"No," said Giovanni, and smiled, "the maid is I don't know where. You could certainly tell that there was no maid if you ever saw my room."

"I would love to," said Jacques.

"Then we will give a party for you one day," said Giovanni.

This, too courteous and too bald to permit any further questioning, nearly forced, nevertheless, a question from my lips. Guillaume looked briefly at Giovanni, who did not look at him but out into the morning, whistling. I had been making resolutions for the last six hours and now I made another one: to have this whole thing "out" with Giovanni as soon as I got him alone at Les Halles. I was going to have to tell him that he had made a mistake but that we could still be friends. But I could not be certain, really, that it might not be I who was making a mistake, blindly misreading everything—and out of necessities, then, too shameful to be uttered. I was in a box for I could see that, no matter how I turned, the hour of confession was upon me and could scarcely be averted; unless, of course, I leaped out of the cab, which would be the most terrible confession of all.

Now the cabdriver asked us where we wanted to go, for we had arrived at the choked boulevards and impassable sidestreets of Les Halles. Leeks, onions, cabbages, oranges, apples, potatoes, cauliflowers, stood gleaming in mounds all over, on the sidewalks, in the streets, before great metal sheds. The sheds were blocks long and within the sheds were piled more fruit, more vegetables, in some sheds, fish, in some sheds, cheese, in some whole animals, lately slaughtered. It scarcely seemed possible that all of this could ever be eaten. But in a few hours it would all be gone and trucks would be arriving from all corners of France—and making their way, to the great profit of a beehive of middlemen, across the city of Paris—to feed the roaring multitude. Who were roaring now, at once wounding and charming the ear, before and behind, and on either side of our taxi—our taxi driver, and Giovanni, too, roared back. The multitude of Paris seems to be dressed in blue every day but Sunday, when, for the most part, they put on an unbelievably festive black. Here they were now, in blue, disputing, every inch, our passage, with their wagons, handtrucks, camions, their bursting baskets carried at an angle steeply self-confident on the back. A red-faced woman, burdened with fruit, shouted—to Giovanni, the driver, to the world—a particularly vivid *cochonnerie,* to which the driver and Giovanni, at once, at the top of their lungs, responded, though the fruit lady had already passed beyond our sight and perhaps no longer even remembered her precisely obscene conjectures. We crawled along, for no one had yet told the driver where to stop, and Giovanni and the driver, who had, it appeared, immediately upon entering Les Halles, been transformed into brothers, exchanged speculations, unflattering in the extreme, concerning the hygiene, language, private parts, and habits, of the citizens of Paris. (Jacques and Guillaume were exchanging speculations, unspeakably less good-natured, concerning every passing male.) The pavements were slick with leavings, mainly cast-off, rotten leaves, flowers, fruit, and vegetables which had met with disaster natural and slow, or abrupt. And the walls and corners were combed with *pissoirs,* dull-burning, make-shift braziers, cafes, restaurants, and smoky yellow bistros—of these last, some so small that they were little more than diamond-shaped, enclosed corners holding bottles and a zinc-covered counter. At all these points, men, young, old, middle-aged, powerful, powerful even in the various fashions in which they had met, or were meeting, their various ruin; and women, more than making up in shrewdness and patience, in an ability to count and weigh—and shout—whatever they might lack in muscle; though they did not, really, seem to lack much. Nothing here reminded me of home, though Giovanni recognized, revelled in it all.

"I know a place," he told the driver, *"très bon marché"*—and told the driver where it was. It developed that it was one of the driver's favorite rendezvous.

"Where is this place?" asked Jacques, petulantly. "I thought we were going to"—and he named another place.

"You are joking," said Giovanni, with contempt. "That place is *very* bad and *very* expensive, it is only for tourists. We are not tourists," and he added, to me, "When I first came to Paris I worked in

Les Halles—a long time, too. *Nom de Dieu, quel boulot!* I pray always never to do that again." And he regarded the streets through which we passed with a sadness which was not less real for being a little theatrical and self-mocking.

Guillaume said, from his corner of the cab: "Tell him who rescued you."

"Ah, yes," said Giovanni, "behold my savior, my *patron*." He was silent a moment. Then: "You do not regret it, do you? I have not done you any harm? You are pleased with my work?"

"Mais oui," said Guillaume.

Giovanni sighed. *"Bien sûr."* He looked out of the window again, again whistling. We came to a corner remarkably clear. The taxi stopped.

"Ici," said the driver.

"Ici," Giovanni echoed.

I reached for my wallet but Giovanni sharply caught my hand, conveying to me with an angry flick of his eyelash the intelligence that the least these dirty old men could do was *pay.* He opened the door and stepped out into the street. Guillaume had not reached for his wallet and Jacques paid for the cab.

"Ugh," said Guillaume, staring at the door of the cafe before which we stood, "I am sure this place is infested with vermin. Do you want to poison us?"

"It's not the outside you're going to eat," said Giovanni. "You are in much more danger of being poisoned in those dreadful, chic places you always go to, where they always have the face clean, *mais, mon Dieu, les fesses!*" He grinned. *"Fais-moi confiance.* Why would I want to poison you? Then I would have no job and I have only just found out that I want to live."

He and Guillaume, Giovanni still smiling, exchanged a look which I would not have been able to read even if I had dared to try; and Jacques, pushing all of us before him as though we were his chickens, said, with that grin: "We can't stand here in the cold and argue. If we can't eat inside, we can drink. Alcohol kills all microbes."

And Guillaume brightened suddenly—he was really remarkable, as though he carried, hidden somewhere on his person, a needle filled with vitamins, which, automatically, at the blackening hour, discharged itself into his veins. *"Il y a les jeunes dedans,"* he said, and we went in.

Indeed there were young people, half a dozen at the zinc counter before glasses of red and white wine, along with others not young at all. A pockmarked boy and a very rough-looking girl were playing the pinball machine near the window. There were a few people sitting at the tables in the back, served by an astonishingly clean-looking waiter. In the gloom, the dirty walls, the sawdust-covered floor, his white jacket gleamed like snow. Behind these tables one caught a glimpse of the kitchen and the surly, obese cook. He lumbered about like one of those overloaded trucks outside, wearing one of those high, white hats, and with a dead cigar stuck between his lips.

Behind the counter sat one of those absolutely inimitable and indomitable ladies, produced only in the city of Paris, but produced there in great numbers, who would be as outrageous and unsettling in any other city as a mermaid on a mountaintop. All over Paris they sit behind their counters like a mother bird in a nest and brood over the cash register as though it were an egg. Nothing occurring under the circle of heaven where they sit escapes their eye, if they have ever been surprised by anything, it was only in a dream—a dream they long ago ceased having. They are neither ill- nor good-natured, though they have their days and styles, and they know, in the way, apparently, that other people know when they have to go to the bathroom, everything about everyone who enters their domain. Though some are white-haired and some not, some fat, some thin, some grandmothers and some but lately virgins, they all have exactly the same, shrewd, vacant, all-registering eye; it is difficult to believe that they ever cried for milk or looked at the sun; it seems they must have come into the world hungry for banknotes, and squinting helplessly, unable to focus their eyes until they came to rest on a cash register.

This one's hair is black and grey, and she has a face which comes from Brittany; and she, like almost everyone else standing at the bar, knows Giovanni and, after her fashion, likes him. She has a big, deep bosom and she clasps Giovanni to it; and a big, deep voice.

"*Ah, mon pote!*" she cries. "*Tu es revenu!* You have come back at last! *Salaud!* Now that you are rich and have found rich friends, you never come to see us anymore! *Canaille!*"

And she beams at us, the "rich" friends, with a friendliness deliciously, deliberately vague; she would have no trouble reconstructing every instant of our biographies from the moment we were born until this morning. She knows exactly who is rich—and how rich—and she knows it isn't me. For this reason, perhaps, there was a click of speculation infinitesimally double behind her eyes when she looked at me. In a moment, however, she knows that she will understand it all.

"You know how it is," says Giovanni, extricating himself and throwing back his hair, "when you work, when you become serious, you have no time to play."

"*Tiens,*" says she, with mockery. "*Sans blague?*"

"But I assure you," says Giovanni, "even when you are a young man like me, you get very tired"—she laughs—"and you go to sleep early"—she laughs again—"and *alone,*" says Giovanni, as though this proved everything, and she clicks her teeth in sympathy and laughs again.

"And now," she says, "are you coming or going? Have you

come for breakfast or have you come for a nightcap? *Nom de Dieu,* you do not *look* very serious; I believe you need a drink."

"*Bien sûr,*" says someone at the bar, "after such hard work he needs a bottle of white wine—and perhaps a few dozen oysters."

Everybody laughs. Everybody, without seeming to, is looking at us and I am beginning to feel like part of a travelling circus. Everybody, also, seems very proud of Giovanni.

Giovanni turns to the voice at the bar. "An excellent idea, friend," he says, "and exactly what I had in mind." Now he turns to us. "You have not met my friends," he says, looking at me, then at the woman. "This is Monsieur Guillaume," he tells her, and with the most subtle flattening of his voice, "my *patron.* He can tell you if I am serious."

"Ah," she dares to say, "but I cannot tell if *he* is," and covers this daring with a laugh.

Guillaume, raising his eyes with difficulty from the young men at the bar, stretches out his hand and smiles. "But you are right, Madame," he says. "He is so much more serious than I am that I fear he will own my bar one day."

He will when lions fly, she is thinking, but professes herself enchanted by him and shakes his hand with energy.

"And Monsieur Jacques," says Giovanni, "one of our finest customers."

"*Enchanté, Madame,*" says Jacques, with his most dazzling smile, of which she, in responding, produces the most artless parody.

"And this is *monsieur l'américain,*" says Giovanni, "otherwise known as: *Monsieur David. Madame Clothilde.*"

And he stands back slightly. Something is burning in his eyes and it lights up all his face, it is joy and pride.

"*Je suis ravie, monsieur,*" she tells me and looks at me and shakes my hand and smiles.

I am smiling too, I scarcely know why; everything in me is jumping up and down. Giovanni carelessly puts an arm around my shoulder. "What have you got good to eat?" he cried. "We are hungry."

"But we must have a drink first!" cried Jacques.

"But we can drink sitting down," said Giovanni, "no?"

"No," said Guillaume, to whom leaving the bar, at the moment, would have seemed like being driven from the promised land, "let us first have a drink, here at the bar, with Madame."

Guillaume's suggestion had the effect—but subtly, as though a wind had blown over everything or a light been imperceptibly intensified—of creating among the people at the bar, a *troupe*, who would now play various roles in a play they knew very well. Madame Clothilde would demur, as, indeed, she instantly did, but only for a moment; then she would accept, it would be something expensive; it turned out to be champagne. She would sip it, making the most noncommittal conversation, so that she could vanish out of it a split second before Guillaume had established contact with one of the boys at the bar. As for the boys at the bar, they were each invisibly preening, having already calculated how much money he and his *copain* would need for the next few days, having already appraised Guillaume to within a decimal of that figure, and having already estimated how long Guillaume, as a fountainhead, would last, and also how long they would be able to endure him. The only question left was whether they would be *vache* with him, or *chic*, but they knew that they would probably be *vache*. There was also Jacques, who might turn out to be a bonus, or merely a consolation prize. There was me, of course, another matter altogether, innocent of apartments, soft beds, or food, a candidate, therefore, for affection, but, as Giovanni's *môme*, out of honorable reach. Their only means, practically at least, of conveying their affection for Giovanni and me was to relieve us of these two old men. So that there was added, to the roles they were about to play, a certain jolly aura of conviction and, to self-interest, an altruistic glow.

I ordered black coffee and a cognac, a large one. Giovanni was far from me, drinking *marc* between an old man, who looked like a receptacle of all the world's dirt and disease, and a young boy, a redhead, who would look like that man one day, if one could read, in the dullness of his eye, anything so real as a future. Now, however, he had something of a horse's dreadful beauty; some suggestion, too, of the storm trooper; covertly, he was watching Guillaume; he knew that both Guillaume and Jacques were watching him. Guillaume chatted, meanwhile, with Madame Clothilde; they were agreeing that business was awful, that all standards had been debased by the *nouveau riche,* and that the country needed de Gaulle. Luckily, they had both had this conversation so many times before that it ran, so to speak, all by itself, demanding of them nothing in the way of concentration. Jacques would shortly offer one of the boys a drink but, for the moment, he wished to play uncle to me.

"How do you feel?" he asked me. "This is a very important day for you."

"I feel fine," I said. "How do you feel?"

"Like a man," he said, "who has seen a vision."

"Yes?" I said. "Tell me about this vision."

"I am not joking," he said. "I am talking about you. *You* were the vision. You should have seen yourself tonight. You should see yourself now."

I looked at him and said nothing.

"You are—how old? Twenty-six or seven? I am nearly twice that and, let me tell you, you are lucky. You are lucky that what is happening to you now is happening *now* and not when you are forty, or something like that, when there would be no hope for you and you would simply be destroyed."

"What is happening to me?" I asked. I had meant to sound sardonic, but I did not sound sardonic at all.

He did not answer this, but sighed, looking briefly in the direction of the redhead. Then he turned to me. "Are you going to write to Hella?"

"I very often do," I said. "I suppose I will again."

"That does not answer my question."

"Oh. I was under the impression that you had asked me if I was going to write to Hella."

"Well. Let's put it another way. Are you going to write to Hella about this night and this morning?"

"I really don't see what there is to write about. But what's it to you if I do or I don't?"

He gave me a look full of a certain despair which I had not, till that moment, known was in him. It frightened me. "It's not," he said, "what it is to *me*. It's what it is to *you*. And to her. And to that poor boy, yonder, who doesn't know that when he looks at you the way he does, he is simply putting his head in the lion's mouth. Are you going to treat them as you've treated me?"

"*You?* What have *you* to do with all this? How have I treated *you?*"

"You have been very unfair to me," he said. "You have been very dishonest."

This time I did sound sardonic. "I suppose you mean that I would have been fair, I would have been honest if I had—if—"

"I mean you could have been fair to me by despising me a little less."

"I'm sorry. But I think, since you bring it up, that a lot of your life *is* despicable."

"I could say the same about yours," said Jacques. "There are so many ways of being despicable it quite makes one's head spin. But the way to be really despicable is to be contemptuous of other people's pain. You ought to have some apprehension that the man you see before you was once even younger than you are now and arrived at his present wretchedness by imperceptible degrees."

There was silence for a moment, threatened, from a distance, by that laugh of Giovanni's.

"Tell me," I said at last, "is there really no other way for you but this? To kneel down forever before an army of boys for just five dirty minutes in the dark?"

"Think," said Jacques, "of the men who have kneeled before you while you thought of something else and pretended that nothing was happening down there in the dark between your legs."

I stared at the amber cognac and at the wet rings on the metal. Deep below, trapped in the metal, the outline of my own face looked upward hopelessly at me.

"You think," he persisted, "that my life is shameful because my encounters are. And they are. But you should ask yourself *why* they are."

"Why are they—shameful?" I asked him.

"Because there is no affection in them, and no joy. It's like putting an electric plug in a dead socket. Touch, but no contact. All touch, but no contact and no light."

I asked him: "Why?"

"That you must ask yourself," he told me, "and perhaps one day, this morning will not be ashes in your mouth."

I looked over at Giovanni, who now had one arm around the ruined-looking girl, who could have once been very beautiful but who never would be now.

Jacques followed my look. "He is very fond of you," he said, "already. But this doesn't make you happy or proud, as it should. It makes you frightened and ashamed. Why?"

"I don't understand him," I said at last. "I don't know what his friendship means; I don't know what he means by friendship."

Jacques laughed. "You don't know what he means by friendship but you have the feeling it may not be safe. You are afraid it may change you. What kind of friendships have you had?"

I said nothing.

"Or for that matter," he continued, "what kind of love affairs?"

I was silent for so long that he teased me, saying, "Come out, come out, wherever you are!"

And I grinned, feeling chilled.

"Love him," said Jacques, with vehemence, "love him and let him love you. Do you think anything else under heaven really matters? And how long, at the best, can it last? since you are both men and still have everywhere to go? Only five minutes, I assure you, only five minutes, and most of that, *hélas!* in the dark. And if you think of them as dirty, then they *will* be dirty—they will be dirty because you will be giving nothing, you will be despising your flesh and his. But you can make your time together anything but dirty; you can give each other something which will make both of you better—forever—if you will *not* be ashamed, if you will only *not* play it safe." He paused, watching me, and then looked down to his cognac. "You play it safe long enough," he said, in a different tone, "and you'll end up trapped in your own dirty body, forever and forever and forever—like me." And he finished his cognac, ringing his glass slightly on the bar to attract the attention of Madame Clothilde.

She came at once, beaming; and in that moment Guillaume dared to smile at the redhead. Mme. Clothilde poured Jacques a fresh cognac and looked questioningly at me, the bottle poised over my half full glass. I hesitated.

"Et pourquoi pas?" she asked, with a smile.

So I finished my glass and she filled it. Then, for the briefest of seconds, she glanced at Guillaume; who cried, *"Et le rouquin là!* What's the redhead drinking?"

Mme. Clothilde turned with the air of an actress about to deliver the severely restrained last lines of an exhausting and mighty part. *"On t'offre, Pierre,"* she said, majestically. "What will you have?"—holding slightly aloft meanwhile the bottle containing the most expensive cognac in the house.

"Je prendrai un petit cognac," Pierre mumbled after a moment and, oddly enough, he blushed, which made him, in the light of the pale, just-rising sun, resemble a freshly fallen angel.

Mme. Clothilde filled Pierre's glass and, amid a beautifully resolving tension, as of slowly dimming lights, replaced the bottle on the shelf and walked back to the cash register; offstage, in effect, into the wings, where she began to recover herself by finishing the last of the champagne. She sighed and sipped and looked outward contentedly into the slowly rising morning. Guillaume had murmured a *"Je m'excuse un instant, Madame,"* and now passed behind us on his way to the redhead.

I smiled. "Things my father never told me."

"Somebody," said Jacques, "your father or mine, should have told us that not many people have ever died of love. But multitudes have perished, and are perishing every hour—and in the oddest places!—for the lack of it." And then: "Here comes your baby. *Sois sage. Sois chic.*"

He moved slightly away and began talking to the boy next to him.

And here my baby came indeed, through all that sunlight, his face flushed and his hair flying, his eyes, unbelievably, like morning stars. "It was not very nice of me to go off for so long," he said, "I hope you have not been too bored."

"*You* certainly haven't been," I told him. "You look like a kid about five years old waking up on Christmas morning."

This delighted, even flattered him, as I could see from the way he now humorously pursed his lips. "I am sure I cannot look like that," he said. "I was always disappointed on Christmas morning."

"Well, I mean very *early* on Christmas morning, before you saw what was under the tree." But his eyes have somehow made of my last statement a *double entendre,* and we are both laughing.

"Are you hungry?" he asked.

"Perhaps I would be if I were alive and sober. I don't know. Are you?"

"I think we should eat," he said with no conviction whatever, and we began to laugh again.

"Well," I said, "What shall we eat?"

"I scarcely dare suggest white wine and oysters," said Giovanni, "but that is really the best thing after such a night."

"Well, let's do that," I said, "while we can still walk to the dining room." I looked beyond him to Guillaume and the redhead. They had apparently found something to talk about; I could not imagine what it was. And Jacques was deep in conversation with the tall, very young, pockmarked boy, whose turtleneck black sweater made him seem even paler and thinner than he actually was. He had been playing the pinball machine when we came in; his name appeared to be Yves. "Are they going to eat now?" I asked Giovanni.

"Perhaps not now," said Giovanni, "but they are certainly going to eat. Everyone is very hungry." I took this to refer more to the boys than to our friends, and we passed into the dining room, which was now empty, the waiter nowhere in sight.

"Mme. Clothilde!" shouted Giovanni, *"On mange ici, non?"*

This shout produced an answering shout from Mme. Clothilde and also produced the waiter, whose jacket was less spotless, seen in closeup, than it had seemed from a distance. It also officially announced our presence in the dining room to Jacques and Guillaume and must have definitely increased, in the eyes of the boys they were talking to, a certain tigerish intensity of affection.

"We'll eat quickly and go," said Giovanni. "After all, I have to work tonight."

"Did you meet Guillaume here?" I asked him.

He grimaced, looking down. "No. That is a long story." He grinned. "No, I did not meet him here. I met him"—he laughed—"in a cinema!" We both laughed. *"C'était un film du far west, avec Gary Cooper."* This seemed terribly funny, too; we kept laughing until the waiter came with our bottle of white wine.

"Well," said Giovanni, sipping the wine, his eyes damp, "after the last gun shot had been fired and all the music came up to celebrate the triumph of goodness and I came up the aisle, I bumped into this man—Guillaume—and I excused myself and walked into the lobby. Then here he came, after me, with a long story about leaving his scarf in *my* seat because, it appeared, he had been sitting *behind* me, you understand, with his coat and his scarf on the seat *before* him and when I sat down I pulled his scarf down with me. Well, I told him I didn't work for the cinema and I told him what he could do with his scarf—but I did not really get angry because he made me want to laugh. He said that all the people who worked for the cinema were thieves and he was sure that they would keep it if they so much as laid eyes on it, and it was very expensive, and a gift from his mother and—oh, I assure you, not even Garbo ever gave such a performance. So I went back and of course there was no scarf there and when I told him this it seemed he would fall dead right there in the lobby. And by this time, you understand, everybody thought we were together and I didn't know whether to kick him or the people who were looking at us; but he was very well dressed, of course, and I was not and so I thought, well, we had better get out of this lobby. So we went to a cafe and sat on the terrace and when he had got over his grief about the scarf and what his mother would say and so on and so on, he asked me to have supper with him. Well, naturally, I said no; I had certainly had enough of him by that time, but the only way I could prevent another scene, right there on the terrace, was to promise to have supper with him a few days later—I did not intend to go," he said, with a shy grin, "but when the day came, I had not eaten for a long time and I was very hungry." He looked at me and I saw in his face again something which I have fleetingly seen there during these hours: under his beauty and his bravado, terror, and a terrible desire to please; dreadfully, dreadfully moving, and it made me want, in anguish, to reach out and comfort him.

Our oysters came and we began to eat. Giovanni sat in the sun, his black hair gathering to itself the yellow glow of the wine and the many dull colors of the oyster where the sun struck it.

"Well"—with his mouth turned down—"dinner was awful, of course, since he can make scenes in his apartment, too. But by this time I knew he owned a bar and was a French citizen. I am not and I had no job and no *carte de travail.* So I saw that he could be useful if I could only find some way to make him keep his hands off me. I did not, I must say"—this with that look at me—"altogether succeed in remaining untouched by him; he has more hands than an octopus, and no dignity whatever, *but*"—grimly throwing down another oyster and refilling our glasses of wine—"I *do* now have a *carte de travail* and I have a job. Which pays very well," he grinned. "It appears that I am good for business. For this reason, he leaves me mostly alone." He looked out into the bar. "He is really not a man at all," he said, with a sorrow and bewilderment at once child-like and ancient, "I do not know what he is, he is horrible. But I will keep my *carte de travail.* The job is another matter, but"—he knocked wood—"we have had no trouble now for nearly three weeks."

"But you think that trouble is coming," I said.

"Oh, yes," said Giovanni, with a quick, startled look at me, as if he were wondering if I had understood a word of what he had said, "we are certainly going to have a little trouble soon again. Not right away, of course; that is not his style. But he will invent something to be angry at me about."

Then we sat in silence for awhile, smoking cigarettes, surrounded by oyster shells, and finishing the wine. I was all at once
very tired. I looked out into the narrow street, this strange, crooked
corner where we sat, which was brazen now with the sunlight and
heavy with people—people I would never understand. I ached
abruptly, intolerably, with a longing to go home; not to that hotel,
in one of the alleys of Paris, where the concierge barred the way
with my unpaid bill; but home, home across the ocean, to things
and people I knew and understood; to those things, those places,
those people which I would always, helplessly, and in whatever bitterness of spirit, love above all else. I had never realized such a sentiment in myself before, and it frightened me. I saw myself, sharply,
as a wanderer, an adventurer, rocking through the world, unanchored. I looked at Giovanni's face, which did not help me. He belonged to this strange city, which did not belong to me. I began to
see that, while what was happening to me was not so strange as it
would have comforted me to believe, yet it was strange beyond belief. It was not really so strange, so unprecedented, though voices
deep within me boomed, For shame! For shame! that I should be so
abruptly, so hideously entangled with a boy; what was strange was
that this was but one tiny aspect of the dreadful human tangle occurring everywhere, without end, forever.

"*Viens,*" said Giovanni.

We rose and walked back into the bar and Giovanni paid our
bill. Another bottle of champagne had been opened and Jacques
and Guillaume were now really beginning to be drunk. It was going
to be ghastly and I wondered if those poor, patient boys were ever
going to get anything to eat. Giovanni talked to Guillaume for a
moment, agreeing to open up the bar; Jacques was too busy with
the pale tall boy to have much time for me; we said good-morning
and left them.

"I must go home," I said to Giovanni when we were in the
street. "I must pay my hotel bill."

Giovanni stared. *"Mais tu es fou,"* he said mildly. "There is certainly no point in going home now, to face an ugly concierge and then go to sleep in that room all by yourself and then wake up later, with a terrible stomach and a sour mouth, wanting to commit suicide. Come with me; we will rise at a civilized hour and have a gentle aperitif somewhere and then a little dinner. It will be much more cheerful like that," he said with a smile, "you will see."

"But I must get my clothes," I said.

He took my arm. *"Bien sûr.* But you do not have to get them *now."* I held back. He stopped. "Come. I am sure that I am much prettier than your wallpaper—or your concierge. I will smile at you when you wake up. They will not."

"Ah," I could only say, *"tu es vache."*

"It is you who are *vache,"* he said, "to want to leave me alone in this lonely place when you know that I am far too drunk to reach my home unaided."

We laughed together, both caught up in a stinging, teasing sort of game. We reached the Boulevard de Sébastopol. "But we will not any longer discuss the painful subject of how you desired to desert Giovanni, at so dangerous an hour, in the middle of a hostile city." I began to realize that he, too, was nervous. Far down the boulevard a cab meandered toward us, and he put up his hand. "I will show you my room," he said. "It is perfectly clear that you would have to see it one of these days, anyway." The taxi stopped beside us, and Giovanni, as though he were suddenly afraid that I would really turn and run, pushed me in before him. He got in beside me and told the driver: *"Nation."*

The street he lived on was wide, respectable rather than elegant, and massive with fairly recent apartment buildings; the street ended in a small park. His room was in the back, on the ground floor of the last building on this street. We passed the vestibule and the elevator into a short, dark corridor which led to his room. The room was small, I only made out the outlines of clutter and disorder, there was the smell of the alcohol he burned in his stove. He locked the door behind us, and then for a moment, in the gloom, we simply stared at each other—with dismay, with relief, and breathing hard. I was trembling. I thought, if I do not open the door at once and get out of here, I am lost. But I knew I could not open the door, I knew it was too late; soon it was too late to do anything but moan. He pulled me against him, putting himself into my arms as though he were giving me himself to carry, and slowly pulled me down with him to that bed. With everything in me screaming *No!* yet the sum of me sighed *Yes.*

Here in the south of France it does not often snow; but snowflakes, in the beginning rather gently and now with more force, have been falling for the last half hour. It falls as though it might quite possibly decide to turn into a blizzard. It has been cold down here this winter, though the people of the region seem to take it as a mark of ill-breeding in a foreigner if he makes any reference to this fact. They themselves, even when their faces are burning in that wind which seems to blow from everywhere at once, and which penetrates everything, are as radiantly cheerful as children at the seashore. "*Il fait beau bien?*—throwing their faces toward the lowering sky in which the celebrated southern sun has not made an appearance in days.

I leave the window of the big room and walk through the house. While I am in the kitchen, staring into the mirror—I have decided to shave before all the water turns cold—I hear a knocking at the door. Some vague, wild hope leaps in me for a second and then I realize that it is only the caretaker from across the road come to make certain that I have not stolen the silver or smashed the dishes or chopped up the furniture for firewood. And, indeed, she rattles the door and I hear her voice out there, cracking, *M'sieu! M'sieu!*

M'sieu, l'américain!" I wonder, with annoyance, why on earth she should sound so worried.

But she smiles at once when I open the door, a smile which weds the coquette and the mother. She is quite old and not really French; she came many years ago, "when I was a very young girl, sir," from just across the border, out of Italy. She seems, like most of the women down here, to have gone into mourning directly the last child moved out of childhood. Hella thought that they were all widows, but, it turned out, most of them had husbands living yet. These husbands might have been their sons. They sometimes played *belote* in the sunshine in a flat field near our house, and their eyes, when they looked at Hella, contained the proud watchfulness of a father and the watchful speculation of a man. I sometimes played billiards with them, and drank red wine, in the *tabac.* But they made me tense—with their ribaldries, their good-nature, their fellowship, the life written on their hands and in their faces and in their eyes. They treated me as the son who has but lately been initiated into manhood; but at the same time, with great distance, for I did not really belong to any of them; and they also sensed (or I felt they did) something else about me, something which it was no longer worth their while to pursue. This seemed to be in their eyes when I walked with Hella and they passed us on the road, saying, very respectfully, *Salut, Monsieur-dame.* They might have been the sons of these women in black, come home after a lifetime of storming and conquering the world, home to rest and be scolded and wait for death, home to those breasts, now dry, which had nourished them in their beginnings.

Flakes of snow have drifted across the shawl which covers her head; and hang on her eyelashes and on the wisps of black and white hair not covered by the shawl. She is very strong yet, though, now, a little bent, a little breathless.

"Bonsoir, monsieur. Vous n'êtes pas malade?"

"No," I say, "I have not been sick. Come in."

She comes in, closing the door behind her, and allowing the shawl to fall from her head. I still have my drink in my hand and she notices this, in silence.

"Eh bien," she says. *"Tant mieux.* But we have not seen you for several days. You have been staying in the house?"

And her eyes search my face.

I am embarrassed and resentful; yet it is impossible to rebuff something at once shrewd and gentle in her eyes and voice. "Yes," I say, "the weather has been bad."

"It is not the middle of August, to be sure," says she, "but you do not have the air of an invalid. It is not good to sit in the house alone."

"I am leaving in the morning," I say, desperately. "Did you want to take the inventory?"

"Yes," she says, and produces from one of her pockets the list of household goods I signed upon arrival. "It will not be long. Let me start from the back."

We start toward the kitchen. On the way I put my drink down on the night table in my bedroom.

"It doesn't matter to me if you drink," she says, not turning around. But I leave my drink behind anyway.

We walk into the kitchen. The kitchen is suspiciously clean and neat. "Where have you been eating?" she asks, sharply. "They tell me at the *tabac* you have not been seen for days. Have you been going to town?"

"Yes," I say lamely, "sometimes."

"On foot?" she inquires. "Because the bus driver, he has not seen you, either." All this time she is not looking at me but around the kitchen, checking off the list in her hand with a short, yellow pencil.

I can make no answer to her last, sardonic thrust, having forgotten that in a small village almost every move is made under the village's collective eye and ear.

She looks briefly in the bathroom. "I'm going to clean that tonight," I say.

"I should hope so," she says. "Everything was clean when you moved in." We walk back through the kitchen. She has failed to notice that two glasses are missing, broken by me, and I have not the energy to tell her. I will leave some money in the cupboard. She turns on the light in the guest room. My dirty clothes are lying all over.

"Those go with me," I say, trying to smile.

"You could have come just across the road," she says. "I would have been glad to give you something to eat. A little soup, something nourishing. I cook every day for my husband; what difference does one more make?"

This touches me, but I do not know how to indicate it, and I cannot say, of course, that eating with her and her husband would have stretched my nerves to the breaking point.

She is examining a decorative pillow. "Are you going to join your fiancée?" she asks.

I know I ought to lie, but somehow I cannot. I am afraid of her eyes. I wish, now, that I had my drink with me. "No," I say, flatly, "she has gone to America."

"*Tiens!*" she says. "And you—do you stay in France?" She looks directly at me.

"For awhile," I say. I am beginning to sweat. It has come to me that this woman, a peasant from Italy, must resemble, in so many ways, the mother of Giovanni. I keep trying not to hear her howls of anguish, I keep trying not to see in her eyes what would surely be there if she knew that her son would be dead by morning, if she knew what I had done to her son.

But, of course, she is not Giovanni's mother.

"It is not good," she says, "it is not right for a young man like you to be sitting alone in a great big house with no woman." She looks, for a moment, very sad; starts to say something more and thinks better of it. I know she wants to say something about Hella, whom neither she nor any of the other women here had liked. But she turns out the light in the guest room and we go into the big bedroom, the master bedroom, which Hella and I had used, not the one in which I have left my drink. This, too, is very clean and orderly. She looks about the room and looks at me, and smiles.

"You have not been using this room lately," she says.

I feel myself blushing painfully. She laughs.

"But you will be happy again," she says. "You must go and find yourself another woman, a *good* woman, and get married, and have babies. *Yes,* that is what you ought to do," she says, as though I had contradicted her, and before I can say anything, "Where is your *maman?*"

"She is dead."

"Ah!" She clicks her teeth in sympathy. "That is sad. And your Papa—is he dead, too?"

"No. He is in America."

"Pauvre bambino!" She looks at my face. I am really helpless in front of her and if she does not leave soon, she will reduce me to tears or curses. "But you do not have the intention of just wandering through the world like a sailor? I am sure that would make your mother very unhappy. You will make a home someday?"

"Yes, surely. Someday."

She puts her strong hand on my arm. "Even if your *maman,* she is dead—that is very sad!—your Papa will be very happy to see bambinos from you." She pauses, her black eyes soften; she is looking at me, but she is looking beyond me, too. "We had three sons. Two of them were killed in the war. In the war, too, we lost all our money. It is sad, is it not, to have worked so hard all one's life in order to have a little peace in one's old age and then to have it all taken away? It almost killed my husband; he has never been the same since." Then I see that her eyes are not merely shrewd; they are also bitter and very sad. She shrugs her shoulders. "Ah! What can one do? It is better not to think about it." Then she smiles. "But our last son, he lives in the north; he came to see us two years ago, and he brought with him his little boy. His little boy, he was only four years old then. He was so beautiful! Mario, he is called." She gestures. "It is my husband's name. They stayed about ten days and we felt young again." She smiles again. "Especially my husband." And she stands there a moment with this smile on her face. Then she asks, abruptly, "Do you pray?"

I wonder if I can stand this another moment. "No," I stammer. "No. Not often."

"But you are a believer?"

I smile. It is not even a patronizing smile, though, perhaps, I wish it could be, "Yes."

But I wonder what my smile could have looked like. It did not reassure her. "You must pray," she says, very soberly. "I assure you. Even just a little prayer, from time to time. Light a little candle. If it were not for the prayers of the blessed saints, one could not live in this world at all. I speak to you," she says, drawing herself up slightly, "as though I were your *maman*. Do not be offended."

"But I am not offended. You are very nice. You are very nice to speak to me this way."

She smiles a satisfied smile. "Men—not just babies like you, but old men, too—they always need a woman to tell them the truth. *Les hommes, ils sont impossibles.*" And she smiles, and forces me to smile at the cunning of this universal joke, and turns out the light in the master bedroom. We go down the hall again, thank heaven, to my drink. This bedroom, of course, is quite untidy, the light burning, my bathrobe, books, dirty socks, and a couple of dirty glasses, and a coffee cup half full of stale coffee—lying around, all over the place; and the sheets on the bed a tangled mess.

"I'll fix this up before morning," I say.

"Bien sûr." She sighs. "You really must take my advice, monsieur, and get married." At this, suddenly, we both laugh. Then I finish my drink.

The inventory is almost done. We go into the last room, the big room, where the bottle is, before the window. She looks at the bottle, then at me. "But you will be drunk by morning," she says.

"Oh, no! I'm taking the bottle *with* me."

It is quite clear that she knows this is not true. But she shrugs her shoulders again. Then she becomes, by the act of wrapping the shawl around her head, very formal, even a little shy. Now that I see she is about to leave, I wish I could think of something to make her stay. When she has gone back across the road, the night will be blacker and longer than ever. I have something to say to her—to her?—but of course it will never be said. I feel that I want to be forgiven; I want *her* to forgive me. But I do not know how to state my crime. My crime, in some odd way, is in being a man and she knows all about this already. It is terrible how naked she makes me feel, like a half-grown boy, naked before his mother.

She puts out her hand. I take it, awkwardly.

"Bon voyage, monsieur. I hope that you were happy while you were here and that, perhaps, one day, you will visit us again." She is smiling and her eyes are kind but now the smile is purely social, it is the graceful termination of a business deal.

"Thank you," I say. "Perhaps I will be back next year." She releases my hand and we walk to the door.

"Oh!" she says, at the door, "please do not wake me up in the morning. Put the keys in my mailbox. I do not, any more, have any reason to get up so early."

"Surely." I smile and open the door. "Good-night, Madame."

"Bonsoir, Monsieur. Adieu!" She steps out into the darkness. But there is a light coming from my house and from her house across the road. The town lights glimmer beneath us and I hear, briefly, the sea again.

She walks a little away from me, and turns. *"Souvenez-vous,"* she tells me. "One must make a little prayer from time to time."

And I close the door.

She has made me realize that I have much to do before morning. I decide to clean the bathroom before I allow myself another drink. And I begin to do this, first scrubbing out the tub, then running water into the pail to mop the floor. The bathroom is tiny and square, with one frosted window. It reminds me of that claustrophobic room in Paris. Giovanni had had great plans for remodelling the room and there was a time, when he had actually begun to do this, when we lived with plaster all over everything and bricks piled on the floor. We took packages of bricks out of the house at night and left them in the streets.

I suppose they will come for him early in the morning, perhaps just before dawn, so that the last thing Giovanni will ever see will be that grey, lightless sky over Paris, beneath which we stumbled homeward together so many desperate and drunken mornings.

PART TWO

O N E

I REMEMBER THAT LIFE in that room seemed to be occurring beneath the sea. Time flowed past indifferently above us; hours and days had no meaning. In the beginning, our life together held a joy and amazement which was newborn every day. Beneath the joy, of course, was anguish and beneath the amazement was fear; but they did not work themselves to the beginning until our high beginning was aloes on our tongues. By then anguish and fear had become the surface on which we slipped and slid, losing balance, dignity, and pride. Giovanni's face, which I had memorized so many mornings, noons, and nights, hardened before my eyes, began to give in secret places, began to crack. The light in the eyes became a glitter; the wide and beautiful brow began to suggest the skull beneath. The sensual lips turned inward, busy with the sorrow overflowing from his heart. It became a stranger's face—or it made me so guilty to look on him that I wished it were a stranger's face. Not all my memorizing had prepared me for the metamorphosis which my memorizing had helped to bring about.

Our day began before daybreak, when I drifted over to Guillaume's bar in time for a preclosing drink. Sometimes, when Guillaume had closed the bar to the public, a few friends and Giovanni and myself stayed behind for breakfast and music. Sometimes Jacques was there—from the time of our meeting with Giovanni he seemed to come out more and more. If we had breakfast with Guillaume, we usually left around seven o'clock in the morning. Sometimes, when Jacques was there, he offered to drive us home in the car which he had suddenly and inexplicably bought, but we almost always walked the long way home along the river.

Spring was approaching Paris. Walking up and down this house tonight, I see again the river, the cobblestoned *quais,* the bridges. Low boats passed beneath the bridges and on those boats one sometimes saw women hanging washing out to dry. Sometimes we saw a young man in a canoe, energetically rowing, looking rather helpless, and also rather silly. There were yachts tied up along the banks from time to time, and houseboats, and barges; we passed the firehouse so often on our way home that the firemen got to know us. When winter came again and Giovanni found himself in hiding in one of these barges, it was a fireman who, seeing him crawl back into hiding with a loaf of bread one night, tipped off the police.

The trees grew green those mornings, the river dropped, and the brown winter smoke dropped downward out of it, and fishermen appeared. Giovanni was right about the fishermen; they certainly never seemed to catch anything, but it gave them something to do. Along the *quais* the bookstalls seemed to become almost festive, awaiting the weather which would allow the passerby to leaf idly through the dog-eared books, and which would inform the tourist with a passionate desire to carry off to the United States, or Denmark, more colored prints than he could afford, or, when he got home, know what to do with. Also, the girls appeared on their bicycles, along with boys similarly equipped; and we sometimes saw them along the river, as the light began to fade, their bicycles put away until the morrow. This was after Giovanni had lost his job and we walked around in the evenings. Those evenings were bitter. Giovanni knew that I was going to leave him, but he did not dare accuse me for fear of being corroborated. I did not dare to tell him. Hella was on her way back from Spain and my father had agreed to send me money, which I was not going to use to help Giovanni, who had done so much to help me. I was going to use it to escape his room.

Every morning the sky and the sun seemed to be a little higher and the river stretched before us with a greater haze of promise. Every day the bookstall keepers seemed to have taken off another garment, so that the shape of their bodies appeared to be undergoing a most striking and continual metamorphosis. One began to wonder what the final shape would be. It was observable, through open windows on the *quais* and sidestreets, that *hôteliers* had called in painters to paint the rooms; the women in the dairies had taken off their blue sweaters and rolled up the sleeves of their dresses, so that one saw their powerful arms; the bread seemed warmer and fresher in the bakeries. The small school children had taken off their capes and their knees were no longer scarlet with the cold. There seemed to be more chatter—in that curiously measured and vehement language, which sometimes reminds me of stiffening egg white and sometimes of stringed instruments but always of the underside and aftermath of passion.

But we did not often have breakfast in Guillaume's bar because Guillaume did not like me. Usually I simply waited around, as inconspicuously as possible, until Giovanni had finished cleaning up the bar and had changed his clothes. Then we said good-night and left. The habitués had evolved toward us a curious attitude, composed of an unpleasant maternalism, and envy, and disguised dislike. They could not, somehow, speak to us as they spoke to one another, and they resented the strain we imposed on them of speaking in any other way. And it made them furious that the dead center of their lives was, in this instance, none of their business. It made them feel their poverty again, through the narcotics of chatter, and dreams of conquest, and mutual contempt.

Wherever we ate breakfast and wherever we walked, when we got home we were always too tired to sleep right away. We made coffee and sometimes drank cognac with it; we sat on the bed and talked and smoked. We seemed to have a great deal to tell—or Giovanni did. Even at my most candid, even when I tried hardest to give myself to him as he gave himself to me, I was holding something back. I did not, for example, really tell him about Hella until I had been living in the room a month. I told him about her then because her letters had begun to sound as though she would be coming back to Paris very soon.

"What is she doing, wandering around through Spain alone?" asked Giovanni.

"She likes to travel," I said.

"Oh," said Giovanni, "nobody likes to travel, especially not women. There must be some other reason." He raised his eyebrows suggestively. "Perhaps she has a Spanish lover and is afraid to tell you—? Perhaps she is with a *torero*."

Perhaps she is, I thought. "But she wouldn't be afraid to tell me."

Giovanni laughed. "I do not understand Americans at all," he said.

"I don't see that there's anything very hard to understand. We aren't married, you know."

"But she is your mistress, no?" asked Giovanni.

"Yes."

"And she is still your mistress?"

I stared at him. "Of course," I said.

"Well then," said Giovanni, "I do not understand what she is doing in Spain while you are in Paris." Another thought struck him. "How old is she?"

"She's two years younger than I am." I watched him. "What's that got to do with it?"

"Is she married? I mean to somebody else, naturally."

I laughed. He laughed too. "Of course not."

"Well, I thought she might be an older woman," said Giovanni, "with a husband somewhere and perhaps she had to go away with him from time to time in order to be able to continue her affair with you. That would be a nice arrangement. Those women are sometimes *very* interesting and they usually have a little money. If *that* woman was in Spain, she would bring back a wonderful gift for you. But a young girl, bouncing around in a foreign country by herself—I do not like that at all. You should find another mistress."

It all seemed very funny. I could not stop laughing. "Do *you* have a mistress?" I asked him.

"Not now," he said, "but perhaps I will again one day." He half frowned, half smiled. "I don't seem to be very interested in women right now—I don't know why. I used to be. Perhaps I will be again." He shrugged. "Perhaps it is because women are just a little more trouble than I can afford right now. *Et puis*—" He stopped.

I wanted to say that it seemed to me that he had taken a most peculiar road out of his trouble; but I only said, after a moment, cautiously: "You don't seem to have a very high opinion of women."

"Oh, women! There is no need, thank heaven, to have an opinion about *women*. Women are like water. They are tempting like that, and they can be that treacherous, and they can seem to be that bottomless, you know?—and they can be that shallow. And that dirty." He stopped. "I perhaps don't like women very much, that's true. That hasn't stopped me from making love to many and loving one or two. But most of the time—most of the time I made love only with the body."

"That can make one very lonely," I said. I had not expected to say it.

He had not expected to hear it. He looked at me and reached out and touched me on the cheek. "Yes," he said. Then: "I am not trying to be *méchant* when I talk about women. I respect women—very much—for their inside life, which is not like the life of a man."

"Women don't seem to like that idea," I said.

"Oh, well," said Giovanni, "these absurd women running around today, full of ideas and nonsense, and thinking themselves equal to men—*quelle rigolade!*—they need to be beaten half to death so that they can find out who rules the world."

I laughed. "Did the women you knew like to get beaten?"

He smiled. "I don't know if they liked it. But a beating never made them go away." We both laughed. "They were not, anyway, like that silly little girl of yours, wandering all over Spain and sending postcards back to Paris. What does she think she is doing? Does she want you or does she not want you?"

"She went to Spain," I said, "to find out."

Giovanni opened his eyes wide. He was indignant. "To Spain? Why not to China? What is she doing, testing all the Spaniards and comparing them with you?"

I was a little annoyed. "You don't understand," I said. "She is a very intelligent, very complex girl; she wanted to go away and think."

"What is there to think about? She sounds rather silly, I must say. She just can't make up her mind what bed to sleep in. She wants to eat her cake and she wants to have it all."

"If she were in Paris now," I said, abruptly, "then I would not be in this room with you."

"You would possibly not be living here," he conceded, "but we would certainly be seeing each other, why not?"

"Why *not*? Suppose she found out?"

"Found *out*? Found out what?"

"Oh, stop it," I said. "You know what there is to find out."

He looked at me very soberly. "She sounds more and more impossible, this little girl of yours. What does she do, follow you everywhere? Or will she hire detectives to sleep under our bed? And what business is it of hers, anyway?"

"You can't possibly be serious," I said.

"I certainly can be," he retorted, "and I am. You are the incomprehensible one." He groaned and poured more coffee and picked up our cognac from the floor. "*Chez toi* everything sounds extremely feverish and complicated, like one of those English murder mysteries. To find out, to find out, you keep saying, as though we were accomplices in a crime. We have not committed any crime." He poured the cognac.

"It's just that she'll be terribly hurt if she does find out, that's all. People have very dirty words for—for this situation." I stopped. His face suggested that my reasoning was flimsy. I added, defensively, "Besides, it *is* a crime—in my country and, after all, I didn't grow up here, I grew up *there*."

"If dirty words frighten you," said Giovanni, "I really do not know how you have managed to live so long. People are full of dirty words. The only time they do not use them, most people I mean, is when they are describing something dirty." He paused and we watched each other. In spite of what he was saying, he looked rather frightened himself. "If your countrymen think that privacy is a crime, so much the worse for your country. And as for this girl of yours—are you always at her side when she is here? I mean, all day, every day? You go out sometimes to have a drink alone, no? Maybe you sometimes take a walk without her—to think, as you say. The Americans seem to do a great deal of thinking. And perhaps while you are thinking and having that drink, you look at another girl who passes, no? Maybe you even look up at that sky and feel your own blood in you? Or does everything stop when Hella comes? No drinks alone, no looks at other girls, no sky? Eh? Answer me."

"I've told you already that we're not married. But I don't seem to be able to make you understand anything at all this morning."

"But anyway—when Hella is here you do sometimes see other people—without Hella?"

"Of course."

"And does she make you tell her everything you have done while you were not with her?"

I sighed. I had lost control of the conversation somewhere along the line and I simply wanted it to end. I drank my cognac too fast and it burned my throat. "Of course not."

"Well. You are a very charming and good-looking and civilized boy and, unless you are impotent, I do not see what she has to complain about, or what you have to worry about. To arrange, *mon cher, la vie pratique,* is very simple—it only has to be done." He reflected. "Sometimes things go wrong, I agree; then you have to arrange it another way. But it is certainly not the English melodrama you make it. Why, that way, life would simply be unbearable." He poured more cognac and grinned at me, as though he had solved all my problems. And there was something so artless in this smile that I had to smile back. Giovanni liked to believe that he was hard-headed and that I was not and that he was teaching me the stony facts of life. It was very important for him to feel this: it was because he knew, unwillingly, at the very bottom of his heart, that I, helplessly, at the very bottom of mine, resisted him with all my strength.

Eventually we grew still, we fell silent, and we slept. We awoke around three or four in the afternoon, when the dull sun was prying at odd corners of the cluttered room. We arose and washed and shaved, bumping into each other and making jokes and furious with the unstated desire to escape the room. Then we danced out into the streets, into Paris, and ate quickly somewhere, and I left Giovanni at the door to Guillaume's bar.

Then I, alone, and relieved to be alone, perhaps went to a movie, or walked, or returned home and read, or sat in a park and read, or sat on a cafe terrace, or talked to people, or wrote letters. I wrote to Hella, telling her nothing, or I wrote to my father asking for money. And no matter what I was doing, another me sat in my belly, absolutely cold with terror over the question of my life.

Giovanni had awakened an itch, had released a gnaw in me. I realized it one afternoon, when I was taking him to work via the Boulevard Montparnasse. We had bought a kilo of cherries and we were eating them as we walked along. We were both insufferably childish and high-spirited that afternoon and the spectacle we presented, two grown men jostling each other on the wide sidewalk and aiming the cherry pits, as though they were spitballs, into each other's faces, must have been outrageous. And I realized that such childishness was fantastic at my age and the happiness out of which it sprang yet more so; for that moment I really loved Giovanni, who had never seemed more beautiful than he was that afternoon. And, watching his face, I realized that it meant much to me that I could make his face so bright. I saw that I might be willing to give a great deal not to lose that power. And I felt myself flow toward him, as a river rushes when the ice breaks up. Yet, at that very moment, there passed between us on the pavement another boy, a stranger, and I invested him at once with Giovanni's beauty and what I felt for Giovanni I also felt for him. Giovanni saw this and saw my face and it made him laugh the more. I blushed and he kept laughing and then the boulevard, the light, the sound of his laughter turned into a scene from a nightmare. I kept looking at the trees, the light fall-ing through the leaves. I felt sorrow and shame and panic and great bitterness. At the same time—it was part of my turmoil and also outside it—I felt the muscles in my neck tighten with the effort I was making not to turn my head and watch that boy diminish down the bright avenue. The beast which Giovanni had awakened in me would never go to sleep again; but one day I would not be with Giovanni anymore. And would I then, like all the others, find myself turning and following all kinds of boys down God knows what dark avenues, into what dark places?

With this fearful intimation there opened in me a hatred for Giovanni which was as powerful as my love and which was nour-ished by the same roots.

TWO

I scarcely know how to describe that room. It became, in a way, every room I had ever been in and every room I find myself in hereafter will remind me of Giovanni's room. I did not really stay there very long—we met before the spring began and I left there during the summer—but it still seems to me that I spent a lifetime there. Life in that room seemed to be occurring underwater, as I say, and it is certain that I underwent a sea change there.

To begin with, the room was not large enough for two. It looked out on a small courtyard. "Looked out" means only that the room had two windows, against which the courtyard malevolently pressed, encroaching day by day, as though it had confused itself with a jungle. We, or rather Giovanni, kept the windows closed most of the time. He had never bought any curtains; neither did we buy any while I was in the room. To insure privacy, Giovanni had obscured the window panes with a heavy, white cleaning polish.

We sometimes heard children playing outside our window, some-times strange shapes loomed against it. At such moments, Gio-vanni, working in the room, or lying in bed, would stiffen like a hunting dog and remain perfectly silent until whatever seemed to threaten our safety had moved away.

He had always had great plans for remodelling this room, and before I arrived he had already begun. One of the walls was a dirty, streaked white where he had torn off the wallpaper. The wall facing it was destined never to be uncovered, and on this wall a lady in a hoop skirt and a man in knee breeches perpetually walked together, hemmed in by roses. The wallpaper lay on the floor, in great sheets and scrolls, in dust. On the floor also lay our dirty laundry, along with Giovanni's tools and the paint brushes and the bottles of oil and turpentine. Our suitcases teetered on top of something, so that we dreaded ever having to open them and sometimes went without some minor necessity, such as clean socks, for days.

No one ever came to see us, except Jacques, and he did not come often. We were far from the center of the city and we had no phone.

I remembered the first afternoon I woke up there, with Gio-vanni fast asleep beside me, heavy as a fallen rock. The sun filtered through the room so faintly that I was worried about the time. I stealthily lit a cigarette, for I did not want to wake Giovanni. I did not yet know how I would face his eyes. I looked about me. Gio-vanni had said something in the taxi about his room being very dirty. "I'm sure it is," I had said lightly, and turned away from him, looking out of the window. Then we had both been silent. When I woke up in his room, I remembered that there had been something strained and painful in the quality of that silence, which had been broken when Giovanni said, with a shy, bitter smile: "I must find some poetic figure."

And he spread his heavy fingers in the air, as though a metaphor were tangible. I watched him.

"Look at the garbage of this city," he said, finally, and his fingers indicated the flying street, "all of the garbage of this city? Where do they take it? I don't know where they take it—but it might very well be my room."

"It's much more likely," I said, "that they dump it into the Seine."

But I sensed, when I woke up and looked around the room, the bravado and the cowardice of his figure of speech. This was not the garbage of Paris, which would have been anonymous: this was Giovanni's regurgitated life.

Before and beside me and all over the room, towering like a wall, were boxes of cardboard and leather, some tied with string, some locked, some bursting, and out of the topmost box before me spilled down sheets of violin music. There was a violin in the room, lying on the table in its warped, cracked case—it was impossible to guess from looking at it whether it had been laid to rest there yesterday or a hundred years before. The table was loaded with yellowing newspapers and empty bottles and it held a single brown and wrinkled potato in which even the sprouting eyes were rotten. Red wine had been spilled on the floor; it had been allowed to dry and it made the air in the room sweet and heavy. But it was not the room's disorder which was frightening; it was the fact that when one began searching for the key to this disorder, one realized that it was not to be found in any of the usual places. For this was not a matter of habit or circumstance or temperament; it was a matter of punishment and grief. I do not know how I knew this, but I knew it at once; perhaps I knew it because I wanted to live. And I stared at the room with the same, nervous, calculating extension of the intelligence and of all one's forces which occurs when gauging a mortal and unavoidable danger: at the silent walls of the room with its distant, archaic lovers trapped in an interminable rose garden, and the staring windows, staring like two great eyes of ice and fire, and the ceiling which lowered like those clouds out of which fiends have sometimes spoken and which obscured but failed to soften its malevolence behind the yellow light which hung like a diseased and undefinable sex in its center. Under this blunted arrow, this smashed flower of light lay the terrors which encompassed Giovanni's soul. I understood why Giovanni had wanted me and had brought me to his last retreat. I was to destroy this room and give to Giovanni a new and better life. This life could only be my own, which, in order to transform Giovanni's, must first become a part of Giovanni's room.

In the beginning, because the motives which led me to Giovanni's room were so mixed, had so little to do with his hopes and desires, and were so deeply a part of my own desperation, I invented in myself a kind of pleasure in playing the housewife after Giovanni had gone to work. I threw out the paper, the bottles, the fantastic accumulation of trash; I examined the contents of the innumerable boxes and suitcases and disposed of them. But I am not a housewife—men never can be housewives. And the pleasure was never real or deep, though Giovanni smiled his humble, grateful smile and told me in as many ways as he could find how wonderful it was to have me there, how I stood, with my love and my ingenuity, between him and the dark. Each day he invited me to witness how he had changed, how love had changed him, how he worked and sang and cherished me. I was in a terrible confusion. Sometimes I thought, but this *is* your life. Stop fighting it. Stop fighting. Or I thought, but I am happy. And he loves me. I am safe. Sometimes, when he was not near me, I thought, I will never let him touch me again. Then, when he touched me, I thought, it doesn't matter, it is only the body, it will soon be over. When it was over, I lay in the dark and listened to his breathing and dreamed of the touch of hands, of Giovanni's hands, or anybody's hands, hands which would have the power to crush me and make me whole again.

Sometimes I left Giovanni over our afternoon breakfast, blue smoke from a cigarette circling around his head, and went off to the American Express office at Opéra, where my mail would be, if I had any. Sometimes, but rarely, Giovanni came with me; he said that he could not endure being surrounded by so many Americans. He said they all looked alike—as I am sure they did, to him. But they didn't look alike to me. I was aware that they all had in common something that made them Americans, but I could never put my finger on what it was. I knew that whatever this common quality was, I shared it. And I knew that Giovanni had been attracted to me partly because of it. When Giovanni wanted me to know that he was displeased with me, he said I was a *"vrai américain"*; conversely, when delighted, he said that I was not an American at all; and on both occasions he was striking, deep in me, a nerve which did not throb in him. And I resented this: resented being called an American (and resented resenting it) because it seemed to make me nothing more than that, whatever that was; and I resented being called *not* an American because it seemed to make me nothing.

Yet, walking into the American Express Office one harshly bright, midsummer afternoon, I was forced to admit that this active, so disquietingly cheerful horde struck the eye, at once, as a unit. At home, I could have distinguished patterns, habits, accents of speech—with no effort whatever: now everybody sounded, unless I listened hard, as though they had just arrived from Nebraska. At home I could have seen the clothes they were wearing, but here I only saw bags, cameras, belts, and hats, all clearly from the same department store. At home I would have had some sense of the individual womanhood of the woman I faced: here the most ferociously accomplished seemed to be involved in some ice-cold or sun-dried travesty of sex, and even grandmothers seemed to have had no traffic with the flesh. And what distinguished the men was that they seemed incapable of age; they smelled of soap, which seemed indeed to be their preservative against the dangers and exigencies of any more intimate odor; the boy he had been shone, somehow, unsoiled, untouched, unchanged, through the eyes of the man of sixty, booking passage, with his smiling wife, to Rome. His wife might have been his mother, forcing more oatmeal down his throat, and Rome might have been the movie she had promised to allow him to see. Yet I also suspected that what I was seeing was but a part of the truth and perhaps not even the most important part; beneath these faces, these clothes, accents, rudenesses, was power and sorrow, both unadmitted, unrealized, the power of inventors, the sorrow of the disconnected.

I took my place in the mail line behind two girls who had decided that they wanted to stay on in Europe and who were hoping to find jobs with the American government in Germany. One of them had fallen in love with a Swiss boy; so I gathered, from the low, intense, and troubled conversation she was having with her friend. The friend was urging her to "put her foot down"—on what principle I could not discover; and the girl in love kept nodding her head, but more in perplexity than agreement. She had the choked and halting air of someone who has something more to say but finds no way of saying it. "You mustn't be a fool about this," the friend was saying. "I know, I know," said the girl. One had the impression that, though she certainly did not wish to be a fool, she had lost one definition of the word and might never be able to find another.

There were two letters for me, one from my father and one from Hella. Hella had been sending me only postcards for quite awhile. I was afraid her letter might be important and I did not want to read it. I opened the letter from my father first. I read it, standing just beyond reach of the sunlight, beside the endlessly swinging double doors.

Dear Butch, my father said, *aren't you ever coming home? Don't think I'm only being selfish but it's true I'd like to see you. I think you*

have been away long enough, God knows I don't know what you're do-
ing over there, and you don't write enough for me even to guess. But my
guess is you're going to be sorry one of these fine days that you stayed over
there, looking at your navel, and let the world pass you by. There's
nothing over there for you. You're as American as pork and beans,
though maybe you don't want to think so anymore. And maybe you
won't mind my saying that you're getting a little old for studying, after
all, if that's what you're doing. You're pushing thirty. I'm getting along,
too, and you're all I've got. I'd like to see you.

You keep asking me to send you your money and I guess you think
I'm being a bastard about it. I'm not trying to starve you out and you
know if you really need anything, I'll be the first to help you but I really
don't think I'd be doing you a favor by letting you spend what little
money you've got over there and then coming home to nothing. What
the hell are you doing? Let your old man in on the secret, can't you? You
may not believe this, but once I was a young man, too.

And then he went on about my stepmother and how she wanted
to see me, and about some of our friends and what they were doing.
It was clear that my absence was beginning to frighten him. He did
not know what it meant. But he was living, obviously, in a pit of
suspicions which daily became blacker and vaguer—he would not
have known how to put them into words, even if he had dared. The
question he longed to ask was not in the letter and neither was the
offer: *Is it a woman, David? Bring her on home. I don't care who she*
is. Bring her on home and I'll help you get set up. He could not risk
this question because he could not have endured an answer in the
negative. An answer in the negative would have revealed what
strangers we had become. I folded the letter and put it in my back
pocket and looked out for a moment at the wide, sunlit foreign avenue.

There was a sailor, dressed all in white, coming across the boulevard, walking with that funny roll sailors have and with that aura,

hopeful and hard, of having to make a great deal happen in a hurry. I was staring at him, though I did not know it, and wishing I were he. He seemed—somehow—younger than I had ever been, and blonder and more beautiful, and he wore his masculinity as unequivocally as he wore his skin. He made me think of home—perhaps home is not a place but simply an irrevocable condition. I knew how he drank and how he was with his friends and how pain and women baffled him. I wondered if my father had ever been like that, if I had ever been like that—though it was hard to imagine, for this boy, striding across the avenue like light itself, any antecedents, any connections at all. We came abreast and, as though he had seen some all-revealing panic in my eyes, he gave me a look contemptuously lewd and knowing; just such a look as he might have given, but a few hours ago, to the desperately well-dressed nymphomaniac or trollop who was trying to make him believe she was a lady. And in another second, had our contact lasted, I was certain that there would erupt into speech, out of all that light and beauty, some brutal variation of *Look, baby, I know you.* I felt my face flame, I felt my heart harden and shake as I hurried past him, trying to look stonily beyond him. He had caught me by surprise, for I had, somehow, not really been thinking of him but of the letter in my pocket, of Hella and Giovanni. I got to the other side of the boulevard, not daring to look back, and I wondered what he had seen in me to elicit such instantaneous contempt. I was too old to suppose that it had anything to do with my walk, or the way I held my hands, or my voice—which, anyway, he had not heard. It was something else and I would never see it. I would never dare to see it. It would be like looking at the naked sun. But, hurrying, and not daring now to look at anyone, male or female, who passed me on the wide sidewalks, I knew that what the sailor had seen in my unguarded eyes was envy and desire: I had seen it often in Jacques' eyes and my reaction and the sailor's had been the same. But if I were still able to feel affection and if he had seen it in my eyes, it would not have helped, for affection, for the boys I was doomed to look at, was vastly more frightening than lust.

I walked farther than I had intended, for I did not dare to stop while the sailor might still be watching. Near the river, on rue des Pyramides, I sat down at a cafe table and opened Hella's letter.

Mon cher, she began, *Spain is my favorite country mais ca n'empêche que Paris est toujours ma ville préférée. I long to be again among all those foolish people, running for métros and jumping off of buses and dodging motorcycles and having traffic jams and admiring all that crazy statuary in all those absurd parks. I weep for the fishy ladies in the Place de la Concorde. Spain is not like that at all. Whatever else Spain is, it is not frivolous. I think, really, that I would stay in Spain forever—if I had never been to Paris. Spain is very beautiful, stony and sunny and lonely. But by and by you get tired of olive oil and fish and castanets and tambourines—or, anyway, I do. I want to come home, to come home to Paris. It's funny, I've never felt anyplace was home before.*

Nothing has happened to me here—I suppose that pleases you, I confess it rather pleases me. The Spaniards are nice, but, of course, most of them are terribly poor, the ones who aren't are impossible, I don't like the tourists, mainly English and American dipsomaniacs, paid, my dear, by their families to stay away. (I wish I had a family.) I'm on Mallorca now and it would be a pretty place if you could dump all the pensioned widows into the sea and make dry-martini drinking illegal. I've never seen anything like it! The way these old hags guzzle and make eyes at anything in pants, especially anything about eighteen—well, I said to myself, Hella, my girl, take a good look. You may be looking at your future. The trouble is that I love myself too much. And so I've decided to let two try it, this business of loving me, I mean, and see how that works out. (I feel fine, now that I've made the decision, I hope you'll feel fine, too, dear knight in Gimble's armor.)

I've been trapped into some dreary expedition to Seville with an English family I met in Barcelona. They adore Spain and they want to take me to see a bullfight—I never have, you know, all the time I've been wandering around here. They're really quite nice, he's some kind of poet with the B.B.C. and she's his efficient and adoring spouse. Quite nice, really. They do have an impossibly lunatick *son who imagines himself mad about me, but he's much too English and much, much too young. I leave tomorrow and shall be gone ten days. Then, they to England and I—to you!*

I folded this letter, which I now realized I had been awaiting for many days and nights, and the waiter came and asked me what I wanted to drink. I had meant to order an aperitif but now, in some grotesque spirit of celebration, ordered a Scotch and soda. And over this drink, which had never seemed more American than it did at that moment, I stared at absurd Paris, which was as cluttered now, under the scalding sun, as the landscape of my heart. I wondered what I was going to do.

I cannot say that I was frightened. Or, it would be better to say that I did not feel any fear—the way men who are shot do not, I am told, feel any pain for awhile. I felt a certain relief. It seemed that the necessity for decision had been taken from my hands. I told myself that we both had always known, Giovanni and myself, that our idyll could not last forever. And it was not as though I had not been honest with him—he knew all about Hella. He knew that she would be returning to Paris one day. Now she would be coming back and my life with Giovanni would be finished. It would be something that had happened to me once—it would be something that had happened to many men once. I paid for my drink and got up and walked across the river to Montparnasse.

I felt elated—yet, as I walked down Raspail toward the cafes of Montparnasse, I could not fail to remember that Hella and I had walked here, Giovanni and I had walked here. And with each step, the face that glowed insistently before me was not her face but his. I was beginning to wonder how he would take my news. I did not think he would fight me, but I was afraid of what I would see in his face. I was afraid of the pain I would see there. But even this was not my real fear. My real fear was buried and was driving me to Montparnasse. I wanted to find a girl, any girl at all.

But the terraces seemed oddly deserted. I walked along slowly, on both sides of the street, looking at the tables. I saw no one I knew. I walked down as far as the *Closerie des Lilas* and I had a solitary drink there. I read my letters again. I thought of finding Giovanni at once and telling him I was leaving him but I knew he would not yet have opened the bar and he might be almost anywhere in Paris at this hour. I walked slowly back up the boulevard. Then I saw a couple of girls, French whores, but they were not very attractive. I told myself that I could do better than *that*. I got to the *Sélect* and sat down. I watched the people pass, and I drank. No one I knew appeared on the boulevard for the longest while.

The person who appeared, and whom I did not know very well, was a girl named Sue, blonde and rather puffy, with the quality, in spite of the fact that she was not pretty, of the girls who are selected each year to be Miss Rheingold. She wore her curly blond hair cut very short, she had small breasts and a big behind, and in order, no doubt, to indicate to the world how little she cared for appearance or sensuality, she almost always wore tight blue jeans. I think she came from Philadelphia and her family was very rich. Sometimes, when she was drunk, she reviled them, and, sometimes, drunk in another way, she extolled their virutes of thrift and fidelity. I was both dismayed and relieved to see her. The moment she appeared I began, mentally, to take off all her clothes.

"Sit down," I said. "Have a drink."

"I'm glad to *see* you," she cried, sitting down, and looking about for the waiter. "You'd rather dropped out of sight. How've you been?"—abandoning her search for the waiter and leaning forward to me with a friendly grin.

"I've been fine," I told her. "And you?"

"Oh, *me!* Nothing ever happens to me." And she turned down the corners of her rather predatory and also vulnerable mouth to indicate that she was both joking and not joking. "I'm built like a brick stone wall." We both laughed. She peered at me. "They tell me you're living way out at the end of Paris, near the zoo."

"I found a maid's room out there. Very cheap."

"Are you living alone?"

I did not know whether she knew about Giovanni or not. I felt a hint of sweat on my forehead. "Sort of," I said.

"Sort of? What the hell does *that* mean? Do you have a monkey with you, or something?"

I grinned. "No. But this French kid I know, he lives with his mistress, but they fight a lot and it's really *his* room so sometimes, when his mistress throws him out, he bunks with me for a couple of days."

"Ah!" she sighed. *"Chagrin d'amour!"*

"He's having a good time," I said. "He loves it." I looked at her. "Aren't you?"

"Stone walls," she said, "are impenetrable."

The waiter arrived. "Doesn't it," I dared, "depend on the weapon?"

"What are you buying me to drink?" she asked.

"What do you want?" We were both grinning. The waiter stood above us, manifesting a kind of surly *joie de vivre.*

"I believe I'll have"—she batted the eyelashes of her tight blue eyes—"*un ricard.* With a hell of a lot of ice."

"Deux ricards," I said to the waiter *"avec beaucoup de la glace."*

"Oui, monsieur." I was sure he despised us both. I thought of Giovanni and of how many times in an evening the phrase, *Oui,*

monsieur fell from his lips. With this fleeting thought there came another, equally fleeting: a new sense of Giovanni, his private life and pain, and all that moved like a flood in him when we lay together at night.

"To continue," I said.

"To continue?" She made her eyes very wide and blank. "Where were we?" She was trying to be coquettish and she was trying to be hard-headed. I felt that I was doing something very cruel.

But I could not stop. "We were talking about stone walls and how they could be entered."

"I never knew," she simpered, "that you had any interest in stone walls."

"There's a lot about me you don't know." The waiter returned with our drinks. "Don't you think discoveries are fun?"

She stared discontentedly at her drink. "Frankly," she said, turning toward me again, with those eyes, "no."

"Oh, you're much too young for that," I said. "*Everything* should be a discovery."

She was silent for a moment. She sipped her drink. "I've made," she said, finally, "all the discoveries that I can stand." But I watched the way her thighs moved against the cloth of her jeans.

"But you can't just go on being a brick stone wall forever."

"I don't see why not," she said. "Nor do I see *how* not."

"Baby," I said, "I'm making you a proposition."

She picked up her glass again and sipped it, staring straight outward at the boulevard. "And what's the proposition?"

"Invite me for a drink. *Chez toi*."

"I don't believe," she said, turning to me, "that I've got anything in the house."

"We can pick up something on the way," I said.

She stared at me for a long time. I forced myself not to drop my eyes. "I'm sure that I shouldn't," she said at last.

"Why not?"

She made a small, helpless movement in the wicker chair. "I don't know. I don't know what you want."

I laughed. "If you invite me home for a drink," I said, "I'll show you."

"I think you're being impossible," she said, and for the first time there was something genuine in her eyes and voice.

"Well," I said, "I think *you* are." I looked at her with a smile which was, I hoped, both boyish and insistent. "I don't know what I've said that's so impossible. I've put all my cards on the table. But you're still holding yours. I don't know why you should think a man's being impossible when he declares himself attracted to you."

"Oh, please," she said, and finished her drink, "I'm sure it's just the summer sun."

"The summer sun," I said, "has nothing to do with it." And when she still made no answer, "All you've got to do," I said desperately, "is decide whether we'll have another drink here or at your place."

She snapped her fingers abruptly but did not succeed in appearing jaunty. "Come along," she said. "I'm certain to regret it. But you really will have to buy something to drink. There *isn't* anything in the house. And that way," she added, after a moment, "I'll be sure to get something out of the deal."

It was I, then, who felt a dreadful holding back. To avoid looking at her, I made a great show of getting the waiter. And he came, as surly as ever, and I paid him, and we rose and started walking towards the rue de Sévres, where Sue had a small apartment.

Her apartment was dark and full of furniture. "None of it is mine," she said. "It all belongs to the French lady of a certain age from whom I rented it, who is now in Monte Carlo for her nerves." She was very nervous, too, and I saw that this nervousness could be, for a little while, a great help to me. I had bought a small bottle of cognac and I put it down on her marble-topped table and took her in my arms. For some reason I was terribly aware that it was after seven in the evening, that soon the sun would have disappeared from the river, that all the Paris night was about to begin, and that Giovanni was now at work.

She was very big and she was disquietingly fluid—fluid without, however, being able to flow. I felt a hardness and a constriction in her, a grave distrust, created already by too many men like me ever to be conquered now. What we were about to do would not be pretty.

And, as though she felt this, she moved away from me. "Let's have a drink," she said. "Unless, of course, you're in a hurry. I'll try not to keep you any longer than absolutely necessary."

She smiled and I smiled, too. We were as close in that instant as we would ever get—like two thieves. "Let's have several drinks," I said.

"But not *too* many," she said, and simpered again suggestively, like a broken-down movie queen facing the cruel cameras again after a long eclipse.

She took the cognac and disappeared into her corner of a kitchen. "Make yourself comfortable," she shouted out to me. "Take off your shoes. Take off your socks. Look at my books—I often wonder what I'd do if there weren't any books in the world."

I took off my shoes and lay back on her sofa. I tried not to think. But I was thinking that what I did with Giovanni could not possibly be more immoral than what I was about to do with Sue.

She came back with two great brandy snifters. She came close to me on the sofa and we touched glasses. We drank a little, she watching me all the while, and then I touched her breasts. Her lips parted and she put her glass down with extraordinary clumsiness and lay against me. It was a gesture of great despair and I knew that she was giving herself, not to me, but to that lover who would never come.

And I—I thought of many things, lying coupled with Sue in that dark place. I wondered if she had done anything to prevent herself from becoming pregnant; and the thought of a child belonging to Sue and me, of my being trapped that way—in the very act, so to speak, of trying to escape—almost precipitated a laughing jag. I wondered if her blue jeans had been thrown on top of the cigarette she had been smoking. I wondered if anyone else had a key to her apartment, if we could be heard through the inadequate walls, how much, in a few moments, we would hate each other. I also approached Sue as though she were a job of work, a job which it was necessary to do in an unforgettable manner. Somewhere, at the very bottom of myself, I realized that I was doing something awful to her and it became a matter of my honor not to let this fact become too obvious. I tried to convey, through this grisly act of love, the intelligence, at least, that it was not her, not *her* flesh, that I despised—it would not be her I could not face when we became vertical again. Again, somewhere at the bottom of me, I realized that my fears had been excessive and groundless and, in effect, a lie: it became clearer every instant that what I had been afraid of had nothing to do with my body. Sue was not Hella and she did not lessen my terror of what would happen when Hella came: she increased it, she made it more real than it had been before. At the same time, I realized that my performance with Sue was succeeding even too well, and I tried not to despise her for feeling so little what her laborer felt. I travelled through a network of Sue's cries, of Sue's tom-tom fists on my back, and judged by means of her thighs, by means of her legs, how soon I could be free. Then I thought, *The end is coming soon,* her sobs became even higher and harsher, I was terribly aware of the small of my back and the cold sweat there, I thought, *Well, let her have it for Christ sake, get it over with;* then it was ending and I hated her and me, then it was over, and the dark, tiny room rushed back. And I wanted only to get out of there.

She lay still for a long time. I felt the night outside and it was calling me. I leaned up at last and found a cigarette.

"Perhaps," she said, "we should finish our drinks."

She sat up and switched on the lamp which stood beside her bed. I had been dreading this moment. But she saw nothing in my eyes—she stared at me as though I had made a long journey on a white charger all the way to her prison house. She lifted her glass.

"À la votre," I said.

"À la votre?" She giggled. "À la tienne, chéri!" She leaned over and kissed me on the mouth. Then, for a moment, she felt something; she leaned back and stared at me, her eyes not quite tightening yet; and she said, lightly, "Do you suppose we could do this again sometime?"

"I don't see why not," I told her, trying to laugh. "We carry our own equipment."

She was silent. Then: "Could we have supper together—tonight?"

"I'm sorry," I said. "I'm really sorry, Sue, but I've got a date."

"Oh. Tomorrow, maybe?"

"Look, Sue. I hate to make dates. I'll just surprise you."

She finished her drink. "I doubt that," she said.

She got up and walked away from me. "I'll just put on some clothes and come down with you."

She disappeared and I heard the water running. I sat there, still naked, but with my socks on, and poured myself another brandy. Now I was afraid to go out into that night which had seemed to be calling me only a few moments before.

When she came back she was wearing a dress and some real shoes, and she had sort of fluffed up her hair. I had to admit she looked better that way, really more like a girl, like a schoolgirl. I rose and started putting on my clothes. "You look nice," I said.

There were a great many things she wanted to say, but she

forced herself to say nothing. I could scarcely bear to watch the struggle occurring in her face, it made me so ashamed. "Maybe you'll be lonely again," she said, finally. "I guess I won't mind if you come looking for me." She wore the strangest smile I had ever seen. It was pained and vindictive and humiliated, but she inexpertly smeared across this grimace a bright, girlish gaiety—as rigid as the skeleton beneath her flabby body. If fate ever allowed Sue to reach me, she would kill me with just that smile.

"Keep a candle," I said, "in the window"—and she opened her door and we passed out into the streets.

THREE

I LEFT HER AT the nearest corner, mumbling some schoolboy excuse, and watched her stolid figure cross the boulevard towards the cafes.

I did not know what to do or where to go. I found myself at last along the river, slowly going home.

And this was perhaps the first time in my life that death occurred to me as a reality. I thought of the people before me who had looked down at the river and gone to sleep beneath it. I wondered about them. I wondered how they had done it—it, the physical act. I had thought of suicide when I was much younger, as, possibly, we all have, but then it would have been for revenge, it would have been my way of informing the world how awfully it had made me suffer. But the silence of the evening, as I wandered home, had nothing to do with that storm, that far-off boy. I simply wondered about the dead because their days had ended and I did not know how I would get through mine.

The city, Paris, which I loved so much, was absolutely silent. There seemed to be almost no one on the streets, although it was still very early in the evening. Nevertheless, beneath me—along the river bank, beneath the bridges, in the shadow of the walls, I could almost hear the collective, shivering sigh—were lovers and ruins, sleeping, embracing, coupling, drinking, staring out at the descending night. Behind the walls of the houses I passed, the French nation was clearing away the dishes, putting little Jean Pierre and Marie to bed, scowling over the eternal problems of the sou, the shop, the church, the unsteady State. Those walls, those shuttered windows held them in and protected them against the darkness and the long moan of this long night. Ten years hence, little Jean Pierre or Marie might find themselves out here beside the river and wonder, like me, how they had fallen out of the web of safety. What a long way, I thought, I've come—to be destroyed!

Yet it was true, I recalled, turning away from the river down the long street home, I wanted children. I wanted to be inside again, with the light and safety, with my manhood unquestioned, watching my woman put my children to bed. I wanted the same bed at night and the same arms and I wanted to rise in the morning, knowing where I was. I wanted a woman to be for me a steady ground, like the earth itself, where I could always be renewed. It had been so once; it had almost been so once. I could make it so again, I could make it real. It only demanded a short, hard strength for me to become myself again.

I saw a light burning beneath our door as I walked down the corridor. Before I put my key in the lock the door was opened from within. Giovanni stood there, his hair in his eyes, laughing. He held a glass of cognac in his hand. I was struck at first by what seemed to be the merriment on his face. Then I saw that it was not merriment but hysteria and despair.

I started to ask him what he was doing home, but he pulled me into the room, holding me around the neck tightly, with one hand. He was shaking. "Where have you been?" I looked into his face, pulling slightly away from him. "I have looked for you everywhere."

"Didn't you go to work?" I asked him.

"No," he said. "Have a drink. I have bought a bottle of cognac to celebrate my freedom." He poured me a cognac. I did not seem to be able to move. He came toward me again, thrusting the glass into my hand.

"Giovanni—what happened?"

He did not answer. He suddenly sat down on the edge of the bed, bent over. I saw then that he was also in a state of rage. *"Ils sont sale, les gens, tu sais?"* He looked up at me. His eyes were full of tears. "They are just dirty, all of them, low and cheap and dirty." He stretched out his hand and pulled me down to the floor beside him. "All except you. *Tous, sauf toi.*" He held my face between his hands and I suppose such tenderness has scarcely ever produced such terror as I then felt. *"Ne me laisse pas tomber, je t'en prie,"* he said, and kissed me, with a strange insistent gentleness, on the mouth.

His touch could never fail to make me feel desire; yet his hot, sweet breath also made me want to vomit. I pulled away as gently as I could and drank my cognac. "Giovanni," I said, "please tell me what happened. What's the matter?"

"He fired me," he said. "Guillaume. *Il m'a mis à la porte.*" He laughed and rose and began walking up and down the tiny room. "He told me never to come to his bar anymore. He said I was a gangster and a thief and a dirty little street boy and the only reason I ran after him—I ran after *him*—was because I intended to rob him one night. *Après l'amour. Merde!*" He laughed again.

I could not say anything. I felt that the walls of the room were closing in on me.

Giovanni stood in front of our whitewashed windows, his back to me. "He said all these things in front of many people, right downstairs in the bar. He waited until people came. I wanted to kill him, I wanted to kill them all." He turned back into the center of the room and poured himself another cognac. He drank it at a breath, then suddenly took his glass and hurled it with all his strength against the wall. It rang briefly and fell in a thousand pieces all over our bed, all over the floor. I could not move at once; then, feeling that my feet were being held back by water but also watching myself move very fast, I grabbed him by the shoulders. He began to cry. I held him. And, while I felt his anguish entering into me, like acid in his sweat, and felt that my heart would burst for him, I also wondered, with an unwilling, unbelieving contempt, why I had ever thought him strong.

He pulled away from me and sat against the wall which had been uncovered. I sat facing him.

"I arrived at the usual time," he said. "I felt very good today. He was not there when I arrived and I cleaned the bar as usual and had a little drink and a little something to eat. Then he came and I could see at once that he was in a dangerous mood—perhaps he had just been humiliated by some young boy. It is funny"—and he smiled—"you can tell when Guillaume is in a dangerous mood because he then becomes so respectable. When something has happened to humiliate him and make him see, even for a moment, how disgusting he is, and how alone, then he remembers that he is a member of one of the best and oldest families in France. But maybe, then, he remembers that his name is going to die with him. Then he has to do something, quick, to make the feeling go away. He has to make much noise or have some *very* pretty boy or get drunk or have a fight or look at his dirty pictures." He paused and stood up and began walking up and down again. "I do not know what happened to him today, but when he came in he tried at first to be very business-like—he was trying to find fault with my work. But there was nothing wrong and he went upstairs. Then, by and by, he called me. I hate going up to that little *pied-à-terre* he has up there over the bar, it always means a scene. But I had to go and I found him in his dressing gown, covered with perfume. I do not know why, but the moment I saw him like that, I began to be angry. He looked at me as though he were some fabulous coquette— and he is ugly, ugly, he has a body just like sour milk!—and then he asked me how you were. I was a little astonished, for he never mentions you. I said you were fine. He asked me if we still lived together. I think perhaps I should have lied to him but I did not see any reason to lie to such a disgusting old fairy, so I said, *Bien sûr.* I was trying to be calm. Then he asked me terrible questions and I began to get sick watching him and listening to him. I thought it was best to be very quick with him and I said that such questions were not asked, even by a priest or a doctor, and I said he should be ashamed. Maybe he had been waiting for me to say something like that, for then he became angry and he reminded me that he had taken me out of the streets, *et il a fait ceci et il a fait cela,* everything for me because he thought I was adorable, *parce qu'il m'adorait—* and on and on and that I had no gratitude and no decency. I maybe handled it all very badly, I know how I would have done it even a few months ago, I would have made him scream, I would have made him kiss my feet, *je te jure!*—but I did not want to do that, I really did not want to be dirty with him. I tried to be serious. I told him that I had never told him any lies and I had always said that I did not want to be lovers with him—and—he had given me the job all the same. I said I worked very hard and was very honest with him and that it was not my fault if—if—if I did not feel for him as he felt for me. Then he reminded me that once—one time—and I did not want to say yes, but I was weak from hunger and had had trouble not to vomit. I was still trying to be calm and trying to handle it right. So I said, *Mais à ce moment là je n'avais pas un copain.* I am not alone anymore, *je suis avec un gars maintenant.* I thought he would understand that, he is very fond of romance and the dream of fidelity. But not this time. He laughed and said a few more awful things about you, and he said that you were just an American boy, after all, doing things in France which you would not dare to do at home, and that you would leave me very soon. Then, at last, I got angry and I said that he did not pay me a salary for listening to slander and then I heard someone come into the bar downstairs so I turned around without saying anything more and walked out."

He stopped in front of me. "Can I have some more cognac?" he asked, with a smile. "I won't break the glass this time."

I gave him my glass. He emptied it and handed it back. He watched my face. "Don't be afraid," he said. "We will be alright. I am not afraid." Then his eyes darkened, he looked again toward the windows.

"Well," he said, "I hoped that that would be the end of it. I worked in the bar and tried not to think of Guillaume or of what he was thinking or doing upstairs. It was aperitif time, you know? and I was very busy. Then, suddenly, I heard the door slam upstairs and the moment I heard that I knew that it had happened, the awful thing had happened. He came into the bar, all dressed now, like a French businessman, and came straight to me. He did not speak to anyone as he came in, and he looked white and angry and, naturally, this attracted attention. Everyone was waiting to see what he would do. And, I must say, I thought he was going to strike me, or he had maybe gone mad and had a pistol in his pocket. So I am sure I looked frightened and this did not help matters, either. He came behind the bar and began saying that I was a *tapette* and a thief and told me to leave at once or he would call the police and have me put behind bars. I was so astonished I could not say anything and all the time his voice was rising and people were beginning to listen and, suddenly, *mon cher,* I felt that I was falling, falling from a great, high place. For a long while I could not get angry and I could feel the tears, like fire, coming up. I could not get my breath, I could not *believe* that he was really doing this to me. I kept saying, what have I done? What have I *done*? And he would not answer and then he shouted, very loud, it was like a gun going off, "*Mais tu le sais, salop!* You know very well!" And nobody knew what he meant, but it was just as though we were back in that theatre lobby again, where we met, you remember? Everybody knew that Guillaume was right and I was wrong, that I had done something awful. And he went to the cash register and took out some money—but I knew that he knew that there was not much money *in* the cash register at such an hour—and pushed it at me and said. "Take it! Take it! Better to give it to you than have you steal it from me at night! Now go!" And, oh, the faces in that bar, you should have seen them. They were so wise and tragic and they knew that *now* they knew everything, that they had always known it, and they were so glad that they had never had anything to do with me. "Ah! *Les encules!* The dirty sons of bitches! *Les gonzesses!*" He was weeping again, with rage this time. "Then, at last, I struck him and then many hands grabbed me and now I hardly know what happened, but by and by I was in the street, with all these torn bills in my hand and everybody staring at me. I did not know what to do, I hated to walk away but I knew if anything more happened, the police would come and Guillaume would have me put in jail. But I will see him again, I swear it, and on that day—!"

He stopped and sat down, staring at the wall. Then he turned to me. He watched me for a long time, in silence. Then, "If you were not here," he said, very slowly, "this would be the end of Giovanni."

I stood up. "Don't be silly," I said. "It's not so tragic as all that." I paused. "Guillaume's disgusting. They all are. But it's not the worst thing that ever happened to you. Is it?"

"Maybe everything bad that happens to you makes you

weaker," said Giovanni, as though he had not heard me, "and so you can stand less and less." Then, looking up at me, "No. The worst thing happened to me long ago and my life has been awful since that day. You are not going to leave me, are you?"

I laughed, "Of course not." I started shaking the broken glass off our blanket onto the floor.

"I do not know what I would do if you left me." For the first time I felt the suggestion of a threat in his voice—or I put it there. "I have been alone so long—I do not think I would be able to live if I had to be alone again."

"You aren't alone now," I said. And then, quickly, for I could not, at that moment, have endured his touch: "Shall we go for a walk? Come—out of this room for a minute." I grinned and cuffed him roughly, football fashion, on the neck. Then we clung together for an instant. I pushed him away. "I'll buy you a drink," I said.

"And will you bring me home again?" he asked.

"Yes. I'll bring you home again."

"Je t'aime, tu sais?"

"Je le sais, mon vieux."

He went to the sink and started washing his face. He combed his hair. I watched him. He grinned at me in the mirror, looking, suddenly, beautiful and happy. And young—I had never in my life before felt so helpless or so old.

"But we will be alright!" he cried. *"N'est-ce pas?"*

"Certainly," I said.

He turned from the mirror. He was serious again. "But you know—I do not know how long it will be before I find another job. And we have almost no money. Do you have any money? Did any money come from New York for you today?"

"No money came from New York today," I said, calmly, "but I have a little money in my pocket." I took it all out and put it on the table. "About four thousand francs."

"And I"—he went through his pockets, scattering bills and

change. He shrugged and smiled at me, that fantastically sweet and helpless and moving smile. "*Je m'excuse.* I went a little mad." He went down on his hands and knees and gathered it up and put it on the table beside the money I had placed there. About three thousand francs worth of bills had to be pasted together and we put those aside until later. The rest of the money on the table totalled about nine thousand francs.

"We are not rich," said Giovanni grimly, "but we will eat tomorrow."

I somehow did not want him to be worried. I could not endure that look on his face. "I'll write my father again tomorrow," I said. "I'll tell him some kind of lie, some kind of lie that he'll believe and I'll *make* him send me some money." And I moved toward him as though I were driven, putting my hands on his shoulders and forcing myself to look into his eyes. I smiled and I really felt at that moment that Judas and the Savior had met in me. "Don't be frightened. Don't worry."

And I also felt, standing so close to him, feeling such a passion to keep him from terror, that a decision—once again!—had been taken from my hands. For neither my father nor Hella was real at that moment. And yet even this was not as real as my despairing sense that nothing was real for me, nothing would ever be real for me again—unless, indeed, this sensation of falling was reality.

The hours of this night begin to dwindle and now, with every second that passes on the clock, the blood at the bottom of my heart begins to boil, to bubble, and I know that no matter what I do, anguish is about to overtake me in this house, as naked and silver as that great knife which Giovanni will be facing very soon. My executioners are here with me, walking up and down with me, washing things and packing and drinking from my bottle. They are everywhere I turn. Walls, windows, mirrors, water, the night outside—they are everywhere. I might call—as Giovanni, at this moment lying in his cell, might call. But no one will hear. I might try to explain. Giovanni tried to explain. I might ask to be forgiven—if I could name and face my crime, if there were anything or anybody anywhere with the power to forgive.

No. It would help if I were able to feel guilty. But the end of innocence is also the end of guilt.

No matter how it seems now, I must confess: I loved him. I do not think that I will ever love anyone like that again. And this might be a great relief if I did not also know that, when the knife has fallen, Giovanni, if he feels anything will feel relief.

I walk up and down this house—up and down this house. I think of prison. Long ago, before I had ever met Giovanni, I met a man at a party at Jacques' house who was celebrated because he had spent half his life in prison. He had then written a book about it which displeased the prison authorities and won a literary prize. But this man's life was over. He was fond of saying that, since to be in prison was simply not to live, the death penalty was the only merciful verdict any jury could deliver. I remember thinking that, in effect, he had never left prison. Prison was all that was real to him; he could speak of nothing else. All his movements, even to the lighting of a cigarette, were stealthy, wherever his eyes focused one saw a wall rise up. His face, the color of his face, brought to mind darkness and dampness, I felt that if one cut him, his flesh would be the flesh of mushrooms. And he described to us in avid, nostalgic detail the barred windows, the barred doors, the judas, the guards standing at far ends of corridors, under the light. It is three tiers high inside the prison and everything is the color of gunmetal. Everything is dark and cold, except for those patches of light, where authority stands. There is on the air perpetually the memory of fists against the metal, a dull, booming tom-tom possibility, like the possibility of madness. The guards move and mutter and pace the corridors and boom dully up and down the stairs. They are in black, they carry guns, they are always afraid, they scarcely dare be kind. Three tiers down, in the prison's center, in the prison's great, cold heart, there is always activity: trusted prisoners wheeling things about, going in and out of the offices, ingratiating themselves with the guards for privileges of cigarettes, alcohol, and sex. The night deepens in the prison, there is muttering everywhere, and everybody knows—somehow—that death will be entering the prison courtyard early in the morning. Very early in the morning, before the trusties begin wheeling great garbage cans of food along the corridors, three men in black will come noiselessly down the corridor, one of them will turn the key in the lock. They will lay hands on someone and rush him down the corridor, first to the priest and then to a door which will open only for him, which will allow him, perhaps, one glimpse of the morning before he is thrown forward on his belly on a board and the knife falls on his neck.

I wonder about the size of Giovanni's cell. I wonder if it is bigger than his room. I know that it is colder. I wonder if he is alone or with two or three others; if he is perhaps playing cards, or smoking, or talking, or writing a letter —to whom would he be writing a letter?—or walking up and down. I wonder if he knows that the approaching morning is the last morning of his life. (For the prisoner usually does not know; the lawyer knows and tells the family or friends but does not tell the prisoner.) I wonder if he cares. Whether he knows or not, cares or not, he is certainly afraid. Whether he is with others or not, he is certainly alone. I try to see him, his back to me, standing at the window of his cell. From where he is perhaps he can only see the opposite wing of the prison; perhaps, by straining a little, just over the high wall, a patch of the street outside. I do not know if his hair has been cut, or is long—I should think it would have been cut. I wonder if he is shaven. And now a million details, proof and fruit of intimacy, flood my mind. I wonder, for example, if he feels the need to go to the bathroom, if he has been able to eat today, if he is sweating, or dry. I wonder if anyone has made love to him in prison. And then something shakes me, I feel shaken hard and dry, like some dead thing in the desert, and I know that I am hoping that Giovanni is being sheltered in someone's arms tonight. I wish that someone were here with me. I would make love to whoever was here all night long, I would labor with Giovanni all night long.

Those days after Giovanni had lost his job, we dawdled; dawdled as doomed mountain climbers may be said to dawdle above the chasm, held only by a snapping rope. I did not write my father—I put it off from day to day. It would have been too definitive an act. I knew which lie I would tell him and I knew the lie would work—only—I was not sure that it would be a lie. Day after day we lingered in that room and Giovanni began to work on it again. He had some weird idea that it would be nice to have a bookcase sunk in the wall and he chipped through the wall until he came to the brick and began pounding away at the brick. It was hard work, it was insane work, but I did not have the energy or the heart to stop him. In a way he was doing it for me, to prove his love for me. He wanted me to stay in the room with him. Perhaps he was trying, with his own strength, to push back the encroaching walls, without, however, having the walls fall down.

Now—now, of course, I see something very beautiful in those days, which were such torture then. I felt, then, that Giovanni was dragging me with him to the bottom of the sea. He could not find a job. I knew that he was not really looking for one, that he could not. He had been bruised, so to speak, so badly that the eyes of strangers lacerated him like salt. He could not endure being very far from me for very long. I was the only person on God's cold, green earth who cared about him, who knew his speech and silence, knew his arms, and did not carry a knife. The burden of his salvation seemed to be on me and I could not endure it.

And the money dwindled—it went, it did not dwindle, very fast. Giovanni tried to keep panic out of his voice when he asked me each morning, "Are you going to American Express today?"

"Certainly," I would answer.

"Do you think your money will be there today?"

"I don't know."

"What are they *doing* with your money in New York?"

Still, still I could not act. I went to Jacques and borrowed ten thousand francs from him again. I told him that Giovanni and I were going through a difficult time but that it would be over soon.

"He was very nice about it," said Giovanni.

"He *can,* sometimes, be a very nice man." We were sitting on a terrace near Odéon. I looked at Giovanni and thought for a moment how nice it would be if Jacques would take him off my hands.

"What are you thinking?" asked Giovanni.

For a moment I was frightened and I was also ashamed. "I was thinking," I said, "that I'd like to get out of Paris."

"Where would you like to go?" he asked.

"Oh, I don't know. Anywhere. I'm sick of this city," I said suddenly, with a violence that surprised us both. "I'm tired of this ancient pile of stone and all these goddam smug people. Everything you put your hands on here comes to pieces in your hands."

"That," said Giovanni gravely, "is true." He was watching me with a terrible intensity. I forced myself to look at him and smile.

"Wouldn't you like to get out of here for awhile?" I asked.

"Ah!" he said, and raised both hands briefly, palms outward, in a kind of mock resignation. "I would like to go wherever you go. I do not feel so strongly about Paris as you do, suddenly. I have never liked Paris very much."

"Perhaps," I said—I scarcely knew what I was saying—"we could go to the country. Or to Spain."

"Ah," he said, lightly, "you are lonely for your mistress."

I was guilty and irritated and full of love and pain. I wanted to kick him and I wanted to take him in my arms. "That's no reason to go to Spain," I said sullenly. "I'd just like to see it, that's all. This city is expensive."

"Well," he said brightly, "let us go to Spain. Perhaps it will remind me of Italy."

"Would you rather go to Italy? Would you rather visit your home?"

He smiled. "I do not think I have a home there anymore." And then: "No. I would not like to go to Italy—perhaps, after all, for the same reason you do not want to go to the United States."

"But I *am* going to the United States," I said, quickly. And he looked at me. "I mean, I'm certainly going to go back there one of these days."

"One of these days," he said. "Everything bad will happen—one of these days."

"Why is it bad?"

He smiled, "Why, you will go home and then you will find that home is not home anymore. Then you will really be in trouble. As long as you stay here, you can always think: One day I will go home." He played with my thumb and grinned. *"N'est-ce pas?"*

"Beautiful logic," I said. "You mean I have a home to go to as long as I don't go there?"

He laughed. "Well, isn't it true? You don't have a home until you leave it and then, when you have left it, you never can go back."

"I seem," I said, "to have heard this song before."

"Ah, *yes*," said Giovanni, "and you will certainly hear it again. It is one of those songs that somebody somewhere will always be singing."

We rose and started walking. "And what would happen," I asked, idly, "if I shut my ears?"

He was silent for a long while. Then: "You do, sometimes, remind me of the kind of man who is tempted to put himself in
prison in order to avoid being hit by a car."

"That," I said, sharply, "would seem to apply much more to
you than to me."

"What do you mean?" he asked.

"I'm talking about that room, that hideous room. Why have
you buried yourself there so long?"

"Buried myself? Forgive me, *mon cher Américain,* but Paris is
not like New York; it is not full of palaces for boys like me. Do you
think I should be living in Versailles instead?"

"There must—there must," I said, "be other rooms."

"*Ça ne manque pas, les chambres.* The world is full of rooms—
big rooms, little rooms, round rooms, square ones, rooms high up,
rooms low down—all kinds of rooms! What kind of room do you
think Giovanni should be living in? How long do you think it took
me to find the room I have? And since when, since when"—he
stopped and beat with his forefinger on my chest—"have you so
hated the room? Since when? Since yesterday, since always? *Dis-
moi.*"

Facing him, I faltered. "I don't hate it. I—I didn't mean to hurt
your feelings."

His hands dropped to his sides. His eyes grew big. He laughed.
"Hurt my *feelings*! Am I now a stranger that you speak to me like
that, with such an American politeness?"

"All I mean, baby, is that I wish we could move."

"We can move. Tomorrow! Let us go to a hotel. Is that what you
want? *Le Crillon peut-être?*"

I sighed, speechless, and we started walking again.

"I know," he burst out, after a moment, "I know! You want to
leave Paris, you want to leave the room—ah! you are wicked.
Comme tu es méchant!"

"You misunderstand me," I said. "You misunderstand me."

He smiled grimly, to himself. *"J'espère bien."*

Later, when we were back in the room putting the loose bricks Giovanni had taken out of the wall into a sack, he asked me, "This girl of yours—have you heard from her lately?"

"Not lately," I said. I did not look up. "But I expect her to turn up in Paris almost any day now."

He stood up, standing in the center of the room under the light, looking at me. I stood up, too, half smiling, but also, in some strange, dim way, a little frightened.

"Viens m'embrasser," he said.

I was vividly aware that he held a brick in his hand, I held a brick in mine. It really seemed for an instant that if I did not go to him, we would use these bricks to beat each other to death.

Yet, I could not move at once. We stared at each other across a narrow space that was full of danger, that almost seemed to roar, like flame.

"Come," he said.

I dropped my brick and went to him. In a moment I heard his fall. And at moments like this I felt that we were merely enduring and committing the longer and lesser and more perpetual murder.

FOUR

At last there came the note which I had been waiting for, from Hella, telling me what day and hour she would arrive in Paris. I did not tell this to Giovanni but walked out alone that day and went to the station to meet her.

I had hoped that when I saw her something instantaneous, definitive, would have happened in me, something to make me know where I should be and where I was. But nothing happened. I recognized her at once, before she saw me. She was wearing green, her hair was a little shorter, and her face was tan, and she wore the same brilliant smile. I loved her as much as ever and I still did not know how much that was.

When she saw me she stood stock-still on the platform, her hands clasped in front of her, with her wide-legged, boyish stance, smiling. For a moment we simply stared at each other.

"*Eh bien,*" she said, "*t'embrasse pas ta femme?*"

Then I took her in my arms and something happened then. I was terribly glad to see her. It really seemed, with Hella in the circle of my arms, that my arms were home and I was welcoming her back there. She fitted in my arms, she always had, and the shock of holding her caused me to feel that my arms had been empty since she had been away.

I held her very close in that high, dark shed, with a great confusion of people all about us, just beside the breathing train. She smelled of the wind and the sea and of space and I felt in her marvellously living body the possibility of legitimate surrender.

Then she pulled away. Her eyes were damp. "Let me look at you," she said. She held me at arm's length, searching my face. "Ah. You look wonderful. I'm so happy to see you again."

I kissed her lightly on the nose and felt that I had passed the first inspection. I picked up her bags and we started towards the exit. "Did you have a good trip? And how was Seville? And how do you like bullfights? Did you meet any bullfighters? Tell me everything."

She laughed. "Everything is a very tall order. I had a terrible trip, I hate trains, I wish I'd flown but I've been in one Spanish airplane and I swore never, never again. It rattled, my dear, in the middle of the air just like a model T Ford—it had probably *been* a model T Ford at one time—and I just sat there, praying and drinking brandy. I was sure I'd never see land again." We passed through the barrier, into the streets. Hella looked about delightedly at all of it, the cafes, the self-contained people, the violent snarl of the traffic, the blue-caped traffic policeman and his white, gleaming club. "Coming back to Paris," she said, after a moment, "is always so lovely, no matter where you've been." We got into a cab and our driver made a wide, reckless circle into the stream of traffic. "I should think that even if you returned here in some awful sorrow, you might—well, you might find it possible here to begin to be reconciled."

"Let's hope," I said, "that we never have to put Paris to that test."

Her smile was at once bright and melancholy. "Let's hope." Then she suddenly took my face between her hands and kissed me. There was a great question in her eyes and I knew that she burned to have this question answered at once. But I could not do it yet. I held her close and kissed her, closing my eyes. Everything was as it had been between us, and at the same time everything was different.

I told myself I would not think about Giovanni yet, I would not worry about him yet; for tonight, anyway, Hella and I should be together with nothing to divide us. Still, I knew very well that this was not really possible: he had already divided us. I tried not to think of him sitting alone in that room, wondering why I stayed away so long.

Then we were sitting together in Hella's room on the rue de Tournon, sampling Fundador. "It's much too sweet," I said. "Is this what they drink in Spain?"

"I never saw any Spaniards drinking it," she said, and laughed. "*They* drink wine. *I* drank gin-fizz—in Spain I somehow had the feeling that it was healthy," and she laughed again.

I kept kissing her and holding her, trying to find my way in her again, as though she were a familiar, darkened room in which I fumbled to find the light. And, with my kisses, I was trying also to delay the moment which would commit me to her, or fail to commit me to her. But I think she felt that the indefinitive constraint between us was of her doing and all on her side. She was remembering that I had written her less and less often while she had been away. In Spain, until near the end, this had probably not worried her; not until she herself had come to a decision did she begin to be afraid that I might also have arrived at a decision, opposite to hers. Perhaps she had kept me dangling too long.

She was by nature forthright and impatient; she suffered when things were not clear; yet she forced herself to wait for some word or sign from me and held the reins of her strong desire tightly in her hands.

I wanted to force her to relinquish reins. Somehow, I would be tongue-tied until I took her again. I hoped to burn out, through Hella, my image of Giovanni and the reality of his touch—I hoped to drive out fire with fire. Yet, my sense of what I was doing made me double-minded. And at last she asked me, with a smile, "Have I been away too long?"

"I don't know," I said. "It's been a long time."

"It was a very lonely time," she said, unexpectedly. She turned slightly away from me, lying on her side, looking toward the window. "I felt so aimless—like a tennis ball, bouncing, bouncing—I began to wonder where I'd land. I began to feel that I'd, somewhere, missed the boat." She looked at me. "You know the boat I'm talking about. They make movies about it where I come from. It's the boat that, when you miss it, it's a boat, but when it comes in, it's a ship." I watched her face. It was stiller than I had ever known it to be before.

"Didn't you like Spain," I asked, nervously, "at all?"

She ran one hand, impatiently, through her hair. "Oh. Of course, I liked Spain, why not? It's very beautiful. I just didn't know what I was doing there. And I'm beginning to be tired of being in places for no particular reason."

I lit a cigarette and smiled. "But you went to Spain to get away from me—remember?"

She smiled and stroked my cheek. "I haven't been very nice to you, have I?"

"You've been very honest." I stood up and walked a little away from her. "Did you get much thinking done, Hella?"

"I told you in my letter—don't *you* remember?"

For a moment everything seemed perfectly still. Even the faint street noises died. I had my back to her but I felt her eyes. I felt her waiting—everything seemed to be waiting.

"I wasn't sure about that letter." I was thinking. *Perhaps I can get out of it without having to tell her anything.* "You were so sort of—offhand—I couldn't be sure whether you were glad or sorry to be throwing in with me."

"Oh," she said, "but we've always been offhand. It's the only way I could have said it. I was afraid of embarrassing you—don't you understand that?"

What I wanted to suggest was that she was taking me out of desperation, less because she wanted me than because I was there. But I could not say it. I sensed that, though it might be true, she no longer knew it.

"But, perhaps," she said, carefully, "you feel differently now. Please say so if you do." She waited for my answer for a moment. Then: "You know, I'm not really the emancipated girl I try to be at all. I guess I just want a man to come home to me every night. I want to be able to sleep with a man without being afraid he's going to knock me up. Hell, I want to be knocked up. I want to start having babies. In a way, it's really all I'm good for." There was silence again. "Is that what you want?"

"Yes," I said, "I've always wanted that."

I turned to face her, very quickly, or as though strong hands on my shoulders had turned me around. The room was darkening. She lay on the bed watching me, her mouth slightly open and her eyes like lights. I was terribly aware of her body, and of mine. I walked over to her and put my head on her breast. I wanted to lie there, hidden and still. But then, deep within, I felt her moving, rushing to open the gates of her strong, walled city and let the king of glory come in.

Dear Dad, I wrote, *I won't keep any secrets from you anymore, I found a girl and I want to marry her and it wasn't that I was keeping secrets from you, I just wasn't sure she wanted to marry me. But she's finally agreed to risk it, poor soft-headed thing that she is, and we're planning to tie the knot while we're still over here and make our way home by easy stages. She's not French, in case you're worried (I know you don't dislike the French, it's just that you don't think they have our virtues— I might add, they don't.) Anyway, Hella—her name is Hella Lincoln, she comes from Minneapolis, her father and mother still live there, he's a corporation lawyer, she's just the little woman—Hella would like us to honeymoon here and it goes without saying that I like anything she likes. So. Now will you send your loving son some of his hard-earned money.* Tout de suite. *That's French for pronto.*

Hella—the photo doesn't really do her justice—came over here a couple of years ago to study painting. Then she discovered she wasn't a painter and just about the time she was ready to throw herself into the Seine, we met, and the rest, as they say, is history. I know you'll love her, Dad, and she'll love you. She's already made me a very happy man.

Hella and Giovanni met by accident, after Hella had been in Paris for three days. During those three days I had not seen him and I had not mentioned his name.

We had been wandering about the city all day and all day Hella had been full of a subject which I had never heard her discuss at such length before: women. She claimed it was hard to be one.

"I don't see what's so hard about being a woman. At least, not as long as she's got a man."

"That's just it," said she. "Hasn't it ever struck you that that's a sort of humiliating necessity?"

"Oh, please," I said. "It never seemed to humiliate any of the women I knew."

"Well," she said, "I'm sure you never thought about any of them—in that way."

"I certainly didn't. I hope they didn't, either. And why are *you*? What's *your* beef?"

"I've got no *beef*," she said. She hummed, low in her throat, a kind of playful Mozart tune. "I've got no beef at all. But it does seem—well, difficult—to be at the mercy of some gross, unshaven stranger before you can begin to be yourself."

"I don't know if I like *that*," I said. "Since when have I been gross? or a stranger? It may be true that I need a shave but that's *your* fault, I haven't been able to tear myself away from you." And I grinned and kissed her.

"Well," she said, "you may not be a stranger *now*. But you were once and I'm sure you will be again—many times."

"If it comes to that," I said, "so will you be, for me."

She looked at me with a quick, bright smile. "Will I?" Then: "But what I mean about being a woman is, we might get married now and stay married for fifty years and I might be a stranger to you every instant of that time and you might never know it."

"But if *I* were a stranger—*you* would know it?"

"For a woman," she said, "I think a man is always a stranger. And there's something awful about being at the mercy of a stranger."

"But men are at the mercy of women, too. Have you never thought of that?"

"Ah!" she said, "men may be at the mercy of women—I think men like that idea, it strokes the misogynist in them. But if a particular *man* is ever at the mercy of a particular *woman*—why, he's somehow stopped being a man. And the lady, then, is more neatly trapped than ever."

"You mean, I can't be at your mercy? But you can be at mine?" I laughed. "I'd like to see you at *anybody's* mercy, Hella."

"You may laugh," she said, humorously, "but there is something in what I say. I began to realize it in Spain—that I wasn't free, that I couldn't be free until I was attached—no, *committed*—to someone."

"To someone? Not some*thing?*"

She was silent. "I don't know," she said at last, "but I'm beginning to think that women get attached to some*thing* really by default. They'd give it up, if they could, anytime, for a man. Of course they can't admit this, and neither can most of them let go of what they have. But I think it kills them—perhaps I only mean," she added, after a moment, "that it would have killed *me.*"

"What do you want, Hella? What have you got now that makes such a difference?"

She laughed. "It isn't what I've *got.* It isn't even what I *want.* It's that *you've* got *me.* So now I can be—your obedient and most loving servant."

I felt cold. I shook my head in mock confusion. "I don't know what you're talking about."

"Why," she said, "I'm talking about my life. I've got you to take care of and feed and torment and trick and love—I've got you to put up with. From now on, I can have a wonderful time complaining about being a woman. But I won't be terrified that I'm *not* one." She looked at my face, and laughed. "Oh, I'll be doing other *things,*" she cried. "I won't stop being intelligent. I'll read and argue and *think* and all that—and I'll make a great point of not thinking *your* thoughts—and you'll be pleased because I'm sure the resulting confusion will cause you to see that I've only got a finite woman's mind, after all. And, if God is good, you'll love me more and more and we'll be quite happy." She laughed again. "Don't bother your head about it, sweetheart. Leave it to me."

Her amusement was contagious and I shook my head again, laughing with her. "You're adorable," I said. "I don't understand you at all."

She laughed again. "There," she said, "that's fine. We're both taking to it like ducks to water."

We were passing a bookstore and she stopped. "Can we go in for just a minute?" she asked. "There's a book I'd like to get. Quite," she added, as we entered the shop, "a trivial book."

I watched her with amusement as she went over to speak to the woman who ran the shop. I wandered idly over to the farthest book shelf, where a man stood, his back to me, leafing through a magazine. As I stood beside him, he closed the magazine and put it down, and turned. We recognized each other at once. It was Jacques.

"Tiens!" he cried. "Here you are! We were beginning to think that you had gone back to America."

"Me?" I laughed. "No, I'm still in Paris. I've just been busy." Then, with a terrible suspicion, I asked, "Who's *we?*"

"Why," said Jacques, with a hard, insistent smile, "your baby. It seems you left him alone in that room without any food, without any money, without, even, any cigarettes. He finally persuaded his concierge to allow him to put a phone call on his bill and called me. The poor boy sounded as though he would have put his head in the gas oven. If," he laughed, "he had *had* a gas oven."

We stared at each other. He, deliberately, said nothing. I did not know what to say.

"I threw a few provisions in my car," said Jacques, "and hurried out to get him. He thought we should drag the river for you. But I assured him that he did not know Americans as well as I and that you had not drowned yourself. You had only disappeared in order—to think. And I see that I was right. You have thought so much that now you must find what others have thought before you. One book," he said, finally, "that you can surely spare yourself the trouble of reading is the Marquis de Sade."

"Where is Giovanni now?" I asked.

"I finally remembered the name of Hella's hotel," said Jacques. "Giovanni said that you were more or less expecting her and so I gave him the bright idea of calling you there. He has stepped out for an instant to do just that. He'll be along presently."

Hella had returned, with her book.

"You two have met before," I said, awkwardly. "Hella, you remember Jacques."

She remembered him and also remembered that she disliked him. She smiled politely and held out her hand. "How are you?"

"*Je suis ravi, mademoiselle,*" said Jacques. He knew that Hella disliked him and this amused him. And, to corroborate her dislike, and also because at that moment he really hated me, he bowed low over her outstretched hand and became, in an instant, outrageously and offensively effeminate. I watched him as though I were watching an imminent disaster from many miles away. He turned playfully to me. "David has been hiding from us," he murmured, "now that you are back."

"Oh?" said Hella, and moved closer to me, taking my hand, "that was very naughty of him. I'd never have allowed it—if I'd known we were hiding." She grinned. "But, then, he never tells me anything."

Jacques looked at her. "No doubt," he said, "he finds more fascinating topics when you are together than why he hides from old friends."

I felt a great need to get out of there before Giovanni arrived. "We haven't eaten supper yet," I said, trying to smile. "Perhaps we can meet you later?" I knew that my smile was begging him to be kind to me.

But at that moment the tiny bell which announced every entry into the shop rang, and Jacques said, "Ah. Here is Giovanni." And, indeed, I felt him behind me, standing stock-still, staring, and felt in Hella's clasp, in her entire body, a kind of wild shrinking and not all of her composure kept this from showing in her face. When Giovanni spoke, his voice was thick with fury and relief and unshed tears.

"Where have you been?" he cried. "I thought you were dead! I thought you had been knocked down by a car or thrown into the river—what have you been doing all these days?"

I was able, oddly enough, to smile. And I was astonished at my calm. "Giovanni," I said, "I want you to meet my fiancée. Mlle Hella. Monsieur Giovanni."

He had seen her before his outburst ended and now he touched her hand with a still, astounded politeness and stared at her with black, steady eyes as though he had never seen a woman before.

"Enchanté, mademoiselle," he said. And his voice was dead and cold. He looked briefly at me, then back at Hella. For a moment we, all four, stood there as though we were posing for a tableau.

"Really," said Jacques, "now that we are all together, I think we should have one drink together. A very short one," he said to Hella, cutting off her attempt at polite refusal and taking her arm. "It's not every day," he said, "that old friends get together." He forced us to move, Hella and he together, Giovanni and I ahead. The bell rang viciously as Giovanni opened the door. The evening air hit us like a blaze. We started walking away from the river, toward the boulevard.

"When I decide to leave a place," said Giovanni, "I tell the concierge, so that at least she will know where to forward my mail."

I flared briefly, unhappily. I had noticed that he was shaven and wore a clean, white shirt and tie—a tie which surely belonged to Jacques. "I don't see what you've got to complain about," I said. "You sure knew where to go."

But with the look he gave me then my anger left me and I wanted to cry. "You are not nice," he said. *"Tu n'est pas chic du tout.*" Then he said no more and we walked to the boulevard in silence. Behind us I could hear the murmur of Jacques' voice. On the corner we stood and waited for them to catch up with us.

"Darling," said Hella, as she reached me, "you stay and have a drink if you want to, I can't, I really can't, I don't feel well at all." She turned to Giovanni. "Please forgive me," she said, "but I've just come back from Spain and I've hardly sat down a moment since I got off the train. Another time, truly—but I *must* get some sleep tonight." She smiled and held out her hand but he did not seem to see it.

"I'll walk Hella home," I said, "and then I'll come back. If you'll tell me where you're going to be."

Giovanni laughed, abruptly. "Why, we will be in the quarter," he said. "We will not be difficult to find."

"I am sorry," said Jacques, to Hella, "that you do not feel well. Perhaps another time." And Hella's hand, which was still uncertainly outstretched, he bowed over and kissed a second time. He straightened and looked at me. "You must bring Hella to dinner at my house one night." He made a face. "There is no need to hide your fiancée from us."

"No need whatever," said Giovanni. "She is very charming. And we"—with a grin, to Hella —"will try to be charming, too."

"Well," I said, and took Hella by the arm, "I'll see you later."

"If I am not here" said Giovanni, both vindictive and near tears, "by the time you come back again, I will be at home. You remember where that is—? It is near a zoo."

"I remember," I said. I started backing away, as though I were backing out of a cage. "I'll see you later. *A tout à l'heure.*"

"*À la prochaine,*" said Giovanni.

I felt their eyes on our backs as we walked away from them. For a long while Hella was silent—possibly because, like me, she was afraid to say anything. Then: "I really can't stand that man. He gives me the creeps." After a moment: "I didn't know you'd seen so much of him while I was away."

"I didn't," I said. To do something with my hands, to give myself a moment of privacy, I stopped and lit a cigarette. I felt her eyes. But she was not suspicious; she was only troubled.

"And who is Giovanni?" she asked, when we started walking again. She gave a little laugh. "I just realized that I haven't even asked you where you were living. Are you living with him?"

"We've been sharing a maid's room out at the end of Paris," I said.

"Then it wasn't very nice of you," said Hella, "to go off for so long without any warning."

"Well, my God," I said, "he's only my roommate. How was I to know he'd start dragging the river just because I stayed out a couple of nights?"

"Jacques said you left him there without any money, without any cigarettes, or anything, and you didn't even tell him you were going to be with me."

"There are lots of things I didn't tell Giovanni. But he's never made any kind of scene before—I guess he must be drunk. I'll talk to him later."

"Are you going to go back there later?"

"Well," I said, "if I don't go back there later, I'll go on over to the room. I've been meaning to do that anyway." I grinned. "I have to get shaved."

Hella sighed. "I didn't mean to get your friends mad at you," she said. "You ought to go back and have a drink with them. You said you were going to."

"Well, I may, I may not. I'm not married to them, you know."

"Well, the fact that you're going to be married to *me* doesn't mean you have to break your word to your friends. It doesn't even mean," she added, shortly, "that I have to *like* your friends."

"Hella," I said, "I am perfectly aware of that."

We turned off the boulevard, toward her hotel.

"He's very intense, isn't he?" she said. I was staring at the dark mound of the Senate, which ended our dark, slightly uphill street.

"Who is?"

"Giovanni. He's certainly very fond of you."

"He's Italian," I said. "Italians are theatrical."

"Well, this one," she laughed, "must be special, even in Italy! How long have you been living with him?"

"A couple of months." I threw away my cigarette. "I ran out of money while you were away—you know, I'm still waiting for money—and I moved in with him because it was cheaper. At that time he had a job and was living with his mistress most of the time."

"Oh?" she said. "He has a mistress?"

"He had a mistress," I said. "He also had a job. He's lost both."

"Poor boy," she said. "No wonder he looks so lost."

"He'll be alright," I said, briefly. We were before her door. She pressed the night bell.

"Is he a very good friend of Jacques?" she asked.

"Perhaps," I said, "not quite good enough to please Jacques."

She laughed. "I always feel a cold wind go over me," she said, "when I find myself in the presence of a man who dislikes women as much as Jacques does."

"Well, then," I said, "we'll just keep him away from you. We don't want no cold winds blowing over this girl." I kissed her on the tip of her nose. At the same moment there was a rumble from deep within the hotel and the door unlocked itself with a small, violent shudder. Hella looked humorously into the blackness. "I always wonder," she said, "if I *dare* go in." Then she looked up at me. "Well? Do you want to have a drink upstairs before you go back to join your friends?"

"Sure," I said. We tiptoed into the hotel, closing the door gently behind us. My fingers finally found the *minuterie,* and the weak, yellow light spilled over us. A voice, completely unintelligible, shouted out at us and Hella shouted back her name, which she tried to pronounce with a French accent. As we started up the stairs, the light went out and Hella and I began to giggle like two children. We were unable to find the minute-switch on any of the landings— I don't know why we both found this so hilarious, but we did, and we held on to each other, giggling, all the way to Hella's top-floor room.

"Tell me about Giovanni," she asked, much later, while we lay in bed and watched the black night tease her stiff, white curtains. "He interests me."

"That's a pretty tactless thing to say at this moment," I told her. "What the hell do you mean, he interests you?"

"I mean who he is, what he thinks about. How he got that face."

"What's the matter with his face?"

"Nothing. He's very beautiful, as a matter of fact. But there's something in that face—so old-fashioned."

"Go to sleep," I said. "You're babbling."

"How did you meet him?"

"Oh. In a bar one drunken night, with lots of other people."

"Was Jacques there?"

"I don't remember. Yes, I guess so. I guess he met Giovanni at the same time I did."

"What made you go to live with him?"

"I told you. I was broke and he had this room—"

"But that can't have been the *only* reason."

"Oh, well," I said, "I liked him."

"And don't you like him any more?"

"I'm very fond of Giovanni. You didn't see him at his best to-night, but he's a very nice man." I laughed; covered by the night, emboldened by Hella's body and my own, and protected by the tone of my voice, I found great relief in adding: "I love him, in a way. I really do."

"He seems to feel that you have a funny way of showing it."

"Oh, well," I said, "these people have another style from us. They're much more demonstrative. I can't help it. I just can't—do all that."

"Yes," she said, thoughtfully, "I've noticed that."

"You've noticed what?"

"Kids here—they think nothing of showing a lot of affection for each other. It's sort of a shock at first. Then you begin to think it's sort of nice."

"It *is* sort of nice," I said.

"Well," said Hella, "I think we ought to take Giovanni out to dinner or something one of these days. After all, he did sort of rescue you."

"That's a good idea," I said. "I don't know what he's doing these days but I imagine he'll have a free evening."

"Does he hang around with Jacques much?"

"No, I don't think so. I think he just ran into Jacques tonight." I paused. "I'm beginning to see," I said, carefully, "that kids like Giovanni are in a difficult position. This isn't, you know, the land of opportunity—there's no provision made for them. Giovanni's poor, I mean he comes from poor folks, and there isn't really much that he can do. And for what he *can* do, there's terrific competition. And, at that, very little money, not enough for them to be able to think of building any kind of future. That's why so many of them wander the streets and turn into gigolos and gangsters and God knows what."

"It's cold," she said, "out here in the Old World."

"Well, it's pretty cold out there in the New One, too," I said. "It's cold out here, period."

She laughed. "But we—we have our love to keep us warm."

"We're not the first people who thought that as they lay in bed."

Nevertheless, we lay silent and still in each other's arms for awhile. "Hella," I said at last.

"Yes?"

"Hella, when the money gets here, let's take it and get out of Paris."

"Get out of Paris? Where do you want to go?"

"I don't care. Just out. I'm sick of Paris. I want to leave it for awhile. Let's go south. Maybe there'll be some sun."

"Shall we get married in the south?"

"Hella," I said, "you have to believe me, I can't do anything or decide anything. I can't even see straight until we get out of this town. I don't want to get married here; I don't even want to think about getting married here. Let's just get out."

"I didn't know you felt this way," she said.

"I've been living in Giovanni's room for months," I said, "and I just can't stand it anymore. I have to get out of there. Please."

She laughed nervously and moved slightly away from me. "Well, I really don't see why getting out of Giovanni's room means getting out of Paris."

I sighed. "Please, Hella. I don't feel like going into long explanations now. Maybe it's just that if I stay in Paris I'll keep running into Giovanni and—" I stopped.

"Why should that disturb you?"

"Well—I can't do anything to help him and I can't stand having him watch me—as though—I'm an American, Hella, he thinks I'm *rich*." I paused and sat up, looking outward. She watched me. "He's a very nice man, as I say, but he's very persistent—and he's got this *thing* about me, he thinks I'm God. And that room is so stinking and dirty. And soon winter'll be here and it's going to be cold—" I turned to her again and took her in my arms. "Look. Let's just go. I'll explain a lot of things to you later—later—when we get out."

There was a long silence.

"And you want to leave right away?" she said.

"Yes. As soon as that money comes, let's rent a house."

"You're sure," she said, "that you don't just want to go back to the States?"

I groaned. "No. Not yet. That isn't what I mean."

She kissed me. "I don't care where we go," she said, "as long as we're together." Then she pushed me away. "It's almost morning," she said. "We'd better get some sleep."

I got to Giovanni's room very late the next evening. I had been walking by the river with Hella and, later, I drank too much in several bistros. The light crashed on as I came into the room and Giovanni sat up in bed, crying out in a voice of terror, *"Qui est là? Qui est là?"*

I stopped in the doorway, weaving a little in the light, and I said, "It's me, Giovanni. Shut up."

Giovanni stared at me and turned on his side, facing the wall, and began to cry.

I thought, *Sweet Jesus!* and I carefully closed the door. I took my cigarettes out of my jacket pocket and hung my jacket over the chair. With my cigarettes in my hand I went to the bed and leaned over Giovanni. I said, "Baby, stop crying. Please stop crying."

Giovanni turned and looked at me. His eyes were red and wet, but he wore a strange smile, it was composed of cruelty and shame and delight. He held out his arms and I leaned down, brushing his hair from his eyes.

"You smell of wine," said Giovanni, then.

"I haven't been drinking wine. Is that what frightened you? Is that why you are crying?"

"No."

"What is the matter?"

"Why have you gone away from me?"

I did not know what to say. Giovanni turned to the wall again. I had hoped, I had supposed that I would feel nothing: but I felt a tightening in a far corner of my heart, as though a finger had touched me there.

"I have never reached you," said Giovanni. "You have never really been here. I do not think you have ever lied to me, but I know that you have never told me the truth—why? Sometimes you were here all day long and you read or you opened the window or you cooked something—and I watched you—and you never said anything—and you looked at me with such eyes, as though you did not see me. All day, while I worked, to make this room for you."

I said nothing. I looked beyond Giovanni's head at the square windows which held back the feeble moonlight.

"What are you doing all the time? And why do you say nothing? You are evil, you know, and sometimes when you smiled at me, I hated you. I wanted to strike you. I wanted to make you bleed. You smiled at me the way you smiled at everyone, you told me what you told everyone—and you tell nothing but lies. What are you always hiding? And do you think I did not know when you made love to me, you were making love to no one? *No one!* Or everyone—but not *me,* certainly. I am nothing to you, nothing, and you bring me fever but no delight."

I moved, looking for a cigarette. They were in my hand. I lit one. In a moment, I thought, I will say something. I will say something and then I will walk out of this room forever.

"You know I cannot be alone. I have told you. What is the matter? Can we never have a life together?"

He began to cry again. I watched the hot tears roll from the corners of his eyes onto the dirty pillow.

"If you cannot love me, I will die. Before you came I wanted to die, I have told you many times. It is cruel to have made me want to live only to make my death more bloody."

I wanted to say so many things. Yet, when I opened my mouth, I made no sound. And yet—I do not know what I felt for Giovanni. I felt nothing for Giovanni. I felt terror and pity and a rising lust.

He took my cigarette from my lips and puffed on it, sitting up in bed, his hair in his eyes again.

"I have never known anyone like you before. I was never like this before you came. Listen. In Italy I had a woman and she was very good to me. She loved me, she loved *me,* and she took care of me and she was always there when I came in from work, in from the vineyards, and there was never any trouble between us, never. I was young then and did not know the things I learned later or the terrible things you have taught me. I thought all women were like that. I thought all men were like me—I thought I was like all other men. I was not unhappy then and I was not lonely—for she was there—and I did not want to die. I wanted to stay forever in our village and work in the vineyards and drink the wine we made and make love to my girl. I have told you about my village—? It is very old and in the south, it is on a hill. At night, when we walked by the wall, the world seemed to fall down before us, the whole, far-off, dirty world. I did not ever want to see it. Once we made love under the wall.

"Yes, I wanted to stay there forever and eat much spaghetti and drink much wine and make many babies and grow fat. You would not have liked me if I had stayed. I can see you, many years from now, coming through our village in the ugly, fat, American motor car you will surely have by then and looking at me and looking at all of us and tasting our wine and shitting on us with those empty smiles Americans wear everywhere and which you wear all the time and driving off with a great roar of the motors and a great sound of tires and telling all the other Americans you meet that they must come and see our village because it is so picturesque. And you will have no idea of the life there, dripping and bursting and beautiful and terrible, as you have no idea of my life now. But I think I would have been happier there and I would not have minded your smiles. I would have had my life. I have lain here many nights, waiting for you to come home, and thought how far away is my village and how terrible it is to be in this cold city, among people whom I hate, where it is cold and wet and never dry and hot as it was there, and where Giovanni has no one to talk to, and no one to be with, and where he has found a lover who is neither man nor woman, nothing that I can know or touch. You do not know, do you, what it is like to lie awake at night and wait for someone to come home? But I am sure you do not know. You do not know anything. You do not know any of the terrible things—that is why you smile and dance the way you do and you think that the comedy you are playing with the short-haired, moon-faced little girl is love."

He dropped the cigarette to the floor, where it lay burning faintly. He began to cry again. I looked at the room, thinking: I cannot bear it.

"I left my village one wild, sweet day. I will never forget that day. It was the day of my death—I wish it had been the day of my death. I remember the sun was hot and scratchy on the back of my neck as I walked the road away from my village and the road went upward and I walked bent over. I remember everything, the brown dust at my feet, and the little pebbles which rushed before me, and the short trees along the road and all the flat houses and all their colors under the sun. I remember I was weeping, but not as I am weeping now, much worse, more terrible—since I am with you, I cannot even cry as I cried then. That was the first time in my life that I wanted to die. I had just buried my baby in the churchyard where my father and my father's fathers were and I had left my girl screaming in my mother's house. Yes, I had made a baby but it was born dead. It was all grey and twisted when I saw it and it made no sound—and we spanked it on the buttocks and we sprinkled it

James Baldwin

with holy water and we prayed but it never made a sound, it was dead. It was a little boy, it would have been a wonderful, strong man, perhaps even the kind of man *you* and Jacques and Guillaume and all your disgusting band of fairies spend all your days and nights looking for, and dreaming of—but it was dead, it was my baby and we had made it, my girl and I, and it was dead. When I knew that it was dead, I took our crucifix off the wall and I spat on it and I threw it on the floor and my mother and my girl screamed and I went out. We buried it right away, the next day, and then I left my village and I came to this city where surely God has punished me for all my sins and for spitting on His holy Son, and where I will surely die. I do not think that I will ever see my village again."

I stood up. My head was turning. Salt was in my mouth. The room seemed to rock, as it had the first time I had come here, so many lifetimes ago. I heard Giovanni's moan behind me. "*Chéri. Mon très cher.* Don't leave me. Please don't leave me." I turned and held him in my arms, staring above his head at the wall, at the man and woman on the wall who walked together among roses. He was sobbing, it would have been said, as though his heart would break. But I felt that it was my heart which was broken. Something had broken in me to make me so cold and so perfectly still and far away.

Still, I had to speak.

"Giovanni," I said. "Giovanni."

He began to be still, he was listening; I felt, unwillingly, not for the first time, the cunning of the desperate.

"Giovanni," I said, "you always knew that I would leave one day. You knew my fiancée was coming back to Paris."

"You are not leaving me for her," he said. "You are leaving me for some other reason. You lie so much, you have come to believe all your own lies. But I, *I* have senses. You are not leaving me for a *woman*. If you were really in love with this little girl, you would not have had to be so cruel to me."

"She's not a little girl," I said. "She's a woman and no matter what you think, I *do* love her—"

"You do not," cried Giovanni, sitting up, "love anyone! You never have loved anyone, I am sure you never will! You love your purity, you love your mirror—you are just like a little virgin, you walk around with your hands in front of you as though you had some precious metal, gold, silver, rubies, maybe *diamonds* down there between your legs! You will never give it to anybody, you will never let anybody *touch it*—man *or* woman. You want to be *clean.* You think you came here covered with soap and you think you will go out covered with soap—and you do not want to *stink,* not even for five minutes, in the meantime." He grasped me by the collar, wrestling and caressing at once, fluid and iron at once, saliva spraying from his lips and his eyes full of tears, but with the bones of his face showing and the muscles leaping in his arms and neck. "You want to leave Giovanni because he makes you stink. You want to despise Giovanni because he is not afraid of the stink of love. You want to *kill* him in the name of all your lying little moralities. And you—you are *immoral.* You are, by far, the most immoral man I have met in all my life. Look, *look* what you have done to me. Do you think you could have done this if I did not love you? Is *this* what you should do to love?"

"Giovanni, stop it! For God's sake, *stop* it! What in the world do you want me to do? I can't *help* the way I feel."

"Do you *know* how you feel? *Do* you feel? *What* do you feel?"

"I feel nothing now," I said, "nothing. I want to get out of this room, I want to get away from you, I want to end this terrible scene."

"You want to get away from me." He laughed; he watched me; the look in his eyes was so bottomlessly bitter it was almost benevolent. "At last you are beginning to be honest. And do you know *why* you want to get away from me?"

Inside me something locked. "I—I cannot have a life with you,"

I said. "But you can have a life with Hella. With that moon-faced little girl who thinks babies come out of cabbages—or Frigidaires, I am not acquainted with the mythology of your country. You can have a life with her."

"Yes," I said, wearily, "I can have a life with her." I stood up. I was shaking. "What kind of life can we have in this room?—this filthy little room. What kind of life can two men have together, anyway? All this love you talk about—isn't it just that you want to be made to feel strong? You want to go out and be the big laborer and bring home the money, and you want me to stay here and wash the dishes and cook the food and clean this miserable closet of a room and kiss you when you come in through that door and lie with you at night and be your little *girl*. That's what you want. That's what you mean and that's *all* you mean when you say you love me. You say I want to kill *you*. What do you think you've been doing to me?"

"I am not trying to make you a little girl. If I wanted a little girl, I would be *with* a little girl."

"Why aren't you? Isn't it just that you're afraid? And you take *me* because you haven't got the guts to go after a woman, which is what you *really* want?"

He was pale. "You are the one who keeps talking about *what* I want. But I have only been talking about *who* I want."

"But I'm a man," I cried, "a man! What do you think can *happen* between us?"

"You know very well," said Giovanni slowly, "what can happen between us. It is for that reason you are leaving me." He got up and walked to the window and opened it. *"Bon,"* he said. He struck his fist once against the window sill. *"If* I could make you stay, I would," he shouted. "If I had to beat you, chain you, starve you—*if* I could make you stay, I would." He turned back into the room; the wind blew his hair. He shook his finger at me, grotesquely playful. "One day, perhaps, you will wish I had."

"It's cold," I said. "Close the window."

He smiled. "Now that you are leaving—you want the windows closed. *Bien sûr.*" He closed the window and we stood staring at each other in the center of the room. "We will not fight any more," he said. "Fighting will not make you stay. In French we have what is called *une séparation de corps*—not a divorce, you understand, just a separation. Well. We will separate. But I know you belong with me. I believe, I must believe—that you will come back."

"Giovanni," I said, "I'll not be coming back. You know I won't be back."

He waved his hand. "I said we would not fight any more. The Americans have no sense of doom, none whatever. They do not recognize doom when they see it." He produced a bottle from beneath the sink. "Jacques left a bottle of cognac here. Let us have a little drink—for the road, as I believe you people say sometimes."

I watched him. He carefully poured two drinks. I saw that he was shaking—with rage, or pain, or both.

He handed me my glass.

"*À la tienne,*" he said.

"*À la tienne.*"

We drank. I could not keep myself from asking: "Giovanni. What are you going to do now?"

"Oh," he said, "I have friends. I will think of things to do. To-night, for example, I shall have supper with Jacques. No doubt, to-morrow night I shall also have supper with Jacques. He has become very fond of me. He thinks you are a monster."

"Giovanni," I said, helplessly, "be careful. Please be careful."

He gave me an ironical smile. "Thank you," he said. "You should have given me that advice the night we met."

That was the last time we really spoke to one another. I stayed with him until morning and then I threw my things into a bag and took them away with me, to Hella's place.

I will not forget the last time he looked at me. The morning light filled the room, reminding me of so many mornings and of the morning I had first come there. Giovanni sat on the bed, completely naked, holding a glass of cognac between his hands. His body was dead white, his face was wet and grey. I was at the door with my suitcase. With my hand on the knob, I looked at him. Then I wanted to beg him to forgive me. But this would have been too great a confession; any yielding at that moment would have locked me forever in that room with him. And in a way this was exactly what I wanted. I felt a tremor go through me, like the beginning of an earthquake, and felt, for an instant, that I was drowning in his eyes. His body, which I had come to know so well, glowed in the light and charged and thickened the air between us. Then something opened in my brain, a secret, noiseless door swung open, frightening me: it had not occurred to me until that instant that, in fleeing from his body, I confirmed and perpetuated his body's power over me. Now, as though I had been branded, his body was burned into my mind, into my dreams. And all this time he did not take his eyes from me. He seemed to find my face more transparent than a shop window. He did not smile, he was neither grave, nor vindictive, nor sad; he was still. He was waiting, I think, for me to cross that space and take him in my arms again—waiting, as one waits at a deathbed for the miracle one dare not disbelieve, which will not happen. I had to get out of there for my face showed too much, the war in my body was dragging me down. My feet refused to carry me over to him again. The wind of my life was blowing me away.

"*Au revoir, Giovanni.*"

"*Au revoir, mon cher.*"

I turned from him, unlocked the door. The weary exhale of his breath seemed to ruffle my hair and brush my brow like the very wind of madness. I walked down the short corridor, expecting every instant to hear his voice behind me, passed through the vestibule, passed the *loge* of the still sleeping concierge, into the morning streets. And with every step I took it became more impossible for me to turn back. And my mind was empty—or it was as though my mind had become one enormous, anaesthetized wound. I thought only, *One day I'll weep for this. One of these days I'll start to cry.*

At the corner, in a faint patch of the morning sun, I looked in my wallet to count my bus tickets. In the wallet I found three hundred francs, taken from Hella, my *carte d'identité,* my address in the United States, and paper, paper, scraps of paper, cards, photographs. On each piece of paper I found addresses, telephone numbers, memos of various rendezvous made and kept—or perhaps not kept—people met and remembered, or perhaps not remembered, hopes probably not fulfilled: certainly not fulfilled, or I would not have been standing on that street corner.

I found four bus tickets in my wallet and I walked to the *arrêt.* There was a policeman standing there, his blue hood, weighted, hanging down behind, his white club gleaming. He looked at me and smiled and cried, *"ça va?"*

"Oui, merci. And you?"

"Toujours. It's a nice day, no?"

"Yes." But my voice trembled. "The autumn is beginning."

"C'est ça." And he turned away, back to his contemplation of the boulevard. I smoothed my hair with my hand, feeling foolish for feeling shaken. I watched a woman pass, coming from the market, her string bag full; at the top, precariously, a liter of red wine. She was not young but she was clear-faced and bold, she had a strong, thick body and strong, thick hands. The policeman shouted something to her and she shouted back—something bawdy and good-natured. The policeman laughed; but refused to look at me again. I watched the woman continue down the street—home, I thought, to her husband, dressed in blue working clothes, dirty, and to her children. She passed the corner where the patch of sun-

light fell and crossed the street. The bus came and the policeman and I, the only people waiting, got on—he stood on the platform, far from me. The policeman was not young, either, but he had a gusto which I admired. I looked out of the window and the streets rolled by. Ages ago, in another city, on another bus, I sat so at the windows, looking outward, inventing for each flying face which trapped my brief attention some life, some destiny, in which I played a part. I was looking for some whisper, or promise, of my possible salvation. But it seemed to me that morning that my ancient self had been dreaming the most dangerous dream of all.

The days that followed seemed to fly. It seemed to turn cold overnight. The tourists in their thousands disappeared, conjured away by timetables. When one walked through the gardens, leaves fell about one's head and sighed and crashed beneath one's feet. The stone of the city, which had been luminous and changing, faded slowly, but with no hesitation, into simple grey stone again. It was apparent that the stone was hard. Daily, fishermen disappeared from the river until, one day, the river banks were clear. The bodies of young boys and girls began to be compromised by heavy underwear, by sweaters and mufflers, hoods and capes. Old men seemed older, old women slower. The colors on the river faded, the rain began, and the river began to rise. It was apparent that the sun would soon give up the tremendous struggle it cost her to get to Paris for a few hours every day.

"But it will be warm in the south," I said.

The money had come. Hella and I were busy every day, on the track of a house in Eze, in Cagnes-sur-Mer, in Vence, in Monte Carlo, in Antibes, in Grasse. We were scarcely ever seen in the quarter. We stayed in her room, we made love a lot, we went to the movies and had long, frequently rather melancholy dinners in strange restaurants on the right bank. It is hard to say what produced this melancholy, which sometimes settled over us like the shadow of some vast, some predatory, waiting bird. I do not think that Hella was unhappy, for I had never before clung to her as I clung to her during that time. But perhaps she sensed, from time to time, that my clutch was too insistent to be trusted, certainly too insistent to last.

And from time to time, around the quarter, I ran into Giovanni. I dreaded seeing him, not only because he was almost always with Jacques, but also because, though he was often rather better dressed, he did not look well. I could not endure something at once abject and vicious which I began to see in his eyes, nor the way he giggled at Jacques' jokes, nor the mannerisms, a fairy's mannerisms, which he was beginning, sometimes, to affect. I did not want to know what his status was with Jacques; yet the day came when it was revealed to me in Jacques' spiteful and triumphant eyes. And Giovanni, during this short encounter, in the middle of the boulevard as dusk fell, with people hurrying all about us, was really amazingly giddy and girlish, and very drunk—it was as though he were forcing me to taste the cup of his humiliation. And I hated him for this.

The next time I saw him it was in the morning. He was buying a newspaper. He looked up at me insolently, into my eyes, and looked away. I watched him diminish down the boulevard. When I got home, I told Hella about it, trying to laugh.

Then I began to see him around the quarter without Jacques, with the street boys of the quarter, whom he had once described to me as *"lamentable."* He was no longer so well dressed, he was beginning to look like one of them. His special friend among them seemed to be the same, tall, pockmarked boy, named Yves, whom I remembered having seen briefly, playing the pinball machine, and, later, talking to Jacques on that first morning in Les Halles. One night, quite drunk myself, and wandering about the quarter alone, I ran into this boy and bought him a drink. I did not mention Giovanni but Yves volunteered the information that he was not with Jacques anymore. But it seemed that he might be able to get back his old job in Guillaume's bar. It was certainly not more than a week after this that Guillaume was found dead in the private quarters above his bar, strangled with the sash of his dressing gown.

F I V E

IT WAS A TERRIFIC scandal. If you were in Paris at the time you
certainly heard of it, and saw the picture printed in all the newspapers, of Giovanni just after he was captured. Editorials were written and speeches were made, and many bars of the genre of
Guillaume's bar were closed. (But they did not stay closed long.)
Plainclothes policemen descended on the quarter, asking to see everyone's papers, and the bars were emptied of *tapettes*. Giovanni
was nowhere to be found. All of the evidence, above all, of course,
his disappearance, pointed to him as the murderer. Such a scandal
always threatens, before its reverberations cease, to rock the very
foundations of the state. It is necessary to find an explanation, a
solution, and a victim with the utmost possible speed. Most of the
men picked up in connection with this crime were not picked up
on suspicion of murder. They were picked up on suspicion of having what the French, with a delicacy I take to be sardonic, call *les*

goûts particuliers. These "tastes," which do not constitute a crime in
France, are nevertheless regarded with extreme disapprobation by
the bulk of the populace, which also looks on its rulers and "betters" with a stony lack of affection. When Guillaume's corpse was
discovered, it was not only the boys of the street who were frightened; they, in fact, were a good deal less frightened than the men
who roamed the streets to buy them, whose careers, positions, aspi-
rations, could never have survived such notoriety. Fathers of families, sons of great houses, and itching adventurers from Belleville
were all desperately anxious that the case be closed, so that things
might, in effect, go back to normal and the dreadful whiplash of
public morality not fall on their backs. Until the case was closed
they could not be certain which way to jump, whether they should
cry out that they were martyrs, or remain what, at heart, of course,
they were: simple citizens, bitter against outrage and anxious to see
justice done and the health of the state preserved.

It was fortunate, therefore, that Giovanni was a foreigner. As
though by some magnificently tacit agreement, with every day that
he was at large, the press became more vituperative against him and
more gentle towards Guillaume. It was remembered that there perished with Guillaume one of the oldest names in France. Sunday
supplements were run on the history of his family; and his old, aris-
tocratic mother, who did not survive the trial of his murderer, testified to the sterling qualities of her son and regretted that corruption
had become so vast in France that such a crime could go so long
unpunished. With this sentiment the populace was, of course,
more than ready to agree. It is perhaps not as incredible as it certainly seemed to me, but Guillaume's name became fantastically
entangled with French history, French honor, and French glory,
and very nearly became, indeed, a symbol of French manhood.

"But listen," I said to Hella, "he was just a disgusting old fairy.
That's *all* he was!"

"Well, how in the world do you expect the people who read newspapers to know that? *If* that's what he was, I'm sure he didn't advertise it—and he must have moved in a pretty limited circle."

"Well—*somebody* knows it. Some of the people who write this drivel know it."

"There doesn't seem to be much point," she said, quietly, "in defaming the dead."

"But isn't there some point in telling the truth?"

"They're telling the truth. He's a member of a very important family and he's been murdered. I know what *you* mean. There's another truth they're *not* telling. But newspapers never do, that's not what they're for."

I sighed. "Poor, poor, poor Giovanni."

"Do you believe he did it?"

"I don't know. It certainly *looks* as though he did it. He was there that night. People saw him go upstairs before the bar closed and they don't remember seeing him come down."

"Was he working there that night?"

"Apparently not. He was just drinking. He and Guillaume seemed to have become friendly again."

"You certainly made some peculiar friends while I was away."

"They wouldn't seem so damn peculiar if one of them hadn't got murdered. Anyway, none of them were my friends—except Giovanni."

"You lived with him. Can't you tell whether he'd commit murder or not?"

"How? You live with me. Can I commit a murder?"

"You? Of course not."

"How do you *know* that? You don't know that. How do you know I'm what you see?"

"Because—" she leaned over and kissed me—"I love you."

"Ah! I loved Giovanni—"

"Not as I love you," said Hella.

"I might have committed murder already, for all you know. How do you know?"

"Why are you so upset?"

"Wouldn't *you* be upset if a friend of yours was accused of murder and was hiding somewhere? What do you mean, why am I so upset? What do you want me to do, sing Christmas carols?"

"Don't shout. It's just that I never realized he meant so much to you."

"He was a nice man," I said finally. "I just hate to see him in trouble."

She came to me and put her hand lightly on my arm. "We'll leave this city soon, David. You won't have to think about it anymore. People get into trouble, David. But don't act as though it were, somehow, your fault. It's not your fault."

"*I* know it's not my fault!" But my voice, and Hella's eyes, astounded me into silence. I felt, with terror, that I was about to cry.

Giovanni stayed at large nearly a week. As I watched, from Hella's window, each night creeping over Paris, I thought of Giovanni somewhere outside, perhaps under one of those bridges, frightened and cold and not knowing where to go. I wondered if he had, perhaps, found friends to hide him—it was astonishing that in so small and policed a city he should prove so hard to find. I feared, sometimes, that he might come to find me—to beg me to help him or to kill me. Then I thought that he probably considered it beneath him to ask me for help; he no doubt felt by now that I was not worth killing. I looked to Hella for help. I tried to bury each night, in her, all my guilt and terror. The need to act was like a fever in me, the only act possible was the act of love.

He was finally caught, very early one morning, in a barge tied up along the river. Newspaper speculation had already placed him in Argentina, so it was a great shock to discover that he had got no farther than the Seine. This lack, on his part, of "dash" did nothing to endear him to the public. He was a criminal, Giovanni, of the dullest kind, a bungler; robbery, for example, had been insisted on as the motive for Guillaume's murder; but, though Giovanni had taken all the money Guillaume had in his pockets, he had not touched the cash register and had not even suspected, apparently, that Guillaume had over one hundred thousand francs hidden in another wallet at the bottom of his closet. The money he had taken from Guillaume was still in his pockets when he was caught; he had not been able to spend it. He had not eaten for two or three days and was weak and pale and unattractive. His face was on newsstands all over Paris. He looked young, bewildered, terrified, depraved; as though he could not believe that he, Giovanni, had come to this, had come to this and would go no further, his short road ending in a common knife. He seemed already to be rearing back, every inch of his flesh revolting before that icy vision. And it seemed, as it had seemed so many times, that he looked to me for help. The newsprint told the unforgiving world how Giovanni repented, cried for mercy, called on God, wept that he had not meant to do it. And told us, too, in delicious detail, *how* he had done it: but not why. Why was too black for the newsprint to carry and too deep for Giovanni to tell.

I may have been the only man in Paris who knew that he had not meant to do it, who could read *why* he had done it beneath the details printed in the newspapers. I remembered again the evening I had found him at home and he told me how Guillaume had fired him. I heard his voice again and saw the vehemence of his body and saw his tears. I knew his bravado, how he liked to feel himself *débrouillard,* more than equal to any challenge, and saw him swagger into Guillaume's bar. He must have felt that, having surrendered to Jacques, his apprenticeship was over, love was over, and he could do with Guillaume anything he liked. He could, indeed, have done with Guillaume anything at all—but he could not do anything about being Giovanni. Guillaume certainly knew, Jacques would have lost no time in telling him, that Giovanni was no longer with *le jeune Américain;* perhaps Guillaume had even attended one or two of Jacques' parties, armed with his own entourage; and he certainly knew, all his circle knew, that Giovanni's new freedom, his loverless state, would turn into license, into riot—it had happened to every one of them. It must have been a great evening for the bar when Giovanni swaggered in alone.

I could hear the conversation:

"Alors, tu es revenu?" This from Guillaume, with a seductive, sardonic, speaking look.

Giovanni sees that he does not wish to be reminded of his last, disastrous tantrum, that he wishes to be friendly. At the same moment Guillaume's face, voice, manner, smell, hit him; he is actually facing Guillaume, not conjuring him up in his mind; the smile with which he responds to Guillaume almost causes him to vomit. But Guillaume does not see this, of course, and offers Giovanni a drink.

"I thought you might need a barman," Giovanni says.

"But are you looking for work? I thought your American would have bought you an oil well in Texas by now."

"No. My American"—he makes a gesture—"has flown!" They both laugh.

"The Americans always fly. They are not serious," says Guillaume.

"C'est vrai," says Giovanni. He finishes his drink, looking away from Guillaume, looking dreadfully self-conscious, perhaps almost unconsciously, whistling. Guillaume, now, can hardly keep his eyes off him, or control his hands.

"Come back, later, at closing, and we will talk about this job," he says at last.

And Giovanni nods and leaves. I can imagine him, then, finding some of his street cronies, drinking with them, and laughing, stiffening up his courage as the hours tick by. He is dying for someone to tell him not to go back to Guillaume, not to let Guillaume touch him. But his friends tell him how rich Guillaume is, how he is a silly old queen, how much he can get out of Guillaume if he will only be smart.

No one appears on the boulevards to speak to him, to save him. He feels that he is dying.

Then the hour comes when he must go back to Guillaume's bar. He walks there alone. He stands outside awhile. He wants to turn away, to run away. But there is no place to run. He looks up the long, dark, curving street as though he were looking for someone. But there is no one there. He goes into the bar. Guillaume sees him at once and discreetly motions him upstairs. He climbs the stairs. His legs are weak. He finds himself in Guillaume's rooms, surrounded by Guillaume's silks, colors, perfumes, staring at Guillaume's bed.

Then Guillaume enters and Giovanni tries to smile. They have a drink. Guillaume is precipitate, flabby, and moist, and, with each touch of his hand, Giovanni shrinks further and more furiously away. Guillaume disappears to change his clothes and comes back in his theatrical dressing gown. He wants Giovanni to undress—

Perhaps at this moment Giovanni realizes that he cannot go through with it, that his will cannot carry him through. He remembers the job. He tries to talk, to be practical, to be reasonable, but, of course, it is too late. Guillaume seems to surround him like the sea itself. And I think that Giovanni, tortured into a state like madness, feels himself going under, is overcome, and Guillaume has his will. I think if this had not happened, Giovanni would not have killed him.

For, with his pleasure taken, and while Giovanni still lies suffocating, Guillaume becomes a business man once more and, walking up and down, gives excellent reasons why Giovanni cannot work for him anymore. Beneath whatever reasons Guillaume invents, the real one lies hidden, and they both, dimly, in their different fashions, see it: Giovanni, like a falling movie star, has lost his drawing power. Everything is known about him, his secrecy has been discovered. Giovanni certainly feels this and the rage which has been building in him for many months begins to be swollen now with the memory of Guillaume's hands and mouth. He stares at Guillaume in silence for a moment and then begins to shout. And Guillaume answers him. With every word exchanged Giovanni's head begins to roar and a blackness comes and goes before his eyes. And Guillaume is in seventh heaven and begins to prance about the room—he has scarcely ever gotten so much for so little before. He plays this scene for all it's worth, deeply rejoicing in the fact that Giovanni's face grows scarlet, and his voice thick, watching with pure delight the bone-hard muscles in his neck. And he says something, for he thinks the tables have been turned; he says something, one phrase, one insult, one mockery too many; and in a split second, in his own shocked silence, in Giovanni's eyes, he realizes that he has unleashed something he cannot turn back.

Giovanni certainly did not mean to do it. But he grabbed him, he struck him. And with that touch, and with each blow, the intolerable weight at the bottom of his heart began to lift: now it was Giovanni's turn to be delighted. The room was overturned, the fabrics were shredded, the odor of perfume was thick. Guillaume struggled to get out of the room, but Giovanni followed him everywhere: now it was Guillaume's turn to be surrounded. And perhaps at the very moment Guillaume thought he had broken free, when he had reached the door perhaps, Giovanni lunged after him and caught him by the sash of the dressing gown and wrapped the sash around his neck. Then he simply held on, sobbing, becoming lighter every moment as Guillaume grew heavier, tightening the sash and cursing. Then Guillaume fell. And Giovanni fell—back into the room, the streets, the world, into the presence and the shadow of death.

By the time we found this great house it was clear that I had no right to come here. By the time we found it, I did not even want to see it. But by this time, also, there was nothing else to do. There was nothing else I wanted to do. I thought, it is true, of remaining in Paris in order to be close to the trial, perhaps to visit him in prison. But I knew there was no reason to do this. Jacques, who was in constant touch with Giovanni's lawyer and in constant touch with me, had seen Giovanni once. He told me what I knew already, that there was nothing I, or anyone, could do for Giovanni anymore.

Perhaps he wanted to die. He pleaded guilty, with robbery as the motive. The circumstances under which Guillaume had fired him received great play in the press. And from the press one received the impression that Guillaume had been a good-hearted, a perhaps somewhat erratic philanthropist who had had the bad judgment to befriend the hardened and ungrateful adventurer, Giovanni. Then the case drifted downward from the headlines. Giovanni was taken to prison to await trial.

And Hella and I came here. I may have thought—I am sure I thought in the beginning—that, though I could do nothing for Giovanni, I might, perhaps, be able to do something for Hella. I must have hoped that there would be something Hella could do for me. And this might have been possible if the days had not dragged by, for me, like days in prison. I could not get Giovanni out of my mind, I was at the mercy of the bulletins which sporadically arrived from Jacques. All that I remember of the autumn is waiting for Giovanni to come to trial. Then, at last, he came to trial, was found guilty, and placed under sentence of death. All winter long I counted the days. And the nightmare of this house began.

Much has been written of love turning to hatred, of the heart growing cold with the death of love. It is a remarkable process. It is far more terrible than anything I have ever read about it, more terrible than anything I will ever be able to say.

I don't know, now, when I first looked at Hella and found her stale, found her body uninteresting, her presence grating. It seemed to happen all at once—I suppose that only means that it had been happening for a long time. I trace it to something as fleeting as the tip of her breast lightly touching my forearm as she leaned over me to serve my supper. I felt my flesh recoil. Her underclothes, drying in the bathroom, which I had often thought of as smelling even rather improbably sweet and as being washed much too often, now began to seem unaesthetic and unclean. A body which had to be covered with such crazy, catty-cornered bits of stuff began to seem grotesque. I sometimes watched her naked body move and wished that it were harder and firmer, I was fantastically intimidated by her breasts, and when I entered her I began to feel that I would never get out alive. All that had once delighted me seemed to have turned sour on my stomach.

I think—I think that I have never been more frightened in my life. When my fingers began, involuntarily, to loose their hold on Hella, I realized that I was dangling from a high place and that I had been clinging to her for my very life. With each moment, as my fingers slipped, I felt the roaring air beneath me and felt everything in me bitterly contracting, crawling furiously upward against that long fall.

I thought that it was only, perhaps, that we were alone too much and so, for a while, we were always going out. We made expeditions to Nice and Monte Carlo and Cannes and Antibes. But we were not rich and the south of France, in the wintertime, is a playground for the rich. Hella and I went to a lot of movies and found ourselves, very often, sitting in empty, fifth-rate bars. We walked a lot, in silence. We no longer seemed to see things to point out to each other. We drank too much, especially me. Hella, who had been so brown and confident and glowing on her return from Spain, began to lose all this; she began to be pale and watchful and uncertain. She ceased to ask me what the matter was, for it was borne in on her that I either did not know or would not say. She watched me. I felt her watching and it made me wary and it made me hate her. My guilt, when I looked into her closing face, was more than I could bear.

We were at the mercy of bus schedules and often found ourselves in the wintry dawn huddled sleepily together in a waiting room or freezing on the street corner of some totally deserted town. We arrived home in the grey morning, crippled with weariness, and went straight to bed.

I was able, for some reason, to make love in the mornings. It may have been due to nervous exhaustion; or wandering about at night engendered in me a curious, irrepressible excitement. But it was not the same, something was gone: the astonishment, the power, and the joy were gone, the peace was gone.

I had nightmares and sometimes my own cries woke me up and sometimes my moaning made Hella shake me awake.

"I wish," she said, one day, "you'd tell me what it is. Tell me what it is; let me help you."

I shook my head in bewilderment and sorrow and sighed. We were sitting in the big room, where I am standing now. She was sitting in the easy chair, under the lamp, with a book open on her lap.

"You're sweet," I said. Then: "It's nothing. It'll go away. It's probably just nerves."

"It's Giovanni," she said.

I watched her.

"Isn't it," she asked, carefully, "that you think you've done something awful to him by leaving him in that room? I think you blame yourself for what happened to him. But, darling, nothing you could have done would have helped him. Stop torturing yourself."

"He was so beautiful," I said. I had not meant to say it. I felt myself beginning to shake. She watched me while I walked to the table—there was a bottle there then as now—and poured myself a drink.

I could not stop talking, though I feared at every instant that I would say too much. Perhaps I wanted to say too much.

"I can't help feeling that I placed him in the shadow of the knife. He wanted me to stay in that room with him; he begged me to stay. I didn't tell you—we had an awful fight the night I went there to get my things." I paused. I sipped my drink. "He cried."

"He was in love with you," said Hella. "Why didn't you tell me that? Or didn't you know it?"

I turned away, feeling my face flame.

"It's not your fault," she said. "Don't you understand that? You couldn't keep him from falling in love with you. You couldn't have kept him from—from killing that awful man."

"You don't know anything about it," I muttered. "You don't know anything about it."

"I know how you feel—"

"You *don't* know how I feel."

"David. Don't shut me out. Please don't shut me out. Let me help you."

"Hella. Baby. I know you want to help me. But just let me be for awhile. I'll be all right."

"You've been saying that now," she said, wearily, "for a long time." She looked at me steadily for awhile and then she said, "David. Don't you think we ought to go home?"

"Go home? What for?"

"What are we staying here for? How long do you want to sit in this house, eating your heart out? And what do you think it's doing to me?" She rose and came to me. "Please. I want to go home. I want to get married. I want to start having kids. I want us to live someplace, I want *you*. Please David. What are we marking time over here for?"

I moved away from her, quickly. At my back she stood perfectly still.

"What's the *matter*, David? What do you *want*?"

"I don't know. I don't *know*."

"What is it you're not telling me? Why don't you tell me the truth? Tell me the *truth*."

I turned and faced her. "Hella—bear with me, *bear* with me—a little while."

"I want to," she cried, "but where *are* you? You've gone away somewhere and I can't find you. If you'd only let me reach you—!"

She began to cry. I held her in my arms. I felt nothing at all.

I kissed her salty tears and murmured, murmured I don't know what. I felt her body straining, straining to meet mine and I felt my own contracting and drawing away and I knew that I had begun the long fall down. I stepped away from her. She swayed where I had left her, like a puppet dangling from a string.

"David, please let me be a woman. I don't care what you do to me. I don't care what it costs. I'll wear my hair long, I'll give up cigarettes, I'll throw away the books." She tried to smile; my heart turned over. "Just let me be a woman, take me. It's what I want. It's *all* I want. I don't care about anything else." She moved toward me. I stood perfectly still. She touched me, raising her face, with a desperate and terribly moving trust, to mine. "Don't throw me back into the sea, David. Let me stay here with you." Then she kissed me, watching my face. My lips were cold. I felt nothing on my lips. She kissed me again and I closed my eyes, feeling that strong chains were dragging me to fire. It seemed that my body, next to her warmth, her insistence, under her hands, would never awaken. But when it awakened, I had moved out of it. From a great height, where the air all around me was colder than ice, I watched my body in a stranger's arms.

It was that evening, or an evening very soon thereafter, that I left her sleeping in the bedroom and went, alone, to Nice.

I roamed all the bars of that glittering town, and at the end of the first night, blind with alcohol and grim with lust, I climbed the stairs of a dark hotel in company with a sailor. It turned out, late the next day, that the sailor's leave was not yet ended and that the sailor had friends. We went to visit them. We stayed the night. We spent the next day together, and the next. On the final night of the sailor's leave, we stood drinking together in a crowded bar. We faced the mirror. I was very drunk. I was almost penniless. In the mirror, suddenly, I saw Hella's face. I thought for a moment that I had gone mad, and I turned. She looked very tired and drab and small.

For a long time we said nothing to each other. I felt the sailor staring at both of us.

"Hasn't she got the wrong bar?" he asked me, finally.

Hella looked at him. She smiled.

"It's not the only thing I got wrong," she said.

Now the sailor stared at me.

"Well," I said to Hella, "now you know."

"I think I've known it for a long time," she said. She turned and started away from me. I moved to follow her. The sailor grabbed me.

"Are you—is she—?"

I nodded. His face, open-mouthed, was comical. He let me go and I passed him and, as I reached the doors, I heard his laughter.

We walked for a long time in the stone-cold streets, in silence.

There seemed to be no one on the streets at all. It seemed inconceivable that the day would ever break.

"Well," said Hella, "I'm going home. I wish I'd never left it."

"If I stay here much longer," she said, later that same morning, as she packed her bag, "I'll forget what it's like to be a woman."

She was extremely cold, she was very bitterly handsome.

"I'm not sure any woman *can* forget that," I said.

"There are women who have forgotten that to be a woman doesn't simply mean humiliation, doesn't simply mean bitterness. I haven't forgotten it yet," she added, "in spite of you. I'm not going to forget it. I'm getting out of this house, away from you, just as fast as taxis, trains, and boats will carry me."

And in the room which had been our bedroom in the beginning of our life in this house, she moved with the desperate haste of someone about to flee—from the open suitcase on the bed, to the chest of drawers, to the closet. I stood in the doorway, watching her. I stood there the way a small boy who has wet his pants stands before his teacher. All the words I wanted to say closed my throat, like weeds, and stopped my mouth.

"I wish, anyway," I said at last, "that you'd believe me when I say that, if I was lying, I wasn't lying to *you*."

She turned toward me with a terrible face. "I was the one you were talking to. *I* was the one you wanted to come with you to this terrible house in the middle of nowhere. I was the one you said you wanted to marry!"

"I mean," I said, "I was lying to myself."

"Oh," said Hella, "I see. That makes everything different, of course."

"I only mean to say," I shouted, "that whatever I've done to hurt you, I didn't mean to do!"

"Don't shout," said Hella. "I'll soon be gone. Then you can

shout it to those hills out there, shout it to the peasants, how guilty you are, how you love to be guilty!"

She started moving back and forth again, more slowly, from the suitcase to the chest of drawers. Her hair was damp and fell over her forehead, and her face was damp. I longed to reach out and take her in my arms and comfort her. But that would not be comfort anymore, only torture, for both of us.

She did not look at me as she moved, but kept looking at the clothes she was packing, as though she were not sure they were hers.

"But I *knew*," she said, "I knew. This is what makes me so ashamed. I knew it every time you looked at me. I knew it every time we went to bed. If only you had told me the truth *then*. Don't you see how unjust it was to wait for *me* to find it out? To put all the burden on *me*? I had the *right* to expect to hear from you—women are always waiting for the *man* to speak. Or hadn't you heard?"

I said nothing.

"I wouldn't have had to spend all this time in this *house;* I wouldn't be wondering how in the name of God I'm going to stand that long trip back. I'd *be* home by now, dancing with some man who wanted to make me. And I'd *let* him make me, too, why not?" And she smiled bewilderedly at a crowd of nylon stockings in her hand and carefully crushed them in the suitcase.

"Perhaps *I* didn't know it then. I only knew I had to get out of Giovanni's room."

"Well," she said, "you're out. And now I'm getting out. It's only poor Giovanni who's—lost his head."

It was an ugly joke and made with the intention of wounding me; yet she couldn't quite manage the sardonic smile she tried to wear.

"I'll never understand it," she said at last, and she raised her eyes to mine as though I could help her to understand. "That sordid little gangster has wrecked your life. I think he's wrecked mine, too.

Americans should never come to Europe," she said, and tried to laugh and began to cry, "it means they never can be happy again. What's the good of an American who isn't happy? Happiness was all we had." And she fell forward into my arms, into my arms for the last time, sobbing.

"Don't believe it," I muttered, "don't believe it. We've got much more than that, we've always had much more than that. Only—only—it's sometimes hard to bear."

"Oh, God, I wanted you," she said. "Every man I come across will make me think of you." She tried to laugh again. "Poor man! Poor men! Poor *me*!"

"Hella. Hella. One day, when you're happy, try to forgive me."

She moved away. "Ah. I don't know anything about happiness anymore. I don't know anything about forgiveness. But if women are supposed to be led by men and there aren't any men to lead them, what happens then? What happens then?" She went to the closet and got her coat; dug in her handbag and found her compact and, looking into the tiny mirror, carefully dried her eyes and began to apply her lipstick. "There's a difference between little boys and little girls, just like they say in those little blue books. Little girls want little boys. But little boys—!" She snapped her compact shut. "I'll never again, as long as I live, know *what* they want. And now I know they'll never tell me. I don't think they know how." She ran her fingers through her hair, brushing it back from her forehead, and, now, with the lipstick, and in the heavy, black coat, she looked again cold, brilliant, and bitterly helpless, a terrifying woman. "Mix me a drink," she said, "we can drink to old times' sake before the taxi comes. No, I don't want you to come to the station with me. I wish I could drink all the way to Paris and all the way across that criminal ocean."

We drank in silence, waiting to hear the sound of tires on gravel. Then we heard it, saw the lights, and the driver began honking his horn. Hella put down her drink and wrapped her coat around her and started for the door. I picked up her bags and followed. The driver and I arranged the baggage in the car; all the time I was trying to think of some last thing to say to Hella, something to help wipe away the bitterness. But I could not think of anything. She said nothing to me. She stood very erect beneath the dark winter sky, looking far out. And when all was ready, I turned to her.

"Are you sure you wouldn't like me to come with you as far as the station, Hella?"

She looked at me and held out her hand.

"Good-bye, David."

I took her hand. It was cold and dry, like her lips.

"Good-bye, Hella."

She got into the taxi. I watched it back down the drive, onto the road. I waved one last time, but Hella did not wave back.

Outside my window the horizon begins to lighten, turning the grey sky a purplish blue.

I have packed my bags and I have cleaned the house. The keys to the house are on the table before me. I have only to change my clothes. When the horizon has become a little lighter the bus which will take me to town, to the station, to the train which will take me to Paris, will appear at the bend of the highway. Still, I cannot move.

On the table, also, is a small, blue envelope, the note from Jacques informing me of the date of Giovanni's execution.

I pour myself a very little drink, watching, in the window pane, my reflection, which steadily becomes more faint. I seem to be fading away before my eyes—this fancy amuses me, and I laugh to myself.

It should be now that gates are opening before Giovanni and clanging shut behind him, never, for him, to be opened or shut anymore. Or perhaps it is already over. Perhaps it is only beginning.

Perhaps he still sits in his cell, watching, with me, the arrival of the morning. Perhaps now there are whispers at the end of the corridor, three heavy men in black taking off their shoes, one of them holding the ring of keys, all of the prison silent, waiting, charged with dread. Three tiers down, the activity on the stone floor has become silent, is suspended, someone lights a cigarette. Will he die alone? I do not know if death, in this country, is a solitary or a mass-produced affair. And what will he say to the priest?

Take off your clothes, something tells me, *it's getting late.*

I walk into the bedroom where the clothes I will wear are lying on the bed and my bag lies open and ready. I begin to undress. There is a mirror in this room, a large mirror. I am terribly aware of the mirror.

Giovanni's face swings before me like an unexpected lantern on a dark, dark night. His eyes—his eyes, they glow like a tiger's eyes, they stare straight out, watching the approach of his last enemy, the hair of his flesh stands up. I cannot read what is in his eyes: if it is terror, then I have never seen terror, if it is anguish, then anguish has never laid hands on me. Now they approach, now the key turns in the lock, now they have him. He cries out once. They look at him from far away. They pull him to the door of his cell, the corridor stretches before him like the graveyard of his past, the prison spins around him. Perhaps he begins to moan, perhaps he makes no sound. The journey begins. Or, perhaps, when he cries out, he does not stop crying; perhaps his voice is crying now, in all that stone and iron. I see his legs buckle, his thighs jelly, the buttocks quiver, the secret hammer there begins to knock. He is sweating, or he is dry. They drag him, or he walks. Their grip is terrible, his arms are not his own anymore.

Down that long corridor, down those metal stairs, into the heart of the prison and out of it, into the office of the priest. He kneels. A candle burns, the Virgin watches him.

Mary, blessed mother of God.

My own hands are clammy, my body is dull and white and dry. I see it in the mirror, out of the corner of my eye.

Mary, blessed mother of God.

He kisses the cross and clings to it. The priest gently lifts the cross away. Then they lift Giovanni. The journey begins. They move off, toward another door. He moans. He wants to spit, but his mouth is dry. He cannot ask that they let him pause for a moment to urinate—all that, in a moment, will take care of itself. He knows that beyond the door which comes so deliberately closer, the knife is waiting. That door is the gateway he has sought so long out of this dirty world, this dirty body.

It's getting late.

The body in the mirror forces me to turn and face it. And I look at my body, which is under sentence of death. It is lean, hard, and cold, the incarnation of a mystery. And I do not know what moves in this body, what this body is searching. It is trapped in my mirror as it is trapped in time and it hurries toward revelation.

When I was a child, I spake as a child, I understood as a child, I thought as a child: but when I became a man, I put away childish things.

I long to make this prophecy come true. I long to crack that mirror and be free. I look at my sex, my troubling sex, and wonder how it can be redeemed, how I can save it from the knife. The journey to the grave is already begun, the journey to corruption is, always, already, half over. Yet, the key to my salvation, which cannot save my body, is hidden in my flesh.

Then the door is before him. There is darkness all around him, there is silence in him. Then the door opens and he stands alone, the whole world falling away from him. And the brief corner of the sky seems to be shrieking, though he does not hear a sound. Then the earth tilts, he is thrown forward on his face in darkness, and his journey begins.

I move at last from the mirror and begin to cover that nakedness which I must hold sacred, though it be never so vile, which must be scoured perpetually with the salt of my life. I must believe, I must believe, that the heavy grace of God, which has brought me to this place, is all that can carry me out of it.

And at last I step out into the morning and I lock the door behind me. I cross the road and drop the keys into the old lady's mailbox. And I look up the road, where a few people stand, men and women, waiting for the morning bus. They are very vivid beneath the awakening sky, and the horizon beyond them is beginning to flame. The morning weighs on my shoulders with the dreadful weight of hope and I take the blue envelope which Jacques has sent me and tear it slowly into many pieces, watching them dance in the wind, watching the wind carry them away. Yet, as I turn and begin walking toward the waiting people, the wind blows some of them back on me.

IF BEALE STREET COULD TALK

Told through the eyes of Tish, a nineteen-year-old girl in love with Fonny, a young sculptor who is the father of her child, Baldwin's story mixes the sweet and the sad. Tish and Fonny have pledged to get married, but Fonny is falsely accused of a terrible crime and imprisoned. Their families set out to clear his name, and as they face an uncertain future, the young lovers experience a kaleidoscope of emotions—affection, despair, and hope. In a love story that evokes the blues, where passion and sadness are inevitably intertwined, Baldwin has created two characters so alive and profoundly realized that they are unforgettably ingrained in the American psyche.

Fiction

Praise for

James Baldwin

"He is thought-provoking, tantalizing, irritating, abusing, and amusing. And he uses words as the sea uses waves, to flow and beat, advance and retreat, rise and take a bow in disappearing . . . the thought becomes poetry and the poetry illuminates thought."
—Langston Hughes

"Baldwin's gift to our literary tradition is that rarest of treasures, a rhetoric of fiction and the essay that is, at once, Henry Jamesian and King Jamesian."   —Henry Louis Gates, Jr.

"This author retains a place in an extremely select group; that composed of the few genuinely indispensable American writers."
—*Saturday Review*

"Moralistic fervor, a high literary seriousness, the authority of the survivor, of the witness—these qualities made Baldwin unique."
—*The New York Review of Books*

"If Van Gogh was our nineteenth-century artist-saint, James Baldwin is our twentieth-century one."   —Michael Ondaatje

"Baldwin refused to hold anyone's hand. He was both direct and beautiful all at once. He did not seem to write to convince you. He wrote beyond you."   —Ta-Nehisi Coates

"What style! What intensity! What religious feeling! . . . He's a marvel!"   —John Cheever

JAMES BALDWIN

Go Tell It on the Mountain

James Baldwin was born in 1924 and educated in New York. He is the author of more than twenty works of fiction and nonfiction, including *Go Tell It on the Mountain*; *Notes of a Native Son*; *Giovanni's Room*; *Nobody Knows My Name*; *Another Country*; *The Fire Next Time*; *Nothing Personal*; *Blues for Mister Charlie*; *Going to Meet the Man*; *The Amen Corner*; *Tell Me How Long the Train's Been Gone*; *One Day When I Was Lost*; *No Name in the Street*; *The Devil Finds Work*; *Little Man, Little Man*; *Just Above My Head*; *The Evidence of Things Not Seen*; *Jimmy's Blues*; and *The Price of the Ticket*. Among the awards he received are a Eugene F. Saxon Memorial Trust Award, a Rosenwald Fellowship, a Guggenheim Fellowship, a *Partisan Review* Fellowship, and a Ford Foundation grant. He was made a Commander of the Legion of Honor in 1986. He died in 1987.

INTERNATIONAL

Books by
JAMES BALDWIN

NOTES OF A NATIVE SON

GIOVANNI'S ROOM

NOBODY KNOWS MY NAME

ANOTHER COUNTRY

THE FIRE NEXT TIME

NOTHING PERSONAL

BLUES FOR MISTER CHARLIE

GOING TO MEET THE MAN

THE AMEN CORNER

TELL ME HOW LONG THE TRAIN'S BEEN GONE

ONE DAY WHEN I WAS LOST

NO NAME IN THE STREET

IF BEALE STREET COULD TALK

THE DEVIL FINDS WORK

LITTLE MAN, LITTLE MAN

JUST ABOVE MY HEAD

THE EVIDENCE OF THINGS NOT SEEN

JIMMY'S BLUES AND OTHER POEMS

THE CROSS OF REDEMPTION

Go Tell It
on the
Mountain

JAMES BALDWIN

Go Tell It

on the

Mountain

A NOVEL

Introduction by
ROXANE GAY

VINTAGE INTERNATIONAL
Vintage Books
A Division of Penguin Random House LLC
New York

FIRST VINTAGE INTERNATIONAL DELUXE EDITION 2024

Copyright © 1952, 1953 by James Baldwin
Copyright renewed 1980, 1981 by James Baldwin
Introduction copyright © 2024 by Roxane Gay

All rights reserved. Published in the United States by Vintage Books,
a division of Penguin Random House LLC, New York, and distributed
in Canada by Penguin Random House Canada Limited, Toronto.
Originally published in hardcover in slightly different form
in the United States by Alfred A. Knopf, a division of
Penguin Random House LLC, New York, in 1953.

Vintage is a registered trademark and Vintage International
and colophon are trademarks of Penguin Random House LLC.

This is a work of fiction. Names, characters, places, and incidents either
are the product of the author's imagination or are used fictitiously. Any resemblance
to actual persons, living or dead, events, or locales is entirely coincidental.

Cataloging-in-Publication Data is on file at the Library of Congress.

Vintage International Deluxe Edition ISBN: 978-0-593-68897-7
Vintage International Trade Paperback ISBN: 978-0-375-70187-0
eBook ISBN: 978-0-345-80655-0

vintagebooks.com

Printed in the United States of America
10 9 8 7 6 5 4 3 2 1

For my Mother and Father

Contents

There are three ways of reading James Baldwin's exceptional debut novel, *Go Tell It on the Mountain*. In one reading, this novel is a parable. The young man at the heart of this novel, John Grimes, is trying to make sense of his place in the world, in the storefront church his family attends, and even in his own family. The narrative details a day in John's life, on his fourteenth birthday. His is a somewhat grim life, but he carries the faith and optimism of youth, the belief that better things await despite so much evidence to the contrary. And this optimism is a feeling he has long held, since a teacher praised him for his intellectual gifts when he was five years old. "That moment gave him, from that time on, if not a weapon at least a shield; he apprehended totally, without belief or understanding, that he had in himself a power that other people lacked; that he could use this to save himself, to raise himself; and that, perhaps, with this power he might one day win that love which he so longed for." These are prescient words because by the end of the novel, John will need to do all these things—save himself, raise himself, and even love himself.

Over the course of that long day, we witness John's hopes and yearnings (a birthday present from his mother, an acknowledgment of his special day, the love of his father, salvation), and how elusive those hopes are, despite his best efforts. And still, he persists. He carries his hope as a shield because there is no safe harbor in John's life. Whether it is the cruel indifference and heavy fists of his father, or the cruel indifference and heavy fists of police treating him more as menace than young man, the angst and guilt he feels for his fleshly desires or his despair at not finding rapture in church, he is in a constant state of vulnerability. That's what makes his story so compelling. He wears such tender flesh while moving through a harsh world that refuses to grant him shelter.

This is also the story of the adults in John's life—his mother, Elizabeth, his stepfather Gabriel, Gabriel's sister Florence, and Gabriel's first wife, Deborah. In a series of flashbacks, we learn who each of these people were before and how they arrived to the present. They are all part of the Great Migration, generations of Black people moving from the South to the North over six decades, in the hopes of securing better futures for themselves and their families. What befalls them in the North, however, certainly complicates the notion of what better looks like. In *The Warmth of Other Suns*, Isabelle Wilkerson writes of those who made the decision to leave, "They were all stuck in a caste system as hard and unyielding as the red Georgia clay, and they each had a decision before them." For John, Elizabeth, Florence, and Gabriel in particular, in making the difficult decision to leave everything they've ever known, they move from one caste system to another.

The fulcrum of this story is Gabriel, his mother's favorite, a young man who finds all kinds of trouble before and after he is saved. He is a preacher, threatening hell and damnation to anyone who will listen. He exists in a state of perpetual judgment, disapproving of everyone and everything that doesn't suit him or his inconsistent sensibilities. He is a sinner who believes he has been forgiven for his sins without applying that same standard of forgiveness to others, which is to say he is a holy hypocrite. And thus, the parable—not everyone who is saved is sanctified.

Read another way, this is a novel about women with dreams and desires deferred, women whose lives and happiness are contingent upon the whims and moods of the men in their lives, women who are forced to sacrifice so much of themselves while receiving little in return. They are held to impossible standards, are asked to satisfy impossible expectations. When a woman dares to live life on her own terms, a high price is exacted. Take Esther, a young woman who becomes Gabriel's mistress. Their affair sets in motion the series of events that lead to her death. Esther becomes one of many examples in the novel of people who love Gabriel paying the highest of prices for his often cruel, always self-serving choices.

The men in this novel are desperately seeking salvation. They want absolution for their mortal sins, for the masculine desires they are unable or unwilling to suppress. They act without thinking, and rarely consider the consequences of their actions. They take and take and offer nothing in return. They hold the women in their lives in low regard while holding themselves in the highest esteem. They are, largely, infuriating and infuriatingly lacking self-awareness.

There are similarities between John Grimes's life and the one lived by James Baldwin. Both John and James were raised in the church, raised by brutal and indifferent fathers. They both experienced the hardships of poverty and the precarity of Black masculinity. They both harbored desires for men, desires they knew they could not express or act on for fear of ostracization, or worse. And they both, for a time, were young men of profound faith who had to shield themselves when no one else would.

In the third and final part of the novel, "The Threshing Floor,"

John and his family have been in their church for hours praying and singing. John realizes he is on the floor, in the middle of a spiritual battle. Eventually, he emerges, having found salvation; he gives himself over to Christ and hopes that finally, he will earn Gabriel's approval. But nothing John can do will ever be good enough for his stepfather. Perhaps Gabriel knows, on some level, that he is a false prophet, knows that he has never practiced what he preaches, and assumes the same is true of John. Perhaps this is but further evidence of how irredeemable Gabriel actually is. And so, the family makes their way home after a long, exhausting night of worship. John is buoyed by his newfound faith, despite Gabriel's skepticism. He continues to have hope, to believe in the potential of his future, to be his own shield.

In his essay "Everybody's Protest Novel," Baldwin incisively critiques Harriet Beecher Stowe's *Uncle Tom's Cabin* and Richard Wright's *Native Son*. In doing so, Baldwin illuminates his issues with the genre more broadly. All too often, he notes, the importance of the issues a protest novel addresses becomes a convenient excuse for aesthetic flaws. "They are forgiven, on the strength of these good intentions, whatever violence they do to language, whatever excessive demands they make of credibility," Baldwin writes. He uses the term "protest novel" derisively because, to his mind, such novels are often "badly written and wildly improbable." They reflect the biases and condescension of their authors and reinforce the very prejudices they are meant to combat. A true protest novel, then, should defy the traditional conventions of the protest novels Baldwin writes of with such disdain. Instead of reinforcing stereotypes and making facile arguments, they should be nuanced, offering original insights into the human condition. They should make readers uncomfortable. They should resist categorization. They should not offer easy or tidy conclusions. They should reflect the complexity of the real world we live in rather than the convenient simplicities of fictional worlds where there is no need for nuance.

And so, read a third way, *Go Tell It on the Mountain* is a protest novel as a protest novel should be. It embodies what a protest novel can be at its very best. Ostensibly, readers might understand this as a story of a young man on a harrowing spiritual quest, but if this novel is read as a true protest novel, *Go Tell It on the Mountain* is a repudiation of hypocrisy and double standards and false prophets and those who wield faith as a weapon rather than a shield.

ROXANE GAY

2024

Roxane Gay is a writer. Her most recent book is *Opinions: A Decade of Arguments, Criticism, and Minding Other People's Business.*

Go Tell It
on the
Mountain

PART ONE

The Seventh Day

And the Spirit and the bride say, Come.
And let him that heareth say, Come.
And let him that is athirst come.
And whosoever will, let him take the water of life freely.

I looked down the line,
And I wondered.

Everyone had always said that John would be a preacher when
he grew up, just like his father. It had been said so often that John,
without ever thinking about it, had come to believe it himself. Not
until the morning of his fourteenth birthday did he really begin to
think about it, and by then it was already too late.

His earliest memories—which were in a way, his only memories—were of the hurry and brightness of Sunday mornings. They all
rose together on that day; his father, who did not have to go to work,
and led them in prayer before breakfast; his mother, who dressed up
on that day, and looked almost young, with her hair straightened,
and on her head the close-fitting white cap that was the uniform of
holy women; his younger brother, Roy, who was silent that day because his father was home. Sarah, who wore a red ribbon in her hair

that day, and was fondled by her father. And the baby, Ruth, who was dressed in pink and white, and rode in her mother's arms to church.

The church was not very far away, four blocks up Lenox Avenue, on a corner not far from the hospital. It was to this hospital that his mother had gone when Roy, and Sarah, and Ruth were born. John did not remember very clearly the first time she had gone, to have Roy; folks said that he had cried and carried on the whole time his mother was away; he remembered only enough to be afraid every time her belly began to swell, knowing that each time the swelling began it would not end until she was taken from him, to come back with a stranger. Each time this happened she became a little more of a stranger herself. She would soon be going away again, Roy said—he knew much more about such things than John. John had observed his mother closely, seeing no swelling yet, but his father had prayed one morning for the "little voyager soon to be among them," and so John knew that Roy spoke the truth.

Every Sunday morning, then, since John could remember, they had taken to the streets, the Grimes family on their way to church. Sinners along the avenue watched them—men still wearing their Saturday-night clothes, wrinkled and dusty now, muddy-eyed and muddy-faced; and women with harsh voices and tight, bright dresses, cigarettes between their fingers or held tightly in the corners of their mouths. They talked, and laughed, and fought together, and the women fought like the men. John and Roy, passing these men and women, looked at one another briefly, John embarrassed and Roy amused. Roy would be like them when he grew up, if the Lord did not change his heart. These men and women they passed on Sunday mornings had spent the night in bars, or in cat houses, or on the streets, or on rooftops, or under the stairs. They had been drinking. They had gone from cursing to laughter, to anger, to lust. Once he and Roy had watched a man and woman in the basement of a condemned house. They did it standing up. The woman had wanted fifty cents, and the man had flashed a razor.

John had never watched again; he had been afraid. But Roy had watched them many times, and he told John he had done it with some girls down the block.

And his mother and father, who went to church on Sundays, they did it too, and sometimes John heard them in the bedroom behind him, over the sound of rats' feet, and rat screams, and the music and cursing from the harlot's house downstairs.

Their church was called the Temple of the Fire Baptized. It was not the biggest church in Harlem, nor yet the smallest, but John had been brought up to believe it was the holiest and best. His father was head deacon in this church—there were only two, the other a round, black man named Deacon Braithwaite—and he took up the collection, and sometimes he preached. The pastor, Father James, was a genial, well-fed man with a face like a darker moon. It was he who preached on Pentecost Sundays, and led revivals in the summertime, and anointed and healed the sick.

On Sunday mornings and Sunday nights the church was always full; on special Sundays it was full all day. The Grimes family arrived in a body, always a little late, usually in the middle of Sunday school, which began at nine o'clock. This lateness was always their mother's fault—at least in the eyes of their father; she could not seem to get herself and the children ready on time, ever, and sometimes she actually remained behind, not to appear until the morning service. When they all arrived together, they separated upon entering the doors, father and mother going to sit in the Adult Class, which was taught by Sister McCandless, Sarah going to the Infant's Class, John and Roy sitting in the Intermediate, which was taught by Brother Elisha.

When he was young, John had paid no attention in Sunday school, and always forgot the golden text, which earned him the wrath of his father. Around the time of his fourteenth birthday, with all the pressures of church and home uniting to drive him to the altar, he strove to appear more serious and therefore less conspicuous. But he was distracted by his new teacher, Elisha, who was the pastor's nephew and who had but lately arrived from Georgia. He was not much older than John, only seventeen, and he was already saved and was a preacher. John stared at Elisha all during the lesson, admiring the timbre of Elisha's voice, much deeper and manlier than his own, admiring the leanness, and grace, and strength, and darkness of Elisha in his Sunday suit, wondering if he would ever be holy as Elisha was holy. But he did not follow the lesson, and when, sometimes, Elisha paused to ask John a question, John was ashamed and confused, feeling the palms of his hands become wet and his heart pound like a hammer. Elisha would smile and reprimand him gently, and the lesson would go on.

Roy never knew his Sunday school lesson either, but it was different with Roy—no one really expected of Roy what was expected of John. Everyone was always praying that the Lord would change Roy's heart, but it was John who was expected to be good, to be a good example.

When Sunday school service ended there was a short pause before morning service began. In this pause, if it was good weather, the old folks might step outside a moment to talk among themselves. The sisters would almost always be dressed in white from crown to toe. The small children, on this day, in this place, and oppressed by their elders, tried hard to play without seeming to be disrespectful of God's house. But sometimes, nervous or perverse, they shouted, or threw hymn-books, or began to cry, putting their parents, men or women of God, under the necessity of proving—by harsh means or tender—who, in a sanctified household, ruled. The older children, like John or Roy, might wander down the avenue, but not too far. Their father never let John and Roy out of his sight, for Roy had often disappeared between Sunday school and morning service and had not come back all day.

The Sunday morning service began when Brother Elisha sat down at the piano and raised a song. This moment and this music had been with John, so it seemed, since he had first drawn breath. It seemed that there had never been a time when he had not known this moment of waiting while the packed church paused—the sisters in white, heads raised, the brothers in blue, heads back; the white caps of the women seeming to glow in the charged air like crowns, the kinky, gleaming heads of the men seeming to be lifted up—and the rustling and the whispering ceased and the children were quiet; perhaps someone coughed, or the sound of a car horn, or a curse from the streets came in; then Elisha hit the keys, beginning at once to sing, and everybody joined him, clapping their hands, and rising, and beating the tambourines.

The song might be: *Down at the cross where my Saviour died!*

Or: *Jesus, I'll never forget how you set me free!*

Or: *Lord, hold my hand while I run this race!*

They sang with all the strength that was in them, and clapped their hands for joy. There had never been a time when John had not sat watching the saints rejoice with terror in his heart, and wonder. Their singing caused him to believe in the presence of the Lord; indeed, it was no longer a question of belief, because they made that presence real. He did not feel it himself, the joy they felt, yet he could not doubt that it was, for them, the very bread of life—could not doubt it, that is, until it was too late to doubt. Something happened to their faces and their voices, the rhythm of their bodies, and to the air they breathed; it was as though wherever they might be became the upper room, and the Holy Ghost were riding on the air. His father's face, always awful, became more awful now; his father's daily anger was transformed into prophetic wrath. His mother, her eyes raised to heaven, hands arced before her, moving, made real for John that patience, that endurance, that long suffering, which he had read of in the Bible and found so hard to imagine.

On Sunday mornings the women all seemed patient, all the men seemed mighty. While John watched, the Power struck someone, a man or woman; they cried out, a long, wordless crying, and, arms outstretched like wings, they began the Shout. Someone moved a chair a little to give them room, the rhythm paused, the singing stopped, only the pounding feet and the clapping hands were heard;

then another cry, another dancer; then the tambourines began again, and the voices rose again, and the music swept on again, like fire, or flood, or judgment. Then the church seemed to swell with the Power it held, and, like a planet rocking in space, the temple rocked with the Power of God. John watched, watched the faces, and the weightless bodies, and listened to the timeless cries. One day, so everyone said, this Power would possess him; he would sing and cry as they did now, and dance before his King. He watched young Ella Mae Washington, the seventeen-year-old granddaughter of Praying Mother Washington, as she began to dance. And then Elisha danced.

At one moment, head thrown back, eyes closed, sweat standing on his brow, he sat at the piano, singing and playing; and then, like a great, black cat in trouble in the jungle, he stiffened and trembled, and cried out. *Jesus, Jesus, oh Lord Jesus!* He struck on the piano one last, wild note, and threw up his hands, palms upward, stretched wide apart. The tambourines raced to fill the vacuum left by his silent piano, and his cry drew answering cries. Then he was on his feet, turning, blind, his face congested, contorted with this rage, and the muscles leaping and swelling in his long, dark neck. It seemed that he could not breathe, that his body could not contain this passion, that he would be, before their eyes, dispersed into the waiting air. His hands, rigid to the very fingertips, moved outward and back against his hips, his sightless eyes looked upward, and he began to dance. Then his hands closed into fists, and his head snapped downward, his sweat loosening the grease that slicked down his hair; and the rhythm of all the others quickened to match Elisha's rhythm; his thighs moved terribly against the cloth of his suit, his heels beat on the floor, and his fists moved beside his body as though he were beating his own drum. And so, for a while, in the center of the dancers, head down, fists beating, on, on, unbearably, until it seemed the walls of the church would fall for very sound; and then, in a moment, with a cry, head up, arms high in the air, sweat pouring from his forehead, and all his body dancing as though it would never stop. Sometimes he did not stop until he fell—until he dropped like some animal felled by a hammer—moaning, on his face. And then a great moaning filled the church.

There was sin among them. One Sunday, when regular service was over, Father James had uncovered sin in the congregation of the righteous. He had uncovered Elisha and Ella Mae. They had been "walking disorderly"; they were in danger of straying from the truth. And as Father James spoke of the sin that he knew they had not committed yet, of the unripe fig plucked too early from the tree—to set the children's teeth on edge—John felt himself grow dizzy in his seat and could not look at Elisha where he stood, beside Ella Mae, before the altar. Elisha hung his head as Father James spoke, and the congregation murmured. And Ella Mae was not so beautiful now as she was when she was singing and testifying, but looked like a sullen, ordinary girl. Her full lips were loose and her eyes were black—with shame, or rage, or both. Her grandmother, who had raised her, sat watching quietly, with folded hands. She was one of the pillars of the church, a powerful evangelist and very widely known. She said nothing in Ella Mae's defense, for she must have felt, as the congregation felt, that Father James was only exercising his clear and painful duty; he was responsible, after all, for Elisha, as Praying Mother Washington was responsible for Ella Mae. It was not an easy thing, said Father James, to be the pastor of a flock. It might look easy to just sit up there in the pulpit night after night, year in, year out, but let them remember the awful responsibility placed on his shoulders by almighty God—let them remember that God would ask an accounting of him one day for every soul in his flock. Let them remember this when they thought he was hard, let them remember that the Word was hard, that the way of holiness was a hard way. There was no room in God's army for the coward heart, no crown awaiting him who put mother, or father, sister, or brother, sweetheart, or friend above God's will. Let the church cry amen to this! And they cried: "Amen! Amen!"

The Lord had led him, said Father James, looking down on the boy and girl before him, to give them a public warning before it was too late. For he knew them to be sincere young people, dedicated to the service of the Lord—it was only that, since they were young, they did not know the pitfalls Satan laid for the unwary. He knew that sin was not in their minds—not yet; yet sin was in the flesh; and should they continue with their walking out alone together, their secrets and laughter, and touching of hands, they would surely sin a sin beyond all forgiveness. And John wondered what Elisha was thinking—Elisha, who was tall and handsome, who played basketball, and who had been saved at the age of eleven in the improbable fields down south. *Had* he sinned? Had he been tempted? And the girl beside him, whose white robes now seemed the merest, thinnest covering for the nakedness of breasts and insistent thighs—what was her face like when she was alone with Elisha, with no singing, when they were not surrounded by the saints? He was afraid to think of it, yet he could think of nothing else; and the fever of which they stood accused began also to rage in him.

After this Sunday Elisha and Ella Mae no longer met each other each day after school, no longer spent Saturday afternoons wandering through Central Park, or lying on the beach. All that was over for them. If they came together again it would be in wedlock. They would have children and raise them in the church.

This was what was meant by a holy life, this was what the way of the cross demanded. It was somehow on that Sunday, a Sunday shortly before his birthday, that John first realized that this was the life awaiting him—realized it consciously, as something no longer far off, but imminent, coming closer day by day.

John's birthday fell on a Saturday in March, in 1935. He awoke on this birthday morning with the feeling that there was menace in the air around him—that something irrevocable had occurred in him. He stared at a yellow stain on the ceiling just above his head. Roy was still smothered in the bedclothes, and his breath came and went with a small, whistling sound. There was no other sound anywhere; no one in the house was up. The neighbors' radios were all silent, and his mother hadn't yet risen to fix his father's breakfast. John wondered at his panic, then wondered about the time; and then (while the yellow stain on the ceiling slowly transformed itself into a woman's nakedness) he remembered that it was his fourteenth birthday and that he had sinned.

His first thought, nevertheless, was: "Will anyone remember?" For it had happened, once or twice, that his birthday had passed entirely unnoticed, and no one had said "Happy Birthday, Johnny," or given him anything—not even his mother.

Roy stirred again and John pushed him away, listening to the silence. On other mornings he awoke hearing his mother singing in the kitchen, hearing his father in the bedroom behind him grunting and muttering prayers to himself as he put on his clothes; hearing, perhaps, the chatter of Sarah and the squalling of Ruth, and the radios, the clatter of pots and pans, and the voices of all the folk nearby. This morning not even the cry of a bed-spring disturbed the silence, and John seemed, therefore, to be listening to his own unspeaking doom. He could believe, almost, that he had awakened late on that great getting-up morning; that all the saved had been transformed in the twinkling of an eye, and had risen to meet Jesus in the clouds, and that he was left, with his sinful body, to be bound in Hell a thousand years.

He had sinned. In spite of the saints, his mother and his father, the warnings he had heard from his earliest beginnings, he had sinned with his hands a sin that was hard to forgive. In the school lavatory, alone, thinking of the boys, older, bigger, braver, who made bets with each other as to whose urine could arch higher, he had watched in himself a transformation of which he would never dare to speak.

And the darkness of John's sin was like the darkness of the church on Saturday evenings; like the silence of the church while he was there alone, sweeping, and running water into the great bucket, and overturning chairs, long before the saints arrived. It was like his thoughts as he moved about the tabernacle in which his life had been spent; the tabernacle that he hated, yet loved and feared. It was like Roy's curses, like the echoes these curses raised in John: he remembered Roy, on some rare Saturday when he had come to help John clean the church, cursing in the house of God, and making obscene gestures before the eyes of Jesus. It was like all this, and it was like the walls that witnessed and the placards on the walls which testified that the wages of sin was death. The darkness of his sin was in the hardheartedness with which he resisted God's power; in the scorn that was often his while he listened to the crying, breaking voices, and watched the black skin glisten while they lifted up their arms and fell on their faces before the Lord. For he had made his decision. He would not be like his father, or his father's fathers. He would have another life.

For John excelled in school, though not, like Elisha, in mathematics or basketball, and it was said that he had a Great Future. He might become a Great Leader of His People. John was not much interested in his people and still less in leading them anywhere, but the phrase so often repeated rose in his mind like a great brass gate, opening outward for him on a world where people did not live in the darkness of his father's house, did not pray to Jesus in the darkness of his father's church, where he would eat good food, and wear fine clothes, and go to the movies as often as he wished. In this world John, who was, his father said, ugly, who was always the smallest boy in his class, and who had no friends, became immediately beautiful, tall, and popular. People fell all over themselves to meet John Grimes. He was a poet, or a college president, or a movie star; he drank expensive whisky, and he smoked Lucky Strike cigarettes in the green package.

It was not only colored people who praised John, since they could not, John felt, in any case really know; but white people also said it, in fact had said it first and said it still. It was when John was five years old and in the first grade that he was first noticed; and since he was noticed by an eye altogether alien and impersonal, he began to perceive, in wild uneasiness, his individual existence.

They were learning the alphabet that day, and six children at a time were sent to the blackboard to write the letters they had memorized. Six had finished and were waiting for the teacher's judgment when the back door opened and the school principal, of whom everyone was terrified, entered the room. No one spoke or moved. In the silence the principal's voice said:

"Which child is that?"

She was pointing at the blackboard, at John's letters. The possibility of being distinguished by her notice did not enter John's mind, and so he simply stared at her. Then he realized, by the immobility of the other children and by the way they avoided looking at him, that it was he who was selected for punishment.

"Speak up, John," said the teacher, gently.

On the edge of tears, he mumbled his name and waited. The principal, a woman with white hair and an iron face, looked down at him.

"You're a very bright boy, John Grimes," she said. "Keep up the good work."

Then she walked out of the room.

That moment gave him, from that time on, if not a weapon at least a shield; he apprehended totally, without belief or understanding, that he had in himself a power that other people lacked; that he could use this to save himself, to raise himself; and that, perhaps, with this power he might one day win that love which he so longed for. This was not, in John, a faith subject to death or alteration, nor yet a hope subject to destruction; it was his identity, and part, therefore, of that wickedness for which his father beat him and to which he clung in order to withstand his father. His father's arm, rising and falling, might make him cry, and that voice might cause him to tremble; yet his father could never be entirely the victor, for John cherished something that his father could not reach. It was his hatred and his intelligence that he cherished, the one feeding the other. He lived for the day when his father would be dying and he, John, would curse him on his deathbed. And this was why, though he had been born in the faith and had been surrounded all his life by the saints and by their prayers and their rejoicing, and though the tabernacle in which they worshipped was more completely real to him than the several precarious homes in which he and his family had lived, John's heart was hardened against the Lord. His father was God's minister, the ambassador of the King of Heaven, and John could not bow before the throne of grace without first kneeling to his father. On his refusal to do this had his life depended, and John's secret heart had flourished in its wickedness until the day his sin first overtook him.

In the midst of all his wonderings he fell asleep again, and when he woke up this time and got out of his bed his father had gone to the factory, where he would work for half a day. Roy was sitting in the kitchen, quarreling with their mother. The baby, Ruth, sat in her high chair banging on the tray with an oatmeal-covered spoon. This meant that she was in a good mood; she would not spend the day howling, for reasons known only to herself, allowing no one but her mother to touch her. Sarah was quiet, not chattering today, or at any rate not yet, and stood near the stove, arms folded, staring at Roy with the flat black eyes, her father's eyes, that made her look so old.

Their mother, her head tied up in an old rag, sipped black coffee and watched Roy. The pale end-of-winter sunlight filled the room and yellowed all their faces; and John, drugged and morbid and wondering how it was that he had slept again and had been allowed to sleep so long, saw them for a moment like figures on a screen, an effect that the yellow light intensified. The room was narrow and dirty; nothing could alter its dimensions, no labor could ever make it clean. Dirt was in the walls and the floorboards, and triumphed beneath the sink where roaches spawned; was in the fine ridges of the pots and pans, scoured daily, burnt black on the bottom, hanging above the stove; was in the wall against which they hung, and revealed itself where the paint had cracked and leaned outward in stiff squares and fragments, the paper-thin underside webbed with black.

Dirt was in every corner, angle, crevice of the monstrous stove, and lived behind it in delirious communion with the corrupted wall. Dirt was in the baseboard that John scrubbed every Saturday, and roughened the cupboard shelves that held the cracked and gleaming dishes. Under this dark weight the walls leaned, under it the ceiling, with a great crack like lightning in its center, sagged. The windows gleamed like beaten gold or silver, but now John saw, in the yellow light, how fine dust veiled their doubtful glory. Dirt crawled in the gray mop hung out of the windows to dry. John thought with shame and horror, yet in angry hardness of heart: *He who is filthy, let him be filthy still.* Then he looked at his mother, seeing, as though she were someone else, the dark, hard lines running downward from her eyes, and the deep, perpetual scowl in her forehead, and the downturned, tightened mouth, and the strong, thin, brown, and bony hands; and the phrase turned against him like a two-edged sword, for was it not he, in his false pride and his evil imagination, who was filthy? Through a storm of tears that did not reach his eyes, he stared at the yellow room; and the room shifted, the light of the sun darkened, and his mother's face changed. Her face became the face that he gave her in his dreams, the face that had been hers in a photograph he had seen once, long ago, a photograph taken before he was born. This face was young and proud, uplifted, with a smile that made the wide mouth beautiful and glowed in the enormous eyes. It was the face of a girl who knew that no evil could undo her, and who could laugh, surely, as his mother did not laugh now. Between the two faces there stretched a darkness and a mystery that John feared, and that some-times caused him to hate her.

Now she saw him and she asked, breaking off her conversation with Roy: "You hungry, little sleepyhead?"

"Well! About time you was getting up," said Sarah.

He moved to the table and sat down, feeling the most bewilder-ing panic of his life, a need to touch things, the table and chairs and the walls of the room, to make certain that the room existed and that he was in the room. He did not look at his mother, who stood up and went to the stove to heat his breakfast. But he asked, in order to say something to her, and to hear his own voice:

"What we got for breakfast?"

He realized, with some shame, that he was hoping she had prepared a special breakfast for him on his birthday.

"What you *think* we got for breakfast?" Roy asked scornfully. "You got a special craving for something?"

John looked at him. Roy was not in a good mood.

"I ain't said nothing to you," he said.

"Oh, I *beg* your pardon," said Roy, in the shrill, little-girl tone he knew John hated.

"What's the *matter* with you today?" John asked, angry, and trying at the same time to lend his voice as husky a pitch as possible.

"Don't you let Roy bother you," said their mother. "He cross as two sticks this morning."

"Yeah," said John, "I reckon." He and Roy watched each other. Then his plate was put before him: hominy grits and a scrap of bacon. He wanted to cry, like a child: "But, Mama, it's my birthday!" He kept his eyes on his plate and began to eat.

"You can *talk* about your daddy all you want to," said his mother, picking up her battle with Roy, "but *one* thing you can't say—you can't say he ain't always done his best to be a father to you and to see to it that you ain't never gone hungry."

"I been hungry plenty of times," Roy said, proud to be able to score this point against his mother.

"Wasn't *his* fault, then. Wasn't because he wasn't *trying* to feed you. That man shoveled snow in zero weather when he ought've been in bed just to put food in your belly."

"Wasn't just *my* belly," said Roy indignantly. "He got a belly, too, I *know* it's a *shame* the way that man eats. I sure ain't asked him to shovel no snow for me." But he dropped his eyes, suspecting a flaw in his argument. "I just don't want him beating on me all the time," he said at last. "I ain't no dog."

She sighed, and turned slightly away, looking out of the window. "Your daddy beats you," she said, "because he loves you."

Roy laughed. "That ain't the kind of love I understand, old lady. What you reckon he'd do if he didn't love me?"

"He'd let you go right on," she flashed, "right on down to hell where it looks like you is just determined to go anyhow! Right on, Mister Man, till somebody puts a knife in you, or takes you off to jail!"

"Mama," John asked suddenly, "is Daddy a good man?"

He had not known that he was going to ask the question, and he watched in astonishment as her mouth tightened and her eyes grew dark.

"That ain't no kind of question," she said mildly. "You don't know no better man, do you?"

"Looks to me like he's a mighty good man," said Sarah. "He sure is praying all the time."

"You children is young," their mother said, ignoring Sarah and sitting down again at the table, "and you don't know how lucky you is to have a father what worries about you and tries to see to it that you come up right."

"Yeah," said Roy, "we don't know how lucky we *is* to have a father what don't want you to go to movies, and don't want you to play in the streets, and don't want you to have no friends, and he don't want this and he don't want that, and he don't want you to do *nothing*. We so *lucky* to have a father who just wants us to go to church and read the Bible and beller like a fool in front of the altar and stay home all nice and quiet, like a little mouse. Boy, we sure is lucky, all right. Don't know what I done to be so lucky."

She laughed. "You going to find out one day," she said, "you mark my words."

"Yeah," said Roy.

"But it'll be too late, then," she said. "It'll be too late when you come to be . . . sorry." Her voice had changed. For a moment her eyes met John's eyes, and John was frightened. He felt that her words, after the strange fashion God sometimes chose to speak to men, were dictated by Heaven and were meant for him. He was fourteen—was it too late? And this uneasiness was reinforced by the impression, which at that moment he realized had been his all along, that his mother was not saying everything she meant. What, he wondered, did she say to Aunt Florence when they talked together? Or to his father? What were her thoughts? Her face would never tell. And yet, looking down at him in a moment that was like a secret, passing sign, her face did tell him. Her thoughts were bitter.

"I don't care," Roy said, rising. "When *I* have children I ain't going to treat them like this." John watched his mother; she watched Roy. "I'm *sure* this ain't no way to be. Ain't got no right to have a houseful of children if you don't know how to treat them."

"You mighty grown up this morning," his mother said. "You be careful."

"And tell me something else," Roy said, suddenly leaning over his mother, "tell me how come he don't never let me talk to him like I talk to you? He's my father, ain't he? But he don't never listen to me—no, I all the time got to listen to him."

"Your father," she said, watching him, "knows best. You listen to your father, I guarantee you, you won't end up in no jail."

Roy sucked his teeth in fury. "I ain't looking to go to no *jail.* You think that's all that's in the world is jails and churches? You ought to know better than that, Ma."

"I know," she said, "there ain't no safety except you walk humble before the Lord. You going to find it out, too, one day. You go on, hardhead. You going to come to grief."

And suddenly Roy grinned. "But you be there, won't you, Ma—when I'm in trouble?"

"You don't know," she said, trying not to smile, "how long the Lord's going to let me stay with you."

Roy turned and did a dance step. "That's all right," he said. "I know the Lord ain't as hard as Daddy. Is he, boy?" he demanded of John, and struck him lightly on the forehead.

"Boy, let me eat my breakfast," John muttered—though his plate had long been empty, and he was pleased that Roy had turned to him.

"That sure is a crazy boy," ventured Sarah, soberly.

"Just listen," cried Roy, "to the little saint! Daddy ain't never going to have no trouble with her—*that* one, she was born holy. I bet the first words she ever said was: 'Thank you, Jesus.' Ain't that so, Ma?"

"You stop this foolishness," she said, laughing, "and go on about your work. Can't nobody play the fool with you all morning."

"Oh, is you got work for me to do this morning? Well, I declare," said Roy, "what you got for me to do?"

"I got the woodwork in the dining-room for you to do. And you going to do it, too, before you set foot out of *this* house."

"Now, why you want to talk like that, Ma? Is I said I wouldn't do it? You know I'm a right good worker when I got a mind. After I do it, can I go?"

"You go ahead and do it, and we'll see. You better do it right."

"I *always* do it right," said Roy. "You won't know your old woodwork when *I* get through."

"John," said his mother, "you sweep the front room for me like a good boy, and dust the furniture. I'm going to clean up in here."

"Yes'm," he said, and rose. She *had* forgotten about his birthday. He swore he would not mention it. He would not think about it any more.

To sweep the front room meant, principally, to sweep the heavy red and green and purple Oriental-style carpet that had once been that room's glory, but was now so faded that it was all one swimming color, and so frayed in places that it tangled with the broom. John hated sweeping this carpet, for dust rose, clogging his nose and sticking to his sweaty skin, and he felt that should he sweep it forever, the clouds of dust would not diminish, the rug would not be clean. It became in his imagination his impossible, lifelong task, his hard trial, like that of a man he had read about somewhere, whose curse it was to push a boulder up a steep hill, only to have the giant who guarded the hill roll the boulder down again—and so on, forever, throughout eternity; he was still out there, that hapless man, somewhere at the other end of the earth, pushing his boulder up the hill. He had John's entire sympathy, for the longest and hardest part of his Saturday mornings was his voyage with the broom across this endless rug; and, coming to the French doors that ended the living-room and stopped the rug, he felt like an indescribably weary traveler who sees his home at last. Yet for each dustpan he so laboriously filled at the doorsill demons added to the rug twenty more; he saw in the expanse behind him the dust that he had raised settling again into the carpet; and he gritted his teeth, already on edge because of the dust that filled his mouth, and nearly wept to think that so much labor brought so little reward.

Nor was this the end of John's labor; for, having put away the broom and the dustpan, he took from the small bucket under the sink the dustrag and the furniture oil and a damp cloth, and returned to the living-room to excavate, as it were, from the dust that threatened to bury them, his family's goods and gear. Thinking bitterly of his birthday, he attacked the mirror with the cloth, watching his face appear as out of a cloud. With a shock he saw that his face had not changed, that the hand of Satan was as yet invisible. His father had always said that his face was the face of Satan—and was there not something—in the lift of the eyebrow, in the way his rough hair formed a V on his brow—that bore witness to his father's words? In the eye there was a light that was not the light of Heaven, and the mouth trembled, lustful and lewd, to drink deep of the wines of Hell. He stared at his face as though it were, as indeed it soon appeared to be, the face of a stranger, a stranger who held secrets that John could never know. And, having thought of it as the face of a stranger, he tried to look at it as a stranger might, and tried to discover what other people saw. But he saw only details: two great eyes, and a broad, low forehead, and the triangle of his nose, and his enormous mouth, and the barely perceptible cleft in his chin, which was, his father said, the mark of the Devil's little finger. These details did not help him, for the principle of their unity was undiscoverable, and he could not tell what he most passionately desired to know: whether his face was ugly or not.

And he dropped his eyes to the mantelpiece, lifting one by one the objects that adorned it. The mantelpiece held, in brave confusion, photographs, greeting cards, flowered mottoes, two silver candlesticks that held no candles, and a green metal serpent, poised to strike. Today in his apathy John stared at them, not seeing; he began to dust them with the exaggerated care of the profoundly preoccupied. One of the mottoes was pink and blue, and proclaimed in raised letters, which made the work of dusting harder:

> *Come in the evening, or come in the morning,*
> *Come when you're looked for, or come without warning,*
> *A thousand welcomes you'll find here before you,*
> *And the oftener you come here, the more we'll adore you.*

And the other, in letters of fire against a background of gold, stated:

> *For God so loved the world, that He gave His only begotten*
> *Son, that whosoever should believe in Him should not per-*
> *ish, but have everlasting life.*
>
> *John iii, 16*

These somewhat unrelated sentiments decorated either side of the mantelpiece, obscured a little by the silver candlesticks. Between these two extremes, the greeting cards, received year after year, on Christmas, or Easter, or birthdays, trumpeted their glad tidings; while the green metal serpent, perpetually malevolent, raised its head proudly in the midst of these trophies, biding the time to strike. Against the mirror, like a procession, the photographs were arranged.

These photographs were the true antiques of the family, which seemed to feel that a photograph should commemorate only the most distant past. The photographs of John and Roy, and of the two girls, which seemed to violate this unspoken law, served only in fact to prove it most iron-hard: they had all been taken in infancy, a time and a condition that the children could not remember. John in his photograph lay naked on a white counterpane, and people laughed and said that it was cunning. But John could never look at it without feeling shame and anger that his nakedness should be here so unkindly revealed. None of the other children was naked; no, Roy lay in his crib in a white gown and grinned toothlessly into the camera, and Sarah, somber at the age of six months, wore a white bonnet, and Ruth was held in her mother's arms. When people looked at these photographs and laughed, their laughter differed from the laughter with which they greeted the naked John. For this reason, when visitors tried to make advances to John he was sullen, and they, feeling that for some reason he disliked them, retaliated by deciding that he was a "funny" child.

Among the other photographs there was one of Aunt Florence, his father's sister, in which her hair, in the old-fashioned way, was worn high and tied with a ribbon; she had been very young when this photograph was taken, and had just come North. Sometimes, when she came to visit, she called the photograph to witness that she had indeed been beautiful in her youth. There was a photograph of his mother, not the one John liked and had seen only once, but one taken immediately after her marriage. And there was a photograph of his father, dressed in black, sitting on a country porch with his hands folded heavily in his lap. The photograph had been taken on a sunny day, and the sunlight brutally exaggerated the planes of his father's face. He stared into the sun, head raised, unbearable, and though it had been taken when he was young, it was not the face of a young man; only something archaic in the dress indicated that this photograph had been taken long ago. At the time this picture was taken, Aunt Florence said, he was already a preacher, and had a wife who was now in Heaven. That he had been a preacher at that time was not astonishing, for it was impossible to imagine that he had ever been anything else; but that he had had a wife in the so distant past who was now dead filled John with a wonder by no means pleasant. If she had lived, John thought, then he would never have been born; his father would never have come North and met his mother. And this shadowy woman, dead so many years, whose name he knew had been Deborah, held in the fastness of her tomb, it seemed to John, the key to all those mysteries he so longed to unlock. It was she who had known his father in a life where John was not, and in a country John had never seen. When he was nothing, nowhere, dust, cloud, air, and sun, and falling rain, *not even thought of,* said his mother, *in Heaven with the angels,* said his aunt, she had known his father, and shared his father's house. She had loved his father. She had known his father when lightning flashed and thunder rolled through Heaven, and his father said: "Listen. God is talking." She had known him in the mornings of that far-off country when his father turned on his bed and opened his eyes, and she had looked into those eyes, seeing what they held, and she had not been afraid. She had seen him baptized, *kicking like a mule and howling,* and she had seen him weep when his mother died; *he was a right young man then,* Florence said. Because she had looked into those eyes before they had looked on John, she knew what John would never know— the purity of his father's eyes when John was not reflected in their depths. She could have told him—had he but been able from his hiding-place to ask!—how to make his father love him. But now it was too late. She would not speak before the judgment day. And among those many voices, and stammering with his own, John would care no longer for her testimony.

When he had finished and the room was ready for Sunday, John felt dusty and weary and sat down beside the window in his father's easy chair. A glacial sun filled the streets, and a high wind filled the air with scraps of paper and frosty dust, and banged the hanging signs of stores and storefront churches. It was the end of winter, and the garbage-filled snow that had been banked along the edges of sidewalks was melting now and filling the gutters. Boys were playing stickball in the damp, cold streets; dressed in heavy woolen sweaters and heavy pants, they danced and shouted, and the ball went *crack!* as the stick struck it and sent it speeding through the air. One of them wore a bright-red stocking cap with a great ball of wool hanging down behind that bounced as he jumped, like a bright omen above his head. The cold sun made their faces like copper and brass, and through the closed window John heard their coarse, irreverent voices. And he wanted to be one of them, playing in the streets, unfrightened, moving with such grace and power, but he knew this could not be. Yet, if he could not play their games, he could do something they could not do; he was able, as one of his teachers said, to think. But this brought him little in the way of consolation, for today he was terrified of his thoughts. He wanted to be with these boys in the street, heedless and thoughtless, wearing out his treacherous and bewildering body.

But now it was eleven o'clock, and in two hours his father would be home. And then they might eat, and then his father would lead them in prayer, and then he would give them a Bible lesson. By and by it would be evening and he would go to clean the church, and remain for tarry service. Suddenly, sitting at the window, and with a violence unprecedented, there arose in John a flood of fury and tears, and he bowed his head, fists clenched against the windowpane, crying, with teeth on edge: "What shall I do? What shall I do?"

Then his mother called him; and he remembered that she was in the kitchen washing clothes and probably had something for him to do. He rose sullenly and walked into the kitchen. She stood over the washtub, her arms wet and soapy to the elbows and sweat standing on her brow. Her apron, improvised from an old sheet, was wet where she had been leaning over the scrubbing-board. As he came in, she straightened, drying her hands on the edge of the apron.

"You finish your work, John?" she asked.

He said: "Yes'm," and thought how oddly she looked at him; as though she were looking at someone else's child.

"That's a good boy," she said. She smiled a shy, strained smile. "You know you your mother's right-hand man?"

He said nothing, and he did not smile, but watched her, wondering to what task this preamble led.

She turned away, passing one damp hand across her forehead, and went to the cupboard. Her back was to him, and he watched her while she took down a bright, figured vase, filled with flowers only on the most special occasions, and emptied the contents into her palm. He heard the chink of money, which meant that she was going to send him to the store. She put the vase back and turned to face him, her palm loosely folded before her.

"I didn't never ask you," she said, "what you wanted for your birthday. But you take this, son, and go out and get yourself something you think you want."

And she opened his palm and put the money into it, warm and wet from her hand. In the moment that he felt the warm, smooth coins and her hand on his, John stared blindly at her face, so far above him. His heart broke and he wanted to put his head on her belly where the wet spot was, and cry. But he dropped his eyes and looked at his palm, at the small pile of coins.

"It ain't much there," she said.

"That's all right." Then he looked up, and she bent down and kissed him on the forehead.

"You getting to be," she said, putting her hand beneath his chin and holding his face away from her, "a right big boy. You going to be a mighty fine man, you know that? Your mama's counting on you."

And he knew again that she was not saying everything she meant; in a kind of secret language she was telling him today something that he must remember and understand tomorrow. He watched her face, his heart swollen with love for her and with an anguish, not yet his own, that he did not understand and that frightened him.

"Yes, Ma," he said, hoping that she would realize, despite his stammering tongue, the depth of his passion to please her.

"I know," she said, with a smile, releasing him and rising, "there's a whole lot of things you don't understand. But don't you fret. The Lord'll reveal to you in His own good time everything He wants you to know. You put your faith in the Lord, Johnny, and He'll surely bring you out. Everything works together for good for them that love the Lord."

He had heard her say this before—it was her text, as *Set thine house in order* was his father's—but he knew that today she was saying it to him especially; she was trying to help him because she knew he was in trouble. And this trouble was also her own, which she would never tell to John. And even though he was certain that they could not be speaking of the same things—for them, surely, she would be angry and no longer proud of him—this perception on her part and this avowal of her love for him lent to John's bewilderment a reality that terrified and a dignity that consoled him. Dimly, he felt that he ought to console her, and he listened, astounded, at the words that now fell from his lips:

"Yes, Mama. I'm going to try to love the Lord."

At this there sprang into his mother's face something startling, beautiful, unspeakably sad—as though she were looking far beyond him at a long, dark road, and seeing on that road a traveler in perpetual danger. Was it he, the traveler? or herself? or was she thinking of the cross of Jesus? She turned back to the washtub, still with this strange sadness on her face.

"You better go on now," she said, "before your daddy gets home."

In Central Park the snow had not yet melted on his favorite hill. This hill was in the center of the park, after he had left the circle of the reservoir, where he always found, outside the high wall of crossed wire, ladies, white, in fur coats, walking their great dogs, or old, white gentlemen with canes. At a point that he knew by instinct and by the shape of the buildings surrounding the park, he struck out on a steep path overgrown with trees, and climbed a short distance until he reached the clearing that led to the hill. Before him, then, the slope stretched upward, and above it the brilliant sky, and beyond it, cloudy, and far away, he saw the skyline of New York. He did not know why, but there arose in him an exultation and a sense of power, and he ran up the hill like an engine, or a madman, willing to throw himself headlong into the city that glowed before him.

But when he reached the summit he paused; he stood on the crest of the hill, hands clasped beneath his chin, looking down. Then he, John, felt like a giant who might crumble this city with his anger; he felt like a tyrant who might crush this city beneath his heel; he felt like a long-awaited conqueror at whose feet flowers would be strewn, and before whom multitudes cried, Hosanna! He would be, of all, the mightiest, the most beloved, the Lord's anointed; and he would live in this shining city which his ancestors had seen with longing from far away. For it was his; the inhabitants of the city had told him it was his; he had but to run down, crying, and they would take him to their hearts and show him wonders his eyes had never seen.

And still, on the summit of that hill he paused. He remembered the people he had seen in that city, whose eyes held no love for him. And he thought of their feet so swift and brutal, and the dark gray clothes they wore, and how when they passed they did not see him, or, if they saw him, they smirked. And how their lights, unceasing, crashed on and off above him, and how he was a stranger there. Then he remembered his father and his mother, and all the arms stretched out to hold him back, to save him from this city where, they said, his soul would find perdition.

And certainly perdition sucked at the feet of the people who walked there; and cried in the lights, in the gigantic towers; the marks of Satan could be found in the faces of the people who waited at the doors of movie houses; his words were printed on the great movie posters that invited people to sin. It was the roar of the damned that filled Broadway, where motor cars and buses and the hurrying people disputed every inch with death. *Broadway:* the way that led to death *was* broad, and many could be found thereon; but narrow was the way that led to life eternal, and few there were who found it. But he did not long for the narrow way, where all his people walked; where the houses did not rise, piercing, as it seemed, the unchanging clouds, but huddled, flat, ignoble, close to the filthy ground, where the streets and the hallways and the rooms were dark, and where the unconquerable odor was of dust, and sweat, and urine, and homemade gin. In the narrow way, the way of the cross, there awaited him only humiliation forever; there awaited him, one day, a house like his father's house, and a church like his father's, and a job like his father's, where he would grow old and black with hunger and toil. The way of the cross had given him a belly filled with wind and had bent his mother's back; they had never worn fine clothes, but here, where the buildings contested God's power and where the men and women did not fear God, here he might eat and drink to his heart's content and clothe his body with wondrous fabrics, rich to the eye and pleasing to the touch. And then what of his soul, which would one day come to die and stand naked before the judgment bar? What would his conquest of the city profit him on that day? To hurl away, for a moment of ease, the glories of eternity!

These glories were unimaginable—but the city was real. He stood for a moment on the melting snow, distracted, and then began to run down the hill, feeling himself fly as the descent became more rapid, and thinking: "I can climb back up. If it's wrong, I can always climb back up." At the bottom of the hill, where the ground abruptly leveled off onto a gravel path, he nearly knocked down an old white man with a white beard, who was walking very slowly and leaning on his cane. They both stopped, astonished, and looked at one another. John struggled to catch his breath and apologize, but the old man smiled. John smiled back. It was as though he and the old man had between them a great secret; and the old man moved on. The snow glittered in patches all over the park. Ice, under the pale, strong sun, melted slowly on the branches and the trunks of trees.

He came out of the park at Fifth Avenue where, as always, the old-fashioned horse-carriages were lined along the curb, their drivers sitting on the high seats with rugs around their knees, or standing in twos and threes near the horses, stamping their feet and smoking pipes and talking. In summer he had seen people riding in these carriages, looking like people out of books, or out of movies in which everyone wore old-fashioned clothes and rushed at nightfall over frozen roads, hotly pursued by their enemies who wanted to carry them back to death. *"Look back, look back,"* had cried a beautiful woman with long blonde curls, *"and see if we are pursued!"*—and she had come, as John remembered, to a terrible end. Now he stared at the horses, enormous and brown and patient, stamping every now and again a polished hoof, and he thought of what it would be like to have one day a horse of his own. He would call it Rider, and mount it at morning when the grass was wet, and from the horse's back look out over great, sun-filled fields, his own. Behind him stood his house, great and rambling and very new, and in the kitchen his wife, a beautiful woman, made breakfast, and the smoke rose out of the chimney, melting into the morning air. They had children, who called him Papa and for whom at Christmas he bought electric trains. And he had turkeys and cows and chickens and geese, and other horses besides Rider. They had a closet full of whisky and wine; they had cars—but what church did they go to and what would he teach his children when they gathered around him in the evening? He looked straight ahead, down Fifth Avenue, where graceful women in fur coats walked, looking into the windows that held silk dresses, and watches, and rings. What church did they go to? And what were their houses like when in the evening they took off these coats, and these silk dresses, and put their jewelry in a box, and leaned back in soft beds to think for a moment before they slept of the day gone by? Did they read a verse from the Bible every night and fall on their knees to pray? But no, for their thoughts were not of God, and their way was not God's way. They were in the world, and of the world, and their feet laid hold on Hell.

Yet in school some of them had been nice to him, and it was hard to think of them burning in Hell forever, they who were so gracious and beautiful now. Once, one winter when he had been very sick with a heavy cold that would not leave him, one of his teachers had bought him a bottle of cod liver oil, especially prepared with heavy syrup so that it did not taste so bad: this was surely a Christian act. His mother had said that God would bless that woman; and he had got better. They were kind—he was sure that they were kind—and on the day that he would bring himself to their attention they would surely love and honor him. This was not his father's opinion. His father said that all white people were wicked, and that God was going to bring them low. He said that white people were never to be trusted, and that they told nothing but lies, and that not one of them had ever loved a nigger. He, John, was a nigger, and he would find out, as soon as he got a little older, how evil white people could be. John had read about the things white people did to colored people; how, in the South, where his parents came from, white people cheated them of their wages, and burned them, and shot them—and did worse things, said his father, which the tongue could not endure to utter. He had read about colored men being burned in the electric chair for things they had not done; how in riots they were beaten with clubs; how they were tortured in prisons; how they were the last to be hired and the first to be fired. Niggers did not live on these streets where John now walked; it was forbidden; and yet he walked here, and no one raised a hand against him. But did he dare to enter this shop out of which a woman now casually walked, carrying a great round box? Or this apartment before which a white man stood, dressed in a brilliant uniform? John knew he did not dare, not today, and he heard his father's laugh: *"No, nor tomorrow neither!"* For him there was the back door, and the dark stairs, and the kitchen or the basement. This world was not for him. If he refused to believe, and wanted to break his neck trying, then he could try until the sun refused to shine; they would never let him enter. In John's mind then, the people and the avenue underwent a change, and he feared them and knew that one day he could hate them if God did not change his heart.

He left Fifth Avenue and walked west toward the movie houses. Here on 42nd Street it was less elegant but no less strange. He loved this street, not for the people or the shops but for the stone lions that guarded the great main building of the Public Library, a building filled with books and unimaginably vast, and which he had never yet dared to enter. He might, he knew, for he was a member of the branch in Harlem and was entitled to take books from any library in the city. But he had never gone in because the building was so big that it must be full of corridors and marble steps, in the maze of which he would be lost and never find the book he wanted. And then everyone, all the white people inside, would know that he was not used to great buildings, or to many books, and they would look at him with pity. He would enter on another day, when he had read all the books uptown, an achievement that would, he felt, lend him the poise to enter any building in the world. People, mostly men, leaned over the stone parapets of the raised park that surrounded the library, or walked up and down and bent to drink water from the public drinking-fountains. Silver pigeons lighted briefly on the heads of the lions or the rims of fountains, and strutted along the walks. John loitered in front of Woolworth's, staring at the candy display, trying to decide what candy to buy—and buying none, for the store was crowded and he was certain that the salesgirl would never notice him—and before a vender of artificial flowers, and crossed Sixth Avenue where the Automat was, and the parked taxis, and the shops, which he would not look at today, that displayed in their windows dirty postcards and practical jokes. Beyond Sixth Avenue the movie houses began, and now he studied the stills carefully, trying to decide which of all these theaters he should enter. He stopped at last before a gigantic, colored poster that represented a wicked woman, half undressed, leaning in a doorway, apparently quarreling with a blond man who stared wretchedly into the street. The legend above their heads was: "There's a fool like him in every family—and a woman next door to take him over!" He decided to see this, for he felt identified with the blond young man, the fool of his family, and he wished to know more about his so blatantly unkind fate.

And so he stared at the price above the ticket-seller's window and, showing her his coins, received the piece of paper that was charged with the power to open doors. Having once decided to enter, he did not look back at the street again for fear that one of the saints might be passing and, seeing him, might cry out his name and lay hands on him to drag him back. He walked very quickly across the carpeted lobby, looking at nothing, and pausing only to see his ticket torn, half of it thrown into a silver box and half returned to him. And then the usherette opened the doors of this dark palace and with a flashlight held behind her took him to his seat. Not even then, having pushed past a wilderness of knees and feet to reach his designated seat, did he dare to breathe; nor, out of a last, sick hope for forgiveness, did he look at the screen. He stared at the darkness around him, and at the profiles that gradually emerged from this gloom, which was so like the gloom of Hell. He waited for this darkness to be shattered by the light of the second coming, for the ceiling to crack upward, revealing, for every eye to see, the chariots of fire on which descended a wrathful God and all the host of Heaven. He sank far down in his seat, as though his crouching might make him invisible and deny his presence there. But then he thought: *"Not yet. The day of judgment is not yet,"* and voices reached him, the voices no doubt

of the hapless man and the evil woman, and he raised his eyes helplessly and watched the screen.

The woman was most evil. She was blonde and pasty white, and
she had lived in London, which was in England, quite some time
ago, judging from her clothes, and she coughed. She had a terrible
disease, tuberculosis, which he had heard about. Someone in his
mother's family had died of it. She had a great many boyfriends, and
she smoked cigarettes and drank. When she met the young man,
who was a student and who loved her very much, she was very cruel
to him. She laughed at him because he was a cripple. She took his
money and she went out with other men, and she lied to the student—who was certainly a fool. He limped about, looking soft and
sad, and soon all John's sympathy was given to this violent and unhappy woman. He understood her when she raged and shook her
hips and threw back her head in laughter so furious that it seemed
the veins of her neck would burst. She walked the cold, foggy streets,
a little woman and not pretty, with a lewd, brutal swagger, saying to
the whole world: "You can kiss my ass." Nothing tamed or broke
her, nothing touched her, neither kindness, nor scorn, nor hatred,
nor love. She had never thought of prayer. It was unimaginable that
she would ever bend her knees and come crawling along a dusty floor
to anybody's altar, weeping for forgiveness. Perhaps her sin was so
extreme that it could not be forgiven; perhaps her pride was so great
that she did not need forgiveness. She had fallen from that high es-
tate which God had intended for men and women, and she made
her fall glorious because it was so complete. John could not have
found in his heart, had he dared to search it, any wish for her redemption. He wanted to be like her, only more powerful, more thor-
ough, and more cruel; to make those around him, all who hurt him,
suffer as she made the student suffer, and laugh in their faces when
they asked pity for their pain. *He* would have asked no pity, and his
pain was greater than theirs. Go on, girl, he whispered, as the student, facing her implacable ill will, sighed and wept. Go on, girl.

One day he would talk like that, he would face them and tell them how much he hated them, how they had made him suffer, how he would pay them back!

Nevertheless, when she came to die, which she did eventually, looking more grotesque than ever, as she deserved, his thoughts were abruptly arrested, and he was chilled by the expression on her face. She seemed to stare endlessly outward and down, in the face of a wind more piercing than any she had left on earth, feeling herself propelled with speed into a kingdom where nothing could help her, neither her pride, nor her courage, nor her glorious wickedness. In the place where she was going, it was not these things that mattered but something else, for which she had no name, only a cold intimation, something that she could not alter in any degree, and that she had never thought of. She began to cry, her depraved face breaking into an infant's grimace; and they moved away from her, leaving her dirty in a dirty room, alone to face her Maker. The scene faded out and she was gone; and though the movie went on, allowing the student to marry another girl, darker, and very sweet, but by no means so arresting, John thought of this woman and her dreadful end. Again, had the thought not been blasphemous, he would have thought that it was the Lord who had led him into this theater to show him an example of the wages of sin. The movie ended and people stirred around him; the newsreel came on, and while girls in bathing suits paraded before him and boxers growled and fought, and baseball players ran home safe and presidents and kings of countries that were only names to him moved briefly across the flickering square of light John thought of Hell, of his soul's redemption, and struggled to find a compromise between the way that led to life everlasting and the way that ended in the pit. But there was none, for he had been raised in the truth. He could not claim, as African savages might be able to claim, that no one had brought him the gospel. His father and mother and all the saints had taught him from his earliest childhood what was the will of God. Either he arose from this theater, never to return, putting behind him the world and its pleasures, its honors, and its glories, or he remained here with the wicked and partook of their certain punishment. Yes, it was a narrow way—and John stirred in his seat, not daring to feel it God's injustice that he must make so cruel a choice.

As John approached his home again in the late afternoon, he saw little Sarah, her coat unbuttoned, come flying out of the house and run the length of the street away from him into the far drugstore. Instantly, he was frightened; he stopped a moment, staring blankly down the street, wondering what could justify such hysterical haste. It was true that Sarah was full of self-importance, and made any errand she ran seem a matter of life or death; nevertheless, she had been sent on an errand, and with such speed that her mother had not had time to make her button up her coat.

Then he felt weary; if something had really happened it would be very unpleasant upstairs now, and he did not want to face it. But perhaps it was simply that his mother had a headache and had sent Sarah to the store for some aspirin. But if this were true, it meant that he would have to prepare supper, and take care of the children, and be naked under his father's eyes all the evening long. And he began to walk more slowly.

There were some boys standing on the stoop. They watched him as he approached, and he tried not to look at them and to approximate the swagger with which they walked. One of them said, as he mounted the short, stone steps and started into the hall: "Boy, your brother was hurt real bad today."

He looked at them in a kind of dread, not daring to ask for details; and he observed that they, too, looked as though they had been in a battle; something hangdog in their looks suggested that they had been put to flight. Then he looked down, and saw that there was blood at the threshold, and blood spattered on the tile floor of the vestibule. He looked again at the boys, who had not ceased to watch him, and hurried up the stairs.

The door was half open—for Sarah's return, no doubt—and he walked in, making no sound, feeling a confused impulse to flee.

There was no one in the kitchen, though the light was burning—the lights were on all through the house. On the kitchen table stood a shopping-bag filled with groceries, and he knew that his Aunt Florence had arrived. The washtub, where his mother had been washing earlier, was open still, and filled the kitchen with a sour smell.

There were drops of blood on the floor here too, and there had been small, smudged coins of blood on the stairs as he walked up.

All this frightened him terribly. He stood in the middle of the kitchen, trying to imagine what had happened, and preparing himself to walk into the living-room, where all the family seemed to be. Roy had been in trouble before, but this new trouble seemed to be the beginning of the fulfillment of a prophecy. He took off his coat, dropping it on a chair, and was about to start into the living-room when he heard Sarah running up the steps.

He waited, and she burst through the door, carrying a clumsy parcel.

"What happened?" he whispered.

She stared at him in astonishment, and a certain wild joy. He thought again that he really did not like his sister. Catching her breath, she blurted out, triumphantly: "Roy got stabbed with a knife!" and rushed into the living-room.

Roy got stabbed with a knife. Whatever this meant, it was sure that his father would be at his worst tonight. John walked slowly into the living-room.

His father and mother, a small basin of water between them, knelt by the sofa where Roy lay, and his father was washing the blood from Roy's forehead. It seemed that his mother, whose touch was so much more gentle, had been thrust aside by his father, who could not bear to have anyone else touch his wounded son. And now she watched, one hand in the water, the other, in a kind of anguish, at her waist, which was circled still by the improvised apron of the morning. Her face, as she watched, was full of pain and fear, of tension barely supported, and of pity that could scarcely have been expressed had she filled all the world with her weeping. His father muttered sweet, delirious things to Roy, and his hands, when he dipped them again in the basin and wrung out the cloth, were trembling. Aunt Florence, still wearing her hat and carrying her handbag, stood a little removed, looking down at them with a troubled, terrible face.

Then Sarah bounded into the room before him, and his mother looked up, reached out for the package, and saw him. She said nothing, but she looked at him with a strange, quick intentness, almost as though there were a warning on her tongue which at the moment she did not dare to utter. His Aunt Florence looked up, and said: "We been wondering where you was, boy. This bad brother of yours done gone out and got hisself hurt."

But John understood from her tone that the fuss was, possibly, a little greater than the danger—Roy was not, after all, going to die. And his heart lifted a little. Then his father turned and looked at him.

"Where you been, boy," he shouted, "all this time? Don't you know you's needed here at home?"

More than his words, his face caused John to stiffen instantly with malice and fear. His father's face was terrible in anger, but now there was more than anger in it. John saw now what he had never seen there before, except in his own vindictive fantasies: a kind of wild, weeping terror that made the face seem younger, and yet at the same time unutterably older and more cruel. And John knew, in the moment his father's eyes swept over him, that he hated John because John was not lying on the sofa where Roy lay. John could scarcely meet his father's eyes, and yet, briefly, he did, saying nothing, feeling in his heart an odd sensation of triumph, and hoping in his heart that Roy, to bring his father low, would die.

His mother had unwrapped the package and was opening a bottle of peroxide. "Here," she said, "you better wash it with this now." Her voice was calm and dry; she looked at his father briefly, her face unreadable, as she handed him the bottle and the cotton.

"This going to hurt," his father said—in such a different voice, so sad and tender!—turning again to the sofa. "But you just be a little man and hold still; it ain't going to take long."

John watched and listened, hating him. Roy began to moan. Aunt Florence moved to the mantelpiece and put her handbag down near the metal serpent. From the room behind him, John heard the baby begin to whimper.

"John," said his mother, "go and pick her up like a good boy." Her hands, which were not trembling, were still busy: she had opened the bottle of iodine and was cutting up strips of bandage.

John walked into his parents' bedroom and picked up the squalling baby, who was wet. The moment Ruth felt him lift her up she stopped crying and stared at him with a wide-eyed, pathetic stare, as though she knew that there was trouble in the house. John laughed at her so ancient-seeming distress—he was very fond of his baby sister—and whispered in her ear as he started back to the living-room: "Now, you let your big brother tell you something, baby. Just as soon as you's able to stand on your feet, you run away from *this* house, run far away." He did not quite know why he said this, or where he wanted her to run, but it made him feel instantly better.

His father was saying, as John came back into the room: "I'm sure going to be having some questions to ask you in a minute, old lady. I'm going to be wanting to know just how come you let this boy go out and get half killed."

"Oh, no, you ain't," said Aunt Florence. "You ain't going to be starting none of that mess this evening. You know right doggone well that Roy don't never ask *nobody* if he can do *nothing*—he just go right ahead and do like he pleases. Elizabeth sure can't put no ball and chain on him. She got her hands full right here in this house, and it ain't her fault if Roy got a head just as hard as his father's."

"You got a awful lot to say, look like for once you could keep from putting your mouth in my business." He said this without looking at her.

"It ain't my fault," she said, "that you was born a fool, and always done been a fool, and ain't never going to change. I swear to my Father you'd try the patience of Job."

"I done told you before," he said—he had not ceased working over the moaning Roy, and was preparing now to dab the wound with iodine—"that I didn't want you coming in here and using that gutter language in front of my children."

"Don't you worry about my language, brother," she said with spirit, "you better start worrying about your *life*. What these children hear ain't going to do them near as much harm as what they *see*."

"What they *see*," his father muttered, "is a poor man trying to serve the Lord. *That's* my life."

"Then I guarantee *you*," she said, "that they going to do their best to keep it from being *their* life. *You* mark my words."

He turned and looked at her, and intercepted the look that passed between the two women. John's mother, for reasons that were not at all his father's reasons, wanted Aunt Florence to keep still. He looked away, ironically. John watched his mother's mouth tighten bitterly as she dropped her eyes. His father, in silence, began bandaging Roy's forehead.

"It's just the mercy of God," he said at last, "that this boy didn't lose his eye. Look here."

His mother leaned over and looked into Roy's face with a sad, sympathetic murmur. Yet, John felt, she had seen instantly the extent of the danger to Roy's eye and to his life, and was beyond that worry now. Now she was merely marking time, as it were, and preparing herself against the moment when her husband's anger would turn, full force, against her.

His father now turned to John, who was standing near the French doors with Ruth in his arms.

"You come here, boy," he said, "and see what them white folks done done to your brother."

John walked over to the sofa, holding himself as proudly beneath his father's furious eyes as a prince approaching the scaffold.

"Look here," said his father, grasping him roughly by one arm, "look at your brother."

John looked down at Roy, who gazed at him with almost no expression in his dark eyes. But John knew by the weary, impatient set of Roy's young mouth that his brother was asking that none of this be held against him. It wasn't his fault, or John's, Roy's eyes said, that they had such a crazy father.

His father, with the air of one forcing the sinner to look down into the pit that is to be his portion, moved away slightly so that John could see Roy's wound.

Roy had been gashed by a knife, luckily not very sharp, from the center of his forehead where his hair began, downward to the bone just above his left eye: the wound described a kind of crazy half-moon and ended in a violent, fuzzy tail that was the ruin of Roy's eyebrow. Time would darken the half-moon wound into Roy's dark skin, but nothing would bring together again the so violently divided eyebrow. This crazy lift, this question, would remain with him forever, and emphasize forever something mocking and sinister in Roy's face. John felt a sudden impulse to smile, but his father's eyes were on him and he fought the impulse back. Certainly the wound was now very ugly, and very red, and must, John felt, with a quickened sympathy toward Roy, who had not cried out, have been very painful. He could imagine the sensation caused when Roy staggered into the house, blinded by his blood; but just the same, he wasn't dead, he wasn't changed, he would be in the streets again the moment he was better.

"You see?" came now from his father. "It was white folks, some of them white folks *you* like so much that tried to cut your brother's throat."

John thought, with immediate anger and with a curious contempt for his father's inexactness, that only a blind man, however white, could possibly have been aiming at Roy's throat; and his mother said with a calm insistence:

"And he was trying to cut theirs. Him and them bad boys."

"Yes," said Aunt Florence, "I ain't heard you ask that boy nary a question about how all this happened. Look like you just determined to raise cain any*how* and make everybody in this house suffer because something done happened to the apple of your eye."

"I done asked you," cried his father in a fearful exasperation, "to stop running your *mouth*. Don't none of this concern you. This is *my* family and this is my house. You want me to slap you side of the head?"

"You slap me," she said, with a placidity equally fearful, "and I *do* guarantee you you won't do no more slapping in a hurry."

"Hush now," said his mother, rising, "ain't no need for all this. What's done is done. We ought to be on our knees, thanking the Lord it weren't no worse."

"Amen to that," said Aunt Florence, "*tell* that foolish nigger something."

"You can tell that foolish *son* of yours something," he said to his wife with venom, having decided, it seemed, to ignore his sister, "him standing there with them big buckeyes. You can tell him to take this like a warning from the Lord. *This* is what white folks does to niggers. I been telling you, now you see."

"He better take it like a warning?" shrieked Aunt Florence. "He better take it? Why, Gabriel, it ain't *him* went halfway across this city to get in a fight with white boys. This boy on the sofa went *deliberately,* with a whole lot of other boys, all the way to the west side, just *looking* for a fight. I declare, I do wonder what goes on in your head."

"You know right well," his mother said, looking directly at his father, "that Johnny don't travel with the same class of boys as Roy goes with. You done beat Roy too many times, here, in this very room for going out with them bad boys. Roy got hisself hurt this afternoon because he was out doing something he didn't have no business doing, and that's the end of it. You ought to be thanking your Redeemer he ain't dead."

"And for all the care you take of him," he said, "he might as well be dead. Don't look like you much care whether he lives, or dies."

"*Lord,* have mercy," said Aunt Florence.

"He's my son, too," his mother said, with heat. "I carried him in my belly for nine months and I know him just like I know his daddy, and they's just *exactly* alike. Now. You ain't got no *right* in the world to talk to me like that."

"I reckon you *know,*" he said, choked, and breathing hard, "all about a mother's love. I sure reckon on you telling me how a woman can sit in the house all day and let her own flesh and blood go out and get half butchered. Don't you tell me you don't know no way to stop him, because I remember *my* mother, God rest her soul, and *she'd* have found a way."

"She was my mother, too," said Aunt Florence, "and I recollect, if you don't, you being brought home many a time more dead than alive. She didn't find no way to stop *you.* She wore herself out beating on you, just like you been wearing yourself out beating on this boy here."

"My, my, *my,*" he said, "you got a lot to say."

"I ain't doing a thing," she said, "but trying to talk some sense into your big, black, hardhead. You better stop trying to blame everything on Elizabeth and look to your own wrongdoings."

"Never mind, Florence," his mother said, "it's all over and done with now."

"I'm out of this house," he shouted, "every day the Lord sends, working to put the food in these children's mouths. Don't you think I got a right to ask the mother of these children to look after them and see that they don't break their necks before I get back home?"

"You ain't got but one child," she said, "that's liable to go out and break his neck, and that's Roy, and you know it. And I don't know how in the world you expect me to run this house, and look after these children, and keep running around the block after Roy. *No,* I can't stop him, I done told you that, and you can't stop him neither. You don't know *what* to do with this boy, and that's why you all the time trying to fix the blame on somebody. Ain't nobody to *blame,* Gabriel. You just better pray God to stop him before somebody puts another knife in him and puts him in his grave."

They stared at each other a moment in an awful pause, she with a startled, pleading question in her eyes. Then, with all his might, he reached out and slapped her across the face. She crumpled at once, hiding her face with one thin hand, and Aunt Florence moved to hold her up. Sarah watched all this with greedy eyes. Then Roy sat up, and said in a shaking voice:

"Don't you slap my mother. That's my *mother.* You slap her again, you black bastard, and I swear to God I'll kill you."

In the moment that these words filled the room, and hung in the room like the infinitesimal moment of hanging, jagged light that precedes an explosion, John and his father were staring into each other's eyes. John thought for that moment that his father believed the words had come from him, his eyes were so wild and depthlessly malevolent, and his mouth was twisted into such a snarl of pain. Then, in the absolute silence that followed Roy's words, John saw that his father was not seeing him, was not seeing anything unless it were a vision. John wanted to turn and flee, as though he had encountered in the jungle some evil beast, crouching and ravenous, with eyes like Hell unclosed; and exactly as though, on a road's turning, he found himself staring at certain destruction, he found that he could not move. Then his father turned and looked down at Roy.

"What did you say?" his father asked.

"I told you," said Roy, "not to touch my mother."

"You cursed me," said his father.

Roy said nothing; neither did he drop his eyes.

"Gabriel," said his mother, "Gabriel. Let us pray. . . ."

His father's hands were at his waist, and he took off his belt. Tears were in his eyes.

"Gabriel," cried Aunt Florence, "ain't you done playing the fool for tonight?"

Then his father raised his belt, and it fell with a whistling sound on Roy, who shivered, and fell back, his face to the wall. But he did not cry out. And the belt was raised again, and again. The air rang with the whistling, and the *crack!* against Roy's flesh. And the baby, Ruth, began to scream.

"My Lord, my Lord," his father whispered, *"my Lord, my Lord."*

He raised the belt again, but Aunt Florence caught it from behind, and held it. His mother rushed over to the sofa and caught Roy in her arms, crying as John had never seen a woman, or anybody, cry before. Roy caught his mother around the neck and held on to her as though he were drowning.

His Aunt Florence and his father faced each other.

"Yes, Lord," Aunt Florence said, "you was born wild, and you's going to die wild. But ain't no use to try to take the whole world with you. You can't change nothing, Gabriel. You ought to know that by now."

John opened the church door with his father's key at six o'clock. Tarry service officially began at eight, but it could begin at any time, whenever the Lord moved one of the saints to enter the church and pray. It was seldom, however, that anyone arrived before eight thirty, the Spirit of the Lord being sufficiently tolerant to allow the saints time to do their Saturday-night shopping, clean their houses, and put their children to bed.

John closed the door behind him and stood in the narrow church aisle, hearing behind him the voices of children playing, and ruder voices, the voices of their elders, cursing and crying in the streets. It was dark in the church; street lights had been snapping on all around him on the populous avenue; the light of the day was gone. His feet seemed planted on this wooden floor; they did not wish to carry him one step farther. The darkness and silence of the church pressed on him, cold as judgment, and the voices crying from the window might have been crying from another world. John moved forward, hearing his feet crack against the sagging wood, to where the golden cross on the red field of the altar cloth glowed like smothered fire, and switched on one weak light.

In the air of the church hung, perpetually, the odor of dust and sweat; for, like the carpet in his mother's living-room, the dust of this church was invincible; and when the saints were praying or rejoicing, their bodies gave off an acrid, steamy smell, a marriage of the odors of dripping bodies and soaking, starched white linen. It was a storefront church and had stood, for John's lifetime, on the corner of this sinful avenue, facing the hospital to which criminal wounded and dying were carried almost every night. The saints, arriving, had rented this abandoned store and taken out the fixtures; had painted the walls and built a pulpit, moved in a piano and camp chairs, and bought the biggest Bible they could find. They put white curtains in the show window, and painted across this window TEMPLE OF THE FIRE BAPTIZED. Then they were ready to do the Lord's work.

And the Lord, as He had promised to the two or three first gathered together, sent others; and these brought others and created a church. From this parent branch, if the Lord blessed, other branches might grow and a mighty work be begun throughout the city and throughout the land. In the history of the temple the Lord had raised up evangelists and teachers and prophets, and called them out into the field to do His work; to go up and down the land carrying the gospel, or to raise other temples—in Philadelphia, Georgia, Boston, or Brooklyn. Wherever the Lord led, they followed. Every now and again one of them came home to testify of the wonders the Lord had worked through him, or her. And sometimes on a special Sunday they all visited one of the nearer churches of the Brotherhood.

There had been a time, before John was born, when his father had also been in the field; but now, having to earn for his family their daily bread, it was seldom that he was able to travel farther away than Philadelphia, and then only for a very short time. His father no longer, as he had once done, led great revival meetings, his name printed large on placards that advertised the coming of a man of God. His father had once had a mighty reputation; but all this, it seemed, had changed since he had left the South. Perhaps he ought now to have a church of his own—John wondered if his father wanted that; he ought, perhaps, to be leading, as Father James now led, a great flock to the Kingdom. But his father was only a caretaker in the house of God. He was responsible for the replacement of burnt-out light bulbs, and for the cleanliness of the church, and the care of the Bibles, and the hymn-books, and the placards on the walls. On Friday night he conducted the Young Ministers' Service and preached with them. Rarely did he bring the message on a Sunday morning; only if there was no one else to speak was his father called upon. He was a kind of fill-in speaker, a holy handyman.

Yet he was treated, so far as John could see, with great respect. No one, none of the saints in any case, had ever reproached or rebuked his father, or suggested that his life was anything but spotless. Nevertheless, this man, God's minister, had struck John's mother, and John had wanted to kill him—and wanted to kill him still.

John had swept one side of the church and the chairs were still piled in the space before the altar when there was a knocking at the door. When he opened the door he saw that it was Elisha, come to help him.

"Praise the Lord," said Elisha, standing on the doorstep, grinning.

"Praise the Lord," said John. This was the greeting always used among the saints.

Brother Elisha came in, slamming the door behind him and stamping his feet. He had probably just come from a basketball court; his forehead was polished with recent sweat and his hair stood up. He was wearing his green woolen sweater, on which was stamped the letter of his high school, and his shirt was open at the throat.

"You ain't cold like that?" John asked, staring at him.

"No, little brother, I ain't cold. You reckon everybody's frail like you?"

"It ain't only the little ones gets carried to the graveyard," John said. He felt unaccustomedly bold and lighthearted; the arrival of Elisha had caused his mood to change.

Elisha, who had started down the aisle toward the back room, turned to stare at John with astonishment and menace. "Ah," he said, "I see you fixing to be sassy with Brother Elisha tonight—I'm going to have to give you a little correction. You just wait till I wash my hands."

"Ain't no need to wash your hands if you come here to work. Just take hold of that mop and put some soap and water in the bucket."

"Lord," said Elisha, running water into the sink, and talking, it seemed, to the water, "that sure is a sassy nigger out there. I sure hope he don't get hisself hurt one of these days, running his mouth thataway. Look like he just *won't* stop till somebody busts him in the eye."

He sighed deeply, and began to lather his hands. "Here I come running all the way so he wouldn't bust a gut lifting one of them chairs, and all he got to say is 'put some water in the bucket.' Can't do nothing with a nigger nohow." He stopped and turned to face John. "Ain't you got no manners, boy? You better learn how to talk to old folks."

"You better get out here with that mop and pail. We ain't got all night."

"Keep on," said Elisha. "I see I'm going to have to give you your lumps tonight."

He disappeared. John heard him in the toilet, and then over the thunderous water he heard him knocking things over in the back room.

"*Now* what you doing?"

"Boy, leave me alone. I'm fixing to work."

"It sure sounds like it." John dropped his broom and walked into the back. Elisha had knocked over a pile of camp chairs, folded in the corner, and stood over them angrily, holding the mop in his hand.

"I keep telling you not to hide that mop back there. Can't nobody get at it."

"I always get at it. Ain't everybody as clumsy as you."

Elisha let fall the stiff gray mop and rushed at John, catching him off balance and lifting him from the floor. With both arms tightening around John's waist he tried to cut John's breath, watching him meanwhile with a smile that, as John struggled and squirmed, became a set, ferocious grimace. With both hands John pushed and pounded against the shoulders and biceps of Elisha, and tried to thrust with his knees against Elisha's belly. Usually such a battle was soon over, since Elisha was so much bigger and stronger and as a wrestler so much more skilled; but tonight John was filled with a determination not to be conquered, or at least to make the conquest dear. With all the strength that was in him he fought against Elisha, and he was filled with a strength that was almost hatred. He kicked, pounded, twisted, pushed, using his lack of size to confound and exasperate Elisha, whose damp fists, joined at the small of John's back, soon slipped. It was a deadlock; he could not tighten his hold, John could not break it. And so they turned, battling in the narrow room, and the odor of Elisha's sweat was heavy in John's nostrils. He saw the veins rise on Elisha's forehead and in his neck; his breath became jagged and harsh, and the grimace on his face became more cruel; and John, watching these manifestations of his power, was filled with a wild delight. They stumbled against the folding-chairs, and Elisha's foot slipped and his hold broke. They stared at each other, half grinning. John slumped to the floor, holding his head between his hands.

"I didn't hurt you none, did I?" Elisha asked.

John looked up. "Me? No, I just want to catch my breath."

Elisha went to the sink, and splashed cold water on his face and neck. "I reckon you going to let me work now," he said.

"It wasn't *me* that stopped you in the first place." He stood up. He found that his legs were trembling. He looked at Elisha, who was drying himself on the towel. "You teach me wrestling one time, okay?"

"No, boy," Elisha said, laughing, "I don't want to wrestle with *you.* You too strong for me." And he began to run hot water into the great pail.

John walked past him to the front and picked up his broom. In a moment Elisha followed and began mopping near the door. John had finished sweeping, and he now mounted to the pulpit to dust the three thronelike chairs, purple, with white linen squares for the headpieces and for the massive arms. It dominated all, the pulpit: a wooden platform raised above the congregation, with a high stand in the center for the Bible, before which the preacher stood. There faced the congregation, flowing downward from this height, the scarlet altar cloth that bore the golden cross and the legend: JESUS SAVES. The pulpit was holy. None could stand so high unless God's seal was on him.

He dusted the piano and sat down on the piano stool to wait until Elisha had finished mopping one side of the church and he could replace the chairs. Suddenly Elisha said, without looking at him:

"Boy, ain't it time you was thinking about your soul?"

"I guess so," John said with a quietness that terrified him.

"I know it looks hard," said Elisha, "from the outside, especially when you young. But you believe me, boy, you can't find no greater joy than you find in the service of the Lord."

John said nothing. He touched a black key on the piano and it made a dull sound, like a distant drum.

"You got to remember," Elisha said, turning now to look at him, "that you think about it with a carnal mind. You still got Adam's mind, boy, and you keep thinking about your friends, you want to do what they do, and you want to go to the movies, and I bet you think about girls, don't you, Johnny? Sure you do," he said, half smiling, finding his answer in John's face, "and you don't want to give up all that. But when the Lord saves you He burns out all that old Adam, He gives you a new mind and a new heart, and then you don't find no pleasure in the world, you get all your joy in walking and talking with Jesus every day."

He stared in a dull paralysis of terror at the body of Elisha. He saw him standing—had Elisha forgotten?—beside Ella Mae before the altar while Father James rebuked him for the evil that lived in the flesh. He looked into Elisha's face, full of questions he would never ask. And Elisha's face told him nothing.

"People say it's hard," said Elisha, bending again to his mop, "but, let me tell you, it ain't as hard as living in this wicked world and all the sadness of the world where there ain't no pleasure nohow, and then dying and going to Hell. Ain't nothing as hard as that." And he looked back at John. "You see how the Devil tricks people into losing their souls?"

"Yes," said John at last, sounding almost angry, unable to bear his thoughts, unable to bear the silence in which Elisha looked at him.

Elisha grinned. "They got girls in the school I go to"—he was finished with one side of the church and he motioned to John to re-place the chairs—"and they nice girls, but their minds ain't on the Lord, and I try to tell them the time to repent ain't tomorrow, it's today. They think ain't no sense to worrying now, they can sneak into Heaven on their deathbed. But I tell them, honey, ain't every-body lies down to die—people going all the time, just like that, to-day you see them and tomorrow you don't. Boy, they don't know what to make of old Elisha because he don't go to the movies, and he don't dance, and he don't play cards, and he don't go with them be-hind the stairs." He paused and stared at John, who watched him helplessly, not knowing what to say. "And boy, some of them is real nice girls, I mean *beautiful* girls, and when you got so much power that *they* don't tempt you then you know you saved sure enough. I just look at them and I tell them Jesus saved me one day, and I'm going to go all the way with *Him.* Ain't no woman, no, nor no man neither going to make me change my mind." He paused again, and smiled and dropped his eyes. "That Sunday," he said, "that Sunday, you remember?—when Father got up in the pulpit and called me and Ella Mae down because he thought we was about to commit sin—well, boy, I don't want to tell no lie, I was mighty hot against the old man that Sunday. But I thought about it, and the Lord made me to see that he was right. Me and Ella Mae, we didn't have nothing on our minds at all, but look like the Devil is just everywhere— sometime the Devil he put his hand on you and look like you just can't breathe. Look like you just a-burning up, and you got to do something, and you can't do nothing; I been on my knees many a time, weeping and wrestling before the Lord—*crying*, Johnny—and calling on Jesus' name. That's the only name that's got power over Satan. That's the way it's been with *me* sometime, and I'm *saved*. What you think it's going to be like for you, boy?" He looked at John, who, head down, was putting the chairs in order. "Do you want to be saved, Johnny?"

"I don't know," John said.

"Will you try him? Just fall on your knees one day and ask him to help you to pray?"

John turned away, and looked out over the church, which now seemed like a vast, high field, ready for the harvest. He thought of a First Sunday, a Communion Sunday not long ago when the saints, dressed all in white, ate flat, unsalted Jewish bread, which was the body of the Lord, and drank red grape juice, which was His blood. And when they rose from the table, prepared especially for this day, they separated, the men on the one side, and the women on the other, and two basins were filled with water so that they could wash each other's feet, as Christ had commanded His disciples to do. They knelt before each other, woman before woman, and man before man, and washed and dried each other's feet. Brother Elisha had knelt before John's father. When the service was over they had kissed each other with a holy kiss. John turned again and looked at Elisha.

Elisha looked at him and smiled. "You think about what I said, boy."

When they were finished Elisha sat down at the piano and played to himself. John sat on a chair in the front row and watched him.

"Don't look like nobody's coming tonight," he said after a long while. Elisha did not arrest his playing of a mournful song: "Oh, Lord, have mercy on me."

"They'll be here," said Elisha.

And as he spoke there was a knocking on the door. Elisha stopped playing. John went to the door, where two sisters stood, Sister McCandless and Sister Price.

"Praise the Lord, son," they said.

"Praise the Lord," said John.

They entered, heads bowed and hands folded before them around their Bibles. They wore the black cloth coats that they wore all week and they had old felt hats on their heads. John felt a chill as they passed him, and he closed the door.

Elisha stood up, and they cried again: "Praise the Lord!" Then the two women knelt for a moment before their seats to pray. This was also passionate ritual. Each entering saint, before he could take part in the service, must commune for a moment alone with the Lord. John watched the praying women. Elisha sat again at the piano and picked up his mournful song. The women rose, Sister Price first, and then Sister McCandless, and looked around the church.

"Is we the first?" asked Sister Price. Her voice was mild, her skin was copper. She was younger than Sister McCandless by several years, a single woman who had never, as she testified, known a man.

"No, Sister Price," smiled Brother Elisha, "Brother Johnny here was the first. Him and me cleaned up this evening."

"Brother Johnny is mighty faithful," said Sister McCandless. "The Lord's going to work with him in a mighty way, you mark my words."

There were times—whenever, in fact, the Lord had shown His favor by working through her—when whatever Sister McCandless said sounded like a threat. Tonight she was still very much under the influence of the sermon she had preached the night before. She was an enormous woman, one of the biggest and blackest God had ever made, and He had blessed her with a mighty voice with which to sing and preach, and she was going out soon into the field. For many years the Lord had pressed Sister McCandless to get up, as she said, and move; but she had been of timid disposition and feared to set herself above others. Not until He laid her low, before this very altar, had she dared to rise and preach the gospel. But now she had buckled on her traveling shoes. She would cry aloud and spare not, and lift up her voice like a trumpet in Zion.

"Yes," said Sister Price, with her gentle smile, "He says that he that is faithful in little things shall be made chief over many."

John smiled back at her, a smile that, despite the shy gratitude it was meant to convey, did not escape being ironic, or even malicious. But Sister Price did not see this, which deepened John's hidden scorn.

"Ain't but you two who cleaned the church?" asked Sister McCandless with an unnerving smile—the smile of the prophet who sees the secrets hidden in the hearts of men.

"Lord, Sister McCandless," said Elisha, "look like it ain't never but us two. I don't know what the other young folks does on Saturday nights, but they don't come nowhere near here."

Neither did Elisha usually come anywhere near the church on Saturday evenings; but as the pastor's nephew he was entitled to certain freedoms; in him it was a virtue that he came at all.

"It sure is time we had a revival among our young folks," said Sister McCandless. "They cooling off something terrible. The Lord ain't going to bless no church what lets its young people get so lax, no sir. He said, because you ain't neither hot or cold I'm going to spit you outen my mouth. That's the Word." And she looked around sternly, and Sister Price nodded.

"And Brother Johnny here ain't even saved yet," said Elisha. "Look like the saved young people would be ashamed to let him be more faithful in the house of God than they are."

"He said that the first shall be last and the last shall be first," said Sister Price with a triumphant smile.

"Indeed, He did," agreed Sister McCandless. "This boy going to make it to the Kingdom before any of them, you wait and see."

"Amen," said Brother Elisha, and he smiled at John.

"Is Father going to come and be with us tonight?" asked Sister McCandless after a moment.

Elisha frowned and thrust out his lower lip. "I don't reckon so, sister," he said. "I believe he going to try to stay home tonight and preserve his strength for the morning service. The Lord's been speaking to him in visions and dreams and he ain't got much sleep lately."

"Yes," said Sister McCandless, "that sure is a praying man. I tell you, it ain't every shepherd tarries before the Lord for his flock like Father James does."

"Indeed, that is the truth," said Sister Price, with animation. "The Lord sure done blessed us with a good shepherd."

"He mighty hard sometimes," said Sister McCandless, "but the Word is hard. The way of holiness ain't no joke."

"He done made me to know that," said Brother Elisha with a smile.

Sister McCandless stared at him. Then she laughed. "Lord," she cried, "I *bet* you can say so!"

"And I loved him for that," said Sister Price. "It ain't every pastor going to set down his own nephew—in front of the whole church, too. And Elisha hadn't committed no big fault."

"Ain't no such thing," said Sister McCandless, "as a little fault or a big fault. Satan get his foot in the door, he ain't going to rest till he's in the room. You is in the Word or you *ain't*—ain't no halfway with God."

"You reckon we ought to start?" asked Sister Price doubtfully, after a pause. "Don't look to me like nobody else is coming."

"Now, don't you sit there," laughed Sister McCandless, "and be of little faith like that. I just believe the Lord's going to give us a great service tonight." She turned to John. "Ain't your daddy coming out tonight?"

"Yes'm," John replied, "he said he was coming."

"There!" said Sister McCandless. "And your mama—is she coming out, too?"

"I don't know," John said. "She mighty tired."

"She ain't so tired she can't come out and pray a *little* while," said Sister McCandless.

For a moment John hated her, and he stared at her fat, black profile in anger. Sister Price said:

"But I declare, it's a wonder how that woman works like she does, and keeps those children looking so neat and clean and all, and gets out to the house of God almost every night. Can't be nothing but the Lord that bears her up."

"I reckon we might have a little song," said Sister McCandless, "just to warm things up. I sure hate to walk in a church where folks is just sitting and talking. Look like it takes all my spirit away."

"Amen," said Sister Price.

Elisha began a song: "This may be my last time," and they began to sing:

> *"This may be the last time I pray with you,*
> *This may be my last time, I don't know."*

As they sang, they clapped their hands, and John saw that Sister McCandless looked about her for a tambourine. He rose and mounted the pulpit steps, and took from the small opening at the bottom of the pulpit three tambourines. He gave one to Sister McCandless, who nodded and smiled, not breaking her rhythm, and he put the rest on a chair near Sister Price.

> *"This may be the last time I sing with you*
> *This may be my last time, I don't know."*

He watched them, singing with them—because otherwise they would force him to sing—and trying not to hear the words that he forced outward from his throat. And he thought to clap his hands, but he could not; they remained tightly folded in his lap. If he did not sing they would be upon him, but his heart told him that he had no right to sing or to rejoice.

> *"Oh, this*
> *May be my last time*
> *This*
> *May be my last time*
> *Oh, this*
> *May be my last time . . ."*

And he watched Elisha, who was a young man in the Lord; who, a priest after the order of Melchizedek, had been given power over death and Hell. The Lord had lifted him up, and turned him around, and set his feet on the shining way. What were the thoughts of Elisha when night came, and he was alone where no eye could see, and no tongue bear witness, save only the trumpetlike tongue of God? Were his thoughts, his bed, his body foul? What were his dreams?

> *"This may be my last time,*
> *I don't know."*

Behind him the door opened and the wintry air rushed in. He turned to see, entering the door, his father, his mother, and his aunt. It was only the presence of his aunt that shocked him, for she had never entered this church before: she seemed to have been summoned to witness a bloody act. It was in all her aspect, quiet with a dreadful quietness, as she moved down the aisle behind his mother and knelt for a moment beside his mother and father to pray. John knew that it was the hand of the Lord that had led her to this place, and his heart grew cold. The Lord was riding on the wind tonight. What might that wind have spoken before the morning came?

PART TWO

The Prayers
of the Saints

And they cried with a loud voice, saying,
How long, O Lord, holy and true,
dost thou not judge and avenge our blood
on them that dwell on the earth?

ONE

Florence's Prayer

Light and life to all He brings,
Risen with healing in His wings!

F<small>LORENCE RAISED HER</small> voice in the only song she could remember that her mother used to sing:

> *"It's me, it's me, it's me, oh, Lord.*
> *Standing in the need of prayer."*

Gabriel turned to stare at her, in astonished triumph that his sister should at last be humbled. She did not look at him. Her thoughts were all on God. After a moment, the congregation and the piano joined her:

> *"Not my father, not my mother,*
> *But it's me, oh, Lord."*

She knew that Gabriel rejoiced, not that her humility might lead her to grace, but only that some private anguish had brought her low: her song revealed that she was suffering, and this her brother was glad to see. This had always been his spirit. Nothing had ever changed it; nothing ever would. For a moment her pride stood up; the resolution that had brought her to this place tonight faltered, and she felt that if Gabriel was the Lord's anointed, she would rather die and endure Hell for all eternity than bow before His altar. But she strangled her pride, rising to stand with them in the holy space before the altar, and still singing:

"Standing in the need of prayer."

Kneeling as she had not knelt for many years, and in this company before the altar, she gained again from the song the meaning it had held for her mother, and gained a new meaning for herself. As a child, the song had made her see a woman, dressed in black, standing in infinite mists alone, waiting for the form of the Son of God to lead her through that white fire. This woman now returned to her, more desolate; it was herself, not knowing where to put her foot; she waited, trembling, for the mists to be parted that she might walk in peace. That long road, her life, which she had followed for sixty groaning years, had led her at last to her mother's starting-place, the altar of the Lord. For her feet stood on the edge of that river which her mother, rejoicing, had crossed over. And would the Lord now reach out His hand to Florence and heal and save? But, going down before the scarlet cloth at the foot of the golden cross, it came to her that she had forgotten how to pray.

Her mother had taught her that the way to pray was to forget everything and everyone but Jesus; to pour out of the heart, like water from a bucket, all evil thoughts, all thoughts of self, all malice for one's enemies; to come boldly, and yet more humbly than a little child, before the Giver of all good things. Yet, in Florence's heart tonight hatred and bitterness weighed like granite, pride refused to abdicate from the throne it had held so long. Neither love nor humility had led her to the altar, but only fear. And God did not hear the prayers of the fearful, for the hearts of the fearful held no belief. Such prayers could rise no higher than the lips that uttered them.

Around her she heard the saints' voices, a steady, charged murmur, with now and again the name of *Jesus* rising above, sometimes like the swift rising of a bird into the air of a sunny day, sometimes like the slow rising of the mist from swamp ground. Was this the way to pray? In the church that she had joined when she first came North one knelt before the altar once only, in the beginning, to ask forgiveness of sins; and this accomplished, one was baptized and became a Christian, to kneel no more thereafter. Even if the Lord should lay some great burden on one's back—as He had done, but never so heavy a burden as this she carried now—one prayed in silence. It was indecent, the practice of common niggers to cry aloud at the foot of the altar, tears streaming for all the world to see. She had never done it, not even as a girl down home in the church they had gone to in those days. Now perhaps it was too late, and the Lord would suffer her to die in the darkness in which she had lived so long.

In the olden days God had healed His children. He had caused the blind to see, the lame to walk, and He had raised dead men from the grave. But Florence remembered one phrase, which now she muttered against the knuckles that bruised her lips: "Lord, help my unbelief."

For the message had come to Florence that had come to Hezekiah: *Set thine house in order, for thou shalt die and not live.* Many nights ago, as she turned on her bed, this message came to her. For many days and nights the message was repeated; there had been time, then, to turn to God. But she had thought to evade him, seeking among the women she knew for remedies; and then, because the pain increased, she had sought doctors; and when the doctors did no good she had climbed stairs all over town to rooms where incense burned and where men or women in traffic with the Devil gave her white powders, or herbs to make tea, and cast spells upon her to take the sickness away. The burning in her bowels did not cease—that burning which, eating inward, took the flesh visibly from her bones and caused her to vomit up her food. Then one night she found death standing in the room. Blacker than night, and gigantic, he filled one corner of her narrow room, watching her with eyes like the eyes of a serpent when his head is lifted to strike. Then she screamed and called on God, turning on the light. And death departed, but she knew he would be back. Every night would bring him a little closer to her bed.

And after death's first silent vigil her life came to her bedside to curse her with many voices. Her mother, in rotting rags and filling the room with the stink of the grave, stood over her to curse the daughter who had denied her on her deathbed. Gabriel came, from all his times and ages, to curse the sister who had held him to scorn and mocked his ministry. Deborah, black, her body as shapeless and hard as iron, looked on with veiled, triumphant eyes, cursing the Florence who had mocked her in her pain and barrenness. Frank came, even he, with that same smile, the same tilt of his head. Of them all she would have begged forgiveness, had they come with ears to hear. But they came like many trumpets; even if they had come to hear and not to testify it was not they who could forgive her, but only God.

The piano had stopped. All around her now were only the voices of the saints.

"Dear Father"—it was her mother praying—"we come before You on our knees this evening to ask You to watch over us and hold back the hand of the destroying angel. Lord, sprinkle the doorpost of this house with the blood of the lamb to keep all the wicked men away. Lord, we praying for every mother's son and daughter everywhere in the world but we want You to take special care of this girl here to-night, Lord, and don't let no evil come nigh her. We know You's able to do it, Lord, in Jesus' name, Amen."

This was the first prayer Florence heard, the only prayer she was ever to hear in which her mother demanded the protection of God more passionately for her daughter than she demanded it for her son. It was night, the windows were shut tightly with the shades drawn, and the great table was pushed against the door. The kerosene lamps burned low and made great shadows on the newspaper-covered wall. Her mother, dressed in the long, shapeless, colorless dress that she wore every day but Sunday, when she wore white, and with her head tied up in a scarlet cloth, knelt in the center of the room, her hands hanging loosely folded before her, her black face lifted, her eyes shut. The weak, unsteady light placed shadows under her mouth and in the sockets of her eyes, making the face impersonal with majesty, like the face of a prophetess, or like a mask. Silence filled the room after her "Amen," and in the silence they heard, far up the road, the sound of a horse's hoofs. No one moved. Gabriel, from his corner near the stove, looked up and watched his mother.

"I ain't afraid," said Gabriel.

His mother turned, one hand raised. "You hush, now!"

Trouble had taken place in town today. Their neighbor Deborah, who was sixteen, three years older than Florence, had been taken away into the fields the night before by many white men, where they did things to her to make her cry and bleed. Today, Deborah's father had gone to one of the white men's houses, and said that he would kill him and all the other white men he could find. They had beaten him and left him for dead. Now, everyone had shut their doors, praying and waiting, for it was said that the white folks would come tonight and set fire to all the houses, as they had done before.

In the night that pressed outside they heard only the horse's hoofs, which did not stop; there was not the laughter they would have heard had there been many coming on this road, and no calling out of curses, and no one crying for mercy to white men, or to God. The hoofbeats came to the door and passed, and rang, while they listened, ever more faintly away. Then Florence realized how frightened she had been. She watched her mother rise and walk to the window. She peered out through a corner of the blanket that covered it.

"They's gone," she said, "whoever they was." Then: "Blessed be name of the Lord," she said.

Thus had her mother lived and died; and she had often been brought low, but she had never been forsaken. She had always seemed to Florence the oldest woman in the world, for she often spoke of Florence and Gabriel as the children of her old age, and she had been born, innumerable years ago, during slavery, on a plantation in another state. On this plantation she had grown up as one of the field workers, for she was very tall and strong; and by and by she had married and raised children, all of whom had been taken from her, one by sickness and two by auction; and one, whom she had not been allowed to call her own, had been raised in the master's house. When she was a woman grown, well past thirty as she reckoned it, with one husband buried—but the master had given her another— armies, plundering and burning, had come from the North to set them free. This was in answer to the prayers of the faithful, who had never ceased, both day and night, to cry out for deliverance.

For it had been the will of God that they should hear, and pass thereafter, one to another, the story of the Hebrew children who had been held in bondage in the land of Egypt; and how the Lord had heard their groaning, and how His heart was moved; and how He bid them wait but a little season till He should send deliverance. Florence's mother had known this story, so it seemed, from the day that she was born. And while she lived—rising in the morning before the sun came up, standing and bending in the fields when the sun was high, crossing the fields homeward while the sun went down at the gates of Heaven far away, hearing the whistle of the foreman and his eerie cry across the fields; in the whiteness of winter when hogs and turkeys and geese were slaughtered, and lights burned bright in the big house, and Bathsheba, the cook, sent over in a napkin bits of ham and chicken and cakes left over by the white folks—

in all that befell: in her joys, her pipe in the evening, her man at night, the children she suckled, and guided on their first short steps; and in her tribulations, death, and parting, and the lash, she did not forget that deliverance was promised and would surely come. She had only to endure and trust in God. She knew that the big house, the house of pride where the white folks lived, would come down: it was written in the Word of God. They, who walked so proudly now, had not fashioned for themselves or their children so sure a foundation as was hers. They walked on the edge of a steep place and their eyes were sightless—God would cause them to rush down, as the herd of swine had once rushed down, into the sea. For all that they were so beautiful, and took their ease, she knew them, and she pitied them, who would have no covering in the great day of His wrath.

Yet, she told her children, God was just, and He struck no people without first giving many warnings. God gave men time, but all the times were in His hand, and one day the time to forsake evil and do good would all be finished: then only the whirlwind, death riding on the whirlwind, awaited those people who had forgotten God. In all the days that she was growing up, signs failed not, but none heeded. "Slaves done ris," was whispered in the cabin and at the master's gate: slaves in another county had fired the masters' houses and fields and dashed their children to death against the stones. "Another slave in Hell," Bathsheba might say one morning, shooing the pickaninnies away from the great porch: a slave had killed his master, or his overseer, and had gone down to Hell to pay for it. "I ain't got long to stay here," someone crooned beside her in the fields, someone who would be gone by morning on his journey North. All these signs, like the plagues with which the Lord had afflicted Egypt, only hardened the hearts of these people against the Lord. They thought the lash would save them, and they used the lash; or the knife, or the gallows, or the auction block; they thought that kindness would save them, and the master and mistress came down, smiling, to the cabins, making much of the pickaninnies and bearing gifts. These were great days, and they all, black and white, seemed happy together. But when the Word has gone forth from the mouth of God nothing can turn it back.

The word was fulfilled one morning, before she was awake. Many of the stories her mother told meant nothing to Florence; she knew them for what they were, tales told by an old black woman in a cabin in the evening to distract her children from their cold and hunger. But the story of this day she was never to forget; it was a day for which she lived. There was a great running and shouting, said her mother, everywhere outside, and, as she opened her eyes to the light of that day, so bright, she said, and cold, she was certain that the judgment trumpet had sounded. While she still sat, amazed, and wondering what, on the judgment day, would be the best behavior, in rushed Bathsheba, and behind her many tumbling children and field hands and house niggers, all together, and Bathsheba shouted: "Rise up, rise up, Sister Rachel, and see the Lord's deliverance! He done brought us out of Egypt, just like He promised, and we's free at last!" Bathsheba grabbed her, tears running down her face; she, dressed in the clothes in which she had slept, walked to the door to look out on the new day God had given them.

On that day she saw the proud house humbled; green silk and velvet blowing out of windows, and the garden trampled by many horsemen, and the big gate open. The master and mistress, and their kin, and one child she had borne were in that house—which she did not enter. Soon it occurred to her that there was no longer any reason to tarry here. She tied her things in a cloth that she put on her head, and walked out through the big gate, never to see that country any more.

And this became Florence's deep ambition: to walk out one morning through the cabin door, never to return. Her father, whom she scarcely remembered, had departed that way one morning not many months after the birth of Gabriel. And not only her father; every day she heard that another man or woman had said farewell to this iron earth and sky, and started on the journey North. But her mother had no wish to go North where, she said, wickedness dwelt and death rode mighty through the streets. She was content to stay in this cabin and do washing for the white folks, though she was old and her back was sore. And she wanted Florence, also, to be content—helping with the washing, and fixing meals and keeping Gabriel quiet.

Gabriel was the apple of his mother's eye. If he had never been born, Florence might have looked forward to a day when she would be released from her unrewarding round of labor, when she might think of her own future and go out to make it. With the birth of Gabriel, which occurred when she was five, her future was swallowed up. There was only one future in that house, and it was Gabriel's— to which, since Gabriel was a man-child, all else must be sacrificed. Her mother did not, indeed, think of it as sacrifice, but as logic: Florence was a girl, and would by and by be married, and have children of her own, and all the duties of a woman; and this being so, her life in the cabin was the best possible preparation for her future life. But Gabriel was a man; he would go out one day into the world to do a man's work, and he needed, therefore, meat, when there was any in the house, and clothes, whenever clothes could be bought, and the strong indulgence of his womenfolk, so that he would know how to be with women when he had a wife. And he needed the education that Florence desired far more than he, and that she might have got if he had not been born. It was Gabriel who was slapped and scrubbed each morning and sent off to the one-room schoolhouse—which he hated, and where he managed to learn, so far as Florence could discover, almost nothing at all. And often he was not at school, but getting into mischief with other boys. Almost all of their neighbors, and even some of the white folks, came at one time or another to complain of Gabriel's wrongdoing. Their mother would walk out into the yard and cut a switch from a tree and beat him—beat him, it seemed to Florence, until any other boy would have fallen down dead; and so often that any other boy would have ceased his wickedness. Nothing stopped Gabriel, though he made Heaven roar with his howling, though he screamed aloud, as his mother approached, that he would never be such a bad boy again. And, after the beating, his pants still down around his knees and his face wet with tears and mucus, Gabriel was made to kneel down while his mother prayed. She asked Florence to pray, too, but in her heart Florence never prayed. She hoped that Gabriel would break his neck. She wanted the evil against which their mother prayed to overtake him one day.

In those days Florence and Deborah, who had become close friends after Deborah's "accident," hated all men. When men looked at Deborah they saw no further than her unlovely and violated body. In their eyes lived perpetually a lewd, uneasy wonder concerning the night she had been taken in the fields. That night had robbed her of the right to be considered a woman. No man would approach her in honor because she was a living reproach, to herself and to all black women and to all black men. If she had been beautiful, and if God had not given her a spirit so demure, she might, with ironic gusto, have acted out that rape in the fields forever. Since she could not be considered a woman, she could only be looked on as a harlot, a source of delight more bestial and mysteries more shaking than any a proper woman could provide. Lust stirred in the eyes of men when they looked at Deborah, lust that could not be endured because it was so impersonal, limiting communion to the area of her shame. And Florence, who was beautiful but did not look with favor on any of the black men who lusted after her, not wishing to exchange her mother's cabin for one of theirs and to raise their children and so go down, toil-blasted, into as it were a common grave, reinforced in Deborah the terrible belief against which no evidence had ever presented itself: that all men were like this, their thoughts rose no higher, and they lived only to gratify on the bodies of women their brutal and humiliating needs.

One Sunday at a camp-meeting, when Gabriel was twelve years old and was to be baptized, Deborah and Florence stood on the banks of a river along with all the other folks and watched him. Gabriel had not wished to be baptized. The thought had frightened and angered him, but his mother insisted that Gabriel was now of an age to be responsible before God for his sins—she would not shirk the duty, laid on her by the Lord, of doing everything within her power to bring him to the throne of grace. On the banks of a river, under the violent light of noon, confessed believers and children of Gabriel's age waited to be led into the water. Standing out, waist-deep and robed in white, was the preacher, who would hold their heads briefly under water, crying out to Heaven as the baptized held his breath: "I indeed have baptized you with water: but He shall baptize you with the Holy Ghost." Then, as they rose sputtering and blinded and were led to the shore, he cried out again: "Go thou and sin no more." They came up from the water, visibly under the power of the Lord, and on the shore the saints awaited them, beating their tambourines. Standing near the shore were the elders of the church, holding towels with which to cover the newly baptized, who were then led into the tents, one for either sex, where they could change their clothes.

At last, Gabriel, dressed in an old white shirt and short linen pants, stood on the edge of the water. Then he was slowly led into the river, where he had so often splashed naked, until he reached the preacher. And the moment that the preacher threw him down, crying out the words of John the Baptist, Gabriel began to kick and sputter, nearly throwing the preacher off balance; and though at first they thought that it was the power of the Lord that worked in him, they realized as he rose, still kicking and with his eyes tightly shut, that it was only fury, and too much water in his nose. Some folks smiled, but Florence and Deborah did not smile. Though Florence had also been indignant, years before when the slimy water entered her incautiously open mouth, she had done her best not to sputter, and she had not cried out. But now, here came Gabriel, floundering and furious up the bank, and what she looked at, with an anger more violent than any she had felt before, was his nakedness. He was drenched, and his thin, white clothes clung like another skin to his black body. Florence and Deborah looked at one another, while the singing rose to cover Gabriel's howling, and Deborah looked away.

Years later, Deborah and Florence had stood on Deborah's porch at night and watched a vomit-covered Gabriel stagger up the moonlit road, and Florence had cried out: "I hate him! I hate him! Big, black, prancing tomcat of a nigger!" And Deborah had said, in that heavy voice of hers: "You know, honey, the Word tell us to hate the sin but not the sinner."

In nineteen hundred, when she was twenty-six, Florence walked out through the cabin door. She had thought to wait until her mother, who was so ill now that she no longer stirred out of bed, should be buried—but suddenly she knew that she would wait no longer, the time had come. She had been working as cook and serving-girl for a large white family in town, and it was on the day her master proposed that she become his concubine that she knew her life among these wretched had come to its destined end. She left her employment that same day (leaving behind her a most vehement conjugal bitterness), and with part of the money that with cunning, cruelty, and sacrifice she had saved over a period of years, bought a railroad ticket to New York. When she bought it, in a kind of scarlet rage, she held like a talisman at the back of her mind the thought: "I can give it back, I can sell it. This don't mean I got to go." But she knew that nothing could stop her.

And it was this leave-taking that came to stand, in Florence's latter days, and with many another witness, at her bedside. Gray clouds obscured the sun that day, and outside the cabin window she saw that mist still covered the ground. Her mother lay in bed, awake; she was pleading with Gabriel, who had been out drinking the night before, and who was not really sober now, to mend his ways and come to the Lord. And Gabriel, full of the confusion, and pain, and guilt that were his whenever he thought of how he made his mother suffer, but that became nearly insupportable when she taxed him with it, stood before the mirror, head bowed, buttoning his shirt. Florence knew that he could not unlock his lips to speak; he could not say yes to his mother, and to the Lord; and he could not say no.

"Honey," their mother was saying, "don't you *let* your old

mother die without you look her in the eye and tell her she going to see you in glory. You hear me, boy?"

In a moment, Florence thought with scorn, tears would fill his eyes, and he would promise to "do better." He had been promising to "do better" since the day he had been baptized.

She put down her bag in the center of the hateful room.

"Ma," she said, "I'm going. I'm a-going this morning."

Now that she had said it, she was angry with herself for not having said it the night before, so that they would have had time to be finished with their weeping and their arguments. She had not trusted herself to withstand the night before; but now there was almost no time left. The center of her mind was filled with the image of the great, white clock at the railway station, on which the hands did not cease to move.

"You going where?" her mother asked sharply. But she knew that her mother had understood, had indeed long before this moment known that this time would come. The astonishment with which she stared at Florence's bag was not altogether astonishment, but a startled, wary attention. A danger imagined had become present and real, and her mother was already searching for a way to break Florence's will. All this Florence knew in a moment, and it made her stronger. She watched her mother, waiting.

But at the tone of his mother's voice Gabriel, who had scarcely heard Florence's announcement, so grateful had he been that something had occurred to distract from him his mother's attention, dropped his eyes and saw Florence's traveling-bag. And he repeated his mother's question in a stunned, angry voice, understanding it only as the words hit the air:

"Yes, girl. Where you think you going?"

"I'm going," she said, "to New York. I got my ticket."

And her mother watched her. For a moment no one said a word. Then, Gabriel, in a changed and frightened voice, asked:

"And when you done decide that?"

She did not look at him, nor answer his question. She continued to watch her mother. "I got my ticket," she repeated. "I'm going on the morning train."

"Girl," asked her mother, quietly, "is you sure you know what you's doing?"

She stiffened, seeing in her mother's eyes a mocking pity. "I'm a woman grown," she said. "I know what I'm doing."

"And you going," cried Gabriel, "this morning—just like that? And you going to walk off and leave your mother —just like that?"

"You hush," she said, turning to him for the first time, "she got you, ain't she?"

This was indeed, she realized as he dropped his eyes, the bitter, troubling point. He could not endure the thought of being left alone with his mother, with nothing whatever to put between himself and his guilty love. With Florence gone, time would have swallowed up all his mother's children, except himself; and *he,* then, must make amends for all the pain that she had borne, and sweeten her last moments with all his proofs of love. And his mother required of him one proof only, that he tarry no longer in sin. With Florence gone, his stammering time, his playing time, contracted with a bound to the sparest interrogative second, when he must stiffen himself, and answer to his mother, and all the host of Heaven, yes or no.

Florence smiled inwardly a small, malicious smile, watching his slow bafflement, and panic, and rage; and she looked at her mother again. "She got you," she repeated. "She don't need me."

"You going North," her mother said, then. "And when you reckon on coming back?"

"I don't reckon on coming back," she said.

"You come crying back soon enough," said Gabriel, with malevolence, "soon as they whip your butt up there four or five times."

She looked at him again. "Just don't you try to hold your breath till then, you hear?"

"Girl," said her mother, "you mean to tell me the Devil's done made your heart so hard you can just leave your mother on her dying bed, and you don't care if you don't never see her in this world no more? Honey, you can't tell me you done got so evil as all that?"

She felt Gabriel watching her to see how she would take this question—the question that, for all her determination, she had dreaded most to hear. She looked away from her mother, and straightened, catching her breath, looking outward through the small, cracked window. There, outside, beyond the slowly rising mist, and farther off than her eyes could see, her life awaited her. The woman on the bed was old, her life was fading as the mist rose. She thought of her mother as already in the grave; and she would not let herself be strangled by the hands of the dead.

"I'm going, Ma," she said. "I got to go."

Her mother leaned back, face upward to the light, and began to cry. Gabriel moved to Florence's side and grabbed her arm. She looked up into his face and saw that his eyes were full of tears.

"You can't go," he said. "You can't go. You can't go and leave your mother thisaway. She need a woman, Florence, to help look after her. What she going to do here, all alone with me?"

She pushed him from her and moved to stand over her mother's bed.

"Ma," she said, "don't be like that. Ain't a blessed thing for you to cry about so. Ain't a thing can happen to me up North can't happen to me here. God's everywhere, Ma. Ain't no need to worry."

She knew that she was mouthing words; and she realized suddenly that her mother scorned to dignify these words with her attention. She had granted Florence the victory—with a promptness that had the effect of making Florence, however dimly and unwillingly, wonder if her victory was real. She was not weeping for her daughter's future, she was weeping for the past, and weeping in an anguish in which Florence had no part. And all of this filled Florence with a terrible fear, which was immediately transformed into anger. "Gabriel can take care of you," she said, her voice shaking with malice. "Gabriel ain't never going to leave you. Is you, boy?" and she looked at him. He stood, stupid with bewilderment and grief, a few inches from the bed. "But me," she said, "I got to go." She walked to the center of the room again, and picked up her bag.

"Girl," Gabriel whispered, "ain't you got no feelings at all?"

"Lord!" her mother cried; and at the sound her heart turned over; she and Gabriel, arrested, stared at the bed. "Lord, Lord, Lord! Lord, have mercy on my sinful daughter! Stretch out your hand and hold her back from the lake that burns forever! Oh, my Lord, my Lord!" and her voice dropped, and broke, and tears ran down her face. "Lord, I done my best with all the children what you give me. Lord, have mercy on my children, and my children's children."

"Florence," said Gabriel, "please don't go. Please don't go. You ain't really fixing to go and leave her like this?"

Tears stood suddenly in her own eyes, though she could not have said what she was crying for. "Leave me be," she said to Gabriel, and picked up her bag again. She opened the door; the cold, morning air came in. "Good-bye," she said. And then to Gabriel: "Tell her I said good-bye." She walked through the cabin door and down the short steps into the frosty yard. Gabriel watched her, standing frozen between the door and the weeping bed. Then, as her hand was on the gate, he ran before her, and slammed the gate shut.

"Girl, where you going? What you doing? You reckon on finding some men up North to dress you in pearls and diamonds?"

Violently, she opened the gate and moved out into the road. He watched her with his jaw hanging, and his lips loose and wet. "If you ever see me again," she said, "I won't be wearing rags like yours."

All over the church there was only the sound, more awful than the deepest silence, of the prayers of the saints of God. Only the yellow, moaning light shone above them, making their faces gleam like muddy gold. Their faces, and their attitudes, and their many voices rising as one voice made John think of the deepest valley, the longest night, of Peter and Paul in the dungeon cell, one praying while the other sang; or of endless, depthless, swelling water, and no dry land in sight, the true believer clinging to a spar. And, thinking of tomorrow, when the church would rise up, singing, under the booming Sunday light, he thought of the light for which they tarried, which, in an instant, filled the soul, causing (throughout those iron-dark, unimaginable ages before John had come into the world) the newborn in Christ to testify: Once I was blind and now I see.

And then they sang: "Walk in the light, the beautiful light. Shine all around me by day and by night, Jesus, the light of the world." And they sang: "Oh, Lord, Lord, I want to be ready, I want to be ready. I want to be ready to walk in Jerusalem just like John."

To *walk in Jerusalem just like John.* Tonight, his mind was awash with visions: nothing remained. He was ill with doubt and searching. He longed for a light that would teach him, forever and forever, and beyond all question, the way to go; for a power that would bind him, forever and forever, and beyond all crying to the love of God. Or else he wished to stand up now, and leave this tabernacle and never see these people any more. Fury and anguish filled him, unbearable, unanswerable; his mind was stretched to breaking. For it was time that filled his mind, time that was violent with the mysterious love of God. And his mind could not contain the terrible stretch of time that united twelve men fishing by the shores of Galilee, and black men weeping on their knees tonight, and he, a witness.

My soul is a witness for my Lord. There was an awful silence at the bottom of John's mind, a dreadful weight, a dreadful speculation. And not even a speculation, but a deep, deep turning, as of something huge, black, shapeless, for ages dead on the ocean floor, that now felt its rest disturbed by a faint, far wind, which bid it: "Arise." And this weight began to move at the bottom of John's mind, in a silence like the silence of the void before creation, and he began to feel a terror he had never felt before.

And he looked around the church, at the people praying there. Praying Mother Washington had not come in until all of the saints were on their knees, and now she stood, the terrible, old, black woman, above his Aunt Florence, helping her to pray. Her granddaughter, Ella Mae, had come in with her, wearing a mangy fur jacket over her everyday clothes. She knelt heavily in a corner near the piano, under the sign that spoke of the wages of sin, and now and again she moaned. Elisha had not looked up when she came in, and he prayed in silence: sweat stood on his brow. Sister McCandless and Sister Price cried out every now and again: "Yes, Lord!" or: "Bless your name, Jesus!" And his father prayed, his head lifted up and his voice going on like a distant mountain stream.

But his Aunt Florence was silent; he wondered if she slept. He had never seen her praying in a church before. He knew that different people prayed in different ways: had his aunt always prayed in such a silence? His mother, too, was silent, but he had seen her pray before, and her silence made him feel that she was weeping. And why did she weep? And why did they come here, night after night after night, calling out to a God who cared nothing for them—if, above this flaking ceiling, there was any God at all? Then he remembered that the fool has said in his heart, There is no God—and he dropped his eyes, seeing that over his Aunt Florence's head Praying Mother Washington was looking at him.

Frank sang the blues, and he drank too much. His skin was the color of caramel candy. Perhaps for this reason she always thought of him as having candy in his mouth, candy staining the edges of his straight, cruel teeth. For a while he wore a tiny mustache, but she made him shave it off, for it made him look, she thought, like a half-breed gigolo. In details such as this he was always very easy—he would always put on a clean shirt, or get his hair cut, or come with her to Uplift meetings where they heard speeches by prominent Negroes about the future and duties of the Negro race. And this had given her, in the beginning of their marriage, the impression that she controlled him. This impression had been entirely and disastrously false.

When he had left her, more than twenty years before, and after more than ten years of marriage, she had felt for that moment only an exhausted exasperation and a vast relief. He had not been home for two days and three nights, and when he did return they quarreled with more than their usual bitterness. All of the rage she had accumulated during their marriage was told him in that evening as they stood in their small kitchen. He was still wearing overalls, and he had not shaved, and his face was muddy with sweat and dirt. He had said nothing for a long while, and then he had said: "All right, baby. I guess you don't never want to see me no more, not a miserable, black sinner like me." The door closed behind him, and she heard his feet echoing down the long hall, away. She stood alone in the kitchen, holding the empty coffeepot that she had been about to wash. She thought: "He'll come back, and he'll come back drunk." And then she had thought, looking about the kitchen: "Lord, wouldn't it be a blessing if he didn't never come back no more." The Lord had given her what she said she wanted, as was often, she had found, His bewildering method of answering prayer. Frank never did come back. He lived for a long while with another woman, and when the war came he died in France.

Now, somewhere at the other end of the earth, her husband lay buried. He slept in a land his fathers had never seen. She wondered often if his grave were marked—if there stood over it, as in pictures she had seen, a small white cross. If the Lord had ever allowed her to cross that swelling ocean she would have gone, among all the millions buried there, to seek out his grave. Wearing deep mourning, she would have laid on it, perhaps, a wreath of flowers, as other women did; and stood for a moment, head bowed, considering the unspeaking ground. How terrible it would be for Frank to rise on the day of judgment so far from home! And he surely would not scruple, even on that day, to be angry at the Lord. "Me and the Lord," he had often said, "don't always get along so well. He running the world like He thinks I ain't got good sense." How had he died? Slow or sudden? Had he cried out? Had death come creeping on him from behind, or faced him like a man? She knew nothing about it, for she had not known that he was dead until long afterward, when boys were coming home and she had begun searching for Frank's face in the streets. It was the woman with whom he had lived who had told her, for Frank had given this woman's name as his next of kin. The woman, having told her, had not known what else to say, and she stared at Florence in simpleminded pity. This made Florence furious, and she barely murmured: "Thank you," before she turned away. She hated Frank for making this woman official witness to her humiliation. And she wondered again what Frank had seen in this woman, who, though she was younger than Florence, had never been so pretty, and who drank all the time, and who was seen with many men.

But it had been from the first her great mistake—to meet him, to marry him, to love him as she so bitterly had. Looking at his face, it sometimes came to her that all women had been cursed from the cradle; all, in one fashion or another, being given the same cruel destiny, born to suffer the weight of men. Frank claimed that she got it all wrong side up: it was men who suffered because they had to put up with the ways of women—and this from the time that they were born until the day they died. But it was she who was right, she knew; with Frank she had always been right; and it had not been her fault that Frank was the way he was, determined to live and die a common nigger.

But he was always swearing that he would do better; it was, perhaps, the brutality of his penitence that had kept them together for so long. There was something in her which loved to see him bow—when he came home, stinking with whisky, and crept with tears into her arms. Then he, so ultimately master, was mastered. And holding him in her arms while, finally, he slept, she thought with the sensations of luxury and power: "But there's lots of good in Frank. I just got to be patient and he'll come along all right." To "come along" meant that he would change his ways and consent to be the husband she had traveled so far to find. It was he who, unforgivably, taught her that there are people in the world for whom "coming along" is a perpetual process, people who are destined never to arrive. For ten years he came along, but when he left her he was the same man she had married. He had not changed at all.

He had never made enough money to buy the home she wanted, or anything else she really wanted, and this had been part of the trouble between them. It was not that he could not make money, but that he would not save it. He would take half a week's wages and go out and buy something he wanted, or something he thought she wanted. He would come home on Saturday afternoons, already half drunk, with some useless object, such as a vase, which, it had occurred to him, she would like to fill with flowers—she who never noticed flowers and who would certainly never have bought any. Or a hat, always too expensive or too vulgar, or a ring that looked as though it had been designed for a whore. Sometimes it occurred to him to do the Saturday shopping on his way home, so that she would not have to do it; in which case he would buy a turkey, the biggest and most expensive he could find, and several pounds of coffee, it being his belief that there was never enough in the house, and enough breakfast cereal to feed an army for a month. Such foresight always filled him with such a sense of his own virtue that, as a kind of reward, he would also buy himself a bottle of whisky; and—lest she should think that he was drinking too much—invite some ruffian home to share it with him. Then they would sit all afternoon in her parlor, playing cards and telling indecent jokes, and making the air foul with whisky and smoke. She would sit in the kitchen, cold with rage and staring at the turkey, which, since Frank always bought them unplucked and with the head on, would cost her hours of exasperating, bloody labor. Then she would wonder what on earth had possessed her to undergo such hard trials and travel so far from home, if all she had found was a two-room apartment in a city she did not like, and a man yet more childish than any she had known when she was young.

Sometimes from the parlor where he and his visitor sat he would call her:

"Hey, Flo!"

And she would not answer. She hated to be called "Flo," but he never remembered. He might call her again, and when she did not answer he would come into the kitchen.

"What's the matter with you, girl? Don't you hear me a-calling you?"

And once when she still made no answer, but sat perfectly still, watching him with bitter eyes, he was forced to make verbal recognition that there was something wrong.

"What's the matter, old lady? You mad at me?"

And when in genuine bewilderment he stared at her, head to one side, the faintest of smiles on his face, something began to yield in her, something she fought, standing up and snarling at him in a lowered voice so that the visitor might not hear:

"I wish you'd tell me just how you think we's going to live all week on a turkey and five pounds of coffee?"

"Honey, I ain't bought nothing we didn't *need*!"

She sighed in helpless fury, and felt tears springing to her eyes.

"I done told you time and again to give *me* the money when you get paid, and let *me* do the shopping—'cause you ain't got the sense that you was born with."

"Baby, I wasn't doing a thing in the world but trying to help you out. I thought maybe you wanted to go somewhere tonight and you didn't want to be bothered with no shopping."

"Next time you want to do me a favor, you tell me first, you hear? And how you expect me to go to a show when you done brought this bird home for me to clean?"

"Honey, I'll clean it. It don't take no time at all."

He moved to the table where the turkey lay and looked at it critically, as though he were seeing it for the first time. Then he looked at her and grinned. "That ain't nothing to get mad about."

She began to cry. "I declare I don't know what gets into you. Every week the Lord sends you go out and do some more foolishness. How do you expect us to get enough money to get away from here if you all the time going to be spending your money on foolishness?"

When she cried, he tried to comfort her, putting his great hand on her shoulder and kissing her where the tears fell.

"Baby, I'm sorry. I thought it'd be a nice surprise."

"The only surprise I want from you is to learn some sense! *That'd* be a surprise! You think I want to stay around here the rest of my life with these dirty niggers you all the time bring home?"

"Where you expect us to live, honey, where we ain't going to be with niggers?"

Then she turned away, looking out of the kitchen window. It faced an elevated train that passed so close she always felt that she might spit in the faces of the flying, staring people.

"I just don't like all that ragtag . . . looks like you think so much of."

Then there was silence. Although she had turned her back to him, she felt that he was no longer smiling and that his eyes, watching her, had darkened.

"And what kind of man you think you married?"

"I thought I married a man with some get up and go to him, who didn't just want to stay on the bottom all his life!"

"And what you want me to do, Florence? You want me to turn white?"

This question always filled her with an ecstasy of hatred. She turned and faced him, and, forgetting that there was someone sitting in the parlor, shouted:

"You ain't got to be white to have some self-respect! You reckon I slave in this house like I do so you and them common niggers can sit here every afternoon throwing ashes all over the floor?"

"And who's common now, Florence?" he asked, quietly, in the immediate and awful silence in which she recognized her error. "Who's acting like a common nigger now? What you reckon my friend is sitting there a-thinking? I declare, I wouldn't be surprised none if he wasn't a-thinking: 'Poor Frank, he sure found him a common wife.' Anyway, he ain't putting his ashes on the floor—he putting them in the ashtray, just like he knew what a ashtray was." She knew that she had hurt him, and that he was angry, by the habit he had at such a moment of running his tongue quickly and incessantly over his lower lip. "But we's a-going now, so you can sweep up the parlor and sit there, if you want to, till the judgment day."

And he left the kitchen. She heard murmurs in the parlor, and then the slamming of the door. She remembered, too late, that he had all his money with him. When he came back, long after night-fall, and she put him to bed and went through his pockets, she found nothing, or almost nothing, and she sank helplessly to the parlor floor and cried.

When he came back at times like this he would be petulant and penitent. She would not creep into bed until she thought that he was sleeping. But he would not be sleeping. He would turn as she stretched her legs beneath the blankets, and his arm would reach out, and his breath would be hot and soursweet in her face.

"Sugar-plum, what you want to be so evil with your baby for? Don't you know you done made me go out and get drunk, and I wasn't a-fixing to do that? I wanted to take you out somewhere to-night." And, while he spoke, his hand was on her breast, and his moving lips brushed her neck. And this caused such a war in her as could scarcely be endured. She felt that everything in existence be-tween them was part of a mighty plan for her humiliation. She did not want his touch, and yet she did: she burned with longing and froze with rage. And she felt that he knew this and inwardly smiled to see how easily, on this part of the battlefield, his victory could be assured. But at the same time she felt that his tenderness, his passion, and his love were real.

"Let me alone, Frank. I want to go to sleep."

"No you don't. You don't want to go to sleep so soon. You want me to talk to you a little. You know how your baby loves to talk. Listen." And he brushed her neck lightly with his tongue. "You hear that?"

He waited. She was silent.

"Ain't you got nothing more to say than that? I better tell you something else." And then he covered her face with kisses; her face, neck, arms, and breasts.

"You stink of whisky. Let me alone."

"Ah. I ain't the only one got a tongue. What you got to say to this?" And his hand stroked the inside of her thigh.

"Stop."

"I ain't going to stop. This is sweet talk, baby."

Ten years. Their battle never ended; they never bought a home. He died in France. Tonight she remembered details of those years which she thought she had forgotten, and at last she felt the stony ground of her heart break up; and tears, as difficult and slow as blood, began to trickle through her fingers. This the old woman above her somehow divined, and she cried: "Yes, honey. You just let go, honey. Let Him bring you low so He can raise you up." And was this the way she should have gone? Had she been wrong to fight so hard? Now she was an old woman, and all alone, and she was going to die. And she had nothing for all her battles. It had all come to this: she was on her face before the altar, crying to God for mercy. Behind her she heard Gabriel cry: "Bless your name, Jesus!" and, thinking of him and the high road of holiness he had traveled, her mind swung like a needle, and she thought of Deborah.

Deborah had written her, not many times, but in a rhythm that seemed to remark each crisis in her life with Gabriel, and once, during the time she and Frank were still together, she had received from Deborah a letter that she had still: it was locked tonight in her handbag, which lay on the altar. She had always meant to show this letter to Gabriel one day, but she never had. She had talked with Frank about it late one night while he lay in bed whistling some ragtag tune and she sat before the mirror and rubbed bleaching cream into her skin. The letter lay open before her and she sighed loudly, to attract Frank's attention.

He stopped whistling in the middle of a phrase; mentally, she finished it. "What you got there, sugar?" he asked, lazily.

"It's a letter from my brother's wife." She stared at her face in the mirror, thinking angrily that all these skin creams were a waste of money, they never did any good.

"What's them niggers doing down home? It ain't no bad news, is it?" Still he hummed, irrepressibly, deep in his throat.

"No . . . well, it ain't no good news neither, but it ain't nothing to surprise *me* none. She say she think my brother's got a bastard living right there in the same town what he's scared to call his own."

"No? And I thought you said your brother was a preacher."

"Being a preacher ain't never stopped a nigger from doing his dirt."

Then he laughed. "You sure don't love your brother like you should. How come his wife found out about this kid?"

She picked up the letter and turned to face him. "Sound to *me* like she *been* knowing about it but she ain't never had the nerve to say nothing." She paused, then added, reluctantly: "Of course, she ain't really what you might call *sure*. But she ain't a woman to go around thinking things. She mighty worried."

"Hell, what she worried about it now for? Can't nothing be done about it now."

"She wonder if she ought to ask him about it."

"And do she reckon if she ask him, he going to be fool enough to say yes?"

She sighed again, more genuinely this time, and turned back to the mirror. "Well . . . he's a preacher. And if Deborah's right, he ain't got no right to be a preacher. He ain't no better'n nobody else. In *fact*, he ain't no better than a murderer."

He had begun to whistle again; he stopped. "Murderer? How so?"

"Because he done let this child's mother go off and die when the child was born. That's how so." She paused. "And it sound just like Gabriel. He ain't never thought a minute about nobody in this world but himself."

He said nothing, watching her implacable back. Then: "You going to answer this letter?"

"I reckon."

"And what you going to say?"

"I'm going to tell her she ought to let him know she know about his wickedness. Get up in front of the congregation and tell them too, if she has to."

He stirred restlessly, and frowned. "Well, you know more about it than me. But I don't see where that's going to do no good."

"It'll do *her* some good. It'll make him treat her better. You don't know my brother like I do. There ain't but one way to get along with him, you got to scare him half to death. That's all. He ain't *got* no right to go around running his mouth about how holy he is if he done turned a trick like that."

There was silence; he whistled again a few bars of his song; and then he yawned, and said: "Is you coming to bed, old lady? Don't know why you keep wasting all your time and *my* money on all them old skin whiteners. You as black now as you was the day you was born."

"You wasn't there the day I was born. And I know you don't want a coal-black woman." But she rose from the mirror, and moved toward the bed.

"I ain't never said nothing like that. You just kindly turn out that light and I'll make you to know that black's a mighty pretty color."

She wondered if Deborah had ever spoken; and she wondered if she would give to Gabriel the letter that she carried in her handbag tonight. She had held it all these years, awaiting some savage opportunity. What this opportunity would have been she did not know; at this moment she did not want to know. For she had always thought of this letter as an instrument in her hands which could be used to complete her brother's destruction. When he was completely cast down she would prevent him from ever rising again by holding before him the evidence of his blood-guilt. But now she thought she would not live to see this patiently awaited day. She was going to be cut down.

And the thought filled her with terror and rage; the tears dried on her face and the heart within her shook, divided between a terrible longing to surrender and a desire to call God into account. Why had He preferred her mother and her brother, the old, black woman, and the low, black man, while she, who had sought only to walk upright, was come to die, alone and in poverty, in a dirty, furnished room? She beat her fists heavily against the altar. He, *he* would live, and, smiling, watch her go down into the grave! And her mother would be there, leaning over the gates of Heaven, to see her daughter burning in the pit.

As she beat her fists on the altar, the old woman above her laid hands on her shoulders, crying: "Call on Him, daughter! Call on the Lord!" And it was as though she had been hurled outward into time, where no boundaries were, for the voice was the voice of her mother, but the hands were the hands of death. And she cried aloud, as she had never in all her life cried before, falling on her face on the altar, at the feet of the old, black woman. Her tears came down like burning rain. And the hands of death caressed her shoulders, the voice whispered and whispered in her ear: "God's got your number, knows where you live, death's got a warrant out for you."

T W O

Gabriel's Prayer

Now I been introduced
To the Father and the Son,
And I ain't
No stranger now.

WHEN FLORENCE CRIED, Gabriel was moving outward in fiery darkness, talking to the Lord. Her cry came to him from afar, as from unimaginable depths; and it was not his sister's cry he heard, but the cry of the sinner when he is taken in his sin. This was the cry he had heard so many days and nights, before so many altars, and he cried tonight, as he had cried before: "Have your way, Lord! Have your way!"

Then there was only silence in the church. Even Praying Mother Washington had ceased to moan. Soon someone would cry again, and the voices would begin again; there would be music by and by, and shouting, and the sound of the tambourines. But now in this waiting, burdened silence it seemed that all flesh waited—paused, transfixed by something in the middle of the air—for the quickening power.

This silence, continuing like a corridor, carried Gabriel back to the silence that had preceded his birth in Christ. Like a birth indeed, all that had come before this moment was wrapped in darkness, lay at the bottom of the sea of forgetfulness, and was not now counted against him, but was related only to that blind, and doomed, and stinking corruption he had been before he was redeemed.

The silence was the silence of the early morning, and he was returning from the harlot's house. Yet all around him were the sounds of the morning: of birds, invisible, praising God; of crickets in the vines, frogs in the swamp, or dogs miles away and close at hand, roosters on the porch. The sun was not yet half awake; only the utmost tops of trees had begun to tremble at his turning; and the mist moved sullenly, before Gabriel and all around him, falling back before the light that rules by day. Later, he said of that morning that his sin was on him; then he knew only that he carried a burden and that he longed to lay it down. This burden was heavier than the heaviest mountain and he carried it in his heart. With each step that he took his burden grew heavier, and his breath became slow and harsh, and, of a sudden, cold sweat stood out on his brow and drenched his back.

All alone in the cabin his mother lay waiting; not only for his return this morning, but for his surrender to the Lord. She lingered only for this, and he knew it, even though she no longer exhorted him as she had in days but shortly gone by. She had placed him in the hands of the Lord, and she waited with patience to see how He would work the matter.

For she would live to see the promise of the Lord fulfilled. She would not go to her rest until her son, the last of her children, he who would place her in the winding-sheet, should have entered the communion of the saints. Now she, who had been impatient once, and violent, who had cursed and shouted and contended like a man, moved into silence, contending only, and with the last measure of her strength, with God. And this, too, she did like a man: knowing that she had kept the faith, she waited for Him to keep His promise. Gabriel knew that when he entered she would not ask him where he had been; she would not reproach him; and her eyes, even when she closed her lids to sleep, would follow him everywhere.

Later, since it was Sunday, some of the brothers and sisters would come to her, to sing and pray around her bed. And she would pray for him, sitting up in bed unaided, her head lifted, her voice steady; while he, kneeling in a corner of the room, trembled and almost wished that she would die; and trembled again at this testimony to the desperate wickedness of his heart; and prayed without words to be forgiven. For he had no words when he knelt before the throne. And he feared to make a vow before Heaven until he had the strength to keep it. And yet he knew that until he made the vow he would never find the strength.

For he desired in his soul, with fear and trembling, all the glories that his mother prayed he should find. Yes, he wanted power—he wanted to know himself to be the Lord's anointed, His well-beloved, and worthy, nearly, of that snow-white dove which had been sent down from Heaven to testify that Jesus was the Son of God. He wanted to be master, to speak with that authority which could only come from God. It was later to become his proud testimony that he hated his sins—even as he ran toward sin, even as he sinned. He hated the evil that lived in his body, and he feared it, as he feared and hated the lions of lust and longing that prowled the defenseless city of his mind. He was later to say that this was a gift bequeathed him by his mother, that it was God's hand on him from his earliest beginnings; but then he knew only that when each night came, chaos and fever raged in him; the silence in the cabin between his mother and himself became something that could not be borne; not looking at her, facing the mirror as he put on his jacket, and trying to avoid his face there, he told her that he was going to take a little walk—he would be back soon.

Sometimes Deborah sat with his mother, watching him with eyes

that were no less patient and reproachful. He would escape into the
starry night and walk until he came to a tavern, or to a house that he
had marked already in the long daytime of his lust. And then he
drank until hammers rang in his distant skull; he cursed his friends
and his enemies, and fought until blood ran down; in the morning
he found himself in mud, in clay, in strange beds, and once or twice
in jail; his mouth sour, his clothes in rags, from all of him arising the
stink of his corruption. Then he could not even weep. He could not
even pray. He longed, nearly, for death, which was all that could release him from the cruelty of his chains.

And through all this his mother's eyes were on him; her hand,
like fiery tongs, gripped the lukewarm ember of his heart; and caused
him to feel, at the thought of death, another, colder terror. To go
down into the grave, unwashed, unforgiven, was to go down into the
pit forever, where terrors awaited him greater than any the earth, for
all her age and groaning, had ever borne. He would be cut off from
the living, forever; he would have no name forever. Where he had
been would be silence only, rock, stubble, and no seed; for him, forever, and for his, no hope of glory. Thus, when he came to the harlot, he came to her in rage, and he left her in vain sorrow—feeling
himself to have been, once more, most foully robbed, having spent
his holy seed in a forbidden darkness where it could only die. He
cursed the betraying lust that lived in him, and he cursed it again in
others. But: "I remember," he was later to say, "the day my dungeon
shook and my chains fell off."

And he walked homeward, thinking of the night behind him. He
had seen the woman at the very beginning of the evening, but she
had been with many others, men and women, and so he had ignored
her. But later, when he was on fire with whisky, he looked again directly at her, and saw immediately that she had also been thinking of
him. There were not so many people with her—it was as though she
had been making room for him. He had already been told that she
was a widow from the North, in town for only a few days to visit her
people. When he looked at her she looked at him and, as though it

were part of the joking conversation she was having with her friends, she laughed aloud. She had the lie-gap between her teeth, and a big mouth; when she laughed, she belatedly caught her lower lip in her teeth, as though she were ashamed of so large a mouth, and her breasts shook. It was not like the riot that occurred when big, fat women laughed—her breasts rose and fell against the tight cloth of her dress. She was much older than he—around Deborah's age, perhaps thirty-odd—and she was not really pretty. Yet the distance between them was abruptly charged with her, and her smell was in his nostrils. Almost, he felt those moving breasts beneath his hand. And he drank again, allowing, unconsciously, or nearly, his face to fall into the lines of innocence and power which his experience with women had told him made their love come down.

Well (walking homeward, cold and tingling) yes, they did the thing. Lord, how they rocked in their bed of sin, and how she cried and shivered; Lord, how her love came down! Yes (walking homeward through the fleeing mist, with the cold sweat standing on his brow), yet, in vanity and the pride of conquest, he thought of her, of her smell, the heat of her body beneath his hands, of her voice, and her tongue, like the tongue of a cat, and her teeth, and her swelling breasts, and how she moved for him, and held him, and labored with him, and how they fell, trembling and groaning, and locked together, into the world again. And, thinking of this, his body freezing with his sweat, and yet altogether violent with the memory of lust, he came to a tree on a gentle rise, beyond which, and out of sight, lay home, where his mother lay. And there leaped into his mind, with the violence of water that has burst the dams and covered the banks, rushing uncontrolled toward the doomed, immobile houses—on which, on roof-tops and windows, the sun yet palely shivers—the memory of all the mornings he had mounted here and passed this tree, caught for a moment between sins committed and sins to be committed. The mist on this rise had fled away, and he felt that he stood, as he faced the lone tree, beneath the naked eye of Heaven.

Then, in a moment, there was silence, only silence, everywhere—the very birds had ceased to sing, and no dogs barked, and no rooster crowed for day. And he felt that this silence was God's judgment; that all creation had been stilled before the just and awful wrath of God, and waited now to see the sinner—*he* was the sinner—cut down and banished from the presence of the Lord. And he touched the tree, hardly knowing that he touched it, out of an impulse to be hidden; and then he cried: "Oh, Lord, have mercy! Oh, Lord, have mercy on me!"

And he fell against the tree, sinking to the ground and clutching the roots of the tree. He had shouted into silence and only silence answered—and yet, when he cried, his cry had caused a ringing to the outermost limits of the earth. This ringing, his lone cry rolling through creation, frightening the sleeping fish and fowl, awakening echoes everywhere, river, and valley, and mountain wall, caused in him a fear so great that he lay for a moment silent and trembling at the base of the tree, as though he wished to be buried there. But that burdened heart of his would not be still, would not let him keep silence—would not let him breathe until he cried again. And so he cried again; and his cry returned again; and still the silence waited for God to speak.

And his tears began—such tears as he had not known were in him. "I wept," he said later, "like a little child." But no child had ever wept such tears as he wept that morning on his face before Heaven, under the mighty tree. They came from deeps no child discovers, and shook him with an ague no child endures. And presently, in his agony, he was screaming, each cry seeming to tear his throat apart, and stop his breath, and force the hot tears down his face, so that they splashed his hands and wet the root of the tree: "Save me! Save me!" And all creation rang, but did not answer. "I couldn't hear nobody pray."

Yes, he was in that valley where his mother had told him he would find himself, where there was no human help, no hand outstretched to protect or save. Here nothing prevailed save the mercy of

God—here the battle was fought between God and the Devil, between death and everlasting life. And he had tarried too long, he had turned aside in sin too long, and God would not hear him. The appointed time had passed and God had turned His face away.

"Then," he testified, "I heard my mother singing. She was a-singing for me. She was a-singing low and sweet, right there beside me, like she knew if she just called Him, the Lord would come." When he heard this singing, which filled all the silent air, which swelled until it filled all the waiting earth, the heart within him broke, and yet began to rise, lifted of its burden; and his throat unlocked; and his tears came down as though the listening skies had opened. "Then I praised God, Who had brought me out of Egypt and set my feet on the solid rock." When at last he lifted up his eyes he saw a new Heaven and a new earth; and he heard a new sound of singing, for a sinner had come home. "I looked at my hands and my hands were new. I looked at my feet and my feet were new. And I opened my mouth to the Lord that day and Hell won't make me change my mind." And, yes, there was singing everywhere; the birds and the crickets and the frogs rejoiced, the distant dogs leaping and sobbing, circled in their narrow yards, and roosters cried from every high fence that here was a new beginning, a blood-washed day!

And this was the beginning of his life as a man. He was just past twenty-one; the century was not yet one year old. He moved into town, into the room that awaited him at the top of the house in which he worked, and he began to preach. He married Deborah in that same year. After the death of his mother, he began to see her all the time. They went to the house of God together, and because there was no one, any more, to look after him, she invited him often to her home for meals, and kept his clothes neat, and after he had preached they discussed his sermons; that is, he listened while she praised.

He had certainly never intended to marry her; such an idea was no more in his mind, he would have said, than the possibility of flying to the moon. He had known her all his life; she had been his older sister's older friend, and then his mother's faithful visitor; she had never, for Gabriel, been young. So far as he was concerned, she might have been born in her severe, her sexless, long and shapeless habit, always black or gray. She seemed to have been put on earth to visit the sick, and to comfort those who wept, and to arrange the last garments of the dying.

Again, there was her legend, her history, which would have been enough, even had she not been so wholly unattractive, to put her forever beyond the gates of any honorable man's desire. This, indeed, in her silent, stolid fashion, she seemed to know: where, it might be, other women held as their very charm and secret the joy that they could give and share, she contained only the shame that she had borne—shame, unless a miracle of human love delivered her, was all she had to give. And she moved, therefore, through their small community like a woman mysteriously visited by God, like a terrible example of humility, or like a holy fool. No ornaments ever graced her body; there was about her no tinkling, no shining, and no softness. No ribbon falsified her blameless and implacable headgear; on her woolen head there was only the barest minimum of oil. She did not gossip with the other women—she had nothing, indeed, to gossip about—but kept her communication to yea and nay, and read her Bible, and prayed. There were people in the church, and even men carrying the gospel, who mocked Deborah behind her back; but their mockery was uneasy; they could never be certain but that they might be holding up to scorn the greatest saint among them, the Lord's peculiar treasure and most holy vessel.

"You sure is a godsend to me, Sister Deborah," Gabriel would sometimes say. "I don't know what I'd do without you."

For she sustained him most beautifully in his new condition; with her unquestioning faith in God, and her faith in him, she, even more than the sinners who came crying to the altar after he had preached, bore earthly witness to his calling; and speaking, as it were, in the speech of men she lent reality to the mighty work that the Lord had appointed to Gabriel's hands.

And she would look up at him with her timid smile. "You hush, Reverend. It's me that don't never kneel down without I thank the Lord for *you*."

Again: she never called him Gabriel or "Gabe," but from the time that he began to preach she called him Reverend, knowing that the Gabriel whom she had known as a child was no more, was a new man in Christ Jesus.

"You ever hear from Florence?" she sometimes asked.

"Lord, Sister Deborah, it's me that ought to be asking *you*. That girl don't hardly never write to me."

"I ain't heard from her real lately." She paused. Then: "I don't believe she so happy up there."

"And serve her right, too—she ain't had no business going away from here like she did, just like a crazy woman." And then he asked, maliciously: "She tell you if she married yet?"

She looked at him quickly, and looked away. "Florence ain't thinking about no husband," she said.

He laughed. "God bless you for your pure heart, Sister Deborah. But if that girl ain't gone away from here a-looking for a husband, my name ain't Gabriel Grimes."

"If she'd a-wanted a husband look to me like she could a just picked one out right here. You don't mean to tell me she done traveled all the way North just for that?" And she smiled strangely, a smile less gravely impersonal. He, seeing this, thought that it certainly did a strange thing to her face: it made her look like a frightened girl.

"You know," he said, watching her with more attention, "Florence ain't never thought none of these niggers around here was good enough for her."

"I wonder," she ventured, "if she *ever* going to find a man good enough for her. She so proud—look like she just won't let nobody come near her."

"Yes," he said, frowning, "she so proud the Lord going to bring her low one day. You mark my words."

"Yes," she sighed, "the Word sure do tell us that pride goes before destruction."

"And a haughty spirit before a fall. That's the Word."

"Yes," and she smiled again, "ain't no shelter against the Word of God, is there, Reverend? You is just got to be in it, that's all—'cause every word is true, and the gates of Hell ain't going to be able to stand against it."

He smiled, watching her, and felt a great tenderness fill his heart. "You just *stay* in the Word, little sister. The windows of Heaven going to open up and pour down blessings on you till you won't know where to put them."

When she smiled now it was a heightened joy. "He done blessed me already, Reverend. He blessed me when He saved your soul and sent you out to preach His gospel."

"Sister Deborah," he said, slowly, "all that sinful time—was you a-praying for me?"

Her tone dropped ever so slightly. "We sure was, Reverend. Me and your mother, we was a-praying all the time."

And he looked at her, full of gratitude and a sudden, wild conjecture: he had been real for her, she had watched him, and prayed for him during all those years when she, for him, had been nothing but a shadow. And she was praying for him still; he would have her prayers to aid him all his life long—he saw this, now, in her face. She said nothing, and she did not smile, only looked at him with her grave kindness, now a little questioning, a little shy.

"God bless you, sister," he said at last.

It was during this dialogue, or hard on the heels of it, that the town was subjected to a monster revival meeting. Evangelists from all the surrounding counties, from as far south as Florida and as far north as Chicago, came together in one place to break the bread of life. It was called the Twenty-Four Elders Revival Meeting, and it was the great occasion of that summer. For there were twenty-four of them, each one given his night to preach—to shine, as it were, before men, and to glorify his Heavenly Father. Of these twenty-four, all of them men of great experience and power, and some of them men of great fame, Gabriel, to his astonished pride, was asked to be one. This was a great, a heavy honor for one so young in the faith, and in years—who had but only yesterday been lying, vomit-covered, in the gutters of sin—and Gabriel felt his heart shake with fear as his invitation came to him. Yet he felt that it was the hand of God that had called him out so early to prove himself before such mighty men.

He was to preach on the twelfth night. It was decided, in view of his possible failure to attract, to support him on either side with a nearly equal number of war horses. He would have, thus, the benefit of the storm they would certainly have stirred up before him; and should he fail to add substantially to the effect they had created, there would be others coming after him to obliterate his performance.

But Gabriel did not want his performance—the most important of his career so far, and on which so much depended—to be obliterated; he did not want to be dismissed as a mere boy who was scarcely ready to be counted in the race, much less to be considered a candidate for the prize. He fasted on his knees before God and did not cease, daily and nightly, to pray that God might work through him a mighty work and cause all men to see that, indeed, God's hand was on him, that he was the Lord's anointed.

Deborah, unasked, fasted with him, and prayed, and took his best black suit away, so that it would be clean and mended and freshly pressed for the great day. And she took it away again, immediately afterward, so that it would be no less splendid on the Sunday of the great dinner that was officially to punctuate the revival. This Sunday was to be a feast day for everyone, but more especially for the twenty-four elders, who were, that day, to be gloriously banqueted at the saints' expense and labor.

On the evening when he was to preach, he and Deborah walked together to the great, lighted lodge hall that had but lately held a dance band, and that the saints had rented for the duration of the revival. The service had already begun; lights spilled outward into the streets, music filled the air, and passers-by paused to listen and to peek in through the half-open doors. He wanted all of them to enter; he wanted to run through the streets and drag all sinners in to hear the Word of God. Yet, as they approached the doors, the fear held in check so many days and nights rose in him again, and he thought how he would stand tonight, so high, and all alone, to vindicate the testimony that had fallen from his lips, that God had called him to preach.

"Sister Deborah," he said, suddenly, as they stood before the doors, "you sit where I can see you?"

"I sure will do that, Reverend," she said. "You go on up there. Trust God."

Without another word he turned, leaving her in the door, and walked up the long aisle to the pulpit. They were all there already, big, comfortable, ordained men; they smiled and nodded as he mounted the pulpit steps; and one of them said, nodding toward the congregation, which was as spirited as any evangelist could wish: "Just getting these folks warmed up for you, boy. Want to see you make them *holler* tonight."

He smiled in the instant before he knelt down at his thronelike chair to pray; and thought again, as he had been thinking for eleven nights, that there was about his elders an ease in the holy place, and a levity, that made *his* soul uneasy. While he sat, waiting, he saw that Deborah had found a seat in the very front of the congregation, just below the pulpit, and sat with her Bible folded on her lap.

When, at last, the Scripture lesson read, the testimonies in, the songs sung, the collection taken up, he was introduced—by the elder who had preached the night before—and found himself on his feet, moving toward the pulpit where the great Bible awaited him, and over that sheer drop the murmuring congregation, he felt a giddy terror that he stood so high, and with this, immediately, a pride and joy unspeakable that God had placed him there.

He did not begin with a "shout" song, or with a fiery testimony; but in a dry, matter-of-fact voice, which trembled only a little, asked them to look with him at the sixth chapter of Isaiah, and the fifth verse; and he asked Deborah to read it aloud for him.

And she read, in a voice unaccustomedly strong: " 'Then said I, Woe is me! for I am undone; because I am a man of unclean lips, and I dwell in the midst of a people of unclean lips: for mine eyes have seen the King, the Lord of hosts.' "

Silence filled the lodge hall after she had read this sentence. For a moment Gabriel was terrified by the eyes on him, and by the elders at his back, and could not think how to go on. Then he looked at Deborah, and began.

These words had been uttered by the prophet Isaiah, who had been called the Eagle-eyed because he had looked down the dark centuries and foreseen the birth of Christ. It was Isaiah also who had prophesied that a man should be as a hiding-place from the wind and tempest, Isaiah who had described the way of holiness, saying that the parched ground should become a pool, and the thirsty lands springs of water: the very desert should rejoice, and blossom as the rose. It was Isaiah who had prophesied, saying: "Unto us a child is born, unto us a son is given; and the government shall be upon His shoulder." This was a man whom God had raised in righteousness, whom God had chosen to do many mighty works, yet this man, be-holding the vision of God's glory, had cried out: "Woe is me!"

"Yes!" cried a woman. *Tell it!*

"There is a lesson for us all in this cry of Isaiah's, a meaning for us all, a hard saying. If we have never cried this cry then we have never known salvation; if we fail to live with this cry, hourly, daily, in the midnight hour, and in the light of the noonday sun, then salvation has left us and our feet have laid hold on Hell. Yes, bless our God forever! When we cease to tremble before Him we have turned out of the way."

"Amen!" cried a voice from far away. "Amen! You preach it, boy!"

He paused for only a moment and mopped his brow, the heart within him great with fear and trembling, and with power.

"For let us remember that the wages of sin is death; that it is written, and cannot fail, the soul that sinneth, it shall die. Let us remember that we are born in sin, in sin did our mothers conceive us—sin reigns in all our members, sin is the foul heart's natural liquid, sin looks out of the eye, amen, and leads to lust, sin is in the hearing of the ear, and leads to folly, sin sits on the tongue, and leads to murder. Yes! Sin is the only heritage of the natural man, sin bequeathed us by our natural father, that fallen Adam, whose apple sickens and will sicken all generations living, and generations yet unborn! It was sin that drove the son of the morning out of Heaven, sin that drove Adam out of Eden, sin that caused Cain to slay his brother, sin that built the tower of Babel, sin that caused the fire to fall on Sodom—sin, from the very foundations of the world, living and breathing in the heart of man, that causes women to bring forth their children in agony and darkness, bows down the backs of men with terrible labor, keeps the empty belly empty, keeps the table bare, sends our children, dressed in rags, out into the whorehouses and dance halls of the world!"

"Amen! Amen!"

"Ah. Woe is me. Woe is *me*. Yes, beloved—there is no righteousness in man. All men's hearts are evil, all men are liars—only God is true. Hear David's cry: 'The Lord is my rock, and my fortress, and my deliverer; my God, my strength, in whom I will trust; my buckler, and the horn of my salvation, and my high tower.' Hear Job, sitting in dust and ashes, his children dead, his substance gone, surrounded by false comforters: 'Yea, though He slay me, yet will I trust Him.' And hear Paul, who had been Saul, a persecutor of the redeemed, struck down on the road to Damascus, and going forth to preach the gospel: 'And if ye be Christ's, then ye are Abraham's seed, and heirs according to the promise!' "

"Oh, yes," cried one of the elders, "bless our God forever!"

"For God had a plan. He would not suffer the soul of man to die, but had prepared a plan for his salvation. In the beginning, way back there at the laying of the foundations of the world, God had a plan, *amen!* to bring all flesh to a knowledge of the truth. In the beginning was the Word and the Word was with God and the Word was God—yes, and in Him was life, *hallelujah!* and this life was the light of men. Dearly beloved, when God saw how men's hearts waxed evil, how they turned aside, each to his own way, how they married and gave in marriage, how they feasted on ungodly meat and drink, and lusted, and blasphemed, and lifted up their hearts in sinful pride against the Lord—oh, then, the Son of God, the blessed lamb that taketh away the sins of the world, this Son of God who was the Word made flesh, the fulfillment of the promise—oh, then, He turned to His Father, crying: 'Father, prepare me a body and I'll go down and redeem sinful man.' "

"So *glad* this evening, praise the Lord!"

"Fathers, here tonight, have you ever had a son who went astray? Mothers, have you seen your daughters cut down in the pride and fullness of youth? Has any man here heard the command which came to Abraham, that he must make his son a living sacrifice on God's altar? Fathers, think of your sons, how you tremble for them, and try to lead them right, try to feed them so they'll grow up strong; think of your love for *your* son, and how any evil that befalls him cracks up the heart, and think of the pain that *God* has borne, sending down His only begotten Son, to dwell among men on the sinful earth, to be persecuted, to suffer, to bear the cross and *die*—not for His *own* sins, like our natural sons, but for the sins of *all* the world, to take away the sins of *all* the world—that we might have the joy bells ringing deep in our hearts tonight!"

"Praise Him!" cried Deborah, and he had never heard her voice so loud.

"Woe is me, for when God struck the sinner, the sinner's eyes were opened, and he saw himself in all his foulness naked before God's glory. Woe is me! For the moment of salvation is a blinding light, cracking down into the heart from Heaven—Heaven so high, and the sinner so low. *Woe is me!* For unless God raised the sinner, he would never rise again!"

"Yes, Lord! I was there!"

How many here tonight had fallen where Isaiah fell? How many had cried—as Isaiah cried? How many could testify, as Isaiah testified, "Mine eyes have seen the King, the Lord of hosts"? Ah, whosoever failed to have this testimony should never see His face, but should be told, on that great day: "Depart from me, ye that work iniquity," and be hurled forever into the lake of fire prepared for Satan and all his angels. Oh, would the sinner rise tonight, and walk the little mile to his salvation, here to the mercy seat?

And he waited. Deborah watched him with a calm, strong smile. He looked out over their faces, their faces all upturned to him. He saw joy in those faces, and holy excitement, and belief—and they all looked up to him. Then, far in the back, a boy rose, a tall, dark boy, his white shirt open at the neck and torn, his trousers dusty and shabby and held up with an old necktie, and he looked across the immeasurable, dreadful, breathing distance up to Gabriel, and began to walk down the long, bright aisle. Someone cried: "Oh, bless the Lord!" and tears filled Gabriel's eyes. The boy knelt, sobbing, at the mercy seat, and the church began to sing.

Then Gabriel turned away, knowing that this night he had run well, and that God had used him. The elders all were smiling, and one of them took him by the hand, and said: "That was mighty fine, boy. Mighty fine."

Then came the Sunday of the spectacular dinner that was to end the revival—for which dinner Deborah and all the other women had baked, roasted, fried, and boiled for many days beforehand. He jokingly suggested, to repay her a little for her contention that he was the best preacher of the revival, that she was the best cook among the women. She timidly suggested that he was here at a flattering disadvantage, for she had heard all of the preachers, but he had not, for a very long time, eaten another woman's cooking.

When the Sunday came, and he found himself once more among the elders, about to go to the table, Gabriel felt a drop in his happy, proud anticipation. He was not comfortable with these men—that was it—it was difficult for him to accept them as his elders and betters in the faith. They seemed to him so lax, so nearly worldly; they were not like those holy prophets of old who grew thin and naked in the service of the Lord. These, God's ministers, had indeed grown fat, and their dress was rich and various. They had been in the field so long that they did not tremble before God any more. They took God's power as their due, as something that made the more exciting their own assured, special atmosphere. They each had, it seemed, a bagful of sermons often preached; and knew, in the careless lifting of an eye, which sermon to bring to which congregation. Though they preached with great authority, and brought souls low before the altar—like so many ears of corn lopped off by the hired laborer in his daily work—they did not give God the glory, nor count it as glory at all; they might as easily have been, Gabriel thought, highly paid circus-performers, each with his own special dazzling gift. Gabriel discovered that they spoke, jokingly, of the comparative number of souls each of them had saved, as though they were keeping score in a pool-room. And this offended him and frightened him. He did not want, ever, to hold the gift of God so lightly.

They, the ministers, were being served alone in the upper room of the lodge hall—the less-specialized workers in Christ's vineyard were being fed at a table downstairs—and the women kept climbing up and down the stairs with loaded platters to see that they ate their fill. Deborah was one of the serving-women, and though she did not speak, and despite his discomfort, he nearly burst each time she entered the room, with the pride he knew she felt to see him sitting there, so serene and manly, among all these celebrated others, in the severe black and white that was his uniform. And if only, he felt, his mother could be there to see—her Gabriel, mounted so high!

But, near the end of the dinner, when the women brought up the pies, and coffee, and cream, and when the talk around the table had become more jolly and more good-naturedly loose than ever, the door had but barely closed behind the women when one of the elders, a heavy, cheery, sandy-haired man, whose face, testifying no doubt to the violence of his beginnings, was splashed with freckles like dried blood, laughed and said, referring to Deborah, that there was a holy woman, all right! She had been choked so early on white men's milk, and it remained so sour in her belly yet, that she would never be able, now, to find a nigger who would let her taste his richer, sweeter substance. Everyone at the table roared, but Gabriel felt his blood turn cold that God's ministers should be guilty of such abominable levity, and that that woman sent by God to comfort him, and without whose support he might readily have fallen by the wayside, should be held in such dishonor. They felt, he knew, that among themselves a little rude laughter could do no harm; they were too deeply rooted in the faith to be made to fall by such an insignificant tap from Satan's hammer. But he stared at their boisterous, laughing faces, and felt that they would have much to answer for on the day of judgment, for they were stumbling-stones in the path of the true believer.

Now the sandy-haired man, struck by Gabriel's bitter, astounded face, bit his laughter off, and said: "What's the matter, son? I hope I ain't said nothing to offend you?"

"She read the Bible for you the night you preached, didn't she?" asked another of the elders, in a conciliatory tone.

"That woman," said Gabriel, feeling a roaring in his head, "is my sister in the Lord."

"Well, Elder Peters here, he just didn't know that," said someone else. "He sure didn't mean no harm."

"Now, you ain't going to get mad?" asked Elder Peters, kindly—yet there remained, to Gabriel's fixed attention, something mocking in his face and voice. "You ain't going to spoil our little dinner?"

"I don't think it's right," said Gabriel, "to talk evil about *no*body. The Word tell me it ain't right to hold nobody up to scorn."

"Now you just remember," Elder Peters said, as kindly as before, "you's talking to your *elders*."

"Then it seem to me," he said, astonished at his boldness, "that if I got to look to you for a example, you ought to *be* a example."

"Now, you know," said someone else, jovially, "you ain't fixing to make that woman your wife or nothing like that—so ain't no need to get all worked up and spoil our little gathering. Elder Peters didn't mean no harm. If *you* don't never say nothing worse than that, you can count yourself already up there in the Kingdom with the chosen."

And at this a small flurry of laughter swept over the table; they went back to their eating and drinking, as though the matter were finished.

Yet Gabriel felt that he had surprised them; he had found them out and they were a little ashamed and confounded before his purity. And he understood suddenly the words of Christ, where it was written: "Many are called but few are chosen." Yes, and he looked around the table, already jovial again, but rather watchful now, too, of him—and he wondered who, of all these, would sit in glory at the right hand of the Father?

And then, as he sat there, remembering again Elder Peters' boisterous, idle remark, this remark shook together in him all those shadowy doubts and fears, those hesitations and tendernesses, which were his in relation to Deborah, and the sum of which he now realized was his certainty that there was in that relationship something foreordained. It came to him that, as the Lord had given him Deborah, to help him to stand, so the Lord had sent him to her, to raise her up, to release her from that dishonor which was hers in the eyes of men. And this idea filled him, in a moment, wholly, with the intensity of a vision: what better woman could be found? *She* was not like the mincing daughters of Zion! She was not to be seen prancing lewdly through the streets, eyes sleepy and mouth half open with just, or to be found mewing under midnight fences, uncovered, uncovering some black boy's hanging curse! No, their married bed would be holy, and their children would continue the line of the faithful, a royal line. And, fired with this, a baser fire stirred in him also, rousing a slumbering fear, and he remembered (as the table, the ministers, the dinner, and the talk all burst in on him again) that Paul had written: "It is better to marry than to burn."

Yet, he thought, he would hold his peace awhile; he would seek to know more clearly the Lord's mind in this matter. For he remembered how much older she was than he—eight years; and he tried to imagine, for the first time in his life, that dishonor to which Deborah had been forced so many years ago by white men: her skirts above her head, her secrecy discovered—by white men. How many? How had she borne it? Had she screamed? Then he thought (but it did not really trouble him, for if Christ to save him could be crucified, he, for Christ's greater glory, could well be mocked) of what smiles would be occasioned, what filthy conjecture, barely sleeping now, would mushroom upward overnight like Jonah's gourd, when people heard that he and Deborah were going to be married. She, who had been the living proof and witness of their daily shame, and who had become their holy fool—and he, who had been the untamable despoiler of their daughters, and thief of their women, their walking prince of darkness! And he smiled, watching the elders' well-fed faces and their grinding jaws—unholy pastors all, unfaithful stewards; he prayed that he would never be so fat, or so lascivious, but that God should work through him a mighty work: to ring, it might be, through ages yet unborn, as sweet, solemn, mighty proof of His everlasting love and mercy. He trembled with the presence that surrounded him now; he could scarcely keep his seat. He felt that light shone down on him from Heaven, on him, the chosen; he felt as Christ must have felt in the temple, facing His so utterly confounded elders; and he lifted up his eyes, not caring for their glances or their clearing of throats, and the silence that abruptly settled over the table, thinking: "Yes. God works in many mysterious ways His wonders to perform."

"Sister Deborah," he said, much later that night as he was walking her to her door, "the Lord done laid something on my heart and I want you to help me to pray over it and ask Him to lead me right."

He wondered if she could divine what was in his mind. In her face there was nothing but patience, as she turned to him, and said: "I'm praying all the time. But I sure will pray extra hard this week if you want me to."

And it was during this praying time that Gabriel had a dream.

He could never afterward remember how the dream began, what had happened, or who he was with in the dream; or any details at all. For there were really two dreams, the first like a dim, blurred, infernal foreshadowing of the second. Of this first dream, the overture, he remembered only the climate, which had been like the climate of his day—heavy, with danger everywhere, Satan at his shoulder trying to bring him down. That night as he tried to sleep, Satan sent demons to his bedside—old friends he had had, but whom he saw no more, and drinking and gambling scenes that he had thought would never rise to haunt him again, and women he had known. And the women were so real that he could nearly touch them; and he heard again their laughter and their sighs, and felt beneath his hands again their thighs and breasts. Though he closed his eyes and called on Jesus— calling over and over again the name of Jesus—his pagan body stiffened and flamed and the women laughed. And they asked why he remained in this narrow bed alone when they waited for him; why he had bound his body in the armor of chastity while they sighed and turned on their beds for him. And he sighed and turned, every movement torture, each touch of the sheets a lewd caress—and more abominable, then, in his imagination, than any caress he had received in life. And he clenched his fists and began to plead the blood, to exorcise the hosts of Hell, but even this motion was like another motion, and at length he fell on his knees to pray. By and by he fell into a troublous sleep—it seemed that he was going to be stoned, and then he was in battle, and then shipwrecked in the water—and suddenly he awoke, knowing that he must have dreamed, for his loins were covered with his own white seed.

Then, trembling, he got out of bed again and washed himself. It was a warning, and he knew it, and he seemed to see before him the pit dug by Satan—deep and silent, waiting for him. He thought of the dog returned to his vomit, of the man who had been cleansed, and who fell, and who was possessed by seven devils, the last state of that man being worse than his first. And he thought at last, kneeling by his cold bedside, but with the heart within him almost too sick for prayer, of Onan, who had scattered his seed on the ground rather than continue his brother's line. *Out of the house of David, the son of Abraham.* And he called again on the name of Jesus; and fell asleep again.

And he dreamed that he was in a cold, high place, like a mountain. He was high, so high that he walked in mist and cloud, but before him stretched the blank ascent, the steep side of the mountain. A voice said: "Come higher." And he began to climb. After a little, clinging to the rock, he found himself with only clouds above him and mist below—and he knew that beyond the wall of mist reigned fire. His feet began to slip; pebbles and rocks began ringing beneath his feet; he looked up, trembling, in terror of death, and he cried: "Lord, I can't come no higher." But the voice repeated after a moment, quiet and strong and impossible to deny: "Come on, son. Come higher." Then he knew that, if he would not fall to death, he must obey the voice. He began to climb again, and his feet slipped again; and when he thought that he would fall there suddenly appeared before him green, spiny leaves; and he caught onto the leaves, which hurt his hand, and the voice said again: "Come higher." And so Gabriel climbed, the wind blowing through his clothes, and his feet began to bleed, and his hands were bleeding; and still he climbed, and he felt that his back was breaking; and his legs were growing numb and they were trembling, and he could not control them; and still before him there was only cloud, and below him the roaring mist. How long he climbed in this dream of his, he did not know. Then, of a sudden, the clouds parted, he felt the sun like a crown of glory, and he was in a peaceful field.

He began to walk. Now he was wearing long, white robes. He heard singing: "Walked in the valley, it looked so fine, I asked my

Lord was all this mine." But he knew that it was his. A voice said: "Follow me." And he walked, and he was again on the edge of a high place, but bathed and blessed and glorified in the blazing sun, so that he stood like God, all golden, and looked down, down, at the long race he had run, at the steep side of the mountain he had climbed. And now up this mountain, in white robes, singing, the elect came. "Touch them not," the voice said, "my seal is on them." And Gabriel turned and fell on his face, and the voice said again: "So shall thy seed be." Then he awoke. Morning was at the window, and he blessed God, lying on his bed, tears running down his face, for the vision he had seen.

When he went to Deborah and told her that the Lord had led him to ask her to be his wife, his holy helpmeet, she looked at him for a moment in what seemed to be speechless terror. He had never seen such an expression on her face before. For the first time since he had known her he touched her, putting his hands on her shoulders, thinking what untender touch these shoulders had once known, and how she would be raised now in honor. And he asked: "You ain't scared, is you, Sister Deborah? You ain't got nothing to be scared of?"

Then she tried to smile, and began, instead, to weep. With a movement at once violent and hesitant, she let her head fall forward on his breast.

"No," she brought out, muffled in his arms, "I ain't scared." But she did not stop weeping.

He stroked her coarse, bowed head. "God bless you, little girl," he said, helplessly. "God bless you."

The silence in the church ended when Brother Elisha, kneeling near the piano, cried out and fell backward under the power of the Lord. Immediately, two or three others cried out also, and a wind, a foretaste of that great downpouring they awaited, swept the church. With this cry, and the echoing cries, the tarry service moved from its first stage of steady murmuring, broken by moans and now and again an isolated cry, into that stage of tears and groaning, of calling aloud and singing, which was like the labor of a woman about to be delivered of her child. On this threshing-floor the child was the soul that struggled to the light, and it was the church that was in labor, that did not cease to push and pull, calling on the name of Jesus. When Brother Elisha cried out and fell back, crying, Sister McCandless rose and stood over him to help him pray. For the rebirth of the soul was perpetual; only rebirth every hour could stay the hand of Satan.

Sister Price began to sing:

> *"I want to go through, Lord,*
> *I want to go through.*
> *Take me through, Lord,*
> *Take me through."*

A lone voice, joined by others, among them, waveringly, the voice of John. Gabriel recognized the voice. When Elisha cried, Gabriel was brought back in an instant to this present time and place, fearing that it was John he heard, that it was John who lay astonished beneath the power of the Lord. He nearly looked up and turned around; but then he knew it was Elisha, and his fear departed.

> *"Have your way, Lord,*
> *Have your way."*

Neither of his sons was here tonight, had ever cried on the threshing-floor. One had been dead for nearly fourteen years—dead in a Chicago tavern, a knife kicking in his throat. And the living son, the child, Roy, was headlong already, and hardhearted: he lay at home, silent now, and bitter against his father, a bandage on his forehead. They were not here. Only the son of the bondwoman stood where the rightful heir should stand.

"I'll obey, Lord,
I'll obey."

He felt that he should rise and pray over Elisha—when a man cried out, it was right that another man should be his intercessor. And he thought how gladly he would rise, and with what power he would pray if it were only his son who lay crying on the floor tonight. But he remained, bowed low, on his knees. Each cry that came from the fallen Elisha tore through him. He heard the cry of his dead son and his living son; one who cried in the pit forever, beyond the hope of mercy; and one who would cry one day when mercy would be finished.

Now Gabriel tried, with the testimony he had held, with all the signs of His favor that God had shown him, to put himself between the living son and the darkness that waited to devour him. The living son had cursed him—*bastard*—and his heart was far from God; it could not be that the curse he had heard tonight falling from Roy's lips was but the curse repeated, so far, so long resounding, that the mother of his first son had uttered as she thrust the infant from her—herself immediately departing, this curse yet on her lips, into eternity. Her curse had devoured the first Royal; he had been begotten in sin, and he had perished in sin; it was God's punishment, and it was just. But Roy had been begotten in the marriage bed, the bed that Paul described as holy, and it was to him the Kingdom had been promised. It could not be that the living son was cursed for the sins of his father; for God, after much groaning, after many years, had given him a sign to make him know he was forgiven. And yet, it came to him that this living son, this headlong, living Royal, might be cursed for the sin of his mother, whose sin had never been truly repented; for that the living proof of her sin, he who knelt tonight, a very interloper among the saints, stood between her soul and God.

Yes, she was hardhearted, stiff-necked, and hard to bend, this Elizabeth whom he had married: she had not seemed so, years ago, when the Lord had moved in his heart to lift her up, she and her nameless child, who bore his name today. And he was exactly like her, silent, watching, full of evil pride—they would be cast out, one day, into the outer darkness.

Once he had asked Elizabeth—they had been married a long while, Roy was a baby, and she was big with Sarah—if she had truly repented of her sin.

And she had looked at him, and said, "You done asked me that before. And I done told you, yes."

But he did not believe her; and he asked: "You mean you wouldn't do it again? If you was back there, where you was, like you was then—would you do it again?"

She looked down; then, with impatience, she looked into his eyes again: "Well, if I was back there, Gabriel, and I was the same girl! . . ."

There was a long silence, while she waited. Then, almost unwillingly, he asked: "And . . . would you let *him* be born again?"

She answered, steadily: "I know you ain't asking me to say I'm sorry I brought Johnny in the world. Is you?" And when he did not answer: "And listen, Gabriel. I ain't going to let you *make* me sorry. Not you, nor nothing, nor nobody in this world. We is got *two* children, Gabriel, and soon we's going to have *three;* and I ain't going to make no difference amongst them and you ain't going to make none either."

But how could there not be a difference between the son of a weak, proud woman and some careless boy, and the son that God had promised him, who would carry down the joyful line his father's name, and who would work until the day of the second coming to bring about His Father's Kingdom? For God had promised him this so many years ago, and he had lived only for this—forsaking the world and its pleasures, and the joys of his own life, he had tarried all these bitter years to see the promise of the Lord fulfilled. He had let Esther die, and Royal had died, and Deborah had died barren—but he had held on to the promise; he had walked before God in true repentance and waited on the promise. And the time of fulfillment was surely at hand. He had only to possess his soul in patience and wait before the Lord.

And his mind, dwelling bitterly on Elizabeth, yet moved backward to consider once again Esther, who had been the mother of the first Royal. And he saw her, with the dumb, pale, startled ghosts of joy and desire hovering in him yet, a thin, vivid, dark-eyed girl, with something Indian in her cheekbones and her carriage and her hair; looking at him with that look in which were blended mockery, affection, desire, impatience, and scorn; dressed in the flamelike colors that, in fact, she had seldom worn, but that he always thought of her as wearing. She was associated in his mind with flame; with fiery leaves in the autumn, and the fiery sun going down in the evening over the farthest hill, and with the eternal fires of Hell.

She had come to town very shortly after he and Deborah were married, and she took a job as serving-girl with the same white family for which he worked. He saw her, therefore, all the time. Young men were always waiting for her at the back door when her work was done: Gabriel used to watch her walk off in the dusk on a young man's arm, and their voices and their laughter floated back to him like a mockery of his condition. He knew that she lived with her mother and stepfather, sinful people, given to drinking and gambling and ragtime music and the blues, who never, except at Christmastime or Easter, appeared in church.

He began to pity her, and one day when he was to preach in the evening he invited her to come to church. This invitation marked the first time she ever really looked at him—he realized it then, and was to remember that look for many days and nights.

"You really going to preach tonight? A pretty man like you?"

"With the Lord's help," he said, with a gravity so extreme that it was almost hostility. At the same time, at her look and voice something leaped in him that he thought had been put down forever.

"Well, I be mighty delighted," she said after a moment, seeming to have briefly regretted the impetuosity that had led her to call him a "pretty" man.

"Can you make yourself free to come tonight?" he could not prevent himself from asking.

And she grinned, delighted at what she took to be an oblique compliment. "Well, I don't know, Reverend. But I'll try."

When the day was ended, she disappeared on the arm of yet another boy. He did not believe that she would come. And this so strangely depressed him that he could scarcely speak to Deborah at dinner, and they walked all the way to church in silence. Deborah watched him out of the corner of her eye, as was her silent and exasperating habit. It was her way of conveying respect for his calling; and she would have said, had it ever occurred to him to tax her with it, that she did not wish to distract him when the Lord had laid something on his heart. Tonight, since he was to preach, it could not be doubted that the Lord was speaking more than usual; and it behooved her, therefore, as the helpmeet of the Lord's anointed, as the caretaker, so to speak, of the sanctified temple, to keep silence. Yet, in fact, he would have liked to talk. He would have liked to ask her—so many things; to have listened to her voice, and watched her face while she told him of her day, her hopes, her doubts, her life, and her love. But he and Deborah never talked. The voice to which he listened in his mind, and the face he watched with so much love and care, belonged not to Deborah, but to Esther. Again he felt this strange chill in him, implying disaster and delight; and then he hoped that she would not come, that something would happen that would make it impossible for him ever to see her again.

She came, however; late, just before the pastor was about to present the speaker of the hour to the congregation. She did not come alone, but had brought her mother with her—promising what spectacle Gabriel could not imagine, nor could he imagine how she had escaped her young man of the evening. But she had; she was here; she preferred, then, to hear him preach the gospel than to linger with others in carnal delight. She was here, and his heart was uplifted; something exploded in his heart when the opening door revealed her, smiling faintly and with eyes downcast, moving directly to a seat in the back of the congregation. She did not look at him at all, and yet he knew immediately that she had seen him. And in a moment he imagined her, because of the sermon that he would preach, on her knees before the altar, and then her mother and that gambling, loud-talking stepfather of hers, brought by Esther into the service of the Lord. Heads turned when they came in, and a murmur, barely audible, of astonishment and pleasure swept over the church. Here were sinners, come to hear the Word of God.

And, indeed, from their apparel the sinfulness of their lives was evident: Esther wore a blue hat, trimmed with many ribbons, and a heavy, wine-red dress; and her mother, massive, and darker than Esther, wore great gold earrings in her pierced ears and had that air, vaguely disreputable, and hurriedly dressed, of women he had known in sporting-houses. They sat in the back, rigid and uncomfortable, like sisters of sin, like a living defiance of the drab sanctity of the saints. Deborah turned to look at them, and in that moment Gabriel saw, as though for the first time, how black and how bony was this wife of his, and how wholly undesirable. Deborah looked at him with a watchful silence in her look; he felt the hand that held his Bible begin to sweat and tremble; he thought of the joyless groaning of their marriage bed; and he hated her.

Then the pastor rose. While he spoke, Gabriel closed his eyes. He felt the words that he was about to speak fly from him; he felt the power of God go out of him. Then the voice of the pastor ceased, and Gabriel opened his eyes in the silence and found that all eyes were on him. And so he rose and faced the congregation.

"Dearly beloved in the Lord," he began—but her eyes were on him, that strange, that mocking light—"let us bow our heads in prayer." And he closed his eyes and bowed his head.

His later memory of this sermon was like the memory of a storm. From the moment that he raised his head and looked out over their faces again, his tongue was loosed and he was filled with the power of the Holy Ghost. Yes, the power of the Lord was on him that night, and he preached a sermon that was remembered in camp-meetings and in cabins, and that set a standard for visiting evangelists for a generation to come. Years later, when Esther and Royal and Deborah were dead, and Gabriel was leaving the South, people remembered this sermon and the gaunt, possessed young man who had preached it.

He took his text from the eighteenth chapter of the second book of Samuel, the story of the young Ahimaaz who ran too soon to bring the tidings of battle to King David. For, before he ran, he was asked by Joab: "Wherefore wilt thou run, my son, seeing that thou hast no tidings ready?" And when Ahimaaz reached King David, who yearned to know the fate of his headlong son, Absalom, he could only say: "I saw a great tumult but I knew not what it was."

And this was the story of all those who failed to wait on the counsel of the Lord; who made themselves wise in their own conceit and ran before they had the tidings ready. This was the story of innumerable shepherds who failed, in their arrogance, to feed the hungry sheep; of many a father and mother who gave to their children not bread but a stone, who offered not the truth of God but the tinsel of this world. This was not belief but unbelief, not humility but pride: there worked in the heart of such a one the same desire that had hurled the son of the morning from Heaven to the depths of Hell, the desire to overturn the appointed times of God, and to wrest from Him who held all power in His hands powers not meet for men. Oh, yes, they had seen it, each brother and sister beneath the sound of his voice tonight, and they had seen the destruction caused by a so lamentable unripeness! Babies, bawling, fatherless, for bread, and girls in the gutters, sick with sin, and young men bleeding in the frosty fields. Yes, and there were those who cried—they had heard it, in their homes, and on the street corner, and from the very pulpit— that they should wait no longer, despised and rejected and spat on as they were, but should rise today and bring down the mighty, establishing the vengeance that God had claimed. But blood cried out for blood, as the blood of Abel cried out from the ground. Not for noth-

ing was it written: "He that believeth will not make haste." Oh, but
sometimes the road was rocky. Did they think sometimes that God
forgot? Oh, fall on your knees and pray for patience; fall on your
knees and pray for faith; fall on your knees and pray for overcoming
power to be ready on the day of His soon appearing to receive the
crown of life. For God did not forget, no word proceeding from his
mouth could fail. Better to wait, like Job, through all the days of our
appointed time until our change comes than to rise up, unready, before God speaks. For if we but wait humbly before Him, He will
speak glad tidings to our souls; if we but wait our change will come,
and that in an instant, in the twinkling of an eye—we will be
changed one day from this corruption into incorruptibility forever,
caught up with Him beyond the clouds. And these are the tidings we
now must bear to all the nations: another son of David was hung
from a tree, and he who knows not the meaning of that tumult shall
be damned forever in Hell! Brother, sister, you may run, but the day
is coming when the King will ask: "What are the tidings that you
bear?" And what will you say on that great day if you know not of
the death of His Son?

"Is there a soul here tonight"—tears were on his face and he
stood above them with arms outstretched—"who knows not the
meaning of that tumult? Is there a soul here tonight who wants to
talk to Jesus? Who wants to wait before the Lord, amen, until He
speaks? Until He makes to ring in your soul, amen, the glad tidings
of salvation? Oh, brothers and sisters"—and still she did not rise; but
only watched him from far away—"the time is running out. One
day He's coming back to judge the nations, to take His children, hallelujah, to their rest. They tell me, bless God, that two shall be working in the fields, and one shall be taken and the other left. Two shall
be lying, amen, in bed, and one shall be taken and the other left.
He's coming, beloved, like a thief in the night, and no man knows
the hour of His coming. It's going to be too late then to cry: 'Lord,
have mercy.' Now is the time to make yourself ready, now, amen,

tonight, before His altar. Won't somebody come tonight? Won't somebody say No to Satan and give their life to the Lord?"

But she did not rise, only looked at him and looked about her with a bright, pleased interest, as though she were at a theater and were waiting to see what improbable delights would next be offered her. He somehow knew that she would never rise and walk that long aisle to the mercy seat. And this filled him for a moment with a holy rage—that she stood, so brazen, in the congregation of the righteous and refused to bow her head.

He said amen, and blessed them, and turned away, and immediately the congregation began to sing. Now, again, he felt drained and sick; he was soaking wet and he smelled the odor of his own body. Deborah, singing and beating her tambourine in the front of the congregation, watched him. He felt suddenly like a helpless child. He wanted to hide himself forever and never cease from crying.

Esther and her mother left during the singing—they had come, then, only to hear him preach. He could not imagine what they were saying or thinking now. And he thought of tomorrow, when he would have to see her again.

"Ain't that the little girl that works at the same place with you?" Deborah asked him on the way home.

"Yes," he said. Now he did not feel like talking. He wanted to get home and take his wet clothes off and sleep.

"She mighty pretty," said Deborah. "I ain't never seen her in church before."

He said nothing.

"Was it you invited her to come out tonight?" she asked, after a bit.

"Yes," he said. "I didn't think the Word of God could do her no harm."

Deborah laughed. "Don't look like it, does it? She walked out just as cool and sinful as she come in—she and that mother of her'n. And you preached a mighty fine sermon. Look like she just ain't thinking about the Lord."

"Folks ain't got no time for the Lord," he said, "one day *He* ain't going to have time for *them*."

When they got home she offered to make him a hot cup of tea, but he refused. He undressed in silence—which she again respected—and got into bed. At length, she lay beside him like a burden laid down at evening which must be picked up once more in the morning.

The next morning Esther said to him, coming into the yard while he was chopping wood for the woodpile: "Good morning, Reverend. I sure didn't look to see you today. I reckoned you'd be all wore out after *that* sermon—does you always preach as hard as that?"

He paused briefly with the axe in the air; then he turned again, bringing the axe down. "I preach the way the Lord leads me, sister," he said.

She retreated a little in the face of his hostility. "Well," she said in a different tone, "it was a mighty fine sermon. Me and Mama was mighty glad we come out."

He left the axe buried in the wood, for splinters flew and he was afraid one might strike her. "You and your ma—you don't get out to service much?"

"Lord, Reverend," she wailed, "look like we just ain't got the time. Mama work so hard all week she just want to lie up in bed on Sunday. And she like me," she added quickly, after a pause, "to keep her company."

Then he looked directly at her. "Does you really mean to say, sister, that you ain't got no time for the Lord? No time at all?"

"Reverend," she said, looking at him with the daring defiance of a threatened child, "I does my best. I really does. Ain't everybody got to have the same spirit."

And he laughed shortly. "Ain't but one spirit you got to have—and that's the spirit of the Lord."

"Well," she said, "that spirit ain't got to work in everybody the same, seems to me."

Then they were silent, each quite vividly aware that they had reached an impasse. After a moment he turned and picked up the axe again. "Well, you go along, sister. I'm praying for you."

Something struggled in her face then, as she stood for yet a moment more and watched him—a mixture of fury and amusement; it reminded him of the expression he had often found on the face of Florence. And it was like the look on the faces of the elders during that far-off and so momentous Sunday dinner. He was too angry, while she thus stared at him, to trust himself to speak. Then she shrugged, the mildest, most indifferent gesture he had ever seen, and smiled. "I'm mighty obliged to you, Reverend," she said. Then she went into the house.

This was the first time they spoke in the yard, a frosty morning. There was nothing in that morning to warn him of what was coming. She offended him because she was so brazen in her sins, that was all; and he prayed for her soul, which would one day find itself naked and speechless before the judgment bar of Christ. Later, she told him that he had pursued her, that his eyes had left her not a moment's peace.

"That weren't no reverend looking at me them mornings in the yard," she had said. "You looked at me just like a man, like a man what hadn't never heard of the Holy Ghost." But he believed that the Lord had laid her like a burden on his heart. And he carried her in his heart; he prayed for her and exhorted her, while there was yet time to bring her soul to God.

But she had not been thinking about God; though she accused him of lusting after her in his heart, it was she who, when she looked at him, insisted on seeing not God's minister but a "pretty man." On her tongue the very title of his calling became a mark of disrespect.

It began on an evening when he was to preach, when they were alone in the house. The people of the house had gone away for three days to visit relatives; Gabriel had driven them to the railroad station after supper, leaving Esther clearing up the kitchen. When he came back to lock up the house, he found Esther waiting for him on the porch steps.

"I didn't think I'd better leave," she said, "till you got back. I ain't got no keys to lock up this house, and white folks is so funny. I don't want them blaming me if something's missing."

He realized immediately that she had been drinking—she was not drunk, but there was whisky on her breath. And this, for some reason, caused a strange excitement to stir in him.

"That was mighty thoughtful, sister," he said, staring hard at her to let her know that he knew she had been drinking. She met his stare with a calm, bold smile, a smile mocking innocence, so that her face was filled with the age-old cunning of a woman.

He started past her into the house; then, without thinking, and without looking at her, he offered: "If you ain't got nobody waiting for you I'll walk you a piece on your way home."

"No," she said, "ain't nobody waiting for me this evening, Reverend, thank you kindly."

He regretted making his offer almost as soon as it was made; he had been certain that she was about to rush off to some trysting-place or other, and he had merely wished to be corroborated. Now, as they walked together into the house, he became terribly aware of her youthful, vivid presence, of her lost condition; and at the same time the emptiness and silence of the house warned him that he was alone with danger.

"You just sit down in the kitchen," he said. "I be as quick as I can."

But his speech was harsh in his own ears, and he could not face her eyes. She sat down at the table, smiling, to wait for him. He tried to do everything as quickly as possible, the shuttering of windows, and locking of doors. But his fingers were stiff and slippery; his heart was in his mouth. And it came to him that he was barring every exit to this house, except the exit through the kitchen, where Esther sat.

When he entered the kitchen again she had moved, and now

stood in the doorway, looking out, holding a glass in her hand. It was a moment before he realized that she had helped herself to more of the master's whisky.

She turned at his step, and he stared at her, and at the glass she held, with wrath and horror.

"I just thought," she said, almost entirely unabashed, "that I'd have me a little drink while I was waiting, Reverend. But I didn't figure on you catching me at it."

She swallowed the last of her drink and moved to the sink to rinse out the glass. She gave a little, ladylike cough as she swallowed—he could not be sure whether this cough was genuine or in mockery of him.

"I reckon," he said, malevolently, "you is just made up your mind to serve Satan all your days."

"I done made up my mind," she answered, "to live all I can *while* I can. If that's a sin, well, I'll go on down to Hell and pay for it. But don't *you* fret, Reverend—it ain't your soul."

He moved and stood next to her, full of anger.

"Girl," he said, "don't you believe God? God don't lie—and He says, plain as I'm talking to you, the soul that sinneth, it shall *die*."

She sighed. "Reverend, look like to me you'd get tired, all the time beating on poor little Esther, trying to make Esther something she ain't. I just don't feel it *here*," she said, and put one hand on her breast. "Now, what you going to do? Don't you know I'm a woman grown, and I ain't fixing to change?"

He wanted to weep. He wanted to reach out and hold her back from the destruction she so ardently pursued—to fold her in him, and hide her until the wrath of God was past. At the same time there rose to his nostrils again her whisky-laden breath, and beneath this, faint, intimate, the odor of her body. And he began to feel like a man in a nightmare, who stands in the path of oncoming destruction, who must move quickly—but who cannot move. "Jesus Jesus Jesus," rang over and over again in his mind, like a bell—as he moved closer to her, undone by her breath, and her wide, angry, mocking eyes.

"You know right well," he whispered, shaking with fury, "you know right well why I keep after you—why I keep after you like I do."

"No, I don't" she answered, refusing, with a small shake of the head, to credit his intensity. "I sure don't know why you can't let Esther have her little whisky, and have her little ways without all the time trying to make her miserable."

He sighed with exasperation, feeling himself begin to tremble. "I just don't want to see you go down, girl, I don't want you to wake up one fine morning sorry for all the sin you done, old, and all by yourself, with nobody to respect you."

But he heard himself speaking, and it made him ashamed. He wanted to have done with talking and leave this house—in a moment they would leave, and the nightmare would be over.

"Reverend," she said, "I ain't done nothing that I'm ashamed of, and I hope I *don't* do nothing I'm ashamed of, ever."

At the word "Reverend," he wanted to strike her; he reached out instead and took both her hands in his. And now they looked directly at each other. There was surprise in her look, and a guarded triumph; he was aware that their bodies were nearly touching and that he should move away. But he did not move—he could not move.

"But I can't help it," she said, after a moment, maliciously teasing, "if you done things that *you's* ashamed of, Reverend."

He held on to her hands as though he were in the middle of the sea and her hands were the lifeline that would drag him in to shore. "Jesus Jesus Jesus," he prayed, "oh, Jesus Jesus. Help me to stand." He thought that he was pulling back against her hands—but he was pulling her to him. And he saw in her eyes now a look that he had not seen for many a long day and night, a look that was never in Deborah's eyes.

"*Yes,* you know," he said, "why I'm all the time worrying about you—why I'm all the time miserable when I look at you."

"But you ain't never told me none of this," she said.

One hand moved to her waist, and lingered there. The tips of her breasts touched his coat, burning in like acid and closing his throat. Soon it would be too late; he wanted it to be too late. That river, his infernal need, rose, flooded, sweeping him forward as though he were a long-drowned corpse.

"*You* know," he whispered, and touched her breasts and buried his face in her neck.

So he had fallen: for the first time since his conversion, for the last time in his life. Fallen: he and Esther in the white folks' kitchen, the light burning, the door half open, grappling and burning beside the sink. Fallen indeed: time was no more, and sin, death, Hell, the judgment were blotted out. There was only Esther, who contained in her narrow body all mystery and all passion, and who answered all his need. Time, snarling so swiftly past, had caused him to forget the clumsiness, and sweat and dirt of their first coupling; how his shaking hands undressed her, standing where they stood, how her dress fell at length like a snare about her feet; how his hands tore at her undergarments so that the naked, vivid flesh might meet his hands; how she protested: "Not here, not here"; how he worried, in some buried part of his mind, about the open door, about the sermon he was to preach, about his life, about Deborah; how the table got in their way, how his collar, until her fingers loosened it, threatened to choke him; how they found themselves on the floor at last, sweating and groaning and locked together; locked away from all others, all heavenly or human help. Only they could help each other. They were alone in the world.

Had Royal, his son, been conceived that night? Or the next night? Or the next? It had lasted only nine days. Then he had come to his senses—after nine days God gave him the power to tell her this thing could not be.

She took his decision with the same casualness, the same near-amusement, with which she had taken his fall. He understood about Esther, during those nine days: that she considered his fear and trembling fanciful and childish, a way of making life more complicated than it need be. She did not think life was like that; she wanted life to be simple. He understood that she was sorry for him because he was always worried. Sometimes, when they were together, he tried to tell her of what he felt, how the Lord would punish them for the sin they were committing. She would not listen: "You ain't in the pulpit now. You's here with me. Even a reverend's got the right to take off his clothes *sometime* and act like a natural man." When he told her that he would not see her any more, she was angry, but she did not argue. Her eyes told him that she thought he was a fool; but that, even had she loved him ever so desperately, it would have been beneath her to argue about his decision—a large part of her simplicity consisted in determining not to want what she could not have with ease.

So it was over. Though it left him bruised and frightened, though he had lost the respect of Esther forever (he prayed that she would never again come to hear him preach) he thanked God that it had been no worse. He prayed that God would forgive him, and never let him fall again.

Yet what frightened him, and kept him more than ever on his knees, was the knowledge that, once having fallen, nothing would be easier than to fall again. Having possessed Esther, the carnal man awoke, seeing the possibility of conquest everywhere. He was made to remember that though he was holy he was yet young; the women who had wanted him wanted him still; he had but to stretch out his hand and take what he wanted—even sisters in the church. He struggled to wear out his visions in the marriage bed, he struggled to awaken Deborah, for whom daily his hatred grew.

He and Esther spoke in the yard again as spring was just beginning. The ground was wet still with melting snow and ice; the sun was everywhere; the naked branches of the trees seemed to be lifting themselves upward toward the pale sun, impatient to put forth leaf and flower. He was standing at the well in his shirtsleeves, singing softly to himself—praising God for the dangers he had passed. She came down the porch steps into the yard, and though he heard the soft step, and knew that it was she, it was a moment before he turned around.

He expected her to come up to him and ask for his help in something she was doing in the house. When she did not speak, he turned around. She was wearing a light, cotton dress of light-brown and dark-brown squares, and her hair was braided tightly all around her head. She looked like a little girl, and he almost smiled. Then: "What's the matter?" he asked her; and felt the heart within him sicken.

"Gabriel," she said, "I going to have a baby."

He stared at her; she began to cry. He put the two pails of water carefully on the ground. She put out her hands to reach him, but he moved away.

"Girl, stop that bellering. What you talking about?"

But, having allowed her tears to begin, she could not stop them at once. She continued to cry, weaving a little where she stood, and with her hands to her face. He looked in panic around the yard and toward the house. "Stop that," he cried again, not daring here and now to touch her, "and tell me what's the matter!"

"I told you," she moaned, "I done told you. I going to have a baby." She looked at him, her face broken up and the hot tears falling. "It's the Lord's truth. I ain't making up no story, it's the Lord's truth."

He could not take his eyes from her, though he hated what he saw. "And when you done find this out?"

"Not so long. I thought maybe I was mistook. But ain't no mistake. Gabriel, what we going to do?"

Then, as she watched his face, her tears began again.

"Hush," he said, with a calm that astonished him, "we *going* to do something, just you be quiet."

"What we going to do, Gabriel? *Tell* me—what you a-fixing in your mind to do?"

"You go on back in the house. Ain't no way for us to talk now."

"Gabriel—"

"Go on in the house, girl. Go *on*!" And when she did not move, but continued to stare at him: "We going to talk about it *tonight*. We going to get to the bottom of *this* thing tonight!"

She turned from him and started up the porch steps. "And dry your *face*," he whispered. She bent over, lifting the front of her dress to dry her eyes, and stood so for a moment on the bottom step while he watched her. Then she straightened and walked into the house, not looking back.

She was going to have his baby—*his* baby? While Deborah, despite their groaning, despite the humility with which she endured his body, yet failed to be quickened by any coming life. It was in the womb of Esther, who was no better than a harlot, that the seed of the prophet would be nourished.

And he moved from the well, picking up, like a man in a trance, the heavy pails of water. He moved toward the house, which now—high, gleaming roof, and spun-gold window—seemed to watch him and to listen; the very sun above his head and the earth beneath his feet had ceased their turning; the water, like a million warning voices, lapped in the buckets he carried on each side; and his mother, beneath the startled earth on which he moved, lifted up, endlessly, her eyes.

They talked in the kitchen as she was cleaning up.

"How come you"—it was his first question—"to be so sure this here's my baby?"

She was not crying now. "Don't you start a-talking that way," she said. "Esther ain't in the habit of lying to *no*body, and I ain't gone with so many men that I'm subject to get my mind confused."

She was very cold and deliberate, and moved about the kitchen with a furious concentration on her tasks, scarcely looking at him.

He did not know what to say, how to reach her.

"You tell your mother yet?" he asked, after a pause. "You been to see a doctor? How come you to be so sure?"

She sighed sharply. "No, I ain't told my mother, I ain't crazy. I ain't told nobody except you."

"How come you to be so sure?" he repeated. "If you ain't seen no doctor?"

"What doctor in this town you want me to go see? I go to see a doctor, I might as well get up and shout it from the housetops. No, I ain't seen no doctor, and I ain't fixing to see one in a hurry. I don't need no doctor to tell me what's happening in my belly."

"And how long you been knowing about this?"

"I been knowing this for maybe a month—maybe six weeks now."

"Six weeks? Why ain't you opened your mouth before?"

"Because I wasn't sure. I thought I'd wait and make sure. I didn't see no need for getting all up in the air before I *knew*. I didn't want to get you all upset and scared and evil, like you is now, if it weren't no need." She paused, watching him. Then: "And you said this morning we was going to do something. What we going to do? That's what we got to figure out now, Gabriel."

"What we going to do?" he repeated at last; and felt that the sustaining life had gone out of him. He sat down at the kitchen table and looked at the whirling pattern on the floor.

But the life had not gone out of her; she came to where he sat, speaking softly, with bitter eyes. "You sound mighty strange to me," she said. "Don't look to me like you thinking of nothing but how you can get shut of this—and me, too—quick as you know how. It wasn't like that always, was it, Reverend? Once upon a time you couldn't think of nothing and nobody *but* me. What you thinking about tonight? I be damned if I think it's *me* you thinking of."

"Girl," he said, wearily, "don't talk like you ain't got good sense. You know I got a wife to think about—" and he wanted to say more, but he could not find the words, and, helplessly, he stopped.

"I know that," she said with less heat, but watching him still with eyes from which the old, impatient mockery was not entirely gone, "but what I mean is, if you was able to forget her once you ought to be able to forget her twice."

He did not understand her at once; but then he sat straight up, his eyes wide and angry. "What you mean, girl? What you trying to say?"

She did not flinch—even in his despair and anger he recognized how far she was from being the frivolous child she had always seemed to him. Or was it that she had been, in so short a space of time, transformed? But he spoke to her at this disadvantage: that whereas he was unprepared for any change in her, she had apparently taken his measure from the first and could be surprised by no change in him.

"You know what I mean," she said. "You ain't never going to have no kind of life with that skinny, black woman—and you ain't never going to be able to make her happy—and she ain't never going to have no children. I be blessed, anyway, if I think you was in your right mind when you married her. And it's *me* that's going to have your baby!"

"You want me," he asked at last, "to leave my wife—and come with you?"

"I thought," she answered, "that you had done thought of that yourself, already, many and many a time."

"You know," he said, with a halting anger, "I ain't never said nothing like that. I ain't never told you I wanted to leave my wife."

"I ain't talking," she shouted, at the end of patience, "about nothing you done *said*!"

Immediately, they both looked toward the closed kitchen doors—for they were not alone in the house this time. She sighed, and smoothed her hair with her hand; and he saw then that her hand was trembling and that her calm deliberation was all a frenzied pose.

"Girl," he said, "does you reckon I'm going to run off and lead a life of sin with you somewhere, just because you tell me you got my baby kicking in your belly? How many kinds of a fool you think I am? I got God's work to do—my life don't belong to you. Nor to that baby, neither—if it *is* my baby."

"It's your baby," she said, coldly, "and ain't no way in the world to get around *that*. And it ain't been so very long ago, right here in

this very *room,* when looked to me like a life of sin was all you was
ready for."

"Yes," he answered, rising, and turning away, "Satan tempted me
and I fell. I ain't the first man been made to fall on account of a
wicked woman."

"You be careful," said Esther, "how you talk to me. I ain't the
first girl's been ruined by a holy man, neither."

"Ruined?" he cried. "You? How you going to be ruined? When
you been walking through this town just like a harlot, and a-kicking
up your heels all over the pasture? How you going to stand there and
tell me you been *ruined*? If it hadn't been me, it sure would have
been somebody else."

"But it *was* you," she retorted, "and what I want to know is what
we's going to do about it."

He looked at her. Her face was cold and hard—ugly; she had
never been so ugly before.

"I don't know," he said, deliberately, "what *we* is going to do.
But I tell you what I think *you* better do: you better go along and get
one of these boys you been running around with to marry you. Because I can't go off with you nowhere."

She sat down at the table and stared at him with scorn and
amazement; sat down heavily, as though she had been struck. He
knew that she was gathering her forces; and now she said what he
had dreaded to hear:

"And suppose I went through town and told your wife, and the
churchfolks, and everybody—suppose I did that, Reverend?"

"And who you think," he asked—he felt himself enveloped by an
awful, falling silence—"is going to believe you?"

She laughed. "Enough folks'd believe me to make it mighty hard
on you." And she watched him. He walked up and down the
kitchen, trying to avoid her eyes. "You just think back," she said, "to
that first night, right here on this damn white folks' floor, and you'll
see it's too late for you to talk to Esther about how holy you is. I

don't care if you want to live a lie, but I don't see no reason for you to make me suffer on account of it."

"You can go around and tell folks if you want to," he said, boldly, "but it ain't going to look so good for you neither."

She laughed again. "But I ain't the holy one. You's a married man, and you's a preacher—and who you think folks is going to blame most?"

He watched her with a hatred that was mixed with his old desire, knowing that once more she had the victory.

"I can't marry you, you know that," he said. "Now, what you want me to do?"

"No," she said, "and I reckon you *wouldn't* marry me even if you *was* free. I reckon you don't want no whore like Esther for your wife. Esther's just for the night, for the dark, where won't nobody see you getting your holy self all dirtied up with Esther. Esther's just good enough to go out and have *your* bastard somewhere in the goddamn woods. Ain't that so, Reverend?"

He did not answer her. He could find no words. There was only silence in him, like the grave.

She rose, and moved to the open kitchen door, where she stood, her back to him, looking out into the yard and on the silent streets where the last, dead rays of the sun still lingered.

"But I reckon," she said slowly, "that I don't want to be with you no more'n you want to be with me. I don't want no man what's ashamed and scared. Can't do me no good, that kind of man." She turned in the door and faced him; this was the last time she really looked at him, and he would carry that look to his grave. "There's just one thing I want you to do," she said. "You do that, and we be all right."

"What you want me to do?" he asked, and felt ashamed.

"I *would* go through this town," she said, "and tell everybody about the Lord's anointed. Only reason I don't is because I don't want my mama and daddy to know what a fool I been. I ain't ashamed of *it*—I'm ashamed of *you*—you done made me feel a shame I ain't never felt before. I shamed before my *God*—to let somebody make me cheap, like you done done."

He said nothing. She turned her back to him again.

"I . . . just want to go somewhere," she said, "*go* somewhere, and *have* my baby, and think all this out of my mind. I want to go somewhere and get my mind straight. *That's* what I want you to do—and that's pretty cheap. I guess it takes a holy man to make a girl a real whore."

"Girl," he said, "I ain't got no *money*."

"Well," she said, coldly, "you damn well better find some."

Then she began to cry. He moved toward her, but she moved away.

"If I go out into the field," he said, helplessly, "I ought to be able to make enough money to send you away."

"How long that going to take?"

"A month maybe."

And she shook her head. "I ain't going to stay around here that long."

They stood in silence in the open kitchen door, she struggling against her tears, he struggling against his shame. He could only think: "Jesus Jesus Jesus. Jesus Jesus."

"Ain't you got nothing saved up?" she asked at last. "Look to me like you been married long enough to've saved something!"

Then he remembered that Deborah had been saving money since their wedding day. She kept it in a tin box at the top of the cupboard. He thought of how sin led to sin.

"Yes," he said, "a little. I don't know how much."

"You bring it tomorrow," she told him.

"Yes," he said.

He watched her as she moved from the door and went to the closet for her hat and coat. Then she came back, dressed for the street and, without a word, passed him, walking down the short steps into the yard. She opened the low gate and turned down the long, silent, flaming street. She walked slowly, head bowed, as though she were cold. He stood watching her, thinking of the many times he had watched her before, when her walk had been so different and her laughter had come ringing back to mock him.

He stole the money while Deborah slept. And he gave it to Esther in the morning. She gave notice that same day, and a week later she was gone—to Chicago, said her parents, to find a better job and to have a better life.

Deborah became more silent than ever in the weeks that followed. Sometimes he was certain she had discovered that the money was missing and knew that he had taken it—sometimes he was certain that she knew nothing. Sometimes he was certain that she knew everything: the theft, and the reason for the theft. But she did not speak. In the middle of the spring he went out into the field to preach, and was gone three months. When he came back he brought the money with him and put it in the box again. No money had been added in the meanwhile, so he still could not be certain whether Deborah knew or not.

He decided to let it all be forgotten, and begin his life again.

But the summer brought him a letter, with no return name or address, but postmarked from Chicago. Deborah gave it to him at breakfast, not seeming to have remarked the hand or the postmark, along with the bundle of tracts from a Bible house which they both distributed each week through the town. She had a letter, too, from Florence, and it was perhaps this novelty that distracted her attention.

Esther's letter ended:

> *What I think is, I made a mistake, that's true, and I'm paying for it now. But don't you think you ain't going to pay for it—I don't know when and I don't know how, but I know you going to be brought low one of these fine days. I ain't holy like you are, but I know right from wrong.*

*I'm going to have my baby and I'm going to bring him
up to be a man. And I ain't going to read to him out of no
Bibles and I ain't going to take him to hear no preaching. If
he don't drink nothing but moonshine all his natural days
he be a better man than his daddy.*

"What Florence got to say?" he asked dully, crumpling this letter
in his fist.

Deborah looked up with a faint smile. "Nothing much, honey.
But she sound like she going to get married."

Near the end of that summer he went out again into the field. He
could not stand his home, his job, the town itself—he could not endure, day in, day out, facing the scenes and the people he had known
all his life. They seemed suddenly to mock him, to stand in judgment on him; he saw his guilt in everybody's eyes. When he stood in
the pulpit to preach they looked at him, he felt, as though he had no
right to be there, as though they condemned him as he had once
condemned the twenty-three elders. When souls came weeping to
the altar he scarce dared to rejoice, remembering that soul who had
not bowed, whose blood, it might be, would be required of him at
judgment.

So he fled from these people, and from these silent witnesses, to
tarry and preach elsewhere—to do, as it were, in secret, his first
works over, seeking again the holy fire that had so transformed him
once. But he was to find, as the prophets had found, that the whole
earth became a prison for him who fled before the Lord. There was
peace nowhere, and healing nowhere, and forgetfulness nowhere. In
every church he entered, his sin had gone before him. It was in the
strange, the welcoming faces, it cried up to him from the altar, it sat,
as he mounted the pulpit steps, waiting for him in his seat. It stared
upward from his Bible: there was no word in all that holy book
which did not make him tremble. When he spoke of John on the isle
of Patmos, taken up in the spirit on the Lord's day, to behold things

past, present, and to come, saying: "He which is filthy, let him be filthy still," it was he who, crying these words in a loud voice, was utterly confounded; when he spoke of David, the shepherd boy, raised by God's power to be the King of Israel, it was he who, while they shouted: "Amen!" and: "Hallelujah!" struggled once more in his chains; when he spoke of the day of Pentecost when the Holy Ghost had come down on the apostles who tarried in the upper room, causing them to speak in tongues of fire, he thought of his own baptism and how he had offended the Holy Ghost. No: though his name was writ large on placards, though they praised him for the great work God worked through him, and though they came, day and night, before him to the altar, there was no word in the Book for him.

And he saw, in this wandering, how far his people had wandered from God. They had all turned aside, and gone out into the wilderness, to fall down before idols of gold and silver, and wood and stone, false gods that could not heal them. The music that filled any town or city he entered was not the music of the saints but another music, infernal, which glorified lust and held righteousness up to scorn. Women, some of whom should have been at home, teaching their grandchildren how to pray, stood, night after night, twisting their bodies into lewd hallelujahs in smoke-filled, gin-heavy dance halls, singing for their "loving man." And their loving man was any man, any morning, noon, or night—when one left town they got another—men could drown, it seemed, in their warm flesh and they would never know the difference. "It's here for you and if you don't get it it ain't no fault of mine." They laughed at him when they saw him—"a pretty man like you?"—and they told him that they knew a long brown girl who could make him lay his Bible down. He fled from them; they frightened him. He began to pray for Esther. He imagined her standing one day where these women stood today.

And blood, in all the cities through which he passed, ran down. There seemed no door, anywhere, behind which blood did not call out, unceasingly, for blood; no woman, whether singing before defiant trumpets or rejoicing before the Lord, who had not seen her father, her brother, her lover, or her son cut down without mercy; who had not seen her sister become part of the white man's great whorehouse, who had not, all too narrowly, escaped that house herself; no man, preaching, or cursing, strumming his guitar in the lone, blue evening, or blowing in fury and ecstasy his golden horn at night, who had not been made to bend his head and drink white men's muddy water; no man whose manhood had not been, at the root, sickened, whose loins had not been dishonored, whose seed had not been scattered into oblivion and worse than oblivion, into living shame and rage, and into endless battle. Yes, their parts were all cut off, they were dishonored, their very names were nothing more than dust blown disdainfully across the field of time—to fall where, to blossom where, bringing forth what fruit hereafter, where?—their very names were not their own. Behind them was the darkness, nothing but the darkness, and all around them destruction, and before them nothing but the fire—a bastard people, far from God, singing and crying in the wilderness!

Yet, most strangely, and from deeps not before discovered, his faith looked up; before the wickedness that he saw, the wickedness from which he fled, he yet beheld like a flaming standard in the middle of the air, that power of redemption to which he must, till death, bear witness; which, though it crush him utterly, he could not deny; though none among the living might ever behold it, *he* had beheld it, and must keep the faith. He would not go back into Egypt for friend, or lover, or bastard son: he would not turn his face from God, no matter how deep might grow the darkness in which God hid His face from him. One day God would give him a sign, and the darkness would all be finished—one day God would raise him, Who had suffered him to fall so low.

Hard on the heels of his return that winter, Esther came home too. Her mother and stepfather traveled North to claim her lifeless body and her living son. Soon after Christmas, on the last, dead days of the year, she was buried in the churchyard. It was bitterly cold and there was ice on the ground, as during the days when he had first possessed her. He stood next to Deborah, whose arm in his shivered incessantly with the cold, and watched while the long, plain box was lowered into the ground. Esther's mother stood in silence beside the deep hole, leaning on her husband, who held their grandchild in his arms. "Lord have mercy, have mercy, have mercy," someone began to chant; and the old mourning women clustered of a sudden around Esther's mother to hold her up. Then earth struck the coffin; the child awakened and began to scream.

Then Gabriel prayed to be delivered from blood guiltiness. He prayed to God to give him a sign one day to make him know he was forgiven. But the child who screamed at that moment in the churchyard had cursed, and sung, and been silenced forever before God gave him a sign.

And he watched this son grow up, a stranger to his father and a stranger to God. Deborah, who became after the death of Esther more friendly with Esther's people, reported to him from the very beginning how shamefully Royal was being spoiled. He was, inevitably, the apple of their eye, a fact that, in operation, caused Deborah to frown, and sometimes, reluctantly, to smile; and, as they said, if there was any white blood in him, it didn't show—he was the spit and image of his mother.

The sun did not rise or set but that Gabriel saw his lost, his disinherited son, or heard of him; and he seemed with every passing day to carry more proudly the doom printed on his brow. Gabriel watched him run headlong, like David's headlong son, toward the disaster that had been waiting for him from the moment he had been conceived. It seemed that he had scarcely begun to walk before he swaggered; he had scarcely begun to talk before he cursed. Gabriel often saw him on the streets, playing on the curbstone with other boys his age. Once, when he passed, one of the boys had said: "Here comes Reverend Grimes," and nodded, in brief, respectful silence. But Royal had looked boldly up into the preacher's face. He had said: "How-de-do, Reverend?" and suddenly, irrepressibly, laughed. Gabriel, wishing to smile down into the boy's face, to pause and touch him on the forehead, did none of these things, but walked on. Behind him, he heard Royal's explosive whisper: "I bet he got a mighty big one!"—and then all the children laughed. It came to Gabriel then how his own mother must have suffered to watch him in the unredeemed innocence that so surely led to death and Hell.

"I wonder," said Deborah idly once, "why she called him Royal? You reckon that's his daddy's name?"

He did not wonder. He had once told Esther that if the Lord ever gave him a son he would call him Royal, because the line of the faithful was a royal line—his son would be a royal child. And this she had remembered as she thrust him from her; with what had perhaps been her last breath she had mocked him and his father with this name. She had died, then, hating him; she had carried into eternity a curse on him and his.

"I reckon," he said at last, "it *must* be his daddy's name—less they just given him that name in the hospital up North after . . . she was dead."

"His grandmama, Sister McDonald"—she was writing a letter, and did not look at him as she spoke—"well, *she* think it must've been one of them boys what's all time passing through here, looking for work, on their way North—you know? them real shiftless niggers—well, *she* think it must've been one of them got Esther in trouble. She say Esther wouldn't never've gone North if she hadn't been a-trying to find that boy's daddy. Because she was in trouble when she left here"—and she looked up from her letter a moment—"*that's* for certain."

"I reckon," he said again, made uncomfortable by her unaccustomed chatter, but not daring, too sharply, to stop her. He was thinking of Esther, lying cold and still in the ground, who had been so vivid and shameless in his arms.

"And Sister McDonald say," she went on, "that she left here with just a little *bit* of money; they had to keep a-sending her money all the time she was up there almost, specially near the end. We was just talking about it yesterday—she say, look like Esther just decided over*night* she had to go, and couldn't nothing stop her. And she say she didn't *want* to stand in the girl's way—but if she'd've *known* something was the matter she wouldn't *never*'ve let that girl away from her."

"Seems funny to *me*," he muttered, scarcely knowing what he was saying, "that she didn't think *something*."

"Why, she didn't think nothing, because Esther always *told* her mother everything—weren't no shame between them—they was just like two women together. She say she never *dreamed* that Esther would run away from her if she got herself in trouble." And she looked outward, past him, her eyes full of a strange, bitter pity. "That poor thing," she said, "she must have suffered *some*."

"I don't see no need for you and Sister McDonald to sit around and *talk* about it all the time," he said, then. "It all been a mighty long time ago; that boy is growing up already."

"That's true," she said, bending her head once more, "but some things, look like, ain't to be forgotten in a hurry."

"Who you writing to?" he asked, as oppressed suddenly by the silence as he had been by her talk.

She looked up. "I'm writing to your sister, Florence. You got anything you want me to say?"

"No," he said. "Just tell her I'm praying for her."

When Royal was sixteen the war came, and all the young men, first the sons of the mighty, and then the sons of his own people, were scattered into foreign lands. Gabriel fell on his knees each night to pray that Royal would not have to go. "But I hear he *want* to go," said Deborah. "His grandmama tell me he giving her a *time* because she won't let him go and sign up."

"Look like," he said sullenly, "that won't none of these young men be satisfied till they can go off and get themselves crippled or killed."

"Well, you know that's the way the young folks is," said Deborah, cheerfully. "You can't never tell them nothing—and when they find out it's too late then."

He discovered that whenever Deborah spoke of Royal, a fear deep within him listened and waited. Many times he had thought to unburden his heart to her. But she gave him no opportunity, never said anything that might allow him the healing humility of confession—or that might, for that matter, have permitted him at last to say how much he hated her for her barrenness. She demanded of him what she gave—nothing—nothing, at any rate, with which she could be reproached. She kept his house and shared his bed; she visited the sick, as she had always done, and she comforted the dying, as she had always done. The marriage for which he had once dreamed the world would mock him had so justified itself—in the eyes of the world—that no one now could imagine, for either of them, any other condition or alliance. Even Deborah's weakness, which grew more marked with the years, keeping her more frequently in her bed, and her barrenness, like her previous dishonor, had come to seem mysterious proofs of how completely she had surrendered herself to God.

He said: "Amen," cautiously, after her last remark, and cleared his throat.

"I declare," she said, with the same cheerfulness, "sometime he remind me of you when you was a young man."

And he did not look at her, though he felt her eyes on him: he reached for his Bible and opened it. "Young men," he said, "is all the same, don't Jesus change their hearts."

Royal did not go to war, but he went away that summer to work on the docks in another town. Gabriel did not see him any more until the war was over.

On that day, a day he was never to forget, he went when work was done to buy some medicine for Deborah, who was in bed with a misery in her back. Night had not yet fallen and the streets were gray and empty—save that here and there, polished in the light that spilled outward from a pool-room or a tavern, white men stood in groups of half a dozen. As he passed each group, silence fell, and they watched him insolently, itching to kill; but he said nothing, bowing his head, and they knew, anyway, that he was a preacher. There were no black men on the streets at all, save him. There had been found that morning, just outside of town, the dead body of a soldier, his uniform shredded where he had been flogged, and, turned upward through the black skin, raw, red meat. He lay face downward at the base of a tree, his fingernails digging into the scuffed earth. When he was turned over, his eyeballs stared upward in amazement and horror, his mouth was locked open wide; his trousers, soaked with blood, were torn open, and exposed to the cold, white air of morning the thick hairs of his groin, matted together, black and rust-red, and the wound that seemed to be throbbing still. He had been carried home in silence and lay now behind locked doors, with his living kinsmen, who sat, weeping, and praying, and dreaming of vengeance, and waiting for the next visitation. Now, someone spat on the sidewalk at Gabriel's feet, and he walked on, his face not changing, and he heard it reprovingly whispered behind him that he was a good nigger, surely up to no trouble. He hoped that he would not be spoken to, that he would not have to smile into any of these so well-known white faces. While he walked, held by his caution more rigid than an arrow, he prayed, as his mother had taught him to pray, for loving kindness; yet he dreamed of the feel of a white man's forehead against his shoe; again and again, until the head wobbled on the broken neck and his foot encountered nothing but the rushing blood. And he was thinking that it was only the hand of the Lord that had taken Royal away, because if he had stayed they would surely have killed him, when, turning a corner, he looked into Royal's face.

Royal was now as tall as Gabriel, broad-shouldered, and lean. He wore a new suit, blue, with broad, blue stripes, and carried, crooked under his arm, a brown-paper bundle tied with string. He and Gabriel stared at one another for a second with no recognition. Royal stared in blank hostility, before, seeming to remember Gabriel's face, he took a burning cigarette from between his lips, and said, with pained politeness: "How-de-do, sir." His voice was rough, and there was, faintly, the odor of whisky on his breath.

But Gabriel could not speak at once; he struggled to get his breath. Then: "How-de-do," he said. And they stood, each as though waiting for the other to say something of the greatest importance, on the deserted corner. Then, just as Royal was about to move, Gabriel remembered the white men all over town.

"Boy," he cried, "ain't you got good sense? Don't you know you ain't got no business to be out here, walking around like this?"

Royal stared at him, uncertain whether to laugh or to take offense, and Gabriel said, more gently: "I just mean you better be careful, son. Ain't nothing but white folks in town today. They done killed . . . last night . . ."

Then he could not go on. He saw, as though it were a vision, Royal's body, sprawled heavy and unmoving forever against the earth, and tears blinded his eyes.

Royal watched him, a distant and angry compassion in his face.

"I know," he said abruptly, "but they ain't going to bother me. They done got their nigger for this week. I ain't going far noway."

Then the corner on which they stood seemed suddenly to rock with the weight of mortal danger. It seemed for a moment, as they stood there, that death and destruction rushed toward them: two black men alone in the dark and silent town where white men prowled like lions—what mercy could they hope for, should they be found here, talking together? It would surely be believed that they were plotting vengeance. And Gabriel started to move away, thinking to save his son.

"God bless you, boy," said Gabriel. "You hurry along now."

"Yeah," said Royal, "thanks." He moved away, about to turn the corner. He looked back at Gabriel. "But you be careful, too," he said, and smiled.

He turned the corner and Gabriel listened as his footfalls moved away. They were swallowed up in silence; he heard no voices raised to cut down Royal as he went his way; soon there was silence everywhere.

Not quite two years later Deborah told him that his son was dead.

And now John tried to pray. There was a great noise of praying all around him, a great noise of weeping and of song. It was Sister McCandless who led the song, who sang it nearly alone, for the others did not cease to moan and cry. It was a song he had heard all his life:

> *"Lord, I'm traveling, Lord,*
> *I got on my traveling shoes."*

Without raising his eyes, he could see her standing in the holy place, pleading the blood over those who sought there, her head thrown back, eyes shut, foot pounding the floor. She did not look, then, like the Sister McCandless who sometimes came to visit them, like the woman who went out every day to work for the white people downtown, who came home at evening, climbing, with such weariness, the long, dark stairs. No: her face was transfigured now, her whole being was made new by the power of her salvation.

"Salvation is real," a voice said to him, "God is real. Death may come soon or late, why do you hesitate? Now is the time to seek and serve the Lord." Salvation was real for all these others, and it might be real for him. He had only to reach out and God would touch him; he had only to cry and God would hear. All these others, now, who cried so far beyond him with such joy, had once been in their sins, as he was now—and they had cried and God had heard them, and delivered them out of all their troubles. And what God had done for others, He could also do for him.

But—out of *all* their troubles? Why did his mother weep? Why did his father frown? If God's power was so great, why were their lives so troubled?

He had never tried to think of their trouble before; rather, he had never before confronted it in such a narrow place. It had always been there, at his back perhaps, all these years, but he had never turned to face it. Now it stood before him, staring, nevermore to be escaped, and its mouth was enlarged without any limit. It was ready to swallow him up. Only the hand of God could deliver him. Yet, in a moment, he somehow knew from the sound of that storm which rose so painfully in him now, which laid waste—forever?—the strange, yet comforting landscape of his mind, that the hand of God would surely lead him into this staring, waiting mouth, these distended jaws, this hot breath as of fire. He would be led into darkness, and in darkness would remain; until in some incalculable time to come the hand of God would reach down and raise him up; he, John, who having lain in darkness would no longer be himself but some other man. He would have been changed, as they said, forever; sown in dishonor, he would be raised in honor: he would have been born again.

Then he would no longer be the son of his father, but the son of his Heavenly Father, the King. Then he need no longer fear his father, for he could take, as it were, their quarrel over his father's head to Heaven—to the Father who loved him, who had come down in the flesh to die for him. Then he and his father would be equals, in the sight, and the sound, and the love of God. Then his father could not beat him any more, or despise him any more, or mock him any more—he, John, the Lord's anointed. He could speak to his father then as men spoke to one another—as sons spoke to their fathers, not in trembling but in sweet confidence, not in hatred but in love. His father could not cast him out, whom God had gathered in.

Yet, trembling, he knew that this was not what he wanted. He did not *want* to love his father; he wanted to hate him, to cherish that hatred, and give his hatred words one day. He did not want his father's kiss—not any more, he who had received so many blows. He could not imagine, on any day to come and no matter how greatly he might be changed, wanting to take his father's hand. The storm that raged in him tonight could not uproot this hatred, the mightiest tree in all John's country, all that remained tonight, in this, John's flood-time.

And he bowed his head yet lower before the altar in weariness and confusion. *Oh, that his father would* die!—and the road before John be open, as it must be open for others. Yet in the very grave he would hate him; his father would but have changed conditions, he would be John's father still. The grave was not enough for punishment, for justice, for revenge. Hell, everlasting, unceasing, perpetual, unquenched forever, should be his father's portion; with John there to watch, to linger, to smile, to laugh aloud, hearing, at last, his father's cries of torment.

And, even then, it would not be finished. *The everlasting father.*

Oh, but his thoughts were evil—but tonight he did not care. Somewhere, in all this whirlwind, in the darkness of his heart, in the storm—was something—something he must find. He could not pray. His mind was like the sea itself: troubled, and too deep for the bravest man's descent, throwing up now and again, for the naked eye to wonder at, treasure and debris long forgotten on the bottom—bones and jewels, fantastic shells, jelly that had once been flesh, pearls that had once been eyes. And he was at the mercy of this sea, hanging there with darkness all around him.

The morning of that day, as Gabriel rose and started out to work, the sky was low and nearly black and the air too thick to breathe. Late in the afternoon the wind rose, the skies opened, and the rain came. The rain came down as though once more in Heaven the Lord had been persuaded of the good uses of a flood. It drove before it the bowed wanderer, clapped children into houses, licked with fearful anger against the high, strong wall, and the wall of the lean-to, and the wall of the cabin, beat against the bark and the leaves of trees, trampled the broad grass, and broke the neck of the flower. The world turned dark, forever, everywhere, and windows ran as though their glass panes bore all the tears of eternity, threatening at every instant to shatter inward against this force, uncontrollable, so abruptly visited on the earth. Gabriel walked homeward through this wilderness of water (which had failed, however, to clear the air) to where Deborah waited for him in the bed she seldom, these days, attempted to leave.

And he had not been in the house five minutes before he was aware that a change had occurred in the quality of her silence: in the silence something waited, ready to spring.

He looked up at her from the table where he sat eating the meal that she had painfully prepared. He asked: "How you feel today, old lady?"

"I feel like about the way I always do," and she smiled. "I don't feel no better and I don't feel no worse."

"We going to get the church to pray for you," he said, "and get you on your feet again."

She said nothing and he turned his attention once more to his plate. But she was watching him; he looked up.

"I hear some mighty bad news today," she said slowly.

"What you hear?"

"Sister McDonald was over this afternoon, and Lord knows she was in a pitiful state." He sat stock-still, staring at her. "She done got a letter today what says her grandson—you know, that Royal—done got hisself killed in Chicago. It sure look like the Lord is put a curse on that family. First the mother, and now the son."

For a moment he could only stare at her stupidly, while the food in his mouth slowly grew heavy and dry. Outside rushed the armies of the rain, and lightning flashed against the window. Then he tried to swallow, and his gorge rose. He began to tremble. "Yes," she said, not looking at him now, "he been living in Chicago about a year, just a-drinking and a-carrying on—and his grandmama, she tell me that look like he got to gambling one night with some of them northern niggers, and one of them got mad because he thought the boy was trying to cheat him, and took out his knife and stabbed him. Stabbed him in the throat, and she tell me he died right there on the floor in that barroom, didn't even have time to get him to no hospital." She turned in bed and looked at him. "The Lord sure give that poor woman a heavy cross to bear."

Then he tried to speak; he thought of the churchyard where Esther was buried, and Royal's first, thin cry. "She going to bring him back home?"

She stared. "Home? Honey, they done buried him already up there in the potter's field. Ain't nobody never going to look on that poor boy no more."

Then he began to cry, not making a sound, sitting at the table, and with his whole body shaking. She watched him for a long while and, finally, he put his head on the table, overturning the coffee cup, and wept aloud. Then it seemed that there was weeping everywhere, waters of anguish riding the world; Gabriel weeping, and rain beating on the roof, and at the windows, and the coffee dripping from the end of the table. And she asked at last:

"Gabriel . . . that Royal . . . he were your flesh and blood, weren't he?"

"Yes," he said, glad even in his anguish to hear the words fall from his lips, "that was my son."

And there was silence again. Then: "And you sent that girl away, didn't you? With the money outen that box?"

"Yes," he said, "yes."

"Gabriel," she asked, "why did you do it? Why you let her go off and die, all by herself? Why ain't you never said nothing?"

And now he could not answer. He could not raise his head.

"Why?" she insisted. "Honey, I ain't never asked you. But I got a right to know—and when you wanted a son so bad?"

Then, shaking, he rose from the table and walked slowly to the window, looking out.

"I asked my God to forgive me," he said. "But I didn't want no harlot's son."

"Esther weren't no harlot," she said quietly.

"She weren't my wife. I couldn't make her my wife. I already had *you*"—and he said the last words with venom—"Esther's mind weren't on the Lord—she'd of dragged me right on down to Hell with her."

"She mighty near has," said Deborah.

"The Lord He held me back," he said, hearing the thunder, watching the lightning. "He put out His hand and held me back." Then, after a moment, turning back into the room: "I *couldn't* of done nothing else," he cried, "what else could I of done? Where could I of gone with Esther, and me a preacher, too? And what could I of done with you?" He looked at her, old and black and patient, smelling of sickness and age and death. "Ah," he said, his tears still falling, "I bet you was mighty happy today, old lady, weren't you? When she told you he, Royal, my son, was dead. *You* ain't never had no son." And he turned again to the window. Then: "How long you been knowing about this?"

"I been knowing," she said, "ever since that evening, way back there, when Esther come to church."

"You got a evil mind," he said. "I hadn't never touched her then."

"No," she said slowly, "but you had already done touched *me*."

He moved a little from the window and stood looking down at her from the foot of the bed.

"Gabriel," she said, "I been praying all these years that the Lord would touch my body, and make me like them women, all them women, you used to go with all the time." She was very calm; her face was very bitter and patient. "Look like it weren't His will. Look like I couldn't nohow forget . . . how they done me way back there when I weren't nothing but a girl." She paused and looked away. "But, Gabriel, if you'd said something even when that poor girl was buried, if you'd wanted to own that poor boy, I wouldn't nohow of cared what folks said, or where we might of had to go, or nothing. I'd have raised him like my own, I swear to my God I would have—and he might be living now."

"Deborah," he asked, "what you been thinking all this time?"

She smiled. "I been thinking," she said, "how you better commence to tremble when the Lord, He gives you your heart's desire." She paused. "I'd been wanting you since I wanted anything. And then I got you."

He walked back to the window, tears rolling down his face.

"Honey," she said, in another, stronger voice, "you better pray God to forgive you. You better not let go until He make you *know* you been forgiven."

"Yes," he sighed, "I'm waiting on the Lord."

Then there was only silence, except for the rain. The rain came down in buckets; it was raining, as they said, pitchforks and nigger babies. Lightning flashed again across the sky and thunder rolled.

"Listen," said Gabriel. "God is talking."

Slowly now, he rose from his knees, for half the church was standing: Sister Price, Sister McCandless, and Praying Mother Washington; and the young Ella Mae sat in her chair watching Elisha where he lay. Florence and Elizabeth were still on their knees; and John was on his knees.

And, rising, Gabriel thought of how the Lord had led him to this church so long ago, and how Elizabeth, one night after he had preached, had walked this long aisle to the altar, to repent before God her sin. And then they had married, for he believed her when she said that she was changed—and she was the sign, she and her nameless child, for which he had tarried so many dark years before the Lord. It was as though, when he saw them, the Lord had returned to him again that which was lost.

Then, as he stood with the others over the fallen Elisha, John rose from his knees. He bent a dazed, sleepy, frowning look on Elisha and the others, shivering a little as though he were cold; and then he felt his father's eyes and looked up at his father.

At the same moment, Elisha, from the floor, began to speak in a tongue of fire, under the power of the Holy Ghost. John and his father stared at each other, struck dumb and still and with something come to life between them—while the Holy Ghost spoke. Gabriel

had never seen such a look on John's face before; Satan, at that moment, stared out of John's eyes while the Spirit spoke; and yet John's
staring eyes tonight reminded Gabriel of other eyes: of his mother's
eyes when she beat him, of Florence's eyes when she mocked him, of
Deborah's eyes when she prayed for him, of Esther's eyes and Royal's
eyes, and Elizabeth's eyes tonight before Roy cursed him, and of
Roy's eyes when Roy said: "You black bastard." And John did not
drop his eyes, but seemed to want to stare forever into the bottom of
Gabriel's soul. And Gabriel, scarcely believing that John could have
become so brazen, stared in wrath and horror at Elizabeth's pre-
sumptuous bastard boy, grown suddenly so old in evil. He nearly
raised his hand to strike him, but did not move, for Elisha lay between them. Then he said, soundlessly, with his lips: "Kneel down."
John turned suddenly, the movement like a curse, and knelt again
before the altar.

THREE

❧

Elizabeth's Prayer

Lord, I wish I had of died
In Egypt land!

W<small>HILE ELISHA WAS SPEAKING</small>, Elizabeth felt that the Lord was speaking a message to her heart, that this fiery visitation was meant for her; and that if she humbled herself to listen, God would give her the interpretation. This certainty did not fill her with exultation, but with fear. She was afraid of what God might say—of what displeasure, what condemnation, what prophesies of trials yet to be endured might issue from His mouth.

Now Elisha ceased to speak, and rose; now he sat at the piano. There was muted singing all around her; yet she waited. Before her mind's eyes wavered, in a light like the light from a fire, the face of John, whom she had brought so unwillingly into the world. It was for this deliverance that she wept tonight: that he might be carried, past wrath unspeakable, into a state of grace.

They were singing:

> *"Must Jesus bear the cross alone,*
> *And all the world go free?"*

Elisha picked out the song on the piano, his fingers seeming to hesitate, almost to be unwilling. She, too, strained against her great unwillingness, but forced her heart to say Amen, as the voice of Praying Mother Washington picked up the response:

> *"No, there's a cross for everyone,*
> *And there's a cross for me."*

She heard weeping near her—was it Ella Mae? or Florence? or the echo, magnified, of her own tears? The weeping was buried beneath the song. She had been hearing this song all her life, she had grown up with it, but she had never understood it as well as she understood it now. It filled the church, as though the church had merely become a hollow or a void, echoing with the voices that had driven her to this dark place. Her aunt had sung it always, harshly, under her breath, in a bitter pride:

> *"The consecrated cross I'll bear*
> *Till death shall set me free,*
> *And then go home, a crown to wear,*
> *For there's a crown for me."*

She was probably an old, old woman now, still in the same harshness of spirit, singing this song in the tiny house down home which she and Elizabeth had shared so long. And she did not know of Elizabeth's shame—Elizabeth had not written about John until long after she was married to Gabriel; and the Lord had never allowed her aunt to come to New York City. Her aunt had always prophesied that Elizabeth would come to no good end, proud, and vain, and foolish as as she was, and having been allowed to run wild all her childhood days.

Her aunt had come second in the series of disasters that had ended Elizabeth's childhood. First, when she was eight, going on nine, her mother had died, an event not immediately recognized by Elizabeth as a disaster, since she had scarcely known her mother and had certainly never loved her. Her mother had been very fair, and beautiful, and delicate of health, so that she stayed in bed most of the time, reading spiritualist pamphlets concerning the benefits of disease and complaining to Elizabeth's father of how she suffered. Elizabeth remembered of her only that she wept very easily and that she smelled like stale milk—it was, perhaps, her mother's disquieting color that, whenever she was held in her mother's arms, made Elizabeth think of milk. Her mother did not, however, hold Elizabeth in her arms very often. Elizabeth very quickly suspected that this was because she was so very much darker than her mother and not nearly, of course, so beautiful. When she faced her mother she was shy, downcast, sullen. She did not know how to answer her mother's shrill, meaningless questions, put with the furious affectation of maternal concern; she could not pretend, when she kissed her mother, or submitted to her mother's kiss, that she was moved by anything more than an unpleasant sense of duty. This, of course, bred in her mother a kind of baffled fury, and she never tired of telling Elizabeth that she was an "unnatural" child.

But it was very different with her father; he was—and so Elizabeth never failed to think of him—young, and handsome, and kind, and generous; and he loved his daughter. He told her that she was the apple of his eye, that she was wound around his heartstrings, that she was surely the finest little lady in the land. When she was with her father she pranced and postured like a very queen: and she was not afraid of anything, save the moment when he would say that it was her bedtime, or that he had to be "getting along." He was always

buying her things, things to wear and things to play with, and taking
her on Sundays for long walks through the country, or to the circus,
when the circus was in town, or to Punch and Judy shows. And he
was dark, like Elizabeth, and gentle, and proud; he had never been
angry with her, but she had seen him angry a few times with other
people—her mother, for example, and later, of course, her aunt. Her
mother was always angry and Elizabeth paid no attention; and, later,
her aunt was perpetually angry and Elizabeth learned to bear it: but
if her father had ever been angry with her—in those days—she
would have wanted to die.

Neither had he ever learned of her disgrace; when it happened,
she could not think how to tell him, how to bring such pain to him
who had had such pain already. Later, when she would have told
him, he was long past caring, in the silent ground.

She thought of him now, while the singing and weeping went on
around her—and she thought how he would have loved his grandson, who was like him in so many ways. Perhaps she dreamed it, but
she did not believe she dreamed when at moments she thought she
heard in John echoes, curiously distant and distorted, of her father's
gentleness, and the trick of his laugh—how he threw his head back
and the years that marked his face fled away, and the soft eyes softened and the mouth turned upward at the corners like a little boy's
mouth—and that deadly pride of her father's behind which he retired when confronted by the nastiness of other people. It was he
who had told her to weep, when she wept, alone; never to let the
world see, never to ask for mercy; if one had to die, to go ahead and
die, but never to let oneself be beaten. He had said this to her on one
of the last times she had seen him, when she was being carried miles
away, to Maryland, to live with her aunt. She had reason, in the years
that followed, to remember his saying this; and time, at last, to discover in herself the depths of bitterness in her father from which
these words had come.

For when her mother died, the world fell down; her aunt, her
mother's older sister, arrived, and stood appalled at Elizabeth's van-

ity and uselessness; and decided, immediately, that her father was no fit person to raise a child, especially, as she darkly said, an innocent little girl. And it was this decision on the part of her aunt, for which Elizabeth did not forgive her for many years, that precipitated the third disaster, the separation of herself from her father—from all that she loved on earth.

For her father ran what her aunt called a "house"—not the house where they lived, but another house, to which, as Elizabeth gathered, wicked people often came. And he had also, to Elizabeth's rather horrified confusion, a "stable." Low, common niggers, the lowest of the low, came from all over (and sometimes brought their women and sometimes found them there) to eat, and drink cheap moonshine, and play music all night long—and to do worse things, her aunt's dreadful silence then suggested, which were far better left unsaid. And she would, she swore, move Heaven and earth before she would let her sister's daughter grow up with such a man. Without, however, so much as looking at Heaven, and without troubling any more of the earth than that part of it which held the courthouse, she won the day: like a clap of thunder, or like a magic spell, like light one moment and darkness the next, Elizabeth's life had changed. Her mother was dead, her father banished, and she lived in the shadow of her aunt.

Or, more exactly, as she thought now, the shadow in which she had lived was fear—fear made more dense by hatred. Not for a moment had she judged her father; it would have made no difference to her love for him had she been told, and even seen it proved, that he was first cousin to the Devil. The proof would not have existed for her, and if it had she would not have regretted being his daughter, or have asked for anything better than to suffer at his side in Hell. And when she had been taken from him her imagination had been wholly unable to lend reality to the wickedness of which he stood accused—*she,* certainly, did not accuse him. She screamed in anguish when he put her from him and turned to go, and she had to be carried to the train. And later, when she understood perfectly all that had happened then, still in her heart she could not accuse him. Perhaps his life had been wicked, but he had been very good to her. His life had certainly cost him enough in pain to make the world's judgment a thing of no account. *They* had not known him as she had known him; *they* did not care as she had cared! It only made her sad that he never, as he had promised, came to take her away, and that while she was growing up she saw him so seldom. When she became a young woman she did not see him at all; but that was her own fault.

No, she did not accuse him; but she accused her aunt, and this from the moment she understood that her aunt had loved her mother, but did not love *him*. This could only mean that her aunt could not love *her,* either, and nothing in her life with her aunt ever proved Elizabeth wrong. It was true that her aunt was always talking of how much she loved her sister's daughter, and what great sacrifices she had made on her account, and what great care she took to see to it that Elizabeth should grow up a good, Christian girl. But Elizabeth was not for a moment fooled, and did not, for as long as she lived with her, fail to despise her aunt. She sensed that what her aunt spoke of as love was something else—a bribe, a threat, an indecent will to power. She knew that the kind of imprisonment that love might impose was also, mysteriously, a freedom for the soul and spirit, was water in the dry place, and had nothing to do with the prisons, churches, laws, rewards, and punishments, that so positively cluttered the landscape of her aunt's mind.

And yet, tonight, in her great confusion, she wondered if she had not been wrong; if there had not been something that she had overlooked, for which the Lord had made her suffer. "You little miss great-I-am," her aunt had said to her in those days, "you better watch your step, you hear me? You go walking around with your nose in the air, the Lord's going to let you fall right on down to the bottom of the ground. *You* mark my words. You'll *see*."

To this perpetual accusation Elizabeth had never replied; she merely regarded her aunt with a wide-eyed, insolent stare, meant at once to register her disdain and to thwart any pretext for punishment. And this trick, which she had, unconsciously, picked up from her father, rarely failed to work. As the years went on, her aunt seemed to gauge in a look the icy distances that Elizabeth had put between them, and that would certainly never be conquered now. And she would add, looking down, and under her breath: " 'Cause God don't like it."

"I sure don't care what God don't like, or you, either," Elizabeth's heart replied. "I'm going away from here. He's going to come and get me, and I'm going away from here."

"He" was her father, who never came. As the years passed, she replied only: "I'm going away from here." And it hung, this determination, like a heavy jewel between her breasts; it was written in fire on the dark sky of her mind.

But, yes—there was something she had overlooked. *Pride goeth before destruction; and a haughty spirit before a fall.* She had not known this: she had not imagined that she could fall. She wondered, tonight, how she could give this knowledge to her son; if she could help him to endure what could now no longer be changed; if while life ran, he would forgive her—for her pride, her folly, and her bargaining with God! For, tonight, those years before her fall, in her aunt's dark house—that house which smelled always of clothes kept too long in closets, and of old women; which was redolent of their gossip, and was pervaded, somehow, by the odor of the lemon her aunt took in her tea, and by the odor of frying fish, and of the still that someone kept in the basement—came before her, entire and overwhelming; and she remembered herself, entering any room in which her aunt might be sitting, responding to anything her aunt might say, standing before her, as rigid as metal and cancerous with hate and fear, in battle every hour of every day, a battle that she continued in her dreams. She knew now of what it was that she had so silently and so early accused her aunt: it was of tearing a bewildered child away from the arms of the father she loved. And she knew now why she had sometimes, so dimly and so unwillingly, felt that her father had betrayed her: it was because he had not overturned the earth to take his daughter away from a woman who did not love her, and whom she did not love. Yet she knew tonight how difficult it was to overturn the earth, for she had tried once, and she had failed. And she knew, too—and it made the tears that touched her mouth more bitter than the most bitter herb—that without the pride and bitterness she had so long carried in her heart against her aunt she could never have endured her life with her.

And she thought of Richard. It was Richard who had taken her out of that house, and out of the South, and into the city of destruction. He had suddenly arrived—and from the moment he arrived until the moment of his death he had filled her life. Not even tonight, in the heart's nearly impenetrable secret place, where the truth is hidden and where only the truth can live, could she wish that she had not known him; or deny that, so long as he was there, the rejoicing of Heaven could have meant nothing to her—that, being forced to choose between Richard and God, she could only, even with weeping, have turned away from God.

And this was why God had taken him from her. It was for all of this that she was paying now, and it was this pride, hatred, bitterness, lust—this folly, this corruption—of which her son was heir.

Richard had not been born in Maryland, but he was working there, the summer that she met him, as a grocery clerk. It was 1919, and she was one year younger than the century. He was twenty-two, which seemed a great age to her in those days. She noticed him at once because he was so sullen and only barely polite. He waited on folks, her aunt said, furiously, as though he hoped the food they bought would poison them. Elizabeth liked to watch him move; his body was very thin, and beautiful, and nervous—*high strung,* thought Elizabeth, wisely. He moved exactly like a cat, perpetually on the balls of his feet, and with a cat's impressive, indifferent aloofness, his face closed, in his eyes no light at all. He smoked all the time, a cigarette between his lips as he added up the figures, and sometimes left burning on the counter while he went to look for stock. When, as someone entered, he said good morning, or good day, he said it barely looking up, and with an indifference that fell just short of insolence. When, having bought what he wanted and counted his change, the customer turned to leave and Richard said: "Thank you," it sounded so much like a curse that people sometimes turned in surprise to stare.

"He sure don't like working in that store," Elizabeth once observed to her aunt.

"He don't like working," said her aunt, scornfully. "He just like you."

On a bright, summer day, bright in her memory forever, she came into the store alone, wearing her best white summer dress and with her hair, newly straightened and curled at the ends, tied with a scarlet ribbon. She was going to a great church picnic with her aunt, and had come in to buy some lemons. She passed the owner of the store, who was a very fat man, sitting out on the sidewalk, fanning himself; he asked her, as she passed, if it was hot enough for her, and she said something and walked into the dark, heavy-smelling store, where flies buzzed, and where Richard sat on the counter reading a book.

She felt immediately guilty about having disturbed him, and muttered apologetically that she only wanted to buy some lemons. She expected him to get them for her in his sullen fashion and go back to his book, but he smiled, and said:

"Is that all you want? You better think now. You sure you ain't forgot nothing?"

She had never seen him smile before, nor had she really, for that matter, ever heard his voice. Her heart gave a dreadful leap and then, as dreadfully, seemed to have stopped forever. She could only stand there, staring at him. If he had asked her to repeat what she wanted she could not possibly have remembered what it was. And she found that she was looking into his eyes and where she had thought there was no light at all she found a light she had never seen before—and he was smiling still, but there was something curiously urgent in his smile. Then he said: "How many lemons, little girl?"

"Six," she said at last, and discovered to her vast relief that nothing had happened: the sun was still shining, the fat man still sat at the door, her heart was beating as though it had never stopped.

She was not, however, fooled; she remembered the instant at which her heart had stopped, and she knew that it beat now with a difference.

He put the lemons into a bag and, with a curious diffidence, she came closer to the counter to give him the money. She was in a terrible state, for she found that she could neither take her eyes off him nor look at him.

"Is that your mother you come in with all the time?" he asked.

"No," she said, "that's my aunt." She did not know why she said it, but she did: "My mother's dead."

"Oh," he said. Then: "Mine, too." They both looked thoughtfully at the money on the counter. He picked it up, but did not move. "I didn't think it was your mother," he said, finally.

"Why?"

"I don't know. She don't look like you."

He started to light a cigarette, and then looked at her and put the pack in his pocket again.

"Don't mind me," she said quickly. "Anyway, I got to go. She's waiting—we going out."

He turned and banged the cash register. She picked up her lemons. He gave her her change. She felt that she ought to say something else—it didn't seem right, somehow, just to walk out—but she could not think of anything. But he said:

"Then *that's* why you so dressed up today. Where you going to go?"

"We going to a picnic—a church picnic," she said, and suddenly, unaccountably, and for the first time, smiled.

And he smiled, too, and lit his cigarette, blowing the smoke carefully away from her. "You like picnics?"

"Sometimes," she said. She was not comfortable with him yet, and still she was beginning to feel that she would like to stand and talk to him all day. She wanted to ask him what he was reading, but she did not dare. Yet: "What's your name?" she abruptly brought out.

"Richard," he said.

"Oh," she said thoughtfully. Then: "Mine's Elizabeth."

"I know," he said. "I heard her call you one time."

"Well," she said helplessly, after a long pause, "Good-bye."

" 'Good-*bye*?' You ain't going away, is you?"

"Oh, no," she said, in confusion.

"Well," he said, and smiled and bowed, "good *day*."

"Yes," she said, "good day."

And she turned and walked out into the streets; not the same streets from which she had entered a moment ago. These streets, the sky above, the sun, the drifting people, all had, in a moment, changed, and would never be the same again.

"You remember that day," he asked much later, "when you come into the store?"

"Yes?"

"Well, you was mighty pretty."

"I didn't think you never looked at me."

"Well, I didn't think you never looked at me."

"You was reading a book."

"Yes."

"What book was it, Richard?"

"Oh, I don't remember. Just a book."

"You smiled."

"You did, too."

"No, I didn't. I remember."

"Yes, you did."

"No, I *didn't*. Not till you did."

"Well, anyway—you was mighty pretty."

She did not like to think of with what hardness of heart, what calculated weeping, what deceit, what cruelty she now went into battle with her aunt for her freedom. And she won it, even though on certain not-to-be-dismissed conditions. The principal condition was that she should put herself under the protection of a distant, unspeakably respectable female relative of her aunt's, who lived in New York City—for when the summer ended, Richard said that he was going there and he wanted her to come with him. They would get married there. Richard said that he hated the South, and this was perhaps the reason it did not occur to either of them to begin their married life there. And Elizabeth was checked by the fear that if her aunt should discover how things stood between her and Richard she would find, as she had found so many years before in the case of her father, some means of bringing about their separation. This, as Elizabeth later considered it, was the first in the sordid series of mistakes which was to cause her to fall so low.

But to look back from the stony plain along the road which led one to that place is not at all the same thing as walking on the road; the perspective, to say the very least, changes only with the journey; only when the road has, all abruptly and treacherously, and with an absoluteness that permits no argument, turned or dropped or risen is one able to see all that one could not have seen from any other place. In those days, had the Lord Himself descended from Heaven with trumpets telling her to turn back, she could scarcely have heard Him, and could certainly not have heeded. She lived, in those days, in a fiery storm, of which Richard was the center and the heart. And she fought only to reach him—only that; she was afraid only of what might happen if they were kept from one another; for what might come after she had no thoughts or fears to spare.

Her pretext for coming to New York was to take advantage of the greater opportunities the North offered colored people; to study in a northern school, and to find a better job than any she was likely to be offered in the South. Her aunt, who listened to this with no diminution of her habitual scorn, was yet unable to deny that from generation to generation, things, as she grudgingly put it, were bound to change—and neither could she quite take the position of seeming to stand in Elizabeth's way. In the winter of 1920, as the year began, Elizabeth found herself in an ugly back room in Harlem in the home of her aunt's relative, a woman whose respectability was immediately evident from the incense she burned in her rooms and the spiritualist seances she held every Saturday night.

The house was still standing, not very far away; often she was forced to pass it. Without looking up, she was able to see the windows of the apartment in which she had lived, and the woman's sign was in the window still: MADAME WILLIAMS, SPIRITUALIST.

She found a job as chambermaid in the same hotel in which Richard worked as elevator boy. Richard said that they would marry as soon as he had saved some money. But since he was going to school at night and made very little money, their marriage, which she had thought of as taking place almost as soon as she arrived, was planned for a future that grew ever more remote. And this presented her with a problem that she had refused, at home in Maryland, to think about, but from which, now, she could not escape: the problem of their life together. Reality, so to speak, burst in for the first time on her great dreaming, and she found occasion to wonder, ruefully, what had made her imagine that, once with Richard, she would have been able to withstand him. She had kept, precariously enough, what her aunt referred to as her pearl without price while she had been with Richard down home. This, which she had taken as witness to her own feminine moral strength, had been due to nothing more, it now developed, than her great fear of her aunt, and the lack, in that small town, of opportunity. Here, in this great city where no one cared, where people might live in the same building for years and never speak to one another, she found herself, when Richard took her in his arms, on the edge of a steep place: and down she rushed, on the descent uncaring, into the dreadful sea.

So it began. Had it been waiting for her since the day she had been taken from her father's arms? The world in which she now found herself was not unlike the world from which she had, so long ago, been rescued. Here were the women who had been the cause of her aunt's most passionate condemnation of her father—hard-drinking, hard-talking, with whisky-and cigarette-breath, and moving with the mystic authority of women who knew what sweet violence might be acted out under the moon and stars, or beneath the tigerish lights of the city, in the raucous hay or the singing bed. And was she, Elizabeth, so sweetly fallen, so tightly chained, one of these women now? And here were the men who had come day and night to visit her father's "stable"—with their sweet talk and their music, and their violence and their sex—black, brown, and beige, who looked on her with lewd, and lustful, and laughing eyes. And these were Richard's friends. Not one of them ever went to church—one might scarcely have imagined that they knew that churches existed—they all, hourly, daily, in their speech, in their lives, and in their hearts, cursed God. They all seemed to be saying, as Richard, when she once timidly mentioned the love of Jesus, said: "You can tell that puking bastard to kiss my big black ass."

She, for very terror on hearing this, had wept; yet she could not deny that for such an abundance of bitterness there was a positive fountain of grief. There was not, after all, a great difference between the world of the North and that of the South which she had fled; there was only this difference: the North promised more. And this similarity: what it promised it did not give, and what it gave, at length and grudgingly with one hand, it took back with the other. Now she understood in this nervous, hollow, ringing city, that nervousness of Richard's which had so attracted her—a tension so total, and so without the hope, or possibility of release, or resolution, that she felt it in his muscles, and heard it in his breathing, even as on her breast he fell asleep.

And this was perhaps why she had never thought to leave him, frightened though she was during all that time, and in a world in which, had it not been for Richard, she could have found no place to put her feet. She did not leave him, because she was afraid of what might happen to him without her. She did not resist him, because he needed her. And she did not press about marriage because, upset as he was about everything, she was afraid of having him upset about her, too. She thought of herself as his strength; in a world of shadows, the indisputable reality to which he could always repair. And, again, for all that had come, she could not regret this. She had tried, but she had never been and was not now, even tonight, truly sorry. Where, then, was her repentance? And how could God hear her cry?

They had been very happy together, in the beginning; and until the very end he had been very good to her, had not ceased to love her, and tried always to make her know it. No more than she had been able to accuse her father had she ever been able to accuse him. His weakness she understood, and his terror, and even his bloody end. What life had made him bear, her lover, this wild, unhappy boy, many another stronger and more virtuous man might not have borne so well.

Saturday was their best day, for they only worked until one o'clock. They had all the afternoon to be together, and nearly all of the night, since Madame Williams had her séances on Saturday night and preferred that Elizabeth, before whose silent skepticism departed spirits might find themselves reluctant to speak, should not be in the house. They met at the service entrance. Richard was always there before her, looking, oddly, much younger and less anonymous without the ugly, tight-fitting, black uniform that he had to wear when working. He would be talking, or laughing with some of the other boys, or shooting craps, and when he heard her step down the long, stone hall he would look up, laughing; and wickedly nudging one of the other boys, he would half shout, half sing: "He-y! Look-a-there, ain't she pretty?"

She never failed, at this—which was why he never failed to do it—to blush, half smiling, half frowning, and nervously to touch the collar of her dress.

"*Sweet* Georgia Brown!" somebody might say.

"*Miss* Brown to you," said Richard, then, and took her arm.

"Yeah, that's right," somebody else would say, "you *better* hold on to little Miss Bright-eyes, don't somebody sure going to take her away from you."

"Yeah," said another voice, "and it might be me."

"*Oh,* no," said Richard, moving with her toward the street, "ain't nobody going to take *my* Little-bit away from *me.*"

Little-bit: it had been his name for her. And sometimes he called her Sandwich Mouth, or Funnyface, or Frog-eyes. She would not, of course, have endured these names from anyone else, nor, had she not found herself, with joy and helplessness (and a sleeping panic), living it out, would she ever have suffered herself so publicly to become a man's property—"concubine," her aunt would have said, and at night, alone, she rolled the word, tart like lemon rind, on her tongue.

She was descending with Richard to the sea. She would have to climb back up alone, but she did not know this then. Leaving the boys in the hall, they gained the midtown New York streets.

"And what we going to do today, Little-bit?" With that smile of his, and those depthless eyes, beneath the towers of the white city, with people, white, hurrying all around them.

"I don't know, honey. What you want to do?"

"Well, maybe, we go to a *museum.*"

The first time he suggested this, she demanded, in panic, if they would be allowed to enter.

"Sure, they let niggers in," Richard said. "Ain't we got to be educated, too—to live with the motherfuckers?"

He never "watched" his language with her, which at first she took as evidence of his contempt because she had fallen so easily, and which later she took as evidence of his love.

And when he took her to the Museum of Natural History, or the Metropolitan Museum of Art, where they were almost certain to be the only black people, and he guided her through the halls, which never ceased in her imagination to be as cold as tombstones, it was then she saw another life in him. It never ceased to frighten her, this passion he brought to something she could not understand.

For she never grasped—not at any rate with her mind—what, with such incandescence, he tried to tell her on these Saturday afternoons. She could not find, between herself and the African statuette, or totem pole, on which he gazed with such melancholy wonder, any point of contact. She was only glad that she did not look that way. She preferred to look, in the other museum, at the paintings; but still she did not understand anything he said about them. She did not know why he so adored things that were so long dead; what sustenance they gave him, what secrets he hoped to wrest from them. But she understood, at least, that they *did* give him a kind of bitter nourishment, and that the secrets they held for him were a matter of his life and death. It frightened her because she felt that he was reaching for the moon and that he would, therefore, be dashed down against the rocks; but she did not say any of this. She only listened, and in her heart she prayed for him.

But on other Saturdays they went to see a movie; they went to see a play; they visited his friends; they walked through Central Park. She liked the park because, however spuriously, it re-created something of the landscape she had known. How many afternoons had they walked there! She had always, since, avoided it. They bought peanuts and for hours fed the animals at the zoo; they bought soda pop and drank it on the grass; they walked along the reservoir and Richard explained how a city like New York found water to drink. Mixed with her fear for him was a total admiration: that he had learned so young, so much. People stared at them but she did not mind; he noticed, but he did not seem to notice. But sometimes he would ask, in the middle of a sentence—concerned, possibly, with ancient Rome:

"Little-bit—d'you love me?"

And she wondered how he could doubt it. She thought how infirm she must be not to have been able to make him know it; and she raised her eyes to his, and she said the only thing she could say:

"I wish to God I may die if I don't love you. There ain't no sky above us if I don't love you."

Then he would look ironically up at the sky, and take her arm with a firmer pressure, and they would walk on.

Once, she asked him:

"Richard, did you go to school much when you was little?"

And he looked at her a long moment. Then:

"Baby, I done told you, my mama died when I was born. And my daddy, he weren't nowhere to be found. Ain't nobody never took care of me. I just moved from one place to another. When one set of folks got tired of me they sent me down the line. I didn't hardly go to school at all."

"Then how come you got to be so smart? How come you got to know so much?"

And he smiled, pleased, but he said: "Little-bit, I don't know so much." Then he said, with a change in his face and voice which she had grown to know: "I just decided me one day that I was going to get to know everything them white bastards knew, and I was going to get to know it better than them, so could no white son-of-a-bitch *nowhere* never talk *me* down, and never make me feel like *I* was dirt, when I could read him the alphabet, back, front, and sideways. Shit—he weren't going to beat my ass, then. And if he tried to kill me, I'd take him with me, I swear to my mother I would." Then he looked at her again, and smiled and kissed her, and he said: "That's how I got to know so much, baby."

She asked: "And what you going to do, Richard? What you want to be?"

And his face clouded. "I don't know. I got to find out. Looks like I can't get my mind straight nohow."

She did not know *why* he couldn't—or she could only dimly face it—but she knew he spoke the truth.

She had made her great mistake with Richard in not telling him that she was going to have a child. Perhaps, she thought now, if she had told him everything might have been very different, and he would be living yet. But the circumstances under which she had discovered herself to be pregnant had been such to make her decide, for his sake, to hold her peace awhile. Frightened as she was, she dared not add to the panic that overtook him on the last summer of his life.

And yet perhaps it was, after all, this—this failure to demand of his strength what it might then, most miraculously, have been found able to bear; by which—indeed, how could she know?—his strength might have been strengthened, for which she prayed tonight to be forgiven. Perhaps she had lost her love because she had not, in the end, believed in it enough.

She lived quite a long way from Richard—four subway stops; and when it was time for her to go home, he always took the subway uptown with her and walked her to her door. On a Saturday when they had forgotten the time and stayed together later than usual, he left her at her door at two o'clock in the morning. They said good night hurriedly, for she was afraid of trouble when she got upstairs—though, in fact, Madame Williams seemed astonishingly indifferent to the hours Elizabeth kept—and he wanted to hurry back home and go to bed. Yet, as he hurried off down the dark, murmuring street, she had a sudden impulse to call him back, to ask him to take her with him and never let her go again. She hurried up the steps, smiling a little at this fancy: it was because he looked so young and defenseless as he walked away, and yet so jaunty and strong.

He was to come the next evening at suppertime, to make at last, at Elizabeth's urging, the acquaintance of Madame Williams. But he did not come. She drove Madame Williams wild with her sudden sensitivity to footsteps on the stairs. Having told Madame Williams that a gentleman was coming to visit her, she did not dare, of course, to leave the house and go out looking for him, thus giving Madame Williams the impression that she dragged men in off the streets. At ten o'clock, having eaten no supper, a detail unnoticed by her hostess, she went to bed, her head aching and her heart sick with fear;

fear over what had happened to Richard, who had never kept her waiting before; and fear involving all that was beginning to happen in her body.

And on Monday morning he was not at work. She left during the lunch hour to go to his room. He was not there. His landlady said that he had not been there all weekend. While Elizabeth stood trembling and indecisive in the hall, two white policemen entered.

She knew the moment she saw them, and before they mentioned his name, that something terrible had happened to Richard. Her heart, as on that bright summer day when he had first spoken to her, gave a terrible bound and then was still, with an awful, wounded stillness. She put out one hand to touch the wall in order to keep standing.

"This here young lady was just looking for him," she heard the landlady say.

They all looked at her.

"You his girl?" one of the policemen asked.

She looked up at his sweating face, on which a lascivious smile had immediately appeared, and straightened, trying to control her trembling.

"Yes," she said. "Where is he?"

"He's in jail, honey," the other policeman said.

"What for?"

"For robbing a white man's store, black girl. That's what for."

She found, and thanked Heaven for it, that a cold, stony rage had entered her. She would, otherwise, certainly have fallen down, or begun to weep. She looked at the smiling policeman.

"Richard ain't robbed no store," she said. "Tell me where he is."

"And *I* tell you," he said, not smiling, "that your boy-friend robbed a store and he's in jail for it. He's going to stay there, too—now, what you got to say to that?"

"And he probably did it for you, too," the other policeman said. "You look like a girl a man could rob a store for."

She said nothing; she was thinking how to get to see him, how to get him out.

One of them, the smiler, turned now to the landlady and said: "Let's have the key to his room. How long's he been living here?"

"About a year," the landlady said. She looked unhappily at Elizabeth. "He seemed like a real nice boy."

"Ah, yes," he said, mounting the steps, "they all seem like real nice boys when they pay their rent."

"You going to take me to see him?" she asked of the remaining policeman. She found herself fascinated by the gun in his holster, the club at his side. She wanted to take that pistol and empty it into his round, red face; to take that club and strike with all her strength against the base of his skull where his cap ended, until the ugly, silky, white man's hair was matted with blood and brains.

"Sure, girl," he said, "you're coming right along with us. The man at the station house wants to ask you some questions."

The smiling policeman came down again. "Ain't nothing up there," he said. "Let's go."

She moved between them, out into the sun. She knew that there was nothing to be gained by talking to them any more. She was entirely in their power; she would have to think faster than they could think; she would have to contain her fear and her hatred, and find out what could be done. Not for anything short of Richard's life, and not, possibly, even for that, would she have wept before them, or asked of them a kindness.

A small crowd, children and curious passers-by, followed them as they walked the long, dusty, sunlit street. She hoped only that they would not pass anyone she knew; she kept her head high, looking straight ahead, and felt the skin settle over her bones as though she were wearing a mask.

And at the station she somehow got past their brutal laughter. *(What was he doing with you, girl, until two o'clock in the morning?— Next time you feel like that, girl, you come by here and talk to me.)* She felt that she was about to burst, or vomit, or die. Though the sweat stood out cruelly, like needles, on her brow, and she felt herself, from every side, being covered with a stink and filth, she found out, in their own good time, what she wanted to know: he was being held in a prison downtown called the Tombs (the name made her heart turn over), and she could see him tomorrow. The state, or the prison, or someone, had already assigned him a lawyer; he would be brought to trial next week.

But the next day, when she saw him, she wept. He had been beaten, he whispered to her, and he could hardly walk. His body, she later discovered, bore almost no bruises, but was full of strange, painful swellings, and there was a welt above one eye.

He had not, of course, robbed the store, but, when he left her that Saturday night, had gone down into the subway station to wait for his train. It was late, and trains were slow; he was all alone on the platform, only half awake, thinking, he said, of her.

Then, from the far end of the platform, he heard a sound of running; and, looking up, he saw two colored boys come running down the steps. Their clothes were torn, and they were frightened; they came up the platform and stood near him, breathing hard. He was about to ask them what the trouble was when, running across the tracks toward them, and followed by a white man, he saw another colored boy; and at the same instant another white man came running down the subway steps.

Then he came full awake, in panic; he knew that whatever the trouble was, it was now his trouble also; for these white men would make no distinction between him and the three boys they were after: they were all colored, they were about the same age, and here they stood together on the subway platform. And they were all, with no questions asked, herded upstairs, and into the wagon and to the station house.

At the station Richard gave his name and address and age and occupation. Then for the first time he stated that he was not involved, and asked one of the other boys to corroborate his testimony.

This they rather despairingly did. They might, Elizabeth felt, have done it sooner, but they probably also felt that it would be useless to speak. And they were not believed; the owner of the store was being brought there to make the identification. And Richard tried to relax: the man *could* not say that he had been there if he had never seen him before.

But when the owner came, a short man with a bloody shirt—for they had knifed him—in the company of yet another policeman, he looked at the four boys before him and said: "Yeah, that's them, all right."

Then Richard shouted: "But *I* wasn't there! Look at me, god-dammit—I wasn't *there!*"

"You black bastards," the man said, looking at him, "you're all the same."

Then there was silence in the station, the eyes of the white men all watching. And Richard said, but quietly, knowing that he was lost: "But all the same, mister, I wasn't there." And he looked at the white man's bloody shirt and thought, he told Elizabeth, at the bottom of his heart: "I wish to God they'd killed you."

Then the questioning began. The three boys signed a confession at once, but Richard would not sign. He said at last that he would die before he signed a confession to something he hadn't done. "Well then," said one of them, hitting him suddenly across the head, "maybe you *will* die, you black son-of-a-bitch." And the beating began. He would not, then, talk to her about it; she found that, before the dread and the hatred that filled her mind, her imagination faltered and held its peace.

"What we going to do?" she asked at last.

He smiled a vicious smile—she had never seen such a smile on his face before. "Maybe you ought to pray to that Jesus of yours and get Him to come down and tell these white men something." He looked at her a long, dying moment. "Because I don't know nothing *else* to do," he said.

She suggested: "Richard, what about another lawyer?"

And he smiled again. "I declare," he said, "Little-bit's been holding out on me. She got a fortune tied up in a sock, and she ain't never told me nothing about it."

She had been trying to save money for a whole year, but she had only thirty dollars. She sat before him, going over in her mind all the things she might do to raise money, even to going on the streets. Then, for very helplessness, she began to shake with sobbing. At this, his face became Richard's face again. He said in a shaking voice: "Now, look here, Little-bit, don't you be like that. We going to work this out all right." But she could not stop sobbing. "Elizabeth," he whispered, "Elizabeth, Elizabeth." Then the man came and said that it was time for her to go. And she rose. She had brought two packs of cigarettes for him, and they were still in her bag. Wholly ignorant of prison regulations, she did not dare to give them to him under the man's eyes. And, somehow, her failure to remember to give him the cigarettes, when she knew how much he smoked, made her weep the harder. She tried—and failed—to smile at him, and she was slowly led to the door. The sun nearly blinded her, and she heard him whisper behind her: "So long, baby. Be good."

In the streets she did not know what to do. She stood awhile before the dreadful gates, and then she walked and walked until she came to a coffee shop where taxi drivers and the people who worked in nearby offices hurried in and out all day. Usually she was afraid to go into downtown establishments, where only white people were, but today she did not care. She felt that if anyone said anything to her she would turn and curse him like the lowest bitch on the streets. If anyone touched her, she would do her best to send his soul to Hell.

But no one touched her; no one spoke. She drank her coffee, sitting in the strong sun that fell through the window. Now it came to her how alone, how frightened she was; she had never been so frightened in her life before. She knew that she was pregnant—knew it, as the old folks said, in her bones; and if Richard should be sent away, what, under Heaven, could she do? Two years, three years—she had no idea how long he might be sent away for—what would she do? And how could she keep her aunt from knowing? And if her aunt should find out, then her father would know, too. The tears welled up, and she drank her cold, tasteless coffee. And what would they do with Richard? And if they sent him away, what would he be like, then, when he returned? She looked out into the quiet, sunny streets, and for the first time in her life, she hated it all—the white city, the white world. She could not, that day, think of one decent white person in the whole world. She sat there, and she hoped that one day God, with tortures inconceivable, would grind them utterly into humility, and make them know that black boys and black girls, whom they treated with such condescension, such disdain, and such good humor, had hearts like human beings, too, more human hearts than theirs.

But Richard was not sent away. Against the testimony of the three robbers, and her own testimony, and, under oath, the storekeeper's indecision, there was no evidence on which to convict him. The courtroom seemed to feel, with some complacency and some disappointment, that it was his great good luck to be let off so easily. They went immediately to his room. And there—she was never all her life long to forget it—he threw himself, face downward, on his bed and wept.

She had only seen one other man weep before—her father—and it had not been like this. She touched him, but he did not stop. Her own tears fell on his dirty, uncombed hair. She tried to hold him, but for a long while he would not be held. His body was like iron; she could find no softness in it. She sat curled like a frightened child on the edge of the bed, her hand on his back, waiting for the storm to pass over. It was then that she decided not to tell him yet about the child.

By and by he called her name. And then he turned, and she held him against her breast, while he sighed and shook. He fell asleep at last, clinging to her as though he were going down into the water for the last time.

And it was the last time. That night he cut his wrists with his razor and he was found in the morning by his landlady, his eyes staring upward with no light, dead among the scarlet sheets.

And now they were singing:

> *"Somebody needs you, Lord,*
> *Come by here."*

At her back, above her, she heard Gabriel's voice. He had risen and was helping the others to pray through. She wondered if John were still on his knees, or had risen, with a child's impatience, and was staring around the church. There was a stiffness in him that would be hard to break, but that, nevertheless, would one day surely be broken. As hers had been, and Richard's—there was no escape for anyone. God was everywhere, terrible, the living God; and so high, the song said, you couldn't get over Him; so low you couldn't get under Him; so wide you couldn't get around Him; but must come in at the door.

And she, she knew today that door: a living, wrathful gate. She knew through what fires the soul must crawl, and with what weeping one passed over. Men spoke of how the heart broke up, but never spoke of how the soul hung speechless in the pause, the void, the terror between the living and the dead; how, all garments rent and cast aside, the naked soul passed over the very mouth of Hell. Once there, there was no turning back; once there, the soul remembered, though the heart sometimes forgot. For the world called to the heart, which stammered to reply; life, and love, and revelry, and, most falsely, hope, called the forgetful, the human heart. Only the soul, obsessed with the journey it had made, and had still to make, pursued its mysterious and dreadful end; and carried, heavy with weeping and bitterness, the heart along.

And, therefore, there was war in Heaven, and weeping before the throne: the heart chained to the soul, and the soul imprisoned within the flesh—a weeping, a confusion, and a weight unendurable filled all the earth. Only the love of God could establish order in this chaos; to Him the soul must turn to be delivered.

But what a turning! How could she fail to pray that He would have mercy on her son, and spare him the sin-born anguish of his father and his mother. And that his heart might know a little joy before the long bitterness descended.

Yet she knew that her weeping and her prayers were in vain. What was coming would surely come; nothing could stop it. She had tried, once, to protect someone and had only hurled him into prison. And she thought tonight, as she had thought so often, that it might have been better, after all, to have done what she had first determined in her heart to do—to have given her son away to strangers, who might have loved him more than Gabriel had ever loved him. She had believed him when he said that God had sent him to her for a sign. He had said that he would cherish her until the grave, and that he would love her nameless son as though he were his own flesh. And he had kept the letter of his promise: he had fed him and clothed him and taught him the Bible—but the spirit was not there. And he cherished—*if* he cherished her—only because she was the mother of his son, Roy. All of this she had through the painful years divined. He certainly did not know she knew it, and she wondered if he knew it himself.

She had met him through Florence. Florence and she had met at work in the middle of the summer, a year after Richard's death. John was then over six months old.

She was very lonely that summer, and beaten down. She was living alone with John in a furnished room even grimmer than the room that had been hers in Madame Williams's apartment. She had, of course, left Madame Williams's immediately upon the death of Richard, saying that she had found a sleep-in job in the country. She had been terribly grateful that summer for Madame Williams's indifference; the woman had simply not seemed to see that Elizabeth, overnight, had become an old woman and was half mad with fear and grief. She wrote her aunt the driest, and briefest, and coldest of notes, not wishing in any way to awaken whatever concern might yet slumber in her breast, telling her the same thing she had told Madame Williams, and telling her not to worry, she was in the hands of God. And she certainly was; through a bitterness that only the hand of God could have laid on her, this same hand brought her through.

Florence and Elizabeth worked as cleaning-women in a high, vast, stony office-building on Wall Street. They arrived in the evening and spent the night going through the great deserted halls and the silent offices with mops and pails and brooms. It was terrible work, and Elizabeth hated it; but it was at night, and she had taken it joyfully, since it meant that she could take care of John herself all day and not have to spend extra money to keep him in a nursery. She worried about him all night long, of course, but at least at night he was sleeping. She could only pray that the house would not burn down, that he would not fall out of bed or, in some mysterious way, turn on the gas-burner, and she had asked the woman next door, who unhappily drank too much, to keep an eye out for him. This woman, with whom she sometimes spent an hour or so in the afternoons, and her landlady, were the only people she saw. She had stopped seeing Richard's friends because, for some reason, she did not want them to know about Richard's child; and because, too, the moment that he was dead it became immediately apparent on both sides how little they had in common. And she did not seek new people; rather, she fled from them. She could not bear, in her changed and fallen state, to submit herself to the eyes of others. The Elizabeth that she had been was buried far away—with her lost and silent father, with her aunt, in Richard's grave—and the Elizabeth she had become she did not recognize, she did not want to know.

But one night, when work was ended, Florence invited her to share a cup of coffee in the all-night coffee shop near by. Elizabeth had, of course, been invited before by other people—the night watchman, for example—but she had always said no. She pleaded the excuse of her baby, whom she must rush home to feed. She was pretending in those days to be a young widow, and she wore a wedding ring. Very shortly, fewer people asked her, and she achieved the reputation of being "stuck up."

Florence had scarcely ever spoken to her before she arrived at this merciful unpopularity; but Elizabeth had noticed Florence. She moved in a silent ferocity of dignity which barely escaped being ludicrous. She was extremely unpopular also and she had nothing whatever to do with any of the women she worked with. She was, for one thing, a good deal older, and she seemed to have nothing to laugh or gossip about. She came to work, and she did her work, and she left. One could not imagine what she was thinking as she marched so grimly down the halls, her head tied up in a rag, a bucket and a mop in her hands. Elizabeth thought that she must once have been very rich, and had lost her money; and she felt for her, as one fallen woman for another, a certain kinship.

A cup of coffee together, as day was breaking, became in time their habit. They sat together in the coffee shop, which was always empty when they arrived and was crowded fifteen minutes later when they left, and had their coffee and doughnuts before they took the subway uptown. While they had their coffee, and on the ride uptown, they talked, principally about Florence, how badly people treated her, and how empty her life was now that her husband was dead. He had adored her, she told Elizabeth, and satisfied her every whim, but he had tended to irresponsibility. If she had told him once, she had told him a hundred times: "Frank, you better take out life insurance." But he had thought—and wasn't it just like a man!—that he would live forever. Now here she was, a woman getting along in years, forced to make her living among all the black scum of this wicked city. Elizabeth, a little astonished at the need for confession betrayed by this proud woman, listened, nevertheless, with great sympathy. She was very grateful for Florence's interest. Florence was so much older and seemed so kind.

It was no doubt this, Florence's age and kindness, that led Elizabeth, with no premeditation, to take Florence into her confidence. Looking back, she found it hard to believe that she could have been so desperate, or so childish; though, again, on looking back, she was able to see clearly what she then so incoherently felt: how much she needed another human being, somewhere, who knew the truth about her.

Florence had often said how glad she would be to make the acquaintance of little Johnny; she was sure, she said, that any child of Elizabeth's must be a wonderful child. On a Sunday near the end of that summer, Elizabeth dressed him in his best clothes and took him to Florence's house. She was oddly and fearfully depressed that day; and John was not in a good mood. She found herself staring at him darkly, as though she were trying to read his future in his face. He would grow big one day, he would talk, and he would ask her questions. What questions would he ask her, what answers would she give? She surely would not be able to lie to him indefinitely about his father, for one day he would be old enough to realize that it was not his father's name he bore. Richard had been a fatherless child, she helplessly, bitterly remembered as she carried John through the busy, summer, Sunday streets. *When one set of folks got tired of me they sent me down the line.* Yes, down the line, through poverty, hunger, wandering, cruelty, fear, and trembling, to death. And she thought of the boys who had gone to prison. Were they there still? Would John be one of these boys one day? These boys, now, who stood before drugstore windows, before poolrooms, on every street corner, who whistled after her, whose lean bodies fairly rang, it seemed, with idleness, and malice, and frustration. How could she hope, alone, and in famine as she was, to put herself between him and this so wide and raging destruction? And then, as though to confirm her in all her dark imaginings, he began, as she reached the subway steps, to whimper, and moan, and cry.

And he kept this up, too, all the way uptown—so that, what with the impossibility of pleasing him that day, no matter what she did, what with his restless weight, and the heat, and the smiling, staring people, and the strange dread that weighed on her so heavily, she was nearly ready to weep by the time she arrived at Florence's door.

He, at that moment, to her exasperated relief, became the most cheerful of infants. Florence was wearing a heavy, old-fashioned garnet brooch, which, as she opened the door, immediately attracted John's eye. He began reaching for the brooch and babbling and spitting at Florence as though he had known her all of his short life.

"Well!" said Florence, "when he get big enough to *really* go after the ladies you going to have your hands full, girl."

"That," said Elizabeth, grimly, "is the Lord's truth. He keep me so busy now I don't know half the time if I'm coming or going."

Florence, meanwhile, attempted to distract John's attention from the brooch by offering him an orange; but he had seen oranges before; he merely looked at it a moment before letting it fall to the floor. He began again, in his disturbingly fluid fashion, to quarrel about the brooch.

"He likes you," said Elizabeth, finally, calmed a little by watching him.

"You must be tired," said Florence, then. "Put him down there." And she dragged one large easy chair to the table so that John could watch them while they ate.

"I got a letter from my brother the other day," she said, bringing the food to the table. "His wife, poor ailing soul, done passed on, and he thinking about coming North."

"You ain't never told me," said Elizabeth, with a quick and rather false interest, "you had a brother! And he coming up here?"

"So he say. Ain't nothing, I reckon, to keep him down home no more—now Deborah's gone." She sat down opposite Elizabeth. "I ain't seen him," she said, musingly, "for more than twenty years."

"Then it'll be a great day," Elizabeth smiled, "when you two meet again."

Florence shook her head, and motioned for Elizabeth to start eating. "No," she said, "we ain't never got along, and I don't reckon he's changed."

"Twenty years is a mighty long time," Elizabeth said, "he's bound to have changed *some*."

"That man," said Florence, "would have to do a whole *lot* of changing before him and me hit it off. No,"—she paused, grimly, sadly—"I'm mighty sorry he's coming. I didn't look to see him no more in this world—or in the next one, neither."

This was not, Elizabeth felt, the way a sister ought to talk about her brother, especially to someone who knew him not at all, and who would, probably, eventually meet him. She asked, helplessly:

"What do he do—your brother?"

"He some kind of preacher," said Florence. "I ain't never heard him. When *I* was home he weren't doing nothing but chasing after women and lying in the ditches, drunk."

"I hope," laughed Elizabeth, "he done changed his *ways* at least."

"Folks," said Florence, "can change their ways much as they want to. But I don't care how many times you change your ways, what's in you is in you, and it's got to come out."

"Yes," said Elizabeth, thoughtfully. "But don't you think," she hesitantly asked, "that the Lord can change a person's heart?"

"I done heard it said often enough," said Florence, "but I got yet to see it. These niggers running around, talking about the Lord done changed their hearts—ain't nothing happened to them niggers. They got the same old black hearts they was born with. I reckon the Lord done give them *those* hearts—and, honey, the Lord don't give out no second helpings, *I'm* here to tell you."

"No," said Elizabeth heavily, after a long pause. She turned to look at John, who was grimly destroying the square, tasseled doilies that decorated Florence's easy chair. "I reckon that's the truth. Look like it go around once, and that's that. You miss it, and you's fixed for fair."

"Now you sound," said Florence, "mighty sad all of a sudden. What's the matter with you?"

"Nothing," she said. She turned back to the table. Then, helplessly, and thinking that she must not say too much: "I was just thinking about this boy here, what's going to happen to him, how I'm going to raise him, in this awful city all by myself."

"But you ain't fixing, is you," asked Florence, "to stay single all your days? You's a right young girl, and a right pretty girl. I wouldn't be in no hurry if I was you to find no new husband. I don't believe the nigger's been born what knows how to treat a woman right. You got time, honey, so *take* your time."

"I ain't," said Elizabeth, quietly, "got so much time." She could not stop herself; though something warned her to hold her peace, the words poured out. "You see this wedding ring? Well, I bought this ring myself. This boy ain't got no daddy."

Now she had said it: the words could not be called back. And she felt, as she sat, trembling, at Florence's table, a reckless, pained relief.

Florence stared at her with a pity so intense that it resembled anger. She looked at John, and then back at Elizabeth.

"You poor thing," said Florence, leaning back in her chair, her face still filled with this strange, brooding fury, "you *is* had a time, ain't you?"

"I was *scared*," Elizabeth brought out, shivering, still compelled to speak.

"I ain't never," said Florence, "seen it to fail. Look like ain't no woman born what don't get walked over by some no-count man. Look like ain't no woman nowhere but ain't been dragged down in the dirt by some man, and left there, too, while he go on about his business."

Elizabeth sat at the table, numb, with nothing more to say.

"What he do," asked Florence, finally, "run off and leave you?"

"Oh, no," cried Elizabeth, quickly, and the tears sprang to her eyes, "he weren't like that! He died, just like I say—he got in trouble, and he died—a long time before this boy was born." She began to weep with the same helplessness with which she had been speaking. Florence rose and came over to Elizabeth, holding Elizabeth's head against her breast. "He wouldn't never of left me," said Elizabeth, "but he *died*."

And now she wept, after her long austerity, as though she would never be able to stop.

"Hush now," said Florence, gently, "hush now. You going to frighten the little fellow. He don't want to see his mama cry. All right," she whispered to John, who had ceased his attempts at destruction, and stared now at the two women, "all right. Everything's all right."

Elizabeth sat up and reached in her handbag for a handkerchief, and began to dry her eyes.

"Yes," said Florence, moving to the window, "the menfolk, they die, all right. And it's us women who walk around, like the Bible says, and mourn. The menfolk, they die, and it's over for them, but we women, we have to keep on living and try to forget what they done to us. Yes, Lord—" and she paused; she turned and came back to Elizabeth. "Yes, Lord," she repeated, "don't *I* know."

"I'm mighty sorry," said Elizabeth, "to upset your nice dinner this way."

"Girl," said Florence, "don't you say a word about being sorry, or I'll show you to this door. You pick up that boy and sit down there in that easy chair and pull yourself together. I'm going out in the kitchen and make us something cold to drink. You try not to fret, honey. The Lord, He ain't going to let you fall but so low."

Then she met Gabriel, two or three weeks later, at Florence's house on a Sunday.

Nothing Florence had said had prepared her for him. She had expected him to be older than Florence, and bald, or gray. But he seemed considerably younger than his sister, with all his teeth and hair. There he sat, that Sunday, in Florence's tiny, fragile parlor, a very rock, it seemed to the eye of her confusion, in her so weary land.

She remembered that as she mounted the stairs with John's heavy weight in her arms, and as she entered the door, she heard music, which became perceptibly fainter as Florence closed the door behind her. John had heard it, too, and had responded by wriggling, and moving his hands in the air, and making noises, meant, she supposed, to be taken for a song. "You's a nigger, all right," she thought with amusement and impatience—for it was someone's gramophone, on a lower floor, filling the air with the slow, high, measured wailing of the blues.

Gabriel rose, it seemed to her, with a speed and eagerness that were not merely polite. She wondered immediately if Florence had told him about her. And this caused her to stiffen with a tentative anger against Florence, and with pride and fear. Yet when she looked into his eyes she found there a strange humility, an altogether unexpected kindness. She felt the anger go out of her, and her defensive pride; but somewhere, crouching, the fear remained.

Then Florence introduced them, saying: "Elizabeth, this here's my brother I been telling you so much about. He's a preacher, honey—so we got to be mighty careful what we talk about when *he's* around."

Then he said, with a smile less barbed and ambiguous than his sister's remark: "Ain't no need to be afraid of me, sister. I ain't nothing but a poor, weak vessel in the hands of the Lord."

"You *see*!" said Florence, grimly. She took John from his mother's arms. "And this here's little Johnny," she said, "shake hands with the preacher, Johnny."

But John was staring at the door that held back the music; toward which, with an insistence at once furious and feeble, his hands were still outstretched. He looked questioningly, reproachfully, at his mother, who laughed, watching him, and said, "Johnny want to hear some more of that music. He like to started dancing when he was coming up the stairs."

Gabriel laughed, and said, circling around Florence to look into John's face: "Got a man in the Bible, son, who liked music, too. He used to play on his harp before the king, and he got to dancing one day before the Lord. You reckon you going to dance for the Lord one of these days?"

John looked with a child's impenetrable gravity into the preacher's face, as though he were turning this question over in his mind and would answer when he had thought it out. Gabriel smiled at him, a strange smile—strangely, she thought, loving—and touched him on the crown of the head.

"He a mighty fine boy," said Gabriel. "With them big eyes he ought to see everything *in* the Bible."

And they all laughed. Florence moved to deposit John in the easy chair that was his Sunday throne. And Elizabeth found that she was watching Gabriel, unable to find in the man before her the brother whom Florence so despised.

They sat down at the table, John placed between herself and Florence and opposite Gabriel.

"So," Elizabeth said, with a nervous pleasantness, it being necessary, she felt, to say something, "you just getting to this big city? It must seem mighty strange to you."

His eyes were still on John, whose eyes had not left him. Then he looked again at Elizabeth. She felt that the air between them was beginning to be charged, and she could find no name, or reason, for the secret excitement that moved in her.

"It's mighty big," he said, "and looks to me—and *sounds* to me—like the Devil's working every day."

This was in reference to the music, which had not ceased, but she felt, immediately, that it included her; this, and something else in Gabriel's eyes, made her look down quickly to her plate.

"He ain't," said Florence, briskly, "working no harder up here than he worked down home. Them niggers down home," she said to Elizabeth, "they think New York ain't nothing but one long, Sunday drunk. They don't *know.* Somebody better tell them—they can get

better moonshine right there where they is than they likely to here—
and cheaper, too."

"But I *do* hope," he said, with a smile, "that you ain't taken to
drinking moonshine, sister."

"It wasn't never *me,*" she said, promptly, "had *that* habit."

"Don't know," he persisted, still smiling, and still looking at
Elizabeth, "tell me folks do things up North they wouldn't think
about doing down home."

"Folks got their dirt to do," said Florence. "They going to do it,
no matter where they is. Folks do lots of things down home they
don't want nobody to know about."

"Like my aunt used to say," Elizabeth said, smiling timidly, "she
used to say, folks sure better not do in the dark what they's scared to
look at in the light."

She had meant it as a kind of joke; but the words were not out of
her mouth before she longed for the power to call them back. They
rang in her own ears like a confession.

"That's the Lord's truth," he said, after the briefest pause. "Does
you really believe that?"

She forced herself to look up at him, and felt at that moment the
intensity of the attention that Florence fixed on her, as though she
were trying to shout a warning. She knew that it was something in
Gabriel's voice that had caused Florence, suddenly, to be so wary
and so tense. But she did not drop her eyes from Gabriel's eyes. She
answered him: "Yes. That's the way I want to live."

"Then the Lord's going to bless you," he said, "and open up the
windows of Heaven for you—for you, and that boy. He going to
pour down blessings on you till you won't know where to put them.
You mark my words."

"Yes," said Florence, mildly, "you *mark* his words."

But neither of them looked at her. It came into Elizabeth's mind,
filling her mind: *All things work together for good to them that love the
Lord.* She tried to obliterate this burning phrase, and what it made
her feel. What it made her feel, for the first time since the death of

Richard, was hope; his voice had made her feel that she was not altogether cast down, that God might raise her again in honor; his eyes had made her know that she could be again—this time in honor—a woman. Then, from what seemed to be a great, cloudy distance, he smiled at her—and she smiled.

The distant gramophone stuck now, suddenly, on a grinding, wailing, sardonic trumpet-note; this blind, ugly crying swelled the moment and filled the room. She looked down at John. A hand somewhere struck the gramophone arm and sent the silver needle on its way through the whirling, black grooves, like something bobbing, anchorless, in the middle of the sea.

"Johnny's done fell asleep," she said.

She, who had descended with such joy and pain, had begun her upward climb—upward, with her baby, on the steep, steep side of the mountain.

She felt a great commotion in the air around her—a great excitement, muted, waiting on the Lord. And the air seemed to tremble, as before a storm. A light seemed to hang—just above, and all around them—about to burst into revelation. In the great crying, the great singing all around her, in the wind that gathered to fill the church, she did not hear her husband; and she thought of John as sitting, silent now and sleepy, far in the back of the church—watching, with that wonder and that terror in his eyes. She did not raise her head. She wished to tarry yet a little longer, that God might speak to her.

It had been before this very altar that she had come to kneel, so many years ago, to be forgiven. When the fall came, and the air was dry and sharp, and the wind high, she was always with Gabriel. Florence did not approve of this, and Florence said so often; but she never said more than this, for the reason, Elizabeth decided, that she had no evil to report—it was only that she was not fond of her brother. But even had Florence been able to find a language unmistakable in which to convey her prophecies, Elizabeth could not have heeded her because Gabriel had become her strength. He watched over her and her baby as though it had become his calling; he was very good to John, and played with him, and bought him things, as though John were his own. She knew that his wife had died childless, and that he had always wanted a son—he was praying still, he told her, that God would bless him with a son. She thought sometimes, lying on her bed alone, and thinking of all his kindness, that perhaps John was that son, and that he would grow one day to comfort and bless them both. Then she thought how, now, she would embrace again the faith she had abandoned, and walk again in the light from which, with Richard, she had so far fled. Sometimes, thinking of Gabriel, she remembered Richard—his voice, his breath, his arms— with a terrible pain; and then she felt herself shrinking from Gabriel's anticipated touch. But this shrinking she would not countenance. She told herself that it was foolish and sinful to look backward when her safety lay before her, like a hiding-place hewn in the side of the mountain.

"Sister," he asked one night, "don't you reckon you ought to give your heart to the Lord?"

They were in the dark streets, walking to church. He had asked her this question before, but never in such a tone; she had never before felt so compelling a need to reply.

"I reckon," she said.

"If you call on the Lord," he said, "He'll lift you up, He'll give you your heart's desire. I'm a witness," he said, and smiled at her, "you call on the Lord, you wait on the Lord, He'll answer. God's promises don't never fail."

Her arm was in his, and she felt him trembling with his passion.

"Till you come," she said, in a low, trembling voice, "I didn't never hardly go to church at all, Reverend. Look like I couldn't see my way nohow—I was all bowed down with shame . . . and sin."

She could hardly bring the last words out, and as she spoke tears were in her eyes. She had told him that John was nameless; and she had tried to tell him something of her suffering, too. In those days he had seemed to understand, and he had not stood in judgment on her. When had he so greatly changed? Or was it that he had not changed, but that her eyes had been opened through the pain he had caused her?

"Well," he said, "I done come, and it was the hand of the Lord what sent me. He brought us together for a sign. You fall on your knees and see if that ain't so—you fall down and ask Him to speak to you tonight."

Yes, a sign, she thought, a sign of His mercy, a sign of His forgiveness.

When they reached the church doors he paused, and looked at her and made his promise.

"Sister Elizabeth," he said, "when you go down on your knees tonight, I want you to ask the Lord to speak to your heart, and tell you how to answer what I'm going to say."

She stood a little below him, one foot lifted to the short, stone step that led to the church entrance, and looked up into his face. And looking into his face, which burned—in the dim, yellow light that hung about them there—like the face of a man who has wrestled with angels and demons and looked on the face of God, it came to her, oddly, and all at once, that she had become a woman.

"Sister Elizabeth," he said, "the Lord's been speaking to my heart, and I believe it's His will that you and me should be man and wife."

And he paused; she said nothing. His eyes moved over her body.

"I know," he said, trying to smile, and in a lower voice, "I'm a lot older than you. But that don't make no difference. I'm a mighty strong man yet. I done been down the line, Sister Elizabeth, and maybe I can keep you from making . . . some of my mistakes, bless the Lord . . . maybe I can help keep your foot from stumbling . . . again . . . girl . . . for as long as we's in this world."

Still she waited.

"And I'll love you," he said, "and I'll honor you . . . until the day God calls me home."

Slow tears rose to her eyes: of joy, for what she had come to; of anguish, for the road that had brought her here.

"And I'll love your son, your little boy," he said at last, "just like he was my own. He won't never have to fret or worry about nothing; he won't never be cold or hungry as long as I'm alive and I got my two hands to work with. I swear this before my God," he said, "because He done give me back something I thought was lost."

Yes, she thought, a sign—a sign that He is mighty to save. Then she moved and stood on the short step, next to him, before the doors.

"Sister Elizabeth," he said—and she would carry to the grave the memory of his grace and humility at that moment, "will you pray?"

"Yes," she said. "I been praying. I'm going to pray."

They had entered this church, these doors; and when the pastor made the altar call, she rose, while she heard them praising God, and walked down the long church aisle; down this aisle, to this altar, before this golden cross; to these tears, into this battle—would the battle end one day? When she rose, and as they walked once more through the streets, he had called her God's daughter, handmaiden to God's minister. He had kissed her on the brow, with tears, and said that God had brought them together to be each other's deliverance. And she had wept, in her great joy that the hand of God had changed her life, had lifted her up and set her on the solid rock, alone.

She thought of that far-off day when John had come into the world—that moment, the beginning of her life and death. Down she had gone that day, alone, a heaviness intolerable at her waist, a secret in her loins, down into the darkness, weeping and groaning and cursing God. How long she had bled, and sweated, and cried, no language on earth could tell—how long she had crawled through darkness she would never, never know. There, her beginning, and she fought through darkness still; toward that moment when she would make her peace with God, when she would hear Him speak, and He would wipe all tears from her eyes; as, in that other darkness, after eternity, she had heard John cry.

As now, in the sudden silence, she heard him cry: not the cry of the child, newborn, before the common light of earth; but the cry of the man-child, bestial, before the light that comes down from Heaven. She opened her eyes and stood straight up; all of the saints surrounded her; Gabriel stood staring, struck rigid as a pillar in the temple. On the threshing-floor, in the center of the crying, singing saints, John lay astonished beneath the power of the Lord.

PART THREE

The Threshing-Floor

Then said I, Woe is me! for I am undone;
because I am a man of unclean lips,
and I dwell in the midst of a people
of unclean lips; for mine eyes have seen the King,
seen the King, the Lord of hosts.

Then I buckled up my shoes,
And I started.

HE KNEW, WITHOUT knowing how it had happened, that he lay on the floor, in the dusty space before the altar which he and Elisha had cleaned; and knew that above him burned the yellow light which he had himself switched on. Dust was in his nostrils, sharp and terrible, and the feet of the saints, shaking the floor beneath him, raised small clouds of dust that filmed his mouth. He heard their cries, so far, so high above him—he could never rise that far. He was like a rock, a dead man's body, a dying bird, fallen from an awful height; something that had no power of itself, any more, to turn.

And something moved in John's body which was not John. He was invaded, set at naught, possessed. This power had struck John, in the head or in the heart; and, in a moment, wholly, filling him with an anguish that he could never in his life have imagined, that he surely could not endure, that even now he could not believe, had opened him up; had cracked him open, as wood beneath the axe cracks down the middle, as rocks break up; had ripped him and felled him in a moment, so that John had not felt the wound, but only the agony, had not felt the fall, but only the fear; and lay here, now, helpless, screaming, at the very bottom of darkness.

He wanted to rise—a malicious, ironic voice insisted that he rise—and, at once, to leave this temple and go out into the world.

He wanted to obey the voice, which was the only voice that spoke to him; he tried to assure the voice that he would do his best to rise; he would only lie here a moment, after his dreadful fall, and catch his breath. It was at this moment, precisely, that he found he could not rise; something had happened to his arms, his legs, his feet—ah, something had happened to John! And he began to scream again in his great, bewildered terror, and felt himself, indeed, begin to move—not upward, toward the light, but down again, a sickness in his bowels, a tightening in his loin-strings; he felt himself turning, again and again, across the dusty floor, as though God's toe had touched him lightly. And the dust made him cough and retch; in his turning the center of the whole earth shifted, making of space a sheer void and a mockery of order, and balance, and time. Nothing remained: all was swallowed up in chaos. And: *Is this it?* John's terrified soul inquired—*What is it?*—to no purpose, receiving no answer. Only the ironic voice insisted yet once more that he rise from that filthy floor if he did not want to become like all the other niggers.

Then the anguish subsided for a moment, as water withdraws briefly to dash itself once more against the rocks: he knew that it subsided only to return. And he coughed and sobbed in the dusty space before the altar, lying on his face. And still he was going down, farther and farther from the joy, the singing, and the light above him.

He tried, but in such despair!—the utter darkness does not present any point of departure, contains no beginning, and no end—to rediscover, and, as it were, to trap and hold tightly in the palm of his hand, the moment preceding his fall, his change. But that moment was also locked in darkness, was wordless, and would not come forth. He remembered only the cross: he had turned again to kneel at the altar, and had faced the golden cross. And the Holy Ghost was speaking—seeming to say, as John spelled out the so abruptly present and gigantic legend adorning the cross: *Jesus Saves.* He had stared at this, an awful bitterness in his heart, wanting to curse—and the Spirit spoke, and spoke in him. Yes: there was Elisha, speaking from the floor, and his father, silent, at his back. In his heart there was a sudden yearning tenderness for holy Elisha; desire, sharp and awful as a reflecting knife, to usurp the body of Elisha, and lie where Elisha lay; to speak in tongues, as Elisha spoke, and, with that authority, to confound his father. Yet this had not been the moment; it was as far back as he could go, but the secret, the turning, the abysmal drop was farther back, in darkness. As he cursed his father, as he loved Elisha, he had, even then, been weeping; he had already passed his moment, was already under the power, had been struck, and was going down.

Ah, down!—and to what purpose, where? To the bottom of the sea, the bowels of the earth, to the heart of the fiery furnace? Into a dungeon deeper than Hell, into a madness louder than the grave? What trumpet sound would awaken him, what hand would lift him up? For he knew, as he was struck again, and screamed again, his throat like burning ashes, and as he turned again, his body hanging from him like a useless weight, a heavy, rotting carcass, that if he were not lifted he would never rise.

His father, his mother, his aunt, Elisha—all were far above him, waiting, watching his torment in the pit. They hung over the golden barrier, singing behind them, light around their heads, weeping, perhaps, for John, struck down so early. And, no, they could not help him any more—nothing could help him any more. He struggled, to rise up, and meet them—he wanted wings to fly upward and meet them in that morning, that morning where they were. But his struggles only thrust him downward, his cries did not go upward, but rang in his own skull.

Yet, though he scarcely saw their faces, he knew that they were there. He felt them move, every movement causing a trembling, an astonishment, a horror in the heart of darkness where he lay. He could not know if they wished him to come to them as passionately as he wished to rise. Perhaps they did not help him because they did not care—because they did not love him.

Then his father returned to him, in John's changed and low condition; and John thought, but for a moment only, that his father had come to help him. In the silence, then, that filled the void, John looked on his father. His father's face was black—like a sad, eternal night; yet in his father's face there burned a fire—a fire eternal in an eternal night. John trembled where he lay, feeling no warmth for him from this fire, trembled, and could not take his eyes away. A wind blew over him, saying: "Whosoever loveth and maketh a lie." And he knew that he had been thrust out of the holy, the joyful, the blood-washed community, that his father had thrust him out. His father's will was stronger than John's own. His power was greater because he belonged to God. Now, John felt no hatred, nothing, only a bitter, unbelieving despair: all prophecies were true, salvation was finished, damnation was real!

Then death is real, John's soul said, and death will have his moment.

"Set thine house in order," said his father, "for thou shalt die and not live."

And then the ironic voice spoke again, saying: "Get up, John. Get up, boy. Don't let him keep you here. You got everything your daddy got."

John tried to laugh—John thought that he was laughing—but found, instead, that his mouth was filled with salt, his ears were full of burning water. Whatever was happening in his distant body now, he could not change or stop; his chest heaved, his laughter rose and bubbled at his mouth, like blood.

And his father looked on him. His father's eyes looked down on

him, and John began to scream. His father's eyes stripped him naked, and hated what they saw. And as he turned, screaming, in the
dust again, trying to escape his father's eyes, those eyes, that face, and
all their faces, and the far-off yellow light, all departed from his vision as though he had gone blind. He was going down again. There
is, his soul cried out again, no bottom to the darkness!

He did not know where he was. There was silence everywhere—
only a perpetual, distant, faint trembling far beneath him—the roaring, perhaps, of the fires of Hell, over which he was suspended, or
the echo, persistent, invincible still, of the moving feet of the saints.
He thought of the mountaintop, where he longed to be, where the
sun would cover him like a cloth of gold, would cover his head like a
crown of fire, and in his hands he would hold a living rod. But this
was no mountain where John lay, here, no robe, no crown. And the
living rod was uplifted in other hands.

"I'm going to beat sin out of him. I'm going to beat it out."

Yes, he had sinned, and his father was looking for him. Now,
John did not make a sound, and did not move at all, hoping that his
father would pass him by.

"Leave him be. Leave him alone. Let him pray to the Lord."

"Yes, Mama. I'm going to try to love the Lord."

"He done run off somewhere. I'm going to find him. I'm going
to beat it out."

Yes, he had sinned: one morning, alone, in the dirty bathroom, in
the square, dirt-gray cupboard room that was filled with the stink of
his father. Sometimes, leaning over the cracked, "tattle-tale gray"
bathtub, he scrubbed his father's back; and looked, as the accursed
son of Noah had looked, on his father's hideous nakedness. It was
secret, like sin, and slimy, like the serpent, and heavy, like the rod.
Then he hated his father, and longed for the power to cut his father
down.

Was this why he lay here, thrust out from all human or heavenly
help tonight? This, and not that other, his deadly sin, having looked

on his father's nakedness and mocked and cursed him in his heart? Ah, that son of Noah's had been cursed, down to the present groaning generation: *A servant of servants shall he be unto his brethren.*

Then the ironic voice, terrified, it seemed, of no depth, no darkness, demanded of John, scornfully, if he believed that he was cursed. All niggers had been cursed, the ironic voice reminded him, all niggers had come from this most undutiful of Noah's sons. How could John be cursed for having seen in a bathtub what another man—*if* that other man had ever lived—had seen ten thousand years ago, lying in an open tent? Could a curse come down so many ages? Did it live in time, or in the moment? But John found no answer for this voice, for he was in the moment, and out of time.

And his father approached. "I'm going to beat sin out of him. I'm going to beat it out." All the darkness rocked and wailed as his father's feet came closer; feet whose tread resounded like God's tread in the garden of Eden, searching the covered Adam and Eve. Then his father stood just above him, looking down. Then John knew that a curse was renewed from moment to moment, from father to son. Time was indifferent, like snow and ice; but the heart, crazed wanderer in the driving waste, carried the curse forever.

"John," said his father, "come with me."

Then they were in a straight street, a narrow, narrow way. They had been walking for many days. The street stretched before them, long, and silent, going down, and whiter than the snow. There was no one on the street, and John was frightened. The buildings on this street, so near that John could touch them on either side, were narrow, also, rising like spears into the sky, and they were made of beaten gold and silver. John knew that these buildings were not for him—not today—*no, nor tomorrow, either!* Then, coming up this straight and silent street, he saw a woman, very old and black, coming toward them, staggering on the crooked stones. She was drunk, and dirty, and very old, and her mouth was bigger than his mother's mouth, or his own; her mouth was loose and wet, and he had *never* seen anyone so black. His father was astonished to see her, and beside himself with anger; but John was glad. He clapped his hands and cried:

"See! She's uglier than Mama! She's uglier than me!"

"You mighty proud, ain't you," his father said, "to be the Devil's son?"

But John did not listen to his father. He turned to watch the woman pass. His father grabbed his arm.

"You see that? That's sin. That's what the Devil's son runs after."

"Whose son are you?" John asked.

His father slapped him. John laughed, and moved a little away.

"I seen it. I seen it. I ain't the Devil's son for nothing."

His father reached for him, but John was faster. He moved backward down the shining street, looking at his father—his father who moved toward him, one hand outstretched in fury.

"And I *heard* you—all the nighttime long. I know what you do in the dark, black man, when you think the Devil's son's asleep. I heard you, spitting, and groaning, and choking—and I *seen* you, riding up and down, and going in and out. I ain't the Devil's son for nothing."

The listening buildings, rising upward yet, leaned, closing out the sky. John's feet began to slip; tears and sweat were in his eyes; still moving backward before his father, he looked about him for deliverance; but there was no deliverance in this street for him.

"And I hate you. I hate you. I don't care about your golden crown. I don't care about your long white robe. I seen you under the robe, I seen you!"

Then his father was upon him; at his touch there was singing, and fire. John lay on his back in the narrow street, looking up at his father, that burning face beneath the burning towers.

"I'm going to beat it out of you. I'm going to beat it out."

His father raised his hand. The knife came down. John rolled away, down the white, descending street, screaming:

"Father! Father!"

These were the first words he uttered. In a moment there was silence, and his father was gone. Again, he felt the saints above him—

and dust was in his mouth. There was singing somewhere; far away, above him; singing slow and mournful. He lay silent, racked beyond endurance, salt drying on his face, with nothing in him any more, no lust, no fear, no shame, no hope. And yet he knew that it would come again—the darkness was full of demons crouching, waiting to worry him with their teeth again.

Then I looked in the grave and I wondered.

Ah, down!—what was he searching here, all alone in darkness? But now he knew, for irony had left him, that he was searching something, hidden in the darkness, that must be found. He would die if it was not found; or, he was dead already, and would never again be joined to the living, if it was not found.

And the grave looked so sad and lonesome.

In the grave where he now wandered—he knew it was the grave, it was so cold and silent, and he moved in icy mist—he found his mother and his father, his mother dressed in scarlet, his father dressed in white. They did not see him: they looked backward, over their shoulders, at a cloud of witnesses. And there was his Aunt Florence, gold and silver flashing on her fingers, brazen earrings dangling from her ears; and there was another woman, whom he took to be that wife of his father's called Deborah—who had, as he had once believed, so much to tell him. But she, alone, of all that company, looked at him and signified that there was no speech in the grave. He was a stranger there—they did not see him pass, they did not know what he was looking for, they could not help him search. He wanted to find Elisha, who knew, perhaps, who would help him—but Elisha was not there. There was Roy: Roy also might have helped him, but he had been stabbed with a knife, and lay now, brown and silent, at his father's feet.

Then there began to flood John's soul the waters of despair. *Love is as strong as death, as deep as the grave.* But love, which had, perhaps, like a benevolent monarch, swelled the population of his neighboring kingdom, Death, had not himself descended: they owed him no allegiance here. Here there was no speech or language, and there was no love; no one to say: You are beautiful, John; no one to forgive him, no matter what his sin; no one to heal him, and lift him up. No one: father and mother looked backward, Roy was bloody, Elisha was not here.

Then the darkness began to murmur—a terrible sound—and John's ears trembled. In this murmur that filled the grave, like a thousand wings beating on the air, he recognized a sound that he had always heard. He began, for terror, to weep and moan—and this sound was swallowed up, and yet was magnified by the echoes that filled the darkness.

This sound had filled John's life, so it now seemed, from the moment he had first drawn breath. He had heard it everywhere, in prayer and in daily speech, and wherever the saints were gathered, and in the unbelieving streets. It was in his father's anger, and in his mother's calm insistence, and in the vehement mockery of his aunt; it had rung, so oddly, in Roy's voice this afternoon, and when Elisha played the piano it was there; it was in the beat and jangle of Sister McCandless's tambourine, it was in the very cadence of her testimony, and invested that testimony with a matchless, unimpeachable authority. Yes, he had heard it all his life, but it was only now that his ears were opened to this sound that came from darkness, that could only come from darkness, that yet bore such sure witness to the glory of the light. And now in his moaning, and so far from any help, he heard it in himself—it rose from his bleeding, his cracked-open heart. It was a sound of rage and weeping which filled the grave, rage and weeping from time set free, but bound now in eternity; rage that had no language, weeping with no voice—which yet spoke now, to John's startled soul, of boundless melancholy, of the bitterest patience, and the longest night; of the deepest water, the strongest chains, the most cruel lash; of humility most wretched, the dungeon most absolute, of love's bed defiled, and birth dishonored, and most bloody, unspeakable, sudden death. Yes, the darkness hummed with murder: the body in the water, the body in the fire, the body on the tree. John looked down the line of these armies of darkness, army upon army, and his soul whispered: *Who are these? Who are they?* And wondered: *Where shall I go?*

There was no answer. There was no help or healing in the grave, no answer in the darkness, no speech from all that company. They looked backward. And John looked back, seeing no deliverance.

I, John, saw the future, way up in the middle of the air.

Were the lash, the dungeon, and the night for him? And the sea for him? And the grave for him?

I, John, saw a number, way in the middle of the air.

And he struggled to flee—out of this darkness, out of this company—into the land of the living, so high, so far away. Fear was upon him, a more deadly fear than he had ever known, as he turned and turned in the darkness, as he moaned, and stumbled, and crawled through darkness, finding no hand, no voice, finding no door. *Who are these? Who are they?* They were the despised and rejected, the wretched and the spat upon, the earth's offscouring; and he was in their company, and they would swallow up his soul. The stripes they had endured would scar his back, their punishment would be his, their portion his, his their humiliation, anguish, chains, their dungeon his, their death his. *Thrice was I beaten with rods, once I was stoned, thrice I suffered shipwreck, a night and a day I have been in the deep.*

And their dread testimony would be his!

In journeyings often, in perils of waters, in perils of robbers, in perils by mine own countrymen, in perils by the heathen, in perils in the city, in perils in the wilderness, in perils in the sea, in perils among false brethren.

And their desolation, his:

In weariness and painfulness in watchings often, in hunger and thirst, in fastings often, in cold and nakedness.

And he began to shout for help, seeing before him the lash, the fire, and the depthless water, seeing his head bowed down forever, he, John, the lowest among these lowly. And he looked for his mother, but her eyes were fixed on this dark army—she was claimed

by this army. And his father would not help him, his father did not
see him, and Roy lay dead.

Then he whispered, not knowing that he whispered: "Oh, Lord,
have mercy on me. Have mercy on me."

And a voice, for the first time in all his terrible journey, spoke to
John, through the rage and weeping, and fire, and darkness, and
flood:

"Yes," said the voice, "go through. Go through."

"Lift me up," whispered John, "lift me up. I can't go through."

"Go through," said the voice, "go through."

Then there was silence. The murmuring ceased. There was only
this trembling beneath him. And he knew there was a light somewhere.

"Go through."

"Ask Him to take you through."

But he could never go through this darkness, through this fire
and this wrath. He never could go through. His strength was finished, and he could not move. He belonged to the darkness—the
darkness from which he had thought to flee had claimed him. And
he moaned again, weeping, and lifted up his hands.

"Call on Him. Call on Him."

"Ask Him to take you through."

Dust rose again in his nostrils, sharp as the fumes of Hell. And he
turned again in the darkness, trying to remember something he had
heard, something he had read.

Jesus saves.

And he saw before him the fire, red and gold, and waiting for
him—yellow, and red, and gold, and burning in a night eternal, and
waiting for him. He must go through this fire, and into this night.

Jesus saves.

Call on Him.

Ask Him to take you through.

He could not call, for his tongue would not unlock, and his heart
was silent, and great with fear. In the darkness, how to move?—with

death's ten thousand jaws agape, and waiting in the darkness. On any turning whatsoever the beast may spring—to move in the darkness is to move into the waiting jaws of death. And yet, it came to him that he must move; for there was a light somewhere, and life, and joy, and singing—somewhere, somewhere above him.

And he moaned again: "Oh, Lord, have mercy. Have mercy, Lord."

There came to him again the communion service at which Elisha had knelt at his father's feet. Now this service was in a great, high room, a room made golden by the light of the sun; and the room was filled with a multitude of people, all in long, white robes, the women with covered heads. They sat at a long, bare, wooden table. They broke at this table flat, unsalted bread, which was the body of the Lord, and drank from a heavy silver cup the scarlet wine of His blood. Then he saw that they were barefoot, and that their feet were stained with this same blood. And a sound of weeping filled the room as they broke the bread and drank the wine.

Then they rose, to come together over a great basin filled with water. And they divided into four groups, two of women and two of men; and they began, woman before woman, and man before man, to wash each other's feet. But the blood would not wash off; many washings only turned the crystal water red; and someone cried: *"Have you been to the river?"*

Then John saw the river, and the multitude was there. And now they had undergone a change: their robes were ragged, and stained with the road they had traveled, and stained with unholy blood; the robes of some barely covered their nakedness; and some indeed were naked. And some stumbled on the smooth stones at the river's edge, for they were blind; and some crawled with a terrible wailing, for they were lame; some did not cease to pluck at their flesh, which was rotten with running sores. All struggled to get to the river, in a dreadful hardness of heart: the strong struck down the weak, the ragged spat on the naked, the naked cursed the blind, the blind crawled over the lame. And someone cried: *"Sinner, do you love my Lord?"*

Then John saw the Lord—for a moment only; and the darkness, for a moment only, was filled with a light he could not bear. Then, in a moment, he was set free; his tears sprang as from a fountain; his heart, like a fountain of waters, burst. Then he cried: "Oh, blessed Jesus! Oh, Lord Jesus! Take me through!"

Of tears there was, yes, a very fountain—springing from a depth never sounded before, from depths John had not known were in him. And he wanted to rise up, singing, singing in that great morning, the morning of his new life. Ah, how his tears ran down, how they blessed his soul!—as he felt himself, out of the darkness, and the fire, and the terrors of death, rising upward to meet the saints.

"Oh, yes!" cried the voice of Elisha. "Bless our God forever!"

And a sweetness filled John as he heard this voice, and heard the sound of singing: the singing was for him. For his drifting soul was anchored in the love of God; in the rock that endured forever. The light and the darkness had kissed each other, and were married now, forever, in the life and the vision of John's soul.

> *I, John, saw a city, way in the middle of the air,*
> *Waiting, waiting, waiting up there.*

He opened his eyes on the morning, and found them, in the light of the morning, rejoicing for him. The trembling he had known in darkness had been the echo of their joyful feet—these feet, blood-stained forever, and washed in many rivers—they moved on the bloody road forever, with no continuing city, but seeking one to come: a city out of time, not made with hands, but eternal in the heavens. No power could hold this army back, no water disperse them, no fire consume them. One day they would compel the earth to heave upward, and surrender the waiting dead. They sang, where the darkness gathered, where the lion waited, where the fire cried, and where blood ran down:

My soul, don't you be uneasy!

They wandered in the valley forever; and they smote the rock, forever; and the waters sprang, perpetually, in the perpetual desert. They cried unto the Lord forever, and lifted up their eyes forever, they were cast down forever, and He lifted them up forever. No, the fire could not hurt them, and yes, the lion's jaws were stopped; the serpent was not their master, the grave was not their resting-place, the earth was not their home. Job bore them witness, and Abraham was their father, Moses had elected to suffer with them rather than glory in sin for a season. Shadrach, Meshach, and Abednego had gone before them into the fire, their grief had been sung by David, and Jeremiah had wept for them. Ezekiel had prophesied upon them, these scattered bones, these slain, and, in the fulness of time, the prophet, John, had come out of the wilderness, crying that the promise was for them. They were encompassed with a very cloud of witnesses: Judas, who had betrayed the Lord; Thomas, who had doubted Him; Peter, who had trembled at the crowing of a cock; Stephen, who had been stoned; Paul, who had been bound; the blind man crying in the dusty road, the dead man rising from the grave. And they looked unto Jesus, the author and the finisher of their faith, running with patience the race He had set before them; they endured the cross, and they despised the shame, and waited to join Him, one day, in glory, at the right hand of the Father.

My soul! don't you be uneasy!

Jesus going to make up my dying bed!

"Rise up, rise up, Brother Johnny, and talk about the Lord's deliverance."

It was Elisha who had spoken; he stood just above John, smiling; and behind him were the saints—Praying Mother Washington, and Sister McCandless, and Sister Price. Behind these, he saw his mother, and his aunt; his father, for the moment, was hidden from his view.

"Amen!" cried Sister McCandless, "rise up, and praise the Lord!"

He tried to speak, and could not, for the joy that rang in him this morning. He smiled up at Elisha, and his tears ran down; and Sister McCandless began to sing:

"Lord, I ain't
No stranger now!"

"Rise up, Johnny," said Elisha, again. "Are you saved, boy?"

"Yes," said John, "oh, yes!" And the words came upward, it seemed, of themselves, in the new voice God had given him. Elisha stretched out his hand, and John took the hand, and stood—so suddenly, and so strangely, and with such wonder!—once more on his feet.

"Lord, I ain't
No stranger now!"

Yes, the night had passed, the powers of darkness had been beaten back. He moved among the saints, he, John, who had come home, who was one of their company now; weeping, he yet could find no words to speak of his great gladness; and he scarcely knew how he moved, for his hands were new, and his feet were new, and he moved in a new and Heaven-bright air. Praying Mother Washington took him in her arms, and kissed him, and their tears, his tears and the tears of the old, black woman, mingled. "God bless you, son. Run on, honey, and don't get weary!"

"Lord, I been introduced
To the Father and the Son,
And I ain't
No stranger now!"

Yet, as he moved among them, their hands touching, and tears falling, and the music rising—as though he moved down a great hall, full of a splendid company—something began to knock in that listening, astonished, newborn, and fragile heart of his; something recalling the terrors of the night, which were not finished, his heart seemed to say; which, in this company, were now to begin. And, while his heart was speaking, he found himself before his mother. Her face was full of tears, and for a long while they looked at each other, saying nothing. And once again, he tried to read the mystery of that face—which, as it had never before been so bright and pained with love, had never seemed before so far from him, so wholly in communion with a life beyond his life. He wanted to comfort her, but the night had given him no language, no second sight, no power to see into the heart of any other. He knew only—and now, looking at his mother, he knew that he could never tell it—that the heart was a fearful place. She kissed him, and she said: "I'm mighty proud, Johnny. You keep the faith. I'm going to be praying for you till the Lord puts me in my grave."

Then he stood before his father. In the moment that he forced himself to raise his eyes and look into his father's face, he felt in himself a stiffening, and a panic, and a blind rebellion, and a hope for peace. The tears still on his face, and smiling still, he said: "Praise the Lord."

"Praise the Lord," said his father. He did not move to touch him, did not kiss him, did not smile. They stood before each other in silence, while the saints rejoiced; and John struggled to speak the authoritative, the living word that would conquer the great division between his father and himself. But it did not come, the living word; in the silence something died in John, and something came alive. It came to him that he must testify: his tongue only could bear witness to the wonders he had seen. And he remembered, suddenly, the text of a sermon he had once heard his father preach. And he opened his mouth, feeling, as he watched his father, the darkness roar behind him, and the very earth beneath him seem to shake; yet he gave to his father their common testimony. "I'm saved," he said, "and I know I'm saved." And then, as his father did not speak, he repeated his father's text: "My witness is in Heaven and my record is on high."

"It come from your mouth," said his father then. "I want to see you live it. It's more than a notion."

"I'm going to pray God," said John—and his voice shook,

whether with joy or grief he could not say—"to keep me, and make me strong . . . to stand . . . to stand against the enemy . . . and against everything and everybody . . . that wants to cut down my soul."

Then his tears came down again, like a wall between him and his father. His Aunt Florence came and took him in her arms. Her eyes were dry, and her face was old in the savage, morning light. But her voice, when she spoke, was gentler than he had ever known it to be before.

"You fight the good fight," she said, "you hear? Don't you get weary, and don't you get scared. Because I *know* the Lord's done laid His hands on you."

"Yes," he said, weeping, "yes. I'm going to serve the Lord."

"Amen!" cried Elisha. "Bless our God!" The filthy streets rang with the early-morning light as they came out of the temple.

They were all there, save young Ella Mae, who had departed while John was still on the floor—she had a bad cold, said Praying Mother Washington, and needed to have her rest. Now, in three groups, they walked the long, gray, silent avenue: Praying Mother Washington with Elizabeth and Sister McCandless and Sister Price, and before them Gabriel and Florence, and Elisha and John ahead.

"You know, the Lord is a wonder," said the praying mother. "Don't you know, all this week He just burdened my soul, and kept me a-praying and a-weeping before Him? Look like I just couldn't get no ease nohow—and I *know* He had me a-tarrying for that boy's soul."

"Well, amen," said Sister Price. "Look like the Lord just wanted this church to *rock*. You remember how He spoke through Sister McCandless Friday night, and told us to pray, and He'd work a mighty wonder in our midst? And He done *moved*—hallelujah—He done troubled *everybody's* mind."

"I just tell you," said Sister McCandless, "all you got to do is *listen* to the Lord; He'll lead you right every *time;* He'll move every *time*. Can't nobody tell me *my* God ain't real."

"And you see the way the Lord worked with young Elisha there?" said Praying Mother Washington, with a calm, sweet smile. "Had that boy down there on the floor a-prophesying in *tongues,* amen, just the very *minute* before Johnny fell out a-screaming, and a-crying before the Lord. Look like the Lord was using Elisha to say: 'It's time, boy, come on home.' "

"Well, He is a wonder," said Sister Price. "And Johnny's got *two* brothers now."

Elizabeth said nothing. She walked with her head bowed, hands clasped lightly before her. Sister Price turned to look at her, and smiled.

"I know," she said, "you's a mighty happy woman this morning."

Elizabeth smiled and raised her head, but did not look directly at Sister Price. She looked ahead, down the long avenue, where Gabriel walked with Florence, where John walked with Elisha.

"Yes," she said, at last, "I been praying. And I ain't stopped praying yet."

"Yes, Lord," said Sister Price, "can't none of us stop praying till we see His blessed face."

"But I bet you didn't never think," said Sister McCandless, with a laugh, "that little Johnny was going to jump up so soon, and get religion. *Bless* our God!"

"The Lord's going to bless that boy, you mark my words," said Praying Mother Washington.

"Shake hands with the preacher, Johnny."

"Got a man in the Bible, son, who liked music, too. And he got to dancing one day before the Lord. You reckon you going to dance before the Lord one of these days?"

"Yes, Lord," said Sister Price, "the Lord done raised you up a holy son. He going to comfort your gray hairs."

Elizabeth found that her tears were falling, slowly, bitterly, in the morning light. "I pray the Lord," she said, "to bear him up on every side."

"Yes," said Sister McCandless, gravely, "it's more than a notion. The Devil rises on every hand."

Then, in silence, they came to the wide crossing where the street-car line ran. A lean cat stalked the gutter and fled as they approached; turned to watch them, with yellow, malevolent eyes, from the ambush of a garbage can. A gray bird flew above them, above the electric wires for the streetcar line, and perched on the metal cornice of a roof. Then, far down the avenue, they heard a siren, and the clanging of a bell, and looked up to see the ambulance speed past them on the way to the hospital that was near the church.

"Another soul struck down," murmured Sister McCandless. "Lord have mercy."

"He said in the last days evil would abound," said Sister Price.

"Well, yes, He *did* say it," said Praying Mother Washington, "and I'm so glad He told us He wouldn't leave us comfortless."

"When ye see all these things, know that your salvation is at hand," said Sister McCandless. "A thousand shall fall at thy side, and ten thousand at thy right hand—but it ain't going to come nigh thee. *So* glad, amen, this morning, bless my Redeemer."

"You remember that day when you come into the store?"

"I didn't think you never looked at me."

"Well—you was mighty pretty."

"Didn't little Johnny never say nothing," asked Praying Mother Washington, "to make you think the Lord was working in his heart?"

"He always kind of quiet," said Elizabeth. "He don't say much."

"No," said Sister McCandless, "he ain't like all these rough young ones nowadays—*he* got some respect for his elders. You done raised him mighty well, Sister Grimes."

"It was his birthday yesterday," Elizabeth said.

"No!" cried Sister Price. "How old he got to be yesterday?"

"He done made fourteen," she said.

"You hear that?" said Sister Price, with wonder. "The Lord done saved that boy's soul on his birthday!"

"Well, he got two birthdays now," smiled Sister McCandless, "just like he got two brothers—one in the flesh, and one in the Spirit."

"Amen, bless the Lord!" cried Praying Mother Washington.

"What book was it, Richard?"

"Oh, I don't remember. Just a book."

"You smiled."

"You was mighty pretty."

She took her sodden handkerchief out of her bag, and dried her eyes; and dried her eyes again, looking down the avenue.

"Yes," said Sister Price, gently, "you just *thank* the Lord. You just *let* the tears fall. I know your heart is full this morning."

"The Lord's done give you," said Praying Mother Washington, "a mighty blessing—and what the Lord gives, can't no man take away."

"I open," said Sister McCandless, "and no man can shut. I shut, and no man can open."

"Amen," said Sister Price. "Amen."

"Well, I reckon," Florence said, "your soul is praising God this morning."

He looked straight ahead, saying nothing, holding his body more rigid than an arrow.

"You always been saying," Florence said, "how the Lord would answer prayer." And she looked sideways at him, with a little smile.

"He going to learn," he said at last, "that it ain't all in the singing and the shouting—the way of holiness is a hard way. He got the steep side of the mountain to climb."

"But he got you there," she said, "ain't he, to help him when he stumbles, and to be a good example?"

"I'm going to see to it," he said, "that he walks right before the Lord. The Lord's done put his soul in *my* charge—and I ain't going to have that boy's blood on my hands."

"No," she said, mildly, "I reckon you don't want that."

Then they heard the siren, and the headlong, warning bell. She watched his face as he looked outward at the silent avenue and at the ambulance that raced to carry someone to healing, or to death.

"Yes," she said, "that wagon's coming, ain't it, one day for everybody?"

"I pray," he said, "it finds you ready, sister."

"Is it going to find you ready?" she asked.

"I know my name is written in the Book of Life," he said. "I know I'm going to look on my Saviour's face in glory."

"Yes," she said, slowly, "we's all going to be together there. Mama, and you, and me, and Deborah—and what was the name of that little girl who died not long after I left home?"

"What little girl who died?" he asked. "A *lot* of folks died after *you* left home—you left your *mother* on her dying bed."

"This girl was a mother, too," she said. "Look like she went North all by herself, and had her baby, and died—weren't nobody to help her. Deborah wrote me about it. Sure, you ain't forgotten that girl's name, Gabriel!"

Then his step faltered—seemed, for a moment, to drag. And he looked at her. She smiled, and lightly touched his arm.

"You ain't forgotten her name," she said. "You can't tell me you done forgot her name. Is you going to look on her face, too? Is her name written in the Book of Life?"

In utter silence they walked together, her hand still under his trembling arm.

"Deborah didn't never write," she at last pursued, "about what happened to the baby. Did you ever see him? You going to meet him in Heaven, too?"

"The Word tell us," he said, "to let the dead bury the dead. Why you want to go rummaging around back there, digging up things what's all forgotten now? The Lord, He knows my life—He done forgive me a long time ago."

"Look like," she said, "you think the Lord's a man like you; you think you can fool Him like you fool men, and you think He forgets, like men. But God don't forget nothing, Gabriel—if your name's down there in the Book, like you say, it's got all what you done right down there with it. And you going to answer for it, too."

"I done answered," he said, "already before my God. I ain't got to answer now, in front of you."

She opened her handbag, and took out the letter.

"I been carrying this letter now," she said, "for more than thirty years. And I been wondering all that time if I'd ever talk to you about it."

And she looked at him. He was looking, unwillingly, at the letter, which she held tightly in one hand. It was old, and dirty, and brown, and torn; he recognized Deborah's uncertain, trembling hand, and he could see her again in the cabin, bending over the table, laboriously trusting to paper the bitterness she had not spoken. It had lived in her silence, then, all of those years? He could not believe it. She had been praying for him as she died—she had sworn to meet him in glory. And yet, this letter, her witness, spoke, breaking her long silence, now that she was beyond his reach forever.

"Yes," said Florence, watching his face, "you didn't give her no bed of roses to sleep on, did you?—poor, simple, ugly, black girl. And you didn't treat that other one no better. Who is you met, Gabriel, all your holy life long, you ain't made to drink a cup of sorrow? And you doing it still—you going to be doing it till the Lord puts you in your grave."

"God's way," he said, and his speech was thick, his face was slick with sweat, "ain't man's way. I been doing the will of the Lord, and can't nobody sit in judgment on me but the Lord. The Lord called me out, He chose *me,* and I been running with Him ever since I made a start. You can't keep your eyes on all this foolishness here below, all this wickedness here below—you got to lift up your eyes to the hills and run from the destruction falling on the earth, you got to put your hand in Jesus' hand, and go where *He* says go."

"And if you been but a stumbling-stone here below?" she said. "If you done caused souls right and left to stumble and fall, and lose their happiness, and lose their souls? What then, prophet? What then, the Lord's anointed? Ain't no reckoning going to be called of *you*? What you going to say when the wagon comes?"

He lifted up his head, and she saw tears mingled with his sweat. "The Lord," he said, "He sees the heart—He sees the heart."

"Yes," she said, "but I done read the Bible, too, and it tells me you going to know the tree by its fruit. What fruit I seen from you if it ain't been just sin and sorrow and shame?"

"You be careful," he said, "how you talk to the Lord's anointed. 'Cause my life ain't in that letter—you don't know my life."

"Where *is* your life, Gabriel?" she asked, after a despairing pause. "Where *is* it? Ain't it all done gone for nothing? Where's your branches? Where's your fruit?"

He said nothing; insistently, she tapped the letter with her thumbnail. They were approaching the corner where she must leave him, turning westward to take her subway home. In the light that filled the streets, the light that the sun was now beginning to corrupt with fire, she watched John and Elisha just before them, John's listening head bent, Elisha's arm about his shoulder.

"I got a son," he said at last, "and the Lord's going to raise him up. I know—the Lord has promised—His word is true."

And then she laughed. "*That* son," she said, "that Roy. You going to weep for many a eternity before you see him crying in front of the altar like Johnny was crying tonight."

"God sees the heart," he repeated, "He sees the heart."

"Well, He ought to see it," she cried, "He made it! But don't nobody else see it, not even your own self! *Let* God see it—He sees it all right, and He don't say nothing."

"He speaks," he said, "He speaks. All you got to do is listen."

"I been listening many a nighttime long," said Florence, then, "and He ain't never spoke to me."

"He ain't never spoke," said Gabriel, "because you ain't never wanted to hear. You just wanted Him to tell you your way was right. And that ain't no way to wait on God."

"Then tell me," said Florence, "what He done said to you—that you didn't want to hear?"

And there was silence again. Now they both watched John and Elisha.

"I going to tell you something, Gabriel," she said. "I know you thinking at the bottom of your heart that if you just make *her,* her and her bastard boy, pay enough for her sin, *your* son won't have to pay for yours. But I ain't going to let you do that. You done made enough folks pay for sin, it's time you started paying."

"What you think," he asked, "you going to be able to do—against me?"

"Maybe," she said, "I ain't long for this world, but I got this letter, and I'm sure going to give it to Elizabeth before I go, and if she don't want it, I'm going to find *some* way—some way, I don't know how—to rise up and tell it, tell *everybody,* about the blood the Lord's anointed is got on his hands."

"I done told you," he said, "that's all done and finished; the Lord done give me a sign to make me know I been forgiven. What good you think it's going to do to start talking about it now?"

"It'll make Elizabeth to know," she said, "that she ain't the only sinner . . . in your holy house. And little Johnny, there—he'll know he ain't the only bastard."

Then he turned again, and looked at her with hatred in his eyes.

"You ain't never changed," he said. "You still waiting to see my downfall. You just as wicked now as you was when you was young."

She put the letter in her bag again.

"No," she said, "I ain't changed. You ain't changed neither. You still promising the Lord you going to do better—and you think whatever you done already, whatever you doing right at that *minute,* don't count. Of all the men I *ever* knew, you's the man who ought to be hoping the Bible's all a lie—'cause if that trumpet ever sounds, you going to spend eternity talking."

They had reached her corner. She stopped, and he stopped with her, and she stared into his haggard, burning face.

"I got to take my subway," she said. "You got anything you want to say to me?"

"I been living a long time," he said, "and I ain't never seen nothing but evil overtake the enemies of the Lord. You think you going to use that letter to hurt me—but the Lord ain't going to let it come to pass. You going to be cut down."

The praying women approached them, Elizabeth in the middle.

"Deborah," Florence said, "was cut down—but she left word. She weren't no enemy of *nobody*—and she didn't see nothing but evil. When I go, brother, you better tremble, 'cause I ain't going to go in silence."

And, while they stared at each other, saying nothing more, the praying women were upon them.

Now the long, the silent avenue stretched before them like some gray country of the dead. It scarcely seemed that he had walked this avenue only (as time was reckoned up by men) some few hours ago; that he had known this avenue since his eyes had opened on the dangerous world; that he had played here, wept here, fled, fallen down, and been bruised here—in that time, so far behind him, of his innocence and anger.

Yes, on the evening of the seventh day, when, raging, he had walked out of his father's house, this avenue had been filled with shouting people. The light of the day had begun to fail—the wind was high, and the tall lights, one by one, and then all together, had lifted up their heads against the darkness—while he hurried to the temple. Had he been mocked, had anyone spoken, or laughed, or called? He could not remember. He had been walking in a storm.

Now the storm was over. And the avenue, like any landscape that has endured a storm, lay changed under Heaven, exhausted and clean, and new. Not again, forever, could it return to the avenue it once had been. Fire, or lightning, or the latter rain, coming down from these skies which moved with such pale secrecy above him now, had laid yesterday's avenue waste, had changed it in a moment, in the twinkling of an eye, as all would be changed on the last day, when the skies would open up once more to gather up the saints.

Yet the houses were there, as they had been; the windows, like a thousand, blinded eyes, stared outward at the morning—at the morning that was the same for them as the mornings of John's innocence, and the mornings before his birth. The water ran in the gutters with a small, discontented sound; on the water traveled paper, burnt matches, sodden cigarette-ends; gobs of spittle, green-yellow, brown, and pearly; the leavings of a dog, the vomit of a drunken man, the dead sperm, trapped in rubber, of one abandoned to his lust. All moved slowly to the black grating where down it rushed, to be carried to the river, which would hurl it into the sea.

Where houses were, where windows stared, where gutters ran, were people—sleeping now, invisible, private, in the heavy darknesses of these houses, while the Lord's day broke outside. When John should walk these streets again, they would be shouting here again; the roar of children's roller skates would bear down on him from behind; little girls in pigtails, skipping rope, would establish on the sidewalk a barricade through which he must stumble as best he might. Boys would be throwing ball in these streets again—they would look at him, and call:

"Hey, Frog-eyes!"

Men would be standing on corners again, watching him pass, girls would be sitting on stoops again, mocking his walk. Grandmothers would stare out of windows, saying:

"That sure is a sorry little boy."

He would weep again, his heart insisted, for now his weeping had begun; he would rage again, said the shifting air, for the lions of rage had been unloosed; he would be in darkness again, in fire again, now that he had seen the fire and the darkness. He was free—*whom the Son sets free is free indeed*—he had only to stand fast in his liberty. He was in battle no longer, this unfolding Lord's day, with this avenue, these houses, the sleeping, staring, shouting people, but had entered into battle with Jacob's angel, *with the princes and the powers of the air.* And he was filled with a joy, a joy unspeakable, whose roots, though he would not trace them on this new day of his life, were nourished by the wellspring of a despair not yet discovered. *The joy of the Lord is the strength of His people.* Where joy was, there strength followed; where strength was, sorrow came—forever? Forever and forever, said the arm of Elisha, heavy on his shoulder. And John tried to see through the morning wall, to stare past the bitter houses, to tear the thousand gray veils of the sky away, and look into the heart—that monstrous heart which beat forever, turning the astounded universe, commanding the stars to flee away before the sun's red sandal, bidding the moon to wax and wane, and disappear, and come again; with a silver net holding back the sea, and, out of mysteries abysmal, re-creating, each day, the earth. That heart, that breath, without which *was not anything made which was made.* Tears came into his eyes again, making the avenue shiver, causing the houses to shake—his heart swelled, lifted up, faltered, and was dumb. Out of joy strength came, strength that was fashioned to bear sorrow: sorrow brought forth joy. Forever? This was Ezekiel's wheel, in the middle of the burning air forever—and the little wheel ran by faith, and the big wheel ran by the grace of God.

"Elisha?" he said.

"If you ask Him to bear you up," said Elisha, as though he had read his thoughts, "He won't never let you fall."

"It was you," he said, "wasn't it, who prayed me through?"

"We was all praying, little brother," said Elisha, with a smile, "but yes, I was right over you the whole time. Look like the Lord had put you like a burden on my soul."

"Was I praying long?" he asked.

Elisha laughed. "Well, you started praying when it was night and you ain't stopped praying till it was morning. That's a right smart time, it seems to me."

John smiled, too, observing with some wonder that a saint of God could laugh.

"Was you glad," he asked, "to see me at the altar?"

Then he wondered why he had asked this, and hoped Elisha would not think him foolish.

"I was mighty glad," said Elisha soberly, "to see little Johnny lay his sins on the altar, lay his *life* on the altar and rise up, praising God."

Something shivered in him as the word *sin* was spoken. Tears sprang to his eyes again. "Oh," he said, "I pray God, I *pray* the Lord . . . to make me strong . . . to sanctify me wholly . . . and keep me saved!"

"Yes," said Elisha, "you keep that spirit, and I know the Lord's going to see to it that you get home all right."

"It's a long way," John said slowly, "ain't it? It's a hard way. It's uphill all the way."

"You remember Jesus," Elisha said. "You keep your mind on Jesus. *He* went that way—up the steep side of the mountain—and He was carrying the cross, and didn't nobody help Him. He went that way for us. He carried that cross for us."

"But He was the Son of God," said John, "and He knew it."

"He knew it," said Elisha, "because He was willing to pay the price. Don't you know it, Johnny? Ain't you willing to pay the price?"

"That song they sing," said John, finally, "*if it costs my life*—is that the price?"

"Yes," said Elisha, "that's the price."

Then John was silent, wanting to put the question another way. And the silence was cracked, suddenly, by an ambulance siren, and a crying bell. And they both looked up as the ambulance raced past them on the avenue on which no creature moved, save for the saints of God behind them.

"But that's the Devil's price, too," said Elisha, as silence came again. "The Devil, he don't ask for nothing less than your life. And he take it, too, and it's lost forever. Forever, Johnny. You in darkness while you living and you in darkness when you dead. Ain't nothing but the love of God can make the darkness light."

"Yes," said John, "I remember. I remember."

"Yes," said Elisha, "but you got to remember when the evil day comes, when the flood rises, boy, and look like your soul is going under. You got to remember when the Devil's doing all he can to make you forget."

"The Devil," he said, frowning and staring, "the Devil. How many faces is the Devil got?"

"He got as many faces," Elisha said, "as you going to see between now and the time you lay your burden down. And he got a lot more than that, but ain't nobody seen them all."

"Except Jesus," John said then. "Only Jesus."

"Yes," said Elisha, with a grave, sweet smile, "that's the Man you got to call on. That's the Man who knows."

They were approaching his house—his father's house. In a moment he must leave Elisha, step out from under his protecting arm, and walk alone into the house—alone with his mother and his father. And he was afraid. He wanted to stop and turn to Elisha, and tell him . . . something for which he found no words.

"Elisha—" he began, and looked into Elisha's face. Then: "You pray for me? Please pray for me?"

"I been praying, little brother," Elisha said, "and I sure ain't going to stop praying now."

"For me," persisted John, his tears falling, "for *me*."

"You know right well," said Elisha, looking at him, "I ain't going to stop praying for the brother what the Lord done give me."

Then they reached the house, and paused, looking at each other, waiting. John saw that the sun was beginning to stir, somewhere in the sky; the silence of the dawn would soon give way to the trumpets of the morning. Elisha took his arm from John's shoulder and stood beside him, looking backward. And John looked back, seeing the saints approach.

"Service is going to be mighty late *this* morning," Elisha said, and suddenly grinned and yawned.

And John laughed. "But you be there," he asked, "won't you? This morning?"

"Yes, little brother," Elisha laughed, "I'm going to be there. I see I'm going to have to do some running to keep up with *you*."

And they watched the saints. Now they all stood on the corner, where his Aunt Florence had stopped to say good-bye. All the women talked together, while his father stood a little apart. His aunt and his mother kissed each other, as he had seen them do a hundred times, and then his aunt turned to look for them, and waved.

They waved back, and she started slowly across the street, moving, he thought with wonder, like an old woman.

"Well, *she* ain't going to be out to service this morning, I tell you that," said Elisha, and yawned again.

"And look like *you* going to be half asleep," John said.

"Now don't you *mess* with me this morning," Elisha said, "because you ain't *got* so holy I can't turn you over my knee. I's your *big* brother in the Lord—you just remember *that*."

Now they were on the near corner. His father and mother were saying good-bye to Praying Mother Washington, and Sister McCandless, and Sister Price. The praying women waved to them, and they waved back. Then his mother and his father were alone, coming toward them.

"Elisha," said John, "Elisha."

"Yes," said Elisha, "what you want now?"

John, staring at Elisha, struggled to tell him something more— struggled to say—all that could never be said. Yet: "I was down in the valley," he dared, "I was by myself down there. I won't never forget. May God forget me if I forget."

Then his mother and his father were before them. His mother smiled, and took Elisha's outstretched hand.

"Praise the Lord this morning," said Elisha. "He done give us something to praise Him for."

"Amen," said his mother, "praise the Lord!"

John moved up to the short, stone step, smiling a little, looking down on them. His mother passed him, and started into the house.

"You better come on upstairs," she said, still smiling, "and take off them wet clothes. Don't want you catching cold."

And her smile remained unreadable; he could not tell what it hid. And to escape her eyes, he kissed her, saying: "Yes, Mama. I'm coming."

She stood behind him, in the doorway, waiting.

"Praise the Lord, Deacon," Elisha said. "See you at the morning service, Lord willing."

"Amen," said his father, "praise the Lord." He started up the stone steps, staring at John, who blocked the way. "Go on upstairs, boy," he said, "like your mother told you."

John looked at his father and moved from his path, stepping down into the street again. He put his hand on Elisha's arm, feeling himself trembling, and his father at his back.

"Elisha," he said, "no matter what happens to me, where I go, what folks say about me, no matter what *any*body says, you remember—please remember—I was saved. I was *there*."

Elisha grinned, and looked up at his father.

"He come through," cried Elisha, "didn't he, Deacon Grimes? The Lord done laid him out, and turned him around and wrote his *new* name down in glory. Bless our God!"

And he kissed John on the forehead, a holy kiss.

"Run on, little brother," Elisha said. "Don't you get weary. God won't forget you. You won't forget."

Then he turned away, down the long avenue, home. John stood still, watching him walk away. The sun had come full awake. It was waking the streets, and the houses, and crying at the windows. It fell over Elisha like a golden robe, and struck John's forehead, where Elisha had kissed him, like a seal ineffaceable forever.

And he felt his father behind him. And he felt the March wind rise, striking through his damp clothes, against his salty body. He turned to face his father—he found himself smiling, but his father did not smile.

They looked at each other a moment. His mother stood in the doorway, in the long shadows of the hall.

"I'm ready," John said, "I'm coming. I'm on my way."

I AM NOT YOUR NEGRO
A Companion Edition to the Documentary Film Directed by Raoul Peck

To compose his stunning documentary film *I Am Not Your Negro*, acclaimed filmmaker Raoul Peck mined James Baldwin's published and unpublished oeuvre, selecting passages from his books, essays, letters, notes, and interviews that are every bit as incisive and pertinent now as they have ever been. Weaving these texts together, Peck brilliantly imagines the book that Baldwin never wrote. In his final years, Baldwin had envisioned a book about his three assassinated friends, Medgar Evers, Malcolm X, and Martin Luther King, Jr. His deeply personal notes for the project have never before been published. Peck's film uses them to jump through time, juxtaposing Baldwin's private words with his public statements in a blazing examination of the tragic history of race in America.

Literature

BLUES FOR MISTER CHARLIE

James Baldwin turns a murder into an inquest in which even the most well-intentioned whites are implicated—and in which even a killer receives his share of compassion. In a small Southern town, a white man murders a black man, then throws his body in the weeds. With this act of violence, Baldwin launches an unsparing and at times agonizing probe of the wounds of race. For where once a white storekeeper could have shot a "boy" like Richard Henry with impunity, times have changed. And centuries of brutality and fear, patronage and contempt, are about to erupt in a moment of truth as devastating as a shotgun blast.

Drama/Literature

TELL ME HOW LONG THE TRAIN'S BEEN GONE

At the height of his theatrical career, the actor Leo Proudhammer is nearly felled by a heart attack. As he hovers between life and death, Baldwin shows the choices that have made him enviably famous and terrifyingly vulnerable. For between Leo's childhood on the streets of Harlem and his arrival into the intoxicating world of the theater lies a wilderness of desire and loss, shame and rage. An adored older brother vanishes into prison. There are love affairs with a white woman and a younger black man, each of whom will make irresistible claims on Leo's loyalty. *Tell Me How Long the Train's Been Gone* is overpowering in its vitality and extravagant in the intensity of its feeling.

Fiction/Literature

GIOVANNI'S ROOM

Set in the 1950s Paris of American expatriates, liaisons, and violence, a young man finds himself caught between desire and conventional morality. With a sharp, probing imagination, James Baldwin's now-classic narrative delves into the mystery of loving and creates a moving, highly controversial story of death and passion that reveals the unspoken complexities of the human heart.

Fiction

THE AMEN CORNER

In his first work for the theater, James Baldwin brought all the fervor and majestic rhetoric of the storefront churches of his childhood along with an unwavering awareness of the price those churches exacted from their worshippers. For years Sister Margaret Alexander has moved her Harlem congregation with a mixture of personal charisma and ferocious piety. But when Margaret's estranged husband, a scapegrace jazz musician, comes home to die, she is in danger of losing both her standing in the church and the son she has tried to keep on the godly path.

Drama

GOING TO MEET THE MAN
Stories

In this modern classic, "there's no way not to suffer. But you try all kinds of ways to keep from drowning in it." The men and women in these eight short fictions grasp this truth on an elemental level, and their stories detail the ingenious and often desperate ways in which they try to keep their head above water. It may be the heroin that a down-and-out jazz pianist uses to face the terror of pouring his life into an inanimate instrument. It may be the brittle piety of a father who can never forgive his son for his illegitimacy. Or it may be the screen of bigotry that a redneck deputy has raised to blunt the awful childhood memory of the day his parents took him to watch a black man being murdered by a gleeful mob. By turns haunting, heartbreaking, and horrifying, *Going to Meet the Man* is a major work by one of our most important writers.

Fiction/Literature

THE DEVIL FINDS WORK

Baldwin's personal reflections on movies gathered here in a book-length essay are also a probing appraisal of American racial politics. Offering an incisive look at racism in American movies and a vision of America's self-delusions and deceptions, Baldwin challenges the underlying assumptions in such films as *In the Heat of the Night*, *Guess Who's Coming to Dinner*, and *The Exorcist*. Here are our loves and hates, biases and cruelties, fears and ignorance reflected by the films that have entertained us and shaped our consciousness. *The Devil Finds Work* showcases the stunning prose of a writer whose passion never diminished his struggle for equality, justice, and social change.

Essays/Film Criticism

THE FIRE NEXT TIME

At once a powerful evocation of James Baldwin's early life in Harlem and a disturbing examination of the consequences of racial injustice, *The Fire Next Time* is an intensely personal and provocative document. It consists of two "letters," written on the occasion of the centennial of the Emancipation Proclamation, that exhort Americans, both black and white, to attack the terrible legacy of racism.

Literature/African American Studies

NOBODY KNOWS MY NAME

From one of the most brilliant writers and thinkers of the twentieth century comes a collection of "passionate, probing, controversial" essays (*The Atlantic*) on topics ranging from race relations in the United States to the role of the writer in society. Told with Baldwin's characteristically unflinching honesty, this "splendid book" (*The New York Times*) offers illuminating, deeply felt essays along with personal accounts of Richard Wright, Norman Mailer, and other writers.

Literature/African American Studies

ALSO AVAILABLE
Another Country
The Cross of Redemption
No Name in the Street
One Day When I Was Lost
Vintage Baldwin

VINTAGE INTERNATIONAL
Available wherever books are sold.
vintagebooks.com